GUST FRONT

GUST FRONT

JOHN RINGO

GUST FRONT

A Baen Books Original

Baen Publishing Enterprises
P.O. Box 1403
Riverdale, NY 10471
www.baen.com

ISBN: 0-671-31976-0

Cover art by Dru Blair
Interior maps by John Ringo

First printing, April 2001

Library of Congress Cataloging-in-Publication Data

Ringo, John, 1963-
  Gust front / by John Ringo.
      p.   cm.
  ISBN 0-671-31976-0
  1. Human-alien encounters—Fiction.   2. Life on other planets—Fiction.
  3. Space warfare—Fiction.   I. Title

PS3568.I577   F87   2001
813'6—dc21   00-065077

Distributed by Simon & Schuster
1230 Avenue of the Americas
New York, NY 10020

Production by Windhaven Press, Auburn, NH
Printed in the United States of America

10   9   8   7   6   5   4   3   2

In Memory of
William Pryor Ringo
Engineer Extraordinaire

——————————

◆ PROLOGUE ◆

"Well, Tir, you think your plans for the humans are working?"

The Darhel Ghin waved a stick of incense through the air and placed the message to the Lords on the Altar of Communication. The background of melodiously chiming song-crystals and the mirrored silver colonnades aided his contemplation of the multitudinous alternate futures. At the moment he sorely needed the aid. Most of the futures looked bleak.

His Indowy body attendants lifted his robes as he rose and turned to the attendant Tir. The younger Darhel's foxlike face was the well-trained mien of a senior Darhel manager. He returned the Ghin's ear flick of polite query with total impassivity. In fact better than two-thirds of the overall plan was in total disarray, mostly because of the actions of a single lucky individual. Admitting that, however, was not a route to power. And there was little for this old fossil to pick apart. The entirety of the plan was known only to himself.

"No plan unfolds in perfection," the Tir said smoothly. "That is the purpose of management."

The elfin Ghin flicked his ears again. The gesture was deliberately ambiguous. It might have been polite agreement. Or it might have been polite disbelief. The difference was subtle. "We retain Diess."

The Ghin deliberately did not ascribe that as a positive or a negative trait. Destroying the allied human forces arrayed to defend the planet might or might not have been part of the young pup's plan. Leaving the statement ambiguous was a deliberate trap with overtones he doubted the Tir was aware of.

The Tir flared his nostrils in agreement and glanced at the gathered Indowy. "It is an important world." The corporations of Diess were entirely Darhel-controlled despite the billions of Indowy

1

residents. The laborers of the Federation were as disposable as bacteria. "The revenue is significant."

The Ghin's nostrils flared. As expected the young fool had sidestepped. "And Barwhon as well."

"Regrettably the human loss there has been great." The expression he displayed now was one copied from humans, cat-pupilled vertical-lidded eyes opening wide. The wide mobile mouth turned down, exposing the edge of sharklike teeth. Even the ears drooped. It was a subtle and effective expression and one difficult to copy. Humans would have slumped in apparent defeat as well. Sorrow was not a Darhel emotion. Hatred, yes. Anger, definitely. Sorrow? No.

The Ghin took a moment to contemplate his own plans. The Ghin knew that the road to mastery was not one of plots alone. A clear understanding of reality was paramount. That the young fool had risen to his current place was a sign that the quality of the opposition had fallen off.

Or of a deeply laid plan.

The Ghin gave an internal flare to the nostrils. No. No deep plans here. His own plans had every path to the future open to his own designs, and every path shut to the young fool. There were no flaws in *his* approach. It was a warm feeling.

"Your plan will require further . . . adjustment? You were frustrated on Diess by the actions of a single human."

"Yes, Your Ghin," agreed the Tir. He had set the trap and the old fool had wandered right in. "I fear my presence on Earth will be required for the next phase."

"And that is?" The Ghin set the *targan* trap and waited for the quarry.

The Tir's face settled into even less readable lines. The next phase was obvious. Even to this old fool. "The humans must enter the path to enlightenment. Individuality is an obstacle to oneness that must be overcome."

"And you propose to do that how?" The Ghin flicked his ears again in that deliberately ambiguous manner.

"There are so many paths to success it would take days to describe. Suffice it to say that the humans must be pawns to the Path of Enlightenment. Their myth of individuality shall be crushed and with it their passion. The way of passion is not the way to success in our current endeavors. Nor is it the way to enlightenment."

The Tir paused, trembling slightly. "The time of heroes is past. And the time of *certain* individuals in particular is long past." The Tir was a master of facial control, but his control of body language was still spotty. The deep breath and rippling of muscles along the upper limbs spoke of surging anger.

The young fool was on the edge of *lintatai!* The Ghin schooled his face into immobility. The Tir had been reading his reports and analyses too long. He had forgotten that, hidden deep beneath the veneer of civilization, the heart of the Darhel was the heart of a frustrated warrior. This was the very urge that he now fought. And that heart told the Ghin that his opponent had seriously miscalculated. Humans would not be so easily vanquished as a threat to Darhel control.

"I am joyful that our people have such exquisite leadership," the Ghin said. Then he also copied a human expression as his lips drew back in a broad smile. The glittering teeth of a rending carnivore were exposed for all to see and the watching Indowy shut their eyes and turned away. None of them had the stupidity to actually run or otherwise embarrass the Darhel lords, but none of them would ever forget the sight. "Our future is in good hands."

◈ CHAPTER 1 ◈

Kabul town was ours to take—
Blow the trumpet draw the sword—
I'd ha' left it for 'is sake—
'Im that left me by the ford.
 Ford, ford, ford o' Kabul river,
 Ford o' Kabul river in the dark!

—"Ford O' Kabul River"
Rudyard Kipling

Ttckpt Province, Barwhon V
1625 GMT November 23rd, 2003 AD

A burst of machine gun fire took the lead Posleen in the chest. The orange tracer of the fifth bullet drifted past the crumpling creature as steaming yellow blood stained the purple ferns of the undergrowth. The company of centaurlike aliens began to spread to either side as the remainder of the humans opened fire. The ford behind the humans echoed a liquid chuckle, as if laughing at the poor soldiers called to their deaths by its aberrant presence.

Captain Robert Thomas peered through the ever-present mists and whispered a call for fire as the Posleen deployed. His company was heavily outnumbered by the approaching Posleen battlegroup and low on soldiers, ammunition and morale. But they had also dug in on the soggy, forward side of the ford. The unit had a choice of fight or die. Crossing the ford with the Posleen at their backs would be a losing proposition.

It was a desperate position to take, almost suicidal. But unless someone got their thumbs out and reinforced them, the surprise strike by the Posleen would turn the flank of the entire Fourth Armored Division. In a situation like this Thomas knew his duty. Place his soldiers on the deadliest ground possible; when the choice is death or death, soldiers tend to fight the hardest. It was the oldest military axiom in the book.

The heavy vegetation of Barwhon had prevented engaging the centaurs at maximum range, so it was the sort of point-blank shootout that favored the Posleen. Thomas grunted in anger as his Second platoon's machine gun section was taken out by a wash of plasma fire, then snarled as the first God King made an appearance.

There were several ways to distinguish the God Kings of the Posleen from the combatant "normals" that made up the bulk of the Posleen forces. The first thing was that they were larger than normals, being about seventeen hands at the complex double shoulder versus the normal's fourteen to fifteen hands. The second thing was that they had high feathery crests running along their backs and opening forward like the ceremonial headdress of the plains Indians. But the main way to distinguish a God King from its bonded normals was the silvery ground-effect saucer it rode.

The device was not only transportation. A pintle-mounted heavy weapon—in this case a hypervelocity missile launcher—bespoke its prime reason for existence. In addition the vehicle mounted a mass of sophisticated sensors. Some God Kings used them actively, others passively, but the sensor suite was just as dangerous in its own way as the heavy weapon. Denying information to the enemy is the second oldest lesson of warfare.

However, in the last year of give-and-take in the jungles of Barwhon V humans had learned a few lessons about fighting God Kings. All the heavy weapons of the company redirected their fire to the forces around the saucer as the company's sniper targeted the God King and its vehicle.

Well before the units had left the blue-and-white ball of Terra, the American military had begun modifying their weapons to deal with the changed threat. First the venerable M-16 had been replaced with a heavier caliber rifle capable of stopping the horse-sized Posleen. In addition there had been changes to the sniper force.

Ever since snipers were reactivated as a position in the 1980s there had been debates about the appropriate standard rifle. The debate was ended by a special operations group deployed to Barwhon. The only reason that any of the reconnaissance team survived to see the green hills of Earth was the use of a .50 caliber rifle by the team's sniper.

The debate went on over the use of bolt-action versus semi-automatic. However, that was a debate for military philosophers. The M-82, the semiautomatic "Murfreesboro Five-Oh," had become the weapon of choice.

Now SP4 John Jenkins demonstrated why. He had chosen to set up on a slight mound behind the company and across the gurgling ford from the likely direction of contact. His coverall, sewn all over with dangling strips of burlap, made him invisible to the naked eye. However, the God King's sensors would not be fooled. To avoid having the sniper detected, the company had to cover his actions with mass fire.

As the M-60s of the three line platoons took the forces around the God King under heavy fire the specialist triggered a single round from the thirty-pound sniper rifle. His two-hundred-pound body rocked from the recoil and the saturated ground under him squished in shock.

The round that the rifle used was essentially the same one used by the time-honored M-2 .50 caliber machine gun. Three times the size of a .30-06 round, it had a muzzle velocity normally associated with antiaircraft cannons. A fraction of a second after the recoil shoved the heavy-set sniper backwards, the armor-piercing bullet struck the saucer to the left of the pintle base.

The Teflon-coated tungsten-cored bullet penetrated the cover of an innocuous box at the God King's feet. Then it penetrated the slightly heavier interior wall. After that it passed through a crystalline matrix. It would have passed entirely through the matrix but its passage had disturbed the delicate balance of the power crystals that drove the heavy antigravity sled.

The power crystals used a charge field to hold molecules in a state of high-order flexion which permitted tremendous energy to be stored by the crystals. However, the flexion was maintained by a small field generator embedded deep in the matrix. When the dynamic shock of the bullet shattered the field generator, the energy of the crystals was released in a blast equivalent to half a ton of high explosives.

The God King vanished in a green actinic flash along with better than half his company as the shrapnel from the shattered saucer washed outward. The fireball consumed the two dozen remaining senior normals immediately around the saucer and the blast and shrapnel killed better than a hundred and fifty more.

The first volley of cluster ammunition artillery seemed almost anticlimactic to Captain Thomas. The next wave of Posleen disagreed.

❖   ❖   ❖

"Echo Three Five this is Pappa One Six, over," Thomas whispered hoarsely. The past two hours had been a blur of charging Posleen, hammering artillery and dying soldiers. He felt that they were about done. He blew on his hand to warm it and stared out at the battle-field. The slope down to their position was littered with Posleen corpses but the damn horses just kept coming. As usual, there was no way to tell how many more there were—aerial reconnaissance was a distant memory in the face of the God King sensors and weap-ons. But there were at least two thousand scattered in front of his company. The bare hundred soldiers he had brought to the table had destroyed twenty times their number.

However, the horrific casualty ratios were beside the point. He was down to less than a reinforced platoon and the next push should slice through them like a hot knife through butter. The problem with fighting the Posleen was rarely killing them; the problem was kill-ing enough of them to matter. Unless the promised reinforcements arrived he was going to have destroyed his whole company for nothing. Having been on Barwhon since the first day the Allied Expeditionary Force arrived, the captain could handle killing his entire company. It had happened before and it would happen again; the unit had had two hundred percent turnover in personnel in the last year. But it irked him when it was for nothing.

He dropped back into his water-filled foxhole. The cold, viscous liquid came up to his waist when he sat on the bottom. He ignored the discomfort—mud was as common on Barwhon as death—slid another clip of twenty-millimeter grenades into his AIW and called brigade again. "Echo Three Five this is Pappa One Six, over." No response. He pulled a steel mirror out of his thigh pocket and held it up where he could see the battlefield. The tired officer shook his head, put the mirror away and jacked a grenade into place.

He moved to a kneeling position and took a deep breath. With a convulsive lunge he popped up and fired a string of grenades into a set of normals that looked ready to charge.

In general, once their God Kings were killed the normals gave one burst for glory then ran. But some of them were more aggressive than others. This group was hanging around, exchanging some fairly effec-tive fire and generally being a pain in the ass. Since most of his troops were scrounging ammunition, patching wounds and preparing for the next heavy assault they did not have time to deal with harass-ment. This would have been Jenkins's job, but he had bought it almost an hour before. So the company commander spun another group of grenades at the idiot centaurs, dropped back into his hole and switched out magazines. Again. Overhead flechette rounds flailed his

hole for a moment and then stopped. Posleen normals were so stupid
they had eclipsed all other ethnic jokes.

"Echo Three Five, this is Pappa One Six," he whispered into the
microphone. "We are under heavy attack. Estimate regimental strength
or better. We need reinforcements. Over." His company was good;
after this long they had to be. But ten-to-one odds was a little much
without prepared defenses. Hell, ten-to-one against the Posleen *with*
prepared defenses was a little much. What was needed was a concrete or rubble wall and a moat filled with punji stakes. Not a company on the ass-end of nowhere and barely enough time to dig in.
No mines, no claymores, no concertina and damn sure no support.

The radio crackled. "Pappa One Six, this is Echo Three Five, actual."
At that moment Captain Thomas knew he was screwed. If the brigade commander was calling it could only mean the shit had truly
hit the fan.

"Situation understood. The second of the one-ninety-eighth was
ambushed during movement to reinforce you. We have at least
another regiment moving uncoordinated in the brigade's rear area."

In the pause Thomas closed his eyes in realization of what that
meant. With over two thousand Posleen in the brigade's vulnerable
rear, there was no way they were going to be able to spare reinforcements.

"Your retreat route is impassable, Captain. There are Posleen all
over it." There was another pause. The sigh at the other end was clear
even over the frequency-clipping radio. "It is imperative that you hold
your position. If we have time we can handle this. But if another
oolt'ondar breaks in right now the whole salient will be in jeopardy."
There was another pause as the colonel on the other end of the phone
tried to find something else to say.

Captain Thomas thought about what it must be like to be on the
other end of the phone. The brigade commander had been here as long
as Thomas and they knew each other well; the commander had pinned
on Thomas's first lieutenant and captain's bars. Now he was sitting in
the heated tactical operations center, staring at the radio, telling one
of his subordinate commanders that the situation had just murdered
him. That he and his whole unit were nothing but centaur fodder. And
that they not only had to die, but that they had to die as hard as possible. Die alone and forlorn in the cold purple mists.

Half the unit was veterans, the usual proportion in experienced
combat units. After the first week of firefights most of the non-
survivors were gone. As time went by the occasional veteran would
be killed and the occasional newbie would survive. The two-hundred-
percent turnover generally occurred in the newbies who did not learn

fast enough. At this point in the battle Captain Thomas figured that most of the newbies had already bought it and those remaining were mainly veterans. That meant that they might just die as hard as brigade wanted them to.

He shook his head and stared up into the violet sky. He closed his eyes for just a moment and tried to conjure up the sky over Kansas. The smell of baking wheat and the hot, dry wind of the prairie. The blue bowl of the sky on a cool autumn day as the sky seemed to stretch to infinity. Then with a final sigh he switched the radio to the local frequency and keyed the mike.

Staff Sergeant Bob Duncan closed the sightless eyes of the captain and looked around.

The autoprojector of his helmet system sensed the tensing of his neck muscles and swiveled the viewpoint around the area of the ford. Target points and intelligence information—trickled deep into his eyes by tiny laser diodes—cascaded across his view unnoticed. Calculations of Posleen and human casualties flickered across the top of his view as the artificial intelligence that drove the armor calculated blood stains and damage assessment. The soft puffs of recycled air that drifted across his mouth and nose were, fortunately, devoid of smell. Nannites swarmed across his eyelids, automatically collecting the water that threatened to drown the vision tunnel.

The powered combat armor automatically adjusted the light levels so they remained constant. The resulting lack of shadows gave the scenery a flat look. After a year and a half of combat Duncan had become so used to it the effect was unnoticeable unless he took his armor off. Since that had last happened nearly six weeks before, "real" vision seemed abnormal.

The advancing Posleen forces had done their usual bang-up job of removing all the corpses from the battlefield. Since humans and Posleen were both edible, they considered humans nothing but tactical problems or rations. The Posleen word for human was "threshkreen." It translated more or less as "food with a stinger." Which made the captain's unmolested body all the more unusual.

Duncan picked up the stick thrust into the ground beside the officer. Duncan had seen one exactly twice before, both times when bodies of commanders were left unmolested. This time, however, the body was on a mound of dirt that must have taken some time to construct. Duncan examined the indecipherable writing on the stick for a moment then picked the stiffening corpse up in his arms. The body's weight was as nothing to the powered battle armor, light as a feather with the soul fled to some region beyond this blood-torn realm. He started trotting.

"Duncan," called his platoon sergeant, first noting the movement on sensors then turning to eyeball the retreating suit. "Where the hell do you think you're going?"

Duncan appeared deaf. He continued to trot back along the trail the suits had used to retake the ford. Here was where the Posleen regiment from the ford had made its stand. The gigantic trees of the Barwhon jungle were flayed, their branches stripped of leaves, massive trunks shattered from heavy-weapons fire.

There was where the last of the scattered Posleen regiment had been overrun. A final pile of bodies indicated where the normals piled on their beleaguered God Kings in a last-ditch attempt to save them from the advancing armored monsters. A pile of combat suits attested to their effectiveness when cornered.

There was where the suits had been ambushed in turn. A God King corpse—pooling yellow blood staining the ground—was sprawled across a shattered suit awaiting recovery. No miracles of modern technology for that trooper; the readouts of the armor showed the telltale signs of a penetration.

Once a Posleen penetrator round entered a suit it tended to stay inside, caroming around like a blender blade. The only sign of damage on the armor was a tiny hole. It still leaked red. Private Arnold was a newbie and with his pureeing the company of one hundred and thirty nominal suits was down to fifty-two functional. That fifty-two had been reduced to forty by the time the unit retook the ford.

Duncan continued on in the ground-eating lope of the armored combat suits. His mind was a blank, without purpose or desire, simply cruising on autopilot.

He finally entered the area of the brigade command. The scattered positions were already being reconsolidated. The damaged vehicles were under repair or being towed off as graves' registration teams moved around "taggin' and baggin' " the bodies of the dead soldiers. Each of the casualties was being fitted with a tag indicating name, location, unit and general nature of death; then the bodies were loaded into black plastic body bags for processing and burial. The cleanup crews would get to the swath of destruction from the armored combat suits in their own good time. The swath from the Posleen, of course, would not need them.

Duncan finally slowed as he neared the brigade's tactical operations center. He noted without caring the expressions on the faces of the MPs at the entrance and the platoon of troops dug-in around the command post.

The Galactic-supplied combat suits were made without any face shields; their visual repeaters took the place of that possible weakness. The MPs and security troops were faced with a featureless front of faceted plasteel that was impregnable to any Terrestrial weapon; a similar suit had survived a blast from a nuclear weapon. Although there were a few hypervelocity missile launchers in the area, there were none at the TOC. So there was no stopping this juggernaut unless reason or orders worked.

One of the MPs decided to try. She was either braver or more foolish than her fellow as she stepped out into Duncan's path and held up a hand like a traffic cop.

"Hold it right there, soldier. I don't care if you *are* Fleet, you don't have authorit—" Duncan never even slowed and the half-ton suit tossed her aside like a rag doll. Her fellow MP rushed to her side but other than a bruised rib and an assault on her dignity she was unharmed.

The TOC was three prefabricated structures hooked together. The doors were not designed to accommodate armored combat suits but that was moot. The door and frame resisted his suit as well as wet tissue paper and he continued through the briefing area and down a short hall to the commander's office. The startled brigade staff followed him.

The brigade commander had his door open. He watched the battle-scorched apparition stalk down the hall towards him without expression. The suit was covered in gouges from glancing hits and splattered with drying Posleen blood. It looked like a mechanical demon from some hell devoted to battle. As the commander recognized who was cradled in the arms of the suit his expression altered, becoming terrible and fey.

Duncan walked up to the commander's desk and gently set the captain's husk on the scattered papers. One of Barwhon's ubiquitous beetles hovered over the open mouth and terribly disfigured face. The mortal blow of a Posleen combat blade had opened the side of Thomas's head like an egg.

Duncan tapped a control on the forearm of the suit, activating the surface speakers. "I brought him home," he said.

The colonel continued to stare up at the angled slab of plasteel armor in front of his desk. The suit radiated heat from blows of kinetic energy weapons, and the stink of putrefying Posleen was thick and hot. He started to open his mouth to speak, but stopped and worked his mouth as if trying to clear his throat.

"I brought him home," said Duncan again, and laid the stick across the captain's body.

The symbol was one that had become universally familiar since the landing. Many were to be found among the rear area troopers, each supposedly authentic. In fact there had only been eight confirmed recoveries of them and the real ones were all accounted for, all carefully laid to rest with their owners. Between them the owners of the staffs had collected four Medals of Honor, three Distinguished Service Crosses and Silver Stars innumerable. The staff alone was guarantee of at least the Star. The colonel's hand went over his mouth and unmanly tears coursed down his cheeks at the sight of the ninth. He cleared his throat again and took a deep breath.

"Thank you, Sergeant," he said, tearing his eyes away from the warrior staff. "Thank you." The suit was swaying in front of his eyes and for a moment he thought it was an optical illusion. But it was soon apparent it was not. Duncan dropped to his knees with a rumble that shook the flimsy building and wrapped his arms around himself.

What was going on inside the suit was impossible to discern, but the colonel had a very good idea. He got up and walked around the desk, with a passing pat on the shoulder to his former subordinate now leaking red all over a report titled "Manpower Requirements FY 2003." The colonel crouched down and put his arm around the shoulders of the gigantic suit.

"Come on, Sergeant," he said as tears continued to course down his cheek. "Let's get you out of that suit."

◆ CHAPTER 2 ◆

It shouldn't oughta be this way, thought Lieutenant Colonel Frederic (Fred) Hanson.

The incoming commander of the First Battalion Five-Fifty-Fifth Mobile Infantry Regiment had years before retired from the Army as an Eighty-Second Airborne Division brigade executive officer. He was familiar from long experience with monumental screwups, but this one took the grand prize.

The way a unit is usually activated—from scratch or from "regimental reserve"—is from the top down. The commanders of the activated units would meet with their officers and work through a plan of activation. The plan could either be supplied or one they developed themselves. In good time the various senior noncommissioned officers would arrive, usually with the subordinate commanders and staff. Then the soldiers would arrive, before the staff was ready but after all the officers and NCOs basically had their feet under them. The equipment would arrive, training schedules would be finalized and the units would begin to come together. Slowly they would become a unit instead of a collection of individuals. In time they would be sent off to war—rarely are units pulled from storage in peacetime—and the hard work of the formation would be forgotten in the harder work of combat.

Under the best of circumstances it is a careful dance of supplying the right number of officers and NCOs along with their equipment. In any war the cannon fodder is the easiest to lay your hands on and trained and confident junior officers the hardest.

13

In the case of the First Battalion, Five-Fifty-Fifth MIR—or for that matter any of the battalions forming throughout the world—the process did not occur so smoothly. Fred Hanson thought he had seen every possible combination of mistakes the United States Army had in store. As the borrowed Humvee pulled into the activation area he was forced to admit he was wrong. This time the Army had made one small mistake, actually microscopic, with macroscopic implications.

The Terran Ground Defense Commands—the various national armies of earth—were not worried about trained personnel. In return for humanity's help in battling the Posleen, one of the first technologies offered by the Galactic Federation was a rejuvenation process. A long-retired senior officer could take a graduated series of shots, possibly go through a few simple surgical procedures, and drop away years. Within a few weeks, months at most, the patient would end up an apparent twenty or so. Thus many of the senior military personnel retired over the previous decades were available for recall in a time of planetary need. There was, however, one tiny difficulty.

The rejuvenation program was matrixed on a combination of final rank and present age. An E-9, a Sergeant Major in the Army or a Senior Master Chief in the Navy, would be called up if he or she were within forty years of service, an E-8 within 39. The scale progressed down to the point where a soldier or sailor who left the service as an E-1 could be called up within twenty years of service. Officers followed a similar matrix.

The personnel of the first enlisted and officer ranks who had been out of service longest were the first called up and rejuvenated. Thus, in the United States, there was a sudden influx of extremely senior officers and NCOs, many of whom last heard a shot fired in anger during the Tet Offensive.

Simultaneously there was a general call-up of personnel shortly out of service and a universal draft. This created a rush of lower-ranking officers and NCOs along with a mass of low-rank enlisted. The rejuv program was designed to supply an equivalent number of field-grade officers, the military's equivalent of middle management.

There was a gap, but there would be more than sufficient capacity to provide command structure and unit integrity. For the first time in the history of an emergency call-up, there would be an overabundance of trained enlisted and commissioned personnel.

The two programs were carefully and strategically timed so that there would be enough recalled senior officers and NCOs to fill all the slots allotted to them. If all went well, before the second lieutenants, first lieutenants and captains along with their respective platoon sergeants and first sergeants got to their units, the brigade and battalion commanders and staff would be in place with their feet on the ground, their "warpaint" on, and an activation plan ready to get into gear.

Unfortunately for the plan, about the time the rejuvenation program reached the level of master sergeants and full colonels, brigade commanders and very senior staff officers, the nannites started to run low. While Galactic technology was impressive, Galactic production capacity was hampered by cottage-industry techniques. As with combat technology, human techniques were slowly gaining currency. That did not, however, help with the critical nannite shortage.

There was virtually no way to slow down the training and deployment of the new draft and the recalled prior service that did not need rejuvenation, so suddenly the Army and Navy had a whole bunch of chiefs and quite a few Indians but not many people to help them communicate.

Colonel Hanson had been briefed on the situation so the sight of trailers stretching off into the distance was not a shock, but the conditions were.

The area was a former live-fire range. He had spent one hot nasty week there as an observer/controller and he remembered it well. Now it was the snowy home of two regular infantry divisions and a Fleet Strike Armored Combat Suit battalion along with support for the activated but still widely distributed Twenty-eighth Mechanized Division formerly of the Pennsylvania Army National Guard.

There were twenty-six thousand personnel on the Table of Organization and Equipment of an infantry division and almost eight hundred in an ACS battalion. Hanson was one of the first crop of O-5 and below to be rejuvenated and he knew that this seething mass of humanity was critically short on senior officers.

The trailers were laid out in battalion and brigade formations with the battalion offices to the notional front and the battalion commander's, staff's, and senior NCOs' housing to either side. To either side of this "headshed" formation was a company street. Stretching down one side of the company street behind the battalion area were the company offices surrounded by officers' and senior NCOs' quarters and supply. Across the street were the enlisted barracks. Each enlisted barracks held fourteen personnel in six two-man rooms and two single rooms for squad leaders.

The companies of one battalion backed on a parade field; across the field was another battalion and the process started again. However, there were over nine thousand trailers in a mass a couple of miles on a side. And, although the personnel were theoretically barracked with NCOs nearby, most of these people were not even soldiers yet, much less units, and the senior NCOs, E-6s, -7s and -8s, were virtually absent.

By the time the rejuv situation turned critical, the pipeline was already full of incoming soldiers. Since basic trainees need constant supervision, the majority of the incoming senior NCOs were going to training units. Battalions in that seething mass were being commanded by captains and companies by brand-new second lieutenants. Most of the companies had staff sergeants as first sergeants, if they were lucky, and often only sergeant E-5s. Without the backbone of a solid NCO and officer corps, command and control was spotty. The children were all home but the parents were trickling in late.

So he had been told by the G-1 Personnel Officer of the Fifteenth Mechanized Infantry Division, and the picture was worse than any briefing could paint. He saw sections of the canton where control had obviously broken down completely. There was laundry strung on the walls of the barracks, garbage littering the company streets and soldiers openly fighting. Groups of soldiers huddled around fires, some of them in shreds of uniform that must barely be fighting off the Pennsylvania winter cold. One block was a mass of fire-torn trailers where a party had apparently gotten out of hand. Other areas were orderly, reflecting the attitudes of the junior officers and NCOs put in charge.

Without his battalion commanders and brigade and battalion staffs in place, the activation commander effectively had his hands tied. There was absolutely no way for a few generals, a handful of "bird" colonels and some sergeant majors to police fifty thousand people. The entire activation had been based on the rejuv program and with that prop kicked out it had fallen apart. Food and supplies were arriving and that was all the rampant juvenile delinquents in the cantonment cared about.

As the Humvee pulled into "his" battalion area Colonel Hanson wanted to cry. It was one of the "bad" areas, the kind of block he would have been loath to walk in without a weapon and body armor. He gestured for the driver to pull down a company street and was appalled. The battalion area was nice enough. It had a rock-bordered entrance to the headquarters and the sidewalks were shoveled and swept. But with one exception the company areas were a disgrace. He could see sections of the barracks that had been ripped away in apparently casual vandalism and garbage covered the ground.

As the driver swung around the back side of the battalion area he saw that the last company was quite neat. Furthermore it had posted guards clad in Fleet Strike gray "combat silks" outside the company offices and was running two-man patrols between the barracks. Since the weapons were M-300 grav-guns the show of force was impressive. The M-300 weighed twenty-three pounds—the same as the Vietnam-era M-60 machine gun which it resembled—but most of the soldiers in sight handled them easily. Their obvious fitness and gray combat silks were the first good news he had seen.

The thin uniforms were supposed to be proof against any normal cold and so it seemed; the lightly clad soldiers were handling the windy winter day with aplomb. Although combat silks were officially the daily uniform of Fleet Strike units, most personnel elsewhere in the battalion seemed to be wearing BDUs and field jackets. It also answered the question of whether any GalTech equipment was available. What the acting battalion commander had to say about wearing the uniform might be instructive. Colonel Hanson wondered why the rest of the battalion was out of uniform and where he was going to get his own set of silks.

He gestured for the driver to pull up in front of the company headquarters.

"Go take my bags to my quarters. Then head back to headquarters." He wished he could keep him—the kid seemed well turned out and smart—but the G-1 had been specific, "Send the driver back along with his Humvee, clear?"

"Yes, sir."

"If anybody gives you any flack over at my quarters, come get me. I'll be with the Bravo Company commander." He gestured at the company headquarters with a thumb.

"Yes, sir."

As Colonel Hanson headed up the snowy path to the trailer the two guards came to attention to a barked "Atten-hut" from the right-hand guard. The guard could see that it was just a baby-faced kid walking into the headquarters, but the kid had been riding in a Humvee and wheels were hard to find. Ergo, it was not a kid; it was a rejuvenated officer or NCO and it looked like an officer. When the private first class finally determined that the black rank on the kid's BDU collar was oak leaves, he blessed his prescience. The two dropped back to parade rest at a returned salute and traded shrugs after the colonel entered the trailer. The senior private blew on his frigid hands and gave a quiet smile. By the appearance of the commander, things were going to go either very well or very poorly for Bravo Company. And he was willing to take book which it would be.

Colonel Hanson was surprised and pleased to see a CQ—a sergeant detailed for a twenty-four-hour period to be in charge of the company area—standing behind a table inside the door at the position of attention. The slight, dark-haired sergeant, who did not look old enough to shave, saluted.

"Sir, Sergeant Stewart, Bravo Company, First Battalion, Five-Fifty-Fifth Mobile Infantry. How may I help you, sir?"

The sergeant was either a refurb, or well trained, and Colonel Hanson could not tell off-the-cuff which it was.

"Well, Sergeant," he said, returning the salute, "you can show me to the company commander's office and get me a cup of coffee if it's available. Water if not."

"*Yes, sir,*" said the sergeant, rather too loudly. Fred wondered why, until he realized that it would probably be audible through the paper-thin walls. He smiled internally as the sergeant continued in the same loud tone. "If the *Colonel* will just follow me to the *commander's office,* I'll see about the *coffee!*" Colonel Hanson kept from laughing with only marginal success as a small snort slipped out.

"Pardon, sir?" asked Sergeant Stewart as he led the colonel down a corridor on one side of the trailer.

"Cough."

"Yes, sir."

The narrow passage to one side of the trailer passed one door labeled "Swamp," a second labeled "Latrine" and a third, which showed signs of repair, labeled "First Sergeant." At the end of the corridor the area opened out to reveal a desk with someone who was probably the company clerk behind it at attention. On the table was a cup of coffee and the private's position was ruined by having a pitcher of cream in his left hand. He saluted.

"Cream, sir?"

"Black. Do you have sugar?"

"Sir!" The private held up a handful of packets.

"One, please." The sugar was dumped and stirred as Sergeant Stewart knocked on the door.

"Enter," came a raspy voice from the interior.

Normally on taking over a unit the incoming commander had the option of studying his officers' open records—their 201 files as they were called—and the officers' efficiency reports. In addition he was able to discuss the strengths and weaknesses of his subordinate personnel with the outgoing commander. In this case the G-1 admitted he was only able to provide the officers' names, and that with difficulty. The information systems were as confused as everything else and in most cases officers' files were still in storage in St. Louis. All that Colonel Hanson remembered was that his Bravo Company commander was named O'Neal.

"Sir, a Lieutenant Colonel Hanson is here to see you," Stewart said through the doorway, respectfully.

Colonel Hanson had pegged Stewart immediately as one of those individuals in any command who can make or break a small unit. He would have to be in charge of something and needed to respect his leaders or he would be running all over them in short order. So the deference he showed towards his company commander told Fred something. Of course the condition of the company had told Colonel Hanson something already but that could be due to several causes. This Captain O'Neal could have an enormously effective senior sergeant, he could be a martinet, and so forth. But O'Neal had at least one hard case eating out of his hand and that said everything necessary about his leadership. Now if he only had some tactical sense.

Thus Fred Hanson thought he showed admirable control when a squat juggernaut who, despite the faint sheen of sweat from a recent workout, was immediately recognizable from numerous TV appearances rolled through the door. Hanson noticed in passing the scars still on O'Neal's forearm as the captain saluted.

"Captain Michael O'Neal, sir, Commander, Bravo Company First Battalion, Five-Fifty-Fifth Mobile Infantry Regiment. How may I help you, sir?"

Fred Hanson slowly returned the salute, as properly as he had ever done in his life. That's how you do it when returning the salute of a holder of the Medal of Honor.

"Lieutenant Colonel Frederic Hanson," said the colonel into the silence. "I'm about to assume command of the One-Five-Five-Five and I thought you might like to come along."

Fred thought he saw a brief flash of suppressed glee go across O'Neal's face but the shuffle of Stewart's boots was the only sound in the silence that followed that announcement.

"Yes, sir. I'd like that main well. Stewart, go find the Gunny then come up to battalion."

"Yes, sir."

"Shall we?" asked the baby-faced battalion commander.

"After you, sir," answered O'Neal, his eyes shining.

"I think that went rather well," said the colonel, shutting the door on the departing major.

"Yes, sir. I think Major Stidwell will be a real asset at post headquarters," agreed O'Neal. "Although he might want to be a tad more careful about who he calls a 'snot-nosed kid' next time."

"I also suspect," continued the colonel with a slight grin at the memory, "that despite whatever damage this might have done to his career, any complaints that Major Stidwell might voice will be pro forma."

"Surely you're not questioning the major's, uhm, intestinal fortitude are you, sir?"

"Not really," Colonel Hanson said, glancing over the battalion commander's desk at his most junior company commander. The new battalion commander started taking down the late Major Stidwell's extensive "I-love-me" wall. As a piece or individually it was impressive. From his West Point diploma to his graduation from Command and Staff College Major Stidwell seemed to have all the merit badges any field-grade infantry officer could ever wish. A graduate of both Ranger School and Special Forces Qualification Course, when in uniform Major Stidwell would be entitled to wear the "Tower of Power": the three stacked tabs of Ranger, Special Forces and Airborne qualification. He was a holder of the PT badge and probably could make a fire with only two sticks.

But somewhere along the line the major had somehow missed the whole concept. What was conspicuously absent were plaques from previous commands. There were two possibilities and, without having seen his personnel file, Colonel Hanson could not decide which was more likely. Either Stidwell was so disliked by his commands that they celebrated his leaving without any sign of regret or he had had very few leadership positions. On second thought, it had to be the latter; some sycophant would always gin up a plaque no matter how disastrous your tenure.

"Although Major Stidwell seems to have all the requisite abilities to be a commander," the colonel professed, gesturing at the wall, "sometimes that does not mean a person has command ability. Often an inability to command can be masked in peacetime by an able staff. However, during times of stress when quick and accurate decisions must be made without benefit of objectively correct answers or able staff support, the inability to lead becomes crystal clear. I suspect that Major Stidwell can function as a junior officer quite well and may even be exemplary as a senior staff officer but is incompetent as a commander, especially a combat commander." He concluded the lecture with a shrug. "It happens."

"Are you supposed to discuss the merits of senior officers with junior officers, sir?" Mike asked, leaning back in a rickety armchair, probably acquired from post stores after being rejected by a dayroom as too old and worn out.

"Well, Captain," the colonel responded, "there are junior officers and junior officers. In your case you can be sure that I will discuss with you anything that I believe will help you in your military development and I will in turn solicit your advice on ACS tactics on a regular basis. I don't intend to take everything you say as gospel. But I *will* listen."

"Because of the Medal?" Mike asked with studied casualness as he pulled a cigar out of the sleeve of his gray silks.

It was not the first time Colonel Hanson had heard of Michael O'Neal. He was *That* O'Neal. Mighty Mite. Ironman O'Neal, the hero of Diess. Colonel Hanson had known more than one real hero in his military career and he knew that without being there it was impossible to determine what actions might or might not have occurred when a medal, especially the Medal, was handed out. Sometimes the most heroic stories turned out to be so much bullshit while others that seemed simple turned out to be unexpectedly complex. Some real heroes were braggarts, some quiet. Often heroes were simply in the wrong place and survived. Sometimes everything was exactly as indicated.

In the case of Michael O'Neal, the sequence of events that led to him being showered with medals was as analyzed, dissected and researched as any sequence in the history of military operations. When the media got as carried away as they did with O'Neal's story there was an inevitable reaction. First he was idolized, then the media tried to pick the story apart. It never found any detail to be any less than it appeared at first glance. Arguably the story had been understated.

As an advisor on armored combat suit tactics to the Diess Expeditionary Force, then-Lieutenant O'Neal had taken command of remnants of the Armored Combat Suit battalion to which he was attached after it had a drastic encounter with the first wave of Posleen. The platoon-sized band, initially weaponless due to a fuel-air explosion that had swept away their suit-mounted weaponry, ended up breaking the Posleen siege of the armored divisions of the expeditionary force. Along the way they killed a plurality of the Posleen in the attack and destroyed a Posleen command ship that had come in for close support of the Posleen forces. O'Neal had accomplished this last feat by the simple expedient of flying his command suit up to the ship and detonating an improvised antimatter limpet mine by hand.

The armor enclosing the young man across from him, who was now examining a cigar as if it were a weapon on guard mount, had been blown five kilometers through the air and several buildings. Finally that particular bit of detritus along with what was left of O'Neal had skipped a further two kilometers out to sea and sunk.

Weeks later it was found by a SEAL recovery team homing in on the automated beacon and glad to find a half a billion credits' worth of combat suit partially intact. To their surprise the armor announced that the occupant was viable.

"Not just the medal. More the way you kept your company together. That's the sign of a good commander."

"Good command team, sir, pardon the correction. Gunny Pappas is tops."

"They sent us a Marine? I thought they were mostly going to Fleet." The way that the Galactic Federation fought the war against the Posleen had caused numerous schisms in the way the United States military did its job. The aliens' Federation supported their Fleet from funds drawn on all two hundred-plus planets of the Federation.

However, planets that were actively engaged against the Posleen had to fund their own ground defenses. In the case of established planets, corporations whose trade would be affected drew on multiple planets to fund the defense. The planet Diess, which O'Neal had served on, drew forces from the spectrum of Earth's armies. However, the planet Barwhon, which despite its lack of industry had more monetary resources to draw on, was being defended only by "NATO" troops.

Since Earth had only heard of the Federation three and a half years before, it was without any monetary support other than whatever it could raise by selling its military forces to the highest bidder, which also served to train Earth's forces for its own impending invasion, now less than two years away. Despite the situation, it seemed impossible to become politically cohesive and prepare as one planet for the invasion. This caused a number of compromises.

Some Fleet Strike forces were detailed directly to the Fleet, while others were detailed to the planets either under attack or about to be attacked. In the case of the Earth, those units detailed to Terran defense were to be retained for their parent countries' usage, while still being under the Fleet's regulations and chain of command. However, Fleet personnel were drawn primarily from Terran navies. And Fleet Strike forces—the ground combat, special operations and fighter forces—were drawn from each country's Marine, Aviation and Special Operations units.

Because of the size of the United States and NATO's Navy, Marines, Airborne and Special Operations, the defense Fleet was heavily influenced by NATO with Russia and China a close second. Virtually every Fleet Strike ground unit was found in those four areas with one battalion in Japan. There were howls of outrage over the patent injustice from the Third World, but this time nobody had time to listen.

The force situation and alien technology had modified some long-standing traditions in the United States military. Fleet Strike's American contingent now consisted of the First through Fourth Fleet Strike Divisions, drawn from the Marines, the 82nd, 101st and 11th Divisions along with the 508th, 509th, 555th, and 565th Separate Regiments, all drawn from the Airborne. The Marine and Airborne Units were or would soon be Armored Combat Suit units, mobile infantry units whose personnel fought encased in powered battle armor and wielded grav-guns that hurled depleted uranium teardrops at relativistic speeds or plasma cannons that could go through the side of a World War II battleship.

Since the Fleet Strike personnel placement system no longer recognized a difference between Marine and Airborne there were occasional situations that were extremely nontraditional. A Marine Gunnery Sergeant might be ordered to a unit that was drawn from the Airborne tradition or an Airborne commander put in charge of a Marine unit. There were more Airborne personnel and senior officers than Marine, so to cantilever the Airborne influence all senior battalion and brigade NCOs could be called "Gunny" although the actual rank was being slowly phased out. Fleet Strike's American Command Post, however, was at Twenty Nine Palms, a former Marine base. And their dress uniforms, while drawing heavily on certain well-known science fiction TV shows, were dark blue piped with red, the color of Marine Dress Blues. The Airborne establishment found itself busy playing catch-up.

A small ceremonial contingent of American Marines remained, passing back and forth between Fleet and the Presidential Guard. They were the only Terran forces under the sole and direct command of a country that wore battle armor. America, with not only tremendous economic clout but equally great military renown, was the only country with an off-planet credit high enough to afford the incredibly expensive suits.

"Yes, sir," said O'Neal with a characteristic frown. "An actual Marine Gunny, long, long service. He's a hippie."

"Hippie?"

"What they call a Vietnam vet. *Real* old timer."

"Well, I suppose us hippies will have to talk over old times," said the commander with a smile.

"Jesus, sir!" said Mike, looking at the apparently teenage colonel in surprise. "You're for real?"

"I took a company of the One-Oh-One into Happy Valley in

Vietnam," said the colonel with a suppressed shudder at the memory. "I started off as a butter bar with the One-Eighty-Seventh."

"Hmmm. Well, at least I won't have to explain who Janis Joplin is."

"It is damn strange, isn't it?" said the commander, tossing another piece of "I-Love-Me" claptrap into a box. "How the hell do you separate the wheat from the chaff? The regimental commander is forty years younger than me. When I was retiring he was a second lieutenant. I'm glad I didn't know him; I can imagine what my memories of him would do to our relationship."

"What about his memories of you, sir? Can you imagine if you wrote him a bad OER back when?"

"However, like your first sergeant . . ."

"He's a Marine," said O'Neal with a chuckle. "Yes, sir, I know. Well, as long as we don't have to take any beaches everything should be fine. Actually I kind of prefer a Marine for this."

Colonel Hanson looked at him quizzically as he dropped the last plaque into the box. "*Pourquois?*"

Mike suddenly looked grim as he held up the cigar with his own querying expression. At a nod he lit it with a Zippo emblazoned with a black panther on a rock. Drawing in a series of puffs he said, "Well, sir . . ." puff, "the Airborne has a tradition," puff, puff, "of in and out. Wham-bam-thank-you-ma'am." Puff. "Also, the Airborne tradition is, practically, for hit and run." Deep draw, puff. "Hmmm, El Sol Imperials. Damn hard to find, what with the shortages." He dropped the affectation with a sudden intensity, stabbing the cigar as if to drive in the points.

"This situation is much more like the Marine tradition, especially the tradition of World War II and Korea. Take a hard objective. Hold it against all comers, against human-wave attacks with critical shortages and damn little support. Hold at all cost and die to the last stinking soldier if necessary, killing as many as humanly possible the whole time. No retreat, no surrender, no quarter. Sir."

Mike had a sudden vision of a narrow clay street with towering skyscrapers to either side. The street was packed with yellow centaurs, the horse-sized invaders in a bayonet to boma-blade battle with a beleaguered German panzer grenadier division. The bodies of the Posleen and Germans were piled in mounds, blocking his way. Their red and yellow bloods had commingled and an orange river was flowing into the alien sea.

He tilted his head down and fiddled for a moment with his cigar as he struggled to throw off the flashback. "Damn, it went out."

Colonel Hanson dropped into his swivel chair as Mike pulled the

Zippo back out. He reached into his breast pocket and produced a pack of Marlboro Reds. It had taken him years to break the habit, but the Galactics had a pill to do that now and besides they had eliminated cancer, heart disease and emphysema for military personnel so . . . "You okay, Captain?" he asked as he tapped out a coffin nail.

"Yes, sir. I am just peachy-keen," said Mike, meeting his eye steadily.

"I . . . we cannot afford a shell-shocked commander."

"Sir, I'm not shell-shocked," disagreed O'Neal, against the cacophony of internal voices. "What I am is one of the damn few people you are going to meet short of Barwhon or Diess who is prepared, mentally, for this invasion. I had gamed it for thousands of hours, before Diess. Diess was, so to speak, just the icing on the cake. When you get your AID you can cross-check me on it." He took a pull on the cigar. Since Diess he had been hitting both tobacco and alcohol kind of hard. One of these days it was gonna catch up with him. "This war is going to be a form of hell, sir, for every single American. The shit just doesn't get any deeper than this."

Colonel Hanson nodded thoughtfully. That made a lot of sense. "Which brings us to the here and now. Now that I have that obnoxious oaf cleared out of my headquarters, what's the situation? The G-1 didn't even know the players and he had no ideas about ACS equipment, but he did say the supply situation is as confused as could be expected. Who are the acting staff? And since this headquarters seems to be absolutely empty, where the fuck are they?" he concluded.

"Major Stidwell was acting as his own G-3, sir, since that was his slot anyway. Actually, he was doubling up on everything except the -4."

"Maybe I should have given him the benefit of the doubt if he was that overwhelmed," the colonel mused.

"Actually, I wouldn't go so far as to say that, sir. The only reason there is an S-4 is that we got sent a supply officer, a mustang L-T, to the assistant −4 slot. Otherwise, Major My-Lot-In-Life-Is-To-Micromanage Stidwell would undoubtedly have taken that slot as well."

"Oh," said the colonel with a grimace.

"We also have a full set of captains as company commanders, sir, any of whom could have taken a second hat if Stidwell was overwhelmed. We're better off than the Line and Guard units from the point of view of company-grade officers.

"However, if *he* made the decisions he could be absolutely sure that they were the right decisions," the captain said with a snort. "God knows what decisions might have been made by mere captains that did not have his years of experience. They might have, oh, 'taken

excessive initiative with the training schedule,' or, God forbid, 'begun
ACS training before all the meetings about how to implement it were
completed.' "

"If I remember my recent history, you have been there and done
that as well, haven't you?" said the colonel neutrally.

"Yes, sir, I have," said O'Neal with instant seriousness. "As a matter
of fact, he was trying very hard to have me court-martialed for
insubordination."

"Were you insubordinate?" asked the new commander, wondering what sort of answer he would get. He shouldn't have wondered.

"Sir, I disobeyed not one direct order, but so many I can't begin
to count," O'Neal stated definitively.

"Why?"

"I did not think anyone would dare court-martial me, sir, and if
it was disobey them or have my company die in combat it was a no-
brainer."

"Why would they have died?" asked Hanson.

"Sir, he was starting training exactly as they did with the Two
Falcon on Diess. Yes, sir, I have been there and done that before and
I was *not* going to do it again; that was an oath I swore on the souls
of my dead. We had, have, a critical suit shortage, the unit has not
received its issue and only a few of the troops, ones transferred from
other ACS units, have them. So he wanted everyone to memorize all
the parts to the suits, do Posleen flash cards, and all the rest of that.
In other words, bore them to death. What I tried to explain to him
was that I obtained a shit-load of Milspecs, VR glasses for training,
through . . . some secondary channels." Mike cleared his throat and
took a puff of his cigar.

Colonel Hanson smiled. He had to remember that although this
officer had extensive experience with suits and even suit combat, he
did not have extensive experience as an *officer*. Needs must when
devils drive. Since time immemorial, units that were not properly
supplied had found ways of obtaining the equipment they needed.
As long as it was kept to a minimum and under control it was not
a problem.

"We could have been training in the field simulating eighty percent reality combat weeks ago," Mike continued after determining that
the colonel was not going to question him on the source of the
Milspecs. Mike was prepared to back his personnel, but it had surprised him as much as the losing company when second squad
showed up with a truck full of GalTech equipment. Since then, of
course, he had learned all about Sergeant Stewart and "The Squad
From Hell." Now nothing surprised him.

"But that wasn't by the book—which is not my fault, I wanted to include it—so he wouldn't buy it. Then we started having problems with shit being stolen out of the barracks, rioters, vandalism, and all the other fun stuff that has been going down around here. I broke out the 'nail-guns' and got rounds for them from the ammo dump out of the training budget. Forget the rants about extremism; I thought, still do, that it made sense to at least put the weapons in the troop's hands, give them a feel for those big bastards and get in some physical training that made more sense than long slow distance runs. But he wasn't worried about the image or whatever, he was most upset that the rounds couldn't be returned to the dump and were going to be charged against his training budget before he was ready to use them for training."

"Well, I can empathize," said the colonel with a frown. "Live-fire training is expensive."

"Oh, Jesus, sir, not you too!" Mike could feel the iron bite of anger on his tongue and tried to keep under control. The last two months with Stidwell had strained his already damaged patience to the limits. This colonel was an entirely different kettle of fish, though. All he had to do was keep in control and present the situation rationally. Right. And then maybe the dreams would stop?

"Captain, training budgets are just that, budgets. You have to stay in them, especially when everybody is having to make sacrifices for this goddamn war."

"Sir, what we will actually spend for training this year can come out of my pay," Mike answered reasonably.

"What? How much do you make?" asked Hanson, surprised.

"Well, in case you haven't noticed, Fleet makes a hell of a lot more, rank per rank, than the Army, sir, but what I meant was: What is included in a training budget?"

"Well, vehicle fuel, expended rounds, consumable expenditures, food, special field equipment, that sort of thing."

"Yes, sir. The first thing to remember is that the Army had no idea what training budgets for an ACS unit would be, so they kept the budgets that they would have had as Airborne, Marines, whatever. What wasn't considered is that the suits are fueled off a dedicated fusion plant at company level that is rated for forty years use with on-board fuels. The cost is part of our *capital* budget including the fuel, just like suits. Suit food is cheap, a basic supply comes with the suit and recycles itself so the cost of the whole battalion's food for the year, if we stayed in suits, would come out of my pay, easy. No field toilet paper, no MREs, no vehicle fuel, no disposable plastics, the suits take care of it all, garbage in garbage out. For that matter, food comes out of the general battalion expenditure. And no ammunition costs."

"What do you mean, no ammo costs?" Colonel Hanson replied, still trying to assimilate all his other assumptions about training costs being stood on their ear.

"When we start suit training, or even VR training, you'll see, sir. The suits are absolutely awesome training vehicles; there is virtually, pun intended, no point in having a live-fire. So, we are so far overbudgeted that we could all buy Cadillacs out of the ammo budget and leave plenty to go around. So, anyway," he concluded, "the big problem is not that we don't have equipment, it's that we haven't received all of our personnel."

"I wasn't aware that, except for senior officers and NCOs, there was a personnel shortage. It sounds like you're talking about troops or company-grade officers."

"Yes, sir, that's exactly what I'm talking about. We're still waiting on twenty percent of our junior personnel consisting of females and recalled enlisted and current training cadre."

"You did say females? Females?"

"It was recently decided to open the Combat Arms to females," O'Neal answered with another puff. He was tempted to chuckle, since the colonel had gotten quite red faced at the concept of females in his battalion. But he finally decided that discretion was called for. "We are expecting four female junior officers, that I am aware of, two transfer first lieutenants from other arms and two butter bars; hell, I am getting two of them. We're also getting a slew of privates and rejuv or current-service NCOs including one of my platoon sergeants. All the girls are going through infantry training at the moment. The others are either going through retraining if they're recalled or still at their units."

"Oh, joy."

"Yes, sir. Better now than when we were having the riots; I hate to think of what would have happened then. And then when they get here we have to retrain in ACS. There is still no ACS training center."

"Right, well I do not intend to wear myself ragged trying to be my entire staff. Until there is a qualified replacement, you are the acting G-3. Get the other company commanders up here one at a time. I am taking them all on sufferance given the condition of the battalion."

"It's only partially their fault, sir. In many cases conditions resulted from direct orders of Major Stidwell."

"Well, we'll see if I agree. Okay, who is senior?"

"Captain Wolf, Charlie Company."

"Get him up here."

"Yes, sir."

"Then get started on revising the training schedule. We don't have any duties to interfere and I believe in training. As soon as the new chums arrive, I want us out in the field, twenty-four/seven until Momma makes us come in from the rain. Create a training schedule beyond your wildest dreams."

"Yes, sir!"

"And in your planning, keep one thing in mind. Our job is to put ourselves between the Posleen and civilians. The mission is to save our people. And we will *not* fail."

◆ CHAPTER 3 ◆

Said England unto Pharaoh, "I must make a man of you,
   That will stand upon his feet and play the game;
That will Maxim his oppressor as a Christian ought to do,"
   And she sent old Pharaoh Sergeant Whatisname.
It was not a Duke nor Earl, nor yet a Viscount—
   It was not a big brass General that came;
      But a man in khaki kit who could handle men a bit,
     With his bedding labeled Sergeant Whatisname.
                —"Pharaoh and the Sergeant"
                  Rudyard Kipling, 1897

Atlanta, GA, United States of America, Sol III
1025 EST January 15th, 2004 AD

"My name is Sergeant Major Jake Mosovich." The lights of the hall
glinted from the silver badge on his green beret.

It was, Jake had decided, a singularly inappropriate environment.
But the reception hall of the First American All Episcopal United
African Church was packed to overflowing with a mixture of the very
old, the very young, and women. All of them were gathered at tables
piled with an odd assortment of weapons, household items and
general bric-a-brac. The new Special Forces team, with a few old faces,
was scattered throughout the room prepared to train or intervene,
whichever seemed necessary. There was a jarring note to the room;
there were no young men. Virtually every male of military age in
the United States was already inducted into the military and if any
of the local teens had gone AWOL, they certainly were not going to

turn up at a Special Forces local defense training clinic. Even if it did mean a hot meal on a cold day.

"I am a twenty-five-year veteran of the United States Army Special Forces: We're called The Green Berets. We are one of the special operations units your tax dollars have supported for years, so now you get to get some of your own back." As usual that was good for a small laugh.

"The mission of the Special Forces is to train indigenous forces in irregular tactics. What that means is that we are supposed to go into countries and teach guerillas that are friendly to the United States how to be better guerillas. Officially, we have never performed our stated mission." He smiled grimly and there was another chuckle. Some of them got it.

"But it is what we are trained to do. And guerillas, in general, do not have access to regular weapons or equipment. They have to make do with what's around. And they don't work with huge supply systems, the 'tail' as we military folks call it."

His face turned grim. Combined with the scars it made him look like something from a nightmare. "We all know what's coming," he said, gesturing at the ceiling and by extension into space. "And we all know that the Fleet won't be ready when it hits. The ships are taking a long time to build. And unless they are all ready, throwing the few that *are* ready at the attacks would not help us at all and *would* set the plans back for years.

"And the politicians have finally admitted that there won't be much of a chance of defending the coastal plains." He chuckled grimly at the simple term. "In case any of you are not aware, that includes Atlanta. And Washington and L.A. and Baltimore and Philly and just about every other major city in America." He didn't completely agree, and he wondered who thought that it wasn't political suicide. But the decision had been made.

He shook his head again. "And I know that most won't be leaving." He looked around the room at the assembled faces. Old women and men, boys and girls. A smattering of women between twenty and fifty. Two men in the same range, one with both legs missing and the other showing signs of palsy. "At least not right up until the invasion. I've seen more wars than most of you have seen movies and don't nobody leave until right up to the last minute. Then there's always a mad scramble. Something always gets left or forgotten. Somebody is always at the back of the line." He shook his head again, face gray and grim.

"So, we are here to teach you all we can about how to survive at the back of the line. How to live and fight without much in the way of support or regular weapons. We're hoping that it will give you an edge if it comes time that you are at the wall. Maybe it will, maybe it won't." He he tapped his camouflage-clad chest, looking at one little girl. "That is right in here.

"We will also be teaching you about how to spread mayhem with regular equipment in case you get access to it," he continued, returning to parade rest.

"Let me say this, I hope I don't have to but we are required to by our orders, what we are teaching you is absolutely and strictly illegal to use outside of time of war. We are going to be at the First American for five days, by the grace of Pastor Williams, and when we get done you are going to know how to make weapons that make Oklahoma City look like a firecracker. But so help me God—and I say that without taking the Lord in vain, this is an oath before Our Lord—if so much as one of you uses this against another American citizen I will hunt you down if it takes the rest of my life." He looked around the room and his scarred face was molded granite.

"You will not use my teaching against your fellow man. You must swear that now, on the Ever-loving God, before we will teach the first lesson. Do you swear?"

There was a sober muttering of general assent. He thought it would be enough. The pastor seemed to understand his flock and most of those present were his congregation.

The training actually served two purposes. It was not expected— and this lesson would be drummed in over the next few days— that these people could hold their neighborhoods. Shelters were being constructed that should be able to hold most of the displaced population. But as he had said, it was human nature to leave it until just a little too late. In addition to teaching a few techniques that might help some of these citizens against the enemy, they would, together with the pastor, designate locals to be official evacuation coordinators. Evac coordinators would hold a semiofficial position, analogous to World War II Air Raid Wardens. In the event of a Posleen landing, they would direct their neighbors towards the most efficient evacuation routes and, if necessary, organize local defenses.

Statistically some of these people they were training would be caught behind Posleen lines. In that sad event, viewed coldly, the more Posleen they could take down the better. Vietnam taught the American Army that even a baby can plant a mine if properly trained. These people would be as well trained as Mosovich could arrange in five short days.

"We are going to start today with basic weapons training. I know that many of you have had bad experiences with guns. Until the call-up sucked up all the gangs, this neighborhood was basically a write-off. I know that bullets flew around practically at random and there were some terrible acts committed. Well, we are going to teach you how to handle guns the right way and how to use them effectively. Not randomly.

"The police department is setting up a firing range for this neighborhood and it will be manned during the day. You are encouraged to go over there and shoot. The training ammunition is free and there will be standard weapons available, you just can't take any with you. When the Posleen are scheduled to start landing, weapons and ammunition will be issued as requested—we have plenty of rifles and ammunition—and if there is a local scatter landing before then you can draw your allotment from the local police station. In the meantime, it is feared that weapons would be stolen from you if they were generally distributed.

"I personally think that is a crock, but all of us occasionally have to live with city hall, or in this case the federal government. I find it easier to think of it this way; soldiers don't take their rifles home, either, they leave them in an armory. Same thing, basically. Anyway . . .

"We are going to take a look at two weapons today, the M-16 and the AK-47."

Sergeant First Class David Mueller watched the lecture bemusedly. It was almost impossible to imagine that an SF team was teaching lower-income city dwellers about urban terrorism techniques. It made sense in abstract. But later he was going to be teaching the first class in a series that would put every one of these people on an FBI register of potential urban terrorists. It was a list that every member of the SF team was on as well.

Yeah, it made sense in a cruel way, but there was one little black girl, hair in pigtails and not more than twelve, who was staring at the AK like it gave milk. This was a group of people who had not seen much in the way of power, and a lot of power was about to be put in their hands. These techniques would work even better against the government than against the Posleen.

"Okay, what's this?" Mueller asked the group of churchgoers, holding up a white plastic bottle of a name-brand cleaner. They had broken up into groups for specialized sessions and analysis. They would be looking for leaders and individuals who showed special talents. So far Mueller was pretty sure he had picked out a team leader. And he suspected the little twelve-year-old would turn out to be pretty talented at mayhem.

"Bleach," the little girl blurted, with a "what, you don't know bleach when you see it, whitey?" look in her eye.

"Really? Okay, and what's this?" he asked, holding up a translucent bottle of clear liquid.

" 'Monia?"

"Right. And what do you use 'em for?"

"Cleanin' stuff," said an older gentleman in the second row.

"Well, I admit I've used them for that, but what I usually use them for is blowin' stuff up." He could see he got their attention then. "You can use these, and some other common products, to produce explosives." To their obvious amazement, he then proceeded to demonstrate the entire process of making a pipe bomb from start to finish.

"Now, you can get slow fuse for the detonator from a gun shop, they use it for hobby cannons and some muzzle loaders, or I'll show you a couple of ways to make it yourself. Also, later on I'll be showing you ways to make a nifty trip-wire booby trap with a pistol or rifle cartridge and some string. If you put more liquid in the mix you get slurry, and I'll show you some neat stuff to do with slurry later. But first, I want you all to make your own pipe bombs, being very careful to follow the steps exactly as I showed you. Afterwards, we'll go over to that old house on the corner, the one that was a crack joint, and blow that SOB sky-high."

Most of them seemed to like that idea.

"You need to brush your teeth more often, young man," said the medic, peering at the ten-year-old's molars. "How long has that tooth been aching?"

"A'out a mo'h, ah 'ess."

"Well, you need a filling, maybe a root canal." A portion of the mission that had just evolved was providing medical support to the communities they trained. It disgusted Sergeant First Class Gleason that her country—with the best health care system in the world— would permit the degree of health neglect that existed in these communities. They should have sent in the Berets long before now; some of their "hearts and minds" techniques might even have done something for the gang problem.

Not that there was one now. That problem had loomed large in the minds of early planners, but it turned out to be basically moot. All the gang members were in the Guard and generally stayed there. Local Guard commanders, when first faced with desertion problems, took a cut a la the Gordian Knot solution. The death penalty had never been removed from the books and local commanders resorted to it more often than not in situations where a soldier had deserted as opposed to taking an extended AWOL.

It was not hard to spot deserters. Police forces were exempt from call-up, being effectively an extension of the war effort when the Posleen landed, and they were on the lookout. Military personnel were, as in the old days, required to be in uniform at all times and, although the local commanders were lenient about weekend passes, if there was a male of military age not in uniform who was spotted by the police he was invariably stopped and asked for his deferment card. Since deferment was now a line on the driver's license, a false deferment card turned up with a simple call to the station or a check of the carcomp. It was a nerve-wracking stop for the cops; the deserters knew what could await them, and most reacted violently. Usually if a suspected deserter was spotted the cop would call for backup and shadow; only when enough force was in place would the stop would be made.

It occasionally made for a comic opera when some poor unsuspecting policeman from another force would find himself suddenly surrounded by fellow officers with drawn guns. But it made the cops pretty damn mad at the Guard commanders when the suspect just said "Fuck you," and pulled out a pistol, suicide being preferable to hanging.

So now the gangs were extinct and only the young, old, female and frail were left. And those people needed better health care than they were getting. The medic looked in question at the boy's mother.

"Ain't no dentist, no doctors neither. They either in the Army or they too expensive. It's a all-day wait at Grady, an' maybe they do something, maybe they don'. So, what you say, soldier-girl?"

The matronly Sergeant Gleason, a recent graduate of the all-inclusive Special Forces Medic course and mother of four, smiled pleasantly. "I say I pull the tooth and do an implant. That way he'll grow back a new, good one. While I'm in there, I'll do any fillings he needs and a general preventive work-over.

"For you, son, since I see your eyes getting round at the thought, I'll be putting you under, so you won't feel a thing. And for you, Mom, I'll tell you it won't cost you a blessed dime." A military nurse for fourteen years, Gleason jumped at the first chance to move to Combat Arms. The choice of Special Forces was difficult for her family, her children especially, to understand, but if she was going to be a combat medic it was going to be the best there was to offer.

Special Forces was designed from its very inception to be a unit that spent most of its time away from the regular force structure and logistic tail. That meant that the team must be self-reliant when it came to medical support. Since it was generally difficult to find an MD willing to go through Special Forces Q course, the SF had to grow their own. While SF medics were not and never would be MDs, they were nearly as well-trained as Physician's Assistants in the area of trauma medicine.

While on a mission they were authorized to perform minor surgery, prescribe drugs and perform minor dental procedures. What actually went on was something else. Although every medic really did know that they were not the equal of a drunk MD on his worst day, sometimes they were all that was available. In situations just like this, throughout the world, SF medics had saved lives with emergency appendectomies, tonsillectomies, tumor removal, benign and malignant, and other actions that would have them burned at the stake by the American Medical Association.

Sergeant First Class Gleason was acting in the best tradition of SF canker mechanics since the Berets had been in existence.

"Thank you, soldier-girl. He says, Okay!" said the relieved mother.

"I do not!"

"Don't you sass your mother. That tooth's just gonna hurt worse if'n you don't get it fixed."

"She's right, you know," said Gleason. "Always trust your mother."

"Okay, I guess," said the child, nervously. "You gonna put me out, right?"

"Yep, with new Galactic medicines so I don't have to worry about dosage and you don't have to worry about aftereffects. When you want to do it?"

"Can it wait 'til tomorrow?" asked the mother. "I gotta go to work an' I wanna be there."

"Sure, anytime. In the meantime, son, you brush good tonight with this toothbrush, and rinse your mouth with this rinse. I'll see you tomorrow at, say, ten?"

"Dat be fine, doctor," said the mother.

"That is one thing I am not. I am, however, licensed to perform minor procedures and I put this in that category. See you tomorrow." The two walked out, the youngster clutching his toothbrush and mouthwash like talismans.

"Last client, doc," said the team leader, Captain Thompson, stepping aside to let the pair through the door.

"Good, I'm about done for. We got any new orders?"

"Yeah, I'll detail it at the team meeting, but we're supposed to wrap up Atlanta. We're going to Richmond next."

"I wondered if they'd consider sending us overseas."

"I think, given our area of responsibility, that we'll probably stay in country."

"Meaning let Africa go hang?" asked Gleason with a grimace.

"Hell," said Master Sergeant Mark Ersin, wandering into the room and the conversation, "let Africa hang. We've got enough to do here."

"Agree," said Captain Thompson, his ebony face somber. "The cities are going to get hit hard. The more prepared our own people are, the better. The Mideast is bristling with weapons and not really attractive and Africa will never get its shit together in time. Let 'em hang."

Ersin's scarred Eurasian face creased in a grim smile. "Trust me, we do not want to be away from supports if the Posleen land early."

Along with Mueller and Mosovich, Ersin was a survivor of humanity's first contact with the oncoming threat. The three were members of a joint service special operations force sent to recon the planet Barwhon. They had survived when the mission was changed from reconnaissance to snatch, had survived when the other five members did not. And along the way they had gathered an immense fund of information about the Posleen rear areas and how they organized themselves. One piece of information all three reinforced was that fighting the Posleen was not a pleasant proposition.

"When the Posleen land," he continued, "we want to be somewhere we can go to ground behind defenses. Once they are down and deployed, I'll be happy to go mess around in their rear. Until then, I want a roof over my head and a wall around me."

"Well," continued Captain Thompson, "after Richmond we'll be finished with our outreach program. We're slated to come back here and act as command and control skeleton for the militias. Cadre."

"What?" gasped both Gleason and Ersin. It was the first time that the cadre idea had been mentioned.

"Apparently the militia training program is working well, but they want professionals in place," the captain explained with a shrug.

"I thought that was what the Guard was for!" Ersin snarled.

"Hey, Sergeant, these are the civilians you are supposed to protect!"

"Excuse me, sir, but I don't think I can do that if I'm dead! If I fight the Posleen again, I want it to be from fixed defenses!"

"Whatever your wants might be, Sergeant, those are our orders," the captain answered with an iron clang to his voice.

"Our orders friggin' stink, sir. Oh, Jesus! We have just been royally corn-cobbed. Have Jake or Mueller heard this yet?"

"No. I didn't realize you would have such an extreme reaction," said the captain with a tone of bemusement.

"Oh my word, sir, you haven't *seen* extreme reaction yet."

✧   ✧   ✧

"*What pissant son of a bitch came up with this fuckin' cadre bullshit?*" shouted the irate sergeant major.

This is not the sort of language normally heard between sergeant majors and four-star generals; however, the Ground Forces Chief of Staff had been more or less expecting the call. When his aide allowed that Sergeant Major Mosovich was on the phone and would like to have a brief word with the General, the General acceded, after making sure no one else would hear the conversation.

"Hello, Jake. Nice to hear from you. Yes, I'm fine, overworked but aren't we all."

"*Fuck that! Who? I will personally frag their ass! Is this some slimy regular-army plot to be done with SF for once and for all?!*"

"Okay, Jake, that is just about enough," General Taylor said, coldly. "It was my fucking plan."

"*What?!*" If General Taylor thought the previous volume was extreme he now discovered a new meaning to the word.

"Okay, you've been teaching them. What chance do those people have if the Posleen land before the evacuation is complete?"

"So you're going to throw the goddamn SF away? Is that it?"

"No. I am going to use them up as carefully as possible. But they are going to be between Posleen and civilians. Where they damn well belong. Clear?"

"Clear. We are not armed, or trained for the mission. We have limited tactical mobility. We are trained to be behind-the-lines, hit-and-run fighters or cadre for that type of force but we will make our stands and be overrun to buy the civilians a few minutes that they will undoubtedly squander." The sergeant major hissed the last words.

"Jake, how do you fight Posleen?" the general asked in a reasonable tone.

"What?"

"I thought the question was in English. How do you fight Posleen?" he repeated.

"My best idea is with artillery and fixed defenses," the sergeant major replied.

"How about mortars and firebases?"

"And then what, sir? We'll be in scattered firebases, cut off and without support. And where are the firebases coming from?"

"Well, in the case of Atlanta, there are several major geographic positions to choose from. The mission will be to form firebases along evacuation routes and man them with indigenous nonmilitary personnel who have some limited training: American Strikers.

The teams will form and train these militias and design and construct the fixed defenses from available local materials and using local assets. Now, in what way is this *not* in the SF tradition, Sergeant Major?"

"Shit." There was a long pause. "We are not going to survive this, Jim. Among other things, our 'militias' will consist of old men and teenage women."

"When the Posleen are down and their deployment is clear, when all civilians are effectively evacuated or hors d'combat, when the fuckin' job is damn well done, SF personnel may make their way to secure areas using any means available."

"There won't be any means, Jim. None."

"Sure there will, dammit. 'If you ain't cheatin' you ain't tryin.' "

" 'If you get caught, you ain't SF.' Understood. I still think this is a Guard function."

"There's gonna be plenty of targets to go around."

"My point was not lack of targets, sir."

"Okay," said Mueller, "we are fucked."

"Sergeant Mueller," said Warrant Officer First Class Andrews, "attitude will not help."

Warrant Officer Andrews and Sergeant First Class Mueller did not get along well. Whether Mr. Andrews knew it or not, in this instance that was going to affect him more than Mueller. Most of the SF warrant officers were ninety-day wonders, junior SF NCOs or even non-SF NCOs who were sent through a warrant officer's course to become the second-in-command of a team. In the new Special Forces, essentially reborn since the oncoming Posleen threat, when a veteran NCO has a problem with a junior officer, the junior officer goes. That tradition had wavered in the last couple of decades. But in the face of adversity old habits die hard.

"I don't see the problem. We build a firebase and secure it. We have a massive amount of building materials to draw on. This is a basic Special Forces mission. What is your problem, Sergeant?"

"It's not his problem solely, sir," interjected Sergeant Major Mosovich, rather harshly. "I made some of the same points to High Command. They had the same attitude. Maybe you just have to see the Posleen in action to realize that this plan is pretty much pissing in the wind."

"Yeah," remarked Ersin. "I wouldn't mind if it made any sense. But it doesn't."

"Pardon me, perhaps it's being a junior officer," started Andrews, meaning "maybe it is my being a little more intelligent than you old fogies," "but we just establish a strong outpost and slow the Posleen advance with indirect fire."

"Yes, sir. And then what?" asked Mosovich. Mueller was uncharacteristically quiet, perhaps realizing how close he was to losing his cool.

"Well, then we E and E out, I suppose. If we can't escape or evade, we go down as hard as possible. It's happened before and it will happen again. Bataan, for example."

"All right, sir. Point one, the Posleen do not slow in the face of indirect or, for that matter, direct fire. They move as fast under fire as not under fire. If you kill enough they stop but only because they're dead. Point two, there will be virtually no way to E and E out. The Posleen will closely invest the strong point and then probably overrun it with mass attacks. If we could build large curtain walls, maybe it would work, but I don't think we have the time and we couldn't supply it for a multiyear siege." He paused and mentally counted.

"Point three, we don't know where they will be coming from or going to. They land more or less randomly and their objectives are more or less random. We will be a focal point for attack without any reasonable chance of killing enough to matter. Now, does the situation make a little more sense, sir?"

"I can't believe that the Posleen will be that great a threat, Sergeant Major," said the warrant officer, somewhat smugly. "While I know you have experience fighting them, that was without fixed defenses. I think we should be able to hold them for a time and then escape."

"Yeah, well, keep dreamin', Mister," Mueller finally interjected, then walked away in disgust.

◆ CHAPTER 4 ◆

Ft. Indiantown Gap, PA, United States of America, Sol III
0900 EST January 22nd, 2004 AD

"For those of you just arrived, welcome to Bravo Company First Battalion Five-Fifty-Fifth Fleet Infantry, my name is Captain Michael O'Neal. And the unit you have joined is called the 'Triple-Nickle.' "

Mike looked the final draft of soldiers over. Already they were scattered through the formation, but they were noticeable by their BDUs and Gortex as opposed to the rest of the company's gray silks. They were also noticeable by being either female, or older than the norm or both. None of them were actually rejuvs, although most had been recalled out of the inactive reserve. Unlike the colonel, Mike had an AID and although the local personnel officers might not be able to call up 201s, he could. He had quickly perused the draft and was generally satisfied. He had a couple of hard cases, including one private second class who had been a sergeant not once but twice, but mostly they were good troops on paper. When he got done with them they would be better. Now for The Lecture, so that they would be absolutely clear where their company commander stood.

"If you're wondering, yes, I'm that Captain O'Neal. That is all I am going to say on the subject. What I am going to talk about you will hear me say today, and on numerous occasions until you have the unpleasant opportunity to see what I mean.

"Those of you, most of you, who have never been in combat, you are not ready for the Posleen. Those few of you who have previous combat experience, you are not ready for the Posleen. The way you fight Posleen, the way we will fight Posleen, is brutally simple. You get a good position, hunker down, call for all the artillery and mortar

41

fire available and kill as many of them as you can until you are almost overwhelmed, then move as fast as you can back to the next position. Since the situation is a binary solution set, win or lose, there is only one choice. We will win. Whether any individual present survives to see that victory is going to be a combination of training and luck." At the back of the formation he could see First Sergeant Pappas looking over the group. Mike suspected that the senior NCO was doing the same thing as Mike: scanning the group of mist-puffing soldiers and wondering where the losses would come from. Would it be the tall guy in Third platoon? The cut-up in First? The wiry, deadly Sergeant Stewart of fame and legend? Sergeant Ampele, his stolid antithesis? New guy? Old? Mike nodded internally and went on.

"Many of us are going to pay the ferryman. But, as George Patton said: 'Your job is not to die for your country. Your job is to make sure the other poor bastard dies for *his* country.' Do not concentrate on the ferryman, he will be there in the end for all of us, whether it is next week, on the plains of battle or at an advanced age at the hands of an outraged spouse.

"Until you meet the ferryman your only thought should be to kill Posleen. If you love your family, put them out of your mind. I have two daughters and a wife. Except in a small compartment deep within myself, I could care less. I live, breathe and eat killing the Posleen. Not because I particularly hate them, not because of Diess, but because anything less is not my all. We have to kill and kill and kill until there are no more Posleen. Until then no one is safe. Until then put away your emotions, unless hate helps you to drive on, and prepare for training harder than anything in your miserable lives." Mike inhaled through his nose and felt the cold burn his sinuses. He couldn't wait to get *suits*!

"Until the suits arrive we will train on Milspecs sixteen hours a day with one half-day off a week for personal business. Once the suits arrive we will take to the field for the same regimen. You can send e-mail during personal stand down. Your pay is direct deposit; there is no other option. If your family needs a larger allotment, see your squad leader; he can show you how to manage your pay through your AID.

"To those of you who are prior service: you are no longer Airborne or Marine, you are Fleet Strike. You may respond 'Airborne' or 'Semper Fi' as you wish, but remember, the persons you are training with, whether they come from your background or not, are the people you will be fighting beside. Don't make judgements on the basis of their prior service or you will find yourself sorry and sore.

Fleet Strike is an entirely new organization, drawing, I hope, on the best of the Army elite and the Marines. Each of you volunteered for this unit, but I doubt you understand what a radical change you have made in your lives. If you are in the Line or Guard, you are first a citizen of the United States, then of Earth and only last of the Federation, operating under basically the strictures with which you are familiar. As a member of the Fleet, your first line of control is the Federation military.

"The Federation treats its military in a way very different from the United States military. You will shortly have a briefing in the high points of Federation military law. I say the high points, because the Federation military operates under a set of strictures more complicated than anything on Earth. You swore an oath to that law and are now bound to it. But there is no way you could possibly understand it.

"For example, as your commander, I can shoot any one of you dead, for no reason whatsoever, and suffer no adverse consequences. To the Federation the military is a separate caste, exempt from most laws while bound by a hedge of others. You may kill a civilian nonmilitary human without legal consequences, with one tiny caveat: as your commander, I absolutely forbid you to violate any American law outside of time of conflict.

"However, the American branch of Fleet Strike operates under a secondary set of regulations which is essentially the Uniform Code of Military Justice. There are massive loopholes; I *can* shoot you dead and get off scott free, but for your purposes following the UCMJ will do.

"One last word. I expect nothing less than one hundred percent of your mind, body and soul. Those of you who are prior service may have heard that one before, too. Do not fuck with me. If you play games, I will have you in a 'prison-unit' so fast the paperwork will take a year to catch up. You all volunteered to be here. If you want out, say so at any time and I guarantee it will be acted on.

"Officers fall into my office after you turn over your troops. First Sergeant, post."

Mike looked coldly over his officers, those already attached and those just arrived. There had been three officers with the new draft: a tall, blond female first lieutenant with the unlikely name of Teri Nightingale, slated to become his XO; a greyhound slender brunette female second lieutenant named Karen Slight headed for Third Platoon; and a dark stocky male second lieutenant, Mike Fallon, who was that rarest of birds, a ring knocker, slated for Second Platoon leader. In Mike's experience service academy officers came in two extreme brands, good and bad. Good West Pointers were very good indeed, but bad West Pointers were simply very good at kissing the boss's ass and covering their own. Only time would tell with this one.

Tim Arnold, previously the acting XO, was a first lieutenant and the weapons platoon leader. A tall, goofy-looking fellow, he was a Mustang like Mike, with prior service as an enlisted man in the Twenty-Fourth Mechanized Infantry Division, then the Eighty-Second Airborne Division as a lieutenant. The goofy personality hid a head full of simple wisdom about the military and people. Mike would miss him as an exec because on at least a couple of occasions it had been Arnold who had kept Mike from losing his famous temper in a very public way.

Dave Rogers, the First Platoon leader, was the odd duck. Rarely do you have a first lieutenant as a grunt platoon leader but with the overabundance of first lieutenants, and being junior, he was stuck. Tall and aristocratic, he seemed to be resigned but offended by the position and Mike suspected there was going to be bad blood between him and Nightingale. Unlike Arnold, he was lightning quick to correct deficiencies, real or imagined, and had nearly as short a temper as Mike's. For all that, he was experienced and sharp. Mike read him as hard but brittle; once Rogers had his first taste of fighting the Posleen, he would find a job as an aide or something similar in short order.

"As those of you who have been here have discovered, what I told the troops goes double for the officers. Despite the spectacularly fucked-up supply situation we should be getting our full equipment loadout next week in one abysmally confused shipment. If the new battalion commander hadn't arrived we would be truly up shit's creek getting it sorted out, but he's detailed me as acting Three, so I'll have some impact on the plan, especially since I get along with Wilson, the Four.

"Once the suits are uncrated we have to adjust them to the troops. As far as I know, I am the only qualified suiter in the battalion, so they'll have to send a tech or techs. I can find no mention of that in the mails, either general or GalTech, and none of my contacts have heard a word, so who knows when the techs will arrive. Whoever and whenever they are sent, it will take two, three, maybe even four weeks thereafter to get everyone suited. Command suits will be first, then platoon sergeants, but then it will be first through weapons. I have already discussed this with Top and he will pass it to the NCOs.

"In the meantime, we have four tactical exercises without troops next week. The first will be an open-field skirmish as a lone company, the second will be integrated with the other companies in a larger open-field encounter, the third a company defense with good to fair terrain and light opposition, and the last will be my personal favorite, the Spartan scenario. Since there's been a shakeup at battalion, that means I can take the aggressor. Nightingale, you'll run the company, you need to learn the ropes; Arnold, brief Nightingale on what that entails."

"Brief Nightingale on the playbook."

"Right." Mike looked at the newly arrived officers. "Combat against the Posleen requires swift fluidity and total concentration. So we're stealing a page from football and soccer and using 'plays' at the squad and platoon level. This serves two purposes.

"The first purpose is to reduce the time it takes to give orders. A series of simple two-part commands covers the vast majority of instructions given in combat.

"The second purpose is to overcome 'combat lock.' I want our troops so conditioned that when the time comes every single one of them opens fire without hesitation. Stopping a Posleen charge is like stopping an avalanche with fire hoses; you can do it, but it takes all the water in the world. We need every single son of a bitch firing."

"Most of that will be up to the NCOs. I want the officers to remain as hands-off as possible unless we are in active company or platoon-level training. If there is an issue with one of your platoons' readiness, bring it up with First Sergeant Pappas or myself."

"Get your shit squared away this afternoon, because as of tomorrow there aren't enough hours in the day. We have a Tactical Exercise Without Troops scheduled for tomorrow and sixteen hours per day of training from here on out until our Fleet Strike Readiness Evaluation Series. So you'd better get cracking.

"Dismissed."

◆ CHAPTER 5 ◆

As the car dropped over the ridge into the pocket valley in the Georgia hills, Sharon O'Neal almost turned around.

She had never understood her reaction to Mike's father. A gruff but fair man, he occasionally called her "Lieutenant" and treated her like a chief would a junior officer, courteous if occasionally salty. At her request, he refrained from relating war stories to the children and rarely did so around her, but she had heard enough over the years to understand him somewhat.

Perhaps it related to her Navy experience, where she felt so exceedingly rejected by the "old-boy" establishment. Mike Senior would drop without a ripple into a group of Navy chiefs, without much of a ripple into a group of Navy officers, especially a group of surface-warfare types. He would be indistinguishable from a group of SEALs. Whether it was real or not, she always felt a trace of contempt or perhaps superiority emanating from the old war-horse.

After a long career related to the unfortunate brevity of human life and the means to arrange for reducing it, Michael O'Neal, Sr., returned to the family farm to raise crops like generations before him, and to raise his family. Since then, with the exception of collecting weapons, some of them illegal, and a group of retirees with a similar bent, he appeared to have put that earlier phase of his life behind him. She knew he had left the Army under somewhat mysterious circumstances—the failure to be recalled along with all his buddies was confirmation of that—and that he had spent some time overseas doing things of a military nature, but what really bothered her

46

was the old-boy feeling. Now he seemed tailor-made for her needs and she was going to have a hard time looking him in the eye and saying that.

She glanced at Cally beside her. If she had to choose which of her children might survive on a world consumed by war, she would have chosen Cally. Usually the older child is more reserved and prissy, but with her children it was reversed. If Michelle scratched her finger, she broke into paroxysms of tears; if Cally ran into a wall, she stood up, wiped the blood off her nose and kept running. But she was still only seven, would only be nine when the Posleen landed, and her mommy and daddy were both going to be far away.

Michelle was already gone, consumed by a colony ship packed with dependents headed for safety. That program had come under fire, both in the United States and overseas. Called racist, supremacist and every other –ist anyone could come up with, it still made too much sense to stop. If a human gene pool was going to be moved off-planet (and given the situation, it made sense to create such a backup), it made sense to choose from the gene pool that represented the necessary skills. Right now, the Federation did not need scientists and it did not need politicians and it did not need engineers; what it needed was soldiers. It might not be nice, it might not be politically correct, but it made sense and that was all the Federation cared about.

The house was stone, unusual in this part of the mountains, and dated to well before the Civil War. The O'Neals were among the first settlers in the area after the Cherokee were forcibly relocated, and the house was designed to protect against the understandably angry stragglers. The first O'Neal was an Irish immigrant who mined gold for a few years then decided that there was more money to be made selling food to the miners than mining. He marked out a stake, broke the ground and built the farmhouse with the occasional help of his fellow miners.

It presided regally over a small valley so filled with good things that it seemed that God had touched it. On the south-facing slope was an orchard of apples and below that an orchard of pecans. The fields were broken into tillage and pasture with hay in portions. It was a tidy and productive six hundred acres that satisfied the financial and nutritional needs of the O'Neal family even in these hard times.

The government was gathering all the foodstuffs it could and caching them in hardened shelters throughout the Rockies and Appalachians. The survivors of America might be on the run, but the United States government was determined that they be well-fed runners. Unfortunately, even with new ground being broken, genetically modified crops and the modern American agricultural engine getting into high gear for the first time, that meant shortages. Shortages were something that happened to other people, not Americans.

When Americans walk into a grocery store, they expect cheerful, smiling bag boys and fresh produce. Now the bag boys were all in uniform and the produce fields were producing wheat and corn crops that were going into holes in the mountains. America's wheat yield the previous year had been twenty-five percent higher than at any time in history but there was a bread shortage.

Even small farmers such as Papa O'Neal were required to report their production and adhere to crop rotas, but the government did not expect or desire to control every acre. The O'Neal garden had kept the family in fresh vegetables throughout the long summer as Sharon awaited her summons to uniform and Mike sat through endless speeches and parades.

The simple numbers meant that one of them would not be coming back, probably Mike, and that Cally's chances were less than good. As a mechanical engineer specializing in maintenance support requirements, Sharon fully expected a glorified clerk's position on Titan Base. Her chances were better than fair. Unfortunately she could take neither her husband nor her eldest daughter with her.

As they pulled up in the twilight the simian shape of her father-in-law, the man from whom Mike had derived his innate strength, if not height, stood silhouetted in the doorway.

"Papa O'Neal?"

"Uhn?" They were sitting in the living room of the farmhouse. It had a bachelor-pad look to it, the feeling that there were no women resident in the house, for all that it was neat as a pin. An oak-wood fire blazed on the hearth against the winter chill while Sharon nursed a glass of white wine that was growing quite warm. She wondered if she dared ask for ice, while Mike Senior nursed a beer gone much the same way. Both of them had been sitting that way since getting Cally off to bed, more unspoken between them than might ever be possible to say.

"I have to ask. It doesn't have a thing to do with this, with Cally, but it's important to me." She paused, wondering how to go on. Wondering if she should. Did she really want to know the answer? "Why'd you leave the Army?"

"Shit," he said, getting up and going to a sideboard. He threw away the warm beer, pulled out an ice bucket, walked over and plunked two cubes in her glass then walked back over and pulled out a Mason jar. He poured two fingers in a small glass mug, knocked it back with a "pah!" and a grimace, then poured two more and walked back over to his chair carrying the jar.

The chair, with its cowhide cover, complete with coarse hair, had the look of much of the house: rough, dependable, marginally comfortable but not by any means aesthetic. He flumped into it with a sigh and continued, "I just knew you were working up to that."

"How?" she asked, swirling the wine and ice with her forefinger. She took a sip as it slowly cooled.

"You'd never asked. And I could tell that you'd never asked Mike."

"I did. He told me to ask you."

"When?" he asked, pouring another hit of the fiery moonshine.

"Shortly after I first met you. I asked him what was with you, you know, why you were so . . ."

"Loony?" he asked.

"No, just . . . well . . ."

"Eccentric then," he prompted with a shrug.

"Okay, eccentric. And he told me you'd had an interesting career. And you've talked about other stuff, but never that. And hardly at all about Vietnam." She cocked her head to one side.

"You were born in, what? Seventy-two?" he asked roughly.

"Three," she corrected.

"Lessee," he said scratching his chin. The action reminded her so strongly of Mike Junior for a moment that she caught her breath. "In nineteen seventy-three," he continued, "I was at Bragg, but I went back in seventy-four."

"I thought we pulled out of Vietnam in seventy-two and three," she said, puzzled.

"Oh, we did, sure." He smiled slyly. " . . . all except the 'Studies and Observation Group.' "

"The what?"

"The SOG. What was the SOG?" he asked rhetorically. "Well, first of all, we were guys that you absolutely could not introduce to mother, or to Congress, which amounts to the same damn thing. We were a bunch of major bad-ass hard cases for which the war just could not be over. It could not be a loss; therefore, they created a way for us to go back into the jungle.

"SEALs, LRPS, Rangers, Phoenix, SF, Marine Recon, they all contributed. Its purpose was, basically, payback. The brass knew the war was lost. Hell, officially and effectively we had pulled out, but there were some targets that we just felt should not survive the experience, a few situations that needed cleansing in a big way." He took a pull from the two-hundred-proof liquor and stared at the crackling fire, mind far away in time and space.

"I really didn't understand the fuckin' Vietnamese then. I mean, the fuckin' VC were such absolute stone-cold motherfuckers. They would do things to people I still wake up in a cold sweat over. But some of them, hell, maybe most of them, did it because they were patriots. Maybe some of them got their rocks off, but quite a few of them were as sickened by it as I was. They did it because the mission was to unite Vietnam under communism, and they believed in that with the same hard cold light that I believed it was evil incarnate. It took me damn near fifteen years to come to that conclusion." He shook his head over old wounds, bone deep.

"Anyway, we were there to arrange permanent solutions for some of the more unpleasant examples of dialectical materialism as manifest on Earth.

"There were two targets that stand out in my mind. It was one of those situations when there was a fine dividing line. There are a lot of situations that are black and white, but most are shades of gray. This was a situation where two people disagreed on what shade one of the targets was. They were both consummate motherfuckers, no disagreement there, but one motherfucker was, officially, on our side and the other motherfucker was, officially, on the other side.

"Well, I finally decided that I was tired of distinctions like that, so I killed them both."

She looked at the glass clutched in his hand, thick crystal formed into a handleless mug. On it was a legend so chipped and marred as to be illegible, but from a faint outline of a shield and arrow she knew what the inscription would be: *De Oppresso Liber*, "To Liberate the Oppressed." It was such a high-minded motto, dropped in the Devil's cauldron of Southeast Asia, where the oppressed seemed to seek oppression over freedom, where enemies were friends and friends were enemies. For the lesser soldiers it was the moment-to-moment fear of the booby trap, the mine and the sniper. For those who ruled the jungle, it was the fear of betrayal, the knife in the back. Across more than thirty years, the jungle of the mind seemed to reach out and touch the tough old man across from her.

"Anyway, it really pissed off the brass. However, giving the real reason it pissed them off wouldn't work. But everybody was into something, back then. Some of them were smuggling drugs back to the World, some of them were moving comfort rations out to the front. Whatever.

"Me? I had been moving some equipment back to the World for the last few tours, the kind of equipment guaranteed to not make the ATF very damn happy. Anyway, they put that together with a couple of other things and whomped up a court-martial for smuggling and black market. Twenty years in Leavenworth was the verdict. I got shipped off about when Mike was born. After three years a particular appeal worked and I was out." He snorted faintly at some remembrance and Sharon realized that the hits of white lightning were finally starting to have some effect.

"Now, I could have, probably should have, come home. But I never was into the story of the prodigal son; if I found myself shoveling pig shit I wasn't going home until I was chief pig-shit shoveler.

"A buddy clued me that there were positions available for someone with my skills. Positions where I'd probably meet a few old friends. The Feds wouldn't care for it, but, hell, they don't like anything they don't directly control while being spot on any evil they do. So I went back to being a soldier. On my own side." He shook his head again at the futility of the long war between East and West. It was fought on battlefields throughout the world, most undeclared. And it killed more than bodies.

"But you know, me and my buddies, we sure could win the goddamn battles but we could never win the goddamn wars! It was Vietnam all over again. In Rhodesia, my unit, the RSAS, we had one team rack up the highest kill ratio in history. Five guys wiped out a guerilla regiment, poof! Gone! And we still lost the goddamn war.

"It was then, after Rhodesia, that I just got fed up. I was making a living, but I sure as hell wasn't making a difference; the gooks won every fuckin' time. So I came home and became a farmer like my father, and his father, and his father. And someday, God willing, Mike will come through that door again and only leave horizontal."

He turned blazing eyes on his daughter-in-law and she realized that he was finally talking to her as a fellow soldier, not just a civilian in uniform. "Know this, Sharon—and this may be the last time I get a chance to teach a young officer—it really is true that you have to pay more attention to your friends than your enemies. You can defend against the enemy, but it is *damn* hard to defend yourself against your own side." He shook his leonine head again and poured more moonshine, the fire of his soul suddenly damped.

"Papa O'Neal?" she said, after some thought.

"Yeah, L-T?" He did not look up from swirling his moonshine.

"I'm glad you shot him. If you hadn't, you wouldn't be here for us." She smiled faintly. "God works in mysterious ways."

"Hmmph," he commented. "Well, in any case I didn't shoot him. I used a knife. I wanted to see his eyes." He shook his head again and threw the fresh white lightning onto the fire where it blazed like a beacon in the night.

◆ CHAPTER 6 ◆

Washington, DC, United States of America, Sol III
0812 EDT May 23rd, 2004 AD

The President hunched forward in his chair, watching the video from Barwhon. The scene was a large, dry open area in the towering forests and swamps. Debris was scattered across the field, bits of cloth and torn tents. Ripped packages of combat meals could be discerned in the foreground, the Mylar linings reflecting the omnipresent purple sky.

The voiceover from the reporter was unnecessary. A clip taken the week before of the same crew's visit to the command center of the First Infantry Division had preceded the current view. Where the brigade of logistics and management personnel had been was now a wasteland of shredded equipment and camouflage uniforms. There was not a body to be seen.

The mistake had been trivial, a battalion being rotated out of the line, their relief missing the "handoff" by a slim margin, an unanticipated Posleen assault. Suddenly a mass of Posleen equivalent to a division was in the rear area. While the flanked line brigades of the division had struggled for existence, the Posleen had sliced through the lightly armed and undertrained rear area personnel like a buzz saw through balsa.

The final casualties were still being counted. As always with the Posleen, it was the Missing In Action column that was the largest. Virtually all of them could be counted on as dead. Many would be rations for aliens, others bits and pieces lost in the ruck the Armored Combat Suits had made of the Posleen.

The ACSs, a British battalion this time, had led the rescue divisions.

The suits, heavily reinforced with fire from the oncoming support, had slashed through the centaurs and relieved the survivors of the American infantry division. Then they had led the French reinforcements into their positions and hunted the Posleen into the ground.

But the losses were enormous. Most of the division was missing, which meant dead. And during the primaries, he was not in a position to take the heat from this debacle.

He flipped off the television and spun in his chair to face the secretary of defense.

"Well?" the President asked.

"It's not as if it hasn't happened before—" said the secretary, only to be cut off.

"Not in the last year. We lost heavily in the first year's fighting, but this is the first big loss anyone has had this year."

"The Chinese just took a big hit on Irmansul, Mister President," commented his national security advisor. The former infantry commander rubbed the side of his nose. He had made his suggestions the first week he had been with the administration. Now to see if they would take fruit.

"But not NATO forces," the President snapped. The treaty was nearly moribund, but the term was still used to indicate the units from "First World" countries. NATO forces commanded far higher funding from the Galactics than counterparts from other areas of the world; a NATO division cost the Galactics twelve times as much as a Chinese division. "Let the Irmansul consortium get what they paid for! But we cannot afford these sorts of losses. And they have to stop!"

"It's war, Mister President," said the secretary, casting a sidelong glance at the NSA. "You win some and you lose some."

"Well, I've never been a 'loser,' Robby," the President snapped, angrily. "And I've got to wonder if that's the case with all of our commanders?"

"Do you have a problem with the chain of command, Mister President?" asked the secretary.

"I don't know," said the President, snidely. "Do you think we have a problem? First we have all these news reports about training and discipline problems. Then we're still reeling from the arguments over whether we should defend the coastal plains or not. Then we have this. I have to wonder if we have the right people in the right jobs!"

"There are several issues currently—" the secretary started and was cut off again.

"I don't want to hear about issues!" the President snapped. "I want to hear about results! Now, do you have any suggestions?"

The secretary of defense finally understood what the President wanted. The President wanted a "policy-maker's" head. With the campaigning already started, he wanted to be distanced from the failure on Barwhon, while having the blame pinned precisely. That meant placing it at a high enough level that the administration could be seen as "doing something." The secretary suddenly realized that he should only offer his own resignation if he *really* meant it.

"I think we need to consider a new command team for Ground Forces," said the secretary, carefully.

"I think we need to consider more than that," said the President. "I think we need to completely replace the upper command and change the command structure..."

The NSA hid a small smile. Fertile ground indeed.

The general gave a broad and humorless smile. It was a well-known mannerism that countless subordinates had fallen victim to. "He did what?"

General Jim Taylor, Chief of Staff to the Ground Forces High Commander, gave a huge grin and balanced the Fairbairn combat knife he was playing with on one finger. "He canned the commander and the vice." Jim Taylor had dealt with plenty of Marines in his time, and as far as he was concerned, the vice commander was just a guy wearing a Marine's hat. "And he's completely changed the command structure. The High Commander will command Training Command, Intelligence, Logistics, what have you. Including 'Base Support Command.'"

"CONARC," said the other general. He gave a resigned sigh. At least his position had finally been given its correct name. He had held the position of CONARC for the past two years, ever since completing his assignment as head of the Infantry branch of the Galactic Technology Board. It had been an intensely frustrating period. Not only was his background as one of the most experienced combat commanders in the Army being squandered, he was responsible for bases that were out of his control. He was the "commander" of the base personnel and "owned" the bases, but he did not have command of the units assigned to those bases. And those units were halfway mutinous and engaging in almost daily riots. Then the cost of the cleanup for those riots came out of *his* budget. So he was watching a previously stellar career come crashing down because of others' failures.

"Nope," said General Taylor. "Continental Army Command is the biggest change. There will be two 'Force' commands under the High Commander: CONARC and ExForC. Continental Army Command and Expeditionary Force Command. The commander of CONARC will have direct command and control of all combat forces in the continental United States."

The silver-haired general Taylor had been addressing sat bolt upright in his chair and pinned his ebony-skinned superior with a glacial-blue gaze. "Are you kidding?"

"Nope," said Taylor with a grin. "And, before you even ask. Yeah, Jack, you get to keep the position. I say that as the new High Commander," he added with an even wider grin.

General Jack Horner sat back in his chair and a rare, real smile violated his normally serious mien. "Congratulations. Jesus, there *is* a God."

Taylor shrugged and expertly threw the knife into a cork dartboard with a picture of Jar-Jar Binks pinned on it. "There are other problems. He wanted to switch back to Ridicuplan, but I talked him out of it, I think. But we have to maintain forces on the coastal plains during the main invasion."

"Oh," said Horner with another thin smile. "Great."

"Yeah. He's got a point; public opinion is dead set against losing the plains completely. It would tear us apart as a country to fall back on the Appalachians and the Rockies, giving up all the major cities . . ."

"Nice recitation," commented Horner. "Are you considering running for Congress?"

"Say that and smile, partner," said Taylor, with a warning grin. "No, but it's also true."

"Sir," said Horner, formally. "There is no way to defend the plains."

"Oh, don't get me wrong, Jack. I know that and I'm not gonna piss away boys' lives trying. And I'm not gonna let the President, either. What we have to do is come up with a plan to defend certain key cities."

"Which ones?" asked General Horner, frowning slightly in agreement. "That I can live with, if we don't have to defend too far out."

"Well, we're going to decide which ones and where. But I more or less promised that if it is 'historic' it would get defended."

Horner nodded. "You know, I played around with that a while back. Defend the inner part of all the 'major' cities that we were planning on losing. But we don't want to do it with a normal population."

"I told him that, too." Taylor nodded. "We'll plan on evacuating all but the military and an essential civilian presence. No children stay."

Horner nodded with another positive frown. "Good. This will actually be a better defense plan, you know."

Taylor nodded with a grim smile. "The cities will pull some of the heat off of the mountain defenses."

"That and it will keep some of the Posleen where those refurbished battleships can reach them," Horner noted. "I'll have a list of recommended cities for defense by the end of the week. Count on Norfolk, DC, San Francisco and New York."

"Okay," said Taylor. "And start thinking about ways to pull out the defenders if it gets too hot. They'll have to be planning on staying for five years, without external support. But if they're going to get overrun, there will have to be a plan."

"Something else for the ACS to handle," Horner said with a frown. He had just the person in mind to write that part of the plan. Always call on an expert.

◆ CHAPTER 7 ◆

Washington, DC, United States of America, Sol III
0605 EDT May 28th, 2004 AD

"Good morning, professor!" came the call from the door.

Monsignor Nathan O'Reilly, Ph.D., the Reagan Chair of Archae-
ology and Ancient History, looked up from the computer screen and
his eyes lit. The young lady in the doorway was not only one of his
favorite former students, she was a notorious gossip. Since her new
job often included gossip that he wanted to hear, it was always a
pleasure to see her.

"Kari! Come in," he said, rising to his feet to rearrange chairs. "Sit,"
he commanded, pointing at the comfortable armchair placed by the
desk. "Coffee?"

"Oh, no!" she gasped. "I couldn't hold another drop. I've been up
practically the whole night and I'm headed to bed!"

"Since when does the White House Protocol Office work swing
shift?" he asked with raised white eyebrows. He took a sip of his own
coffee and glanced at the cesium-quartz clock on the wall. Among
the bric-a-brac of ancient alembics, archeological relics and old books
it stuck out like a nuclear reactor in a Roman coliseum.

The clock had been a gift from another former student. The newly
promoted Vice Admiral with the Federation Fleet had presented it
to his old mentor with the joke that now he could always be sure
what century he was in. It indicated that Kari was returning home
shortly after six in the morning. While he was habitually early to work,
he knew from experience that Kari, while quite beautiful and intellectually brilliant, was a tad lazy. Her working through the night was
something he would have deemed impossible.

"Oh!" she exclaimed, tossing her head to clear an errant blonde hair. "It is just *so* exciting! The Tir Lord Dol Nok is coming on a state visit! And the *first* place he is visiting is *right here!*"

"Kari, Kari," the professor soothed, "calm yourself. Precision, darling. By right here are you referring to George Mason University or Washington?"

"Washington! He's going to hold a summit with President Edwards to finalize the sale of the heavy weapons for the planetary defense centers in the U.S.!"

The professor shook his head. Kari was a wonderful girl, but it was early for her particular brand of cheerleader enthusiasm. "That is wonderful news. But why were you up all night?"

"Oh," she said, letting out an exaggerated sigh. "The summit won't be for months, but the protocols for the High Tir are just *sooo* complex. Previously the WHoPo thought that the only significant similar human protocols seemed to be among the Mandarin. But that was just being narrow-minded. I was able to convincingly demonstrate that there were more similarities with observed Egyptian motifs. . . ."

O'Reilly leaned forward and gave her every bit of his attention. While in many ways Kari epitomized the image of the dumb blonde, she was one of the most brilliant young ladies it had been his privilege to teach. Her insights into early societies' interactions probably exceeded his own. If she were not such a natter-head or had an inkling about what was actually happening in the world around her, she would be a perfect recruit for the Société.

He nodded his head as she made a point about the surprising similarity between Minoan court protocols and the protocols of the Darhel. He was aware of the similarity, had in fact pointed it out to her on a previous visit. Unlike Kari, however, he had a pretty good idea why the similarity existed. The protocols of the court of Minos derived from both Egypt and Phoenicia. Since becoming a member of the Société, what he had to say about Maya, Egypt and Phoenicia was no longer printable. He could not, unfortunately, teach the truth. That was the part that stuck furthest into his craw.

"So, anyway," she finished her dissertation, "we had to completely restructure the plan. I swear, those idiots from the State Department think that the Darhel are just funny-looking Chinese or something! They had no idea at all that the manner of precedence is reversed with the Tir. They had no idea about food protocols; they were going to serve *roast beef* to *vegetarians!*"

"State is usually more competent than *that,*" commented the professor, chuckling. "Surely they have dealt with the Darhel's idiosyncrasies before this?" He knew that they had. Kari was not the only former student who came back for occasional "chats."

"I don't know what moron concocted the menu," she answered. "But we got it straight. The precedence thing has apparently been overlooked before."

"Well, not this time," the professor said with a smile. "You seem to be doing well?"

"Oh, I don't know." She sighed, her normally vivacious face deflated. "What the heck is the point? We're still going to have hell on earth, no matter *how* good I am at protocol."

"We each must do our small part for the future," he said with a reassuring smile. "Think of the poor people who labor in factories or even work in a convenience store. At least you work at the White House."

"Hmm," she said with a pensive frown. "But, lately I feel like I should be doing more."

"Such as?"

"Larry offered me a position on his staff," she said.

"You want to enlist in Fleet?" he asked, surprised.

"Not enlist. Get a commission. They need officers who can be liaisons with the Indowy and Darhel."

He regarded her somberly for a moment. If she left the White House not only would he lose a very good source, she would be like a fish out of water. She simply had no concept of how different military life was from anything she had ever previously experienced.

"Kari," he said carefully, "why did you say the Tir was coming to visit?"

She wrinkled her brow prettily and cocked her head. "There's a problem with the heavy grav-guns going into the planetary defense centers. The Galactics can't produce as many as had been planned for before the invasion. Also, the new plan to defend the cities is going to require more than the Pentagon had planned for. The Tir is coming to decide the final apportionment not only for the United States but worldwide."

"Hmm," the professor murmured, nodding his head. "Do you think that the Tir would have been more or less favorably disposed to the United States for more grav-guns if the President had shaken his hand, walked at his side to dinner and fed him beef?"

Kari's eyes widened. "Oh."

The old man's face creased in an engaging smile. Kari thought that when he did that it took thirty years off him. He still had the greenest eyes she had ever seen. She wondered for a moment what he was like as a young man. She knew he had come late to his current profession. And he had flaming red hair before it turned white. He was probably a pistol as a kid, she thought.

"So," he asked, "still planning on taking that position with Fleet?"

"No," she said, shaking her head. "Your logic, as usual, is perfect." She smiled back. "What about you?"

It was his turn to look rueful. "Well. The Ministry did not feel it necessary to reactivate a former subaltern, whatever his later accomplishments."

She shook her head. "What idiots. They could use you in Fleet Intelligence. You seem to understand more about the Galactics and the Posleen than anyone I've ever met in the military."

His face displayed none of the terror that little admission fired in him. He had thought his understanding of both their Galactic "allies" and their putative enemies was carefully hidden. Apparently he had been insufficiently circumspect.

"Well, it seems to me that knowledge of humanity and its many foibles gives more than enough background to understand our allies and enemies. We are, after all, not so terribly different."

She nodded and yawned. "Oh!" she exclaimed with a hand over her mouth. "Sorry!"

"No problem, dear," he said with a twinkle in his eye. "I think you need some rest."

"Mmm," she agreed, getting up and heading to the door as he stood in anachronistic gentility. She paused at the open door. "I'm going to be busy for a while, so I may not be able to see you. Take care, Monsignor."

"And you, my dear," he said as she walked out. "And you. Most definitely take care."

He sat down and went back to parsing out the Sanskrit tablet on the screen as his mind worked on many different tracks. He began to mutter a tune that had nearly fallen out of favor except as a corrupted nursery rhyme.

"Yankee Doodle went to town a-ridin' on a pony..."

◆ CHAPTER 8 ◆

Ft. Indiantown Gap, PA, United States of America, Sol III
1023 EDT June 6th, 2004 AD

"Does he ever lighten up?" asked Lieutenant Nightingale as she stepped onto the covered porch of the company headquarters. Tall and greyhound thin, the blonde XO had just been the victim of an O'Neal smoking. She now took a moment in the shade out of sight of the troops to regain her composure.

"I don't think so," said Lieutenant Arnold, her fellow sufferer. The tall, balding thirty-two-year-old weapons platoon leader shook his head.

Until the arrival of the second draft, he had been the executive officer of Bravo Company. He knew exactly how stringent their commander's standards were. He had come to grips with them. Teri, on the other hand, was having problems.

In the captain's eyes, the faults of the two lieutenants were too numerous to list.

The job of an executive officer was usually to ensure that the unit was functioning smoothly first and learn to be a company commander second. O'Neal, however, had put "tuning" the company in the lap of their extremely competent first sergeant and insisted that Nightingale become as competent as he was at maneuvering the company in combat. She had thus far failed miserably.

She was having a hard time adjusting her command style to combat troops. The gentle cajoling that worked well with the techs who had been in her previous intelligence company was perceived as weakness by grunts. She also seemed to have no tactical sense at all. The fact that she was for all practical purposes a neophyte was beside

61

the point. From Captain O'Neal's uncluttered point of view she was one heartbeat away from having his company in her hands and either she could cut the mustard or she could not.

In Arnold's case, the new weaponry and employment techniques were the problem. He was having to adjust to ranges of fire and maneuver he had previously never considered. At the same time he was overseeing the training of troops in a variety of weapons beyond their dreams.

The military had learned some lessons on Diess and Barwhon, and the ACS weapons platoons now packed so much firepower they were jokingly referred to as the Grim Reapers. They had initially been deployed with 75mm automortars and terawatt lasers. Diess had proven that the standard suit grenade systems were superior to the automortars at short ranges while the lasers were too bulky and awkward for the sort of rapid movement ACS had adopted. The mortars and lasers were effectively retired, but in their wake came a diversity of suit-mounted special weapons. From this diversity the platoon leader was supposed to choose which would be appropriate for the probable mission. Since no mission ever went as planned, there were far more wrong choices than right.

If the probable mission was indirect fire-support, the platoon packed individual multimortars. These were enhanced grenade launchers and each weapon-suit packed four: one on each shoulder and one on each arm. They threw 60mm rounds up to five miles with pinpoint accuracy and had fourteen separate munition types from which to choose.

The basic munition was a standard high-explosive (HE) round that could be set for airburst, surface detonation or delay. The weapons graded up from there through "enhanced conventional munitions," i.e., cluster bombs, to antimatter rounds with a "soft kill" radius larger than the range of the mortar. Thus any unarmored humans, or Posleen, in the immediate area of the mortar platoon would be fried if these were used. Unfortunately, for everyone involved, these heavy weapons suits could run through the available onboard rounds in twenty seconds. The "Reapers" joked that they all needed one platoon of grunts apiece, just to carry ammunition.

If the probable mission was close support there were three separate weapons systems to chose from, depending on how close and how personal. The simplest was a set of super shotguns with multiple types of rounds from which to choose. From there it got complicated.

Unfortunately each suit could only mount one type of weapon and choosing the right weapons mix could make or break an engagement.

The Old Man was actually beginning to perfect some beautiful sucker moves for the playbook that involved the heavy weapons platoon. But they required that the platoon leader be able to read his mind. As the playbook got firmed up it might be a little easier but in the meantime there were far more wrong mixes than right.

"Well, I don't care what anybody says," continued Nightingale, angrily, "there's such a thing as— What the hell is that?" she broke off.

"Those are Indowy, I think," said Arnold seriously.

Outside the headquarters the Pennsylvania summer sun stirred up the yard of the company area in playful dust devils. Emerging from the swirling dust was a group of squat green humanoids. Looking superficially like fat children, their coloring derived from a chlorophyllic symbiont that wavered across their lightly clad skin like green fur. Their faces were nightmarishly batlike but their eyes were large and round, giving them an ingenuous expression that actually went well with their personalities. In their midst they towed a large crate on an anti-grav dolly.

"No, that. It looks like a coffin," said Nightingale.

"Little coffin," commented Arnold. Neither of them had ever seen the traveling carton for an armored combat suit.

The nine Indowy were led by an individual with somewhat more ornamentation, but otherwise indistinguishable to the pair of officers. When the lead Indowy reached the bottom of the rickety metal stairs leading to the company headquarters it stopped and bowed. The following Indowy set the box down and shuffled nervously.

"Is this the clan of the most illustrious Michael O'Neal?" The AID translation was in a higher pitch than the two were used to, almost off the audible scale.

Arnold nudged Nightingale.

"Yes," she said. "Yes, it is. I am Lieutenant Nightingale," she continued more firmly, "his second-in-command."

"I bear a gift from my master, the Indowy Aenaol," said the leader with a deep bow. At a gesture the remaining Indowy righted the sarcophagus and touched a button. The box opened to reveal a small combat suit that sported some notable modifications from the standard command suit.

The first thing the officers noticed was the ornamentation. The suit was covered in complex designs that at first appeared to be three-dimensional, an absolute no-no when dealing with penetrating fire. On closer examination they appeared to be holograms somehow incorporated into the armor. There were some elegant fins running down the arms and legs that might help with heat dissipation, a major fault of most combat suits. The helmet was formed into the face of some sort of demon or horrific alien creature, smooth to the front with pointed demon-ears and fangs dangling nearly to the suit's chest. Both arms sported underarm daggers and more weapons peeped from unlikely places. It appeared that if it was surrounded the whole suit might start blasting. More of the company were gathering around to look at the apparition as First Sergeant Pappas stepped through the door.

"Okay, what the hell is . . . that?" the tall, Herculean Samoan NCO said, uncharacteristically dumbfounded.

"The captain's new suit, Top," chuckled Arnold. "Why don't you go get him?"

Mike walked through the door a moment later to the relief of the Indowy team, who were becoming nervous at being surrounded by humans. For the Indowy, dealing with humans had much the same effect as a human dealing with a tiger. The trainer can tell you all day it is harmless, but once you're in the cage it is just a damn big carnivore.

"Top, clear these people out," Mike said, instantly analyzing the situation. He turned a bit of dip between his lip and gum, then spat in the dust to the side of the porch.

"What the hell does this look like, a fuckin' circus?" the first sergeant said, rounding on the first NCO in sight. "Sergeant Stewart! Move your squad out of here before I find something useful for you rag-bags to do! What? None of you have anything better to do? Maybe we need to GI a few barracks?" The crowd rapidly dispersed leaving only the captain, the lieutenants and the first sergeant.

"Indowy Aelool, *taon*, I see you," said Mike, making a fractional bow. He had not dealt with any Indowy since Diess, but he had kept current with the position of the human military ranks in the complex hierarchy of the Federation. However, the decorations marked the Indowy as a senior craftsman. As a Fleet Strike captain Mike outranked the Indowy by several degrees despite the fact that it might command thousands of Indowy. In the Federation scheme of things, Indowy had incredibly low caste.

O'Neal was not certain but he suspected the senior craftsman was a transfer/neuter. That Indowy sex had a natural advantage career-wise, since they were only peripherally involved in childbirth; they also were a strong political force within the Indowy ranks. That made his assignment to a fitting team unusual to say the least. Mike would have expected a lower-rank female craftsman.

"Inspired Lord O'Neal, I see you," the Indowy intoned.

"Inspired Lord?" asked Mike. It was an Indowy rank equivalent to a clan leader; he was not aware that it was ever bestowed on non-Indowy. He could not immediately determine a human equivalent, but there was rarely more than one per planet, sometimes none on a minor planet.

"It was the determination of the grouped clans that such would be your rank among the Indowy, henceforth until time should end. Never has one done so much for so many. I grieve that no greater lord than my humble self could greet you as fit."

"I understand the difficulty." And he did. The Darhel would probably look poorly on this example of Indowy independent thought. "But," he continued determinedly, "the success on Diess was the result of the actions of many."

"So you have said, repeatedly," the Indowy Master agreed. "Yet the strategy for success did not exist until you showed your own commanders the Way. The forces necessary for success were freed by the action of men under your command. The final action, protecting the assembling defenses by single-handed destruction of a command ship, was not done by others." It wrinkled its jowls, an Indowy head shake. "Your humility is in keeping with the finer traits of the humans, but it is false. Argue not, you are an Inspired Lord, in thought as well as deed.

"In keeping with your new assumption," it continued, "it was found mete to gift you with this token of our gratitude. A free gift, freely given as you gave so freely to our brothers." He gestured grandly at the suit. "It incorporates every aspect of suit design that you called for, that was possible to construct."

"Power source?" asked Mike glancing quickly at the suit. He moved the bit of dip to the side as a slight smile violated his face.

"Class Two antimatter reactor, as you specified. Equivalent to a five-kiloton antimatter warhead, but small enough to armor against almost any strike. Just such a warhead could go off next to the armor and not penetrate the energy core, so strongly is it protected."

"Armor?" Mike asked on a rising tone.

"Sixty-millimeter frontal monomolecular uranium-silicon alloy with energetic reinforcement. The energetic reinforcement is logarithmically autocontrolled against nonrelativistic–velocity projectiles. As the round comes closer to a penetrating angle, the deflection energy increases logarithmically."

Mike stepped gingerly down the steps and ran his hand down the front of the suit. "Inertial systems?"

"Two hundred eighty gravities with full lift and drive, seven inertial sump points. Sorry," he said with a shrug. The gesture was shared by Indowy and humans. "It was the best the Tchpth could do."

Mike turned with a closed-mouth smile—he knew what the sight of teeth did to the Indowy—and gleaming eyes. "Tell the Indowy that I accept with thanks!"

"Umm, sir?" interjected Nightingale.

"Yes, Lieutenant?"

"Is that legal? I mean, isn't there some law against it?" she asked.

"No," he responded definitively. His face was quite closed as he turned slightly to spit out another stream of tobacco juice.

"Sir? I mean, conflict of interest? And gifts from contractors? I know there are Army regulations, sir." She finished with a moue of distaste. He was the commander and could have any filthy habit he wanted to have. But he could at least have the decency to keep it private. Her former unit had a zero-tolerance tobacco policy.

"There aren't any in the Federation laws, Lieutenant. None at all," said the Indowy Master. "We checked quite carefully, and it is entirely within the agreed-upon structure for the Federation Armed Forces remuneration process. Also, since it is a necessary piece of equipment for the captain's function, it is not taxed."

"Oh." The group of officers and NCOs shared looks. The Indowy had just handed their captain nearly half a billion credits worth of suit, untaxed. In perspective, an Indowy junior craftsman earned less than five credits a month.

"Again, my thanks," Mike said to the Indowy.

"It is little. My team will be staying to fit your clan. I guarantee you the best fitting possible."

"Why don't you come inside out of the dust and we can talk," said Mike, gesturing towards the headquarters. "There are a few things I've been hoping to talk to a good technician about."

"Thank you. And my team?"

"Top," O'Neal said.

"Right you are, sir. Beds for the Indowy, coming right up. I think a trailer to themselves?"

"Reading my mind again, Top."

"Yes, sir," said the darkly tanned mountain with a smile. "That and training is what NCOs is for."

◆ CHAPTER 9 ◆

Rabun County, GA, United States Of America, Sol III
1023 EDT June 17ᵗʰ, 2004 AD

"Okay, honey, now turn the cam a quarter twist, carefully, while making sure the pin don't come out."

"Like this?" asked Cally, her forehead wrinkling in concentration.

"Just right. Now, can you feel any resistance to the pin?" asked Papa O'Neal, watching the exercise from the shade of a tree. The heat of Georgia's summer enveloped them here at the edge of the fields and every little scrap of shade was appreciated. He worked the massive wad of Redman in one cheek then moved it to the other side.

"No," she said, licking a drop of sweat off her lip. "There's no resistance at all," she confirmed, barely moving the cotter pin.

"Okay, pull it out, carefully. Don't move the trip wire and for dang sure if you feel any resistance, stop."

Cally was taking to demolitions like a duck to water. She had incredible hand-eye coordination for an eight-year-old, and took infinite pains. It only took Papa O'Neal blowing up one cow for her to decide she wanted to be real careful. This was the most advanced technique yet: a claymore directional mine on a trip wire, with the trip wire booby-trapped. Okay, so it was not a real claymore, yet. It was, however, a real blasting cap.

"Okay," he said, continuing the lesson, "so you're walking along a trail . . ."

"No, I'm not, 'cause trail is spelled D-E-A . . . T-H . . . uh . . . T-R-A-P," she contradicted.

"Okay, you're having a bad day."

67

" 'Pay more attention if you're having a bad day, you make more mistakes, not less,' " she recited pedantically.

"Okay, your target is walking along a trail," said O'Neal with a shake of his head. He took a pull from the Gatorade at his side and nodded at her canteen.

"Posleen or human?" she asked, taking a large swig of water. Papa O'Neal's house had the best water in the entire world.

"Well, human this time."

"Okay," she agreed with equanimity. Humans were generally smarter than Posleen according to both Papa O'Neal and her daddy, who ought to know. If you trained to kill humans you were bound to be better at killing Posleen.

"And he's smart . . ." continued Mike Senior, turning slightly to the side to spit. The stream of brown juice nailed a grasshopper as it slumbered on a grass stem.

"No, he's not," she disagreed, putting away her canteen. "He's on a trail."

"Sometimes you gotta use the trails," said Papa O'Neal.

"Not me, I'm in the trees."

"Okay, a target is walking along the trail, a not-very-smart human target."

"Okay," she agreed.

"And he's smart enough to be looking for trip wires."

"Dogs?"

"Feelers."

"Okay."

"And he spots the trip wire . . ."

"Feels."

"Right. And what does he do?"

"Not-very-smart?"

"Right."

" 'Always assume your target is smarter than you.' "

"Would you stop throwing my statements back in my face and go with the exercise!" He worked the Redman back over to the other side and spat again. A beetle started to burrow, thinking it was raining.

"Okay," she agreed. If that was how he wanted to do it, fine.

"Okay, what does mister not-so-smart do?"

"Cuts the wire."

"Go ahead."

"No way!" she disagreed. "You cut the wire. I'm not taking your word on that being a practice claymore!"

"Okay, pull the blasting cap, then cut the wire."

"Okay." She crept over to the camouflaged claymore, sweeping carefully ahead of her with a long piece of grass; you never knew when Papa O'Neal was going to booby-trap his exercises. Then, with a glance over her shoulder to make certain that Grandpa was not going to mess with the detonator, she pulled the blasting cap out.

There was a series of sharp retorts behind her as the training claymores that were hooked to the booby trap on the blasting cap went off in a daisy chain sequence. If all of the claymores had been real, a hundred-meter swath of the edge of the fields would have erupted in fire.

"And the moral of today's lesson?" asked Papa O'Neal dryly. The wad of chewing tobacco distended his grin.

"You are an obnoxious prick, Grandpa!" she retorted.

"And I'm teaching you bad language."

"Hey!" she shouted indignantly, holding up the blasting cap. "This isn't even real!"

"Like I'm going to let you handle a live cap hooked to a trip wire," said the old man. "Get real. I promised to return you in one piece."

"You pull caps all the time," she said, puzzled.

"Not once I've set an antitamper device on it. If I can't blow it in place, I go around. Handling live traps is for fools and damn fools. Which kind are you?"

"Oh, okay. Enough demo for today?"

"Enough for today, except I want you to repeat after me. I will not . . ."

"I will not . . ."

"Attempt to disable . . ." Spit.

"Attempt to disable . . ."

"Any demo . . ."

"Any demo . . ."

"So help me, God."

"So help me, God."

"Amen." Spit.

"Amen."

"Let's go bust some caps," he said with a smile. Cally was good at demo but shooting pistols was her real love.

"Okay, but I want a five-point handicap this time," she said, checking the Walther in the skeleton holster at her back.

"No way. I'm getting old, my hands are all palsied," he quavered, holding out a shaking left hand. "I think *I* should have a handicap."

"You do have a handicap, Grandpa; you're getting senile. Remember last week? Fourteen points ahead on the twenty-meter range? You know what they say: short-term memory . . ."

"Are you sure you're eight?" he asked. A moment later an ant was smashed to its knees by a descending mass of mucus and vegetable matter. After a moment it shook its head and looked around in ant wonder at the largess from the sky.

◆ CHAPTER 10 ◆

For heathen heart that puts her trust
In reeking tube and iron shard,
All valiant dust that builds on dust,
And, guarding, calls not Thee to guard,
For frantic boast and foolish word—
Thy mercy on Thy People, Lord!

—"Recessional"
Rudyard Kipling, 1897

Ft. Indiantown Gap, PA, United States of America, Sol III
2237 EDT July 28th, 2004 AD

Stewart's second squad sprinted forward and dropped to the prone, their grav-guns tracking and firing on the advancing virtual Posleen the whole time. Wherever the silver beams of relativistic-velocity teardrops intersected the Posleen wall, racking explosions tore deep gaps in the oncoming line. In response, hypervelocity flechettes and missiles tore at the defenders' armor, most of the hipshot rounds missing high. But with millions of penetrator rounds coming at the relatively few suits, losses were a statistical certainty.

"Ten–twenty-two, ten–twenty-two, execute!" Stewart said in a steady voice as Private Simmons's data lead went blank. Half the team checked fire just long enough to reach into a side compartment and pull out a small ball. Flicking off the cover and thumbing the switch they set it offset to their right and went back to firing.

"Clear Ten–Alpha," said the Alpha team leader as Bravo team duplicated the maneuver.

71

As Bravo resumed firing, the cratering charges emplaced by the Alpha team went off. They again checked fire only long enough to slither into the impromptu foxholes, then took the Posleen back under fire. "Clear Twenty-Two–Alpha," called the team leader.

Moments later the entire platoon was under cover.

"So that's your playbook," said Colonel Hanson.

"Yes, sir," said O'Neal, watching Second platoon perform an advance under fire. The hasty defense presented by second squad was temporarily impregnable to the Posleen who were advancing on a narrow strip between a ridge and the Manada River, a much larger body of water than reality for the purposes of the exercise. "We've got about two hundred plays, so far, with the various levels of the company trained in their own actions under each play. It's more or less analogous to the bugle calls the cavalry used. In this case, the squads are performing a Ten–Twenty-Two, 'form hasty fighting positions and take cover.' Not that it will help them for long on this exercise." He worked a bit of dip and spat it into a pocket in the biotic underlayer of the all-enveloping helmet. The saliva and tobacco products were rapidly ingested by the system like all wastes. To the underlayer it was all grist for the mill.

"Is this a fair test?" asked Colonel Hanson, noting how Second platoon was dissolving as inexorably as rock candy in hot water. He wished he could have a cigarette, but they were a bitch to smoke in the suits.

"I think so. By the time Nightingale noticed the flanking maneuver, it was nearly too late for Second to establish the optimum conditions, which was for the Posleen to be a hundred meters farther up river. There the chokepoint is only thirty meters wide, and Lieutenant Fallon could have held them indefinitely. As it is, I don't think they'll make it."

"What would you do?"

"I'd probably try a charge, maybe with some psychological refinements, and try to push them back to the chokepoint," said O'Neal. He swiveled his viewpoint down into the river for a moment then back to the fighting. "It's really not a time thing; the length of time they hold is moot. If the Posleen break through now or three hours from now they'll crack the company defense down the river."

"Would it work?" asked Colonel Hanson, now paying much more attention to the briefer than the essentially finished engagement.

"According to the scenario, it will work on an irregular basis, dependent on a number of factors not available to adjustment by the tested," O'Neal answered precisely. Whether any of it would work in the real world was the question in his mind. Every time he looked back at Diess he got cold chills. The chances he had taken were insane. Every single action had been long-ball odds and only incredible good luck had carried the platoon through. His own survival was still placed, by everyone, in the "miraculous" category. And he was afraid he'd used up not only his own quota of luck, but his company's. If these plans were wrong, it was going to be a massacre. And the fault would rest squarely on his shoulders.

He worked the dip around in thought and spat again. "The Posleen might have a wimpy God King, they might not have enough muscle to the front, minute factors of surface structure on the squad's armor affects penetration, and so forth. But if you're this far back you have to hammer them like the hinges of hell, and Lieutenant Fallon's not a hinges-of-hell kind of guy."

"So the mistake on Lieutenant Nightingale's part was farther back?"

"Yes, sir," Mike answered, in a distracted tone. Something about the scenario was playing false to his experienced senses.

"I almost always leave First platoon in reserve, which pisses the other two platoons off," he continued automatically. "But Rogers always goes around with such a head full of steam, when I use him to reinforce or blitz it gets hammered home with a vengeance."

The First platoon leader was a tall, broad, good-looking first lieutenant. As a first lieutenant he would normally have either a heavy weapons platoon or a staff position. Filling a slot for a second lieutenant was beginning to eat him alive; Mike had forwarded four requests for transfer in the last six months.

"Nightingale believes in distributing the load. I am trying to disabuse her of that. The only thing that matters is the mission. You have to pick your units on that basis, not on the basis of 'fair.' I finally decided that what she needed was more of a helping hand. But I'd backed myself into a corner being overcorrective." He grimaced at admitting the mistake.

"Finally I took over most of the stuff the first sergeant had been handling for both of us and sicced him on her. They've been spending a hell of a lot of time together and she's starting to get the hang of it; Gunny Pappas is a top-notch trainer. But I'm still not totally comfortable with her tactical sense."

"It takes time to learn that," Hanson admitted.

"Yes, sir. And I hope we've got it." Mike kicked up a probability graph of the engagement if it continued on the current course and fed it to the battalion commander. The casualty graph looked like a mountainside.

For Hanson, who came to his military maturity in the cauldron of Southeast Asia and the Army of the '70s, the Virtual Reality gear the unit trained with was the next best thing to science fiction.

He had been nearly seventy when recalled and although he had continued in business after the Army, he was one of those executives for whom computers were Greek. These systems, however, were as far from modern computers as a Ferrari from a chariot.

Taking his lead from the resident expert, he started calling his artificial intelligence device, a Galactic-supplied supercomputer the size of a pack of cigarettes, "Little Nag." He now used her for all his official correspondence and, now that he had gotten her over the annoying literalness of a new AID, she was better than any secretary he'd ever had. In the regular exercises the battalion was conducting, Little Nag kept better track of friendly and enemy disposition, personnel and equipment levels, and all the other minutiae that made for a successful military operation, than any staff in history. The newly arrived S-3 and the other battalion staff officers were getting used to their own AIDs and the staff was approaching a level of perfection seldom to be dreamed.

There was a rapid shuffling below as second squad left their positions and the others moved to cover the extended front. The reduced fire pressure permitted the Posleen to begin moving slowly forward, piling up windrows of their dead but willing to take the sacrifice to overrun the position. However, what remained of second squad eeled past the other positions and, using a gully that kept them more or less out of Posleen sight, slipped one by one into the river and out of Virtual sight.

"Oh, God damn," whispered Mike, cutting in an overlay of positions to track second as they moved up current. He smiled and spit into the vacuole again.

"What?" asked Colonel Hanson. "It looks like a forlorn hope to me." He tapped a series of virtual controls to project the course of the unit. The leader, the Sergeant Stewart he had met his first day at the unit, had entered orders for his team and the group of eight survivors was headed for a point in the river opposite the narrow chokepoint the platoon had been unable to reach.

"Not necessarily, sir. Even with the few that remain, second squad could take and hold that chokepoint for a moment, given the right conditions. Maybe long enough for the rest of the platoon to charge forward and relieve them. Damn, I didn't think that by-the-book Long-Grey-Line son of a gun had it in him."

Mike watched as the squad formed under the cover of the green waters then erupted upward. As they moved, the water began to hump and wriggle as if infested by snakes. What surfaced was not a group of suits, but a swarming mass of worms, each gray body surmounted with a fang-filled maw. As lines of silver explosive lightning flicked God Kings out of existence, the worms snatched Posleen from the banks and dragged them screaming into the suddenly yellow-stained water. The air, at the same time, was filled with an evil caterwaul and the thunder of drums.

"Is that what I think it is?" asked Colonel Hanson. His own half-smile was unseen. The flair of their company commander was obviously rubbing off on some of the members of the company. O'Neal's own use of music in battle had become legendary almost overnight.

"If you think that's the Seventy-Eighth Fraser Highlanders' bag-pipes slamming out 'Cumha na Cloinne' it is. Stewart's been listening to my CDs again."

"Your idea?"

"No, sir, but now I know what infested Lieutenant Fallon's mind. That would be Sergeant Stewart." The smile of the company commander was hidden by the faceless armor but the battalion commander could clearly hear it in his voice. "You remember him, sir."

"Mmm," was the only comment. The battalion commander had recently returned a request from the Ground Force Criminal Investigation Division for an investigation into various items of equipment that had gone missing around post. His basis was insufficient evidence of it being traced to Bravo Company. In fact, he was fairly certain that the diminutive second squad leader was responsible.

"You know," the battalion commander commented. "Bravo had a fairly shabby reputation before you took over. You might want to ensure that it doesn't get one again."

Mike's abbreviated nod was unseen. Prior to the nearly simultaneous arrival of First Sergeant Pappas and Lieutenant Arnold, the company had been a center for black marketeering at the post. The easy and unquestioned availability of technology that was centuries ahead of current had created a tremendous profit for the former first sergeant. Stewart and his squad of recent basic trainees, along with the first sergeant and Arnold, had been instrumental in cleaning up the situation. The former first sergeant was now serving time in the Fleet military prison on Titan Base. The prisoners were used for work out in the vacuum that was considered particularly hazardous.

"I'll point that out at the next leaders' meeting," was Mike's only comment. He let out another stream of tobacco juice and smiled at the course the battle was taking. Stewart was definitely a subordinate worth having around. Too bad he was only a squad leader.

Their God King lords dead, and under assault from a creature of an evil mythology, the Posleen advancing through the gap turned and tried to fight their way to the rear as the mass of worms humped itself up onto the ground and began attacking in both directions.

"How are they snatching the Posleen?" asked Colonel Hanson, watching one struggling centaur being dragged below the water.

"Well, sir, you've got me there, unless they've retrofitted the suits somehow." Mike keyed into a higher level of oversight, on channels poorly understood by most of the AIDs, much less humans.

O'Neal had been in on the design of the suits from the very beginning and had been fighting in them from the first contact on Diess. He knew more about the real abilities of the weapon than any other human in the Federation. His last suit had more hours on it when it was lost than any two others in the armed forces, and his new suit was climbing in hours fast. Single-mindedly devoted to the mission, he spent virtually every waking hour, and a significant amount of sleep time, in armor. He had, as far as Hanson could tell, no social life and interacted with the other battalion officers only on business matters or at required social functions.

Not that there were many of those. Indiantown Gap did not present many amenities to the units forming there. The clubs, officer, NCO and enlisted, were overrun with activating units, and the town of Annville, which was the only civilian area reachable without a personal vehicle, was equally overrun with servicemen. In addition, with the limited training costs of the suits the unit could train 24/7 if so desired. The colonel was taking full advantage of these facts, and the battalion had been in the field nearly every day since they completed fitting.

"Okay," Mike said in a distant voice, consciousness deep in an electronic world. "I see what they're doing. They're grabbing them with space grapples. Could work."

"The AIDs are going with it," said the colonel, overlooking the lack of a "sir" in the sentence. "They're not disallowing it anyway."

"I don't know if it would work or not, I've never tried it," Captain O'Neal continued in a distant tone. "That's odd." He had finally found what was bothering him.

"What?"

"The Posleen are being run at only eighty percent efficiency."

"What do you mean?"

"Well, you can adjust these scenarios to the user. It's kind of like levels in a computer game. You don't want to kick the ass of a basic trainee; it takes their edge off to get beat all the time. So, you set the level of difficulty."

"What level was this set to?" asked the battalion commander. Sometimes the things he did not know about his job frightened him and most things like that were not in any manual. With the exception of a few people like this captain, there were no "old hands" with suits. He wondered how the battalions without an O'Neal were able to prepare at all.

"I set it at a hundred percent," answered the captain. "These are trained troops and we could expect real-world landings at any time. The problem with fighting at a lower level is that it doesn't simulate reality well. You want to train harder than real combat, not easier."

The months since he had taken over the battalion had flown by; Hanson could hardly believe how fast. The first wave of Posleen was only six months away, but they were expecting a few scouting Battle Dodecahedrons any day. And before that there would be a few tests.

Captain O'Neal did not know it yet, but Colonel Hanson had arranged for an FSTEP, the Fleet Strike Testing and Evaluation Program final exam. He was going to inform the company commanders right after this exercise. One week after the FSTEP would be an Organizational Readiness Survey and an inspection by the Fleet Strike Inspector General's office.

Thanks to his increasingly able staff and the little troll standing next to him he expected to pass all three tests with flying colors. If they got a first-time pass, which had rarely happened with the other units that were already operational, he had been approved for unit leave of one week. O'Neal would take the time off, out of a suit, or the colonel would have him escorted off the post. And the colonel had arranged a little surprise for the unassuming former NCO. One that he would never have asked for, deserving or not.

"There it is," continued the company commander. "Hmm."

"What?" asked the battalion commander, drawn back from pleasant reverie. The surprise had required an unforeseen number of participants. Mike should be astounded.

"There is a command line in the general training software to reduce difficulty levels at some unspecified intervals. The intervals are tied to about a million lines of spaghetti logic."

"What's that mean?" asked the colonel, wondering what pasta had to do with combat suit programs.

"It means someone's been screwing with the code: I didn't call for this. It could only be the Darhel, they wrote the software. There's a communications protocol in it as well. I wonder if it's a bug or a deliberate function. If it's a deliberate function, I can't see the sense. All it could do is lower the readiness of the training units."

"What do you do about it?" asked the colonel with an unseen half-nod. He was still getting used to the lack of head movement caused by the gelatinous underlayer of the suits.

"I'll report it to GalTech; maybe one of the new members called for it," commented O'Neal, coming out of his programming trance. "But we won't be using the training software much longer, will we, sir?" he asked grimly.

"No," agreed the battalion commander. "No, I think the time for training is about over."

The training for the Second platoon was, indeed, about over. Second squad was entirely expended in the attack, but by the time the last trooper fell the rest of the platoon had fought its way into the gap and was in prepared positions. With a limited front to fight through, it would simply be a matter of how long humans could hold on, not how long they could hold out. It was a subtle differentiation that was often a deciding factor in war. This action was a win; the company's role was to drive forward and hold on until "conventional" forces could reinforce. Whether the company would ever be used that way was the question.

"Have they finalized what our role is going to be, sir?" asked O'Neal, hoping against hope that the battalion commander had heard something that he had not.

"Not yet, and, yes, that bothers me."

"I wish to hell Jack would get his shit together," Mike concluded with an unseen grimace. He moved the dip to the other side of his lip and spit. It wasn't like his old boss to jerk around this way.

◆ CHAPTER 11 ◆

The Pentagon, VA, United States of America, Sol III
1523 EDT August 29ᵗʰ, 2004 AD

Jack Horner currently demonstrated the trait that was his trademark; his face was fixed in a tight, nearly friendly smile that stopped dead at his eyes. The general that this mien was directed at was not fooled; he recognized the danger signs. But he also considered it his duty to continue the diatribe he had embarked upon.

"In conclusion, General, the CONARC staff is unanimously of the opinion that the projected distribution of forces is tactically untenable and logistically unsupportable. The stated intent—to place seventy percent of our combat power and nearly eighty percent of our real shock power—on the coastal plains is patently unacceptable."

"To whom?" asked General Horner, tightly.

"To your staff, sir, and to the nation we are sworn to defend," answered his chief of staff, Lieutenant General Bangs, rather pompously.

"Very well, General, I will accept your resignation, if you feel so intent upon protest."

"Pardon me, General?" gasped Bangs in surprise, face suddenly ashen.

"I think I spoke English, didn't I?" asked Horner rhetorically. He smiled like a tiger, lips drawn back in a rictus, and his bright blue eyes were cold as a glacier. "I will accept your resignation if you feel so strongly about it. Because I have *my* orders from the Commander in Chief, and he says we are going to hold the plains. To do that, we have to place the majority of the combat power there, because it is also where the Posleen are going to concentrate. I gave *my* staff,

as you so succinctly put it, their marching orders, through you, two
months ago. And you come back to me, a month and a half late and
more than a dollar short, with the bald statement that you are not
going to support the plan. Fine. I will accept your resignation within
the hour, or I'll relieve you for cause. Your call." And only after more
months of back-room political dickering to make it acceptable to the
critical politicians. It was still amazing to him how many politicians
simply accepted the "Mountain Plan" and now held it close to their
hearts.

"You cannot relieve me for cause," snarled General Bangs, his florid
face broken out in a sweat. "You don't have it."

"Actually, your simple statement could be construed as insubordination, not against me, but against a Direction of the President. I
could care less: I can fire you at will, whether you think so or not.
The President has a declared war on his hands. All your friends in
Congress can do is hold on to his coattails. They're not going to
expend any effort on a broken-down war-horse. Now, unlike some
people, I have work to do. You are dismissed."

As the shaken Lieutenant General Bangs left, Jack shook his head.
He had put up with Bangs for half a year and he was glad to have him
off his back. Besides being well over the range into the "active/stupid"
category of officer, Bangs was the most immoral senior officer Jack
had ever met. Talking about women was, admittedly, a common sport
of all soldiers—J.E.B. Stuart put it succinctly when he said "a soldier
who won't fuck, won't fight"—but senior officers should not openly
brag about their prowess outside the marital bed.

He went back to looking at the logistics distribution report. Bangs
had been nearly accurate when he said that the distribution was
logistically unsupportable, but he and the rest of the staff were
thinking linearly. Jack was as certain as the staff that the plains would
be lost, but how they were lost was important.

The initial concept of the war was to play a giant game of Go.
Since they could not predict where the Posleen landers would come
down, the forces would be widely distributed. It was accepted that
the Posleen would overwhelm some of the forces. By the same token
some forces should be able to defeat the Posleen in their areas. The
standards for open field battle would require nearly four-to-one
superiority on the part of human forces. But if the conditions were
right they could recapture small areas.

The plan was that these survivors would then rally and reduce the
areas that held active Posleen. As in Go, if a human unit was surrounded by Posleen, it was effectively gone. On the other hand, if
the human units could surround the Posleen, the reverse was true.

Take the white and black balls and cast them upon the Go board of Earth. Begin the game.

However, the Go field does not have terrain obstacles. The first and greatest obstacles were the oceans. The Posleen were almost intensively terrestrial. While they were masters of extracting every last bit of resource from land surfaces of terrestrial type worlds, they left oceans alone. Thus as the landers came in on scattered ballistic paths, they had to divert towards the continental landmasses.

The simple orbital mechanics of this maneuver meant that there was a concentration on the eastern and western coastlines and that there was a greater concentration on eastern than western.

Once the landers were down, the invaders had to deal with the terrains of these regions. The Posleen were structured much like horses, except for the arms jutting from a forward double shoulder, and they were fairly dense so they did not swim well. Also—with the notable exception of the God Kings—they did not use anti-grav vehicles for planetary transport and they were useless as combat engineers. This meant that they were stymied by terrain obstacles that had even the lightest defense. They could not climb mountains and they could not swim rivers, ever, in the face of any sort of defense, even a teenager with a .22-caliber rifle.

In addition, they did not land at random. Landers had never been observed landing in extremely built-up areas, such as the center of large urban areas. Instead they landed in clusters around the cities and moved in towards them.

Despite the reluctance of some of his staff, in the months since the meeting with Taylor, Jack had worked out the broad plan for coastal defense. His AID, along with selected lower level staffers, was fleshing it out even as he had the confrontation with his chief of staff.

The suburbs were indefensible; that was an absolute. Evacuate them when the first real incursion was scheduled, but not before. Plan for that, because nobody, realistically, would leave until the last minute. That was one of the things the Interstate system was designed for; use it. Have the people pull out every scrap of food before they left, bring out all the domesticated animals beforehand. Supermarkets, in general, used "Just-In-Time" inventory systems, so the Posleen were going to get, perhaps, two to three days rations from the available resources. All the other food was in production or stored by the various agricultural companies and grocery chains.

Part of the work being done by his staff was compiling a list of all the locations where food was stored in bulk and integrating it, where possible, into the coastal defense plan. Any stocks that could not be easily integrated were going to be either confiscated or destroyed before the landing. The Posleen would not find one iota of harvested food if he could help it.

The inner cities, on the other hand, were a different kettle of fish. The plan called for defense of the inner cities, but only as firetraps, hell holes to slaughter Posleen. The basic plan had worked well for General Houseman on Diess and Jack intended to use it in America. It also meant that the plains were going to be the battlegrounds that the American populace insisted on.

Again, evacuate the cities. Around them in the suburban areas, at locations that were being determined, would be established firebases. Around the inner city construct a wall. The bastions would be the warehouses and skyscrapers of the city itself. Those bastions would be able to interlock fire with the firebases surrounding the city. As the Posleen attacked the city, the firebases would take them under fire from behind. If they turned on the firebases, the city defenders would take them under fire. The city would become a giant octopus of destruction, engulfing the attacking Posleen in its arms.

Certain major boulevards, preferably ones that were in direct line of sight with the outer fortresses, would be left open, but with walls on either side and the ability to close them off if necessary. Such killing fields had worked well on Diess and they might work again. Let the Posleen file into the boulevards, thinking they were advancing, then open up with all the weaponry in the city.

The fortress plan also reduced the logistical argument. The city fortresses could be stocked for a five-year siege if the Army started constructing and filling warehouses and silos immediately. If the urban forces had to retreat they would destroy the remaining stocks of ammunition and food with preplaced charges. If the war took more than five years, they might as well slit their throats and be done with it.

He understood that eventually the coastal plain cities would fall unless the Fleet came in time. But the reduction of the Posleen forces would work in America's favor in phase two.

Phase two involved drawing back to the mountains. When a region or city became untenable the forces would have to be drawn back through secured routes to the mountains. In this more than anything he thought the Armored Combat Suit units would be effective.

The cities' outer fortresses would be designed whenever possible with their heaviest concentration along the side toward the nearest refuge areas. When a city's defense became untenable, large sections of the city would be dropped, then the remaining defenders would gather on the refuge side and perform a breakout. With the interlocking fires of the exurbs and the city bastions, the forces might be able to break through the surrounding Posleen and start on the long route to safety. As they performed their breakout, ACS units could descend on closing Posleen columns and break them up.

In some cases the Navy, the wet arm, might be able to slip in and perform the evacuation or provide fire-support. He expected this in the case of the Florida cities especially. The Navy was reactivating ships long dormant to support those endeavors.

In the long run most of the cities would fall. But the Posleen that were attacking them would break their teeth, reducing the pressure on the mountain defenders and reducing the overall Posleen population. Until the Fleet was completed it came down to a war of attrition.

The initial mountain plan, which called for a complete retreat to the mountains and the turning over of the cities to the Posleen, would have left vast numbers of Posleen virtually untouched and all the resources of those cities at their disposal. Once the Posleen attack on the mountain passes got into high gear those forces would have been available and fresh. Now they would generally be unavailable. And if the Posleen did attack the mountain defenses they would be battered from hammering on the brick wall of the city fortresses.

If the situation dictated, forces could even sally against the Posleen. But he intended to hold that card up his sleeve or three years from now some politician would give away their hard-won gains in a pointless gesture.

In the mountains and in the interior the situation would be slightly different. The Appalachian and Rockies routes had been worked on for the past two years and featured multilayered defenses all the way up to the Continental Divides. In the southeast, heavy defenses had been prepared along the Tennessee River, through the region of and heavily assisted by the Tennessee Valley Authority, guys who knew all about big projects. In addition, along the outer slopes of the Blue Ridge Mountains and the Rockies twenty-seven superfortresses were under construction. These fortresses, once completed, would afford interlocking antiship fire all along the coasts and overlooked strategic cities. In addition their locations provided an umbrella of defensive fire over the entire country. Posleen forces that attacked the mountain defenses from the coastal plains were again going to break their teeth. They would advance, but he doubted they would be able to break through.

In the interior, landings were anticipated to be light. The way that the Posleen assaulted planets, in large more-or-less random swarms, caused them to concentrate the majority of their forces on the seacoasts. As in the coastal areas, defenses were just starting construction around the inner cities and forts were being constructed in the suburbs. In the case of the Midwest, however, the parasite forts were larger and, conversely, less heavily armed. They were larger because these cities were not going to be evacuated and if the Posleen landed in and near them, the civilians were going to run for shelter. The entry systems were being built by amusement park companies and were designed to accept millions of people in a matter of hours.

The fortresses were less heavily armed because there were only so many heavy weapons to go around. The armaments allocated to cities such as Pittsburgh, Minneapolis and Des Moines were based on the lower likelihood of attack and the greater likelihood of external support. The fortresses also were designed similar to traditional "castles" and hosted numerous firing ports on every side.

After the gates shut the "civilians," many of whom had designated militia positions, would be expected to pick up arms from armories scattered throughout the walls and proceed to firing positions. From there, behind fixed defenses, the refugees could become effective fighters. They would have to be; the interior fortresses would have a third of the "conventional" forces allotted to the coastal fortresses. The interior would also be completely without ACS support. The ACS would have other overriding missions.

The Posleen, as a rule, did not care for extreme cold any more than humans. They also were less able to deal with it effectively. Therefore, they landed in temperate or tropical zones. Thus, Canada could be guarded by her own forces and be well off; the northern border was not considered a problem. That did leave Mexico as a failure source.

An argument had been advanced that America should just erect a great wall along the Mexican border, something that some people had wanted for years. Whether it was a valid argument or not was moot; there were insufficient resources to do the job before the Posleen landed. Any Posleen that landed in Mexico were going to have the field day expected in the Third World for the Posleen and most would probably remain there at first. But some of them were going to turn north; how many was anyone's guess.

Unfortunately, as the Border Patrol had often said, there are virtually no terrain obstacles in the southwestern United States. The only forces that could fight the Posleen effectively without either fixed defenses or terrain obstacles were the ACS, so the ACS were going to be committed primarily to the southwestern U.S.

Jack Horner had, effectively, two divisions of ACS. Fleet had left behind in America the Eleventh Mobile Infantry Division, formerly the Eleventh Airborne Division of World War II Pacific fame, and three regimental task forces: the 508th, the 509th and the 555th Mobile

Infantry Regiments. How he distributed these forces might make or break the defense. Some were going to have to be distributed to the coasts, especially the East Coast, with its broader plain and less defensible passes, but most would have to go to the Southwest.

He had a little time to decide on the distribution and he knew only one person on Earth who was more expert in the abilities of the combat suit units than himself. He decided it was time to call in another opinion.

◆ CHAPTER 12 ◆

The grader was a Marine né Mobile Infantry Major from Fourth Fleet Strike Division. The unit was currently deeply involved in the battles on Barwhon. He was a dark-skinned, blue-eyed Iron Man in the square-jawed movie-star Marine fashion, but his armor was commendably battered. Fighting the Posleen left gouges all over. The nannites that maintained it, that existed throughout the underlayer, could, with time, work out all the wounds on the surface. But the process left a faint discoloration, obvious to the trained eye. Repaired gouges and nicks were regarded much as scars were, badges that said that you had been there and done that. Unmarred armor, like Mike's, was a sign that either you had been through total hell, or were a rookie.

The grader had maintained a deadpan through the entire company FSTEP. Mike was not terribly worried about the results; he had more or less written the book and was careful to follow it to the letter at each stage of the exercise. He was wondering, however, what the major made of it all.

They completed the last exercise, a prepared company defense, just as the first of autumn's cold-front thunderstorms came across the ridges. The hurtling cumulus started to darken the air as Mike bounded up to the major on the ridgeline. Mike unsealed his helmet, the molecular seal bright in the afternoon sunlight, pulled it off his head with a sucking sound as the shock gel released, tucked it under his arm, then lifted one eyebrow in question.

"That scenario was designed as a no-win," stated the major,

removing his own helmet with a characteristic slurp. His dark skin could only have come from tanning beds; most ACS personnel were as white as slugs. A wash of cold air suddenly displaced the muggy early fall heat as a swirling wind stirred the dust and leaves on the ridgeline.

"Yes, sir, I know," said Mike carefully. "I wrote it."

"You obviously also know how to beat it," commented the major. "Were you going to tell anyone else?" Mike could see the last of the nannites that had been left on the former Marine's scalp scampering down to the helmet. The silver trickle writhed in the afternoon sun like intelligent water. The elongated droplet reared out from the major's head, apparently sensed its objective below and jumped into the helmet.

"It's not something I am able to teach systematically, sir," O'Neal admitted with a wrinkled brow. "It is a matter of reading the movements of the Posleen and shuffling your subunits to react to them along with careful employment of artillery and positioning of observers. I only break it about one time in ten. This time it was relatively easy and I wonder if the controller didn't adjust it. The Posleen acted . . . uncharacteristically during the final assault phase. They were almost timorous." He spat into his helmet. The juice was a brief brown spot on the writhing gray surface. A moment later the juice disappeared, absorbed into the underlayer and beginning the long journey to becoming rations.

Another blast of wind whipped the yellowing beech trees around them in a frenzy as a distant branch cracked. A rumble of thunder rolled across the valley as lightning played on the ridges in the distance.

"Gust front," commented the major, looking up at the swirling cumulus. The sky was turning black overhead.

"Pardon, sir?" shouted Mike, not quite catching the words over the wind.

"Gust front," the major yelled back, redonning his helmet. When Mike hooked back up, he continued, "It's the term for that blast of wind you get just before a storm." As the heavens opened their sluice gates and water began to pour from the sky Mike shivered for a moment with a wave of cold chills; the shiver was unnoticeable in the armor. "It's often the strongest wind of a storm."

"The adjustment to Posleen actions is a random effect based upon their actions on Barwhon," the grader continued. "Every now and again they do seem to turn timorous, as you put it. Good exercise," concluded the major.

"Thank you, sir, we try."

"Not that I was going to be able to give you a fail, even if you deserved one." The mahogany face was covered with two inches of plasteel and another two inches of underlayer. But Mike could still see the angry grimace.

"I hope that is not the case."

"Don't worry, Captain, your company seems well prepared for the invasion," the major admitted. O'Neal's reputation as a tactical innovator and near-god of suit combat had only grown since Diess. There were plenty of people in Fleet who felt that O'Neal's reputation was so much bull. The major, at least, was starting to be a convert.

Mike watched his company assembling in the valley as visions of silver fire and swarming yellow centaurs swept across his memory. "I wish I could agree, sir. I wish I could agree."

"Captain O'Neal," the battalion commander's voice chirped in his earpiece.

"Yes, sir?"

"Report to battalion, on the double."

"Yes, sir." He saluted the major. "Sir, I have to go."

"Roger, Captain," said the major, returning the salute, "good luck."

"And to you, sir," said Mike. He dropped the salute and took off down the ridgeline, legs blurring into run mode.

The colonel was waiting outside the command vehicle, a converted Humvee since they had not yet received updated combat shuttles. The first generation of combat shuttles was determined to be deficient even before deployment when the humans discovered that one of the Galactic races, the Himmit, had incredibly effective stealth technology.

The Himmit were an inquisitive species of cowards. Although curiosity might have killed the cat, it never killed the Himmit because they were very, very good at hiding. They had reconned multiple Posleen worlds without ever getting caught. It was a success which humans did not even consider until the first human special operations team went to do the same thing and failed miserably. One small note in the resulting multihundred–page report caused more changes in the war effort than the entire rest of the mission.

The weapons that the Posleen God Kings mounted on their saucer jeeps had continental range and autotargeting ability. While they seemed to have a blind spot where ballistic weapons were concerned, they would sweep away any item under power that crested the horizon. Therefore, tactical operations involving aircraft were basically out the window.

The original teams that designed the Galactic equipment that humans would use, such as the combat suits and the space dreadnoughts, designed a combat shuttle that was heavily armored, incredibly fast and surprisingly maneuverable. But on Diess they discovered it was still vulnerable to the God King launchers; of nine combat shuttles sent to succor then-Lieutenant O'Neal's cut-off ACS platoon, only one survived.

The answer was stealth. Using a combination of human and Himmit stealth technologies a new generation of combat shuttles was being created that would be slightly less heavily armed and armored, but even faster and more maneuverable. Best of all it would be extremely stealthy.

The shuttles had a negative radar cross-section to human systems and only showed up as ephemeral ghosts on Galactic detectors; projectors even smoothed turbulence zones at subsonic speeds. The first prototypes had been fielded on Barwhon, where the humans were engaged in a desperate struggle in the swamps. While they continued to take losses, the rate was much more acceptable.

But until Terran Fleet Strike units received them, the battalions used a mixture of modern and futuristic equipment, such as the converted Humvee with a Galactic communications and battle planning center on the back deck. It affected their strategic mobility, but not local combat.

Colonel Hanson high-fived his Bravo Company commander with a resounding metallic *clang!* "Airborne, Captain! They're trying to find a fault to discuss!"

"Well, I think I should have salvoed the third fire mission just a little earlier," said Mike soberly. "The wave that made it through the fire on that one caused about three percent higher casualties than it should have. I have *got* to find somebody to delegate fire control to."

"Well, I'll just have to send you to bed without supper!" laughed the ecstatic battalion commander. All his other companies were performing well within expectations, but O'Neal's performance had definitely been the cherry on the sundae. He had exceeded every pretest estimate of the highest possible marks. "I don't think they're gonna notice that one, frankly, and neither did I. I don't think they can find a thing negative to say."

"I didn't think you could max an FSTEP, sir," Mike said.

"I think you might have set a new standard. But that wasn't what I called you back for." The battalion commander proffered a hardcopy of e-mailed orders. "Nightingale is going to have to deal with the ORS and IG on her own; you've been ordered to CONARC on temporary duty. Your master's voice, I guess."

Mike glanced at the bald prose of the orders. It had Jack Horner's touch all over it.

"Yes, sir, it sure looks that way. Well, the company's as squared away as it's gonna get. When do I leave?"

"There's an evening flight out of Harrisburg direct to D.C.; you're on it."

"Yes, sir. By your leave?" he asked, saluting.

"Get outta here, Captain," chuckled the colonel, returning the salute.

The flight into D.C. turned out to be a connecting flight full of uniforms. If there was a male of military age not in uniform, Mike thought he should be shot, stuffed and put in a museum as a rarity. The variety of uniforms was a surprise. Although most of the military on the flight seemed to come from Ground Force Guard and Line units—notable by their essentially unchanged United States Army greens—there were also "wet" navy officers and chiefs in black uniforms, Air Force in their blue, and Fleet officers in high-collar black uni-seals and beret. Mike was the only one on board in Fleet Strike blue and red, and felt conspicuous. He was glad that his seat companion, a forty-something female Fleet captain, either did not recognize him or did not care.

After the flight reached cruising altitude, the flight attendants came around with drinks. When the flight attendant passed him the requested Coke, she did a double take, but continued on, apparently dismissing the idea that Michael O'Neal would be on her plane. Afterwards, however, as the plane was just beginning its descent into Washington National, she came forward and did the approved stewardess squat by Mike's seat.

"Excuse, me, sir. I was wondering something . . ." she said, diffidently.

"And that was?" Mike had cycled into a foul mood. Although the company was in good shape for an ORS and IG he wanted to be there to smooth out any wrinkles that might come up. He wanted the company to do as well on the inspections as they did in their readiness test. Although he respected Nightingale's organizational abilities, he was worried about how she would manage the "problem children" in the company, even with Gunny Pappas riding herd. In that kind of mood, he didn't give anyone any slack, much less a stewardess who just wanted to rub elbows with notoriety.

It was the very reason his tunic, against regulation, was totally unadorned with ribbons. He was wearing a Combat Infantryman's Badge, with one star, indicating that he had been in two major conflicts, and a pin that was still so unusual as to be nearly unrecognizable:

a half starburst. The pin had been developed by Fleet to recognize persons who had been in the path of a nuclear blast. Despite the fact that it was authorized to both Fleet and Terran personnel, there were not many people vertical who wore them.

"Are you the Michael O'Neal that was on Diess, the one who got the Medal of Honor?" she asked quietly.

"Yes," Mike snapped. "Next question."

"No question," she said with an honest smile. "I just wanted to thank you. My brother is in the Seventh Cavalry. He made it back to the Dantren Perimeter, but he never would have made it out without your platoon arriving when it did. Thank you."

Well, that was an entirely different matter. "Damn, I'm glad to hear that! You know, the armored forces hardly ever get any mention in all the fuss. They stacked the damn Posleen up like cordwood even before we got there and nobody ever gives them any credit. How's he doing? I admit I haven't kept up with the units on Diess."

"They returned his division to the States. He's down with the Texas Guard units, getting ready for The Day."

"Well, when you talk to him, wish him well from me," Mike said with a smile.

"Okay, I'll do that. He'll be happy I stopped."

"Good luck yourself."

"Well, we're from Missouri. From what they're saying on the news, we should be hit lightly. I hope so, but I'm sorry for all the people on the coasts."

"Yeah, most of my people are in the coastal plains. But no place is going to be completely safe, so get yourself a weapon. If they're swarming, you might not even be able to take one with you," he said bluntly. "But if they've been whittled down, it might save your life. I recommend a twelve-gauge riot gun. They've got a kick like a mule, but it's hard to miss with a shotgun at close range and double-ought will take down a Posleen just fine. You may be in the safest spot there is and have the bad luck of a globe landing on you. So get a weapon."

"Okay, I will. Thanks again."

"Take care."

As the stewardess walked away, the Fleet captain looked up from her papers.

"I thought it was you, but I wasn't going to be impolite and ask," she said with a strong English accent. Mike, who had a fair ear for accents and had spent time with the British while developing the ACS program, placed it as Midlands.

"Yeah, well, I'm me, ma'am. I've never been anything else."

"You're going to Washington?"

"Yes, ma'am, apparently General Taylor wants some advice on how to run the war."

"Well, I can't think of a better source for Combat Suit advice. Might I ask you what is causing you to be so caustic, young man?"

Mike let out a sigh, much of his formless anger blowing out with it. The problems he was dealing with weren't the captain's fault. Nor was his own lack of confidence. "Well, Captain, my company is going through an Operational Readiness Inspection and an inspection by the Inspector General's office at the moment and I would much rather be there than giving dog and pony shows in D.C. I gave a bunch of them last year and nobody gave a shit, pardon my French, so I don't know that it'll be any different this time."

"So you're really going to be telling General Taylor how to run the war?" she said with a chuckle.

"I suspect I might be, ma'am, at least from an ACS standpoint. The CONARC commander and I have a long-term acquaintance. The orders came from CONARC at Fort Myer, but I'm supposed to report directly to the Pentagon. Go figure."

"I think you should be happy about a chance for input," she said, puzzled.

"Well, ma'am, the other problem is the difference between tactical and strategic. Although I will admit to being one of *the* experts at tactical employment of ACS, I won't bet dollars to donuts about strategic employment."

"Just remember," she said, " 'an Army travels on its stomach.' Strategic and operational art are better than eighty percent logistics. Approach it from a logistical standpoint and you'll have them eating out of your hands."

"Logistics."

"Logistics."

"Okay, thanks, ma'am," he said with a smile.

"Don't mention it." She laughed.

"Captain Michael O'Neal," said Mike holding out his hand, "Fleet Strike."

"Captain April Weston," said the gray-haired battleaxe, "Fleet Line. Command." The period was easy to hear.

"Oh, you have a ship?" asked Mike, interested. Very few of the ships being built for the defense were on-line or would be before the first few waves of the invasion. It was what would make the coming years such a difficult prospect.

"If you can call it that," she said, with a sour grimace. "It's a converted Galactic frigate."

"Ouch," said Mike, with a grimace of his own. "I saw the specs when I was at GalTech. No armor . . ."

"Light weapons . . ."

"No redundant systems . . ."

"Limited targeting ability . . ."

"Well," said Mike, with another grimace, "at least you'll have Combat Environment space suits."

"Great," she said with a snort. "I spend a career fighting my way up through bloody-mindedness and knowledge of the sea, and now I have to learn to breathe vacuum."

"You're a regular?" Mike said, surprised.

"Actually, I was Royal Navy reserve until I made captain when they finally succumbed to the bloody inevitable and switched me to regular. My last command was the *Sea Sprite*, which, for your general fund of knowledge, is a cruiser. Now I'm off to the boundless depths of space and classes in astrogation. At my age," she concluded, throwing up her hands.

"Well," Mike smiled, "good luck."

"Yes, we'll all need it."

◆ CHAPTER 13 ◆

The Sons of Mary seldom bother,
   for they have inherited that good part;
But the Sons of Martha favour their Mother
   of the careful soul and the troubled heart.
And because she lost her temper once,
   and because she was rude to the Lord her Guest,
Her Sons must wait on Mary's Sons,
   world without end, reprieve or rest.

—"The Sons of Martha"
Rudyard Kipling, 1907

Washington, DC, United States of America, Sol III
2317 EDT September 5th, 2004 AD

Except for the profusion of uniforms, the nation's capital was virtually unchanged. Mike had taken the shuttle bus from Washington National and it went all over town before heading to the relatively nearby Pentagon. He caught brief glimpses of the Mall, and the streets of Georgetown were surprisingly crowded with partyers. Mike finally saw males out of uniform, persons with jobs so vital that they could not be spared as cannon fodder for the war effort. From their suits, age and haircuts, they were mostly attorneys or congressional aides. *Probably for the best,* thought Mike. *God knows what they would be like in uniform.*

In the previous year, while on tour after the Diess victories, Mike had had his fill of politicians, political aides, political military officers and everything else spin-related. Diess had given him such a clear and uncompromising view of the coming storm that he sometimes felt like the one-eyed man in the country of the blind. There had also been much more exposure to the upper echelons of the military than he had been used to and it had not been a successful exposure.

Mike's idea of subtle was to not tell the person, word for word, that they could not find their ass with both hands. Nonetheless the message came across. When a lieutenant, as he had been then, even a lieutenant with The Medal, takes an attitude like that towards officers thirty or more years his senior the lieutenant comes out of the contest the loser.

The problem, from O'Neal's point of view, was that although many of the senior military officers he had met were quite prepared for and capable of, even brilliant at, fighting humans, they still could not get their minds around the Posleen. Despite the ongoing stalemate on Barwhon and the horrendous daily losses it inflicted, they insisted on thinking of the Posleen as simply suicidal humans, something like the Japanese in World War II. And the numbers were not real to them. They thought in terms of weapons systems, tanks and armored personnel carriers, then troops, because waves of humans simply could not stand up to a modern army.

But the Posleen not only boasted incredible masses of troops so fanatical they would happily take any ordered loss to achieve any ordered objective, they also had weapons capable of negating the utility of tanks and armored personnel carriers. Although the weapons of the normal Posleen were unaimed, fired "from the hip" without careful sighting, many Posleen carried heavy railguns, capable of penetrating side armor on an M-1 tank, or hypervelocity missile launchers capable of penetrating frontal armor. And the God King leader caste carried either automatic HVMs, laser cannons or plasma cannons. A plasma cannon, even if it struck a modern tank with a glancing blow, raised the interior temperature so high it cooked the crew to death.

But all that senior officers heard was "wave charges" and "unaimed weaponry" and they assumed it would be like fighting Napoleonic-era human troops. It might even have been true were it not for the God Kings and their systems. It seemed to those senior commanders as if a modern, well-trained and equipped force should be able to slaughter them.

On that point Michael agreed; the Posleen were going to be slaughtered. What he could not get across to the senior leadership was that the Posleen couldn't care less how many they lost. They came in such masses that reducing their numbers by ninety percent often left them still outnumbering defenders, and with superior weaponry. Well, the powers-that-be would discover the error of their ways soon enough. Unfortunately Mike expected blood baths aplenty in the near future.

The bus finally pulled up to the side entrance of the Pentagon, disgorged a mass of uniformed personnel and prepared to take on another mass headed back to the airport. Mike stared at the busy, scurrying officers, so intent on superior performance of their little niches, and wondered what they all did. What in the world were thirty captains, majors and colonels, most of whom wore the Military District of Washington shoulder patch, doing flying out to distant places at ten o'clock at night?

"Their contribution to the war effort, I guess," he muttered as he stomped wearily over to the MP-guarded entrance. His day had begun at 3 A.M. and had included a prepared attack, a hasty defense and a prepared defense. He had fought three virtual "murthering great battles" and it was, in his opinion, getting nigh on to bedtime.

"Can I help you, Captain?" asked the MP lieutenant in an oddly supercilious tone, as he stepped in Mike's way. Mike recognized the symptoms. Many Army and Navy personnel resented the whole concept of Fleet Strike, effectively American units being put under a broader command, some of them removed from America and not directly defending it. And the difference in pay scale did not help matters.

Since Fleet and Fleet Strike were paid by the Federation, as opposed to Terran governments, they were paid in Federation credits. The Federation had a fixed payment scale for every level of worker throughout the Federation and the soldiers and spacemen of Fleet and Fleet Strike were given positions in that hierarchy.

Through one of those quirks of Federation law that was so beneficial to humans, military personnel had an automatically advanced caste position. Federation law legitimized differing legal structures for differing societal rank; what was illegal for a lower-rank Galactic might be legal for a higher-rank Galactic.

Since the Galactics did not recognize the difference between the legality of things civilian and military, most military activities, such as terminating sentient life, required special permissions. These, in turn, required a higher "caste." That being the case, the lowest ranked soldier or spaceman was ranked the same as an Indowy junior master craftsman. The higher ranks were thus extremely advanced in the overall Galactic hierarchy.

Given these advanced ranks, the Galactic pay scales were equivalent. A Fleet Strike captain made as much as a junior Darhel coordinator—nearly as much as an Army major general. On the other hand, with the tax increases for the war he was being taxed at almost eighty-seven percent of his income. It was a reasonable contribution to the war fund by anyone's estimation. Mike had also heard something about a Federation-mandated bonus from the Diess action. That would further add to the disparity in pay scales. Whatever the case there was extreme prejudice over the pay structure.

It was an attitude that would slowly dissipate after the war, if anyone survived, as Army units were subsumed into Fleet Strike. In the meantime it was just another hassle to be shrugged off.

"Yes, you can, Lieutenant. You can check me in. I'm supposed to report to CONARC."

"I'm sorry, Captain, you seem to be in the wrong place. CONARC is based at Fort Myer. There will be a shuttle in about forty-five minutes."

Mike handed over his copy of the e-mail and fingered the AID wrapped around his wrist. "As you can see, the orders clearly state to report to the CONARC commander at the Pentagon, not Fort Myer. So, where am I supposed to go?"

"I don't know, Captain, I'm just the gatekeeper. But these aren't authority for Pentagon entry." He did not seem a bit displeased by the problem. "And in case no one ever explained this sort of thing to you, when it says report to the commander, it actually means report to someone at the command who will report you as arrived." The lieutenant proffered another smug smile, having to explain such a simple item to one of the lords of the Fleet.

Mike fingered the AID for a moment. "Would you care to try to find out?"

"I wouldn't know where to start, Captain. I suppose you could call CONARC," he finished, pointing to a rank of pay phones outside the entrance.

"Okee-dokee." Mike slipped the AID off his wrist and set it on his head. It automatically conformed into a headset/microphone array. "Shelly, get Jack, please."

"Yes, sir," the AID chirped. There was a brief pause, then, "General Horner on the line."

"Mike?" came the clipped tones.

"Yes, sir."

"Where are you?" asked General Horner.

"At the side entrance."

"Tell the MP to clear you through to the High Commander's office, ASAP."

"Yes, sir." He looked at the MP. "Okay, Lieutenant, the Continental Army Commander say, go to dee High Commander's office, ASAP. Whadda you say?"

"I have to have an authorized clearance to permit you entry to the building, sir," said the MP, obviously calling the snotty Fleet jerk's bluff.

"Jack, he says he has to have clearance."

When Mike used the Continental Army Commander's first name, without being rebuked, the MP's face turned as white as milk. It was obviously not a bluff.

"Give him the phone," General Horner said, icily.

Mike handed over the AID, which the MP accepted gingerly, and watched as the lieutenant basically melted into the concrete. After three "yes, sirs" and a "no, sir" he handed the AID back and waved over one of the guards.

"Sergeant Wilson, take the captain directly to the High Commander's office," he said quietly.

"Have a nice day." Mike waved airily as he snapped the shiny, black AID back around his wrist.

"Yes, sir."

REMF, thought Mike.

Although Shelly could have led him through the labyrinth to the HC's office, Mike was just as glad to have the sergeant along. The slightly smiling noncom led him first to a secondary guard room to get him a temporary pass, which was, miraculously, already cleared for him, then to the area formerly dedicated to the Joint Chiefs.

They walked in through the clerks, still hard at work, and up to the desk of the final keeper of the portal, an aged black warrant officer who looked like he ate nails for breakfast. Mike had heard of Warrant Officer Kidd, an SF legend who apparently had decided that General Taylor needed a keeper at all times. He and the general went way back, so it was said, to an unlikely incident involving an annoyed alligator and two bottles of Jack Daniels. The sergeant stopped at the final keeper and saluted. "Chief Kidd, Sergeant Wilson reporting with Captain Michael O'Neal, who is here to see the High Commander."

Warrant Office Fourth Class Kidd returned the salute. "Thank you, Sergeant. Return to your post."

"Yes, sir," said the sergeant, did a perfect about-face and marched out.

"I think I ruined his whole day," said Captain O'Neal.

"Naw. Made it maybe. But you sure as hell ruined that L-T's. Or so I heard," said Kidd with a cruel chuckle. "Did you really call CONARC 'Jack' to his face?"

"And you've never called General Taylor 'Jim'?" Mike answered with a smile.

"Well, not where anyone could hear." The warrant officer stood up and towered over the dwarfish captain. "Damn, you are short," he said and held out his hand. "Warrant Officer Kidd. *You* can call me *Mister* Kidd."

"Captain Michael O'Neal," said Mike as Kidd's hand engulfed his. Kidd went immediately for a crusher grip which Mike deflected through superior gripping power, although it was hard with the size of Kidd's hands. They wrestled for a moment until a look of pain flashed across the warrant's face. "As a special favor, you can call me Mighty Mite," said Mike as he let up, slowly.

"Okay," Kidd gasped.

"Can I go in now?" asked Mike, maintaining a grip.

"Will you let go if I say, 'Yes'?"

"Mike!" said the CONARC, striding across the office with his hand outstretched, "it's good to see you. You look a hell of a lot better than the last time."

"Thank you, sir," said Mike after a perfunctory salute, shaking General Horner's hand. "Belated congratulations on the fourth star. It is well deserved. Sorry, I didn't bring any cigars, I'm flat out."

"Good cigars are getting hard to find," said General Horner, leading him across the office to a sofa set. General Taylor stood up and walked to his desk to retrieve a cigar box.

"Here," the High Commander said, proffering the box to Mike, "on the house. There's a guy in Readiness that flies down to Guantánamo about once a month. What with the warm relations we're developing with Cuba, cigars are no problem. He always brings me a couple of boxes."

Mike extracted one of the long black panatelas. "Thank you, sir."

"Take a handful. I'll get a box sent over to your company next trip."

" 'He said to the captain, just before the axe fell,' " said Mike.

"What gives you that impression?" asked Horner.

"Well, both of you gentlemen are nice guys, but there has to be a reason you're up until after midnight plying me with tobacco," Mike said with a smile.

"Not really," said General Taylor, chuckling as he lit one of the long, black cigars. "We were going to be up anyway and now was as good a time as any to brief you on your temporary mission."

"Which is?" asked Mike as he extracted his Zippo and began to puff.

"Mike," started General Horner, "as you know, as everyone knows, the defense plan that everyone was calling 'The Mountain Plan' has been scrapped. The President and the Congress will not stand for the Armed Forces not defending the coastal plains, especially the coastal plain cities. The President accepts that we cannot fight for every piece of ground, but he insists that we defend every major city. You with me so far?"

"Airborne," said Mike, carefully judging the flame on the end of the cigar. When it was drawing just right he took a deep puff. *Good cigar*, he thought. "Okay, boss, it's a given: The cities will be fought for. Does the President realize that that will probably inflict more damage than if we can come back in two–three years' time with full Fleet backing and kick them out?"

"Yes," said Taylor.

"Oh."

"That has actually been the subject of a series of news magazine reports," said General Taylor, dryly. "I gather you haven't been keeping up with current events."

"No, sir, I haven't," said Mike. "Not even Net news. I've been getting my company as ready as it can be."

"Apparently you succeeded," said General Taylor, chuckling. "I got a rather snippy e-mail to the effect that there must be a bug in the software for your engagement. You were able to score one hundred percent on a no-win situation. There is some question whether you diddled the software."

"I don't think so, sir," said O'Neal with a smile. "It is a well-known fact that only SFers cheat. We happened to luck out and the God King assigned by the software on the final engagement was a wuss and routed. But mostly, it helps to have done the same exercise a couple of hundred times in VR and Tactical Exercises Without Troops. I play those scenarios in my spare time for recreation, sir, something that other leaders need to learn to do. I mean, most of them don't even play Mario Brothers with their kids."

"Are you saying they need to play video games more?" asked the High Commander, surprised at the frivolous approach.

"Basically, sir," said Mike, peering at the cigar blearily. The fatigue from the long day and the days of preparation beforehand had him saying more than he intended at a first meeting with the generals. He still was not too sure of himself.

Preparing his company was at a level he understood. This "strategic" level was something else. But if being in the game had taught him one thing, it was never lose the image of confidence. Sometimes rep was the only thing that would carry your men through. And sometimes the definition of "your men" could get awfully broad.

"This gear creates a video game environment and the wargames

are based on a number of video game archetypes," Mike continued.
"If they would spend less time doing the work of their first sergeants
and pushing hardcopy and more time in the VR environment they
would do better in notional battles."

"Well," said General Horner, "we, and by that I mean General Taylor
and myself and to a lesser extent you, need to decide what that battle
is going to be and how it is going to be fought. I am going to outline
for you, in broad strokes, what the strategic and operational mission of the ACS should be and, over the next two weeks, you suggest how we should do it, in as much detail as possible given the
time. Got it?"

"Got it," answered Mike, leaning back in the chair. After a moment
he leaned forward again. The comfortable armchair was a surefire
way to put him to sleep. If he was going to keep from making an
ass of himself in front of these officers, he was going to have to stay
on his toes.

"Okay." General Horner looked up at the ceiling as if drawing
thoughts from the pooling cigar smoke. "We are required, by order,
to do as much as humanly possible not to lose the cities to the
Posleen. First we have to define what a city is. We have arbitrarily
decided to defend only the city core, because, quite frankly, we don't
see any way to defend into suburbs. Oh, we'll have some depth, and
some outer defenders, besides the parasite forts I'll talk about in a
minute, but basically we're just going to try to hold 'downtown,' the
part with the skyscrapers that Posleen shy away from landing on
anyway.

"Outside the cities, near the beltway that is around most of them,
now, we are going to construct modern fortresses. They won't be
'state-of-the-art' like the planetary defense centers, but they'll have
some sort of curtain wall and moat system along with massive conventional firepower. We are going to give the fort commanders pretty
wide leeway on how they want to arm their walls. The idea of these
forts, and the central city fortifications, is to catch the Posleen between
two fires. We call the outer forts 'coral forts' because they are like a
spreading coral.

"The cities and the coral forts will have enough supplies to hold
out for five years, if necessary. Each of them will also be just out
of line of sight of a planetary defense center; that was already in the
PDC plans, so we don't have to worry overmuch about them being
directly assaulted by landers or command ships. If landers or command ships take to the air less than en masse, the planetary defense
centers should be able to sweep them out of the sky.

"If the situation becomes completely untenable for a city's forces, they may attempt to flee to refuge. For the purely coastal cities, we are coming up with plans to evacuate them by sea."

"How, sir?" Mike interrupted. If he had one weakness it was sleep. Without regular doses his brain turned to mush. It had pretty much gone south sometime around the landing in D.C. He was currently well beyond playing guessing games. He took another hit of the nicotine hoping it would clear some cobwebs.

"Partially by subs. We're reactivating a bunch of the nuclear launch boats, boomers, that haven't been scrapped. We're ripping out all the weaponry and upgrading the environmental systems. We figure we can pack nearly a battalion into the missile section alone, more in the torpedo rooms, and so on. We're substituting the nuclear kettle with power crystals to appease the environmentalists."

"Like there's going to be an environment left," snorted General Taylor. He walked over to a sideboard and poured a measure of scotch. "Anyone care to join me in a snort?"

"I'll take a vodka, straight," said General Horner.

"Bourbon on ice, sir, thank you, sir. Much ice, sir."

"Don't be so uptight, Captain. We're all old soldiers here," said the High Commander.

"Yes, sir," Mike answered with a wink. He would rather have asked for coffee, but when the High Commander offers drinks you don't refuse.

General Horner snorted and went on. "The Navy is also reactivating all the battleships that haven't been turned into razor blades. Since there were a bunch of them that have become museums and since there were howls of protest over scrapping the last two of the Iowa class that weren't, it turns out we have eight."

"I heard about that, sir," said Mike. "Can they stand up to Posleen weapons?"

"Well, their belt—that is, the portion of their hull that is above the waterline, and most of their bridge armor—is twelve to fourteen inches of homogenous steel. That would normally be light to stand up to plasma cannons, but the steel that they are made of turned out to be surprisingly resistant. Also they're adding on some lightweight ceramet enhancements that increase their resistance to laser and plasma fire by about twenty-five percent. They'll be able to hold their own, even at short range, and think about the firepower! Each of those things has nine guns, either fourteen or sixteen-inchers."

"Didn't the *Iowa* lose one in an accident?" asked Mike, rubbing his chin and thinking about having a battleship broadside at his beck and call.

"Yes," said General Taylor. "But they are building a new breech at Granite City Steel in St. Louis. It'll be ready in about ten months."

"However, for those cities which cannot be evacuated by sea," continued General Horner, "there must be some alternative means."

"If you mean fighting their way out through the investing Posleen, sir," interrupted Mike, "I don't see any. Are we talking about light infantry, sir?" He hid a yawn and took a deep breath to drive some oxygen into his flagging brain.

"Some, but with enough transport organic to the division to move the whole thing. Basically a motorized infantry regiment. Most will actually be mechanized infantry, Armor or Armored Cav. The tanks and AFVs will be positioned in forward revetments or ready to sally and the troops will be in bunkers. If they have to retreat or sally there will be trucks and other transports to move the entire force and any civilians who've stayed behind. In one sortie."

"Okay, let me give you a situation and a city, sir," said O'Neal, rubbing his chin in thought, flogging his brain. "Let me see if I understand this plan. Let's talk about . . . Sacramento."

"Good choice," said General Horner, leaning back.

"Okay, sir." Mike tapped his AID. "Map menu." He tapped the icons on the hologram until he had the map he wanted and yawned again. "It looks like about a two-hour drive from Sacramento to Placerville, where, I would guess, the first of the mountain defenses would be placed. How am I so far?"

"About right," said General Horner after a moment's thought.

"Okay, sirs. That means about six to ten hours of battle to reach the first defense lines," Mike said, taking another pull on the cigar. He looked at the ceiling and flicked an ash.

"About that," agreed Taylor from the bar.

"Through a Posleen swarm," said Mike, still contemplating the ceiling.

"Yes," the generals chorused.

"Nope," said Mike, shaking his head definitively. "Sirs."

"Really?" asked General Taylor, handing out the drinks.

"Really, sir. Look at Diess or Barwhon. Remember that French armored division on Barwhon that got caught out of prepared positions during a movement?"

"Right, Third Armored Cav," said General Taylor.

"*Troisieme Armore Chevalier*," Mike corrected. "They lasted, what? thirty minutes?"

"There had just been a landing, Mike," pointed out General Horner, "the Posleen numbers were at their maximum."

"We have to assume an outside influence to force the evacuation, sir," O'Neal pointed out and took a sip of the bourbon. He raised an eyebrow at the quality of the sourmash. It had been in an unlabeled decanter, but it was a nice Kentucky distillery, probably an "estate" brand. Obviously being High Commander had a few perks even in these days of universal rationing.

"Okay, I'll give you that," admitted the CONARC. "Now, assume MI support for the retreat and reconfigured roadways to maximize terrain cover. How much MI support would you want to evacuate the remains of a corps out of Sacramento?"

"Oh. You're talking about covering three or four divisions?"

"Yes, or five. I think Sacramento is detailed for five divisions."

"Jesus, sir." Mike shook his head. "I don't think you could lead five of the current standing divisions to a whorehouse on a Sunday morning much less through five hours of battle with the Posleen in open field combat."

General Horner looked at Taylor and raised an eyebrow. "You wanna take that one, General?"

General Taylor smiled and shook his head. "We hope to get that under control, Captain."

Mike snorted. "Better you than me, General. Which particular magic wand are you planning on waving?"

"Mike," said Horner, warningly.

"No," said General Taylor, holding up a hand. "He's right. Things on the ground are totally fucked-up. Every fucking report we get from the IGs says the same thing." He turned to the frowning and bleary-eyed captain. It was always hard to tell if O'Neal was pissed off or not, however, because the frown was plastered on his face at all times. "There's no magic wand. We're getting more and more rejuvs in the pipeline. As we get people into their positions, most of the major problems will correct themselves. When there are officers and NCOs available to lead and be held responsible the directives that are already in place will start to take effect.

"We've got the better part of a year to fix things. And most of the divisions, especially the really bad ones, will be fighting in fixed positions. So even if they crack in places it should be controllable. But we do have one trick left."

"Mike," interjected Horner, "remember back when we were with GalTech we discussed who was going to be called up in what order?"

"Sure," said Mike, thinking back. "Combat background personnel first. Start from the highest ranks and work down. Noncombat experienced last." He thought about it a bit more and smiled faintly. That was in the days before the Galactics' problems with supply became evident. When everything was going to be pure Tech as a salvation. When the plans were perfect and the future was rosy. "Good days," he added.

"Well." General Taylor nodded, with an understanding smile. "That was the plan. But somewhere along the line the plan and the process went astray."

"One of my 'computer geeks,' " said Horner, with a wry aside to General Taylor, "finally got a look at the algorithm the personnel department was using for the call-up. It was based on Officer and Enlisted Evaluation Reports."

"Oh, shit," said Mike, with a chuckle. Although good soldiers generally came out fine on the Army's evaluations, the reports tended to miss the difference between a good leader and a "Lifer." The original plan had been to call up warriors as the first wave, setting a tone for the forces to follow. That had obviously not happened.

"So," said General Taylor, "we've had the software rewritten . . ."

"By my people," General Horner interjected.

"Right," continued Taylor. "From now on combat experience will have a high multiplier along with medals for valor. We're calling it 'The Old Soldier' program."

"Oh, hell," said Mike with a grim chuckle. "No modifier for age, right?" Most of the files that a program like that would spit out would have been formed in the caldrons of World War II, Korea and Vietnam. Old soldiers indeed.

"Right," said Horner. "The program has been in place for a couple of weeks getting the bugs out, but the really big call-up will be during the conference."

There was an unexpected bark of laughter from Taylor. Both of the officers looked at him in puzzlement. Then Horner realized what he was thinking about and frowned in humor.

"What?" said Mike. The fact that something had discomfited his former mentor was obvious even through his fatigue.

"There were . . ." said General Horner, carefully.

"A few bugs," completed Taylor with a laugh. "His computer super geeks forgot that there are certain persons who, shall we say, are unavailable for recall." The senior commander laughed again, uproariously. "Oh, Jesus, the look on his face!"

Horner frowned. Hard. A sure sign he was about to burst out laughing. "The computer was searching for high-ranking officers who were still alive and had combat experience. We felt that if there were bugs, it would be better to make the mistake with senior officers than junior. The program had been deliberately set to ignore whether their experience was *as* the rank they 'retired' at."

"Although in one case it wouldn't have mattered," pointed out Taylor helpfully.

"I still don't get it," said Mike, looking from face to face.

"Mike," said Horner, with a slight snort of his own. "You do realize that Commander in Chief is a rank, don't you?"

"Oh," said Mike, then, "*Oh!*"

"Yep," said Taylor, and howled in laughter, "it called up all the surviving Presidents who had either served during a time of combat at any rank or who were President during a time of war. It recalled them at the rank of four-star general, that being the highest available, and ordered them to report to Fort Myer immediately for inprocessing as same."

"Oh, God," laughed Mike, "that's rich."

"I got a couple of very irate calls from the Secret Service," Taylor laughed. "But what was even funnier were the direct calls. One of 'em even offered to come back as his 'original' rank."

"Did you take him up on it?" asked Mike.

"Nah. I was tempted. God knows Fleet needs every pilot it can get. But it would have been a political nightmare. I hope he was just joking."

"Anyway," said Horner, severely, "right after this conference is the big kickoff. To make sure nothing goes too wrong on one end of the spectrum, we will, with great ceremony, recall every single winner of the Medal of Honor still at large."

"Oh, man," said Mike, quietly. Although he wore the Medal himself, he was sure that most of the other winners were *real* heroes. Whenever he was in their company he felt like a piker. What he had not yet realized was that most of the Medal winners felt the same way about the other holders.

"We're hoping that the infusion of 'heroes' will put some spine in the force," said Taylor, seemingly pulling a knife out of the air and cutting the end off of his own cigar. The knife, after a brief flurry that looked like a simple habit rather than showing off, disappeared as rapidly.

"We're reactivating the 'Strike, Line, Guard' concept as well," the High Commander continued. "The plan of creating 'elite' Line forces that were mobile shock forces fell by the wayside along with a lot of other ideas." He lit the cigar with a silver lighter. The inscription "Who Dares Wins" was faintly visible along with a chased dagger and wings.

Taylor took a drag on the cigar and let out a stream of blue smoke. "Right now, other than the Fleet Strike Forces and Special Operations, the only forces that show overall high readiness are some of the Cavalry regiments. We're going to start the Line concept around them. They will become mostly volunteer and will be moved to locations where they can be used to reinforce defense points and sally against Posleen columns. They're going to take a hell of a lot of casualties, but I expect there will always be volunteers.

"So, most of the 'heroes' will end up in Line units," Horner pointed out. "But they're going to be bearing the brunt so it's the right place to put them."

"Just remember," said Mike, rubbing his eyes, "some of these guys are not going to be tightly wrapped."

"Speaking from experience, Mighty Mite?" asked Horner.

"I've had my bad days, sir," Mike admitted, quietly. "Nights, usually."

"You need a break, son," said Horner. He didn't tell him they already had something in mind.

"I had one, remember, sir," said Mike, sourly. "I was on a Bond Tour."

"That wasn't a break and you know it," said Horner. "And it wasn't my fault. I didn't have a shred of pull back then."

Mike nodded and decided to change the subject. "Apropos of nothing, sir, where is the equipment for all these mechanized and mobile divisions coming from?"

"Chrysler is back in the armor-making business, has been for nearly a year. They and GM have been producing like mad, son," said General Taylor. "They've not only stepped up their production rate beyond anything they expected, they've converted two factories in western Pennsylvania and Utah for M-1 production and four for Bradley production. The Toyota plant in Kentucky is about to get into the business as well. Modern equipment we have out the ass. What we don't have is GalTech."

"And even an Abrams can't stand up to Posleen for very long," continued General Horner.

"Hmm. Any more rabbits in the hat?" asked Mike.

"Like what?" asked Jack.

"Like independent forts along the way?"

"No," said the CONARC. "We've only got so much logistics to go around. Not to mention bodies. We have to concentrate on the cities, not long-ball chances like the evac. There might be some small outposts—we're looking at doing some stuff with militias—but by this time they will probably be swept away. That's where the mobile infantry comes into play." The fate of the defenders was obvious. But the general carefully did not comment on that.

"And in the southwest," interjected General Taylor, flicking an ash from his stogie.

"And in the southwest," agreed Horner, "which is going to be an Eleventh Mobile Infantry show. The other use for the MI will be as support during the initial retreat to the montane defenses and to ensure that the Posleen do not break through the Appalachian defenses especially. What we want you to do is go over the conventional battle plans being developed and set up the MI zones of responsibility.

"Zones of responsibility will not be detailed to units smaller than a battalion," continued Horner. "The units you have to work with are the 508th, 509th and the 555th. The Eleventh will be used as a division to hold the 'underbelly.' "

"Are we going to have all of those?" Although there were plans in the pipeline to supply all those regiments with suits, the schedule of supply had been pushed back and back. Pretty soon they were going to start taking losses and the new suits would be going to replace casualties.

"We have to assume so," Horner stated. His grim smile belied the words. "I've set up an office with a couple of staff and all the necessary clearances. And of course you've got Michelle," said General Horner, gesturing at the captain's AID.

"Shelly," corrected Mike, fingering the bracelet of black intelliplastic. "Michelle died on Diess."

"Sorry," said General Horner, ignoring the inquiring glance from General Taylor, "Shelly. Can you work out the details with just that?"

"I could do it without the staff, if everything is in the network."

"It is," said Horner.

"Then no problem."

"Initial deployments and SOP battle plans for three regiments in wildly varying terrain?" asked General Taylor. "No problem?"

"Yes, sir," said O'Neal with a tired smile. He thought it would be a nightmare, but doable. "After activating a company of multigenerational soldiers being introduced to science fiction technology for the first time, in an encampment that has daily riots, this will be a piece of cake."

"Okay," chuckled General Horner, tossing back the last of his vodka. "You have three weeks. Your company will be on leave by then and you're going on leave as well. Colonel Hanson asked me to make that an order, by the way."

"Yes, sir. I could do with a little time off."

"I agree," said Taylor. "And so did Lieutenant General Left."

Mike looked suspiciously from general to general. "How did the Fleet Strike Commander, who I trust is still safely ensconced on Titan, become involved?"

"Well, Bob seemed like the best point of contact to make with Fleet," said Horner with a frown.

Mike flicked an ash off his cigar and frowned warily. "And why did Fleet get involved?"

"Well, we had to get permission from Vice Admiral Bledspeth," explained Taylor.

"Yes, sir," said Mike, his suspicions fully aroused. "I suppose you did. For *what* is the question?"

"Well, to get them to kick Sharon loose," said Horner.

"And shuttle her down for a break of her own," pointed out Taylor. "That was almost harder."

Mike's jaw dropped. "Sharon's taking leave?" he asked incredulously. "Since when?"

"What time is it?" asked Taylor, ostentatiously looking at his watch.

Horner gave one of his rare true smiles. "Close your mouth, Mike, flies will take advantage. Think of it as having friends in high places. Or, if you prefer, think of it as a reward for maxing your FSTEP."

"Sir," the captain spluttered. "This is not funny. It is completely unfair to everyone else in the world who has a spouse on detached duty! It is the worst case of personal privilege I can imagine!"

"Yes, it is," said Taylor, seriously. "But most of those soldiers have not made the contributions you have. Most of those soldiers are not going to be asked to shoulder the burdens you, and Sharon, will be asked to shoulder. And most of those families, despite the occasional tear-jerker news report, don't have both parents in harm's way."

"Mike," said Horner, seriously also. "It's a done deal. I knew you would react this way which is why I didn't even ask you about it. Take it as a gift from a friend or an order from a general. I don't care which. But Sharon will be on leave a week before you get kicked loose. Then you'll have a week together. After that you'll have a week by yourself. And that will probably be the last break you have for years."

"Yes, sir," said O'Neal, finally getting over the shock. Looked at a different way it was a hell of a compliment. The only part that bothered him was the personal privilege. He finally decided that this was one gift horse where he wasn't gonna look at the teeth.

"Take off, Mighty Mite. It's good to have you around."

" 'Night, sir," said Mike. He paused at the door in thought. "And thanks," he said.

◆ CHAPTER 14 ◆

Lagrange Point Four, Sol III
0510 EDT September 10th, 2004 AD

I wanna pony. Her young face was scrunched in an unhappy frown, her arms crossed over her chest and tears threatening in her eyes. The light wind of the summer afternoon had faded and the trees in the background were dropping their leaves like rain.

I'm sorry, sugar, you can't have a pony. None of us can have ponies.

Why not?

There's no air for them to breathe. As she said it Sharon realized that there really wasn't any air. She began to pant but she couldn't fill her lungs.

Mommy? said the little girl, receding into the blackness. She had fallen out of the air lock and was drifting off into the depths of space, the diamond-hard stars wheeling around her as she fell and fell. Mommy? Mum? Comman'er O'Neal? Commander? Mum? COMMANDER!

Sharon started up in the bunk and banged her head into the bunk above hers. For a moment stars wheeled around her and she nearly screamed at not waking from the nightmare. Instead she took a deep breath and quietly let slip her husband's favorite swearword.

"Are you quite all right, mum?" asked Boatswain Michaels. He squatted by the side of the bunk with a cup of steaming tea in his hand. His thick Midlands accent was, as always, nearly incomprehensible.

"I'll be fine as soon as I figure out how to kill Lieutenant Crowley so I can have his bunk removed," she joked, swinging her legs over the side of the bunk. It was necessary to hunch forward to avoid banging her head again. The ceilings of the converted Indowy fast courier were barely six feet tall. Cramming two bunks in vertically had been challenging.

Everything had been challenging since she'd been assigned to the position of executive officer on the *Agincourt* five months before. During her tenure she had suffered through three different captains as Fleet High Command cycled officers through the few available warships. The first one was fine, a former submariner who had taught her many of the tricks that stood her in good stead since. The other two had been losses, micromanaging assholes who were lost commanding the ship. The last one had been a philanderer to boot, a Russian bigot with wandering hands.

She had firmly quashed a mutiny by the ship's crew that would have led inevitably to a fatal "accident" for the officer. The crew treated her more like an older sister than their XO, and had fiercely defended her. By the time the captain left he had discovered the many pleasures of a badly tuned ship, such as varying air pressure in his cabin, reversing toilets, lighting that remained at constant intensity but slid through the spectrum in varying increments, now red, now purple, now, apparently, out, but really broadcasting in high ultraviolet. The sunburn from the last had actually overwhelmed his antiradiation nannites.

Since he had completely bypassed his executive officer, placed in the position because of her background in astronautic engineering, the systems failures were entirely his fault. He, of course, did not see it that way, blaming everything on Sharon. She, in turn, kept full records of all meetings or even casual encounters.

The past two weeks of inquiries had been . . . interesting. It was not an experience she cared to repeat. However, a new commander was on the way and the Russian was headed back to the land of borscht.

"Ach, you don' wann' remove Lieutenant Crowley now, mum," the boatwsain disagreed. "Thin you'd have'ta con this bitch on your own everytime."

She accepted the cup of tea, then rubbed her forehead before taking a sip. She'd have a knot there. The request for foam rubber had been on the books for nearly four months. Time to send another HEAT round. And then there was the shortage of filters, which was why the ship smelled like a goat-locker. And the forward force screen was acting up. And the number three impeller. And about half the environmental fans, thus the hint of ozone in the goat-locker. And the heat exchangers. And with the main water recovery unit down, the cup of tea she was ingesting was a third of her potable water ration for the day. But with the Russian gone at least they might get some of it fixed. If they could squeeze the parts out of Titan Base.

"Anything I need to know right away?" she asked and reached across the narrow compartment for a bottle of Tylenol. The living compartments were designed for four-feet-tall Indowy. At five feet eleven she fitted in them poorly.

"Aye, mum," said the boatswain soberly. "Wiv finely lost the forward force screen."

"Damn," she muttered, swallowed a handful of the acetaminophen and chased it with a swig of the bitter tea. The "chai" as the NCO insisted on calling it was a thick, nearly black concoction preferred in the British Navy. Sharon had talked the crew out of many things, feeding her pickled herring for breakfast as an example, but she had been unable to adjust the tea. Whatever. It woke you up.

She pulled off her T-shirt and pulled out one that was marginally fresher. Michaels was queer as a three-dollar bill, so it wasn't going to inflame him.

They'd had a couple of problems with sexual harassment and one attempted rape in the first few weeks she was onboard. Not all the countries that had contributed sailors to the Fleet had a tradition of females serving on ships. She had stamped on it hard. Maybe too hard. She sometimes wondered if being left on the ship was punishment for suspending the attempted rapist in microgravity, vacuum and darkness for fourteen hours. With his radio pulled. The sailor had had to be transferred to Ground Forces.

She pulled on a stained coverall and stamped her feet into a pair of shipboots. The emergency belt pack was the last piece of necessary equipment to go on and she was ready to face her day. She was already hot as hell. The backup heat converter must be out again.

"You should at least have a bite," said Michaels reproachfully. He held out a platter with toast on it.

She tilted her head to the side, a habit she had picked up from her husband, and smiled. "You're the bosun, not a steward."

Michaels shrugged. "Cooky's pretty damn busy, mum. I knew you'd not eat if I di'nt insist."

Sharon picked up one of the pieces of toast and took a nibble. It was dry and quite awful. There was no decent bread flour in the ship and the last fresh food they had received had come in nearly a month before.

The ship was on a seemingly endless patrol of near-Earth space. Parts and food, such as reached them, were shipped in by light freighters and transferred by hand from ship to ship. The crew struggled endlessly against the conflicting demands of failing systems and the boring patrols.

Sharon knew they were no better or worse off than the other frigates. The converted fast couriers were the front line of the Federation's defense against the Posleen, but they were frighteningly inadequate from the human's point of view. The ships were ancient, literally centuries old, and lacked every item that humans had come to expect in a warship. There were no redundant systems, no easily switched out spares, not much in the way of defense, and the weapons were nearly useless.

What made matters worse was their customization. Each ship was hand built over nearly a half century by one of a few Indowy families. Since each ship was custom fabricated there were no interchangeable spare parts. For that matter, since the ships were designed to last for a few centuries of blemishless activity, then be taken out of service, there were no parts whatsoever. Every part was solid-state; there was no reason that they would not last a pair of centuries. And the Indowy guaranteed it.

Unfortunately, most of the ships, like their own *Agincourt*, had been in service since the beginning of the war. The losses from the war were straining the production capacity of the Federation beyond the maximum and the shortage of shipping was the most obvious aspect. These ships, which should have been taken out of service a century earlier, were still being used on the front line. And the Indowy technicians attached to the Fleet were learning a new term from the humans: jury-rigging.

She nibbled at her dry toast and had another sip of the bitter tea. Then she tapped the artificial intelligence device on her wrist. "What's the news?" she asked.

"There are twenty-seven messages in your e-mail queue," the AID answered in a melifluous baritone.

"How many of those are the maintenance people on Titan whining about our parts requests?"

"Fourteen."

"Delete."

"Okay. Then there are five denying requests from various crewmembers for a transfer off ship. One of those is a rather snotty question about the leadership of the frigate."

"Send 'em a copy of the transcript from the inquiries and tell them to kiss my ass. Diplomatically. And resubmit the requests. God knows somebody should be able to get off this tub."

"Done. There are six answers to your requests for better food, all of which boil down to quit whining."

"Okay. Send the requests back but increase the requested amount every time until you get to our maximum stores level. Do that once per day or once per denial if they respond within the day. Carbon-copy all requests to Fleet HQ."

"Okay. Most of the rest of it is junk. But there is a message from Titan Base stating that the new CO has been assigned and will be arriving this afternoon."

"Joy," said Michaels. "Bloody joy and happiness. Another one." Part of the problem was that the COs for the frigates were captains. The post would have been one for a lieutenant commander or even a lieutenant in a regular navy but the frigates were the only place for "wet navy" sailors to learn the ins and outs of space command. Because the posting was relatively "simple," the senior officers assigned generally started off assuming that they knew twice as much as the officers and crew in place. Many of them had learned what it was like to breathe vacuum.

Sharon shook her head. "Hey, maybe this one will be different. Who is it?" she asked the AID.

"Captain April Weston," said the AID.

At the name, Michaels sucked in his breath. "Bloody hell."

"You know her?" asked Sharon.

"I've never met her," said Michaels. "But everybody in His Majesty's bloody Fleet knows *about* her."

Sharon made a come-on gesture, indicating a request for enlightenment.

Michaels shook his head. "Well, she's just about the only woman who has ever stood for admiral in the fleet who came out of surface warfare. She's a bloody legend among the swifties. On her mother's side she's related to a dead chappie named Mountbatten." He paused trying to figure out how to explain that to an American.

"I've heard of him," Sharon said dryly. The late Earl Mountbatten had been the last of a breed. Closely related to the Royal Family he had been an officer in the Navy during World War II. After distinguishing himself as commander of a destroyer squadron and having repeated ships shot out from under him he had formed the first combined special operations groups in history. After the war he had been made Earl of Burma and expertly ushered that country into independence. He was a national hero and a treasure whose life was finally snuffed out by the bomb of an Irish terrorist. "So she's related to the Royal Family?"

"Distantly," said Michaels with a shrug. "Us Brits have still got a thing about, well, 'blood.' You know?"

"Lineage," said Sharon.

"Bloody right. Well, this Weston is the sort of person who . . . sort of reinforces that. If there was ever a case of the acorn not falling far from the bloody oak."

Sharon nodded. "So this is good?" she asked cautiously.

"Oh, yeah," said Michaels. "Of course, Mountbatten survived four ships. And most of his chappies never made it back. There was some as would jump ship rather than sail with him."

Sharon snorted and thought about the departed Russian. "I'll take my chances."

The air lock hissed and Captain Weston stepped forward, still fumbling at the catches of her pressure helmet. It annoyed her to demonstrate incompetence in her first moments on the ship, but the only previous time she had worn a battle suit was during the four-hour familiarization class at Titan Base.

One of the petty officers standing at attention stepped forward and unhooked the last recalcitrant fitting and her ears were blasted by the shrill of a recorded boatswain's pipe.

She stepped forward and returned the salute of a good-looking brunette in a slightly soiled coverall. "Captain April Weston," she said and removed a folded piece of paper from a sealed belt-pouch. That maneuver she had managed to practice on the shuttle over and it went off flawlessly.

" 'You are hereby ordered to proceed forthwith to the Fleet Frigate *Agincourt* for purposes of assuming command,' " she quoted. "Signed Hareki Arigara Vice Admiral, Director, Fleet Personnel Department." Weston lowered the paper and nodded at the presumptive executive officer. "I take command, ma'am."

"I stand relieved, ma'am," said the brunette. "Sharon O'Neal, Lieutenant Commander. I'm your XO."

Captain Weston nodded and looked around at the assembled crew. It was a fairly small party. "I am about to betray my ignorance," she admitted. "Is this most of the crew?" she continued, slightly aghast. Normally most of the off-duty crew members would be present for the greeting party. There was more than enough room in the pressure hold for more people, so the group of twenty or so might be it. That would place the upper end of the crew at thirty or so. The crew of a "wet" frigate would number over a hundred. Her previous cruiser command had numbered over a thousand.

"Ma'am, there are four on duty in the tac center," the XO answered, "three in engineering and four more at various other points. There are also six Indowy crewmembers." She hesitated. "They . . . don't usually associate with large groups of humans."

Weston nodded her head. That was one briefing she had gotten. "Understood." She looked around and raised her voice slightly. "I'm sure we'll all get to know each other well over the next few months." The tone was a command voice. It implied that what the speaker said would occur, whatever the universe might throw at the speaker. Compared to the whiny and blustering Russian she replaced it was immensely heartening to the crewmembers. Which was what she had intended.

She looked around at the damaged and dingy interior of the ship. The lighting was purplish and unpleasant and the cargo hold was covered in scuffs and dents. For all that there was little real dirt. The ship was obviously well cared for. But the age and poor condition were clear nonetheless. She smiled and chuckled. "I'm sure we're going to get *real* friendly."

There was an uneasy chuckle in response from the group and she turned to the XO. "Mrs. O'Neal, why don't you show me to my dayroom and we'll get down to business."

"Yes, ma'am," said Sharon. The new commander had obviously gotten a realistic first impression and the response was better than she had hoped. "If you'll follow me?"

The commander's office turned out to be a cramped antechamber of the captain's quarters. It was smaller than the office April had on her first command—also a frigate, as it happened—and very poorly positioned. The captain's quarters were nearly thirty meters away from the bridge through a twisting maze of unusually low corridors. Using this as an office was obviously out of the question.

She turned to her XO, standing at attention behind her. She waved a hand. "This isn't Fleet Headquarters, for God's sake. Simply bowing will suffice." She smiled to assure the XO it was a joke. "Is there anywhere closer to the bridge for me to do my paperwork?"

The XO shook her head. "No, ma'am, there isn't. Believe it or not, engineering and the bridge are almost collocated. The engineering section pretty much wraps the bridge. Then, out from there are a mass of environmental systems. This is as close as any quarters are to the bridge. And there's not anything that can be moved or taken off-line to get you closer. I'm even farther away, which is why I was using the office in the period between the last commander and your arrival."

Captain Weston nodded firmly. "Well, I suppose I shall have to learn to hurry." She sat in the workstation chair and spun it to face the XO standing at parade rest. "Sit," she commanded, pointing at the nearby bunk.

Sharon seated herself carefully, hands on knees.

Weston examined her just as carefully. The officer was attempting to radiate calm but was obviously as nervous as a virgin in the East End. Weston nodded unconsciously.

Sharon wondered what the nod meant. The new commander had been regarding her steadily for nearly a minute. If she thought she could outwait Sharon O'Neal she had another think coming. The stare was, however, disconcerting. The captain had blue eyes so dark as to be almost black. They were like looking into a Highland loch; there was no way to know how deep it might be. They seemed to suck light into them. Sharon almost shook herself, realizing she was becoming half mesmerized.

"Lieutenant Commander Sharon Jerzinsky O'Neal," said the new captain, startling the XO. The captain smiled. "Jerzinsky?"

Sharon shrugged. "Polish, Captain."

"That I recognized. Rensselaer Polytechnic, Class of '91. BS Aeronautic Engineering. Cum Laude. Entered the United States Navy Reserve Officer Training Program in 1989. Why?"

Sharon shrugged again. This was going differently than she expected. Among other things she was amazed at the officer's memory and wondered how far it would stretch.

"I took the ROTC program for the money, Captain. It wasn't much but with a couple of scholarships I only had to have one job on the side." She carefully refrained from discussing what the job was. Modeling was modeling but there were a few pictures around of her that she sure hoped never made it into her official packet. Or the fact that her minor had been in dance.

The new commander nodded and went on. "Commissioned as an ensign and took training as an aeronautics maintenance officer. Assigned USS *Carl Vinson*. Served four years, three on the *Carl Vinson*. Exited regular service in 1995. Why not continue?"

Sharon wondered how to explain to this career officer. How to explain that despite all the pressure being applied to reduce harassment, an aircraft carrier at sea for six months or more at a time was still no place for a former model. How to explain the decline in morale and discipline during those dark days of the American military. How to explain the frustration of not being able to keep birds in the air because of a lack of parts. Or the pressure to put up birds you were not one hundred percent sure were good. Of having a husband knife her in the back so he could get a few more hours in the air. Of having the same son of a bitch leave her for an "LBFM," a "Little-Brown-Fuck-Machine." The Indonesian wife was nice and almost apologetic. But that hadn't helped.

"There was no reason to continue at that time, ma'am," she answered, her stock noncommittal response. "I had never considered the Navy a career."

"Despite a string of 'Excellents' on your Officer Evaluation Reports?" asked the British officer. "Despite, 'this officer manifests maturity and ability far beyond her age and far beyond her peers. Future assignments of this officer should be determined keeping in mind the good of the service and possible future high rank rather than the immediate needs of career placement.' And it was 'enthusiastically endorsed' by the carrier commander." The professional officer cocked her head to the side in puzzlement. "That's better than any evaluation I got at the same rank. So, why leave? You had the possibility of a fine career in front of you."

Sharon raised her hands palm up. "I was never a careerist, Captain. I'm happy that Commander Jensen was so enthusiastic and that Captain Hughes agreed. But I still was not there for a career."

The new commander cracked her fingers and leaned back in the station chair, fingers laced behind her head. "Bullshit."

Sharon stared at her stonily. "Perhaps, Captain. But it is all I am required to discuss with my superiors."

Captain Weston cocked an eyebrow. "Once burned thrice shy?"

Sharon smiled faintly. "More like eternally shy. Ma'am."

"Okay." The officer nodded. "Fair enough. Returned to school, Georgia Technical Institute. Met and married one Michael O'Neal." She stopped. "Parenthetically, I met the Mike O'Neal who won the medal on Diess on a plane just the other day. Nice fellow, if you've never met him. Just as short as he looks on TV."

Sharon smiled thinly. "Yes, he is, ma'am. But I find him quite tall enough."

Captain Weston looked surprised for the first time in the interview. "Seriously? He's your husband?" she asked, her accent for once becoming prominent.

Sharon smiled whimsically. "Seriously. I mean, I know he's not much to look at . . ." she said and smiled again.

The captain shook her head and trudged on. "Took your masters in aeronautic engineering, specializing in determining maintenance cycling. Went to work for Lockheed-Martin in Atlanta on the F-22 project. The project was then in the process of being 'downsized.' I'm surprised you got a job." She cocked an eye for an answer.

"So was I," Sharon admitted. "But they were continuing background developmental work, figuring that sooner or later Congress was going to give up and buy the damn thing. I was fresh out of college and cheaper than the people they were letting go. I wasn't happy about it, but I took the job anyway."

"But you stayed for two more years. Until you were called up, in fact."

"I'd hardly been there any time when We Heard." Sharon finally crossed her legs and interlaced her fingers over her knee. "By then we'd started tinkering with the Peregrine variant. When the parameters came back it looked like the Peregrine would be the answer to our prayers. Now that I've gotten a better look at the data on Posleen weapons I think it's a death trap. But nobody listens to me these days."

"Oh, I wouldn't say that," said Captain Weston, enigmatically. She leaned back and ran her fingers through her hair. They came away greasy and she grimaced. "They listened to you at the Board of Inquiry. And that was with an entirely male board and two Russians on it. Have you ever wondered why you are still on this ship when all the other officers have been cycled through like shit through a goose?"

Sharon snorted at the sudden profanity out of the somber officer. "Yes, Captain, actually I have."

"So, we're back to 'Captain' are we?" asked the officer, with a snort. "As you wish. You realize that none of the officers have been in place long enough to give you an evaluation report."

"Yes, ma'am," Sharon answered, more carefully.

"Captain Stupanovich tried. He submitted your review despite only being in command for sixty days. The minimum is one hundred and eighty."

"Yes, ma'am," replied Sharon with a grimace. "I saw it."

"Not particularly good from what I've heard," admitted Weston. "Well, that was one piece of paper that will never see the light of day. If there is a remaining copy anywhere, Fleet has been unable to find it."

Sharon wrinkled her brow. "I don't understand. Why would Fleet be trying to purge that review? I can understand denying it, but why purge it?"

"Commander," asked Weston, leaning forward and pinning her with that deep, black gaze, "how many systems are currently down on this barge?"

Sharon grimaced. "There are seventeen 'minor' systems down and four 'major' systems, ma'am. The major systems are limited to environmental and defense. All weapon systems and drive systems are on-line." She shrugged. "The crew is doing wonders, especially the Indowy, but we don't have the *spares*! We might have been able to get spares delivered for the heat exchangers and the number six forward fans by now if Captain Stupanovich had bothered to forward the requests!" she finished angrily.

Weston nodded. "Commander, there are seventeen frigates assigned to Earth system defense. You know that, right?"

"Yes, ma'am."

"Do you know how many are *flying*?" she continued, aggressively.

"Twelve, ma'am," said Sharon, wondering where the discussion was going.

Weston nodded again. "Do you know how many have more than fifty percent capability in weapons and drive? The two systems that you correctly pointed out are the most important?" She waved at the air. "It's hot! The exchangers are off-line, right?"

"No, ma'am, I don't know how many are out of service and yes, ma'am, the heat exchangers are out," said Sharon. "Actually, half—" she continued and was cut off.

"I'm not attacking your job, Commander. I'm telling you why you should straighten up your damn shoulders! Having all the heat exchangers off-line can be deadly. But not nearly as deadly as having our lance-launch ability off-line! Do you know what Admiral Bledspeth, whom I have known since I was in diapers, said to me?"

Sharon shook her head, wondering what the Terran System Fleet Commander would have said about this bucket of bolts. She felt like she was being slapped in three different directions by the rapid turns of the new commander.

"He told me to keep my damn comments to myself and listen to Commander O'Neal and I might just live to see Terra again." She shook her head and swore. "This is the only damned frigate circling Earth that has all its weapons on-line and a fully capable drive! And if you don't think Fleet notices that, you're not as smart as they say you are.

"We are currently the only frigate that is more or less ready to sail in harm's way!" continued the captain, seriously. "If there is an emergence of Posleen ships, the fighters and the other frigates will try. But most of the frigates, if they're not limping on one reactor their launch systems are off-line!"

"Oh, joy!" said Sharon as anger built in her system. "So, what you're telling me is I've been stuck in this hell-hole for doing a *good* job?"

"No, Commander!" said the captain, determinedly. "I'm telling you that you are stuck for doing an *incredible* job! And you are now going to have to teach still another sea-sucking regular Navy asshole how the *hell* you do it!"

"Oh, God," said Sharon, with a laugh for the accuracy of the phrasing. The laugh held a note of despair.

"And I, in turn," said the officer quietly, "will give you all the support I can. So, maybe, we can turn this into something other than a flying rat-hole sardine-can."

Sharon nodded and sighed. "Well, ma'am, in that case we'd better get you accustomed to the paperwork."

"Not the systems?" asked the captain. It was a test. The captain might learn a smattering of the equipment, but for the moment getting the parts out off the supply chain was much more important.

"Not if you want to have any running in a month," said Sharon, shortly. "The Fleet floats on electronic paperwork. And my AID is about to give your AID a crash course. Starting with how messed up the parts program is."

◆ CHAPTER 15 ◆

Ft. Indiantown Gap, United States of America, Sol III
1427 EDT September 13th, 2004 AD

"Yes, Ampele?" First Sergeant Pappas looked up at the image of the operations sergeant displayed by his AID. The call had interrupted his attempt to reduce the mass of paperwork that had built up while he was on leave and he suppressed an illogical snarl; the recently promoted ops sergeant was famous for not wasting his time.

"Top, battalion PAC just called and we're getting another E-6."

"We're up to strength," responded Pappas as a knee-jerk reaction.

"No, we're down one, according to PAC, and technically they're right."

"If you're talking about Stewart's squad, you've got to be joking."

"I don't know what else we're going to do with him. He's senior to Stewart and all the other squads have staffs as squad leaders."

"Do we have his two-oh-one? And where are we on getting Stewart his Six?"

"The two-oh-one's still queuing from all the transfers, but PAC is 'very confident' that we will have it in hand by the time he arrives, and he has a hardcopy with him. And there is no way that battalion is going to board Stewart. He's barely out of basic!"

"So are you, and I got you your five stripes. Never mind, I'll take another hammer to the sergeant major. When the new guy arrives, send him straight in."

"Roger."

"Staff Sergeant Duncan," said the new NCO, from the doorway, "reporting to the first sergeant as ordered."

Duncan had been around—he was entering his twelfth year in the military—and he knew that when you reported to your company, whatever the procedure might say, you usually saw other NCOs before you were introduced to your new first sergeant or commander. Because they were very busy people with tight schedules, if you were ordered to report directly to one or the other on arrival, it usually meant trouble. And he really had no interest in trouble. Especially from the big son of a bitch that was his new Top.

"Come on in, Duncan was it? Pull up a chair." Ernie Pappas, who still thought of himself as a gunnery sergeant, could tell when someone was on pins and needles and suspected he knew why.

"No big problem," he continued. "If you're wondering why I asked to see you right away, just a couple of things I wanted you to be aware of. Termites in your new home, so to speak."

First Sergeant Pappas did a quick perusal of his newest NCO and came away with varying first impressions. For one thing, the guy was no rejuv. Pushing thirty probably, though it was hard to tell with his eyes. He had a battered look, kinda shocky, that reminded him of the Old Man when he first arrived, and a pin that he had only ever seen before on the captain, the one that meant that the person had been in nuclear ground combat. Despite how bad it was on Barwhon, the pin had only been earned in one engagement.

He held out his hand for the hardcopy personnel file clutched in the new NCO's hand. "Diess?" he asked, softly.

"Yeah. And I just got back from Barwhon," the staff sergeant replied, surprised. "How'd you know?"

"I've seen the pin before." Pappas let it lie at that and started reading the file. He skipped all the marketing bullshit at the front that was mainly for promotion boards and went straight to the military history file. Several items leaped off the page. After a few moments' scan he closed the file and smiled.

"What?" Duncan asked. He knew that his new first sergeant had seen something that made him adjust his first impressions, probably either the Article 15 just before Diess, or he had read through the lines on his most recent transfer. The smile could mean anything.

"Well, I have the old good news, bad news routine," said Pappas with a slight smile. "And I'll lay it out with the intermediate news first. I wanted you to know that your platoon sergeant is a female.

"Sergeant First Class Bogdanovich was an instructor for the Marines before they opened up the combat arms and she jumped at the chance to go to Strike. She is extremely competent and runs a helluva platoon. I doubt that you're going to have problems, but you're not prejudiced against women, are you? I'd appreciate an honest answer; I can shuffle things if you are."

Like I could say yes? thought Duncan. "No, that's fine. I've never worked with a female boss, but we were having them trickle in as I was leaving Diess. The ones who are professional are fine."

"You got a problem with some that aren't professional?" asked the first sergeant cautiously.

"Top, if one of my troops starts bawling because I told them they fucked up, that's their problem," said Duncan with a frown. "I do not coddle my male troops, I damn sure won't coddle any female ones. Yeah, I had a little problem with that on Diess, not one of my troops. She eventually decided that maybe Fleet Strike wasn't the place for her."

The first sergeant decided to take that one on faith. It sounded like a couple of incidents he'd heard about, but not in Bravo since they'd received their first group of women. Fleet Strike was composed of multiple countries' forces, some of which had a tradition of women in combat. It made no allowances for feminine virtues or perceived weaknesses. It was not that what was generally considered a feminine approach did not have merit, it was just that it had no merit in combat. The Fleet forces were slowly coming to terms with that fact, the American forces generally much slower than others. From Pappas's point of view, it was up to the Bogdanoviches and the Nightingales to prove that they had a place. There were no freebies in the infantry. Not with a war on.

"Okay," he said with a nod, scratching the back of his head with a pen. "I don't think you're going to have a problem with that. Now for the really bad news. We've already completed our FSTEP, and maxed it, so I'm understandably proud of our junior leadership and don't really want to mess with it.

"The only squad that does not have an E-6 squad leader is headed up by an E-5 who is so outstanding I'm considering offing you to keep him in charge." Pappas smiled to show he was joking. "Unfortunately, he is also so incredibly junior—he's practically straight out of boot camp—that you virtually have to take the squad."

"Well, Top," said Duncan, furrowing his brow, "you know that thing about a lazy man? If I can let my Alpha team leader run my whole damn squad . . ." He held up his hands as if taking them off.

"Sure, sure, I believe that. Anyway, I think you can handle Stewart. You'll find this out soon enough, but I came here from the Fleet Basic course at McCall with the skeleton of the company, and Stewart came with me. Nonetheless, he really is extraordinary. Wait'll you deal with him. Last but not least, I think you should know that I doubt I will be able to do anything about it even if you do have problems with Stewart. Or Bogdanovich, for that matter. Or even me."

"Why?" asked Duncan, sensing a trap.

"You know how I said I'd seen that pin . . ."

"Sergeant Bogdanovich," said the first sergeant as he walked into the Swamp, "meet your new second squad leader, Staff Sergeant Duncan. He was in the Old Man's platoon on Diess."

Natalie Bogdanovich hesitated fractionally as she extended her hand, then took Duncan's in a strong grip. "Welcome to O'Neal's Traveling Circus."

Duncan sized up his new platoon sergeant and was immediately impressed. Bogdanovich was a short, heavily muscled blonde with engaging blue eyes and her hair pulled back in a bun. Her fresh good looks were barely undone by a nose that was slightly crooked from being broken some time in the past. But the energy and enthusiasm she exuded quickly drew the attention away from that tiny defect. Duncan could feel a restrained power behind her grip that reminded him of Lieutenant O'Neal.

"I didn't even know he made captain, although I'm not surprised."

"Given the size of Fleet Strike," pointed out Gunny Pappas, "we were bound to get someone who knew him on Diess. There's not that many units."

"Well," Duncan noted with a grim shake of the head, "there were only twelve of us left and three are on permanent disability."

"How do you get permanently disabled?" asked the first sergeant. "Galactic Medical can fix anything that doesn't kill you outright."

"Psychiatric," Duncan and Bogdanovich said together, then looked at each other quizzically.

"Boggle did a tour on Barwhon, first," said Pappas.

Bogdanovich nodded, somberly. "It seems there's still some things they can't cure."

"Yeah," Duncan agreed quietly. "Although I think in the case of Private Buckley, they let him off 'cause they didn't want to put up with the stories." Duncan gave a grim chuckle.

"Private Who?" queried the first sergeant.

"What, Mighty Mite never told that one?" said Duncan with a smile. Two combat vets and Mighty Mite as a commander. It looked like this might be a good place to call home for a while.

◆ CHAPTER 16 ◆

Ft. Myer, VA, United States of America, Sol III
1825 EDT September 13th, 2004 AD

"All work and no play makes Mike a dull boy," said General Horner, leaning casually in the doorway of Mike's tiny office; his junior aide, Captain Jackson, hovered at his side.

"Well, sir, the nightlife in Georgetown ain't what it used to be."

Since being given the almost overwhelming task of writing employment guidelines for the Armored Combat Suit units in the upcoming defense, Mike had been working sixteen to twenty hours a day, seven days a week. Work was actually a relief compared to contemplating the current situation. As the world hurtled to its inevitable rendezvous with the Posleen, society had begun a slow process of meltdown.

Once the full import of the upcoming invasion became apparent, a radical shift in economic and population emphasis occurred. Seventy percent of the world's population and eighty percent of its wealth was concentrated in coastal plain zones or plains contiguous with coastal plains. While these areas had many noteworthy features, defensibility against the Posleen was not one of them.

The developing "Sub-Urbs," underground cities for the refugees from the plains, had been designed with locations for businesses, factories and all the other necessary organs of society. However, like many things Galactic related, they were not being completed as fast as originally anticipated. The waiting list for businesses and manufacturing locations was even longer than the one for residences.

Businessmen, insurance adjusters and the common man could often do enough math to make their own decisions. Areas that had become moribund due to the previous decades' shift away from montane zones suddenly began to experience a rebirth.

The faded industries of Bavaria and the American Rust Belt, especially the cities of Detroit and Pittsburgh, saw a massive influx of new plants, as GalTech and more mundane terrestrial industries relocated their fixed facilities to locations that could be defended.

With this movement of industry and services came a matching movement of labor. The workers, managers and executives of the moving firms followed the jobs, but others could put two and two together and a massive movement of people without any fixed employment flooded the Ohio Valley and the Midwest in the United States, and Switzerland, Austria and the Balkans in Europe. In Asia, more limited infrastructures and disputed borders did not permit mass migrations such as occurred in the United States and Europe, but there was significant movement towards and into the Himalayas, Hindu Kush and Caucasus.

In Japan, meanwhile, all the industry remained on the plains, but massive civilian shelters were being dug and populated throughout the country's many mountain ranges. The Japanese experiences in World War II and their extensive civil engineering infrastructure continued to serve them well.

This mass migration and the flickering disruptions it caused in supply and demand of goods, services and labor were causing every kind of shortage in one area and oversupply in another.

Many individuals were getting rich on these supply problems, most of them ethically. Shortages had always been the creators of fortune. These individuals and anyone else with an income were then faced with the problem of where to put their money.

In most cases this was still the currency of whatever country the transaction occurred in, rather than Federation Credits. However, there was no convincing evidence that banks or even countries would survive the invasion. Thus, the cautious investor would prefer placement in a Galactic bank or a Terrestrial bank in a very secure location. Although most funds were merely electrons, a brick and mortar location remained a necessity. There was more to store than money. People had valuable artworks, personal treasures, precious gems and other items of "real" value. Terrestrial banks had, early on, joined in partnership with Galactic banks and, using this conduit, funds and goods began to flow outward from Earth.

However, the inevitable law of supply and demand again reared its ugly head, and as the flow continued from Terrestrial currencies to FedCreds, the exchange rate went up and up. Now, along with a famine of hope, was the specter of inflation. There were two exceptions to this.

Switzerland, already a renowned financial center, had been given the highest possible Galactic bond rating. Not only was it a major financial center already. Not only was it seventy percent mountains. But the Swiss militia had gone through several tests against notional attacks and every single assault had been beaten off with ease. However, another player had entered the banking market.

The ancient and secretive Buddhist country of Bhutan was briefly conquered by its neighbor, Bangladesh, for the purpose of becoming a leadership haven. A single visit by a British Armored Combat Suit battalion returned things to their original structure, but the Bhutanese had learned their lesson.

Obstructed by their religion from engaging in violence, they could still hire mercenaries, and a new Ghurka regiment was born. Ghurkas were mountain troops from Nepal that had a reputation as the best light infantry in the world.

To pay for it Bhutan opened a few small branch offices of major banks. Since the kingdom was determinedly old-fashioned and environmentally rigorous the bank branches were shoehorned into millennia-old massively built stone monasteries. Now, defended by the most renowned fighters in the world, massive stone walls and terrain obstacles to daunt Hannibal, the banks began to receive a tsunami influx of precious artwork, gems, metals and funds. A fractional tithe of this flood served to pay for the most advanced military equipment on Earth for the Ghurkas. The Ghurkas, and their British mercenary officers, were only too happy to put it to use.

Inflation, deflation and shortages wracked the world, causing famines and plagues in their wake. But through all of it most continued to work and struggle: to labor for a possible victory.

"Actually," said Horner with a smile, "I hear the ratio of unmarried females is even higher than ever."

"As, I said . . ."

"Well, you're getting out of this office tonight. You have to be about done."

"I am done," Mike answered, gesturing at a massive stack of hardcopy on his desk: reports and presentations. "That's it."

"Okay, good," Horner said, pleased but not surprised that everything was just so.

Mike had worked for him for two years when he was in charge of the GalTech infantry team, initially as a civilian TechRep and later as his aide. Horner had learned early that the junior officer had an intense ability to concentrate on getting a job done. He had chosen him for this job for that reason as much as for his ACS experience. Time had been short. There was a tiny list of people who could design the operational strategy for ACS employment in Fortress Forward. And there was a different tiny list of people who could pull something like that together in the bare two weeks he had had at his disposal. The only officer that Jack was aware of who was on both lists was sitting in the chair.

"As long as you're ready for the all-commands conference tomorrow, you don't have a reason not to come to the Fort Myer's club tonight, all spiffy in your Fleet Blues."

"Well, sir," said Mike with a not particularly false yawn, "actually I have about thirty reasons, starting with sleep."

Jack seemed to pay no attention to his rejection. "Besides welcoming all the Army commanders to this official kickoff of 'Fortress Forward' we will be celebrating the visit of the new French Ground Forces commander with a dining-out. I thought you might like to attend."

"Well, sir, as I said . . ."

"His name is Crenaus."

"The Deuxieme Armore commander, sir?" Deuxieme Armore, along with the Tenth Panzergrenadier and a scattering of British, Chinese and American armor units was rescued by then-Lieutenant O'Neal's platoon on Diess, when they had been encircled by Posleen in the Dantren megascraper. The platoon had dropped megascrapers on two sides of the encirclement and cracked the Posleen on the remaining side with a barrage of antimatter grenades. The French general— a gangling firecracker of a man who bore a remarkable resemblance to the scarecrow in *The Wizard of Oz*—had been notably impressed. Mike, in turn, had been impressed with how well the general had held his unit together in such an impossible situation. Deuxieme Armore had come out of the conflict with lower losses than any of the other units in the mobile defense, to a great extent because they retained cohesion when others broke like glass vases. The strongest reason for that cohesion was the guest of the dining-out.

"The same. When he heard you were in town he insisted that you attend," Horner said with a rare true smile.

"Yes, sir." Mike took mental inventory of his wardrobe. He had a pressed set of Fleet Mess Blues and—on the suspicion that someone would require he wear them at some point—his medals.

He had thus far succeeded in not wearing any of them, despite Ground Force regulations to the contrary, by the simple expedient of pointing out that he was not, in fact, a Ground Force officer and, therefore, the regulation did not apply. He had had to endure three more drubbings by overzealous MP officers until a special order was circulated explaining the position of Fleet versus Ground Force personnel. He probably would not have made the issue were it not for the fact that other Fleet personnel assigned to the Pentagon were under constant harassment. If his application of the old-boy network could help to mitigate that in any way he felt it worth the effort. He also hated the looks he got when people saw him with the Medal. But, what the hell, it would be a chance to see some old companions.

"Airborne, General, sir. I'll be there with bells on."

"Just be sure you're there with all your medals on." Jack smiled one of his cold thou-shalt-obey smiles. "Medals, Mike, not ribbons. And all of them."

"Absent companions," toasted Mike, as junior in the group.

"Absent companions," chorused the inebriated crowd huddled around the new French High Commander.

The main ballroom of the Fort Myer Officers' Club was jammed with the Military District of Washington's finest. The bright light of the chandeliers pulled out highlights on gold braid and jewelry throughout the room as the officers and their ladies danced the minuet of power. The room was packed with generals of every rank; full colonels were not much more than waiters. But the entire room's focus was on the small group by the head table where a circle of aides and senior subordinates clustered around four officers. Three of them were four-star generals; one of them was a mere captain.

"By rights, *mon ami*, you should be factored in that toast," said the guest of honor, with a companionable clap on the shoulder to Mike.

"Well, there ain't many left from my impromptu first command, that's for sure." Mike looked around at his company, only faintly uncomfortable with the situation.

In the year after his return from Diess he had been dragged around the United States as a talking head for the Public Information Office. During the tour he had intimate conversations with every kind of senior officer. He was sure at the time that the Curse of the Medal was on him; that for the rest of his career the closest he would come to the front was talking about it with a commentator. He was finally reprieved with his current command. So he was comfortable with senior officers at this point. And he had no problems with uniforms.

Before the tour began the first thing that was required of him by the PIO was the purchase, at fabulous expense, of a set of the new Fleet Strike Mess Blues. The group of designers and forward-thinking military officers that designed it rammed through some wildly successful combinations of Galactic technology and the modern mania for efficient and comfortable clothing. The daily wear uniform, combat silks, was as comfortable a set of clothes as any casual dress maniac could desire and even the standard dress uniform was extremely comfortable compared to the norm. That mania for casual comfort had ended abruptly at Mess Blues.

Designed to highlight several traditions from members of the Fleet Strike amalgam, the uniform also called on futuristic styling. A long mag-sealed tunic of Navy blue, worn flapped open, was lined with the branch color of the wearer, in Mike's case Infantry sky blue. Around the middle was worn a full sash cummerbund of "Redcoat" red (the identical shade was used by, variously, the American Marines, American artillery, French paratroopers and the Red Army) looped with gold. The shoulders and sleeves were again covered in gold loops, the number of loops denoting rank. The pants were piped with red. It was topped by a simple American-ized beret in the color of the different branches of Fleet Strike. This gave the unfortunate impression that all members of the Infantry were on a UN Peacekeeping mission, but that impression would pass with time.

This admittedly flashy uniform was, in Captain O'Neal's case, further highlighted by a frightening set of medals. In the case of most persons with multiple layers of "fruit-salad" the weight was on the lower end, the various commendation medals and other bits of colorful "I Was There" ribbons that say that the wearer has been a good boy and gone where a soldier was supposed to go. In Mike's case, the weight was uncomfortably skewed in the other direction.

Besides the Medal, specifically awarded for single-handedly tak-ing out a Posleen command ship at the Main Line of Resistance on Diess, he had been separately awarded for three other actions dur-ing that forty-eight hours of madness that saw victory snatched from the jaws of defeat. There was a Bronze Star for organizing the demo-lition of Qualtren, despite the accidental consequences, a Bronze Star for organizing the survivors under the rubble left from the explo-sion and a Silver Star for the relief of the Tenth Panzergrenadiers at the Boulevard of Death. He had not wanted any of them and argued that, by tradition, they should all have been lumped into one award. But they came piecemeal instead.

Along with those awards, and two Purple Hearts, there was a mass of foreign decorations from countries as widely varied as England and mainland China (almost three companies of the regi-ment China had sent survived due to O'Neal's platoon). A single

Army commendation medal, a good conduct medal and an I-Was-There medal for Desert Storm huddled at the bottom.

In any other company the combination of uniform and fruit-salad would have looked maniacal, but that was in any other company.

The cluster of officers around Général Crenaus included the American High Commander in Ground Force Mess Dress, a veteran of Just Cause, Desert Storm and Monsoon Thunder along with so many odd little out-of-the-way missions he had long ago stopped trying to remember them all. His "fruit-salad" was also impressively high protein, low fat. General Horner, in Mess Dress, had managed to be involved instrumentally in all three operations and although he was light on "Forgot To Duck" Purple Hearts, his commendations were all about being out front leading troops.

And it turned out that Général Crenaus, in French Mess Dress, tails, stovepipe hat and all, had apparently been involved in every action the French had been able to think up over the last couple of decades. And, apparently, a few they were not quite willing to admit to as well.

Between the Mess Dress on all the senior officers and the medals on every chest, Mike was wondering when the Valkyries were supposed to show up and go violently mezzo-soprano.

"I like that one," said General Taylor rather thickly as he pointed to an unrecognized decoration on Captain O'Neal's chest. He had managed to ingest better than a quart and a half of scotch during the course of the evening. "I didn't think there were any Japs with you on Diess." The decoration worn just above the Combat Infantryman's Badge looked somewhat like a golden rising sun.

Général Crenaus laughed grimly. "That's not for saving Nip ass, *bon homme*. That is simply an award for being there. I have one as well." He pointed to the same medal on his own chest.

"That's not the Diess medal," pointed out General Horner, peering at O'Neal's chest. "*That's* our Diess Expeditionary Force medal," he continued, pointing at a normal-sized medal of tan and red.

"Not for being on Diess, *mon Général*," corrected Général Crenaus's senior aide from the periphery where the aides danced attendance. "It is a Federation recognition device for being in the effect zone of a nuclear blast."

"*Oui*, this one is entirely our young friend's fault," laughed the boisterous French general, thumbing in the direction of the captain. "However, on reflection, I can hardly fault him."

"Fine, great," said Mike, feeling the bourbons the senior officers had been pressing on him. "Next time I'll leave your Frog ass swinging in the breeze."

Général Crenaus laughed uproariously to the apparent relief of the officers in the outer ring. "I sincerely desire that there is never another such incident, my young *capitaine.*"

Mike, in the meantime, was rather drunkenly looking at his Star Burst medal upside down. "You know the bastard part of it, sir?" he asked as he swayed forward and back; trying to maintain balance with his head down was getting harder and harder.

"What?" asked General Horner, knocking back his Absolut and picking another off a passing tray.

"I don't remember a bit of it. I mean, some of the guys got to really groove with the experience. Some of the platoon couldn't find bolt holes in time and they were on the roofs when it went. Now that would be a rush."

"A rush?" gasped one of the colonels in the periphery.

Mike rounded on the officer, with a look of disbelief on his face. "Sure, sir, can't you just see it? That wall of flame coming right at you and all you can do is duck and cover? I mean, like, *what* a rush!" He smiled ferally as the generals laughed. Most of the American aides, none less than a major in rank, were remarkably short on medals indicating combat time. They obviously were not sure to what extent the aggressive captain was joking.

Crenaus's aide, wearing the same medal, snorted and shook his head. Having met the junior officer at his best, and worst, he had no doubt of the little firecracker's sincerity. Deuxieme Armore called him "The Little Shrew" and spoke it in hushed tones. Not for any spitefulness, but because, weight for ferocity, shrews were the most deadly thing on earth. And quite utterly fearless.

"*Oui*, in a suit perhaps," interjected Général Crenaus, genially. "But most of us were not in suits. It was quite unpleasant from my point of view."

"Sure, sir," slurred Mike. "That's why I gave you thirty—hic—seconds warning."

"Twenty. You said thirty and detonated at twenty. *Merci beaucoup*, by the way, and what a surprise that was!"

"*C'est la guerre. Vingt, trente*, who's counting."

"We were, *certainment*. With our, how do you say it? 'pedal to the metal' we were. '*Dix-neuf . . .* ' Wham! Zee Camera of God!" the general continued, mock angrily.

"Bitch, bitch, bitch," Mike snorted and took another slug.

Général Crenaus laughed again, hard, as at another thought. "Your Private Buckley did not think it was, as you say, a 'roosh.' "

"Heh, yeah, I heard that one afterwards. Hah! And I thought *I* was havin' a bad day."

"Would you care to let the rest of us in on the joke?" asked General Taylor, settling rather heavily on the head table.

"*Oui*, it is a good one," said Géneral Crenaus, gesturing at Mike.

"Well, come on in when you want. Where to begin?" mused Mike, taking a sip of bourbon.

"At the beginning is usually best," commented General Horner dryly. The dozen or so Absoluts had seemed to effect Horner not at all. Mike had heard he had a hollow leg. Now he believed it. The only way to tell he was drunk off his ass was that his normally sober expression had become like iron. Way drunk.

"Yeah. Well, Buckley was one of the guys caught under Qualtren. Now, we had to extract ourselves from the rubble, which we did by blowing through with our grenades and stuff, not a technique I suggest to the unarmored."

"*Oui*, they are after all . . ."

" . . . antimatter!" Mike finished. "Right. So, everybody was able to figure out how to do this successfully except the unfortunate Private Buckley, or Lefty as we came to call him. Private 'Lefty' Buckley, on his first try, slipped out his grenade, extended it as far away as he could, since it was, after all . . ."

" . . . antimatter!" chorused Géneral Crenaus and his aide.

"Right. So he sticks his arm out as far as it will go, pushing through the rubble, and thumbs the activator."

"*Oui, oui!* Only to find that he can't retract his arm!" crowed the French general, belly laughing.

"Yeah! The rubble shifted and it's caught. So, like, this is gonna huuurt, right? Actually, it only hurts for a second 'cause of all the suit systems. Blocks the nerve, shuts down the bleeding, debrides and disinfects the wound, all in seconds. But, ya know, ya got to imagine, I mean . . ."

"It's a ten-second count?" asked General Horner, looking grim, which for him was the same as smiling.

"Right, right. So like . . ."

"*Dix, neuf, huit, sept . . .*" interjected Crenaus, with tears of laughter in his eyes.

"Right, ten, nine . . ." Mike translated, "and then . . ."

"Wham!" interjected General Taylor, laughing.

"Right. Like, 'Whoa, is this a Monday or what?' Anyway, it didn't, doesn't really hurt, or it wouldn't be so funny. Just the really brief but memorable sensation of your hand vaporizing."

"So, what does that have to do with the command ship detonation?" asked one of the surrounding aides.

"Well," continued Mike, with another sip of bourbon. "Lefty has made it to the perimeter, and performed a really decent private's job, as well as he can left-handed. And when the command ship lifts he's one of the guys that goes with Sergeant Green." Mike paused and solemnly lifted his glass. "Absent companions . . ."

"Absent companions," the officers chorused.

" . . . he went with Staff Sergeant Alonisus Green to distract the command ship away from the Main Line of Resistance and focus its attention so that I could attempt to plant a friggin' antimatter mine on its side," he ended, quite solemnly.

"There was supposed to be a humorous punch line," said General Horner as the pause became elongated.

"Right, sir," said Captain O'Neal after a sip of his sour mash. " . . . so anyway the whole cockamamie thing works, I get through the defenses, plant the mine and do my now famous imitation of a piece of radioactive fallout . . ."

"Ten seconds early, might I add!" interjected Géneral Crenaus.

"Man, some people wouldn't be happy if you hanged them with a gold rope! I go 'to infinity and beyond' and all the friggin' Frenchie can do is complain about premature detonations. Where was I, sirs?"

"Detonation," answered a very junior aide, a mere stripling of a major.

"Right," said the captain. "Well, the mine works like a charm, except for some minor little secondary effects . . ."

"Another three meters and I would have been steak tartare!" the general shouted, holding his arms in the air.

"With all due respect: Quit interrupting, General, sir. Anyway it packs about the wallop of a Class Three Space Mine and it causes some nasty secondaries, most of which are, fortunately, directed away from the MLR and certain unnamed ungrateful Frenchmen . . ." commented Captain O'Neal, rolling his eyes.

"Did I say I was ungrateful? General Taylor, General Horner, I call you to witness, I never have said I was ungrateful. Nervous? A touch. Frightened? *Merde*, yes! But not ungrateful, you dwarf poltroon!"

"Hah, stork! Anyway, it tears the living shit out of the command ship, but about a third of the ship hangs together. It apparently was really spectacularly visible from some of the positions on the MLR. This big piece of space cruiser describes a beautiful ballistic arc almost straight up, looking like it's moving in slow motion," expounded Captain O'Neal, gesturing with both hands. "You have to remember, this is to the background of a relatively small but quite noticeable nuclear blast . . ."

"About four kilotons," interjected Géneral Crenaus, taking a hard pull on his cognac, "and less than a kilometer away!"

"More like three kilometers. Anyway, it rides up on the mushroom cloud, describes this tremendous vertical arc and comes gracefully back down . . ."

"Right on Buckley," hooted Géneral Crenaus and cracked up.

" . . . right smack dab on Private Second Class Buckley. He was one of the guys who was on the roofs, in the blast radius . . ."

"*Sacré Bleu!* I was in the blast radius!"

"You guys should have hardly felt it in the blast shadow from the buildings!"

"Blast shadow he calls it! *Oui!* They were around our ears!" shouted the general, hands waving on either side of his head. "I know, I know . . ." he continued, holding up a hand.

"Bitch, bitch . . . anyway, here's Buckley, grav-boots clamped to some nice powerful structure, miraculously alive, survives looking right into the shockwave, survives looking right into the neutron pulse, survives looking right into the thermal pulse . . ." Mike paused dramatically.

"It didn't kill him, did it?" asked one of the aides, right on cue.

"In a suit? Nah, but it did knock him clean out. And this time he waited for somebody to come dig him up. He kinda had to since he was about fifty stories down in the building with a quarter kilometer of space cruiser on top of him," ended Captain O'Neal, chuckling.

"To Private Buckley!" roared Géneral Crenaus, raising his brandy on high.

"To Private Buckley!" roared Captain O'Neal. "And all the other poor sods who wear the Mask of Hell!" he ended, a touch bitterly.

"Here, here," chorused General Taylor, after there was a moment's uncomfortable pause, and everyone raised their glasses and drank. "Is that what you call it, Mike?"

"Isn't it, sir?" asked Captain O'Neal, swaying like an oak in the wind. "I may joke about a rush, but it's armor that you can take into a friggin' nuclear blast. As we have, and will have to again. What else is the mission that I have been working on for two weeks? To go where no one else can go, to do what no one else can do and to do that until we are no more.

"For whatever goddamn reason we are going to get hit with *five times* the number of Posleen pointed at Barwhon and Diess. As we are *all* well aware. That level of force will leave us totally invested. No *large* ships are going to be able to sneak through that firepower!

"So, from when the Posleen land until Fleet is strong enough to invest us and take out the landers, we will be cut off from resupply of GalTech. And that means ten little MI troopers . . . nine little MI troopers . . . eight little MI troopers, until 'we're singing Glory be to God that there are no more of us, cause one of us could drink it all alone.' And it is my a-hoo-wah job to take my company into that maelstrom of nukes and gas and hypervelocity missile rounds and fight the Posleen on their own turf at up to one-thousand-to-one odds and cover all the other troops who don't have the equipment to experience it.

"Yes, sir," finished Mike. "I designed it, I made it, I live it and I call it the Mask of Hell. And all who wear it are the Damned!" he ended softly.

◆ CHAPTER 17 ◆

Lunar Orbit, Sol III
2230 EDT September 13th, 2004 AD

"Oh, I will be *God* damned!" If anyone had been present when Captain Weston opened the e-mail from Fleet HQ on Titan Base, they would have been amazed at her command of invective. She managed to curse for a solid pair of minutes without repeating herself once. At the end of the diatribe she cut herself off abruptly, realizing that the stresses of the new command were causing the reaction.

In the short time she had been there, the only thing she had been able to determine was that the situation was worse than expected. She now realized that keeping the systems on-line had meant not only Herculean effort on the part of her XO, but sheer good luck. Any of the jury-rigged repairs, patches and add-ons could cut out at any time. This would make it appear that Captain April Weston was not quite as competent as some had supposed. She doubted it would destroy her career, but it would be awfully embarrassing.

For that matter they might not have to worry too much about embarrassment. With the forward deflector screen out any Posleen missile that made it through the defenses would have a free ride. The detonation of a twenty-kiloton nuclear missile in contact with the hull would erase any need to worry about career advancement.

The parts were bound to turn up sooner or later. And the XO was just as good as advertised at wheedling them out of Titan Base and getting the Indowy to venture out of their quarters and install them. Losing her "immediately" and without any warning for a two-week leave was not good news.

The other side of the ledger, however, was that the XO definitely needed some time off. She had brightened up in the last few days, but it was a brittle brightness. She definitely needed some shore leave.

So be it. Far be it from April Weston to hold someone back from their just deserts. If Uncle Al Bledspeth thought it was a good idea then it was a good idea. But when she found whoever it was pulling the strings in the background, she was going to have their guts for garters. She hated figuring out who was conspiring with whom.

"Nathan!" came the pleased cry.

Monsignor O'Reilly looked over his shoulder and stood up in greeting. "Paul, how are you?"

The short, balding, dapper man was finely dressed in a tailored silk suit shot through with threads of purple and green that caught the soft lighting in the Century Club dining room. He smiled at his old friend and shook his hand vigorously.

"Oh, well, my friend, well." He was accompanied by an Indowy. While they were no longer in the two-headed calf category, it was exceedingly rare to see one in public. Paul des Jardins gestured at the alien. "Monsignor Nathan O'Reilly, I would be pleased to introduce you to the Indowy Aelool."

O'Reilly was aware that Indowy did not consider touching to be an appropriate action. Like the Japanese they engaged in a variety of bows depending on status. Since he had no idea what its status would be to the Galactics and since he had no conception of the Indowy's rank, trying to bow appropriately would be an exercise in futility. He settled for bowing his head fractionally.

He also was unsure of the Indowy's sex. They had male, female and transfer neuter to choose from and there was no discrimination. They also were difficult to discern: The Indowy did not have significant external physical sexual expression such as mammaries. And their subtle expression—their equivalent of softer skin and rounded hips— was notoriously hard to spot. After a moment's introspection he decided that the neuter forms of speech would be best. Male and female Indowy rarely objected to an accidental neuter reference, but transfer neuters tended to treat male/female references with humor.

The Indowy had an aura of peace and calm that was rarely found when they were near humans. Normally the little creatures were as nervous as cats in a room full of rocking chairs. This one did not even flinch at the sight of humans eating meat.

"Indowy Aelool, I see you." He was enough of a student of the Galactics to know their greetings. Actually he was enough of a student of the Galactics to know three of the extraterrestrial languages. He still had no idea why Paul had tracked him down at the Club.

They normally used cut-outs. This was lousy tradecraft and could damage an executive cell. He was furious; Paul had better have a damn good reason for this.

"Please." He gestured at his table. "Sit down." The damage, if any, was done. Might as well play the hand.

"I'm glad you were here, Nathan," said Paul, taking a seat. One of the hovering waiters came forward and replaced the high-backed leather chair with one designed for Indowy. Nathan had not been aware that the club had them, but he was not surprised. The Century Club was one of the most exclusive clubs in Washington. Since it catered to the highest class of clientele, it undoubtedly had preparations for every type of Galactic visitor. "The Indowy Aelool is heading off-planet shortly and I wanted you to get a chance to meet him."

"There was so much to do," said the diminutive alien in a soft, high voice. Monsignor O'Reilly suddenly realized that the Indowy had spoken English rather than use an AID translator and was surprised. As far as he knew, no Indowys spoke the language or any language but Indowy. It was generally believed that their vocal resonance cavities could not form human-style words. What other capabilities might they be hiding? "My team has just completed the armoring of the First Battalion of your Five-Fifty-Fifth Fleet Strike and I was to head back to Irmansul immediately. However, my good friend Monsieur des Jardins insisted that I meet you. As he said, 'A stitch in time saves nine.' "

O'Reilly paid no attention to the code phrase, simply nodding and taking a sip of the fruity Washington State Beaujolais the waiter had delivered earlier. As he did his mind raced and a series of pieces fell into place.

Apparently Paul or someone high among the Fellowship had decided that the Indowy was the perfect conduit into the Galactics. And he was sure enough to possibly burn his sole contact to O'Reilly's Société. The Fellowship and the Société had similar aims, but O'Reilly was, as far as he knew, the sole link. If this little meeting exposed him it would set back the work a decade. On the other hand, access to Galactic technology was imperative. Both groups were hampered by imperfect knowledge of the Galactics' surveillance capabilities.

And the Indowy always insisted on a face-to-face meeting before any serious alliance was joined. From what he had been able to glean from current study, and on the basis of Société records, he could understand why. The Darhel had owned the electronic information systems of the Galactic Federation for thousands of years. That gave them the ability to create any illusion they chose using those systems.

Face-to-face was the only way to be sure you were talking to an actual contact.

The logic complete he nodded to himself internally. The risk was worth the action. He would have to sever himself from Paul as a contact for some time to come. However, they would still be able to use intermediaries. And there was always the Internet. The chaotic system still seemed to have the Darhel confused; they depended upon filtering proxy servers for information control and the American Supreme Court—bless those nine unknowing fools—had recently ruled them unconstitutional.

"Well, Indowy Aelool, if this Yankee dandy felt it necessary, I suppose I have to agree." He delivered the countersign with a broad but toothless smile. A toothed grin was the sign of a predator to the nervous Indowy. Something about this one, though, made him suspect that it could take a full-toothed grin without a flinch. "Will you join me for dinner?"

"I think not," said the alien, his face wrinkling in a complicated expression. After a moment Nathan realized that it was an attempt to copy a smile. The closest Indowy expression was actually a motherly expression of disapproval. "I have a ship to catch. But perhaps we shall meet . . . anon." Again the odd grimace. In this case a few broad ratlike front teeth were exposed.

Nathan thought for a moment. Then he wrinkled his nose as hard as he could, pulled back his upper lip and crossed his eyes. At the incredibly silly expression Paul nearly choked on his own recently delivered wine but the Indowy simply copied it in surprise and emitted a series of high-pitched whines like a kitten with its tail caught in a door. He clapped his furry hand over his mouth but was unable to stop. Heads throughout the room turned at the odd and annoying sound.

"Where did you learn that?" asked the Indowy, having finally managed to stop whining. The sound was Indowy laughter and was as infectious and difficult to stop for them as laughter was for humans. "That was the best human copy of 'ironic agreement' I have ever seen."

"I'm a student of anthropology," said the Jesuit with deprecation. "There is *nothing* that says that 'anthro' must refer only to human beings . . . You ought to see me do Darhel 'unfortunate embarrassment.' I've been practicing."

◆ CHAPTER 18 ◆

Ft. Myer, VA, United States of America, Sol III
0710 EDT September 14th, 2004 AD

"Hangover or no, you're giving the brief this morning," said Captain Jackson as he sauntered into Mike's cubicle.

Mike turned and looked at him with one eye shut, as a piston hammered his head. "I will have you know, I have never had a hangover in my life. This headache that is currently pounding me into the ground is entirely coincidental and based upon nervousness over the briefing. It is *not* the result of trying to drink officers who have far more experience and training in the imbibing of hard alcohol under the table."

"Same for the light sensitivity and the taste in your mouth?" asked the nattily dressed aide. Mike was fairly sure that the tailored uniform had not come off the rack at the Officers' Sales Store. Like Mike's it was probably Brooks Brothers or Halberds. The cloth was noticeably better and the fit was immaculate.

"Correct. Besides, in about three minutes the GalMed I just took will kick in and no more headache. To what do I owe the honor, Captain, sir?"

"Actually," said Captain Jackson, with a smile, "I think you have me by date of rank, Captain, sir."

"Ah, that would explain the confused look you perennially sport."

"Actually, that look comes with the position of aide."

"That I am familiar with," Mike agreed with a wince. "I held the position myself, briefly. Thank God there were no real aide's duties, though; I was basically the wild-hair guy for the GalTech program. But since there were no real aide duties it was a good place to stash me."

"So I've heard. I also heard you fought it tooth and nail."

"Well, the position of aide is one that is strongly political, no offense, and I'm lousy at passing canapés."

"Unlike us ring knockers?" asked the new aide with a raised eyebrow and an almost subconscious gesture of his right hand. The West Point ring briefly caught the light.

"I will admit that I have met only one mediocre West Point graduate," Mike said in oblique agreement.

"Thanks." The captain's brow furrowed. "Why do I suddenly suspect that is not the outstanding advertisement for West Point it at first sounds?"

"As I was saying, to what do I owe the honor?" asked Mike.

"Well, first the general sends his regrets. He won't be able to see you prior to the briefing, other items have suddenly come up, but he will see you at the reception afterwards."

"Tell the general, thank you, I can hold my own pecker just the same."

"You are really in a savage mood this morning, aren't you?" the aide commented with a nervous chuckle.

"Yes. Is there anything else?"

"Do you think the damn medal gives you the right to dispense with common courtesy?"

"No. I was a revolting SOB before I got the medal. Is there anything else?"

Captain Jackson's face worked for a minute. "No. But can I ask you something?"

"You just did." After a moment Mike relented. "Go ahead."

"You are about to go out in front of a bunch of goddamned senior brass, under the direction of CONARC, and tell them how CONARC— really meaning you—thinks they should handle their ACS forces. Now, if you show your ass, it's going to reflect poorly on my boss. Since one of my jobs is to make sure that doesn't happen, I've gotta find out if you're up to this briefing, because right now I am tempted to call General Horner and tell him his fair-haired boy is even more canned than last night and not up to the briefing."

"That would be bearing false witness, Captain," said Mike, casually. He obviously considered it an empty threat. He took a sip of his coffee and swished it around in his mouth. "And isn't there some sort of unwritten code at West Point about ratting?"

"There is a written code about reporting . . . questionable behavior. I would be following the written code. And good sense. I will stop this presentation if I think you can't answer questions civilly. Trust me, I know the system and how to use it. If General Horner doesn't pull you, there are other venues."

Mike smiled calmly for the first time in the encounter; it was like a tiger stretching to work out the kinks and the toothy smile was strangely feline as well.

"Like I said, Captain, to each his own. Very well, my problems are as follows. One." He flicked a finger up, counting. "I am about fed up with professional paper-pushers. It was paper-pushing, political, regular-Army assholes that fed me into a grinder on Diess and that probably will here on Earth. So—remember you pointed out that you are politically connected not me—you were probably the worst possible person to send to buck me up. Since Jack knows this, it was probably a test. I am in no mood for tests, which I will point out the next time I see him.

"Two." He flicked another finger. "I am giving a briefing for the senior commanders of America's defense on the subject of usage of ACS. I figure that there is about one chance in ten of those senior officers paying me any attention, despite the fact that these are the recommendations of their commander. We will undoubtedly institute the strategic logistical plan. After that single bone tossed to us, the ACS will get used in one of two ways: as cannon fodder, or as a last desperate measure.

"In the first case, ACS will be sent out unsupported by artillery or followed by conventional forces and thrown at the Posleen in movement-to-contact environments. They will be expected to make contact and stop the forces, without flank support or logistical tail. Most of the time, they will run out of juice, be surrounded and overrun. That will happen to about three battalions in the first month of skirmishing, on the East and West Coasts. This will be *completely contrary* to recommended doctrine.

"In the other scenario, ACS will be sent into close-contact infernos when all other methods, except nukes, have failed. They will be in close terrain, but, again, not in prepared positions. They will be given orders to hold on like the Spartans at Thermopylae and, by and large, much the same fate will befall them. This will include the fact that the follow-on forces will be ineffectively assembled or completely imaginary. And then the strategic scenario they died for will die with them. That scenario will occur repeatedly throughout the invasion. Again, it will be contrary to recommended doctrine.

"In the meantime, senior officers will complain that the MI are a waste of funds, that the same funds spent on conventional equipment would have given us much more capacity. The ones that complain the worst will be the most pissed off when the ACS are destroyed by improper implementation, and point to those defeats as support for their arguments. The fact that they would not even consider sending a conventional unit into the same environment will be completely overlooked. And the whole time, we, meaning the ACS, will be watching our numbers dwindle, without the ability to reinforce. It is not a pleasant scenario, sort of like suicide by arsenic: slow and painful."

"Well," said Captain Jackson, shaking his head at the Fleet Strike officer's vehemence, "congratulations, you have one last chance to get them to see the light."

"Captain, did you ever read 'The Country of the Blind'?"

"No."

"Well, the one-eyed man did not become king!"

◆ CHAPTER 19 ◆

Richmond, VA, United States of America, Sol III
1232 EDT September 19ᵗʰ, 2004 AD

"My name's John Keene," said the tall, distinguished engineer, taking the hand of the Green Beret sergeant who met him at the airport.

"Sergeant First Class Frank Mueller."

"I could have caught a cab," the engineer continued as they walked through the Richmond airport. It was filled with more smokers than any airport he had ever seen. In fact, the entire airport was a smoking area with the exception of occasional small nonsmoking areas. It almost made him think about having a cigar.

"No you couldn't, there aren't any. Or hardly any. And anyway, I wasn't busy. You got any bags?"

Keene gestured by lifting the small carry-on and briefcase in his hands. "What is the Special Forces role in all this?" he asked.

"The Richmond Defense Project?" asked Mueller, wresting the carry-on out of Keene's grip but leaving him with the briefcase. He gestured with his head towards the front of the airport and started walking. "In the case of our team, not much. Virginia already has a Special Forces group. We were sent to beef up the local defense training program. But Twentieth group has that well in hand, so we were mainly sitting on our thumbs waiting to go back to Atlanta until the 'Fortress Forward' program was announced. The local corps commander knew our team chief 'back when' and he made us a sort of super IG for the time being. When there's a problem, we get sent out to deal with it. Occasionally we lend a helping hand, like picking up a defense engineering specialist at the airport."

"I'm not that much of a specialist . . ." said the engineer in deprecation. Until the project to create the regional defense center in
northwest Georgia was dropped in his lap he had been a well-
respected but otherwise unremarkable civil engineer in the Atlanta
market, one of literally thousands. However, as the project had progressed, his innovative plans and almost fiendish details had vaulted
him to the top of the hierarchy of "continental defense engineers."

"I saw the raw reports from the Fort Mountain Planetary Defense
Center," Mueller disagreed. "You had more innovative recommendations than any seven other engineers involved. Same with Chatta-
nooga. Richmond is going to need innovative ideas to survive."

"So is Atlanta," Keene protested, "where my exwife and daughter
are. So you can understand if I would rather be there."

"You'll be going back. For that matter so will we; Atlanta is where
we are being based. But Richmond needs some input."

"What's the problem?" asked Keene, looking around the area of
the airport. The first thing that came to mind was that the area was
flat, which favored the Posleen. But, heck, airports always were.

"Terrain, or lack of it," said Mueller, as if he was reading Keene's
mind. "When I was a terrain analyst we would call the terrain around
Richmond, with the exception of the James River and a couple of
hills, microterrain. From a military point of view, it's flat as a pan-
cake. I don't know why they chose it for a defense city."

"Politics, history and size," said the engineer, "the same reason they
chose Atlanta, which has the same problems. Hell, Atlanta doesn't
even have the James; the Posleen can cross the Chattahoochee at any
point they choose. And what am I to do about that? I can't bring a
mountain to Mohammed."

"I don't know, why don't you wait and see?" Mueller said as he
walked up to a car parked in a no-parking zone. He tossed the carry-
on in the backseat, pulled the sign that said "Richmond Defense Planning Agency, Official Business" off the dashboard of the unremarkable
white Ford Taurus, pulled a ticket off the window and put it in the
glove compartment. He had to stuff it into a pile of others.

"Okay, any other information before the briefing?" asked Keene
with a smile at the little pantomime.

"Well, we're all staying at the Crowne Plaza hotel."

"Okay, wherever."

"It's a nice enough place with a good view of the James . . ."

John gave Mueller a sidelong look; even in their brief walk from
the gate he was experienced enough with the sergeant to wonder
where the explanation was going.

"It's fairly convenient to the state capitol, which is where most of the meetings are, but not very. However, it is within walking distance of Schockoe Bottom. Which is really important."

"Okay. Why?"

"Well," said Mueller, pulling out onto Williamsburg Avenue, "there's this fantastic microbrewery . . ."

John laughed, the first full belly laugh he had had in a while. He looked around at the sparse traffic for a moment as if someone might have heard the mirth and found it out of place.

"It must help to be military," John commented.

"Huh?"

"You guys are better prepared, mentally, for this than civilians, I guess."

"Man, have you got that wrong," Mueller denied. "There is no way to be prepared for the Posleen. None."

"Well, you can joke about it, anyway."

"Ah, well, that I can. If you can't joke about dyin' you are not suited to the military. So I guess that means we *are* better prepared."

After that they continued in silence through the suburbs of Richmond, heading towards the barely visible city center. Avoiding the fork onto Government Road, Mueller took the more scenic drop into Stony Run, overlooked by the Confederate Memorial. Beyond the juncture with Main Street they touched the outskirts of Schockoe Bottom. Abandoned factories loomed on their left as a giant hill rose on their right.

"This isn't exactly microrelief," commented Keene, looking up at tree-covered Libby Hill looming over the valley of the James. The trees were turning color with the first chill of autumn and the hill was a mix of brown and yellow. "Hell of a lot better than Atlanta."

"Maybe not," replied Mueller, "but it's not like the city is up there. I'm damned if I can think of a way to use it."

"Possibly," mused the engineer, "possibly you are."

"The capitol and city center are that way." Mueller gestured to their right as they dropped into the sector of old brick factories. The dying rays of the sun lit the crowds beginning to come to the area after the work of the day. Music began to pulse as soldiers of the Twenty-Second Cavalry Regiment in BDUs mingled with female office workers, dancing the dance that was old before clothing was born. The city, each night, seemed to empty to Schockoe Bottom. They climbed out of the bottoms and made a series of lefts to intersect the one-way Cary Street. As they approached their hotel Keene took another look around.

"Yes, there's definitely possibility here," Keene whispered, almost inaudibly.

Mueller hid his small, unsurprised smile.

◆ CHAPTER 20 ◆

Ft. Myer, VA, United States of America, Sol III
1650 EDT September 27th, 2004 AD

"General Olds," said O'Neal, nodding his head slightly to the approaching First Army commander, "I hope you enjoyed the conference."

The reception ending the all-commands conference was considered mandatory, a way for the various commanders and their staffs to get together one last time and go over all the things that had been missed at the marathon series of meetings. For the next few weeks, e-mails would fly hot and heavy as everyone came up with questions that they forgot or modifications arose from those questions. However—as the American Army had repeatedly proven—open and complete communication was the key to effective military operations. The left hand not knowing what the right was doing was the quickest road to defeat.

On the other hand, what it meant for Mike was one last run of the gauntlet with some senior officers that in O'Neal's opinion were poster children for the Peter Principle. But once it was over, it was off for two weeks' leave and finding out what bad habits Cally had picked up from Dad.

"O'Neal," said the tall, spare commander, nodding his own head. "I thought I would get a clarification on one item. I believe you stated that the directive of CONARC was that ACS should not be used in a situation where a 'Fortress Forward' or montane defense point had already fallen."

Mike gave it a quick scan for booby traps. "Yes, General, that is correct."

149

"Even if the ACS could permit the survival of the defending units."

"Again, General, that is the intent of the directive."

"So, you, or CONARC through you, equate an ACS battalion to be the same as the units in a 'Fortress Forward' position, equivalent to a corps of trained soldiers? All their support? Some seventy thousand lives balanced against six hundred?"

Mike considered his response carefully. "General, I realize that you disagree with the logic . . ."

"You are correct, Captain, a point that I believe I have made with General Horner. There is no military justification for such a stance, and if Fleet Strike feels that its units are too good to support Army units, then I question why we are funding Fleet Strike!"

Earth provides a fraction of Strike's funding, General. We are almost abysmally poor by Galactic standards. So we are not exactly "funding" Fleet Strike. Of course we do provide one hundred percent of its personnel. "It is not a situation of lack of desire, General, but rather the coldest of military necessities," Mike stated. While the general had been reactivated after one of the longest careers in the history of the United States Army, he had somehow obtained his current rank without ever hearing a shot fired in anger. Furthermore, the primary period during which he was a senior officer was the period of retrenchment by the Army that culminated in Monsoon Thunder, a period during which the Army was often less worried about a unit's readiness than about physical fitness norms and political correctness.

While the general had served during the periods of both Desert Storm and Monsoon Thunder, coincidentally in neither case had he been deployed to the combat zone. Possibly because of that fact he was among those officers who placed the blame for failures during Monsoon Thunder on the forces that were deployed, not the plan or the overall level of military readiness.

Mike was in one way looking forward to the day the general was finally responsible for a real world military operation. Someday the general would be faced with a situation where he was losing lives and territory faster than reinforcements could be thrown into the gaps. But Mike was sorry for the troops that would have to pick up the burden. What *am I thinking?! I* am *the troops that will have to pick up the burden.*

"Let me ask you a question, sir."

"All right."

"I am sure you have examined the reports from Barwhon and Diess, sir. Have you noticed that while conventional forces invariably suffer significant levels of casualties when they venture out from fixed defenses, the ACS is able to roam virtually at will and can often stand and fight or break contact without major levels of loss?"

"I am aware of that fact but I disagree with the conclusion you are about to draw: that therefore, the ACS must be preserved because they are the only mobile force that can take the fight to the enemy. Those casualty levels are primarily a terrain issue as opposed to a tactical, equipment or operational issue. The terrain of both Barwhon and Diess is not suited to modern, mobile combat.

"The swamps of Barwhon hamper our Abrams and Bradleys, while the megascrapers of Diess hamper artillery and deny effective logistical support. Given open terrain, or even broken terrain, mobile cavalry and armored forces would be able to outmaneuver the Posleen forces and subject them to repeated firetraps. That is the way to fight them, on the plains that everyone wishes to avoid!

"Right here in Virginia would be perfect. Everyone says that the plains are lost, but that is bullshit! Once the Posleen are on the plains, in nonrestrictive terrain, our armored columns and artillery will eat them alive. 'Fortress Forward' ought to be called 'Maginot Two Thousand'! We don't need to go back to tactics that were smashed by the Wehrmacht! Apparently everyone has forgotten Military History One-Oh-One!

"And as for the ACS–one-tenth the expense poured into those tin suits would have bought thousands more fighting vehicles. And I have stated my professional analysis of the effect of conventional equipment in the upcoming conflict. So, I beg to differ that one ACS battalion is worth five damn divisions of trained and equipped mechanized infantry, armor and cavalry, I really, really do." The general was practically frothing by the end of the tirade.

"Well, General," said Mike and stopped. He thought for a moment and decided that there was no way to antagonize the officer more than he already was. It was obvious that this was one officer who rejected every concept under which the GalTech and Fortress Forward programs were designed. Furthermore, he was so far out of Mike's chain of command that Mike could do just about anything but punch the officious oaf in the nose and get away with it. Fleet and Ground Force's first official point of contact was somewhere in the morass of Galactic bureaucracies.

"Well, General," he repeated, "that's your opinion . . . and you know the saying about opinions." He grinned coldly to drive the insult home. "Before the primary invasion we will, I fear, both have ample opportunities for vindication. I frankly hope you are correct; it would make my job easier. Now if you'll excuse me, I have a plane to catch. Heaven and hell have been moved so that I can spend one more week with my family. It behooves me to keep them both on my good side."

◆ CHAPTER 21 ◆

Big Pine Key, FL, United States of America, Sol III
1422 EDT October 4ᵗʰ, 2004 AD

The Keys were a scene from the Twilight Zone.

The last time Mike had been down Highway 1—the long strip of asphalt and concrete that linked the beads of the Keys together like the cord in a coral necklace—the traffic had still been heavy at 1 A.M. The occasion was a spring break from college and the party would go on through the night and the next day. Honking cars and pickup trucks crowded the highway, and people packed the shops and restaurants from Largo to Key West.

Mike watched an errant palm frond tumble across the sand-filled parking lot of the Piggly Wiggly and knew in his bones that the world had turned a corner. The strip mall on Big Pine Key had never been a center for bustling tourism, but the islands to the north of it, where once retirees and college students mingled, were just as deserted. The O'Neal family had driven ever southward on the strip of blacktop looking for an open motel, or even a gas station. Instead there had been an unending string of closed shops, abandoned businesses and tumbledown residences. Crossing the Seven Mile Bridge to this ghost town had been the final straw.

The whole trip had been a disaster. The visit to Sharon's parents had been particularly excruciating. Despite the fact that he had faced the Posleen in combat, and still held the scars to prove it, Sharon's parents had retreated into the disbelieving shell that many of the nation shared. In their hearts they truly believed it was all a made-up threat of the "gubermint" and stated the fact in no uncertain terms.

To many of their ilk the world was flat, the sun revolved around it and there were no other worlds. The sociologists were referring to this stance as "societal denial." After the third time his father-in-law had carefully but firmly corrected him on the subject, Mike started referring to it as "total bullshit."

Finally Sharon had cut short the visit and they had continued on their way to the Keys. The locale held special meaning for Mike and Sharon. They had briefly met on Key Largo during school and felt a mutual, undeclared, attraction. When chance happened to throw them together at a later date the mutual attraction had rapidly flowered. Michelle and Cally were the results.

When the opportunity had come to take time together the target of the Keys immediately came to mind. The lure of four-star hotels, pools and diving was almost irresistible. Mike knew that Cally would love it; there would be other kids to play with and the clean green sea to play in. The only thing that would make it perfect would be to have Michelle along. But at least she was safely on her way to Adenast. Whatever happened on Earth, at least one member of the family would survive.

But the vacation might not. They had traveled through the deserted islands looking in vain for a place to lay their heads. Or even refuel. The Chevy Tahoe was a gas guzzler. Since Mike had packed along some items to start prepositioned caches they were able to get all the gas they needed from military rations, but the range of the tank was only so great.

They had filled up in Fort Worth, north of Miami, but they had now reached the point of no return. There was not enough gas to get them to Key West, where Mike was sure he could get refilled at the reactivated Navy base, but if they turned around they could make it back to Miami. If they did that they would stay; the Keys were not worth wandering in the wilderness. And that would put the cap on the trip.

Mike tossed the useless map he had been perusing on the floor and looked at his wife. Even with the travails of the vacation she still looked like a starlet in a low-budget disaster movie. Her hair was just pleasantly mussed, her eyes slightly shadowed, her face lineless and grave. It made him sit back and pause. She had hardly talked about her Fleet position, but he was sure it was no sinecure. He suddenly realized that being lost in a howling wilderness, running out of gas and on the edge of being stranded might look good. What that told him about her last few months was unsettling. He cleared his throat.

"Take the chance on going on or turn around," he said, laying out the options for discussion.

She nodded her head and looked around again. There was nothing more to be revealed by the scenery. The day was one of those "blazing gray days" that south Florida had from time to time. A cold front had petered out to the north but the high-level clouds had continued on, obscuring the sun but permitting the heat to build up underneath. The result was a condition of terribly bright indirect light, combined with a dessicating wind. It was like being in Kansas, except with palm trees and green water.

The scenery matched the conditions. The strip mall had once sported all the usual businesses for such a locale. There was a grocery store, nail kiosk, chiropractor and hair salon. The "random choice" on this particular mall was a small restaurant that professed to sell "Authentic Keys Food." This could be read on the sign that was now swinging from side to side in the hot, dry wind.

Sharon stared at the same palm frond that had caught Mike's eye and snorted. "This isn't going so well, is it?" she asked.

Mike had talked endlessly about his company. And every word was praise for the men, the command and the training. Which just meant that his situation was about as fucked-up as hers. She knew she should talk about it. He might even have some input that would help; he had been bumping around Fleet for a couple of years longer than she. But it would sound like complaining and she just couldn't add that to the unmitigated disaster the trip was becoming.

The days at her parents' house in Orlando had been bad for many reasons. Besides her parents' complete illogic about the Posleen there was also the fact that Cally was used to going to the various amusement parks in the area. Unfortunately, they were all closed "for the duration." Cally had taken it well; she seemed to have developed an almost unhealthy control under her grandfather's influence. But not being able to give her the treat hurt at a subliminal level. The trip to the Keys was as much for Cally as for Sharon and Mike.

Now even that had come apart. The world's greatest natural tourist trap had apparently closed for the duration as well. And that did not leave many alternatives.

"There has to be a way to find a motel or something," she said, fingering her AID.

"We already checked for websites," Mike reminded her, noticing the gesture. The Galactic artificial intelligence devices were connected to the Web and capable of searching it as well as or better than any human-made interface. But they could not produce shelter from thin air. "Heck, we haven't seen a single person except that one lady working in her garden up in Largo." He now regretted not asking directions, but at the time it had not made sense to stop.

"Hmm," she responded noncommitally. "A-I-D?" she queried.

"Yes, Commander O'Neal?" Mike was amused to note that the AID was a baritone. Most males preferred female voices; females appeared to choose the opposite.

"There are no website listings for motels in the Marathon or Big Pine Key area," Sharon stated. "Is that correct?"

"Correct, ma'am. There were such sites, but all are now inactive or specifically indicate that the hotel is closed. The nearest hotel that indicates functionality is on Key West."

Sharon let out a breath and thought for a moment. "AID, is there any other source of information that indicates that an area might offer guest services?"

"Please specify a source, ma'am." The AID actually sounded puzzled.

"Oh, police reports, news articles . . ."

"Infrared satellite imagery," Mike interjected.

"Right," said Sharon, nodding her head. "That sort of thing."

"Commander O'Neal, you are reminded that you do not have access to civil-political intelligence gathering," stated the AID. It was the flat, unaccented response Mike had come to recognize as security protocol response.

"Let me try." He smiled. "AID, check *my* overrides and use the lowest level of intelligence necessary to derive requested information."

The AID did not exactly sniff in disdain, but the tone of voice was distinctly unhappy. "National Technical Means," it said, sarcastically, "indicates that the small fish camp on No-Name-Key is in operation. There is no indication of cabin usage, but it has had cabins for rent in the past. They should still be available."

Mike picked the map back up and searched for No-Name-Key.

"That's right next door," he said in surprise.

"Correct," said the AID. "In addition, imagery indicates that the proprietor has been underreporting fish harvests by about twenty percent, contrary to United States Rationing and Storage Regulation F-S-B-One-Zero-Seven-Five-Eight-Dash-One-A."

Mike rubbed his chin and frowned. "Is that your own analysis or did you pull it out of a file?"

"That is my own analysis, Captain O'Neal," stated the device.

"Well, lock that analysis down unless overridden and remind me at an opportune time to discuss where you developed the information," Mike snapped. The hell if he was going to let a piece of GalJunk drop the dime on some hard-working fishermen.

"Yes, sir, Captain," the AID snapped back.

"Well, that's that settled," said Sharon with a smile.

"Mom?" asked Cally from the back seat.

"Yes?"

"Do you think there will be somewhere to eat?" she asked. There was not a hint of a whine, just a simple question.

Sharon turned and looked at her oldest daughter. Cally lay against the driver's side door, looking out at the abandoned landscape, idly tapping her fingers on her thigh. Her face was somber and grave but the eyes slid across the area outside, constantly questing. For targets or threats, Sharon suddenly realized. The light blouse the eight-year-old wore had ridden up enough to reveal the small automatic in her waistband. Taken all together the image made Sharon want to cry. It was as if disaster had already come to America and they were wanderers in some post-Apocalyptic nightmare. Sharon took a deep breath and forced herself to be calm. Most of the reaction was stress still bleeding off from the *Agincourt* and the disastrous visit to her parents. It would pass. It had to.

"Probably. There should be somewhere to get something. And if not we've got more 'travel rations,' " she finished with a smile. The rations had been Papa O'Neal's suggestion and it had been a good one.

Papa O'Neal had been paying more attention to conditions across the United States than either Sharon or Mike. When they had stated their plans to take a car trip down the Florida Peninsula he had demurred. Even though they had access to unlimited fuel supplies because of the "cache" items Mike had ported along, he pointed out other problems. Without stating anything other than vague reports of lack of services in south Florida he had suggested that staying at the farm would be the best plan. But when Sharon and Mike had been insistent he had made a series of startling suggestions. He had been so adamant about them that the couple had finally given in, figuring that the additional items fell under the category of "better safe than sorry."

Thus, attached to the spare tire on the back was a five-gallon can of gas and a shovel. In the morass of material in the back were three cases of beer and two other cases of mixed liquor. There were more cases of smoked and tinned meats, gathered and prepared on the farm, along with sealed containers of flour, cornmeal and a variety of dried fruits. If they did end up on a desert island they could live comfortably for nearly a month on the stored provisions they had packed along.

In addition to food and liquor, Papa O'Neal had strongly recommended taking along "trade goods." The very thought of taking such ubiquitous items as hooks, heavy monofilament and rubber tubing for sling spears to the Keys was ludicrous. Looking around at the surroundings Mike had had more than one occasion to bless his father's foresight. The Old Man had spent years in Third World hellholes and now it looked like the Keys just about fit that bill. Even if no one was willing to take Galactic credits for room and board, Mike was willing to bet dollars to donuts a case of six gross Number Two hooks would open doors.

"Well, let's go find out, shall we?" said Mike, putting the Tahoe into gear. He deliberately steered to crush the tumbling palm frond, metaphorically spurning the depression caused by the desolation around them. As they turned down the side street towards No-Name-Key, the wind caught the shattered palm frond and tumbled the pieces onto U.S. 1. The hard wind whistled through the abandoned buildings and erased the marks the vehicle had made on the drifting sand in the parking lot.

◆ CHAPTER 22 ◆

"Teri, you have *got* to stop getting into pissing contests with enlisted men."

Teri Nightingale sighed deeply as Ernie Pappas's strong, oil-covered fingers dug out the tensed muscles on her back. The first sergeant's thumbs rolled up along both sides of her spine, smoothing away the accumulated stresses of the day. At the accusation she could feel the muscles try to tense, but forced calm into her system. It was no good getting angry; he was right.

"I know," she said with another resigned sigh. "I know. But I was so goddamn mad at Stewart I couldn't stop myself."

"And now you've ended up looking like an ass," said Pappas with toneless brutality. "And such a nice ass it is," he added, giving it a little pat as he rolled off her back and propped himself up on one fist.

The tiny motel on the outskirts of Hummelstown was as far as they could reasonably get from the post. But Pappas was fairly sure a few of the company suspected something. Which must have really confused them when he quietly corrected his lover after her latest outburst.

The Old Man had left a list of missions to work on in his absence, missions that he specifically felt the unit was weak on. Earlier that day, practicing an envelopment maneuver, the entire exercise fell apart. The Posleen had attacked with more ferocity than normal and exploited a gap between First and Third platoons to roll up the company.

158

Stewart, in the after-action review, had injudiciously pointed out that proper employment of the reserve would have plugged the gap and saved the maneuver. They still would have taken more casualties than their "norm," but less than the total wipeout they had experienced.

It was the casual remark of a young man who was rapidly turning into a brilliant tactician. The formal training of the military had taken an untutored but febrile mind and rocketed it into areas of genius. He proceeded to outline four other simple steps that, either before or during the engagement, would have saved the company's ass. It was a given that he had thought of them in the thick of the action and not as a "Monday Morning Quarterback" reaction after the drill. He was only trying to be helpful, but the XO had taken it as a direct attack and responded at length.

When the harried XO, in front of most of the leaders of the company, had finished describing her opinion of the comments she went on to discuss Stewart's parentage, unfortunately probably with more truth than she realized, education and probable future. Before she realized what she was doing, she had thoroughly poisoned the well.

When she finished, the young NCO had stood up, stone-faced, and left the room without a word. And also without asking permission, which was a legally objectionable action. No one had suggested that he stay. Or be charged for that matter.

Pappas's comment had been pithy, succinct and to the point: "Lieutenant Nightingale, with all due respect, that was a stupid thing to do."

Their discussion of how to rectify her mistake had drifted to bed, as many of their discussions did. The relationship had taken both of them by surprise, but when Nightingale put her hand on his neck the first time and hesitantly drew him towards her, Pappas's sixty-year-old brain had been run over by his freshly rejuvenated twenty-year-old hormones. Although he had been faithful to his wife during his entire previous enlistment, the current situation was just too tough. For Nightingale, the combination of nearly a half century of sexual experience and a twenty-year-old's body had been an intensely pleasant surprise. Pappas not only knew some of the oddest tricks, he was back in condition to be able to use them.

He now ran a finger down her perfect back, hooked a thumb into her armpit and turned her to look at him. He pulled her to him, tucking her leg over his and slid his hand down her back. "You had better get a handle on this, soon, or the Old Man will turn you to paste." He gently caressed her inner thigh then slid his hand upward.

She made a hissed inhalation and arched her back. "I know," she said with a little gasp. She paused for a moment then went on, panting slightly. "I just cannot get a handle on . . ." She paused again, making little inhalations through her nose. The nostrils fluttered in and out prettily.

"On?" asked Pappas, waiting for her to try to answer.

"On . . . uhm . . ." she said as he moved his hand slightly to the side. She stopped trying to talk.

"Are you listening?" he asked, backing away slightly then sliding forward. Docking was abrupt and perfect.

"Umm-hmm," she murmured. "Definitely." She slid her leg up to hook over his hip.

"Stop fighting with Stewart and listen to him. He's better at this than anyone else in the company besides the Old Man."

"Okay," she squeaked, starting to rock back and forth.

"I'm serious," said Pappas, giving a little gasp of his own as well-trained muscles clamped. He was on the losing side of the battle now.

"I'll make up to the shrimp," she said pushing his shoulder to roll him over on his back. She grabbed his short thick black hair in both hands. "Now hang on."

Duncan popped the top off the unlabeled beer bottle with a K-bar combat knife and wordlessly handed it to Stewart. The younger NCO was staring unseeingly at the wall of his tiny room. He took a swig without looking at the product, then stopped and stared at the bottle.

"Damn," he said, looking up at the recently arrived staff sergeant. "I thought *I* had balls. Raiding the Old Man's home brew is a capital offense." Beer was getting harder and harder to find. Materials such as barley and hops were strictly controlled under emergency rationing and storage plans. The easy accessibility of the materials to the company commander was a closely held secret of the company.

"He'd understand," said Duncan, slipping a pack of Marlboro Reds out and lighting one. "He's good people." He took a deep drag on the butt and blew smoke at the ceiling.

"Unlike certain unnamed stuck-up bitches," snarled the younger NCO and clenched both hands. His arms were shaking in anger.

"Who is currently getting her ass fucked off by Top," noted Duncan, with a wry smile.

Stewart shook his head. "I never thought I'd see the day."

"Well, he's a good-looking guy . . ." said Duncan.

"No," interrupted Stewart with a grimace. "I was talking about Top fucking her, not the other way around. I mean, *damn*, the Gunny was always such a straight arrow!" Only then did he realize that the other NCO was jerking his chain.

"Well," mused Duncan with another puff on the cancer stick, "I wouldn't kick her out of bed for eating crackers."

Stewart snorted. "Yeah, neither would I. Gotta admit it. Great set of knockers. Prime slice any way you cut it."

"So," asked Duncan with a smile. "Is your anger with Gunny Pappas because he is fucking your Public Enemy Number One, or because he's getting some and you're not?"

"Who says I'm not getting any?" snapped Stewart, machismo aroused.

"Well, I know you're not getting any from Nightingale, although the way you two fight . . ."

"Oh, fuck you," said Stewart, trying not to laugh.

"And Arnold has already nailed up Lieutenant Slight, so she's right out."

"No!" gasped Stewart, starting to double up in laughter. "Jesus! Arnold and Slight? Are you sure?"

"Well, I suppose he could have been demonstrating mouth to mouth. . . ."

"Oh, shit!" laughed Stewart, finally letting go of the tension of the argument with the XO. "So when are you and Boggle gonna do the dirty deed?"

Duncan's face took on a look of deepest sorrow. "I fear never," he said, placing a hand on his chest in simulated despair. "Methinks that Sergeant Boggle pines for Lieutenant Fallon!"

Stewart laughed so hard that nut-brown ale spurted out of his nose and he started gasping. The battles between the Second platoon leader and his female platoon sergeant were as legendary as his own with the XO. The image of "Boggle" Bogdanovich and the West Pointer wrapped up in Eros's embrace was as implausible as . . . the XO and Top.

"Jesus," he swore again, after regaining control of himself. "You don't think?"

"Well, not yet," said Duncan, leaning forward and taking the home brew for a swig. "If you're just going to waste this blowing it out your nose . . ."

"So," said Stewart with a smile as he wiped beer off his chair, "who are you planning on getting a leg over with?"

"Oh," commented Duncan, handing the bottle back and waiting for Stewart to take another slug, "I was thinking about . . . Summerhour."

Beer blasted across the room again. Summerhour was a nearly

seven-foot, not particularly bright, fairly ugly, male, heavy weapons private. Since Stewart was fairly sure Duncan was straight, the choice could not have been more unlikely.

Stewart finally wiped up the mess, wiped his eyes and gave up on drinking. "You think the Old Man knows?" he asked soberly.

Duncan shook his head. "Everybody thinks I'm some sort of expert on Captain O'Neal. I was only with him for a couple of days. You guys have been training with him for over a year. You answer the question."

Stewart thought about it. "Probably. I've never seen anything surprise him."

"I have," admitted Duncan. "But only when the enemy pisses all over his battle plans. He gets really angry then. *Really* angry." He shook his head and finished the brew to the yeasty dregs. "You don't want to see him when he's angry."

◆ CHAPTER 23 ◆

No-Name-Key, FL, United States of America, Sol III
1440 EDT October 2nd, 2004 AD

Mike was trying very hard not to get angry. "Sir, I understand that you're out of the hotel business. I can even understand you being unhappy with tourists. But I've got my wife and daughter with me and we need someplace to put our heads down."

The man behind the counter was in his fifties, his long graying hair pulled back in a ponytail. He stared down his nose at the short, massively built soldier and wrinkled his nose in distaste. "Look, buddy, you're right. I'm out of the hotel business. There ain't any tourists anymore. How the hell did *you* get leave when everybody else is locked up on a base or working their ass off?"

Mike threw his hands up in despair. "I pulled every string in the book. Is that what you wanted to hear?" In fact, every string in the book had been pulled behind his back. But that would take more explanation than it was worth.

The proprietor's face worked. "Look . . ."

"Harry," said a female voice from the office at the rear. "Calm down."

The No-Name-Key Fish Camp consisted of eight ancient, wooden bungalows bleached gray by a half century of sun, a few rickety docks surrounding a small but deep embayment, a brand new cinder-block icehouse about thirty yards long and the office, a single-story wooden building protruding over the small harbor. The buildings all surrounded an oyster-shell parking lot. The parking lot had a motley assortment of vehicles, mostly pickup trucks, parked at every angle. Most of the trucks appeared to have been abandoned where they sat, palm fronds and dirt encrusting their hoods. The racket of a large diesel generator sounded from somewhere behind the icehouse and an overwhelming scent of fish and rotting weeds was being carried away on the strong southwest wind.

The office was a "T"-shaped building that doubled as a general store. The front area was normally devoted to food and sundries while the back area was devoted to tackle and live bait. On one side of the crossbar was the cash register and an empty cooler. The other side had a door with a sign over it that said "Keep Out." It was from beyond this door that the voice had issued.

Both areas were barren. The live bait tanks were uniformly empty and the tackle shelves were bare while the food and sundries area was nearly empty. There were a few jars of peanut butter and some quart Mason jars for sale. Other than that the store had been picked clean. For all it was nearly abandoned, it had been well cared for. The empty shelves had been covered with plastic sheets, to keep flies and their specks off, and the floor was freshly scrubbed.

The proprietor, propped beside his antique cash register, rolled his eyes and looked out the window as the source of the voice walked into the main area. The woman was fortyish and reminded O'Neal of Sergeant Bogdanovich. She had long, blonde hair tied in a ponytail which hung down her back and wore faded jeans and a peasant blouse. She had one of the darkest tans Mike had ever seen in his life and a nice smile.

"Forgive my husband, sir," she said, sliding behind the counter and knocking that worthy aside with a casual bump of her hip. "He's best suited as a hermit."

"I'm sorry to impose on you . . ." said Mike.

"It is not an imposition," the proprietress said, with another smile. "Harry has a lot on his mind is all. But one of them is the condition of the cabins and about that I've got to be frank—"

"They're a wreck," said Harry with a slight snarl. "We haven't had a visitor for nearly a year. There's only one that the roof doesn't have a leak!" He thought about the admission. "Well, two."

"And those we offer," stated the proprietress with a tight smile.

"We've used up most of our linens for other things!" said Harry.

"We'll improvise," said the proprietress.

"There's no electricity!" the proprietor thundered.

"There's the generator." The blonde smiled.

"It's for the *ice!*"

"These are guests," said the proprietress, reasonably, but with a hint of teeth.

"No! We don't get a *gas ration* for *guests!*"

"We'll improvise."

"There's no food!"

"Oh, pish. There's fish, lobster, crab . . ." She turned to Mike, who was watching the familial argument with amusement. "No one in your family is allergic to shellfish, are they?"

"No," said Mike with a smile at the play. "Look, let me get a word in edgewise." He started ticking things off on his fingers. "One, we don't need electricity. We came prepared to camp out, so we have our own lanterns." He thought about the argument. "Two, we have our own sleeping bags, so we don't need linens. Having a bed, any bed, is better than the floor and a roof is better than a tent. We just want to spend a few days in the Keys and maybe get a little snorkeling and fishing in."

Mike turned to the proprietor as he opened his mouth to argue. "Look, I understand where you're coming from. But let me say a few things. We're prepared to pay and pay handsomely. But if you don't take FedCreds, we brought stuff that people said was in short supply down here. I'm sorry to point it out, but I notice your cupboards are bare. I've got fifty- and twenty-five-pound monofilament, slingspear rubber, five diving masks and two cases of large hooks."

Mike raised an eyebrow as Harry's mouth closed with an audible clop. When he did not say anything Mike went on. "We've also got some other 'comfort rations.' So we'll be okay without all the usual amenities." He looked from proprietor to proprietress. The two exchanged a look and then Harry shrugged his shoulders.

"Sir," said the proprietress with a smile, "welcome to No-Name-Key Fish Camp."

O'Neal smiled back. "Call me Mike."

The cabin was small, old and smelled heavily of the mildew as common in the Keys as mosquitoes. A chameleon had broken off its pursuit of a large antlike insect as Mike opened the door. The cabin had two beds for the adults and another had been prepared for Cally. It was divided into two rooms, the side towards the parking lot being a combination living room/kitchen/dining room, while the rear side towards the bay was the bedroom and bath.

The furniture must have dated from the 1960s. The chairs, gleaming yellow in the fading light from a window, were all tube steel and cracked plastic padding. The countertops and floor were cracked linoleum, the patterns so worn as to be indecipherable. Mike glanced at the nonfunctional stove, television and refrigerator. The bedroom window showed signs of once sporting an air conditioner, but here under the spreading palms and salt-tolerant oaks the wind was relatively cool. There was running water but the proprietress, whose name was Karen, pointed out that it was strictly rationed and not to be trusted for drinking. There was a certain amount of imported bottled water, but the main source for drinking water was the distiller attached to the icehouse.

The icehouse turned out to be the center of the little community, as Mike found out when he left the cabin at dusk. The rising clouds of Keys mosquitoes drove him quickly across the parking lot to the knot of men gathered in the screened porch of the large building. It turned out that they were preparing the day's catch.

With the exception of the baseball caps, sputtering incandescent lantern and modern clothing, the scene could have been from any time in the last thousand years. The men and women were arranged along tables, talking and laughing quietly as they expertly processed the harvest of the seas.

How they kept up with whose was whose was a mystery to Mike as rubber tubs of fish were dumped on the communal table. The piscines would slither outward, some of them still faintly thumping, until they reached an available preparer. There they would be filleted or simply gutted.

Mike was amazed at the speed and technique of the workers. The gutting was different from what he was used to. When he gutted fish he generally inserted the knife into the anus and cut towards the gills. Then the head could be cut off and the guts dragged out with it or the guts could be pulled out by hand and the head left on.

The fish that were being gutted here, mainly yellowtail grunt and mangrove snappers, were being done in the opposite direction. The knife was drawn across the fish's throat just forward of the gills then the belly was slit back to the anus. A twist of the hand brought out gills and guts in a smooth motion and the fish was flipped away and the next one expertly snatched up.

The filleting was, if anything, faster. A cut would be made across the meat of the fish, just behind the pectoral fins down to the backbone. Then a cut would be made along the backbone itself. A third sweeping motion lifted the meat off, leaving a flap of skin attached to the tail. A swift slice along this flap lifted away a clean fillet. Then the fish was flipped over and the same motions cleared its other side. The remains of the fish were going into a bucket; they were useful in traps and for trolling lures. The filleters would stop after every couple of jobs and run the knives over a sharpener, then get back to work.

Once prepared, the harvest slid down the steel table to the tubs at the end. At that point a group of children under the direction of a young teen female sorted them by type, washed them and iced them down. Whenever a tub got full it would be covered and wheeled into the icehouse, only to be replaced by another.

After watching quietly for a few minutes Mike picked up an abandoned knife and gloves and joined in. He chose only the types to be gutted, recognizing that his filleting technique was not up to par. He tried his own gutting technique and quickly found that not only did it require more motions, it left more junk in the body cavity. So he started experimenting with the new technique.

The conversation went on around him, much of it in such a thick cracker accent as to be nearly incomprehensible. The conversation, whether it was the norm or censored for the visitor in their midst, centered around the weather to be expected for the next few days, fair, and the fishing, fair, and the price the fish might fetch when the buyer came through in a few days, poor. Despite price stabilization supports and general inflation the price per pound of all the major fish types, even the prized black grouper and red snapper, had been going consistently down.

Mike kept his face in its habitual frown when Harry and a fisherman called Bob got into another argument about power. Bob was of the opinion that Harry was being stingy in not providing electricity for the regular Saturday-night party at the No-Name-Key Pub. Harry pointed out the consequences of overusing fuel in a way that was so oblique as to be opaque to an outsider. Thereafter the conversation slid to less ominous topics, leaving Mike metaphorically scratching his head.

Finally the last fish was gutted and Mike stripped off the chain mail gloves. The fisherman called Bob looked him up and down and tossed over a cut lime. "Let's get washed up and head to the pub," he said in general. There was a chorus of muttered agreement which Mike decided to take as invitation. The worst that would happen was that someone would try to throw him out.

Good luck.

Harsh, homemade soap and the strong Key limes took away the worst of the fish smell and the crowd headed out of the screening to brave the mosquitoes. The distant pub was lit by kerosene lanterns hung over the doorway, but the path to it was pitch-black darkness. Mike found himself walking between Harry and Bob and decided that he was more or less being escorted.

"It was good of you to help with the cleaning," said Harry, somewhat stiffly.

"The more hands the better," was Mike's only comment.

The walked a little farther in silence.

"You in the Army?" asked Bob, noncomitally.

"Fleet Strike," said Mike and heard a faint snort.

"Really," said Harry in a sarcastic tone. "I bet you've been off-planet and everything, huh? Got a chest full of medals from Barwhon. Pull the other one."

"We had a guy down here a couple of times," said Bob in explanation. "He was a SEAL based at Homestead Airforce Base, or so he said. The cops finally caught up with him. He was a deserter from a Guard unit in Missouri."

"He sure could talk the talk, though," said Harry, bitterly.

"He stiffed Harry for a goodly bill. And ate us out of house and home," Bob commented.

Mike's nod was unseen in the darkness but they stopped when he did. He reached into the depths of his jacket and extracted a card from his wallet. It was easily discerned by the faintly glowing purple stripe around the edges.

"You forgot to ask for my ID," Mike noted, handing it to Bob instead of Harry. As he did he tapped a control on the lower face of the electronic ID.

A full-length hologram of Mike at parade rest in combat silks sprung up as an electronic voice intoned the appropriate statistics. Name, rank, service, Galactic ID number, height, weight, sex and age were all recited by the combination ID and dog tag. The IDs were made of the same refractory material as the suits, designed to take damage and still be able to identify their users. In a pinch they made a dandy weapon in trained hands.

The group had stopped when the hologram blossomed. When the recording ended the only thing that could be heard was the buzz of mosquitoes and the occasional idle swat. Bob handed the ID back.

"Hmmph," said Harry, noncommitally. "Okay, you're really in Fleet Strike. Big deal."

"And my wife's an XO of a frigate in Fleet," said Mike mildly. "And if you give her the same ration of shit I've gotten I'll feed you your left arm."

There was a general chuckle from the group in the darkness and a movement towards the pub. "I think he means it," said Bob, chuckling at the store owner's discomfiture.

"Yeah, well," said the aging hippie. "It's been so long since I had any red meat, it might not be all that bad."

"Things *are* getting a tad complicated," admitted Mike.

◆ CHAPTER 24 ◆

Monsignor O'Reilly regarded the small piece of electronics that had mysteriously appeared in his cassock pocket. It looked like a standard flash memory card, but there were no manufacturer's marks on it. Nor were there any instructions. He finally put it in the flash reader attached to his computer and checked its directories.

The chip was apparently named "Religious Documents." The first directory was titled "Rig Veda," the second "Koran," the third "Talmud" and the fourth "The Franklin Bible." He opened up this directory and stared at the single file titled "Install." He twisted his face a few times, took a deep breath and double-clicked the file.

It asked for a password. He thought about it. He had not been given a password. The likelihood was that if the first guess was wrong, the chip would erase instantly. Finally he typed, "We must all hang together, or assuredly we shall all hang separately." The computer chirped and the installation began.

Either the chip had more memory than any flash card should or the file had been hyper-compressed. The tiny file was expanding to dump a mass of files into his computer. If he had to destroy the evidence it would be nearly impossible to track them all down. He nearly pulled the chip in panic, but the file dump finally ended and a text box popped up.

"WELCOME," it read, "TO THE FRANKLIN BIBLE COMPLETE STUDY OF HUMAN ARCHETYPES AND PRE-HISTORIC MYTHS."

There was a new icon on his taskbar, a tiny blue world with a

169

telephone on it. He drifted the mouse across it and the caption "New Messages" popped up. He clicked it.

"Dear Monsignor O'Reilly," the simple text box read, "in the event that you do not want this program to stay on your computer, simply uninstall it using the uninstall icon on your desktop. Uninstallation will remove all files created with this program, all messages associated with this program and every bit of evidence that it ever existed on your computer. This will take less than fifteen seconds with the system it is currently installed on. You may also do this by simply saying, 'Dump the Post Office.'

"At this time these are the critical messages for the Society of Jesus.

"The Tir Dol Ron is en route to Earth. His first stop will be the United States."

The message that followed was much the same information he had received from Kari. It did, however, include some expansions. Apparently the reason that the Tir was coming to finalize the negotiations was that the humans could not possibly kill this messenger.

The message contained detailed data on requested defensive systems, construction rates for Galactic-supplied weapons and Fleet construction rates. Actual rates were graphed against planned and currently reported rates and the difference was obvious. The bottom line was that less than half the equipment requested for Terran Forces would be available before the invasion. There would, however, be sufficient materials to equip all the expeditionary forces. Those forces, by solemn and binding agreement, came first.

With America asking for more grav-guns and fewer being available, it should be an interesting meeting.

The final piece of information was a note on subsystem suppliers. He nearly overlooked it but a particular note caught his eye. All sixteen Darhel clans were participating in supplying materials for the Fleet and the Terran Defense systems. And all of them were behind on their schedules. However, one particular clan, the Tindar, was farther behind than any of the others.

He narrowed his eyes and wondered about the significance of that bit of information. The list had been intentionally sorted by negative production rates. It was definitely a clue to something. After a moment's introspection and a mental memo he returned to reading the primary message.

"We have no suggestions or requests at this time. The installed software has complete plans for a variety of Galactic systems including descriptions of production and use.

"All messages will completely clear themselves five minutes after reading; there will be no trace of them on the system. The flash card will erase itself in twenty seconds and will dissolve if submerged in water. We are happy to once again be in contact with our human comrades.

"The Bane Sidhe."

◆ CHAPTER 25 ◆

Mike woke to the to sound of the wind-up radio they had brought with them. It was forecasting four more days of perfect weather to be ended in the season's first severe cold front. Hurricane Janice was proceeding to the north of Bermuda and was not expected to make landfall in the United States. The United States Ground Force command had recently upgraded its forecast likelihood of early Posleen landings. The new forecast called for small-scale landings to begin occurring no later than two months from the date of forecast.

Mike snorted and threw aside the poncho liner he had been sleeping in, flipping a small lizard nose-over-tail through the air. The silky, smooth nylon and polyester blanket was a near-perfect camping accessory. It was the one item that Fleet Strike had eliminated from its inventory that Mike disagreed with. Although he understood that the replacement item was supposed to be better in every way, there was an atavistic thrill to the simple polyester fill product that the newer one did not have. In addition to that, there was also the fact that the GalTech version was virtually unavailable, whereas the South Carolina factory that made poncho liners was running three shifts and had ample supplies on hand. It had recently been moved up the waiting list for Sub-Urb production facilities on the basis of the product being designated "critical warfighting supplies." Not bad for an ersatz blanket.

Mike rubbed the stubble on his face and decided that it was acceptable. One of the GalTech products he had fallen in love with was depilatory cream. The product not only removed hair, it inhibited growth for nearly a month thereafter. Of course it was in as short supply as everything else, so Mike eked out his cache by using razors in between. But he was still in the latter stage of inhibition and could more or less ignore shaving for a few days.

He rubbed his face, looked around the dilapidated room crawling with ants, and shook his head. With a snort at the fruition of their plans for the trip he took the two steps necessary to enter the bathroom. The mirror was losing its silvering, giving an impression of leprosy to his face, and had a large chunk cracked out of one corner. He propped up the seat of the toilet and did his morning business, smiling at the handwritten sign the proprietress had posted at eye level.

With the shortage of water, flushing urine was contraindicated. To point this out delicately the sign stated "If it's yellow, it's mellow. If it's brown, it goes down." There was a bottle of bleach on the back of the toilet and Mike carefully measured a capful and tossed it into the bowl to neutralize the ammonia.

When he came out after a sketchy wash-up Sharon had come back to the room.

"If you hurry you can probably still get some breakfast," she said with a smile. She had a bouquet of tropical flowers that she set on the cracked linoleum table.

Mike smiled and shook his head. "Not exactly what we planned, eh?"

"Not the Ritz-Carlton," she admitted.

Although they had both visited the Keys more than once, it had always been on a shoestring. This time they had looked forward to staying in the best hotels in Key Largo. Not only were they both making as much as pre-war generals, Mike was absolutely flush with prize money from Diess.

The Fleet fell under Federation regulations. One of those complex rules related to property captured or recovered by military forces. It had been enacted, along with a slew of other inducements, when the Posleen had first entered Federation space. The monetary inducements were designed to persuade the chronically poor Indowy to renounce their minimalist and nonviolent ways and enter the Galactic military. The various inducements had failed miserably in their intent, but they had never been taken off the books.

Military equipment abandoned by the Posleen, as thousands of ships had been abandoned on Diess, fell under the category of "salvage." It belonged to the forces that had either captured it or permitted its capture.

This was not immediately apparent to the human forces on Diess.

They had simply let the thousands of in-system and interstellar ships sit until a Darhel factor had pointed out that they were responsible for clearing them off the planet. The military had protested that it did not have the equipment to remove the ships, so the Darhel offered to remove them for them.

The commander on Diess was not born yesterday. He decided to put the ships up for bid and was amazed by the response. Both in-system and interplanetary ships were at a premium due to low production rates and war losses. To date, fewer than half the ships had been sold, but the income had exceeded the Federation "payment" for all other NATO forces.

However, the Federation regulations also required "sharing" of the income from the prizes under a complicated scheme. One aspect of it related to "actions of extraordinary nature." Since it was unlikely that any of the ships would have fallen into human hands without the actions of O'Neal and his platoon, a percentage of every ship was detailed to them.

Mike's prize income the previous year had been larger than the Gross National Product of most Terran countries. Not that it did them any good in the Keys.

"Where's breakfast?" he asked, pulling on a pair of multipocketed safari shorts and a light cotton button-down shirt with still more pockets. He tended to get lonely without them.

"Over at the pub," she said, putting the flowers in water. "The locals apparently sell them eggs from free-range chickens. One of mine was . . . a little on the pink side."

Mike grimaced. He hadn't had fertilized eggs since his dad got out of the egg business decades before. He had just opened his mouth to retort when there was a shriek from the direction of the harbor.

Sharon was not sure where the Desert Eagle appeared from, but before she had started to move Mike was outside with the .357 caliber automatic leveled. As she ran out the door she saw him lower the weapon from its two-handed grip and grin sheepishly. Then she realized that the second shriek from their daughter was a cry of surprised delight. It took her a moment to recognize the chittering squeals that responded.

Cally, in the company of Karen the proprietress, was squatting at one end of the closest dock, trading splashes with a dolphin. The small bottlenose was chattering back at her every squeal and she was obviously having the time of her life.

Mike slid the gigantic automatic into the rear of his shorts and stepped out onto the dock. At the creak of the wood, Karen looked over her shoulder and smiled.

"Morning sleepyhead," she quipped and stood up.

The dolphin protested as she stepped away but she just waved and tossed it a handful of fish bits. The bottlenose caught them expertly and went back to charming bits out of Cally.

"Tame dolphin," Sharon commented, squinting against the bright morning sun. "They aren't usually like that, are they?"

"No," Karen said. "I was Shirlie's trainer."

Sharon raised her eyebrows in surprise. "Where? Sea World?"

"No," said the woman, bitterly. "Not anymore anyway. I was at the Marine Mammal Research Facility in Marathon. It was really just a tourist trap for dolphin rides, but I've never had anything against that. I was with Sea World for years as a trainer and really believe that we did good work. Making cetaceans stars kept all sorts of ugly things from happening to them over the years. Heck, if it wasn't for places like Sea World, nobody would care about dolphins and orcas."

"So how'd you end up here?" asked Sharon as Mike walked down the dock to where his daughter continued to converse with the cetacean.

"Well, when the tourists started to fall off, we got a notice from the National Marine Fisheries Board that we were to release all of our specimens. Their reasoning was that there was no way to maintain captive marine mammals in adequate conditions and it was better to release them."

Mike turned and looked behind him. "That's insane!" he stated. "You can't just release a captive mammal and expect it to survive!"

"No duh," Karen said, then smiled sadly to take the sting out of the words. "That was exactly what I said, and two or three dozen other trainers that I kept in contact with. What really pissed me off was that we couldn't even get any press time. The NMFB just shoved the damn ruling down our throats and the press paid no attention."

Mike nodded. "Let me guess. It wasn't 'newsworthy.' "

"Exactly." Karen nodded. "Anyway, I was dating Harry at the time. Instead of going back up north–I'm from Chicago originally–I moved in with him. Shirlie and four other dolphins just sort of 'followed' me here," she concluded with a sly smile.

"Trail of breadcrumbs?" asked Sharon, watching Cally pat the six-hundred-pound sea mammal. She wondered when the inevitable question would hit.

"Something like that," said Karen. "We used to take them out for swims with the boat." She gestured at a well-kept Boston Whaler tied up to the office. Something about it indicated to Mike that it hadn't moved lately. "I just told them to follow me over."

"What happened to all the rest?" asked Mike. "I mean there was

Sea World and the Miami Oceanarium and that one in St. Augustine . . ."

Karen's face pinched up at the thought. "Sea World just went over to the coast and released theirs in the Intercoastal Waterway. I don't know about the dolphins and porpoises, but at least one male orca was later found dead. The rest did pretty much the same thing."

"Damn," said Mike. There didn't seem to be much else to say. Then another thought hit him. "Hey, what about all —"

"The zoos?" Karen interjected. "And animal parks?"

"Yeah," Sharon agreed. "What about them? I remember something about Zoo Atlanta only being able to keep the gorillas."

"There are a couple of big parks in Florida that have taken in some of the animals," Karen said. "The herbivores are free roaming and more or less making it. Most of the carnivores have had to be put down. And anything that can't get into one of the reserve parks is getting put down."

"That's not right," Mike said. "We've got an obligation to those animals! They didn't exactly *ask* to be put in zoos."

"You're preaching to the choir," said Karen sadly. "We've been writing Congress, the President, everybody. But the responses we've gotten have a point. With shortages for humans, where are we going to get food for the animals?"

"Daddy, get real," said Cally, rolling onto her back, then flipping to her feet in the most limber move Mike had ever seen in his life. "It's an obligation, not a suicide pact. Once you kick the Posties' ass, we can gather them back up and recover whatever we find. Until then, we gotta concentrate." She rubbed the small of her back. "Shit. I forgot about the Walther."

"Showoff," Mike laughed. He shook his head. "I suppose you're right, kitten. It still pisses me off."

"Softy," said Sharon with a smile and gave him a thump on the shoulder.

Karen smiled at the byplay then turned to Cally. "You want to swim with Shirlie?" she asked.

"Sure!" said Cally with a grin. "That'd be spar!"

"Go get a suit," Karen said, and smiled as the girl scampered off. "Harry and I don't really think children are a good idea," she commented without looking at them as Cally went around the corner.

Mike grimaced. "I can understand that."

"She carries a pistol with her?" Karen asked, carefully.

"You don't?" Mike snorted. "Yeah. And she knows how to use it. She also knows all about firearm safety. Don't worry about Cally; Dad's turning her into a survivor."

"Our other daughter is off-planet," Sharon said, quietly. She was looking at the dolphin racing around the small harbor. "Could I join you?" she asked.

"Sure!" said Karen. "The more the merrier. The boys'll probably show up around ten, after they're done foraging. Shirlie's just so lazy she'd rather be fed." Karen turned to Mike. "What about you? Want to join us?"

"Maybe later," Mike said. "I think I'm gonna go try to butter Harry up. You guys have got a couple of cases of hooks coming."

Karen exhaled in relief at that the thought. "That would be great. You don't have any idea how bad it's been lately."

"Yeah," growled Mike. "We've got a few things to thank the Posleen for."

Mike set the case of fishhooks on the counter and smiled. "There's another case in the Tahoe, and the other stuff. I've also got a Number-Ten can of coffee, but you can't have all of it."

Harry shook his head and smiled faintly. "You sure know how to make friends," he said. He opened the case and pulled out a box of hooks. "We've been making them out of nails and tearing up lures. But, believe it or not, we've got coffee."

Mike reached behind his back and extracted a hip flask. "I've got some of this out in the Tahoe, too." He took a hit and passed it to Harry. "I'll even give some of it up for some goddamn explanations."

Harry regarded the clear liquid carefully. "Well, it's a little early," he said, then took a swig. He grimaced and coughed. "Oh! Smooth!" he gasped. "Jesus, what is that?"

"Georgia Mountain Dew," Mike answered with a laugh. "Only the finest. Now what the hell is going on around here?"

Mike had never had a conch omelet before. He had to admit it wasn't bad, but the thought would take a little getting used to. He scraped up the last of the grits and wiped his mouth with the provided hand towel. The Key did indeed have coffee, and Mike had to admit that wherever it came from it was better than the issue can he had with him. He took another sip of the excellent brew and cleared his throat.

"So let me get this straight. All fuel is rationed. Okay, got that; it's that way all over. Fuel for the boats is rationed on the basis of their production. High-producing boats get more fuel."

"Right-on so far," said Harry, taking a sip of the java as well.

"And power to the islands has been out for months. So you have to have a generator to distill the water and make the ice. And the fuel for the icehouse has to come out of the pool of fuel for the boats?"

"Right."

"And every month the price of the fish has gone down along with the fuel ration."

"Yep," said Harry. "Next month there won't possibly be enough fuel for all the boats *and* to make ice. If we can't store the fish until the trucks arrive, we might as well give up."

"What about the stuff you've been holding back?" asked Mike, carefully.

Harry was cool. "What stuff?" he said, blandly.

Mike laughed and held up his wrist to reveal the AID. "My AID analyzed satellite imagery of this place for the last year. It says you're holding back about twenty percent of your production."

Harry grimaced and nodded. "Yeah. But that goes to a lot of places. It's not really . . . available."

"Maybe you'd better make it available," said Mike, quietly. Hoarding was becoming a real problem as more and more people reacted to the coming invasion with a panic mentality.

Harry sighed. "If we did that it would take away the only things that make working here worth living." He paused and thought about it for a moment. "The spare isn't just in fish. It's in stuff that's more transportable. It's in dried conch and lobster tails. Shells. Stuff like that."

"What the hell do you use that for?" asked Mike.

"Trade goods, partly," Harry answered, holding up the cup of coffee. "There are small traders who move stuff around the islands and up to the mainland. Conch keeps for a long time. There's a market for it in Florida. The traders get stuff in Miami you can't get in places like Cuba and bring back rum and coffee."

"Oh," said Mike, nodding his head. He was aware that the shortages had created a thriving black market, but this was almost like pioneer days. It sounded like a triangle trade.

"Some of it goes to the dolphins," Harry pointed out. "They do a lot of their own foraging, but we still eke out their feed. And we do a little dealing on the side with the general goods trader that comes through." He grimaced again. "The damn thief."

"That bad?" asked Mike.

"Half the stuff he carries he'll only sell at black market prices. He'll have two cases of corn flour, but officially it's only one case. Once the first case is sold the rest sells at whatever the market will bear."

"Damn," said Mike with a stronger than habitual frown. "That's *not* the way it's supposed to work."

"There's not enough fuel for us to go up to Miami every week or even every month. So we have to depend on the one 'official' trader or the free traders. But the free traders are totally black market and there's no way to be sure what they're going to be carrying."

"And every month the price of the stuff is going up and the price of the fish is going down," said Mike sourly.

"Right," Harry said with the same tone. He looked like he'd bitten a Key lime.

Mike nodded in thought. He had had a thought the night before but it was firming up now. "Let me ask you this, Harry. What happens if you take the icehouse out of the equation?"

"What do you mean?" asked Harry. "We have to run the generator to keep the fish iced. Besides that, the distiller is our only consistent source of fresh water. We can't take it out of the equation."

"But what if you could not use the fuel for the generator?" Mike asked. "What then?"

"Well, that puts off a reckoning," Harry admitted. "We've thought about a windmill or something. We'd be pretty okay then. Hell, I've got an electric car stashed. We could load up on spare batteries and make it to Miami and back with at least some of the stuff we need." He shook his head in despair. "But we don't have a windmill and they're impossible to buy these days. Even if we had the cash. And it wouldn't produce enough electricity to matter. And the first good storm would tear it up."

"Ay-aaaah-ah," Mike whispered and whistled a scrap of melody.

Harry smiled. "It's not quite that bad. We haven't had a Viking raid. Yet."

Mike smiled. "It's an old memory. Who's your electrician?"

Harry wrinkled his brow in question. "Why the twenty questions?"

"I'm getting to that," Mike said. "Is it you?"

"No," admitted Harry. "It's one of the guys on Bob French's long-line boat."

"Okay," Mike said. "Well we'll have to wait for Bob to get back in to get it installed, but let me show you something I just happened to have brought along."

Good day, thought Bob French as he navigated the cut up to No-Name-Key. The world might be going to hell in a handbasket, but the lack of tourists, fuel and markets had reduced fishing pressure to the point of recovery. Since the types of fishing that prevailed put more pressure on the upper end of the food chain, the stocks of feeder fish recovered in the first year of the emergency. Since then the increases in catch size across the board had been phenomenal.

On ledges where he used to be lucky to get one legal-sized snapper he now was taking dozens a day. Lobster pots were coming in brimming with "keeper" langostino and occasionally had a real monster, the sort of lobster that hadn't been seen in the Keys since the '60s. And he had always thought that the tales the old-timers told of multi-square-mile shoals of herring and sardines were sea-stories until he saw one just this year.

This day he was coming in with a boat loaded to the gunnels with giant groupers and snappers. Unfortunately, the thought of what that meant was disheartening. Every month the price was going down for all the fish, even the best cuts. And the official trade company paid in warbucks instead of pre-war dollars or, best of all, FedCreds. The warbuck was deliberately inflationary, so the cost of everything went up nearly as fast as the price of fish went down. It should have been the other way, but it wasn't.

He suspected, hell, all the fishermen suspected, that it wasn't supposed to be that way. But without any way to communicate with the mainland except mail or driving, nothing seemed to be happening. He had finally used up his hoard of gas tickets and gone to Miami to complain. After two days of getting shuffled from one department to the next at the Marine Fisheries offices he had to get back. If he wasn't fishing he'd find himself on the shore.

And he was better off than most of the fishermen. His boat was free and clear and one of the larger ones still operating. Two of the guys working for him had lost their boats to the repo companies after they couldn't make the payments. He couldn't pay his crew much—hell most everybody got paid in fish or supplies—but it was something. The communities had pulled together so nobody starved and everybody had a little something extra. But nobody, not even he or Harry, had much.

What was going to happen when the invasion finally came was another question. But that was a worry for another day. For today there was gutting a bumper haul of fish that would just put him more in the hole for gas.

He made the cut ahead of the tide race and finally saw something to smile about. John Samuels had made harbor, which was the first bright spot he'd seen in a month of Sundays.

They called Samuels "Honest John" as a joke. The free trader ran a sixty-foot sloop that carried small cargoes from Miami to Cuba and back. He stopped at all the islands, buying delicacies "on the left" and trading at prices lower than the "official" black marketers. He and the other traders were practically the only source of tobacco and alcohol in the islands.

The trader was sitting on the dock of the harbor office with Harry and the "visitor" from Fleet Strike. The little fireplug probably was an actual Fleet officer; his casual demonstration of Galactic technology the night before had been impressive. Before everything went south they had watched the video from Barwhon and Diess. Fighting the aliens was going to be hell. He didn't envy the frowning little bastard his job.

The visitor seemed to have mended his fences with Harry. As the boat took the final turn to the dock the sound of their laughter was clear over the quiet chugging of the diesel. He killed the engines and drifted into the dock; every bit of fuel was worth saving. As Harry and Honest John caught his tossed lines the visitor flicked the butt of a cigar into the waters. Unless Bob was mistaken it was one of John's prized Havana Panatellas. The Fleet guy was making friends fast.

"How's the fishing?" John asked, taking the boat captain's hand as he jumped ashore.

"Oh, it was a hell of a haul," Bob answered bitterly. "For what it's gonna fetch."

"Smile, Bob," Harry said with a grin of his own. "We just got a new set of buyers and suppliers."

The fisherman looked from one grinning face to the other in puzzlement. "You want to explain that?"

"FBI agents just performed raids on your suppliers' and buyers' offices along with the offices of the Miami Rationing Board and the Marine Fisheries Board," the visitor answered for them.

"Why the hell would they do that?" he asked in surprise. "And how did we find out so fast?"

"Well," answered the visitor, with a slight smile violating his habitual frown, "they are *required* to perform an investigation at the registered request of a Galactic Enforcement Officer. All Fleet officers are also law officers. A second request from the office of the Continental Army Commander just got them moving faster than you can say '*posse comitatus.*' "

"That black thing around his wrist is a communicator," Harry added with a laugh. "The FBI has already called him back. They said it was the best black market bust they've made since the start of the emergency. It's gonna make national news."

"Things are gonna be screwed up for a while still, man," Honest John cautioned. "They're gonna have to find a replacement that ain't part of the Cubano Mafia that's been controlling it." He shook his head. "Ain't gonna be easy. The Cubanos have gotten used to having their way in South Florida. One raid ain't gonna stop it."

"Cooperate," said the Fleet officer. "The assets of the companies have been seized. Ask the FBI to turn them over pending the completion of the investigation. They don't need the trucks to prosecute the perps. And you can probably get them permanently as the 'victims.' Get some materials and convert the old Piggly Wiggly to a warehouse so you don't have to base in Miami."

"That takes electricity," said Bob, with his own shake of a head. "Which is something we ain't got. We can't afford the diesel to run a generator that big. Even if we're in a co-op with the whole Keys."

"Ah, well, as to that," said the visitor, with a real grin while John and Harry just laughed.

"What?" asked the captain, as the crew started to unload. The four of them joined in as tub after tub of prime grouper and snapper were unloaded. He looked at Harry again, waiting for him to go on. "What's so funny?" he asked again, heaving a hundred-pound tub to the Fleet Strike officer. The heavyset dwarf caught it like it was a feather and slid it across the dock. He was even stronger than he looked.

"Mike had a little present with him," said Harry with a grin.

"It's not a present," said the visitor, seriously. "It isn't even a loan. One of the things I was doing on my vacation was finding places to plant energy caches. We're seeding the coastal plains with power sources to recharge suit units that get caught behind the lines. When I was on Diess it was a pain in the ass trying to find power. So I came down with three antimatter generators. They've got a finite amount of power, but it's enough to run a small city for a year, so . . ." He shrugged and smiled again.

"Damn," said the boat captain, tossing him another tub. "Thanks."

"Well, the priority is any unit that needs it," Mike said severely. "And, technically, you're not supposed to tie into it. But since you don't have a power grid, it's not like the whole Keys are going to be hooked up to it." He shrugged again and frowned. "As screwed up as it is down here, it seems the least I could do for you. Just don't overuse it. It's like a really big battery and once it's gone, it's gone."

"Well, thanks anyway," said Harry, stacking the last tub on the dock. The three hands were already loading up dollies to carry the fish to the icehouse for cleaning. "This means we don't have to waste fuel for generation so the boats can stay out longer. Hell, we've got a satellite dish, so we can hook up a TV in the pub and even get real news."

"Getting news again will be great," said Bob, with a smile. "Hell, before you know it we might even have telephones again!" He laughed. "And then it's faxes . . ."

" . . . and cell phones . . ." laughed Harry. The electronic imped-imentia they had all grown up with was as distant as buggy whips these days.

"Well, enjoy it as long as you can," said Mike grimly. "The first serious invasion will hammer the satellites. And there goes your reception again."

"Yeah," said Bob, "that's true. But it's a hell of a long time since we got any news but radio. I got a question to ask on that, if you don't mind."

"Shoot," said Mike, but there was a hint of wariness.

"You said you were on Diess, right?"

"Right."

"There was this guy that won the Medal. They said he got blown up in a nuclear explosion and lived. What *really* happened?"

Sharon squealed and spun around in the water as Herman goosed her.

Karen laughed in return and slapped the dolphin on the flank as it went by. "You have to watch that one. There's a reason we named him Herman Hesse."

The three of them had been dragged off to a tidal pool by the dolphins. Here, on the Florida Bay side of the island, they had been swimming with the big cetaceans most of the day. Cally had stayed firmly attached to Shirlie, who at less than five hundred pounds was the lightest of the four. The other three were males: Herman, who had more or less attached himself to Sharon, Charlie Brown and Ted. Ted had left for a few hours in the midafternoon, but the others had stuck with them.

The day had not been for pure fun. The pool was home to a vast collection of the sorts of rare marine organisms that could be traded for luxury goods. Seven species of anemones, several more types of urchins, two types of lobster and various other items had been gathered. Sharon watched Cally as she rode the small dolphin to the bottom of the pool. There, in about fifteen feet of water, the eight-year-old let go and began plucking at the reef. A sponge, a spider crab and an anemone found their way into her mesh bag before she began to claw for the surface and air.

"This has been great," said Sharon, finning slightly and spinning in place to keep Herman in sight, "but I'm getting worn out."

Karen smiled. "A little different than what you usually do, huh?"

"A bit," Sharon admitted. She could see the dolphin trying to get into position behind her.

"What do you do?" Karen asked. Most of the conversation of the day had been taken up by the tasks that they had been learning.

Karen had prepared well. The dolphins had taken turns toting the three humans and an inflatable boat full of the necessities of the expedition. She had packed a light lunch of cold lobster salad and some cut fruits along with plenty of fresh water. Sharon had been careful to wear a T-shirt and to insist that Cally wear one as well. The hot South Florida sun would still have burned their legs badly, but Sharon kept Cally well covered with sunscreen. In Sharon's case, the same nannites that scoured Fleet bodies for radiation damage would make short work of the sunburn.

Sharon watched Cally line up for another run at the bottom. She was too worn out to even think about making another try, but the energetic youngster seemed as fresh as when they started. "I'm an XO on a frigate," she answered, watching the quick hands snag a passing shovel-nose lobster. Although they were less plentiful than the more common spiny lobsters, they were prized by the oriental community as an aphrodisiac and fetched a high price among the free traders.

"What's that mean? I mean, what do you do?" asked Karen, interested. She had never met a person who had been off-planet.

Sharon suddenly found herself unable to explain. How could she explain the constant strain of wondering which critical system would fail next? When the hull would suddenly breach? How the ship, and herself, would perform when they were finally in combat?

She paused a moment and smiled faintly. "Mostly I wait for the air to run out."

Karen was a kind and empathetic woman. And she recognized that not only was the answer correct, it was also as much as she could expect to get for the time being. She nodded in agreement instead. "We ought to be getting back." She suited action to words, tossing her nearly full mesh bag into the cooler in the inflatable. She pulled a harness out and winked. "If you waggle your hips do you think you can lure Herman over?"

Mike took another pull on the bottle of beer and a puff from the cigar. The sky was slowly darkening, the famous purple of the Caribbean drifting up from the east as they kept watch over the westward opening. The girls had been gone most of the day and it was about time they turned back up.

"If this isn't paradise," he opined to the trader, "it's within the limits of tolerance."

"It is close," Honest John admitted. "In a lot of ways, life's gotten better. Slower at least."

"Down here," Mike pointed out. "It hasn't been slow for me."

John nodded in agreement. "The margin sure as hell has gotten thinner, though. It used to be there was, I dunno, flex in the system. These days it's sink or swim. Sometimes literally."

"So, how is the Coast Guard these days?" Mike asked with a laugh.

John laughed in return. "Not bad. They keep the pirates in check, at least. But a lot of them have gotten transferred to 'more vital' tasks. So, SAR is spotty." He pronounced the acronym for Search and Rescue "Sahr." It was a military way of phrasing it that caused Mike to cock his head.

"Have you lost many boats?" Mike asked.

"A few. There's two problems. Some of the boats *have* gone to pirates. Or that's the way it looks. Boats just disappear in calm seas. And the free traders are in a constant low-grade war with the *Mariellitos* bastards who think they control the trade down here." The trader frowned and looked over towards his ship as if to ensure it was still intact.

"Have you been having much trouble?" Mike asked.

The trader snorted, gave a grim smile and shook his head. "Not . . . anymore." He seemed disinclined to explain the reference.

"The other problem is a lot of the boats, their GPS and Loran is giving out; they're at sea more than the systems are designed to handle. And most of the traders aren't real sailors, guys who know how to navigate by the wind and the stars. So if they lose their GPS, they get lost: really lost. There was one was just making the crossing from Los Pinos to Key West. The crossing's maybe two hundred miles. Stupid fucker ended up near Bermuda. Dismasted, out of water, half mad. How in the hell anyone could completely *miss* the Bahamas I'll never know." The tall captain took another toke on the joint he held. "Nobody could get that stoned. Hell of it is, he wants to go back to sea."

Mike chuckled grimly. He had his own massive list of screwups that he could detail, starting with the Diess Expeditionary Force. But the situation in the Keys was something of a whole different order.

"I don't understand how it could get this way," said Mike, gesturing around with the beer bottle. "Where the hell is everybody? I can understand the tourists, but where's the retirees?" The whole state of Florida was filled with retirees. Some of them were recalled military, admittedly. But that had to be a small percentage. Where were the rest?

"It happened slowly," Honest John admitted. "Not just here but all over Florida. First, the tourists started trickling off. Then, most of the people who could hold a hammer or run a press without cutting their fingers off went up north to get jobs. The Fisheries Board reinstituted net fishing for the Florida waters about then and there was a small rush to get into that. But when people found out how hard it was most of them moved away too. Then all the young guys got sucked off by the Army."

He smiled and took a big toke. "I was getting recalled my-own-self," he said with a chuckle. "But not only is free trader a 'vital war production position'—and didn't that take some squeeze to a certain congressman—but I convinced the in-process board it would be a waste of perfectly good rehab just to get a drugged-out Petty Officer Three." He grinned again.

"Anyway, before we knew it the entire population of the Keys was below twenty thousand, most of them retirees. The nursing homes and 'managed care' retirement centers started having problems with taking care of their old folks. Some of 'em died cause there just wasn't anybody on duty.

"Then when Hurricane Eloise came through, they took it as an excuse to evacuate all the retirees that were not 'fully capable of self-care.' Down here in the Keys, anyway.

"That meant the only people left, other than in Key West, were the fishermen and their families. There's a federal law that Florida Power had to deliver down here. But after Eloise, they got an 'indefinite suspension' because there was a shortage of parts, or so they said. That was last year.

"So that," the ship captain finished, "is how it got so totally screwed up down here. An' that's the truth."

The trader took another toke on his joint and a pull on the glass of Georgia branch water Mike had supplied. He worked his mouth for a moment. "Cotton mouth. Haven't talked this much in a coon's age.

Mike nodded and took a contemplative puff on the cigar. Papa O'Neal's branch water was awfully smooth. He doubted that the trader had any idea what proof he was knocking back like water. It was eventually going to catch up with him. "Just one thing I don't understand," he mused. "Where'd they put them? The retirees I mean."

"Some of 'em got mixed into the groups up the peninsula. Lots of 'em went to the big underground cities they're building," said John. He took a last puff on the joint and spun the butt into the water. "One nice thing about this war. Not only has it driven the cost of Mary Jane down, the coasties don't give a rat's ass if you're carrying."

"That's crazy," Mike argued, thinking about the first part of the statement.

"Why?" asked John with a laugh. "They've got a real war to worry about. They don't have to worry about the 'War on Drugs.' "

"No," said Mike with a touch of impatience. "I was talking about the Sub-Urbs. The work on them is hardly complete. I don't see them being able to take tens of thousands of geriatric invalids! Who the hell is going to care for them there?"

"Search me," said Honest John, putting words into action as he patted his pockets. "Damn," he muttered, swaying to his feet. "I gotta go back to the ship an' get some more weed." He took one step forward and fell in the water. He came up spluttering and looked around. "Where's those damn dolphins when you need them?" he said blearily.

Mike shaded his eyes against the westering sun and smiled. "Be filled with joy; salvation is at hand," he quipped and pointed at the opening where the group of humans and cetaceans had just hove into view.

"Hey Herman!" shouted Honest John. "Give a poor drunk trader a fin, buddy!" He grabbed a dangling rope and smiled up at Mike happily. "To think I could have been in-processing right now."

Mike nodded in mock soberness. "I gotta agree that might not have been a great idea."

◆ CHAPTER 26 ◆

"You know, General," said General Horner, with a characteristic antihumor frown, "I gotta wonder if this was the greatest idea."

Taking a look around the in-processing station, General Taylor was forced to wonder the same thing. Even if Horner had said it in jest.

Shortly after the change of command structures, one of General Horner's computer geeks pointed out that the recall program had been misdesigned. Any serious student of modern militaries could recognize that there were, of necessity, two general types of officers: warriors and paper pushers. There were a few officers, such as Jack Horner, who were superlative in both areas. But they were few and far between. Most officers were very good at one or the other, but not both.

The reason for a fighting army to have warriors in the officer ranks was obvious. But there was a viable reason for paper pushers as well. Armies float on a sea of paper. The logistic problems of Napoleonic armies had been solved, but only at the expense of constant information flow that required humans in the loop. Humans who were much more comfortable making decisions on the basis of a spreadsheet than a map. Humans who found a more efficient way to load trucks, well, exciting.

But bureaucracies are like hedges: beautiful when pampered and trimmed and ugly as hell when left to run riot. A military filled with warriors slags into a scrapheap as the warriors vie for command slots and neglect their paperwork. A military filled with paper pushers bloats out of control as the paper pushers create new empires to lord over.

The upcoming war with the Posleen was, admittedly, going to require lots and lots of bean counters. But the previous personnel policies had left it with, in both Generals Horner and Taylor's opinion, more than enough bureaucrats at every level. What it desperately needed was leaders and warriors.

However, most of the first "crop" was . . . a little on the moldy side.

"What're you in for?"

The questioner was a tall, trim man in his early seventies. He vaguely recognized the man next to him, but could not quite place the face.

The man in question took a suck off the oxygen tube in his nose and wheezed out a reply. "I got the Medal in Holland," he croaked. The statement set off a paroxysm of coughing that trailed into laughter. "They're gonna have their jobs cut out with me!" The laughter led to more coughing until he was turning blue.

"You gonna be okay?" asked the questioner.

"Sure," said the emphysemic once he had reestablished control. "As long as the damn ceremony don't go on too long. What'd they get you for? I don't recognize you from any of the meetings." The last was accusatory. The group consisted mostly of Medal of Honor winners. The emphysemic former paratrooper knew them all by heart and could list off the missing files along with dates of service and death. He was not so good on what he'd had for breakfast, but he was spot on for fallen comrades.

"I made it on points," said the tall former lieutenant colonel. He'd never thought he'd be wearing Army green again; it was almost ludicrous. Hell, there were more people who wanted him offed in the Puzzle Palace than in the rest of the globe. If they ever organized, his ass was as good as dead.

The emphysemic just grunted and went back to listening to the brass drone. He thought he knew who was who, but then realized that the black guy was in charge. Hell of a world.

"Who's the jig?" the WW II paratrooper asked and coughed for his efforts. He rattled the bottle to get it to deliver a decent amount of oxygen but it didn't help.

His former inquisitor just laughed.

"In conclusion," said General Taylor, "I'll just mention a few things about where you should expect to be placed. Most of you are thinking, 'Hell, I've got the Medal. They don't dare let me get killed.' All I can say to that is, sorry. This is the real and the bad and the scary. I can't afford to waste warriors on bond tours and rear-area paper pushing. You can expect to be placed with Line forces and shuttled from front to front for emergency reaction forces. You are going to be the tip of the spear, always the men in the breach.

"Face it, most of you screwed up over and over again to win the awards that are on your chest." This last brought a note of often hacking laughter from the two hundred or so in the meeting room. "If I had to be there, I couldn't think of a better group to have at my side or behind me. So it is the least I can do for my soldiers."

"There are," he finished, "a lot of things going wrong in the Ground Forces today, and throughout America. Our job is to fix them. And we are going to."

◆ CHAPTER 27 ◆

No-Name-Key, FL, United States of America, Sol III
2022 EDT October 3rd, 2004 AD

With great ceremony Harry pressed the "on" button. There was a buzz from the crowd enjoying alcohol and appetizers as the thirty-inch television blossomed into life, showing the CBS evening news.

He bowed to the humorous applause, then walked to the back of the bar where Mike and Honest John were continuing a running argument.

The weekly party was in full swing as the mosquitoes closed in on the pub. In one corner the youngsters from throughout the mid-Keys region played and argued as the teenagers danced. A table down the middle of the room was half covered with dishes brought in by families. Most of them consisted of various ways to prepare conch. The pièce de résistance, two man-sized black groupers, a butterflied yellow-fin tuna and three bushels of lobster tails, was grilling outside.

Mike and family had contributed to the haul. Honest John had accepted Mike's charter for the remainder of their stay and the boat had sailed out daily for fishing and diving adventures. Mike had returned laden with lobster and a variety of species of fish, while Sharon and Cally had collected inshore species with the dolphins and Karen. Despite his intent to spend time with Cally and Sharon, they had been drawn to the inshore and the dolphins while he had been drawn to the sailing, fishing and diving offshore.

The expert captain proved that it was not necessary to have a "tuna boat" to catch tuna, as he and Mike hit the yellow-fin run in the Stream. Mike had been thrilled by the explosive strikes of the stream-lined eating machines, while John and the Key co-op had been thrilled by the high-quality protein; freshly caught tuna was a valuable trade meat.

Mike had also caught some praise for his diving skills. His GalTech breath-pack was a major reason for that. The small, experimental system included a nitrox rebreather that extracted oxygen and nitrogen from water. The staging bottle was small but high-pressure so the system was good for several days. The depth on it was limited to one hundred twenty feet, but the tiny pack made for such limited drag that it was like diving without gear.

Mike was able to approach normally skittish hog-fish and groupers without disturbing them with bubbles. And if they spooked anyway, he was still usually able to make a kill; the fish had no time to learn that a compact body and giant fins meant incredible burst speeds. Then the blood, turned green by the light filtering of the water column, would flow backwards as the fish made a last desperate dash for safety.

He was even able to make a rare tuna kill on a young fish that was attracted by the strange seal-like creature in the water column. The thirty-pound yellow-fin made a fine contribution to the catch.

He had finally dragged Cally away from the dolphins for a day to go fishing. Floating along a weed patch she had hooked into a big bull dorado and practically been dragged out of the boat. Any lingering resentment at being taken from her cetacean friends was washed away as the rainbow-sparkling fish tail-walked across the wake of the drifting sailboat, taking the line out of the reel with a banshee's shriek.

The nights had been just as good as the days. Mike, Sharon and Cally spent most early evenings at the pub, eating part of the day's catch and discussing the news from the radio with Harry, Bob, Honest John and Karen. By eight o'clock, though, Cally was whipped. Most nights Mike ended up carrying her off to bed. Then the conversation on wide-ranging topics would either continue or Mike and Sharon would retreat to their own room and renew their acquaintance.

The last two evenings the news had been about the war. And it was mostly bad. The goodness mopping up on Diess was countervailed by the opening of the Irmansul campaign, where the Posleen had gained an immediate upper hand over the mostly Asian forces. The Chinese Third Army had suffered over one hundred thousand losses in the first week's fighting and the bets were on that the Darhel would call on European forces to help them out. While European and American forces had suffered horrendous losses at the hands of the Posleen on Barwhon and Diess their superior coordination often

permitted them to avoid the massive casualties that were characteristic of Chinese and Southeast Asian forces.

During the discussions, Mike—and Cally, to everyone's amusement—pointed out that the best units were on Barwhon, not Earth.
The Barwhon units had a high percentage of veterans and were well
drilled in to the needs of battle against the alien centaurs. By comparison the units left "Earthside" were in lousy shape. Units stripped
from France, Germany or the United States would be no better off
at the outset than the Asian units.

The virtual destruction of the first Expeditionary Forces and the
ongoing blindsided slaughter on Barwhon had stripped the NATO
militaries of most of their trained forces. The rejuvenated officers
and NCOs would, eventually, take up some of the slack of their loss.
But the current forces were a rotten branch. Until the reforms that
Horner and Taylor had instituted took effect the units that were
"Stateside" might as well be back in basic training.

All of which was surprisingly hard to explain to the boat captain.

"Look," said the slightly drunk captain, pugnaciously. "They're
soldiers, right?"

"Sure, John," O'Neal said, "but soldiering isn't just about shooting a gun. Most war is about getting the shooters and the backing
for them to where the enemy is. Even the Posleen aren't everywhere.
So getting the right forces to the right place is the problem."

"What's so hard?" asked Harry. "They're right there," he continued, pointing in the general direction of Florida Bay. "What's so hard
about finding them?"

"Oh," Mike said ruefully. "You'll find them. Or, usually, vice versa.
But for regular forces to survive them you have to dig in. Do you
understand that?"

"No," said Harry. "But I'll accept it."

Mike took a pull on a panatela and wondered how to explain.
"Okay, here's the best explanation I can give. You're going to fight
somebody. You've got a one-shot pistol. They turn up with fifty
buddies armed with machine guns. What do you do?"

"Oh," said Harry. He scratched his head for a second. "I guess you
shoot the son of a bitch who called you there."

"True," agreed Mike. "But if you do it from behind a wall you
might be able to reload and kill some more, right? Hell, you might
be able to survive."

"Okay," agreed John, taking a pull on a lemon-dashed rum. "I'll
buy that."

"So, the way to fight is from prepared positions. It's a lot like World
War I that way. But you've either gotta have enough men to man a

huge front or you've gotta guess where the Posleen are coming. And this is realizing that they can drop out of the sky, anywhere, at any time."

"Gooks used to have little antiaircraft batteries all over the damned place," said Honest John with a belch. "Why don't we?" The tone was bitter.

Mike raised an eyebrow but answered the question. "Technology. The 'gooks' got antiaircraft batteries from the Russians. The Russians had scads of gear lying around and lots of production facilities. We're having to teach the Galactics not only what to build but how to mass-produce stuff. Even then what we're really doing is a sort of super cottage industry. So, we don't have many weapons that can hurt the landers."

"So we have to hit them on the ground," Cally interjected, suddenly popping up to snatch a conch fritter. "Until they give mom a real ship and we get some more Class Nine Grav Cannons we're shit out of luck." She popped the tender piece of giant whelk into her mouth and trotted back to the arcane games being played in the corner.

"And you're saying if we hit 'em on the ground, we're screwed," said Honest John. He grinned ferally. "I bet there are ways to hurt 'em that don't involve tactics we gave up after Belleau Wood." He took another pull on the rum and pulled out a joint. "You oughta be able to sneak into the rear area."

"And do what?" asked Mike, curious. Honest John had always been happy to talk about fishing or the sea and he had debated a few military subjects, but this was the first time he had evinced any real knowledge or background. It was like he had dropped a mask or thrown off a cloak and said "Ah, hah!"

"Ambush convoys? Destroy supply depots? Call in artillery strikes? Kidnap cadre?"

Mike shook his head. "There's a fairly robust long-range reconnaissance section on Barwhon. But they don't really strike, they give warning where strikes are going to occur. The Posleen don't have much in the way of convoys, not yet anyway, and they don't have supply depots besides their ships. And those are pretty heavily defended." Mike paused and thought about the question.

"The way that the horses partition stuff, most of their good artillery targets end up being beyond artillery range. Which is why a couple of universities are working on longer-range artillery." Mike shook his head again and puffed on the cigar. "And the Posleen don't care if a 'town' gets wiped out by a special op group. They don't pull forces back from the front to look for the group. They use local forces. So it is generally a net loss. Just ask the combined ops team that we sent to Barwhon before the expeditionary force."

"So we just, what did you call it, 'hunker down and take our licks'?" asked Karen, softly.

"I'm afraid so," said Sharon in reply. "The Fleet is building. I don't know if it could go faster; maybe it could, maybe it couldn't. Once we have a real fleet we'll be safe. But until then we have to fight them on the ground."

"We've tried mobile warfare," said Mike, taking a sip of his beer. "The French tried it a couple of times on Barwhon. It was not successful." He grimaced.

"Well, that was the French," said Harry.

Mike snorted. "Don't let General Crenaus hear you say that. They also ate *our* lunch on Diess, but that was when they had already 'broken the square.' So it's not a fair comparison. But an M-1 is a tin can to their weapons. So I don't see being able to fight them in open field."

"Well," snorted John, drunkenly, "they don't do islands."

"No, they don't," Mike agreed.

"So we blow the Seven Mile Bridge and we're golden," continued John, taking a big hit on the joint.

"And that will be that," said Karen quietly. "We'll be cut off."

"It's already bad enough," said Harry. "Since the clinic in Marathon shut down we've lost two people who should have lived. Tom Robins died from appendicitis and Janey Weaver died of scarlet fever. God help us if there's something like a measles epidemic."

"If there's an epidemic the government will help," said Karen.

Mike took a pull of his beer to make sure his face was covered but John was not so diplomatic. "The government?" he laughed. "What government? The one that saddled you guys with the Cuban Mafia in the first place? Or the one that made Florida Power fix their lines? How about the one that is setting the prices so low nobody can make a dime to set aside then, if you do, taxes the shit out of it?"

Harry held up his hands to forestall further argument. "No, no more!" he intoned. "For tonight, we have power, no one is sick, the leeches have been taken off our backs and there is plenty to eat. Let's worry about which bridges to burn tomorrow."

John nodded his head. "Yeah, man. You're right." He looked at Karen and smiled lopsidedly. "Sorry, gal. Don' mind me. I'm drunk."

"And stoned." She laughed, picking up the smoldering joint and taking a hit herself. "Damn," she said, coughing, "no wonder you're stoned."

John laughed in return and hoisted the glass of rum. "Only the best! Cuba doesn't only make fine cigars!"

"Speaking of which," said Mike, happy to change the subject, "what do you want for a couple of cases of cigars and rum?"

John thought about it for a minute and shook his head. "I know better than to dicker when I've got a load on," he laughed. "But what the hell. How much of that white lightning you got?"

"Two cases of liquor, white lightning and muscadine brandy in liter bottles. I've got a couple of cases of beer as well. Then there's some smoked and tinned wild boar and venison. I've got a five-gallon can of gas. I can give you the gas but I want the can back or an empty."

Honest John nodded. "Well, I think I can give up a box of panatelas for that," he said.

Mike's normal frown turned up in a smile. "Now I know why they call you 'Honest John.'"

"Mike," said Sharon, smiling sweetly, "let me do the dickering."

"Uh, oh," said John, setting down the joint. "I don't like the sound of that."

"Did I mention I spent six months as a procurement officer?" she asked, cracking her knuckles and leaning forward. "Now, I've got to wonder if the local authorities are fully aware of your cargoes . . ."

◆ CHAPTER 28 ◆

No-Name-Key, FL, United States of America, Sol III
0832 EDT October 5th, 2004 AD

Mike carefully set the last case of hand-rolled Imperials on the stack. The cigars were in twine-wrapped bundles of fifty, a gross of bundles to the case. The stack of cigar cases and rum barrels made an awkward fit in the back of the SUV.

Honest John rubbed his face and grimaced. "Christ, I knew I shouldn't dicker when I was drunk."

"And never play poker with her, either," Mike opined. "She'll clean your clock."

"She already did," the trader bemoaned.

"Oh, fiddlesticks," Karen said. "You know how that wine-jerked venison will go over in Havana. Not to mention that muscadine brandy. You're going to make a killing."

The trader just snorted but then smiled. "It's been a good visit, guys," he said to Mike and Sharon. "You guys keep safe. Don't bunch up."

Mike turned from where he was securing the empty gas can and frowned at the trader. "What rank did you say you were?" he asked.

"A third class petty officer," John answered. He smiled faintly and patted the pockets of his floral shirt until he found a panatela and a match. He flicked the match with his thumb and lit the panatela. "Why?"

" 'Don't bunch up' is not a Navy saying," Mike answered.

"Musta heard it somewheres," was the trader's answer.

"Uh-huh," Mike answered. "And didn't you say they just sent you a recall notice?"

" 'Bout two weeks ago," John agreed, warily. "Why?"

"Oh," said Mike, smiling. "Just wondering. Most of the notices went out last year. I can only think of one group that got recalled in the last few months."

"What are you two talking about?" asked Sharon, frowning.

"Nothing," said Mike, closing the back of the Tahoe.

"Guys," said Harry, giving Sharon a hug. "You take care, ya hear?"

"We will," said Sharon.

"Keep in touch," said Karen, smiling. "Herman will want to hear about all your big adventures."

"Okay," said Cally, giving the woman a hug. "I'll make sure to write him."

"Well," said John. "I'm not into soppy good-byes and I've got a tide to catch." He hugged Sharon and Cally and waved at Mike. "Tell that big ugly bastard Kidd that Poison said 'Hey.' "

"I will," said Mike with a smile.

"And tell Taylor he can kiss my fat, white ass."

"Okay," said Mike with a snort.

"Keep your feet and knees together, snake," he finished and walked towards the dock. He started to yell for his two missing crewmen but after the first wince thought better of it and just hopped in the dinghy, untied and started rowing towards the harbor opening.

As he was clearing the opening the two half-clad worthies, trailed by two swearing females, charged out of one of the abandoned bungalows and down the shore towards the retreating rowboat.

"What were those women saying, mom?" asked Cally, ingenuously.

"I think it was 'See you later honey,' " Sharon answered, pushing her towards the back seat.

"Oh," said Cally. " 'Cause, you know, it sounded a lot like, 'What about our money?' "

Mike laughed and shook Harry's hand. "Thanks for having us."

"Anytime," Harry answered. "On the house."

Mike nodded and smiled, then got in the Tahoe. He turned to Sharon and shrugged. "Ready for a long damn drive?"

"Sure. And this time let's bypass my parents."

"Works for me. Actually, if we go by way of Mayport, you can probably catch a shuttle from there. Then Cally and I will drive back to Dad's. I can catch a shuttle out of Atlanta or Greenville."

"Okay," she answered with a sad smile. "And one last night?"

"Yeah," he answered. "One last night. Until the next time."

Sharon nodded. Of course there would be a next time. It had taken the highest possible command authority to pry them both loose for this time. And they were both going to be in the thick of combat.

But, of course there would be a next time. Mike put the Tahoe in gear and they drove out of the parking lot, down the shell-paved path, wrapped each in mirror thoughts.

◆ CHAPTER 29 ◆

"Join the Fleet and see the Universe, eh Takagi?" mused Lieutenant Mike Stinson for the umpteenth time as he looked out the clear plastron of his fighter canopy at the swirling stars.

"Yes, my friend. For once the recruiters didn't lie."

Captain Takao Takagi was the number-one-rated fighter pilot in the Japanese Self-Defense Force when he leaped at the opportunity to transfer to Fleet Strike Fighter Force. He knew the objective realities of the situation, that without dreadnoughts to break up the Posleen battleglobes the fighters could only peck ineffectually at the surface, that the Posleen space-based weapons would probably sweep the limited number of fighters available out of the heavens. He recognized that his chances of ever seeing the snow-capped mountains of Honshu again were slim to none. But he also understood the ancient mantra of the Japanese warrior, the words that every Japanese soldier, airman or sailor carries in his inner heart: *Duty is heavier than mountains, death is lighter than a feather.*

Someone must stand between Earth and the Posleen landings. Until the heavy Fleet forces were ready, that meant a rag-tag band of converted Federation frigates and the space fighters as they came off the assembly line. If it was his day to die, when the Posleen came, then so be it, as long as he could take an offering with him to the ancestors.

And the view didn't hurt.

Working in two fighter Combat Space Patrol teams, the first three fighter squadrons maintained a close Earth patrol. Since the first few scouting Posleen could be expected any day, it was hoped that the CSPs could intercept the Posleen as they exited from hyperspace and began their movement to Earth.

There were two forms of hyperspatial transport known: "ley-line" transport and "quantum tunneling."

The Federation, without exception until recently, used "line" transport. A quirk of quantum theory first proposed by humans in the 1950s turned out to be true. Along the path from star to star was a "valley" or "line" that permitted easy entry into the alternative dimensions of hyperspace. These valleys permitted ships to travel at high "relative" speeds, far exceeding the speed of light. Although it was possible to "quantum tunnel" outside the valleys, it was slower and more power intensive.

The problem from a military perspective with the "valleys" was that the openings were both a known location and they were relatively distant from the inner planets. Therefore, it took hours or sometimes even days for a ship to travel from the habitable world to the "valley entrance." Nor were the entrances necessarily near each other or near planets. So most of a long hyperspatial trip involved movement in star systems from one valley to the next. Furthermore, the approach of a ship in the "valley" set up a harmonic that was detectable outside the "hyperspace dimension," but ships in the valley were blind to the outside. Although the Posleen did not, currently, set up space ambushes, the possibility existed. And that made Fleet dislike "ley-line" hyperspace intensely.

The Posleen, however, used an alternative method. Disdaining the "valley" method they used "quantum tunneling." Quantum tunneling had numerous items to its advantage. It permitted "small" jumps within star systems. It permitted the ships to come out relatively close to their target, be it a planet or some other location. And it was practically undetectable.

However, "tunneling" had two countervailing problems. First, it was slow and energy intensive, compared to the "valley" method. The trip from Diess to Earth took six months using the "valley" method; most of the time spent in systems going from valley to valley. Using the "tunneling" method it took almost a year and seven times as much energy. Second, the "exit" phase was highly random. Ships come out of hyperspace on a random course and at low velocities. But it was the preferred method of the Posleen. Indeed, the species seemed unaware of the "lines" between star systems.

Because of the vagaries of "tunneling," and the low relative velocity of the ships exiting it, if the first few ships were individual Battle Dodecahedrons or Command Dodecahedrons, the combination of fighters for immediate reaction and frigates to pound with marginally heavier weapons *might* keep some of the pre-landings from happening. At least, that was the hope.

In the meantime, what it meant for the pilots of the First, Ninth, and Fifty-Fifth Interplanetary Fighter Squadrons was an up-close and personal view of the world spread out before them. The patrol positions were just beyond geosynchronous orbit—close enough to intercept the Posleen but far enough out to avoid the junk belt surrounding the planet—and the swirling blue globe constantly caught the eye. As Takao rotated his fighter to take in the view again, the terminator was just starting to cross the Atlantic. The pair's current patrol was just ahead of it—maintaining a near geosynchronous orbit—and he could clearly see the American coastline coming up. After the series of cold fronts that had lashed them for the past two weeks it looked like they were having some extraordinary early fall weather.

He had spent some time at Andrews Air Force Base, cross training with the American F-15 wings before anyone had heard the word "Posleen" and he imagined that quite a few people were heading to the mountains or the beaches this weekend. His next leave was several months off, but he might take it there instead of . . .

"Come on, Sally!" shouted Big Tom Sunday as his daughter stepped up to the plate, "keep your eye on the ball!"

The booming voice caused more than one head to turn and Little Tom at his side grinned sheepishly as he saw Wendy Cummings look their way. She gave a slight, disinterested smile and looked back across the diamond. There Ted Kendall was surrounded by a bevy of young ladies like her, sentenced by their parents to watch a Saturday afternoon elementary school softball game.

Tommy followed her eyes and quickly turned back to watching the game. At a moment like this the shadow of his father seemed to overpower him like a rising flood, just as irresistible and as elemental. His father had been a football star, his father had been chased by the girls, his father never had to worry about what to do on a Saturday night. His father was a butthead.

Little Tom pulled his glasses off and wiped them on his shirt. There was a moment's sting in his eyes that he put down to the strong north wind and he took a surreptitious swipe as he redonned them. Just the wind. He need not bother being surreptitious, another check had Wendy halfway around the diamond, headed in the other direction.

Wendy walked slowly and carefully towards the crowd around Ted Kendall. Until the week before he had seemed welded at the hip to

Morgen Bredell, the two the undisputed class king and queen as a classic double whammy: head cheerleader and lead quarterback. Since their spectacular breakup during study hall, the competition for both had become heavy. Morgen had latched onto Ted's number one rival for big man on campus, the school's lead fullback, Wally Parr, but Ted had seemed totally uninterested in female companionship.

Most of the school thought that he was waiting for Morgen to come back. Sooner or later she was bound to discover that Wally had fast hands not only in the backfield. Besides being the quarterback Ted was considered an all-round nice guy. As too many girls had learned, that did not hold for Wally.

Wendy had considered that dissimilarity carefully before deciding to move into the circle around Ted. After a few unpleasant dates with the backfield she had practically sworn off football players, but maybe Ted would be different. She practiced her opening line as she swayed closer.

Little Tom glanced over again as Wendy closed in on the bevy, then looked away as his eyes burned from the sun shining off her long blonde hair. *You'd figure sooner or later they'd learn.* He pulled his glasses off again and took another swipe at his eyes.

"What the hell's wrong now, Tommy?" asked his father.

"Nothin', Dad."

"Allergies?"

"No, just the sun. I should have brought my shades."

"With all I paid for custom sunglasses, you think you would. Stop a Posleen shotgun blast."

"Yep," said Little Tom with an unheard sigh at his dad's total cluelessness. "Pity about the rest of my face, mind you."

His dad laughed and went back to berating his sister. At nine she was already a star athlete and well on the way to erasing Big Tom's shame at having a computer geek for a son. Big Tom unconsciously checked the Glock behind his back as a high, thin line of cirrus clouds swept across the sun.

"Could come any time," he commented just as unconsciously.

"Yep. Anytime," Little Tom agreed. Another sigh and rolled eyes. "Dad, can I go home now?"

"No. We need to stay here and show our support for Sally."

"Dad, Sally's got enough confidence for three of us. She knows we support her. I've got homework and I have to get in two hours range time so I can be in the tournament next week. When am I going to be able to?"

"After the game," answered his father with a frown.

"After the game you are taking Sally and her friends out for sundaes," answered Little Tom with the sort of remorseless logic that always got him in trouble. "You will expect me to participate in that as well. After sundaes we will convey Sally's friends to their various residences. We will return home at approximately nine P.M. You will maintain lights out for ten P.M. I repeat . . ."

"Tommy," Big Tom growled.

"Shut up."

"More or less. You are going to show your support or you can kiss any goddamn computer game tournament good-bye."

Little Tom took a deep breath. "Yes, sir!" he snapped, crossing his arms and tapping one boot.

"When is this damn tournament, anyway?" asked his father.

"Next Saturday, three P.M. until it finishes," said Little Tom, knowing he was in for it.

"You're supposed to be participating in a Youth Militia exercise that night!"

"Chief Jordan excused me," said Little Tom with another roll of the eyes. "I've outgrown the local militia, Dad. Besides, the tournament counts as tactical exercises for military prep credit."

"Who says?" asked Big Tom with a snort of disgust at the asinine idea. As if sitting in front of a computer playing shoot-'em-up games could be considered real combat training.

"Fleet," answered Tommy. "They count national standing in *Death Valley* toward military pre-training."

"Well, I don't. You need to know what the real thing is like, not a Virtual fairy tale. You're going on the Youth Militia exercise."

"Dad!"

"No means no."

"Okay, no means fucking no," said the son furiously. "In that case, what is my motivation for watching this softball bullshit, O Great Master of All Things Military?"

"Watch your mouth, mister!"

"Dad, you are a fuckin' dinosaur!" the teenager finally exploded. "I am *damned* if I'm going to be in any Ground Force unit! I am going to be Fleet Strike or nothing! And Youth Militia does *not* count towards Fleet! I don't mind you acting like I've got two heads and a tail because I don't measure up to your ideal son, but you are not going to screw up my chances of getting into Fleet!"

"You had better calm down and get a civil tongue in your head or you're going to be grounded for the rest of the school year!"

Little Tom met his father's eyes fiercely but he knew the old man would never back down now. With the other parents listening it was going to be a point of pride, something that his father had in over-abundance. His eyes closed and his face worked in anger as he tried to control himself. Finally he opened his eyes.

"I am going to go catch a ride home," he snarled at his father. "And then I am going to cap targets for a couple of hours. And I suspect I am not going to miss."

"Get out of here," his father husked and dismissed him from his attention.

He stepped out of the crowd of parents and started looking for someone, anyone who had a car. As he did he saw the coach of the opposing team charge onto the field towards the umpire.

Wendy waited carefully as Ted warmed to expounding about himself. Until his breakup with Morgen he had been the quietest of all the football players. His humility was rapidly slipping away under the onslaught of female attention and since there was not much he could think of to talk about except football the focus was on recent games.

"Then I handed off to Wally and he ran . . ." he continued.

"Thirty-two yards for a touchdown," interjected Wendy.

"Yeah," he said, momentarily stymied.

"You were down by more than seven, so you decided to go for the double point rather than try for a touchdown and a field goal."

"Uh-huh."

"So you threw to Johnny Grant for a touchdown," continued Wendy, flipping a lock of blonde hair out of the way, "but I was wondering something at the time . . ."

"Yeah?"

"It looked like Jerry Washington was in the open and you had to throw past a safety to get to Johnny. Why didn't you throw to Jerry?"

"You know," he said, chagrined, "Wally, the big son of a bitch, was blocking, was in the way, I couldn't see past him. Everybody asked me that, afterwards, especially Jerry. He was really pissed." He turned towards her as the conversation finally turned to something he could talk about.

"You need to do something about that. That explains the same problem on the next series when you got intercepted," she said with a toss of her hair. She personally thought it was her best feature and decided that subliminally showing it off would help.

"What," he asked, laughing, "you doing a piece for the school newspaper?"

"No," she answered, "do you think we need a better sports section?"

"Oh," he started to respond, "I think the school . . ."

"What is that bozo doing?" asked one of the suddenly snubbed coterie, watching the coach of the opposing team apparently charging the umpire.

"For she's a jolly good fellow, for she's a jolly good fellow, for she's a jolly good fellllow, which nobody can deny!" "Woof! Woof!"

The chorus of male, female and canine voices rang through the Fredericksburg Public Safety Building and out the open windows into the splendid autumn sunshine. A mob of happy faces in jumpsuits and body armor–bulked uniforms were gathered around a conference table to celebrate the thirtieth anniversary of the fire chief.

"Speech! Speech!" cried the usual joker at the back.

"Speech! Speech!"

"Okay! Okay!" said the slight gray-haired female as she stepped up to the head of the table. Her blue, patch-covered coverall bore the nametag "Wilson" over her left breast. One side of her face and the back of her hand on the same side bore the stigma of replaced skin, slick and shiny, but her electric blue eyes were undimmed by age and untrammeled by care. "If I can get you guys to just shut up for once it'll be worth it."

She looked around at the sea of young faces and suddenly grinned. "Now," she cackled, shaking her finger and gumming the words, "lemme tell you about the ooold days, smack, smack, wah in mah day, we had ta carry the water up from the river, yep . . ." At the common, quavered litany the group of firefighters and police—most of them trained and all of them at one time counseled by the wise old woman—laughed uproariously.

"No, really," she continued in a normal voice, shaking her head. "I just want to say that the last thirty years are what living is all about. I don't know how people who don't like their jobs get up in the morning. Every damned day I wake up and spring out of bed more ready to come to work than the last." That the job had eaten two marriages and left her without children she carefully did not mention. There were balances in any life and on the scale she was willing to accept her portion.

"You people, and the generation before you and I hope the generation after are what makes this job so special. That and the chance, every day, to go out and do some good. If there is a better thing to do with your day than to save a life—whether fighting a fire or preventing a crime—I don't know what it is. Someday, someday fairly soon, I suspect, I won't be able to climb the ladders, or carry the stretchers or run the hoses. And the legacy that I will leave is right here in this room." There were a few sniffles in the bunch now and she thought it best to wrap up before it got too sentimental.

"And every day, I want you to keep that in mind. There is nothing more important than saving an innocent life and anything that you have to do, through fire or explosion, it is worth whatever effort. There is just nothing like it." As the crowd was cheering the door to the hall burst open to admit the dispatcher.

One of the opposing team softball players was following her coach, dragging a boombox nearly as big as the player. At the same time, one of the teenaged sisters dragged along by the parents was tugging at her father's arm, leaning into him and proffering the headset from her Walkman. At the coach's first words the umpire waved the game to a halt, leaned over and dialed the boombox's volume to the max.

" . . . not a test, this is an announcement of the Emergency Broadcast System. Posleen ships have been detected exiting hyperspace in near-Earth proximity . . ."

Everyone at the game unconsciously looked up. As they did there was a flash of white light, clear against the crystalline blue sky. The blossom of nuclear fire marked the location of at least one space battle. Tommy looked back towards his dad and, as they caught each other's eye, they both unconsciously checked behind their backs. When they realized the mimicry, they both looked chagrined. For a moment they seemed to connect in a way that they had not felt in years. Then Big Tom headed out to the field to collect his daughter and Tommy headed for the Suburban.

"Earth is under a landing watch. This means that probability of landing in your area within the next four hours is high. All military personnel are ordered to immediately return to their units by the shortest possible means. All aircraft are ordered to ground immediately at the nearest possible landing area. Citizens without military duties are strongly urged to go immediately to their homes and stay there until landing areas are determined.

"All businesses with the exception of essential services, such as groceries and fueling stations, are ordered to close immediately. All citizens are urged to return to their homes and remain there. Stay tuned to your local TV and radio stations for updated watches and warnings. Up-to-date watch and warning information for your local area is available through National Weather Service Broadcasts. . . ."

Wendy listened to the announcement in shock. The group around Ted swayed towards him then started to break up as individual girls sought out their parents. Wendy was the last one to leave and she looked at him for a moment, reached out her hand in farewell then walked away.

"... Citizens are urged to remain off interstate highways which are designated for military troop movements. If you feel it necessary to leave your area, or if your area is ordered to evacuate, follow the designated evacuation routes from your area to refuge areas. There will shortly be a statement from the President...."

The dispatcher had a portable weather radio with her and simply held it over her head. As the dispatch began to repeat Chief Wilson looked around and said, simply, "You all know the drill. Time to get to work."

The mountain of black metal had appeared with a brief flicker of plasma discharge at a range of less than six hundred kilometers—knife-fighting distance in space—and more or less on a collision course. Before Takagi and Stinson could even initiate evasive maneuvers a plasma cannon wiped Stinson from the heavens. Takagi grabbed his stick, flikkered, engaged thrusters and hit the Hammer. The next plasma wash missed his fighter by less than thirty meters.

The fighters conceived of and designed by the GalTech Fighter Board were the most advanced spaceships ever built. Because the Posleen occasionally exhibited a degree of skill at jamming, and because the Galactics required a human in the fire decision loop, there had to be a body in the cockpit. To survive in the expected environment the ships had to mount not only impressive countermeasures but be able to maneuver in ways considered impossible by the first designers.

The primary Posleen weapons that would be used against fighters were either a terawatt laser system on the landers or a similar grade plasma cannon. Galactic reports and information developed on Barwhon and Diess determined that Posleen detection and acquisition systems were state-of-the-art. Indeed, there was mounting evidence that they surpassed the Federation in every respect. Furthermore, a laser beam traveled at the speed of light, a plasma ray only fractionally slower. While over extremely long ranges there was lag, at any practical engagement range the time between firing and impact was effectively instantaneous.

Given these two facts there was little hope for a fighter component, despite their obvious utility against landers. The entire battle would have to be fought by ships that could take a hit and keep coming.

However, in any weapons system there was a slightly longer lag between acquisition of target and firing, the "lock-on" phase. It was this inherent lag that was the single chink designers could foresee in Posleen antiship weapons. What would be required to survive in that type of environment would be a fighter capable of carrying a reasonable payload and sufficient projectors and deflectors to be able to somewhat spoof the Posleen acquisition systems, but most of all it would have to be incredibly maneuverable. It would have to be able to make vector changes that could avoid a light-speed weapon in the time it took that weapon to acquire it and fire; it would have to be able to turn on a dime at a fraction of the speed of light.

The only thing that made this possible was inertial control. Inertial controllers were used in all space craft, otherwise they could not reach reasonable speeds without squashing their crew flat from acceleration forces. After months of research and development the Galactic science/philosophers, the crablike Tchpth, managed to create an inertial stabilization system capable of damping six hundred standard gravities with a reasonable field area and mass. Since the resulting craft would be at least the size of a conventional F-15 it had more than enough room for weapons and jammers. Acceleration, however, remained a problem.

The Federation in general used a reversal of the inertial damping field for reactionless acceleration. While it was a tremendously efficient system, it had some limitations that they had not yet overcome. Specifically, although they could damp six hundred gravities of acceleration, they could not generate them. Thus the fighter's dampers exceeded its actual abilities. This was where human ingenuity came to the fore.

The humans on the design team made a series of points on the subject of reactionary as opposed to reactionless thrust and the utility of some of the materials the Galactics used regularly. After a brief protest over the inherent danger of the system, the antimatter thruster and afterburner were born. Antiprotons and water were squirted into a plenum chamber at a three-to-one mix ratio. When the antimatter hit the water it created a thrust just made for getting down and busy. Dropping more raw antimatter into the thrust plume created an afterburner that gave new meaning to the name "Hammer." The Space Falcons could even do a maneuver previously the sole prerogative of the Harrier jump jet, a VSLP.

This maneuver was discovered, accidentally, by a new Harrier pilot who found himself in a fairly high-altitude battle of maneuver—a dogfight or furball to the military—with an F-16. The F-16 was inarguably the superior aircraft for the situation; it was considered the best dogfighter in the world.

The new pilot was desperate to avoid impending mock doom and not yet instinctive about what not to do in a Harrier. As a mistake, he accidentally pointed all of his vector fans in opposed directions, then somehow recovered. If he had not been high above the ground he would have found out just how unforgiving an aircraft he was flying. Briefly.

Instead, he suddenly found himself going one hundred eighty degrees in the opposite direction, directly at the rapidly encroaching F-16. He fired his own, notional, missiles, dove for the deck and both avoided the nearly inevitable midair collision and "killed" the surprised and momentarily terrified F-16 pilot. Once it was determined what he had done—and a method to successfully and safely replicate it was developed—the maneuver became a regular part of the Harrier's repertoire. All the other pilots suddenly started to give Harrier pilots, mostly semisuicidal Marines, a wide berth in a furball; they were likely to fly right up your nostrils.

What was unusual in an "airbreather" fighter was the norm in a space system and the F-2000 Space Falcon could do the identical maneuver. In spades. With a flip of the pilot's wrist the fighter could be pointed in the opposite direction, but because of inertial forces would continue along its initial vector. However, an application of antimatter thrusters and afterburners slowed all but the most extreme velocities and had the fighter headed in the new direction in no time. In the case of Takao Takagi—up close and personal to a Posleen Battleglobe that had not even existed moments before—he used every trick he knew in that first moment and it spared his life for another day.

He flipped his fighter end for end, a "flikker" maneuver, and fired off his antimatter thrusters. At almost the same instant he kicked in his afterburners. Hitting the Hammer was a desperation maneuver at low relative velocities. At reversed velocities, as he was after the flikker, it was nearly suicide, requiring an extraordinary degree of skill. If the ship already had velocity or acceleration negative to, that is away from, the antimatter mass, the additional punch of the antimatter degrading was absorbable by the ship systems. Although the inertial effects would be high, the dampers could absorb them. All that occurred was extremely rapid acceleration.

However, if the vector was neutral with respect to the location of the antimatter mass or positive to it—as in flying into it—the danger was that not only could the inertial dampers be overloaded, resulting in pilot mush, but portions of the unconverted antimatter might touch the ship itself, with catastrophic results.

As it was, for a moment he sustained over sixty Gs after damping. While likely to kill most human beings, with training and if they are sustained for only an instant, sixty Gs are marginally survivable. In the case of Takao Takagi it was an instant he would remember for the rest of his life. As he came out of momentary shock, he fired a volley of antimatter "lances." The small, "brilliant" weapons were about the size of a conventional AMRAAM that had hypervelocity drivers and penetration aids designed to get inside Posleen defenses. The Class Four antimatter warheads should be able to destroy or severely damage a lander. He knew that his AID would be broadcasting warnings so he didn't even bother.

The battleglobe right in front of him was the only one he could worry about, but he heard scattered reports of others. His globe was on a vector headed away from Earth but it was already maneuvering ponderously back into orbit.

The thing was so large it was incomprehensible as a ship. Up close his fighter, nearly the size of a World War II bomber, was swallowed by the immensity, a gnat pecking at a house. The black globe was kilometers across, and every cubic meter was devoted to killing. As his fighter tossed him through pounding evasion maneuvers, it seemed that every one of those weapons was aimed at him.

The gigantic black globe was comprised of thousands of individual ships. It was not concentrating on the unimportant gnat pecking at its exterior. Indeed, it was throwing missiles and plasma and lasers in every direction. As the Posleen dropped towards Earth they seemed to target everything for destruction. Whether it was wanton violence or calculated experience, nothing escaped their ire. Satellites flickered and died, burning like moths in a flame as gouts of plasma or laser beams touched their fragile skeletons. The nascent International Space Station, a valiant project dropped in favor of more immediate plans and real deep-space work, was good for an antimatter missile. Inoffensive bits of space junk, sections of orbiters, detached skins or deceased satellites that had inhabited useless orbits doing nothing but being in the way since the 1960s were washed from space as the extraterrestrial juggernauts descended.

Light kinetic energy weapons dropped towards the planet below as probable threat locations were spotted or a God King simply wanted to make a pretty explosion. Dozens of the small, smart entry vehicles dropped through the atmosphere striking cities and military bases across Earth. Four of them for some reason struck the Great Pyramids in Cairo and another half dozen were targeted on deserted areas in the Central American jungle. The detonations—equivalent to a ten-kiloton nuclear weapon—were tiny, white pinpricks on the surface of the planet.

After what seemed like days, but was in fact hours, Takao had expended all his lances and was reduced to peppering the globe with his dual terawatt lasers. The globe began to break up, exposing to fire more of the vulnerable landers and the more important command dodecahedrons as it neared the atmosphere.

But despite its increasing vulnerability, Takao had to break off. Space Falcons were exactly that: *Space* falcons. Only vaguely aerodynamic and without a heat shield, they would burn up entering the atmosphere at combat speeds.

Bitterly ashamed at his inability to stop the inevitable, the pilot turned back to Lunar Farbase, watching in his rear camera as the black ball broke apart into a swarm of death descending towards the Pacific and his beloved home islands.

◆ CHAPTER 30 ◆

The Pentagon, VA, United States of America, Sol III
1749 EDT October 9th, 2004 AD

"This is Bob Argent at the Pentagon." The familiar reporter was grim faced. He stood in a nondescript, brightly lit hallway in the background of which figures in green, blue and black uniforms could be seen hurrying in every direction. "While it would be inaccurate to say that the United States military was caught flat-footed by the upcoming Posleen landing, it is true that the Posleen are both earlier and in greater force than anticipated. As the situation progresses, we will be bringing you live feeds from Continental Army Command here in the Pentagon, where their state-of-the-art GalTech landing projector is hard at work determining probable landing areas. The word is that the final landing area will probably be determined only half an hour before the actual landing and we will be standing by live. The Continental Army Commander is expected to have a short press conference within the next hour. He will discuss defense plans and known American and other casualties from the bombardment. This is Bob Argent, live, at the Pentagon."

When the word came over the radio, Shari Reilly took off her apron, handed it to the manager and walked out of the Waffle House without looking back. If he didn't like it he could mail her the check. Most of the customers were walking out and not many were paying. She had wanted to be prepared for this, but when the daycare and the bills and the rent and the groceries were paid for, there was not much left to set by. She had thirty dollars stashed in her purse and she fully intended to write checks that were not good if she had to but first she had to get the babies.

Wherever the Posties landed, it was going to be chaos and she had to hang on to her cash as long as possible. But if she was going to have to get out of town, she needed some stuff. The baby—Susie was hardly a baby anymore, really a big girl at two, almost as big as Kelly, but she still needed diapers—and little Billy was sick and she needed some medicine. They needed some road food, stuff that would keep, and batteries. Some bottled water. After she picked up the kids she would just have to go to Wal-Mart or Target, just like everybody else in Fredericksburg.

She walked to her battered gray 1991 Grand Am, a faded beauty in faded clothes, her fine hair wisping out from under the hairnet, got in and pumped the gas. After several false starts the engine finally caught. Turning out onto VA 3 she debated going to the stores and then getting the babies, but she felt a strong need to have them by her now, when it all came to the wall.

The sitter was frantic, wanting to keep the little ones while Shari shopped, but she finally got the babies away and headed back to the malls. By the time she got out onto 3, the traffic from the malls was backed up to U.S. 1.

She turned around, got around the line of cars and pickup trucks pulling into the Guard Armory and found a gas station. When she got to a pump she filled it up with regular then walked into the 7-Eleven. As she got to the front of the line, she pulled out her checkbook and screwed up her courage. She had used this same store and dealt with Mr. Ramani for over three years and she knew the answer was no.

"Take a check?" she asked, holding up the checkbook.

Mr. Ramani looked at her with the most neutral expression she had ever seen on his coal black face, then nodded. "You postdate it."

"What?"

"Postdate it. And call me to tell me if I can deposit it." He pulled out his card and pressed it into her hand.

She began to tear up then shook herself inside and wrote the check so fast her hand practically cramped.

"You take care, okay?" asked the Hindu as he took the proffered check.

"Okay," she answered, then blurted, "you too. God bless you."

"Thank you, and may your God bless you and your children," he said and gestured at the man behind her. "You pay cash or charge!"

"Why?" asked the startled customer, putting away the checkbook.

"You *got* money. Pay up."

Shari stepped outside trying not to cry and got back in traffic.

Lieutenant Colonel Frank Robertson, battalion commander of the Two Hundred Twenty-Ninth Engineering Battalion (Light, "Sappers Lead!") United States Ground Forces, stood at the head of the battalion conference table at parade rest. His first order on arriving at the Fredericksburg headquarters that afternoon was to have the chairs removed, since "nobody was going to have time to sit down anyway."

"All right, gentlemen," he said to his assembled staff and company commanders, "we've gamed this plenty of times. They're here in more force than we expected and earlier than we expected, but that doesn't really affect us much. We have our full equipment and ammunition load-out, including all necessary demolition charges in the new ammo dump, and by the time we have a probable landing zone the majority of our personnel should have made it in." That would not include the Alpha Company (Equipment) commander or his assistant division engineer. Both of them were out of town on business and would certainly not be back before the landing.

"There are effectively two possibilities. We will be in the landing zone or we will not be in the landing zone. If we are not in the landing zone we respond as ordered to act against Posleen spread and localize them until sufficient forces are available to destroy the infestation. On that highly probable basis I want all of the companies fully loaded and ready to roll on first orders to do so. You have the demolition plans for every bridge in Virginia and your primary, secondary and tertiary targets.

"On orders, if there is a landing in our area of responsibility, which is central Virginia, we will begin rigging all the bridges leading out of the infested zone for demolition. You will *not*, I say again, *not*, destroy any bridge without express order unless the Posleen are in near contact, that means one thousand meters or less."

He paused for a moment, obviously trying to find a good way to say something. "I think that if you haven't talked about this you probably have thought it. It may be, probably will be, that some of those bridges will have . . . refugees on them when the Posleen come into close contact.

"You have all seen the news and official reports from Barwhon and Diess; you know what it is like for refugees with the Posleen. You may be tempted to let the refugees over the bridges and blow the bridge up with Posleen on it. Gentlemen, I will have court-martialed anyone who does that. You have no flexibility in this. You *will* blow the bridge when the Posleen reach five hundred meters distance. We cannot take the risk of the Posleen capturing a bridge.

Is that clear?" There was a muted rumble of ascent from a ring of serious faces. "Very well, are there any questions?"

Only one hand was raised, that of the acting assistant division engineer. A terribly young, recent graduate of the University of Virginia. He was just out of the state-sponsored OCS that was providing most of the new crop of Virginia's officers.

"Yes, Lieutenant Young?"

"And if we are in the interdiction circle, sir?"

The commander paused and looked around the circle of serious older faces. Most of them had known each other off and on for years and he wondered how much longer he would be looking at the same group. "Well, Lieutenant, in that case we die and all of those we love die with us. And all we can do is take as many Posleen with us to hell as we can."

Mueller had driven the quiet engineer around town since just after sunrise. They had done the Fan and the university district in the morning and south Richmond—with its unique intermingled odor of petrochemical plants, paper manufacture and tobacco processing— in the early afternoon. Now, as the afternoon wore on, Mueller had negotiated the tour into Schockoe Bottom. After a brief tour around the Bottom, he intended to head up to Libby Hill and the best view of Richmond around.

Instead the engineer gave his first command of the entire tour, ordering him to turn down Twelfth Street then following it around onto Byrd. After a dizzying series of turns and three stops to consult the U.S. Geological Survey map they had brought, they were stopped under the Schockoe Slip underpass, a stone arch bridge that once connected the city proper to the Kanawaha Canal. Now it connected two trendy office complexes built into and around the nineteenth-century buildings.

"You're thinking of something," stated Mueller, as the engineer again consulted the map, switching between the quadrangle and a larger street map. More detailed maps supplied by the city engineering department littered the backseat of the government sedan.

"Umm," Keene replied, noncommittally. He got out and walked up the gray stone stairs from Canal Street to Schockoe Slip. He stopped at the top and looked down from the overpass into Schockoe Bottom. Mueller looked at the same scene and could see some good positions for a small-unit firefight, but not anything to interest a nationally renowned defense engineer.

None of the major city engineers or officials had been officially available to "sight-see." The strategic plan for Richmond's defense was still up in the air, one of the reasons that Continental Army Command had sent John Keene. Keene's suggestions and use of terrain in the construction of the Tennessee River defenses had brought him to the attention of the chief engineer for Third Army. When Richmond's planning had begun to lag, the chief engineer had offered Keene's services to First Army as a useful addition.

However, despite the enthusiastic reception by the Twelfth Corps Commander, who was tasked with the defense of Richmond and southern Virginia, Keene was less enthusiastically received by the other engineers. Each of them had their own pet projects to advance and the internecine fighting was the fundamental reason that the defenses were lagging.

The Corps Engineer, Colonel Bob Braggly, commander of the Corps Engineering Brigade, preferred turning the Libby and Mosby Hills into a giant firebase and giving up the center of Richmond to the Posleen. The city engineer, given quasimilitary standing by the new "Fortress Forward" stance, absolutely refused to surrender one inch of ground, preferring the concept of a wall enclosing the entire city limits.

Various local engineering firms had been called in to break the deadlock. Instead they offered their own versions or negated each other's effects by weighing in on one side or the other. Either project was going to be the biggest engineering contract in a hundred years of Richmond's history, ten or twenty times as large as the Floodwall project.

The corps commander had flatly stated that there was no way to defend a wall that extensive with the troops at hand. But one of his subordinates, the Twenty-Ninth Infantry Division commander, had bypassed the corps commander in the chain of command and sent staff studies supporting the elongated wall to First Army. John Keene, as a disinterested third party recommended through national command, was a possible way to break the deadlock.

Keene looked at the map again and walked under the Martin Agency building into the circle at one hundred Schockoe Slip. Mueller had never been this way and had gotten slightly turned around but it only took a moment for him to reorient himself when he saw the Richbrau microbrewery. It had been a long day and he was trying to figure out a way to subtly suggest that maybe it was Miller time, when Keene finally responded, "I'm thinking of Diess."

"So am I," remarked Mueller, following his own thought process, "it sure is warm for October." In fact the weather had been unseasonably cool, but he was about to continue in the vein that a cold Ole Nick would go down a treat when he realized that Keene had gone almost catatonic in thought. He waited for him to go on. "Is this when I'm supposed to prompt you," he finally prompted, "or when I'm supposed to shut up and wait?"

Keene looked at the fountain in the middle of the circle without replying and muttered, "Captain Morgan, I am really sorry for what we are going to do to you." Then turning back to Mueller he thumbed across the street. "Time for a cold one, Sergeant."

Once they were seated in the dimness of the microbrewery, having dodged the various street people between themselves and their goal, Keene became abruptly animated.

"Okay," he said taking a sip of the tasty malt and stabbing the map, "how do you kill Posleen?"

"Well, apparently they've ruled out poison gas," Mueller joked, "so I guess that leaves artillery."

"Right, and what is the problem with killing them with artillery?"

"I don't know." Mueller waited for Keene to go on but realized that the engineer was really testing him. "Forward observers I suppose. Seeing them while staying alive yourself," he finally answered testily. He'd had more than enough personal experience with how hard they were to kill.

"In part. And that if you don't contain them, physically, they both do more damage and have the option to figure out how to get to your forces. The best thing is to keep them at arms' reach. Failing that, to have them contained where you have superior terrain advantage, man-made or natural. With me so far?"

"Yep."

"Okee-dokee. On Diess, once the humans got their shit together, they formed the boulevards into tremendous killing grounds. In Tennessee we were doing the same thing with walls and even some tunnels. Lead them by the nose, then corral them and pound them with machine guns, manjacks and artillery."

"Never work here," countered Mueller. He was familiar with the Diess operation where the Third Corps commander had built walls along the boulevards and slaughtered the Posleen. The differences in cities were marked. "The skyscrapers are too flimsy, the distances are shorter and the city engineer would have a cow. Then the governor, who is a buddy of the city engineer and the Twenty-Ninth ID commander and, for that matter, the President, would have a cow."

"Sure," agreed Keene, easily. "But would they give up Schockoe Bottom?"

Mueller thought about that one. "Possibly," he finally answered. "I would have to say probably." The area was half deserted, with only a few businesses and the bars that supplied the local forces with beverages surviving the economic blight.

"On every other planet the Posleen have invaded for the past hundred and fifty years, all the wealth, the production wealth, is in the megascrapers," Keene pointed out. "The Galactics have their factories built right into them. So, the Posleen are expected to go for our skyscrapers; if it's low, it's less of a target to them.

"So when they land near Richmond, from any direction, they're going to head for the city center. Now, Richmond should have been evacuated by then. The city engineer can bitch all he wants, but CONARC has designated the inner cities as the defense zones, screw the suburbs.

"So, using techniques as yet undetermined, we will lure the Posleen forward from every direction, but all the roads will lead to Schockoe Bottom and none of them will lead out. The tough part, the heavy engineering part, will be making sure that, one, they can only get to Schockoe Bottom and, two, they can't get back out."

"Posleen check in . . ." said Mueller with a growing smile.

" . . . but they don't check out. You got it. I want to go look at those heights across the way . . ."

"That's Libby Hill. It was next on the agenda."

"But first I want to get a better look at the Bottom. It would be good if we could set up some sort of direct-fire positions into the pocket. I was thinking of firing from across the river, but maybe we could build a berm."

"What's wrong with the Wall?" asked Mueller, puzzled. "Besides wracking stress. Can't we just backfill?"

"What wall?" asked the puzzled engineer.

John Keene looked up at the thirty feet of reinforced concrete that made up the mile-long Richmond floodwall and grinned like a teenager. "Oh, man," he said, gesturing at the Army Corps of Engineers heraldic device, a two-turreted castle, on the face, "are the Posties ever going to learn to hate that symbol."

For the next two hours he and Mueller walked around the floodwall, Schockoe Bottom and the surrounding area, occasionally driving when something in the distance caught their fancy. Finally they stood in Mosby Park, on Mosby Hill, where a group of children from a nearby preschool played under the careful tutelage of elderly teachers. As Keene looked down his mind was filled with visions of fire.

"We can just pack the back side of this hill with those stubby tube artillery things . . ."

"Do you mean mortars?" asked Mueller, chuckling.

"Yeah, them. Do you know they have more killing power than much larger artillery?" Keene continued animatedly.

"Um, yeah. I knew that."

"It's because they don't need as heavy a casing."

"I know, sir."

"Right. Anyway. We block off exit from the pocket on this side by rubbling those abandoned factories down there and piling the rubble from the wall to this hill."

"Got it," said Mueller, sketching a diagram on his AID.

"On the other side, it's not as good but we have plenty of time and concrete. We'll build a wall connector from the Ethyl Corporation Hill to the wall. Then continue around the terrain of the city, basically down Canal to Twelfth then over to Thirteenth then along the streets to 95."

"Good," Mueller commented.

"Why good?"

"That leaves the Richbrau in the perimeter."

"Yeah," laughed Keene, "I hadn't thought of that."

"Well, we just would have had to change the perimeter."

"Right," laughed Keene again. Then he looked puzzled. "Hey, why are we in the Crowne Plaza instead of the Berkley Hotel? It's right next door to the Richbrau."

"Hardy Boys."

"What?"

"Cyberpunks. They got there first. One of the laws of SpecOps: never mix Cybers and SF, it just doesn't work."

"What the hell are Cyberpunks doing in Richmond?"

" . . . and never ask Cybers what they're doing anywhere."

"Oh." Keene shook his head and returned to the business at hand. "The perimeter will be as follows: 95 to the Franklin exit. Block all entrances into the city. Use all the buildings for direct fire into the pocket. Continue up Thirteenth then cut across to Twelfth at Cary down to Byrd. The old power station is outside, the Federal Reserve and Riverfront Plaza are inside. Maintain the defenses up to around Belvedere Street where it gets carried down to the river and necked off with the only real wall we're going to have to build.

"Whatever direction the Posleen come from, all roads leading to Schockoe Bottom are open and all roads leading elsewhere are closed. Pack the back side of the wall with troops, pack the skyscrapers with troops, all of them firing into the pocket. Artillery and mortars on the heights. If they're only on the north side, we can pack artillery on the south side of the James River and pound them all day long.

"God," John paused for a moment, eyes practically glowing, "it's going to be glorious."

"Just remember," Mueller cautioned, "no plan survives contact with the enemy."

"What?" asked Keene, confused.

"They never told you that in Tennessee?"

"No. Why is that?"

"It's sort of a military axiom," explained Mueller, watching the afternoon traffic build early. "The other side wants to win too, so they try to figure out how to defeat your plan. Although that's less of a problem with Posleen than with humans. And then there are all the little things you didn't think of. There are changes in orders that don't take into account the real situation. There are bad communications that lead to actions like Pickett's Charge. Lee said 'Don't charge' and the message was received 'Charge.' There's the 'fog of war,' making decisions on the basis of what you think is reality when in fact it is not.

"Anyway, you construct your plan and really internalize it, but you also construct alternative plans in case that one goes awry. If your primary plan is internalized, but not really expected to succeed perfectly, you can devise changes on the fly. And then you construct your GOTH Plan."

"A Goth Plan?" asked Keene again, shaking his head at the pessimistic outlook of soldiers. "What? As in getting overrun by Goths?"

"Not 'Goth' as in 'Hun,' 'GOTH' as in G-O-T-H. Your Go-To-Hell plan. Your plan when all your other plans have gone to hell and the wolf is at the door. Your, 'They died with their boots on' plan."

"Oh."

"So what's the GOTH plan?"

"I don't know," answered Keene, musing on the landscape below. "I don't plan for failure very well."

"Then somebody fucked up saying you're a defense expert. 'Expect success, plan for failure' is right up there with 'on dangerous ground maneuver, on deadly ground fight' as a military axiom."

"The only military axioms I was aware of before the Planetary Defense Center program were 'never volunteer for anything' and 'never get involved in a land war in Asia.' "

"Well, now you know," Mueller fiddled his fingers and wrinkled his brow with a grin, "um, three more."

Keene chuckled as Mueller's AID chirped.

"Sergeant Mueller."

"Yes, AID?" Mueller said with a smile.

"Five Posleen globes have just exited hyperspace in near-Earth orbit. TERDEF analysis calls for landings in approximately three hours." The voice was so toneless that the facts took a moment to sink in.

"*What?*" Mueller's eyes momentarily went round and his skin flushed with a cold sweat. He involuntarily looked up, then shook himself thinking the action was futile. Even as he mentally started to berate himself there was a sudden flash of light in the cloudless sky. The detonation of an antimatter reactor was clear even in bright sunlight.

"Five Posleen globes have just exited hyperspace in near-Earth orbit. TERDEF analysis calls for landings in approximately three hours."

Mueller looked at Keene who had continued to look out over the cityscape.

Uh, oh. "AID."

"Yes, Sergeant Mueller?"

"Contact Sergeant Major Mosovich. Tell him to get the corps commander to stall on the defense plan. I think we have a winner."

"Well," said Keene turning back to the sergeant. "I see what you mean about plans now. I suppose I'd better get started on that GOTH plan."

◆ CHAPTER 31 ◆

The Pentagon, VA, United States of America, Sol III
1820 EDT October 9ᵗʰ, 2004 AD

"Have you been getting everything you needed?" asked General Horner as he strode into the conference room. It had been billed as a press conference but, in a rare burst of sanity, the news media agreed to simply have one representative of each major media "type" in the Continental Army Center.

Until the Blue Mountain Planetary Defense Center was completed, the nerve center for the defense of the United States was in the Pentagon. The indefensible building gave Jack Horner the uncomfortable feeling of swinging in the breeze. Being on the front line did not bother him—he had been there and done that—but it was no place to command a continental-scale battle.

His AID would help, but even with it he needed an undistracted staff and that was not going to happen if the Posleen were breathing down their necks. And the latest information made that look pretty likely.

"Well, sir, we really haven't been given *any* access since the first warning," answered Argent, as the unofficial spokesperson. Although the other representatives were all "Pentagon Hands" none of them had Argent's depth of experience or name recognition. His cameraman, another old Pentagon hand, subtly directed his camera towards the general. Although the press conference had not officially been "started" all was fair in a fluid situation like this.

"So I understand," said Horner with a bleak smile of anger. It was not how he had told the Pentagon Public Information Office to handle information flow. As he had just explained to the chief of information's replacement.

"To change that, I'm going to assign you Lieutenant Colonel Tremont, my senior aide." He gestured to the slim, dark lieutenant colonel accompanying him. "He can cut through any red tape you may encounter. We so far have no indication that the Posleen use battlefield intelligence. I've already cut half of the red tape out and decided you can report on just about anything you generate while you're in here. I'm giving you one hundred percent access to my areas of responsibility. You basically have Top Secret clearance and assumed Need-To-Know on anything related to this invasion. If anyone has any questions about that they can direct them to me *after* they have answered your questions."

Argent looked momentarily stunned. "Thank you, sir. Are you sure about that?"

"This was the original plan, believe it or not. I have to communicate effectively not only to my troops, but to the citizens of the United States. It is my job, my duty, to protect them and keep them informed of dangers to the best of my ability. The best way to do that is through you," he gestured at the TV crew, "and your radio friends." He gestured at the representatives from ABC Radio.

"Pardon me," he continued, turning to the print journalists and photographers, "but you guys come last." That got a laugh.

"So, shall we start?" asked Bob.

"What, we haven't already?" Jack said with another cold smile.

"Well . . ." Argent temporized. He hadn't dealt much with the Continental Army commander but he recognized the smile as a bad sign.

"Hasn't your cameraman been filming the whole thing?" asked Horner, shortly. "And unless I'm an idiot, everybody is taking notes."

"Okay," admitted Argent. "In that case: General Horner, it has been an hour since the Posleen came out of hyperspace. What's happening?" The cameraman lifted the minicam to his shoulder to get a steadier shot.

"There've been some space battles between the fighter patrols and the converted frigates that were on station, but this incursion has been outside all the expected parameters," responded Horner formally. "The Posleen are here in greater strength than we anticipated, they are more bunched than we were expecting not only on the basis of Galactic reports but on the basis of our own experience on Barwhon and Diess. Last but not least, they came out unusually close to the Earth; dangerously close in fact.

"Because of all of this the Fleet has been unable to engage them with any sort of strength. They are coming down more or less untouched, while we have lost quite a few of the fighters and frigates that engaged them. I have to say this, those Fleet people did a hell of a job given the disparity of the forces they faced. Their efforts were just outstanding."

"Can we get a look at some video?" asked one of the radio personalities.

"We'll get some of that in from the Operations center in a moment. Having said the other, about total access, I want you to understand that we have a job to do and we need to do it to the best of our ability. Understand?"

"Yes," replied the reporters, wondering when the hammer was going to fall.

"I don't have time to draw any of my people off their duties; so we're going to go into the CIC to meet the players. They are all very busy trying to save our country, so be polite. This is a very quiet, serene place where people concentrate very hard: no disruptions. Think of it like a war library. No shouts for a quote, no flash photography, no camera lights." He fixed them with a blue, basilisk stare until all of them had nodded in compliance. "If any of you do any of those things in CIC, I'll have you thrown out of this building by a suit of combat armor. He will have orders to shot-put you into the Potomac." The river was nearly a mile away. The reporters were fairly sure it was hyperbole, but looking at the grim-faced, cold-eyed general, they were not absolutely sure.

"After the CIC, I'll hook you up with a couple of our technical people who will try to integrate our systems with yours. I want you guys to know where the landings are going to be as fast as I do. But no disruptions. The American people cannot afford them. Your *families* cannot afford them. Clear?"

"Clear," answered the sobered journalists. Never had a situation like this occurred, where the people they were interviewing were in charge of saving not only their lives, but the lives of their families and loved ones. In real time. Usually, rattling a subject or throwing an unanswerable question at them was the best way to get a really juicy quote. Those techniques suddenly seemed like a bad idea. Rattled would be bad. Argent looked around and saw the other reporters coming to the same sobering conclusion.

Horner and his aide led them down a short corridor and over to an MP-guarded door. On the far side was a small antechamber and beyond a large, darkened room filled with a mixture of Terran and Galactic technology. On the far side of the room was a giant Mercator projection showing a number of orbit lines in green, blue and red and five large ovals designating possible landing areas. The outside of the ovals, where they were discrete, was yellow and they shaded inward through orange to red. One was centered on the Atlantic, another on the Pacific, a third on Southeast Asia to India, one on Central Asia and one on Africa. The TV cameramen started filming, not sure if the screens would show well enough to broadcast. The quiet atmosphere reminded him of a surgery, everyone concentrating on their individual tasks for an overall good.

The possible areas for Posleen landings were still vast; the Atlantic oval spread from Chicago to Berlin. The Africa oval overlapped the Southeast Asia oval. The very edge of the Pacific oval overlapped the Southeast Asia oval near the Philippines. In all they nearly circumnavigated the northern hemisphere.

"Full house spread," whispered a reporter from the *Atlanta Journal Constitution*.

"This screen used to be covered with satellite tracks," pointed out Lieutenant Colonel Tremont in a whisper. "The remaining military satellites and facilities are the green tracks, while the blue tracks are remaining commercial facilities."

"Yeah," whispered the CNN producer in return. "We're mainly going out on dedicated landlines to cable operators and on the Internet. Cell, pagers and phones are mostly down."

"This screen is, obviously, not used for tactical operations," Colonel Tremont explained. "But it is useful for getting an overall picture."

"Colonel," Argent asked quietly, putting on his reporter face, "is the loss of the satellites going to degrade the quality of your artillery fire and command and control? I understand that most development in those areas has concentrated on global positioning satellites."

"It would, yes, except for the extraordinary work over the last three years of the United States Geological Survey Service. Using a mixture of military, civilian and volunteer personnel, they have put in survey markers across the country, in most areas no more than a kilometer apart. In turn, the location and elevation of the markers have been put into a universal target database. Now, whenever an artillery unit gets into place, they just find the distance and elevation to the nearest UTD point and input that data. That gives them their location to the millimeter. Other units use a similar although slightly less accurate system. So, yes, it will be a pain, but with the UTD we have effectively replaced GPS."

"What about targeting the enemy? Didn't that depend on the GPS as well?"

"Same thing, only backwards. The forward observer determines his distance and elevation to the nearest UTD and his distance and elevation to the target and sends the raw data to the targeting computers. It all can be done with a special laser range-finding system. The targeting computer crunches the numbers and assigns the fire to the appropriate guns. It's incredibly automatic."

"Will it work?" asked the *Journal Constitution* reporter.

"Ah, well that is the question isn't it?"

"You said something about connecting our equipment up, General," interjected the producer.

"Of course, let me introduce Major George Nix." General Horner gestured for one of the hovering officers and the slight, bespectacled major hurried over from one of the displays.

"Major Nix came out of Space Command and is our tactical systems officer. The TacSO is the officer in charge of making sure all the systems integrate and are maintained, as opposed to the tactical actions officer, Colonel Ford. Colonel Ford—we call him the TacCO— is in charge of making the moment-to-moment tactical decisions.

"Major Nix, can you get these journalists a feeder screen and somehow hook their cameras up? I want to make sure that everyone in the United States has up-to-the-minute access to all the data we are generating."

"Yes, sir, we anticipated this." He turned to one of the video technicians. "Come with me."

Nix led the tech out of the room, the reporters following and quietly making notes about the intense atmosphere in the room. He led them down the corridor and into a well-lit chamber where two specialists and a slightly overweight staff sergeant were arguing at a display.

"Sergeant Folsom, 'One If By Land.' And do it fast."

"Yes, sir." The two specialists hurried out of the room as the sergeant went around configuring displays. As he worked he talked. "Gentlemen, we had anticipated this, so you will get more functionality than you would expect, but less than you are used to. I'm setting up two displays for the print and radio guys, and we'll feed you to your headquarters, ABC, over RealAudio, so you can do your radio thing over the Net. The Net is busy right now, but the usage is not as high as a normal business day so you should have good connectivity.

"The consoles use a simple graphic user interface. Right-click on an area of the map and it will zoom down to a fineness of about six hundred miles on a side. It's not a political map. It's drawn from satellite imagery, so somebody had better be up on their geography."

"Sergeant," asked the CNN producer, appropriating one of the consoles, "is there any way to run a second audio feed back to CNN?"

"Sure, if somebody there has Interphone or NetMeeting."

"Where?"

The sergeant walked over and tapped at the next console. "What's their URL?"

Within minutes the sergeants and the specialists, returned from rerouting Internet T-3 lines to increase the room's available bandwidth, had configured all of the backup CIC consoles to support the media effort. The reporters were practically speechless.

"Sergeant," said the CNN producer, as she finished preparing the headquarters' team for the next round of reports, "when this is all over, if you ever need a job, come see me."

"I'll think about it, when this is all over." The question of when it would be over and whether any of them would be around to see it was unspoken.

"Well, now all we do is wait," said Argent, watching the ovals of probable landing areas reduce on his monitor.

"What about reporting on the personnel being called back to duty?" asked the video technician, watching the feed on his own monitor to ensure the "take" was working.

"That's being reported on in Atlanta."

"Poor bastards."

"Bye, honey," said Mike, shrugging into his silks top.

"Bye, Daddy," said Cally, looking up at him with round eyes.

"You listen to Grandpa, all right? And be a good girl."

"I will, Daddy. When the Posleen come we get a few, then run and hide. Stop, drop and roll, right?"

Unless they're right on top of you.

"And then I'll come dig you out," he promised.

"Right," she said, face twisting as she tried not to cry.

"Take care, son," said his father, proffering a Mason jar for the road.

"Too right, the last time in the body and fender shop was enough. Getting shot smarts."

"Long drive."

"Too long. They'll be down before I'm in South Carolina." He looked at the Mason jar, shrugged and took a hit. The fiery liquor felt good going down. He sealed it and tossed it in his bag.

"How you going?"

"Want to know if I'm going to be in a landing path?"

"Something like that. The Twenty-Fourth Tennessee Volunteers are right up the road as the Tennessee Divide reserve and the whole

Fifty-Third Infantry is holding Rabun Gap. So we're probably going to be fine. You, on the other hand, are driving up to Pennsylvania. So, are you taking the plains or the mountains?"

"I'm still trying to decide. The plains would be faster, even with the interstates doglegging away from the Gap. But, that is a possible landing area according to Shelly, so . . ."

"So. Which way?"

"Mountains," Mike decided. "Up Interstate 81. Better to be caught in traffic jams than in a landing."

"Want a piece?" A Glock 9mm appeared by legerdemain in the old man's hand.

"No, I'm packed. Speaking of which." He reached into his bag and pulled out a finely carved wooden box. The wood was an odd shade of lavender-brown Mike Senior had never seen before. Mike Junior handed it to Cally. "I was going to leave this with your Grandpa as a birthday present, but I think now would be a good time to give it to you."

She was puzzled by the latch, a circular pattern similar in appearance to a maze, with no obvious buttons. Pulling on the sections caused them to lift, and they could be twisted on their axes but none of the actions seemed to open the box.

"It's an Indowy puzzle box, which I don't, unfortunately, have time to let you work through. Watch." He lifted three sections and twisted them until the sections joined together to form a pattern reminiscent of a multiheaded dragon. When slid back into place, the latch released and the top opened as the serpent seemed to writhe off the box and into a circuitous dance. The fire-breathing hologram danced above the open box as Cally gasped at the contents.

"I'm still getting presents from Indowy clans over Diess. Most of them I pass on to the survivors or their families, but this I couldn't resist." In the box, cradled in a lustrous silken foam were a gilded pistol and two magazines.

"I've got a case of ammunition for this out in the truck. The powers-that-be still frown on grav-guns in civilian hands but this is a pulser gun. It fires pulse darts. Each of the darts has an electrical charge in it powerful enough to kill an elephant, much less a Posleen. There are twenty-four darts in a clip. It's accurate to about a hundred yards with a good hand." He pulled a clip out of his cargo pocket. "This is a clip of practice ammunition and you can reuse an expended dart as practice ammo. But to fire it in practice, you have to charge the onboard capacitor." He turned to Mike Senior. "It charges on 220."

"No sweat."

"Thanks, Daddy," said Cally, picking it up and feeling the heft. "It's small."

"It's designed for Indowy, not that they would ever use it. It's made out of lightweight boron polymers. The charge on a dart is adjustable, so it can be nonlethal. And it'll take down a Posleen, unlike your Walther." The small-frame pistol was notorious for jamming, but it was one of the few in the world that both fit her hand and had a decent-sized round. Since the Posleen were not going to be stopped by an itsy-bitsy little .380 low-velocity, Papa O'Neal had tapped and filled its bullets with mercury. The Posleen that caught one might not be killed but it was going to know it had been kissed.

"Umm," she asked, carefully turning it so as not to point at either adult, "how do you clear it and where is the damn safety?"

Mike laughed and pulled out a computer disk. "Here's the manual, read it on your laptop. For the time being you have to trust me that it is empty."

"Thanks, Daddy." She grinned, putting the pistol back in the case. "You're swell."

"Get some practice with it right away. I know you're good with that James Bond gun, but this has more stopping power and is better suited for your hands. I'd prefer you get familiar with it in case you have to use it."

"Okay."

He tousled her hair, thinking that she looked a lot like her mother must have at the same age. "You stay safe, okay, pumpkin?"

"Okay." She was tearing up again, the excitement of the gift giving way to the fear of the moment.

"And you listen to your Grandpa."

"You already said that."

"I'm sorry we didn't get up to the base so you could see my unit."

"It's okay, we can after you kick their asses back into space."

Mike Junior looked significantly at Mike Senior, who shrugged his shoulders, unrepentant. "What do you want, a little lady or a little warrior?"

Mike picked her up and hugged her gently. "G'bye, pumpkin."

"Bye, Daddy." She bucked a little in his arms, holding back the sobs.

He set her down, grabbed his bag and headed out the door.

They followed him downstairs and out the front door where he removed the case of pulser darts from the front of the Tahoe, handed it to his dad and threw in his bag. He took his daughter in his arms one last time.

"And if they land here, what do you do?"

"Shoot, scoot and hide."

"Okay."

"Don't worry about us, Daddy, you're going to be on the sharp end."

"Are you worried about me, pumpkin?" asked Mike, honestly surprised.

"Uh-huh." She started to cry.

"Oh, pumpkin," he smiled, putting on his mission face, "don't worry about me." He slipped on his Milspecs, wrapped Shelly around his head as a hands-free communicator and smiled ferally. "I've finally got the Posleen right where I want them. They don't know it, but they're about to get the whole can of kick-ass." He looked out at the fields he had grown up in and thought for a moment about what he had said. The company was trained and ready. He was trained and ready. They *could* do this. The company believed it. The battalion commander and staff believed it. Regiment was as sure as if it were a steel-hard certainty.

Now if he could only convince himself.

Mueller, meantime, was getting on a different kind of mission face, as were Mosovich, Ersin and Keene. Keene's proposed plan for the defense of Richmond was not meeting with the approval of the mayor or the city engineer.

"We thought you were going to come up with a compromise plan, Mr. Keene, not a new plan to destroy the city," snarled the mayor, banging the conference table.

"It is not intended to destroy the city, Mr. Mayor, only a small portion of it."

"And it does not provide for the defense of the outskirts whatsoever," noted the city engineer, poring over the detailed plan that Mueller's AID had printed out on their arrival.

"Fortress Forward does not intend the defense of the majority of the city," interjected the corps engineer, "as we have pointed out time and again."

The corps commander motioned him subtly to back off, more than familiar with the old argument between the two. "This firesack of Schockoe Bottom actually looks like precisely what the Fortress Forward program is all about, but it only makes provisions for one outer fort," he continued, "instead of the suggested multiple."

"Yes, but it makes best use of the available terrain," noted Keene. "This is really the only area where you have two useable terrain features to emplace on and catch the Posleen in a crossfire. And the outer fortress can provide fire support if the forces are forced to retreat towards Newport News."

"What about the rest of the city? What about south Richmond? Our primary industrial area?"

Colonel Braggly was again waved down by the corps commander as Keene answered. "It is indefensible. Period. With the exception of a few gently rolling knolls, the James is the only noticeable terrain feature.

"There are four scenarios to work with here, gentlemen," Keene said in an iron voice, "and we have to be very clear about what they are. Sergeant First Class Mueller, what is the best-case scenario for Richmond?"

"The Posleen land beyond masking terrain features, effectively out of range to cause us harm."

"Right," agreed Keene. "In which case, a few days later a portion of the corps rolls out to wherever they are needed."

"What?" shouted the mayor. "Why the hell are you going to do that?" he snarled, turning to the corps commander.

"To support those in need, Mr. Mayor," replied the corps commander, calmly. "I would hope that other corps would do the same for us. No, I know they would; it would be the right military decision and so ordered. Of course, if the Posleen land well away from here, other units would react. We're not going anywhere if they land in California."

"Yes, sir, but I was thinking if they landed south of the Broad River or north of the Potomac, for example," noted Keene. "Now, Master Sergeant Ersin, what is the worst-case scenario?"

"They land directly on us," he said to universal grimaces. His own scarred face remained stone-faced, eyes remote.

"And in that case," Keene said, with an almost unnoticeable twinkle in his eyes for the moment of levity, "we activate our GOTH Plan."

"Our what?" asked the city engineer.

"Our Go-To-Hell plan," answered Mosovich, face as stony as Ersin's.

"The plan you use when all your other plans have failed," noted the corps commander, nodding his head at the clued-in civilian engineer.

"Your 'On Deadly Ground Plan,' as it is sometimes called," interjected the otherwise silent corps chief of staff.

"Our 'we are fucked' plan," Keene clarified, "will be to destroy the city, Mr. Mayor, because there will be no survivors anyway and we might as well leave the Posleen a smoking ruin. Mine every building, blow up every block as they come to it. Leave not one edible scrap of food including humans, destroy the bodies as we go. Kill as many Posleen as we can, but most of all, make it very plain that fighting humans is a losing proposition: All you get is sorry, hungry and sore." He looked around the room and for once saw consensus.

"You might make that Virginians," corrected the city engineer with a slight, sad smile.

"As you will. Ah, sir, am from the Great State of Juwjah, Ah will have you know." It was good for a little laugh. "But that is the absolute worst-case scenario. There are two more, anyone care to take a stab?"

"They land either north or south of the James, but not right on us," said the corps commander, "we've gotten that far."

"Right. Now, if they have landed south of the James, my professional recommendation is to pull back across the James and wait for support. Maybe do some things with the bridges and the floodwall on that side, in the way of sucking them in, but basically the south side is open terrain and you'll just have to sit on this side and pound them with artillery. On the other hand, if they land on the north side we probably have the time to implement the fire-trap plan. If we get started right away."

"You already said it is pointless if they don't land between the Potomac and the James. It might not even work if they land north of Fredericksburg," argued the City Engineer. "In that case, I don't think we could get the support of the owners of those facilities for the demolition work."

"We don't need it," pointed out the corps engineer. "Necessary defensive works under the emergency war provisions. We have eminent domain."

"That could be tied up in court for days," bemoaned the mayor.

"They can apply for just reparations," said the corps commander, "but that is all."

"Yes," said Keene, "that has all been covered in the PDC program. The private owner just does not have a leg to stand on if the property falls under the heading of necessary defensive structures as defined by the area commander, which is General Keeton," he noted, gesturing at the Corps Commander at the head of the table. "He can order it with no debate now or in the future, if he, in his sole opinion, feels it militarily justified."

"On the other hand," noted General Keeton, with a frown, "we will absolutely require the help of the entire civilian populace. We cannot afford to antagonize the city and certainly not its leaders," he concluded, gesturing at the mayor and the engineer. "We will need your complete and undivided support."

"Do we really have to destroy Schockoe Bottom?" asked the mayor, plaintively. "It's an eyesore and a crime zone, but there's a lot of history there."

"Mr. Mayor," said Mueller gently, "whether today, or in the next year, a whole new book in the history of Richmond is about to be written. The only question is whether there will be anyone to write it."

The mayor looked at the city engineer, who shook his head in resignation. "I still say we could have circumvalleted the entire city."

"Maybe we could have," nodded Keene, "but we're out of time and it would have thrown away our best terrain features. There is no way, in Fortress Forward, to save the city as a functioning entity. Rather, the idea is to absolutely screw the Posleen while retaining the historic core."

The corps commander nodded. "Correct. Mr. Mayor? Mr. City Engineer? I need your active support in this. Are you with us?"

The mayor nodded his head. "Yes, yes." He looked at the engineer, who nodded his own head mutely. "Yes, we are."

"All right," said the corps commander turning to the corps engineer, "initiate Mr. Keene's plan, modifying as you see fit while staying within the overall plan."

"What do we call it?" asked the Chief of Staff.

"How 'bout Operation Abattoir?" joked Mueller.

"Actually," said the corps commander, who had planned more than one antiarmor defense against aggressor cavalry forces, "I prefer 'Operation Big Horn.' "

The military guys laughed while the civilians looked confused. "Why Big Horn?" asked the mayor.

"First you suck 'em in . . ." answered Mueller in explanation.

"Then you blow the shit out of 'em," finished Ersin with eyes as dead as a shark's.

"Gentlemen," said Sergeant Folsom, poking his head in the room, "you might want to start a feed; the computers are about to give final projections on Posleen landings."

For the past hour the newsmen had been giving almost continuous live reports but, except for the narrowing of the potential landing ovals, it had been much of the same. It amazed the CNN producer that anything could be so terrifying and boring at the same time.

Argent got up and stood in front of the American flag that had been procured from a nearby general's office, preparing to say his piece as the technician checked the live feed from the defensive computers again. All of the ovals were discrete, now, and the Atlantic oval, with the exception of an attenuated end that made it look like a comma, had shifted almost completely away from the European continent. It appeared the Europeans were going to sit this one out.

"In three, two, one . . ."

"We have just been informed that the defensive system computers are about to determine the final Posleen objectives. As we have been telling you, until the Posleen globes definitively commit to a reentry trajectory, the landing areas remain only possibilities. Now, however, there are signs that the Posleen are about to commit to definite targets.

"They have had one orbit of the world, under fire from the available Fleet Fighters, as has been reported from Palo Alto, and by now they must have picked their targets." At a call from the producer he hastily finished, "We now cut to the live feed from the defensive computers . . ."

And Colonel Robertson leaned towards the wardroom TV, taking a pull on his pipe . . .

And Little Tommy Sunday stopped packing his war bag and turned to the radio in his room . . .

And Lieutenant Young stopped compulsively reviewing demolition plans . . .

And General Keeton turned away from the mayor and towards the TV in his office . . .

And throughout the world, people stopped whatever they were doing, pulled over in their cars or set down their burdens and waited for the American Defense Command, or Russian Army Headquarters, or Japanese Defense Forces Headquarters or Chinese Red Army Headquarters, to place the seal on their fates, whether for good or ill.

"The ovals are shrinking rapidly now," continued Argent coolly. "So we are going to zoom in on the American landing. I'll keep you updated on the other zones and when the final points are determined we will zoom back out and note their particular areas.

"We can definitely say, at this time, that there is little or no chance of a landing in Australia, South America, Central America, Europe or Russia. There is very little chance of a landing in the Midwestern United States. It mainly looks like West Africa, India or Bangladesh, Coastal Northern China, the Eastern United States and somewhere around Uzbekistan or Turkmenistan.

"The ovals are shrinking. The American oval is centering on the eastern seaboard between Philadelphia and . . . somewhere in central South Carolina. Getting smaller . . ."

The oval abruptly collapsed and turned a complete malignant red. "The area is now centered on Washington, D.C. . . ." he continued with a note of strain building in his voice as cold adrenaline jetted into his stomach . . .

And shifted south . . .

"Richmond, Virginia . . ."

North and smaller . . .

"Washington . . ."

And finally centered between the two, straddling a river. It began to pulse an evil crimson, the vague outline of a city on the computer-generated map in the center like a pupil. Argent just paused for a moment, shocked by the evil icon blazing out from the console.

"The target," he paused for a moment to compose himself, "the target, ladies and gentlemen, is Fredericksburg, Virginia."

◆ CHAPTER 32 ◆

They send us in front with a fuse an' a mine,
To blow up the gates that are rushed by the Line,
   But bent by Her Majesty's Engineers,
   Her Majesty's Royal Engineers
   With the rank and the Pay of a Sapper!

Now the Line's but a man with a gun in his hand,
An' Cavalry's only what horses can stand,
   When helped by Her Majesty's Engineers,
   Her Majesty's Royal Engineers
   With the rank and the Pay of a Sapper!

Artillery moves by the leave o' the ground,
But we are the men that do something all round,
   For we are Her Majesty's Engineers,
   Her Majesty's Royal Engineers
   With the rank and the Pay of a Sapper!

—From "Sappers"
Rudyard Kipling, 1896

Fredericksburg, VA, United States of America, Sol III
1950 EDT October 9th, 2004 AD

"Dependents are on their way in, Colonel," said the supply officer, the S-4. The "Four" had taken over the job of Civil and Dependent Affairs; he was out of any other job. All the equipment and ammunition was issued and there wasn't going to be a resupply.

"For all the good it will do," noted the Charlie company commander. "They're due to land in fifteen or twenty minutes."

"None of that," said Colonel Robertson. "We do what we can do, and all that we can do. The telemetry looks like the Posleen are going to be spread hither and yon. The probable landing zone stretches from over the Potomac in Maryland to Spotsylvania County. They seem to be spreading out to surround Fredericksburg and the area immediately around the township will be clear. Captain Avery," he turned to the supply officer, "get the dependents who are under sixteen years of age headed into town with their available parent. That will give them a few more minutes. Who knows, the horse might still sing. Put the other ones to work."

"Doing what?" the S-4 asked.

"Setting up our Go-To-Hell Plan. Captain Brown," Robertson turned to the Charlie commander and began snapping out commands, rapier fast, "start entrenching around the city center, with outliers to the interstate but no farther."

"Yes, sir," said the company commander, noting the instructions down in his green leader's notebook.

"Four, have someone call the radio station and tell them to start broadcasting for anyone with heavy equipment to come to—"

"The Mary Washington College parking lot," interjected the executive officer. He and the operations officer had taken over the tactical map from the two privates who normally updated it and were sketching in a battle plan. The battalion staff and company commanders had been together for years, as was common with National Guard units. At this point they could practically read each other's minds.

"Good," said Robertson. He was new to the unit, but he had already recognized that it had a superior staff for a "part-time" unit. And they were coming together beautifully. If he could keep up the momentum and keep them from falling into depression they would teach these centaur bastards a thing or two. "And call for all noncombatants to head for the city center, coordinate with Public Safety on where. Bravo company . . ."

"Start mining the Chatham bridge . . ." said Captain Avery, the Bravo company commander, glancing at the map on the wall.

"And the railroad bridge and the Jeff Davis, but not the I-95 bridge; it's too far out," agreed the commander.

"I'll take some of the older dependents with me for gophers. If any of them have a clue I'm arming them."

"Approved, we're shorthanded." Many of the personnel had chosen to remain home rather than respond to the recall.

"Some of those AWOLs will be coming in now, if they can make it," Avery pointed out. "There's nowhere to run."

"And nowhere to hide," remarked Brown, the Charlie commander, darkly. "Jesus Christ," he whispered, his mind on his wife and two sons gathering with the other dependents on the armory drill floor.

"Gentlemen," said the colonel, glad that his children were grown and well away from here. "Many of you have wives and children out in the armory. There is not a lot I can say. There's just not time for you to run, or I would say 'Run like hell.' The landing will happen in moments; if you tried to get out from under the interdiction circle you would run right into it.

"As I told Lieutenant Young," he said with a nod at the introspected assistant division engineer, "the best we can do is hold them back for as long as possible, make it as painful as possible for them, and ensure that the deaths of our loved ones are quick and relatively painless. We should also try to determine some manner by which we can destroy as many stocks of food as possible before we are overrun. We must, unfortunately, include ourselves in that equation; we've all seen the reports from Diess and Barwhon.

"Stay straight, keep your troops in hand and do the mission. Our only choice is to stand. We shall stand like Americans have always stood at a moment such as this, on our feet, heads up and fighting," he concluded. "Now get out and do it."

As the two company commanders and the staff filed out Lieutenant Young gestured for the battalion commander to remain a moment.

"Sir?" said the young lieutenant.

"Yes, Lieutenant? You've been quiet."

"I have been thinking about what you said at the first briefing, about how in this situation we would all die and all of our loved ones."

"And now it comes to fruition," the colonel snapped. Then he relented. "Your point?"

"That is my point, sir. Does it have to happen?"

"There is nowhere to run, son, and the forces outside the pocket are not going to charge in and rescue us."

"Yes, sir," admitted the lieutenant in a distracted tone. "But eventually, in two or three weeks, maybe a little longer, we, that is the United States, will have retaken this area. And we've got enough demo to destroy every bridge in Virginia."

"We can't hold out for two or three weeks against upwards of four million Posleen with a short battalion of light engineers." The colonel mused for a moment on a couple of terrain features last used in the

Civil War but the situation was fundamentally different and he shook off the unreal idea.

"No, sir, our death is a foregone conclusion, I accept that, intellectually, but what about the dependents?" the acting assistant division engineer continued, abstractedly. His eyes, concealed behind thick glasses, began blinking rapidly.

"Lieutenant . . ."

"That's it!" the junior officer blurted with a snap of fingers.

"What?"

"I was trying to figure out . . . Look, sir . . . damn, this is complicated."

"Hold on, son, what are you talking about?"

"Okay," the ADE paused and nodded his head as the last piece of the puzzle fell into place. "Okay, sir, here goes. I'm from here, most of you officers aren't. I got into the history of Fredericksburg in high school really heavily and one of the things I learned is that there are tunnels under the city, mostly forgotten, connecting into basements. Now, if we just stash the women and children in the tunnels the Posleen will find them, right?"

"Hold on, who knows about these tunnels? I've never heard of them! Where they are and how large are they?" asked the surprised battalion commander, hearing of the feature for the first time.

"I don't know where most of them are, sir, but somebody will," the lieutenant answered. "They were used in the old days, like the nineteenth century, to move supplies up from the river. They're not very well-known, even to locals, but I'm sure that someone in EMS or city engineering will know where they are. They'd practically have to."

"All right, we'll get past that," said the colonel. "The Posleen will still sniff them out."

"Yes, sir, so we have to make the Posleen think there is nothing left to find in Fredericksburg."

"And we do that . . ." asked the colonel, quizzically.

"By setting off a real mother of an explosion," said the junior officer excitedly. "If I had a nuke it would be perfect."

"But we don't have one."

"Quarles Gas is right outside of town, sir," the lieutenant pointed out. "Fill up a couple of the buildings with natural gas and set them off. Can you say, 'F-A-E'?"

The colonel opened his mouth to rebuke the idea then pulled out his pipe and began tamping it in thought.

A fuel-air explosive, FAE, was the next best thing to a nuclear weapon.

During Desert Storm the United States Air Force dropped

pamphlets—helpfully translated into Arabic—on the Iraqi lines explaining that at 10 A.M. on a certain date they would drop a fuel-air bomb on an area which was held by a brigade of the Iraqi Republican Guard. The pamphlets went on to explain that the weapon would have the effect of destroying all the life in a two-square-kilometer area and be severely damaging out to three square kilometers. All personnel in the affected area were urged to evacuate before they dropped the FAE, to reduce needless loss of life.

Naturally, Saddam Hussein—that polite and abstemious gentleman—derided the idea that such a weapon existed. So at 10 A.M., a battalion and a half of soldiers, over eight hundred human beings, were wiped from the face of the earth in a pair of milliseconds. The Air Force spokesperson promptly held a press conference to defuse Saddam's natural reaction that America had initiated first use of weapons of mass destruction.

The next day the United States Air Force dropped pamphlets—helpfully translated into Arabic—on the Iraqi lines explaining that at 10 A.M. on a certain date they would drop a fuel-air bomb on an area which was held by a brigade of the Iraqi Republican Guard. The next FAE took no lives, but did leave a three-mile-wide stretch of the lines open to advances. At least three Iraqi officers, however, are known to have lost their lives trying to stop the mutinying troops from retreating out of the area of effect.

"That's 'Can you say FAE, sir,' " the colonel corrected, distractedly.

"Right, sir."

"Yes, I can. So we hide as many women and children in these tunnels as we can, then we set off an FAE."

"Yes, sir," answered the excited lieutenant.

"Then what?"

"Then it kills a lot of Posleen, they think everything is destroyed and go away in frustration."

"And the women and children dig themselves out of a series of collapsed tunnels? Into a possibly hostile environment? Do you happen to know how they are constructed?"

"No, sir," answered the lieutenant. It was a good question. If the tunnels were not structurally sound, the overpressure from the shock wave would collapse them on the very people they were trying to save.

"What the structural integrity and overburden are?"

"No, sir," said the crestfallen civil engineer.

"Well, neither do I," mused the commander. "Obviously we don't have all the answers. You know, I think that our alien friends have never read Sun Tzu."

The young ADE nodded his head. "'Cast them into positions from which there is nowhere to go and they will die without retreating.'"

"'On dangerous ground one must devise stratagems, but on deadly ground do battle,'" concluded the battalion commander.

The sergeant major stuck his head in the conference room as the colonel nodded his head in turn. "Sir, it's the fire chief, she's here with a group of cops and firefighters to see what they can do."

"Get them to the operations officer . . ."

"Sergeant Major, Colonel," shouted the colonel's driver, running past the sergeant major in the corridor. "You need to come outside and see this." The officers and NCOs, perforce, followed.

Shari finally made it out of Target, after what seemed like hours and she only had half the things she felt like she needed. For once the problem was not money. By prior plan on the part of the Target corporation and the Federal Emergency Management Agency, the store offered everything for free. One person had quipped that that really meant the world was coming to an end. The problem was reaching the merchandise.

Everyone in Fredericksburg seemed to have come to Central Square at once and there were fights breaking out everywhere. Twice she was sure she had lost Billy in the crowds and even as she fought through the crowds she had things snatched from her basket.

Finally she decided that whatever she had was going to have to do. All of her acquisitions were in four shopping bags, three that she carried along with the baby and one that Billy lugged. Two boxes of cereal bars, diapers, wipes, some bottled water and juice, a few batteries. It was not much to make a run for it.

She heard them saying that the Posleen were coming to Fredericksburg but wrapped in her own straitened world she had not assimilated it. As she fought through the crowds towards her distant car, the movement and noise around her dropped off, the crowd in front of her stopped. She was forced to stop as well and looked up with everyone else in the parking lot.

In the east, the sky was on fire. A new sun made up of hundreds of glowing red landing craft tight-packed into a giant disk was an eye of Baal descending upon the Virginia tidewater. The sight was unreal in the dusky afternoon sunshine, a blazing circlet of death picked out among the fleecy clouds and the darkening cerulean blue sky.

Every human in view of the spectacle stood transfixed as the circle grew and grew, swelling from a moon-sized ring to a horizon-spanning wall in moments. In the time it took to scream, the circle went from a speck to a ring to a blazing wall of fire and then snuffed out as the landing craft slowed below orbital velocities. As the meteoric reentry slowed, the individual ships could be picked out, the twelve-sided polygons of the command craft surrounded by their rings of protective landers. Moments later the sonic boom hit.

The sound was too large to be real, an aural Krakatoa beyond the ability for human hearing to accept. Most in the parking lot were driven to their knees and many lost their hearing permanently. None were spared.

Shari screamed with everyone else, her hands flying to her ears, for once matronly protectiveness being driven out by self-preservation. Billy and the other children were writhing on the ground in agony when the crowd began to surge. She snatched her children up, overcoming her own pain, dropped her hard-won possessions and stumbled into the lee of a truck that, for the moment, was stationary.

The crowd around her broke into riot as everyone individually did whatever they thought was the best for themselves. Some tried to get back into the stores, some ran for their cars, some, like Shari, huddled in the shelter of unmoving vehicles and some began firing randomly into the air. She held her babies as the world around her went mad and they screamed in pain and fear, from the riot as much as the sonic boom. Her ears ringing madly, she cradled her children in the space afforded by the shadow of the truck and waited for the panic to subside. Instead it increased, the crowd surging first one way and then the other as more shots rang out. She steeled herself to look, needing to know the cause of the newest panic and was nearly panicked herself as the shadow of an interstellar craft swept across the parking lot.

The lander drifted across the shopping center, like a zeppelin before a zephyr, and settled as gently as a dandelion seed onto Salem Church hill. The appearance of weightlessness was abruptly dispelled as the titanic craft, as tall as a fifteen-story skyscraper, dropped the last few feet.

As the reverberation of the landing crashed across the crowds, the lower fifty feet of the facet facing the parking lot dropped outward with another resounding clang. Moments later the Posleen came pouring out, a yellow tide of hunting centaurs.

Virtually every armed human, the vast majority of the immense crowd, pointed various weapons at the yellow mass and opened fire.

Shari on the other hand took one look at the tide of Posleen pouring out of the landing craft, put Kelly's left hand in Billy's, picked up the baby, took Kelly's right hand and began walking towards town.

It was not hard. Just stand up, drop everything and go. Like the time that Rorie finally got too drunk and crazy. All the other times, the cops would tell her to go to the shelter but she stayed. She told them she would know when it was time. And it was time. Not hard, just pick the babies up, walk out, get in the car and drive. When the time came you just went. Maybe later there would be time to go back and pick up all the things you left behind. And maybe not. As long as you got away alive and unmaimed that was the thing.

Just walk away and keep walking. As guns go off on either side, and a high, whispery racket goes overhead with a *crickety-crack*. As a line of giant holes suddenly appear in a Jeep ahead of you, and the policeman that was firing from behind it flies backwards in a mass of intestines.

Just keep walking and don't look back, as the crowd tries to pluck your babies away faster than the courts, and the chatter of alien voices and boom of alien guns comes closer.

◆ CHAPTER 33 ◆

Richmond, VA, United States of America, Sol III
2025 EDT October 9th, 2004 AD

"The engineering companies of the Thirty-Sixth, Forty-Ninth and Hundred and Fifth Mechanized Divisions are on the way via I-95," said the Twelfth Corps operations officer, looking at a flimsy. "The remainder of the divisions are going to take a back way across the James and blow it behind them. That will be it for Fort A.P. Hill. The dependents are already gone."

The temporary headquarters that Twelfth Corps had set up in the First Union building was coming down. With the Posleen on the north side of the James, the area was going to get untenable fast. Already the sound of folding chairs and collapsing equipment could be heard in the background.

The meeting was taking place in a gorgeous fourth-floor conference room. The wonderful view to the east was about to be surrendered to the infantry. Present were a skeleton staff, the commander, some operations and intelligence officers, the major local commanders and the ubiquitous Special Forces representatives.

"My boys are ready to roll," said Colonel Walter Abrahamson, commander of the First Squadron Twenty-Second Cavalry (Virginians), the armored cavalry unit assigned to the Richmond local area. The commander was as tall and broad as one of his armored behemoths, but his hooked nose and generally saturnine look bespoke his desert heritage. With his current grim and implacable expression he looked like a biblical plague preparing to spring forth upon the enemies of his people. A gold Star of David earring, strictly non-regulation, sparkled on his left earlobe.

"Unfortunately," commented the corps commander, "we don't have a mission for you."

"Then let us go perform our traditional role." The Cav commander smiled confidently. "Eyes and ears."

"He's got a point," said the corps intelligence officer. "We're effectively blind. All we know is that all communication into the Fredericksburg area is cut off. All the wireless communications are being jammed and we lost the last phone trunk about twenty minutes ago. There were a few Spotsylvania County sheriff's deputies that made it out, but they've only been able to tell us where the Posleen aren't. We still don't know exactly where they *are*. We need to find out."

"Sir," said Sergeant Mueller, "they could do more than that. We can hit back."

"Oh?" commented an Intel/Planning officer, looking askance at an NCO devising strategy. "The Cav is in Bradleys and Humvees. The Posleen open those like tin cans."

"Yes, ma'am, if you put them out in the open. But I went out on 95 north and south last month, just nosing around. Coming down from Fredericksburg it's pretty darn flat but there are a few areas where, with improvement, they could fire hull-down. Get them hull-down, fire at max engagement range, which with those twenty-five millimeters is, what two thousand meters?" he asked the Cav commander.

"About that," agreed the Cav officer with a nod at the NCO.

"Call for a volley of fire and boogie out," continued Mueller. "It will require some engineering support but just a couple of bulldozers. That way we both keep the enemy in view and slow them down."

"You'll take casualties," said the corps commander, turning to the battalion commander, "and the few Posleen you kill will be a tithe of a tithe of their main force. Are you for it?"

"Yes, sir," said the cavalry officer with understated enthusiasm. "That is a straightforward Cav mission. My boys are cocked, locked and ready to roll."

"Very well. Sergeant Mueller, you and Master Sergeant Ersin head up the road," said the corps commander. "Get with the corps engineer before you leave. Tell him to assign you some civilian construction equipment. Make a list."

"Yes, sir," said Ersin quietly.

"Colonel Abrahamson," said the corps commander, "we have a battery of mobile one hundred fifty-five millimeter available. They're the new Reaver model. Take it with you. As more come on-line, we'll send the mobile units out to support you; the others we'll be digging into Mosby and Libby Hills. Have your fire-support chief coordinate through corps artillery, since you're effectively cut off from the rest of the Twenty-Second."

The Lieutenant General smiled grimly. "Last, Colonel, I hope I don't have to say this. You are not to become decisively engaged, not for *any* reason. Understand?"

"With upwards of four million Posleen?" The cavalry colonel chuckled dryly, with a rub of his thick, black hair. "General, my name's Walter Jacob Abrahamson, not George Armstrong Custer." The infamous cavalry general had been both blond and balding.

"And remind your men not to try to enter abandoned homes and businesses," the corps commander commented, sadly. "It looks like the 'Scorched Earth' program is going to get an early test."

Parker Williamson closed the front door, blotting out the sight of the Posleen lander that had crushed the Hawkes's house at the end of Bourne Street. He had already closed the curtains on the unpleasant view out the back. He turned to face his wife, down whose face tears cascaded.

"Well," he sighed, "I guess we drew the short straw."

She nodded, unable to speak, as their oldest daughter entered the room.

"Is it gonna boom anymore, Mommy?" the four-year-old asked, dabbing at the passing tears.

"No, sweetie." Jan Williamson gathered her composure, picking up the two-year-old as he toddled into the room, still crying from the painful sonic booms. "Not that we'll notice."

Parker locked the door and turned to a red panel by the standard home security system. The door swung open to reveal a key pad. A yellow light flashed above the pad and a beeping tone started.

"Federally Authorized Home Destruction System Mod One is activated. Posleen emanations detected, predestruct sequencing authorized. Enter code for command authorization."

Parker punched in a code and hit set.

"State your name."

"Parker Williamson."

"Parker Williamson, are you at this moment in your right mind?" the box asked, beginning the federally mandated litany.

"Emergency bypass authorization."

"Please key in second authorization as required by federal law." Jan walked over and keyed in a second sequence.

"What is your name?"

"Jan Williamson."

"Jan Williamson, do you concur in setting the Federally Authorized

Home Destruction System Mod One into function? Be aware that the system is monitoring Posleen emanations in the near area."

"I do."

The panel chuckled for a moment, checking that their voice prints were correct and then the light went red. At the same time the home security system turned on.

"Intruder detection system activated, autodestruct sequence activated." In the basement of the house, two chemicals, harmless when separated, began to mix. "Destruct sequence will auto-activate upon unauthorized entry ... may God protect and keep you."

"Come on, honey," said Jan Williamson, picking up their daughter in a big hug, "let's go read Peter Rabbit ..."

Lieutenant General Arkady Simosin, Tenth Corps Commander, the corps tasked with the defense of Northern Virginia and Maryland, humorously called "The Army of the Potomac," looked at the giant blotch of red on his southern flank and wiped his mouth.

"Tell the Twenty-Ninth to pull his armored battalions back," he told his G-3, pointing at the tactical display. "They're too far forward. Empty Belvoir and Quantico, get them headed north of the Potomac. That's going to be our defensive line."

"Yes, sir. Sir, I called General Bernard. He said that he would only take that order from you directly and that he intended to drive into the Posleen flank to pull them off of Fredericksburg."

"What?" the general asked incredulously.

"I just got off the horn with him."

"Get him back." The general fumed as contact was made with the subordinate commander.

"General Bernard?" he asked on speaker phone.

"Yes, General?"

"I believe the G-3 told you to pull your battalions back. I would like to know why you have refused."

"I believe that I can put enough pressure on the Posleen to pull some of them off of Fredericksburg, possibly give the Two-Twenty-Ninth some time to organize a breakout."

General Simosin considered General Bernard the epitome of the one officer you could do nothing with: active/stupid. A consummate politician, General Bernard had expended sweat and blood to become the Virginia Adjutant General—the senior military commander in the Virginia National Guard—in the days before the Posleen threat. With the rejuvenation of so many senior officers, such as Simosin, advancement had effectively stopped. General Bernard naturally blamed the rejuvenation program for his inability to advance to Lieutenant General.

In fact, the general had been strongly considered for relief for cause. He was chronically insubordinate, jumped the chain of command at every opportunity, was tactically unsound and refused to subordinate his units to either Tenth or Twelfth Corps. Instead he insisted that they remained distributed in penny packets throughout the state.

Now he held true to every negative in his history and it was about to get his troops slaughtered. Unfortunately, General Simosin knew that if he put pressure on him the idiot would just jump to the First Army commander and get the order countermanded. It was worse than the damn Confederates! Well, too bad.

"General, you are ordered to round up your units and pull them across the Potomac. We cannot stop the Posleen short of that natural obstacle and I will not throw units away in a pointless gesture. That is an order, failure to follow it will result in your arrest."

"Dammit, General, do you realize that that will throw away Alexandria, the Pentagon and Arlington Cemetery? Not to mention thousands of American citizens in Fredericksburg!"

"And Washington National Airport and Fort Belvoir. I can read a map. And I'm in that area at the moment, I might add. I am fully aware of those facts as is the Continental Army commander. He is evacuating the area even as we speak."

"We can stop them! This isn't Barwhon or Diess; common people are standing up to them everywhere and wearing them away. We can stop them at any point on the map! Just give me one brigade of the Forty-First Division, and we can stop them before Quantico."

"Since I just ordered you to retreat, I could scarcely authorize a forlorn hope with someone else's troops. General, pull your battalions back and do it now. Failure to do so will constitute violation of a direct order in combat. That is my final word."

Simosin squeezed the tabletop, trying to keep the tension from coming through in his voice. Now, if the First Army commander would only have the sense to see reality. Even if he did not, CONARC was one hundred percent behind pulling across the Potomac.

"If that is your final word, General, very well."

"Then you will pull your troops back? Let me be clear, both General Keeton and I agree that contact should be held until all necessary measures have been emplaced. Do not contact the Posleen without direct and clear orders to do so by either myself or General Keeton. Is that clear?"

"Yes. I will contact you when that withdrawal has been effected."

"Very well, start them back immediately. Out here." He turned back to the assembled staff that had listened to the call.

"And in the real world . . . how is the evacuation going?" General Simosin asked, taking a deep breath and turning to the Federal Emergency Management Agency representative.

"Fairly well, all things considered," the FEMA rep replied. "We've opened up the HOV lanes into Washington and we're routing the refugees through and out of town. It's moving slow, but we should have most of northern Virginia evacuated by morning. It would help if we could open up a few of the lanes the military isn't using.

"I know they are designated for defense use, but they're being underutilized by your military forces. We could maintain one lane and an emergency lane for the military forces and it would more than handle what is moving currently."

He turned to the G-3. "Are we going to have a big increase?"

"No, the convoys are pulling out of Belvoir and Quantico in a steady stream. We planned it that way and it's taking about an hour per battalion to cycle them through beans and bullets. They shouldn't pulse much. Most of them are headed towards D.C. also, but a few are being sent up the Prince William Parkway to Manassas. But I'm worried about civilian vehicles intruding on troop lanes."

"Issue orders to disable any civilian vehicle in a military lane with all appropriate force. Have the order broadcast and displayed on those overhead signs, then turn over unutilized lanes to FEMA. Anything else?"

"No, we're cutting all the corners we can," replied the FEMA rep. "But when the Posleen start coming close, into contact, things could get out of hand."

"Do you need troops?"

"We could use a few. MPs by preference."

"G-3?"

"Three-Twenty-Fifth MP Battalion at your service, Madame."

"Thank you," the FEMA rep said. "That should cover it."

"Get those civilians out of harm's way; we'll try to slow the centaur bastards down." General Simonsin wiped his face and looked at the map projection.

"Now as to that. I don't want to have even cavalry in contact; the Posleen move too fast and hit too hard. We will follow the Reticulan Defense Plan to the letter and pull fully across the Potomac. I have so informed First Army and CONARC. So, to slow them down, what do we do for engineers?" The corps engineering brigade was at Fort Leonard Wood going through a large-scale engineering exercise. The timing of the exercise was exquisite. Exquisitely lousy.

"The engineering companies of the Forty-First and Ninety-Fifth Divisions probably should accompany them, since they'll have to dig in," said the G-3.

"So, what do we use?" the commander asked again.

"Sir," said one of the operations officers. "I called Fort Belvoir and, since they've reactivated the Fifty-Two Echo program there, they have plenty of combat engineering instructors and trainees. And there are the officers going through basic and advanced courses . . ."

" 'And to the strains of Dixie, the cadets marched off the field to war,' " Simosin quoted. "Well, that's a start. Where do we deploy them?"

"The first real terrain obstacle the Posleen will encounter is at the Occoquan Estuary . . ." said the corps intelligence officer.

Second Lieutenant William P. Ryan—being a not quite graduate of the Basic Combat Engineers Officers' course—did not know much about combat engineering. And he knew even less about combat in general. But he was willing to learn, even if this kind of makee-learnee was not particularly survivable. One look at the pitiable stream of refugees headed north on Interstate 95 was enough to make him determined to do his best.

Most of his classmates were rigging the I-95 and U.S. 1 bridges over the Occoquan River under the expert tutelage of their instructors. The senior instructor had decided that Ryan was a good-enough prospect that he was sent to destroy a bridge all on his own, and his "platoon" was rigging the 123 bridge under the guidance of an experienced instructor-sergeant. The platoon was a group of trainees from the enlisted combat engineers course along with their drill instructors and junior technical instructors. The interesting challenge in concrete cutting posed by the bridge he had left up to the much more experienced NCO instructors.

He crossed the river and walked down through the charming little town of Occoquan to get a better look at the far ridge from the Posleen's perspective. The town was nestled along the south side of the river where it passed between two high ridges. The subsurface geology of the ridges created the falls that gave birth to the town and that were integrated into the Occoquan dam. That dam, in turn, created the reservoir that stretched from his location nearly to Manassas, twenty miles away.

As he stood just below Rockledge Manor he noticed a small footbridge crossing over the river just below the waterworks. He made a note to have a squad come over and rig it for demolition as well. The dam, on the other hand, was another matter.

If they dropped the dam, God only knew where the Posleen might be able to cross the Occoquan. After checking his map he guessed it would be somewhere around Yates Ford Road, half the distance they might otherwise have to travel. On the other hand, the Posleen could push forces across the dam itself. Not many or in great force, but any intrusion was to be dissuaded. And there was an older, partially submerged dam as well. He was unsure how to handle that tactical problem and decided to pass it up the line.

Walking rapidly back through the deserted town he got a strange feeling of sadness. He could remember the days before the Posleen were a word, before Earth knew it was in the path of an invasion. Even as America prepared, as more and more shortages occurred and liberties fell by the wayside in the race to get ready, the world was more or less the same as it had always been.

At that moment, striding rapidly back to where engineers under his command were preparing to destroy a major civil structure, he knew that this was truly the end of the golden age. That from now until an unforeseeable future man would be a hunted animal on his own world and that only God knew what the outcome would be.

"Ladies and gentlemen," the loudspeaker boomed, "we need you to remain calm." The crowd gathered behind the Fredericksburg Public Safety Building was mostly women and children. They had run from their homes in fear and fled to the only refuge they knew. There was plenty of room with all of the ambulances and police cars dispatched. The group huddled in the gathering dark, most of them knowing that by coming here they were only delaying the inevitable.

"We are working on a way to get you out," continued the speaker, one of the remaining fire fighters, "and we just need you to remain calm."

"He's dreamin'," said Little Tom Sunday in a monotone. Then, "Hiya, Wendy."

Wendy Cummings spun around. Little Tom stood behind her with a pack on his back and duffel bag at his feet. He was wearing some sort of weird black padding that stretched almost to his knees, a black helmet like the soldiers wore and a pair of sporty sunglasses. Inside she sighed in exasperation. If there was one person she did not want to spend her last hours with, it was Little Tommy Sunday. But she might as well be polite.

"Hi, Tommy. What's that stuff?" she asked out of curiosity, gesturing at the padding.

"Body armor," he answered in a disinterested tone. "It won't stop one of their railguns, but it'll stop the shotgun rounds and spalling."

Her eyes widened as she recognized it from "Real Police" shows. Officers had been shot at point-blank range wearing similar suits and survived. "Do you have any more?" she asked, hopefully.

"Well," he answered, bending down stiffly to rummage in his duffel bag, "I don't have any more Class One, but I've got a Safe-Tee, some T-shirt Kevlar." He pulled the body armor out of the bag, revealing the contents. He glanced at her chest. "It might fit," he ended doubtfully.

"Holy shit," she gasped, "what-all do you have in there?" The bag gleamed with the bluing of lethal purpose. She recognized the shape of some sort of machine gun and other things she thought were grenades.

She had taken the school survival course, but only because it was required. But, since you didn't have to pass, she had spent most of her time doing homework from other classes and passing notes to her friends. She barely recognized the items in the bag from familiarization.

"A few odds and ends," he answered, zipping the bag shut.

"Do you . . . Could I borrow a gun or something?" she asked, trying to figure out the connections on the body armor.

"What would *you* do with it?" he asked, disgustedly, grabbing the Velcro and efficiently connecting first one underarm strap then the other.

"Try?" she asked, looking him in the eye for the first time in years. She suddenly realized that he was far taller than she thought; much taller than she was, which was a surprise. Everyone just thought of him as Little Tommy. He had been self-effacing for so long, it had made him appear short.

"You should have tried years ago," he answered. He reached back into the duffel and brought out a short black pistol in a shoulder holster.

"You ever use one of these things before?" he asked rhetorically, dropping out the magazine and yanking back the slide to eject the round up the spout. He caught the 9mm round in the air like a trout after a fly.

"No," she answered, intimidated by his suddenly revealed expertise.

"Okay." He lifted up the magazine. "This is the gas, you fuel it like this." He slid the magazine back into the well. "It's fueled when you hear the click. You start it like this." He jacked back the slide. "And," he said, laying one finger lightly on the trigger as he pointed the weapon skyward and across the river, "this is the accelerator. You drive it by looking through the rear sights while focusing on the front sights. Place the white dot on the front sight across the V of the rear sights and pull on the accelerator real slow. There, the Tom Sunday School of Glock Driving."

She accepted the weapon gingerly as he ensured she had it pointed up and downrange.

"So where is Park?" she asked dryly.

He took the weapon back, put it into the shoulder holster and handed her the rig. "There is no Park," he said as he easily hefted the weapon-stuffed duffel. "See ya."

"Where are you going?"

He looked at her for a moment and cocked his head to one side. "That stuff," he noted, gesturing with his chin at the body armor, "is really supposed to go under your clothes. I'm heading up to somewhere on Charles or Princess Anne Street that has a good view," he said, throwing the strap of the duffel across one shoulder, "then I'm going to smoke a whole pack of Marlboros waiting for the Posleen to show their heads. Then I'm going to die." He smiled warm and quietly, as if asking her to deny the reality of that statement.

She smoothed the stomach of her armor unconsciously and went through a series of rapid mental readjustments. "Can I come with you? Maybe I can reload or something."

"I sincerely doubt that there will be time to reload," he answered, "but you would be extremely welcome. Now, to find a good spot on Charles Street," he said, turning up the hill.

"How about Worth's?" she suggested.

Bill Worth sat at ease in the rear of his store, a Franklin stove removing the last tinges of chill from the evening of this truly wearisome day. The large front room of the shop was redolent with the scent of old books and fine antiques. It was the scent of home.

He was spending what he considered to be his last few moments perusing an early edition of *Moll Flanders* that included some tracts not usually found outside of the editions published during Defoe's era and sipping a Cóte d'Azur '57 he had traded the previous year for a prototype Colt Peacemaker. As in all good business deals, both parties felt they got the better of the bargain.

He had just reached a condition of maximum comfort, his sockless loafers perched on an ottoman, his wine close at hand, when the door to the shop jingled as, most unexpectedly, a pair of customers entered.

"Feel free to look around, gentlemen," he told the pair of soldiers, officers if his "Uniforms and Insignia of the United States Armed Forces" was any judge. "However, I prefer not to sell anything today. I have decided to maintain my collection intact for old sake's sake."

He chuckled at the reference neither of the soldiers would possibly recognize.

"Hi, Mr. Worth, it's me, Kenny Young," said the younger officer, truly a babe-in-arms as it were.

"Ah, yes, young Mr. Young," he said with another breathy chuckle. "The uniform befits you. I thought you were studying engineering?"

"I'm a military engineer."

"Ah! A Pioneer! Bravo. Where are you based?"

"Here, Mr. Worth. That's what the local Guard unit is, Engineers." Lieutenant Young smiled faintly. It was a well-known fact that Bill Worth hadn't set foot outside of the five or ten blocks of what he termed "historic Fredericksburg" in years.

"Ah, yes, somewhere up Route 3 isn't it?" asked the shopkeeper, quizzically.

"Yeah, about a mile from here," chuckled the lieutenant.

"Ah. Terra Incognita, indeed. So, to what do I owe the honor of your presence on this most gloriously unpleasant evening?"

"Well, we need to find out about the tunnels. We were told you might know something about them."

"Yes," commented the local historian, with a nod of his head. "Well, it would really be Ralph Kodger, you need to talk to about them . . ."

"But he's . . ." noted the lieutenant.

"Dead, yes, but a great historian in his time. Or perhaps Bob Bailey . . ." continued Worth.

" . . . who . . ." said Young.

" . . . moved to Kansas, yes, I see you're ahead of me here."

"Do you know anything about them? Where the openings are?" asked the engineer.

"What their structure is?" asked the other soldier.

"And you are, sir?" Bill asked politely. The older soldier was obviously impatient, one of those people who feel it necessary to continuously rush about as if life wasn't always exactly the same length.

"Captain Brown, sir, Charlie Company commander," said Captain Brown, shortly. "We hope to hide some of the women and children in the tunnels and blow up, well, the city basically, to cover our tracks. We wondered about a '50s-style bomb shelter, but there aren't any. So we're back to the tunnels. Unless you know where a bomb shelter is."

"A valorous endeavor indeed," commented Worth, setting down his Defoe and walking to the desk that was the center of his domain. "Might I ask a few questions?"

"As long as you're quick," snapped the impatient commander.

"How are they to survive?" asked the shopkeeper. "The women and children that is. Without air, food or water? There won't be much room for that sort of thing, I would suppose." He rummaged in the top drawer of the desk and extracted a pad of what appeared to be parchment.

"It turns out that the paramedics have been using a Galactic medication called Hiberzine that can put a person in suspended animation for months," said the lieutenant, excitedly. "Public Safety has plenty of it; we can pack in as many as can fit. Resources are not an issue."

"Ah, and how do you intend to blow up the city?" Mr. Worth asked, beginning to doodle on the pad.

"We're going to fill some of the buildings with natural gas, basically," answered Captain Brown. "It'll do the job; do those centaur bastards anyway. Now, I'm sorry, but if you don't mind, we need to find somewhere to stash the women and children. If you'll excuse us?"

"Actually, I think you might consider my pump house," Worth noted with a world-weary laugh, continuing to sketch.

"We need something larger than a pump house," said the captain, assuming he meant one covering the well for a house. "Thank you just the same. Come on, Lieutenant."

"Captain," the storekeeper drawled, finished scribbling rapidly on his pad, "would something like this suffice?" He held up the sketch. "A two-story underground pump house for an industrial plant? Three-foot-thick concrete walls? Fifty feet long, thirty feet wide? Two levels? Underground?"

"Jesus," whispered Captain Brown, snatching the pad. "Where is this?"

"By the river," Worth answered with a dry smile.

"You own this?" asked Lieutenant Young, peering at the well-drawn sketch.

"Yes, I bought it several years ago and fixed it up," answered the storekeeper.

"Why?" asked Captain Brown, curious despite himself.

"Well," answered Bill Worth, with a sigh, "it's got such a beautiful view of the river.... Captain, if I offer this made-in-heaven facility for your little plan, can I pick *which* building you blow up?"

"Are you sure about this, Captain?" asked the first sergeant of Charlie Company as Second and Third platoons assembled in the parking lot of the Fredericksburg Executive Building. A seven-story block of unimaginative '70s architecture, it had all the aesthetic appeal of a brick, creating a modern eyesore among the pleasant stone seventeenth- and eighteenth-century buildings that predominated in the city center.

"It was Mr. Worth's only condition and it's really the best building for our purpose," answered the captain. "It's got plenty of volume, it's close to the pump house but the railroad embankment will create a blast shadow and I have to agree, not that it matters, that it is one of the *ugliest* buildings I have *ever* seen." He turned back to the assembled troops and raised his voice to carry over the sound of approaching semitrailers.

"Men, we are going to kill two birds with one stone. While some of you prepare a bunker to hide the women and children, others of you are going to prepare a reception for the Posleen they will never forget. We have found an industrial pump house that used to supply water for the old cellophane mill. It is partially buried and has three-foot-thick concrete walls.

"Second platoon, along with these arriving construction guys, is going to finish covering it with as much overburden as we can find, while also preparing the inside. You need to fair over the opening to the pump house proper, you'll see what I mean when you get in there. The radio station is calling for anyone with welding equipment to come here and construction equipment is being diverted from the Interstate lines to assist.

"Get the pump house covered with overburden and get the opening faired over with sheet and structural steel, whatever you can find. When we get as many women and children in as we can, we'll blow the tower and seal them in.

"I've looked it over and there may be room for all the surviving women and children, praise be to God. Since there may not be time or room, the chief of police is starting a lottery for who goes in and the order. Only children under sixteen and their mothers are going in the bunker.

"The problem is that if we just bury the noncombatants, the Posleen will dig them out like anteaters after termites. We need to create as much disruption as possible and try to make it appear that there is nothing left to find in Fredericksburg, and especially not on this side. To do that, we are going to turn this building," he pointed with his thumb at the monstrosity over his shoulder, "into a giant fuel-air bomb.

"Trucks are coming from Quarles Gas to pump it full of propane. But first it has to be prepped. I want Third platoon to get in there and blow holes through all the floors, to increase interior circulation. And before you leave make sure every interior door is open. While the building is being prepped, the first sergeant will rig it for demolition. Don't set any of your charges in his way.

"When you're done, which should take less than forty-five minutes, you'll either go to the bunker work, or up to prepare the town defenses."

He gestured to the arriving lowboys burdened with bulldozers and backhoes. "Second, we're depending on you and those guys to make an impregnable bunker. Get to work. And Third," he gestured to the cases of C-4 at the entrance to the building, "go blow some holes. Keep your helmets on, somebody might be blowing above you."

"Sir," muttered the first sergeant as the platoon pounded into the building, grabbing demo and caps as they went by, "this is bound to cause casualties."

"Well, Top, there are times when you have to balance relative risk. I don't have much idea how much time we have, but I doubt we have much longer."

"We have to slow them down," noted the S-3, desperately. "Charlie is just starting on the bunker and the FAE. It'll take them at least an hour."

"More," noted the fire chief, "it'll take that long just to pump the building full of gas."

The Posleen had taken their time assembling—for which everyone was thankful. But having reduced the last resistance and most of the buildings around Central Square, the nearest B-Dec force was coming down Highway 3. And there was only a scattering of militia and police to stop the six-thousand-odd rampaging aliens. Other Posleen were moving in from the east and west, but by the time those Posleen reached the city center it would be nearly dawn and the bunker and FAE would be prepared.

It was the Central Square force, rolling down the main highway into town, that would be the primary threat to the plan.

"We need something to distract them, to scare them," commented the battalion commander, "something like that dragon that the ACS used on Diess."

"I'll tell you one thing every Earth animal is afraid of," said the scarred chief, getting the glimmering of an idea, "and that's fire."

"What are you thinking?" asked the commander.

"If we had some flamethrowers . . ." said the S-3 and his eyes widened at the same time as the chief's.

"Jerry," said the S-3, turning to his NCOIC, "call Quarles Gas, and tell them we need some more flammables. Some gas trucks, gasoline that is, or kerosene. Any liquid flammables."

"Kerosene is the preference. I'll go get the fire trucks," said the chief, shaking her head.

"Colonel?"

"Yes, Sergeant Major?" Colonel Robertson was mortally tired. The strains of the day were rapidly taking their toll and he wondered what new catastrophe the sergeant major had to report.

"Well, sir, I was checking on the detail that was issuing from the ammo point, and all the parties are out on site, but there's still over a ton of demo and ammunition of one sort or another left."

"Okay, I guess we could blow it in place when the Posleen get here."

"Yes, sir, we could, but I was thinking, the ammo dump isn't far from the armory and I've got that detail still on site . . ."

"And you think there might be better places to put the ammo than in the ammo dump."

"Yes, sir. Face it, the dump is designed to *contain* an explosion," said the sergeant major with a feral smile.

"Well, Sergeant Major, why don't you just take charge of that little detail." The colonel smiled back. Good subordinates were such a treasure.

"Yes, sir!"

Shari stumbled into the crowd behind the Public Safety Building and carefully lowered Kelly and Susie to the ground. Billy let go of her skirt and sat down, his eyes wide and unseeing. She slumped beside him as the two girls huddled into her lap, Susie quietly whimpering from the broken blisters on her feet and the sights glimpsed over her mother's shoulder. A woman coming through the crowd stopped and stared, then walked over.

"Are you in the pool?" she asked abruptly.

Shari looked at her with wide unemotional eyes. It took a long moment to register her question. "What?" she croaked.

"Are you in the basket? Did you enter your name to be drawn?"

"Drawn for what?" she gasped again, mouth and throat dry from dehydration and agonizingly extended fear.

Finally the woman grasped that Shari was suffering from more than the general shock of the loathsome afternoon drawn into evening. "Are you going to be all right?"

Shari started to laugh quietly and the laughs began to segue into sobs.

Every step she took, from the parking lot to where the Army and police were digging in along the interstate, she knew would be their last. Time and again she heard the centaurs drawing closer, only to be delayed by some more interesting target. When she was forced to pick up Susie, drawing her already slow progress to a crawl, she was overcome with the utter certainty that her babies were going to die. And from what she had heard behind her it was going to be one of the worst of all possible deaths.

The pain-racked march was a drawn-out nightmare, in which the monsters were always just behind you and you knew that at any moment they would touch you and then you would die. But this was no nightmare; this was a stark reality as the sun set behind her in a blaze of red and she dropped into the shadows of Salem Hill to the accompaniment of dying screams.

The passing matron waved for one of the tending fire fighters as Shari began to collapse into hysterics. The EMT came over, readying a dose of Hiberzine.

"No," said one of the other paramedics. She grabbed Shari by her shoulders and forced her to look up. "You have to keep together," she snapped. "We need you; we need all the mothers. You're Shari Reilly, right?"

Shari nodded her head, still unable to stop the sobs. The girls started crying softly in response as Billy just sat and rocked, looking into the deepening twilight.

"You came in from Central Park?"

"Uh-huh," Shari sobbed, unable to catch her breath.

"All you have to do is hang on until they call your name, okay? It's a lot easier than walking from Target to the interstate. We got a call on you. Let me see your daughter's feet."

As the paramedic tended to Susie, Shari slowly got herself under a little better control.

"You're going through a normal reaction," said the medic, soothingly. "You've had a shock, Jesus, we all have! But yours was worse. You go through a reaction period. You held out until you were here, which is better than most. You held it together getting out of the . . . the . . ."

"Out of hell," said Billy.

Shari squeezed her son to her. "Are you gonna be okay, baby?"

"I . . . I . . ."

"It's okay, baby, we're safe."

"No, we're not, Mom. Don't lie."

"Son," said the medic firmly, "the engineers are building the best damn shelter they can to protect you, and the rest of us are going to try to make sure there's nothing to draw the Posleen in. We're gonna do our level best to save you, I promise you that."

"Is it gonna work?" asked Shari, catching her breath in a pause between crying spells.

"I won't promise anything," said the paramedic honestly. "But it's a better chance than without it."

"Excuse me," said a woman, looming out of the darkness, "somebody said you were up at Spotsylvania Mall." The woman's voice caught for a moment. "Did you happen to see a man driving," she paused, "driving a hunter green Suburban . . ."

"My husband was a tall man . . ."

"Did you see . . ."

The women rose around her, closing in with desperate questions, but the paramedic rose over her like an enraged lioness. "Look, people, I know you're wondering about your . . . your families, your husbands, but this lady's been through enough already . . ."

"No," said Shari, with a quavering voice, "I have to say it, I have to. . . . There was nobody behind me, nobody at all. I'm sorry . . ." She started crying again, quietly. "There wasn't anything I could do. I, I, just had to walk away, you see? I had to save my babies, I had to walk and keep walking . . . There was this little girl . . . she wouldn't come with me and I was carrying my babies . . . I couldn't, I couldn't . . ."

"Shhh," the medic cried into her hair, "it's all right, it is. There's nothing to do . . ."

"We had to walk," laughed Billy. "We just walked and walked and never ever looked back. You can't look back, you just have to walk and walk . . ." He began to scream.

The paramedic leaned over and pressed an injector against his neck. In a moment he was out cold.

"What was that?" Shari snarled, struggling to her feet.

"Shh, just Hiberzine. He'll sleep quiet. Unfortunately, when he wakes up to him it'll be just a moment from now. So before anyone gives him the antidote, make sure they know he's not tracking very well. We've put quite a few out." The lost wives had faded back into the darkness and another paramedic brought over blankets and soup.

"I put you in the drawing," he said. "The engineers are about to start loading."

"I wonder how they're doing at the interstate?" said the female paramedic.

The chassis of a gas truck, caught on the overpass as the Posleen pounded into view, was silhouetted by the fires of thousands of gallons of kerosene, diesel and gasoline. A fire truck kept up a steady stream of mixed flammables as its counterpart stood at a comfortable distance across Plank Road awaiting its turn to fire. The giant flamethrower had demonstrated truly awesome range from time to time as the Posleen tried to bypass the incendiary barrier. The gushing fuel spouted out at tremendous force and ignited only as it touched the other burning fuel. Occasionally openings would occur. When the Posleen tried to charge through, the fire fighters would get them good and soaked then drift a line of fuel to the nearest patch of flame. The explosion of fire would immolate the group and the massacre would continue. Behind the two fire trucks was a line of fuel trucks, well dispersed, and a spare pair of pumper cars having their seals replaced.

"Damn if this isn't working, Chief," said Colonel Robertson with an amazed smile. The stupid aliens were hell-bent on forcing the passage and getting turned into Posleen Toasties in the process.

"Yes, sir, Colonel. Those holes your boys put in help too." She gestured to the large craters blown into the median, requiring the Posleen to go out of their way by nearly a kilometer on either side. Explosions and shots in both directions showed where skirmishing was occurring on the flanks. The Posleen had not yet pressed in either direction nor did they appear to be interested in pursuing it. When they did the defense would have to fall back.

"It's amazing. They don't seem to have consolidated, yet," the colonel informed her. "They're just coming in piecemeal and we're blowing them away all over the place. We blew the Jeff Davis bridge, but they're pressing up from the south on the Jeff Davis and Tidewater Trail. We're going to be untenable here before the juice runs out."

"Okay, well, we'll pull back when you call it," said the fire chief, wiping at a bit of soot on her cheek. The smell of burning Posleen was like nothing else on earth. The closest she could come was burning rubber and that was about as close as alligator to chicken. The smoke was almost enough to call for breath-packs and who knew what toxins it might contain.

"It won't be soon," he commented with a grim smile as another group tried to charge the fire. The fire fighters had almost made a game of it, opening pockets to allow the enemy to charge forward then cutting off their retreat before filling the hole and incinerating them. Even the God Kings seemed unable to find the source of the fuel as the flames climbed high into the night.

"You probably ought to turn this one over to your second," Colonel Robertson noted. "I'd like you to take a safety look at the fuel-air explosive. It would be a bitch if it prematurely detonated, but we have to fill the building in advance."

"You got it, Colonel. Where are you going to be?"

"Oh, I have an appointment at the armory. Something about preparing a reception."

The old fire fighter smiled. "Well, lay in the punch and I suppose they will come."

"Right down William Street."

"Yup. Welcome to Historic Fredericksburg."

"I think they'll spread out a little from William Street," said Little Tommy, turning away up Princess Anne Street. "Probably as far as Fauquier or Hawk before they blow the Big One."

They walked along Princess Anne in the dusk, crunching the shattered glass from display windows underfoot as the rattle of gunfire sounded in the distance. The quaint shops had taken a big hit from the sonic booms of the landing.

"I was wondering . . ." he said diffidently. "Do you want to take a chance on the bunker? Now that they're going to do that?"

"I'm over sixteen," Wendy pointed out, "and not a mother." The last was somewhat sharp, almost bitter.

"Ahem. Well, there might be more room; they might take, you know, others. Shit, I wish I had a hole to hide in."

"You wouldn't hide if they gave you the chance, would you?"

Tommy thought about it. "No; no, I probably wouldn't. Not until I . . . did some good. And by then it would be too late."

"What is it with all of this?" she asked, gesturing at the body armor and bags. "I mean, I know kids that are in Junior Militia who are less well prepared."

"Yeah, well, my dad's one real regret in life is that he took a scholarship to Clemson to play football instead of West Point to play army. Then he went pro and that ended any chance of going in the military. Instead, he became an armchair soldier. You know, CNN junky, shooting pistols instead of playing golf, playing paintball all weekend. The whole Posleen thing was the greatest thing that ever happened to him; he was finally going to get to be a soldier. He even tried to enlist, but he was outside the range since he wasn't prior service. And then there's the knees . . .

"Anyway, he decided early on, way before we Knew, that I was going to be the next Hannibal . . ."

"Who?" asked Wendy, coughing as a particularly strong swirl of smoke from the interstate wafted down the street.

" . . . the next Robert E. Lee," Tommy translated.

"Oh."

"I've been training to be a soldier since most kids were learning to play T-ball. My dad made a big thing about giving me my first pistol when I was eight. I'd asked for a new computer."

"Yeah," said Wendy, in a questioning tone. "I thought you were a computer geek, not a gun geek."

"Gun geek, that's rich," he said bitterly. "I *am* a computer geek, actually a computer super-geek. I'm nationally ranked number eleven at *Death Valley* and the smart money was on me going into the top five next week. I've been coding practically since I could write. I live for computers. Knowing that, Dad requires that I give equal time to this kind of training. I have to put in exactly as much time on the range or in the field as I do on a computer.

"I was the youngest member of the Junior Militia and basically quit after two years because I was so far ahead of the rest of those slow-assed bozos. I can run well enough to go out for track, but it was track or computer time. And, hell, football? Lifting weights is considered 'military training' so I can press well over my body weight and Dad wanted me to try out for the squad. It was the one time I basically told him to stuff it. If I was a jock it would cut into either range time or computer time and I knew which one my dad would choose."

He shrugged philosophically. "So, here I am, the most dangerous kid in school, and an outcast computer geek. Go figure."

"Well," said Wendy carefully as they stopped by Goolrick's drug-store on the corner of George Street, "I guess you've come to your moment."

"My dad's moment, you mean. He's out there, somewhere, holed up, waiting for the Posleen to come into view and just living for it. Mom and Sally will go into the hole and I'll 'give 'em as good as I get,'" he quoted in a false baritone.

"Fucking bastard," he spat, bitterly. "The bitch of it is, I'm sitting here figuring angles of fire as well as any infantry lieutenant, and as if it's going to do any good." He shrugged and looked around, still figuring the angles.

"What about Alesia's Antiques?" he asked, gesturing across the street with his chin. "It's got a good shot across the courtyard behind it. We might even move into the Bank Museum. That would give us first and second positions. We might even survive three minutes," he finished with a laugh.

"I've been thinking about Alesia's," she answered speculatively. "You know when you asked if I wished I was going in the Bunker?"

"Jesus," said Tommy, as the rebar went through the brick wall next to an antique safe, "it really is here. How did you know about this?"

"Well, your love is computers and the military. Mine is local history and research."

He poked his head through the small hole and into the musty tunnel beyond, shining a Maglite around. "It's about five, five and a half feet high. Brick arch, dry earth floor. Amazing. What were these things for?"

"Nobody's sure. There's no written records about them, but they date to the Eighteenth century at least. The best guess is that they were used to bring cargo up from the docks. The streets back then were dirt and they got awful boggy in the rain. The romantic story is that they were for transporting contraband. Smuggled silk and untaxed tea, stuff like that. The really stupid story is that they were created by the slaves as escape routes. No way. They might have been used as hiding places for the Underground Railroad, but they were not created by it; they're from an earlier period."

He turned and looked at her in the dimness of the antique shop's basement. "I guess I'm not the only one surprising people today."

"I usually get complimented on my intelligence just before I get dumped," she said, frowning.

He swallowed a lump of his own resentment. "Maybe you were hanging out with the wrong guys."

"Yeah," she answered, "maybe I was. Look," she continued, pulling out the Glock, "this isn't going to do me much good against the Posties. You got anything heavier in there?" She gestured at the duffel.

"Yeah, good point. The only problem is these are a little more complicated." He unzipped the duffel and started emptying it. He had set aside his armor and backpack to move the heavy sideboard blocking the tunnel wall and now gestured at the backpack. "Open that up and start laying the stuff out. We'll need to divvy it up."

In a few minutes the two bags were emptied out on the floor and their contents neatly arranged. It made an impressive arsenal.

"We're not going to get to use a third of this stuff, but I believe in being truly prepared."

"I can see that," she said, picking up one of the assault rifles that had been stowed in the duffel bag. "What's this one?"

"That's a Galil .308. It's a good anti-Posleen weapon. Do you want to try it?"

"Okay, it looks less complicated than that one." The other weapon appeared to have more than one rifle on it.

"It is. This one is my baby." He hefted the rifle. "It's an Advanced Infantry Weapon, a 7.62 rifle with a twenty-millimeter grenade launcher underneath. Thirty-round magazine for the rifle and five rounds for the grenade launcher. Laser designator. Definitely the thing."

"I'll take this one," she said, lifting the Galil. "Is it loaded?"

"No." He took it and went through the basic steps to arm, fire, reload and safe it. "Pull it into your shoulder and squeeze the trigger. This one has a laser designator, too, but it's low infrared so you can only see it through the scope."

He safed the weapon and handed it back. "It's empty. Point it at the far wall and squeeze the trigger while you look through the scope." He helped her get a good cheek-to-stock position. "See the dot?"

"Yeah, it's all over the place."

"Take a deep breath," he said, forced to notice the pleasant things it did to her anatomy even under body armor, "let it out and squeeze the trigger gently . . ." He almost continued with the standard line but snorted instead.

"Don't laugh at me!" she snapped, dropping the rifle to waist level. "I'm trying!"

"I know you are. I wasn't laughing at you," he said, snorting again. "I was trying not to continue the saying that goes with that."

"With what?" she asked, confused.

"Look, when you're teaching trigger control the way the saying usually goes is 'let your breath out and squeeze it gentle, like a tit,' okay? That was what I laughed about, I almost said it. Okay?"

"Okay," she said, mollified. "What a crude and stupid thing to say," she continued.

"I tried not to! You badgered me into saying it, okay?"

"Like you would know what squeezing a tit felt like!" She stopped and her hand flew across her mouth as she realized what she had blurted.

"Thanks," he smiled grimly, "thanks a lot. If you must know, I guarantee I know more about squeezing tits gently than you do."

"Oh, sure. I don't think you've gone with a girl since Kathy Smetzer in fifth grade!"

"Jesus, you really *have* been keeping up with my life, haven't you," he snarled.

"It's a small town," she answered, lamely.

"Right. Well, for your general fund of information, my dad also had very . . . different ideas about summer camp . . ."

It took a moment for the gist of what he had said to sink in. "Oh, sure, a camp story."

"The camp I go to is a coed combat-training camp in Montana, run by the National Militia Association," he continued, firmly. "Although sex is not specifically encouraged, sex education, as in, 'this is how you do it, boys and girls' is taught. In detail. And there are no restrictions except those relating to consent. Okay?"

"You're kidding."

"You wish. Every year I get through the year's insults, slights and put-downs knowing that the big man on *that* campus is the best shot, the best at hand-to-hand or the most stealthy. And I generally come out somewhere close to the top. And *all* the girls are in *great* shape."

"You're not kidding."

"No."

"So," she snapped, returning to the crux of the argument, "do the girls at that camp say that, say 'gentle like a tit'?"

"Some do," he said, smiling warmly, obviously cueing on a happy memory, "but most say 'gentle like a dick.'"

◆ CHAPTER 34 ◆

Fredericksburg, VA, United States of America, Sol III
0014 EDT October 10ᵗʰ, 2004 AD

Kenallai, *Kessentai Oolt'ondai* of the *Gamalada Oolt' Po'os'* felt that, after conquering five worlds, after so many years of battles that the lowly fiefs bestowed by the Net upon a Scoutmaster were in the final stages of *orna'adar*, he had seen it all.

"Aarnadaha lost *how* many oolt'os?" He snorted in surprise, drifting his *tenar* absently back and forth in the verge of U.S. 1. The crackle of distant riflery echoed from the north and there was a stink of burning on the light wind. The house across the street was a crater that looked as if a giant had scooped it out.

"He has only a single oolt left," related Ardan'aath, his closest Kessentai. They had been associates for many years and he trusted the old oolt'ondai's advice.

Kenallai's crest rose in defiance of this impossibility. "He landed with a full Oolt' Po'os, did he not?"

"Yes, oolt'ondai. And they landed on the richest booty in the region, the storehouses of these thresh. As it is we hold only a smattering of living quarters. The thresh gathered so far barely will meet our needs for the next day. Furthermore, many of the living quarters were destroyed, either before our oolt'os entered or as they entered. Many of them blew up in their muzzles. Little of the thresh permitted itself to be in-gathered and much of the thresh and booty that was left behind had been damaged or destroyed."

"I have to call him." The senior battlemaster fluffed his crest nastily. "That thrice-damned puppy had it coming, pushing us aside as he did in the landing!"

"Tell it to the Net," grunted Ardan'aath. "He was removed from the Path as he exited his Oolt' Po'os. One shot to the crest!"

"What sort of *Alld'nt* planet is this?" Kenallai wondered aloud.

"I may have an answer to that, my edas'antai," answered one of the other God Kings in the ad hoc council of war.

He turned to his eson'antai, Kenallurial. Ardan'aath had yet to trust him. He was only recently raised from scoutmaster to the lowest level of battlemaster and filled with strange new concepts. Where a Kessentai might develop a few close and trusted allies, as Kenallai had with Ardan'aath, the Path was a Path of fury. In the heat the only call to depend upon was the call of the Blood. To trust an edas'antai was one thing, but to gather a group of like-minded Kessentai, to form wide allegiances and to advocate "thinking like the enemy" was not the Way of the Path.

Many of the other battlemasters advocated returning him to scoutmaster status for more seasoning. More time in the forefront of battle, when his weak allegiances disintegrated on him in the heat of edan, when his "allies" strove to be the first on the finest territory, thus increasing the yield of their fiefs, would, in the eyes of the older Kessentai, prove to him the error of his ways.

Nonetheless, whether because of the ties of blood, or because he suspected merit at the core of the young battlemaster's philosophies, Kenallai maintained him at his side.

Other oolt'ondai turned aside as the young battlemaster looked up from his Net interface. "I have found a reference to these thresh."

"I looked for data on this world," snorted Ardan'aath. "There was nothing. Only widespread reports of it as a fecund world of low technology, ripe for the plucking. We are lucky to have arrived ahead of the main waves. We shall gorge ourselves on territory and booty!" There were feral growls from the assembled God Kings.

"Not reports of these thresh from this world. They were reported on two other worlds within the last *tar*. Edas'antai," he continued, touching a control to send the data to his elder's screen, "this report is most disturbing."

The Posleen DataNet was a morass of poorly sorted information. Without a central control, information robots or any correlated indexes, data that was thousands of years old had identical priority with newer, more appropriate data. Navigating its rocks and shoals was a task few of the Kessentai enjoyed and most used it as little as possible. The Net permitted communication within the local area, distributed resources after conquest and occasionally called for reinforcements, but as a source of intelligence most Posleen found it lacking.

"In the last *tar*, thresh similar in appearance have begun to appear in small numbers. On Aradan 5 the invasion has been effectively repulsed."

"What?" scoffed Ardan'aath. "The Po'oslena'ar have never been defeated!"

"They are on Aradan 5," noted Kenallai quietly. "Many have already left. The few that remain are being pushed back day by day."

"Note the data on the physiology," Kenallurial continued. "They are definitely not modifications of the green ones for all they have some superficial similarities, nor of the thin ones. This is a new species and the first I have been able to find in the Histories with the Will to Battle."

The other Kessentai began perusing the data dredged up by the young battlemaster and murmured among themselves.

"But these reports do not mention dwellings of these thresh," noted the Oolt'pos' Kessentai. The brigade commander shook his crest in disturbed fury. The data from the other planets was ominous.

"No edas'antai, they do not."

"Your analysis?"

"I believe we have landed on their homeworld," the young leader caste answered.

"Then we have truly placed our *esonal* in the *grat's* nest," said the brigade commander.

"We shall sweep them aside like *abat*," said Ardan'aath, confidently blowing out a snort that scattered sputum across the grass of the road verge. "What are a few thresh?"

"Ask Aarnadaha," commented Kenallai grimly. "Well, our scouts are pressing forward from the south. Soon we will have them between us, Sammadar and the remainder of Aarnadaha's forces." He looked at the schematic of the Posleen closing in on the defenseless city. The three-dimensional image showed the flecks of located enemy and the relative locations of the Posleen forces. But the image was not a map; there were no symbols for road, buildings or terrain. Like ants, the Posleen depended on the paths of scouts for finding their way around. The best that they could do was vague images garnered during the landing phase that noted built-up areas and heavy defenses. Usually, unless a God King and his sensors were sitting on it, it was unknown land.

"We shall crush them beneath our talons and move on to the greater prize to the north. This is a sideline. Send forces up the greater highway behind the oolt of Aarnadaha," Kenallai continued. "We can thereby lay claim to the fiefs he would have taken. There is great booty to be had there."

"My scouts report that they are about to contact organized forces," noted one of the oolt'ondai.

"Then let us move forward to observe these thresh. And hope that they are not threshkreen."

"Best hope they are not metal threshkreen," muttered Kenallurial, reviewing the data from the world humans called Diess, quietly so that Ardan'aath would not take notice. But Kenallai fluffed his crest in agreement.

"Is this gonna work, Sarge?" asked Lieutenant Kevin Ray, prepping a remaining claymore.

"Well, that depends on what you mean by work, sir," retorted Staff Sergeant Arthur Van Tri. His Eurasian features creased in a grin at the lieutenant who had reported to the unit only the week before. "If you mean save our lives, no. If you mean kill a whole piss-pot full of Posleen, oh yeah."

The group of mixed engineers and civilians huddled in exhaustion on the ground floor of the Fredericksburg Assembly of God Church. A hole had been knocked high up on the wall, through which Staff Sergeant Tri, perched on a ladder, could look from time to time.

"I just hope they don't realize that fence posts usually have fences attached to them," he continued, peering into the darkness through a night-vision scope.

"I just hope they don't realize that fence posts don't usually have bombs attached to their tops," chuckled one of the civilians, playing with his blisters. "I don't give a shit, as long as you engineers get the bunker ready in time."

"Don't worry, Mr. Sunday," said Lieutenant Ray. "We'll get it done. First we dig 'em, then we die in 'em, right Sergeant Tri?"

"That's the *Seabees*, sir," the sergeant sighed.

"Shouldn't we pull back, Sergeant?" continued the lieutenant, unrepentant. "We could set up another ambush." He flourished the claymore. The clacker was set to one side, already hooked up to a detonator.

"Except for that we're about out of demo, sir. We really should have used it on the ambush."

"Hey, Sergeant, it's like in the old days. Always save a round for yourself!"

"*Echo 39, this is Tango 39, over.*"

Sergeant Tri picked up the handset of the radio. The PRC-77 was an antique, but it could still do the job. "*Tango 39, this is Echo 39, over.*"

"*Echo 39, we are about to initiate. Posrep Lafayette and Old Green-wich, over.*"

"*Roger, Tango 39, understand Posrep Lafayette and Old Greenwich, over. Still negative activity at this site.*"

"*Roger, Echo 39. Well, this is Tango 39, saying nice knowing you yah old chink.*"

Sergeant Tri swallowed as his eyes misted. "*Copy that Tango 39. See ya in hell, Hillbilly. This is Echo 39 out.*"

Sergeant Tri wiped his eyes and peeked out through the opening again.

"Looks like I spoke too soon," he said. "Might as well get your weapons ready." Behind him the mixed force gathered up their rifles and started to move towards other slits cut in the wall.

Coming down the road, just as he had been told they would, was a phalanx of trotting centaurs. Their crocodilian heads swayed from side to side as they scanned the nighttime air, scenting for prey and resources. Well back from the front ranks a God King, notable by his larger form and crested head, rode in his saucer-car.

Sergeant Tri was no slouch with an Advanced Infantry Weapon, but there were a couple of serious shooters among the civilians who were headed up to the roof to take care of the God Kings, along with instructions on when not to fire.

Although the Posleen targeting systems could pick out a sniper no matter how well they were hidden, they got overwhelmed in a general melee, so smart snipers waited until forces were fully involved before firing. Sergeant Tri did not actually expect that to be a problem with the first or even second God King because the human force had just spent a productive hour preparing a fiery welcome.

The Jeff Davis Highway ran practically straight as an arrow from where it met with Interstate 95 south of town until it crossed the Rappahanock River north of town. From Walker Grant Middle School to the church was mostly empty fields. The road that had been virtually unadorned was now lined with oak fence posts.

Although a bush-hog was going to be useless to the city defenses, the posthole digger attachment that one of the civilians brought along was just the thing from Sergeant Tri's point of view. While the battalion was actually low on mines, as opposed to plain explosives, there turned out to be a simple remedy. On the way out of town they stopped by Fredericksburg Hardware.

There, not only were their top shooters able to pick up a few choice boxes of rounds, the rest of them were able to load the back of a pickup truck with cases of nails and duct tape.

Wonderful stuff, duct tape. A quick flick of the wrist and a small charge of Composition Four was bound to a box of one hundred nails. Another flick of the wrist and the package was attached to the top of a fence post, a tree, a sign, rope, mailbox, car door, or virtually any other structure. Although most authorities called for the tenpenny nail in a situation like this, Sergeant Tri found them lacking in imagination. While tacking nails will do the job, roofing nails, the kind for putting down roofing tack, with a wide flat top that tended to land point up, that was his favorite. That way, even if the nail failed to hit a Posleen, it was going to be a real pain to the next one to step on it.

"Is this going to slow them down?" asked Big Tom Sunday, gesturing in the general direction of the advancing Posleen. Tri was willing to give him the benefit of the doubt; he was the guy who thought of the posthole digger.

"Nope."

"Then why the hell did we do all this?" Big Tom asked without heat.

"It's not intended to slow these guys down, Mr. Sunday," said Tri, politely, not taking his eyes from the advancing enemy. "It's intended to kill them."

"Oh. And the ones that follow?"

"Well, it'll take them a little more time stepping over and around the piles of bodies."

Big Tom Sunday smiled and headed for the ladder.

Anarlaralta, Scoutmaster of the Po'oslena'ar swiveled his head from side to side as he moved his *tenar* in a random pattern, tiny touches of his talons slipping it from side to side. He had been warned that other groups were taking tremendous casualties but—with the exception of dwellings seeming to spontaneously combust—he had met with little resistance. A few of the thresh had shown fight, but they were rapidly dispatched. A few had even been captured. It was easier to have them transport themselves to the slaughter than to slaughter and carry them. They showed no fight; most seemed to be nestlings. All of that being the case, he was at a loss to explain the bad feeling in his gut. Perhaps he had not yet adjusted to the new thresh.

His oolt now approached a building where his sensors told him a group of thresh huddled, some of them armed. He thought of spreading his oolt to envelop it in its arms but decided not to bother. He would order a few oolt'os forward, to reduce the loss if the building erupted as others had. But for the rest they would remain between the many highway markers to either side.

These thresh certainly had odd habits. On this stretch not only

were there overhead lines with many objects attached, there were
markers every few feet and they were adorned with the same sort
of odd contraption as the overhead lines . . .

Sergeant Tri watched the first few Posleen normals head for the
church door, hefted his AIW, turned and nodded significantly at
Lieutenant Lee.

As Lee moved the jumper cables into contact with the car battery, a fat blue spark jumped through the shadows of the darkened
church.

Simultaneously, to the human ear, over three hundred improvised
claymores detonated over a four-hundred-yard length of road. Each
of the mines spewed out over a hundred missiles traveling much faster
than a bullet. The mines were on both sides of the road, attached
to ropes slung across the road, on the ground, at every level. Thousands of deadly missiles swarmed the road, and the Posleen were torn
to shreds.

The nails tore the centaurs apart, yellow blood flying through the
air along with bits of flesh and bone. Hundreds of rounds of ammunition detonated and the rear-rank God King's saucer was consumed
in silvery fire as its onboard energy cells shattered. In that first violent
instant, over a hundred Posleen were destroyed and the Battle of
Concord Heights was joined.

"Colonel," said the S-3, "Lieutenant Ray reports they are in contact with the Posleen. The front ranks walked right into the ambush
and they finished off the survivors pretty quick, but the rear ranks
are pushing forward hard and he doesn't think he can hold his
position much longer."

"Right. Well." Colonel Robertson looked around at the figures
hurrying in and out of the armory. The pile in the center of the
armory floor was getting to a respectable size. "We need to pull this
operation back. What's the situation at the interstate?"

"The main Posleen force has basically extinguished itself, pun
intended, but reinforcements are moving in from the north and south.
They're going to be able to hold out for about fifteen minutes more."

"It's better than we had any right to expect. And the bunker?"

"Just about loaded."

"Heaven be praised. Okay, tell the sergeant major this is the last
load."

"Who gets to do the honors?"

"I think I'll leave it up to the sergeant major. You and I need to
head into town."

As they walked out the front of the armory for the last time, the colonel turned and looked at the sign just inside the front door and snorted grimly. "I hope that our enemy at least has enough intelligence to begin to recognize insignia."

"Why?" asked the S-3.

The colonel gestured at the two-turreted castle. "Just imagine how much they'll come to hate that crest."

"I will have the get of these *Alld'nt* threshkreen for my supper!" Kenallai stepped mincingly through the offal clogging the road, having abandoned his saucer for a closer look at the carnage. A haze of dust and smoke still hung over the battlefield and the shattered bodies of the Posleen companies were steaming in the cold night air. "What in the name of the nineteen fuscirt did this?"

"This, my eson'antai," said Kenallurial, gesturing into the building that had been the center of the fighting. He pointed to a large green-clad thresh missing most of his foreparts. An explosion had occurred that ate most of the thresh's mass, leaving little to salvage for rations. From the spray of oolt'os outward from the thresh, it was an explosion designed to kill the oolt'os as they tried to come upon him. Kenallurial tore a bit of the green garment away.

"Note the marking. In the reports it stated that all the green- and gray-clad thresh wore markings. Many await deciphering, but this one is recognized. It translates as something like 'leader of military technicians.' There are others that wear rifles that are leaders of warriors."

"Military technicians?" scoffed Ardan'aath. "What rot! What does war have to do with repairmen? War is for the warriors, not skulkers who use explosives for their weapons! Show me the ones with the rifles and I shall bring you their get on my blade!" He spun his saucer and darted off towards his advancing oolt'ondar.

Kenallai took the proffered piece of cloth in his hand, turning the symbol so that the protrusions were upward. "It appears to be a building."

"Yes, eson'antai. It may be their headquarters. And although their purpose includes construction, they also are the primary artists of explosive destruction," he gestured around, "as you can see."

"Well, do these military technicians have a name of their own?"

"Yes, they call them the 'engineers' or 'sappers.'" Kenallurial's muzzle made a hash of the syllables.

"'Sappers.'" Kenallai tasted the word. "I hope that this encounter is the last that we see of them."

✧   ✧   ✧

"Damn," muttered Colonel Robertson under his breath, "it's working."

The tail end of the line of women and children shuffled forward another few steps as he passed under the railroad bridge over Sophia Street.

He could see Lieutenant Young talking earnestly with a civilian construction worker as he neared the pump house. The power to the city had been lost, and thereby the streetlights, but construction Klieg lights had been set up and the bulldozers and earthmovers worked unabated. The hill that had flanked Frederick Street opposite the train station was leveled and the street was practically gone. There was no trace of the buildings that had been there, or of the Montessori School on the corner. In their place the Rappahanock had a new bluff. The area looked as if it had been attacked by a group of giant gophers.

The pump house had been a low concrete building, about fifty feet long by thirty feet wide, surmounted by what appeared to be a twenty-foot-high silo. The lower building had been partially covered by alluvial deposits, but otherwise was protected overhead and on the river side only by its three-foot-thick reinforced concrete walls. A narrow catwalk had led to the door at the top of the silo where there was a room ringed by windows: the "delightful view of the river." To the side of the catwalk had been another, wider, door with a crane mounted above it. It was through this door that replacement equipment was lifted when the pump house was still in operation.

Now fill dirt reached nearly to the door, as load after load of what the military referred to as overburden was dumped onto the lower building. It was in this lower compartment of the bunker that the noncombatants were being secured. The catwalk had been replaced by a wider ramp constructed of structural steel. Colonel Robertson could see military engineers rigging it to be destroyed as the noncombatants shuffled up. At the top, the wall had been ripped out around the door and other engineers and construction workers were driving holes for demolition charges. The line of women and children, their breath steaming in the air, disappeared into the maw of the beast at the top of the ramp.

As Colonel Robertson waited patiently for the young lieutenant to finish with his conference he found himself starting to nod off. He glanced at his watch and realized that they had successfully held the Posleen back for over six hours. On the other hand, with the Posleen across 95, through the defenses on the Jeff Davis and pressing up Tidewater Trail, it was really all over but the shouting.

Lieutenant Young turned away from the construction worker and nearly walked into the colonel. When the lieutenant finally focused on the obstacle he swayed for a moment and snapped off a salute. Sometime during the hellish evening he had lost his glasses and peered at his superior owlishly.

"Good evening, sir." He looked around and swayed again in fatigue. "I am pleased to report that we have sufficient room for all the remaining women and children." He looked at the line of crying children and worn women who were all that remained of the Fredericksburg noncombatants.

Only hours ago they had been as relatively carefree as any group of people could be in the face of an impending invasion: middleclass matrons and their children, the flower of American suburbia. Now they shivered in the freezing dark as predatory aliens closed in on either side and only a forlorn hope stood between them and an end in the belly of the beast. "This had better work."

"It will," the colonel assured the plan's developer. He had his own dark thoughts about the likelihood, but it was far too late to voice them. And when it came down to cases it was not a choice between this plan and a better one, but a choice between this plan and nothing.

"Well, even if it doesn't, sir, they'll never know."

"You're going to Hiberzine all of them?"

"All except the last few coherent mothers, sir. In the unlikely event that something goes wrong that is fixable, it would be a hell of a note to have the whole group die because nobody was awake to fix it."

"Like a leak or a fire or something?"

"Yeah, or somebody having an allergic reaction, whatever. It just seemed like a good idea. Sir," he added belatedly.

"I think at this point we can more or less dispense with military courtesy, Kenny. Aren't they going to use up too much air? I thought that would be a limiting factor."

"Well, the Public Safety folks and Quarles Gas came through again. They each had some CO_2 scrubbers for work in confined spaces. So, anyway, the bunker will be outfitted with sufficient power and light for a two-week stay, at which point the sentry mothers will be instructed to put themselves under and hope for the best. If they're still alive at that point the Posleen will not have found them, which is good, but on the other hand neither did the Army so it would be a wash."

"Sir," said Colonel Robertson's radio operator, "the XO."

"*Uniform 51, this is Uniform 82-actual, over.*"

"*This is Uniform 51-actual, over.*"

"*Uniform 51, we have penetration to Sunken Road and Kenmore House. Estimate old town entry in five, say again, five minutes. Over.*"

"*Roger, Uniform 82. Am with Uniform 49 at Point Delta. Plan Jackson is nearly complete. Coordinate with . . .*" His mind blanked on the call sign for Charlie company. "*Coordinate with Charlie 6, over.*"

"*Roger, Uniform 51. This is Uniform 82.*" There was a pause then the radio crackled one last time. "*Nice knowing you, Frank.*"

"*Same here, Ricky. God will surely know his own.*"

"*Roger that. Out here.*"

Colonel Robertson handed the mike to the RTO, swallowed and cleared his throat. "Despite all your good work, we need to get a move on," he said, gesturing at the dwindling line.

"Yes, sir, I heard. I'm going to go coordinate some more overburden, but if you want to go chivvy some civvies, well, we work for you."

The colonel chuckled at the weak joke. "I wish we could get some support, any support. Any distraction right now would be a good one."

❖ CHAPTER 35 ❖

"All right, here's the plan, such as it is," said Lieutenant Colonel Augusta Sherman, commander of the Twenty-Second Tactical Fighter Squadron. The squadron ready room at Andrews Air Force Base was heavily soundproofed. The soundproofing was legacy of the days when fighters and supply aircraft thundered into the skies; the padded walls reduced the thunder to a dull rumble. In the face of the grounding of aircraft worldwide it created an eerie silence into which the squadron commander's soprano voice dropped like pebbles in a tomb.

"We know that the Posties are in and around Fredericksburg," she continued. "But we don't have a hard fix on numbers, depth, locations or any other damn intel. Army AirCav Kiowas have fixed a route in that is out of sight of any of the landers by sneaking along with their sensor masts just above the trees. In case you need a reminder, flying in sight of landers is a definite no-no."

She pointed to the snaking course drawn in on the map. "It's pretty close to following the Rappahanock River. But just north of Fort A.P. Hill they ran into solid Posleen forces and really got mauled by the God King's automatic targeting systems."

She looked around the ready room at the group of blue-suited squadron pilots. Until the coming of the Galactics, American military hardware was the crème de la crème and the F-22E was the cutting edge. But with the coming of the Galactics and the Fleet Fighter Force the cream of the world's fighter pilots was sucked off into space. So many fighters were needed for the fleet that virtually

279

anyone with a background in flying or even a strong aptitude was offered a slot.

What was left to fly the hottest plane ever developed through purely Terran technology was a ragbag group of relative losers. There was Kerman, who had his flight license suspended after putting his crop duster into a house then registering a blood alcohol level of .25. The investigator had it retaken because it seemed an impossibility anyone could fly with that much blood in his alcohol. There was Lieutenant Wordly, who spent as much time holding on to a puke bag as he did the stick, Jefferson Washington Jones, plane lover, GED graduate, a functional illiterate until he was twenty-five, whose first solo, at the age of fifty-seven, was in a jet trainer, and all the others.

And there was one antiquated squadron commander who got such a severe case of agoraphobia after one trip out of the atmosphere she could no longer fly above two thousand feet. *It's not the height, General, it's the horizon.*

On the other hand, they had a plane that practically flew itself and every single pilot was bound and determined to do the best job they possibly could.

"They tried sending in Predator drones, but they got mauled too. The powers-that-be hope that the combination of Terran stealth and high speeds will give us some limited survivability. It's really the only reason they produced the Echo, for a situation just like this."

She took a sip of coffee to give an appearance of calm and took another look around the room. Most of the pilots were simply listening, taking it all in. There would be hardly time to breathe on a mission like this one, much less read notes. And the whole mission would be programmed into their birds. This was just so the pilots had some idea what was happening when they had to change the plan. Kerman picked up the sheet of paper in front of him and started to fold it, whistling quietly through his teeth.

"We're going in Nap-Of-The-Earth—sorry Wordly," she said in an aside that produced general chuckles. "Set your terrain-following gear to HARD. And we'll go in one at a time. When the point bird is lost the next in line will follow. Hopefully they will be able to avoid whatever took him out. The alternative, throwing everyone in en masse, is suicide. None of the data we have indicates that we can overwhelm the Posleen systems."

Augusta was getting distracted by Kerman. Whatever the origami was that he was working on, the sound of the folding was interspersed across her words. And she was trying in the back of her mind to remember what the song was that he was whistling. She thought she recognized it, but she couldn't figure out from where.

"Eventually we are going to get a complete look at the Posleen-controlled area or we'll run out of planes, take your pick. We'll be continuously uplinking the take from all of our sensors, but we are going in black otherwise. We'll have to depend on our low-light gear and IR lidar for terrain avoidance and data. I realize how badly the Army needs intel, but the only way to get it is if we can survive the penetration." There was a snort of disbelief at this last suggestion. She thought it was Kerman, who seemed to have almost completed his complicated origami.

Augusta agreed that surviving this mission would be unlikely. However, they had all signed on the dotted line and raised their hands to swear. She still intended to give them a chance to back out.

"Once we are in the basket, into the actual Fredericksburg area, I intend to go full active so we can get the max information possible." There had been some fidgeting and quiet conversation before she said that. When the words were said, the room dropped to total silence.

"Because of the threat and the fact that we are forced to go active on sensors, I personally do not expect to come back. Given that fact, anyone who wants to bow out can do so." She paused and waited for someone to get to their feet. Surprisingly, nobody did. She looked pointedly at Kerman but the older pilot just smiled quietly and kept whistling.

"Okay, with the exception of the first run, we'll draw lots for the order. Oh, and we're going in loaded for ground attack. If you find a juicy target, there's no reason not to pickle the bastard."

"So, who takes the first run?" asked Kerman, slipping on a set of jet-black aviator's shades and popping the origami to full size with a flick of the wrist. He obviously felt that as the aviator with the most experience at this sort of flying it should be him.

"Who do you think, Captain Kerman?"

When the last lingering pilot had quit the room, the origami of a mushroom cloud was left to flutter in the breeze from the air-conditioning.

At over twelve-hundred knots the darkened trees to either side of the river were a blur of gray, even when she was fully conscious. With a setting of HARD on the terrain-following gear, the plane was no longer adjusting itself for human physiology. The only thing that mattered to it was the plane's survivability. Between thrust-vector technology, super-cruise ability and the craft's robust airframe design Colonel Sherman was taking regular hits of over sixteen Gs.

Between her gray- and red-outs she could see bars of silver and red flashing by on either side. At first she put it down to optical illusions from the pounding she was taking, but then she realized what it really was.

"*Base, this is Tigershark 1,*" she gasped. "*Are you copying this fire, over?*"

"*Roger, Tigershark 1. You hanging in there?*"

"*Negative, Base, I'm fading in and oooooooh shiiit.*" She broke off.

"*Sorry, Base,*" she continued after a moment. "*There was a lift by Rufin's Pond.*"

"*Hang in there, Tigershark. You're beyond where the Kiowas took it in the ass.*"

"*Roger, Base. Fire picking up now, there's . . . damn.*" She tapped a command into the low-light TV camera. "*There's Posleen packed onto 17 headed into town. Fredericksburg must still be holding out.*"

The TV revealed masses of the centaurs headed north on U.S. 17 in brief flashes through the trees. The God King's systems were thwarted by the same trees; the plasma, flechettes and lasers attenuated just enough that the Peregrine continued its remarkable survival.

"*Coming up on Fredericksburg, now,*" she continued, pointing the camera forward again. "*Got some tracers, they must still be fighting in there. I'm gonna give them a little room. Don't want to kill anybody with the sonic boom.*" She touched a series of controls and the plane made a hard bank across the Posleen mass on 17. To survive the moment, the bank took her to over twenty Gs and she blacked out despite crunching as hard as she could. The blackout was only momentary, nor did she succumb to the complete loss of blood to the brain that pilots call the "funky chicken." She was back in action in moments. In that time, however, she had flashed across over three miles and was coming up on Concord Heights too fast to target the next likely attack point.

"*They're solid on U.S. 1, too,*" she continued as she recovered. "I guess they're pressing them back into town. Heading for the I-95 interchange and going active now."

It was one of the few required tasks laid on the mission, and one she was certain was going to be her last. Once she crossed into the interchange of I-95 and VA 3 she would be in the open, radiating in multiple spectrums, and that was a deathtrap. She finally understood how the Japanese kamikazes felt. She made a series of adjustments to the weapons controls.

The F-22E Peregrine variant hosted a number of instruments the original F-22 designers would never expect would someday be standard equipment. The plane was originally conceived and designed, in the days of the Global Positioning System, as an air superiority fighter. If there was a ground autotargeting system to be installed, it would naturally be based on the GPS.

However, since the designers modifying the F-22 into a ground-attack variant recognized that there were not going to be any satellites, period, they had to come up with other measures. Eventually they fell back on three old but proven technologies.

First, the Peregrine could fix its position fairly well on the basis of inertial guidance. Given that it knew where it took off from, sensitive devices measured every direction vector on the craft and, on the basis of calculating all of those various vectors, could determine its current location with fair accuracy. It was '60s technology, but with more sophisticated computers, software and sensors, its degree of accuracy far exceeded any previous system. However, the farther the plane went from its starting point, called an IP, the larger the degree of inaccuracy. This was especially true when the plane was performing excessive maneuvers such as max thrusters on a HARD terrain setting.

Second, the plane could "look" at the terrain and match it to a computerized map in its memory. A system originally developed for the much slower Tomahawk cruise missile, with modern computers, radar and software it was more than capable of taking terrain reads at twelve hundred knots. The terrain reads were primarily used to adjust the data from the inertial guidance system, correcting it as it got farther and farther off baseline. Thus, if the terrain was good the inertial guidance became much more accurate.

Last, the plane could fix its position in two dimensions quite well off LORAN radio direction finding.

So when Colonel Sherman programmed all of her cluster bombs to land just east of the 95/3 interchange, she could be fairly certain that that was where they were going to land. All she had to do was live long enough to give the drop command. She had to ensure that the CBU-58s would land on Posleen and not human defenders.

The plane made a hard jink to the left and dropped as a huge explosion occurred behind her and to the right. Slapped by the shockwave, she at first thought she had dropped her load early and looked in her rearview at the wrong moment. As she snapped her head back to the front she got tone just as the Peregrine cleared the woods west of Fredericksburg.

The area in and around the interchange was a seething mass of Posleen. Forces driving from the north and south had met at the interchange and tens of thousands of them were creating a sea of alien centaurs in their haste to enter the city before it could be fully sacked. But that same pileup made for thousands of God Kings and they all swiveled towards the target as Colonel Sherman's fighter rocketed fully into the open.

Before her thumb could complete the fractional movement to the firing button, hundreds of lasers and plasma cannon shredded her aircraft. The high-tech fighter came apart in a shower of carbon fibers, jet fuel and rocking explosions, but before those cannons and lasers tattered her aircraft the last burst of data from her sensor rig, video, radar and all, was received by the ground controller.

"That's a hard target for Showboat, sir," said the technician, stabbing the monitor with her finger in eagerness.

"Concur," said the ANGLICO captain, looking over her shoulder. "Call 'em up. Tell 'em to give it all they've got; there's no humans in that mass."

"Fire mission, continuous!"

With the setting of the sun, the wind had died and the Potomac River was as still as a pond. The ship had already dropped its anchors to hold it in place against the slight current and the huge guns now swiveled westward in their turrets.

"Load M-One-Four-Four!"

Doors opened in the side of turrets and the long green rounds slid across the compartment, up the carriage and into the breeches.

"Elevation twelve-fifty, five bags."

The tubes slowly elevated as teenage seamen and women hurled the heavy bags of powder onto the rammers, doing the same job their great-grandfathers had done over sixty years before. With a sussurant hush the fifty-pound bags were shoved up behind the antipersonnel cluster rounds.

"Warning Light is ON!"

Throughout the ship sailors opened their mouths and clamped hands over ears already stuffed with earplugs.

"Fire!"

And the newly refurbished USS *North Carolina,* one of the seven remaining battleships in the world—pulled from her berth in Wilmington where she had spent nearly fifty years as a state monument—shivered as flame lanced from her sixteen-inch guns for the first time in over sixty years.

◆ CHAPTER 36 ◆

Fredericksburg, VA, United States of America, Sol III
0456 EDT October 10th, 2004 AD

"Jesus Christ!" Lieutenant Young shouted, clamping his hands over his ears, "what the fuck was that?!"

"Had to be one of the new Peregrines to survive this far in," Colonel Robertson surmised, shaking his head to clear the ringing. Just when his hearing was getting back to normal from the noise of landing, the human fighter had slammed it again. "It was definitely a jet."

The mothers, intent on getting into shelter, paid little or no attention to the cries of their children as they carried them, with the help of the many defenders who had gathered in the area, up the ramp to safety. There were fewer than fifty to go, but the line had started to slow.

Lieutenant Young was peering past the Klieg lights in the direction the fighter went when there was a tremendous explosion to the west. Again the group was rocked by a pressure wave as a huge fireball climbed above the trees in the distance. For a moment the city was lit as if it were day, then the magenta and orange flash faded. A split second later there was a second, fairly anticlimactic, explosion to the northwest.

"Well, there goes the fighter," said Lieutenant Young. "So much for support."

"I think that first one was the armory," Colonel Robertson corrected. "The second was probably the fighter. But if he was running a direct feed, we might get some artillery. Depending on how far out the Posleen go, One-Five-Five might reach. And there might be more fighters, there's a whole squadron up at Andrews."

"I don't think they're going to slow them down, though," the lieutenant commented grimly.

"No, probably not," the commander agreed. His tone was fairly philosophical. His unit had done its job and more. When he died he would know that no one could have done more. It was a form of peace. "I think I will go chivvy some civvies."

"Okay, sir. I think I'll head over to the Executive Building and see how that's going."

"Good luck, Lieutenant."

The young officer straightened up and snapped a parade ground salute. The old commander solemnly returned it. Without another word they turned away, each in the direction they felt that duty called them.

Ted Kendall found himself, unfamiliar rifle in hand, in a line of figures shuffling past the Executive Building. Led by a tough old bird from the National Guard armory, they were headed towards the sounds of rifle fire to try to slow down the Posleen. It was their last detail, having spent the previous three hours working on the bunker being prepared for the women and children. He stopped when he saw a familiar figure hunched over a large piece of banner paper.

"Morgen, honey," he rasped, his voice gone from passing commands in the construction around the bunker, "what do you think you're doing?"

"I'm making a sign." Morgen Bredell had been in one cheerleading or pep squad or another since she was eight. She knew she was not as brilliant as she was good-looking, but if there was one thing she could get straight, come hell or high water, it was making a sign out of banner paper and paint. She could even paint a picture, after a fashion. She reached for the Red Brick color as she continued: "When the Posties get here, I think they should have a sign. Don't you?" She started crying as she slowly dabbed in a building on the banner paper.

"Sure, honey, sure," he comforted. "I love you, Morgen."

"I love you too, Ted. Sorry about the fight."

"Yeah, me too, honey. Good luck."

"Yeah." She did not look up. "You too."

"Yeah." He shook his head and hurried to catch up with the last platoon of the militia reserve.

"This is insane," Wendy muttered as they lifted another piece of antique furniture onto the pile under the glassless window.

"Death is lighter than a feather, duty is heavier than furniture," misquoted Tommy, stepping back and dusting his hands off.

"Would you quit with the Zen quotes, already," she snapped.

"Well, you could just blow your brains out and be done with it," he answered serenely. He gestured at the pistol. "That'll do the job nicely."

"What? You want me to kill myself?" she retorted.

"No, I want you to be as happy as you can be in what are probably your last few minutes of life," he answered with a grim smile. "What's the point of getting angry? It just reduces the quality even further."

"Sorry, but I'm not even completely through the denial stage, okay?"

"It's not upsetting me, it's upsetting you. What we have here is a case of pronoun trouble."

"This is a great way to spend the last hour of life," she continued, pulling over a table to lean against as she fired. "Not. Besides, the old thing about, 'you don't want to die a virgin, do you?' keeps running through my head."

He nodded his head, putting a pillow on a table of his own then stopped. "Hold it, does that mean ... ?"

"Yep."

"You're kidding."

"Nope."

"What about ... ?"

"The whole football squad?"

"Yeah. And ... ?"

"Half the other guys in school?"

"Yeah."

"None of them wanted to admit to the rest that I was a tease."

"*Really?*" he asked and guffawed.

"Fuck you. I *wasn't* a tease. I told them all up front that I wasn't that kind of girl. Most of 'em figured they could change my mind, but they were wrong. Now I wish I hadn't held out."

"Well," said Tommy, setting up a command-detonated claymore by the door, "I'd love to help you out and all, but all things considered I think we should concentrate on what we're doing."

"Yeah, what are you doing?" she asked, placing her Galil on the table, pointed out the window.

"Well, the plan is we fire a few rounds from here for glory and boogie out the back door, run into Alesia's and get to our firing point there, right?"

"Right."

"The problem is, I don't think we'll have enough time to get in position in Alesia's. We need something to slow the horses down. Voilà, the claymore. It's a command-detonated mine that can be pointed at the enemy. Then when you're ready to blow it," he pulled the clacker out of his cargo pocket, "you hook this up, clack it three times and BOOM!"

"Oh, okay. Then when are we going to blow it up?"

"As we enter Alesia's. I'll run the detonator line back there and as we run through the door I'll set it off. That should slow them down a few seconds at least. Then we get into position, fire a few more rounds for glory, run down to the basement and hide in the tunnel. With any luck they'll lose the trail when I detonate the other claymore I set up in Alesia's."

"Why do you clack it three times?" she asked, holding out her hand for the device.

"Just to be sure," he said, handing it over and looking out the window.

"Okay, so the wire . . ." There was a sudden massive boom and both of the teenagers slapped hands over their ears moments too late.

"Fuckin' 'ell!" shouted Tommy as a second and third massive explosion erupted.

"What was that?" shouted Wendy through the ringing in her ears.

"The first thing was a sonic boom, a jet, had to be a Peregrine . . ."

"A what?"

"A ground-attack version of the Rapier Stealth Fighter."

"Oh," she said, understanding not a word of the explanation.

"The other two, I don't know what they were."

"Did they blow up the Executive Building already?"

"No. If we're above ground when that goes up we won't have to worry about wondering what the sound was. We'll be dead. And those explosions came from the wrong direction. Actually, one of them was probably the fighter eating a plasma round."

"Okay. If they got a fighter in here, does that mean help might be on the way?"

"No. The reason I think it was an F-22 is that's the only thing that might have survived to get this far. The Posleen are murder on aircraft."

"Oh. Damn."

"Yeah." He looked out the window. "So now we wait. It's supposed to be the worst part."

"Even worse than getting wounded? That's what really scares me."

"Yeah, me too."

"You? You're not scared of anything."

"Yeah, I am. I'm scared of being just bad enough wounded that I'm conscious when the horses get to me. That or being captured alive. You heard about their pens?"

"Yeah. That scares me too." She got a thoughtful look on her face. "Umm . . ."

"Yeah. No problem."

"You know what I was going to say?"

"Well, it was probably going to be that old saw about, 'if they're goin' to take me alive . . . ' And the answer is, 'okay.' "

"Okay. Thanks. . . . What about you?"

"I'd appreciate it," he said and paused. "Oh, my," he said mildly.

"What?" she started and then she heard it approaching.

The sound was a freight train of the gods, tearing the firmament asunder with its roar. All nine of the sixteen-inch, two-ton rounds rumbled over the town with a thunder to drown the Hellbound Train. The culmination was a relatively anticlimactic sound like millions of firecrackers in the direction of the distant mall.

"Fuckin' A!" shouted Tommy, "ICM!"

"What?"

As the Volkswagen-sized shells rumbled over the town, their nose cones began to open and release their submunitions. Each submunition, about the size and shape of a softball, was an onion of destruction. Surrounding the central ball of explosive was layer after layer of notched steel wire and white phosphorus. As the munitions spun gently through the air, a cocking mechanism was engaged by the inertial force. When the cocking mechanism reached a certain point, after some seven hundred spins, the weapon was armed. A moment after impact, the hammer released.

As the bomblets arrived in fan-shaped sprays they first bounced back into the air then detonated individually, giving the weapon its characteristic firecracker sound. Across the length and breadth of the highway interchange, the ground flashed white.

The weapons were designed to detonate at head height on a person, so across the mass of Posleen thousands of grenades began to explode. The explosions hurled the centaurs aside, tearing their yellow bodies asunder, but the worst effect was from the shrapnel. Each bomblet released thousands of tiny bits of metal, each traveling faster than a bullet and along with these bits of shrapnel traveled burning white phosphorus.

The phosphorus and steel wire smashed into the bodies of centaurs throughout the Posleen swarm with terrific effect. Thousands of the Posleen normals were killed, along with their God King commanders, as they drove forward towards the beleaguered defenders of Fredericksburg. Those that were not killed outright were horribly wounded by flying steel and the phosphorus that refused to extinguish even after penetrating the bodies.

The first salvo eliminated the last remnant of Aarnadaha's brigade, which had swept across the mall area only to be decimated at the I-95 interchange. They had paused, fatally, to regroup in the shadow of the melted Quarles Gas truck and were swept away on the tides of destruction. And another salvo followed, and another.

"What are those?" Chief Wilson asked Charlie company's first sergeant, pulling back her Nomex head cover to hear better.

"Artillery," answered the first sergeant, not looking up from the circuit he was installing. "What I don't know is where the hell it could be coming from. And it's big, too. At least as big as one-five-five, sounds like larger."

"It is," said Lieutenant Young, joining the conversation as he arrived from the bunker. "I think it's one of those converted battlewagons they refurbished."

"Damn," laughed the NCO, "with fuckin' sixteen-inch ICM, those Posties are gonna be Post Toasties."

"Yeah," smiled Lieutenant Young grimly, "between this an' that, these fuckers are at least gonna know they've been kissed!"

"Change of mission, boyos," said Captain Kerman over the squadron channel. "Fredericksburg is still holding out. We're going to be going in as ground support, adding our weight to the *North Carolina*'s broadside. In addition, set your ground support radios to settings 96-35 and 98-47. Those are the ground support settings for the engineer unit in Fredericksburg. They may try to contact us. If they come over the radio, don't try to respond, we won't have time, just let it uplink.

"One of the reasons for this strike is to try to get more targeting data. We don't know exactly where the Posties end and the humans start, so we're going to continue to pound the interchange. The battleship has to have had an effect by now, so we might survive the encounter. If you do, return to base for bullets and gas.

"Your flight paths are on your computer; modify them as you see fit." He paused, searching for something to say as the squadron banked out of its figure-eight pattern and lined up to face the embattled city.

"Sir," interjected Lieutenant Wordly, "what about straying into one of the sixteen-inchers. Shouldn't we avoid their path?"

Kerman blanked for a moment on how to answer the question. "I tell you what, Lieutenant. If you run into one of those shells, you may officially complain about having a bad day." There were actually a few chuckles transmitted over the frequency-hopping radios.

"Well," he concluded, "I guess it's time to go back to historic Fredericksburg."

◆ CHAPTER 37 ◆

Fredericksburg, VA, United States of America, Sol III
0524 EDT October 10th, 2004 AD

"Major, they're across the obstacles on Sunken Road," said the civilian runner, a well-set-up football type with blisters on his hands and blood from a head wound dripping down his sweat-streaked face.

Major Witherspoon looked at the dead and wounded piled throughout the Presbyterian church. The dead were rapidly cooling in the unheated vestibule as medics pointlessly worked to repair the wounded. Then he looked through the broken windows to the west. There the inexorable tide of centaurs was clearly visible, pushing through the piles of demolished trucks and cars at Williams and Washington. A rolled-over gas truck—converted to a suicide bomb by the driver—gave its last spiteful luminance to the scene.

"God," he chuckled, "I love it when a plan comes together. Okay," he continued, turning to the now-veteran soldier, "tell First platoon and the militia to pull back and head to the south. We don't want fire directed at the Executive Building. As of now they are detached to whatever means they want to use, just don't get between the Posleen and the Exec. Same general orders to the Second and Third, but tell them to pull straight back."

"Yes, sir." The private now had tears mingled with the blood on his face. "I wish we could do more."

"When you do the best you can, there isn't any more to do, son. We held them through the night; held them longer than the expedition on Diess. You should only have regrets if you have not given your all."

"Yes, sir."

"Good luck."

"Yes, sir." Then Ted Kendall hoisted his AIW, and trotted off into the darkness.

"Ma'am," said Colonel Robertson, proffering a bundle to the last mother entering the bunker. "I'd like you to take this in there with you. When you get your place, just set it down and don't tamper with it. It's booby trapped in case the Posleen try to open it, but it won't injure anything outside the box if it goes off."

Shari looked at the bundle in bemusement, wondering how to juggle it while carrying Kelly.

"I'll take it down with her, sir," said the fireman who was carrying Billy. "And make sure it gets in a secure place."

"It's a record of the defense and the unit's colors. You know, the Flag?"

The fireman nodded, eyes misting slightly, "Yes, sir."

Shari nodded as well, " 'At the twilight's last gleaming,' right?"

"It sounds strange . . ."

"No, it doesn't." She gestured with her chin at the line entering the bunker. "Where else would this happen?"

"Well," said Colonel Robertson, picking up his rifle, "you'd better get down there." He glanced back over his shoulder at a sudden burst of fire due west. "It won't be long, now."

Shari hurried down the steep stairs as best she could. The rungs were pierced steel, but the passage of so many feet had packed the planking with dirt and the steps were slick with mud and other debris.

She passed the first level, where the engineers and civilian workers were welding the last steel in place, and ended up on the muddy bottom floor. The concrete walls rose up around her, dripping condensation from the packed humanity's breath, the water sparkling brightly in the massed Klieg lights.

A firewoman took the sleeping baby from her arms and ducked through a low opening. To either side engineers worked feverishly to shore and strengthen the hasty walls that had been faired over the opening. Following the firewoman out of the echoing chamber Shari entered the vault beyond.

On the left-hand side along the wall was a series of closed ports, apparently the pump outlets. The fifty-foot concrete cellar appeared to be a sepulcher, with the women and children under the Hiberzine resembling corpses in the harsh lights of the medics' headlamps. The bodies were piled throughout the long, low-ceilinged room, children as much as possible on the top, but with little other order. The flaccid limbs, slack jaws and staring eyes made Shari balk for a moment, but the fireman just inside the door was used to the reaction and pulled her through, gently but firmly.

"They're just asleep, promise," he said with an automatic grimace he probably thought was a grin. "It's the Hiberzine that makes them look that way."

Shari skittered sideways and pulled Susie back to her as she stared wide-eyed around the apparent tomb.

"Go feel a pulse, if you want," said the fireman who had brought Billy down, carrying his burden to the front corner.

She bent and felt at the neck of the nearest woman, a lady in her forties, well-dressed as if going to work at a bank. After a long and frightening moment when the vein in her neck remained flaccid, there was a single strong pulse then nothing.

"It works," said the firewoman who preceded her. She gently pulled the protesting Susie away and gracefully put her under; the motion was as automatic as breathing by this point. "Be glad for it."

"Carrie," said the fireman at the door, holding out his arms.

The firewoman wrapped her arms around her compatriot and slapped him on the back. "Sorry, man."

"Hey, just make more good babies, okay?"

"Yeah. Do good."

"Yeah." The fireman ducked through the low opening and was gone.

Carrie repeated the pantomime with the other fireman, then a civilian in a hard hat propped up a steel plate and with a last spiteful burst of an arc welder, the two women were alone among the piled bodies.

"Well," the firewoman said, "it looks like you drew the short straw."

"What?" said Shari, looking for a place to lie down that was not on a body part.

"They decided that there needed to be a few people awake on each level. You're the last one in and I've got a ten-year-old somewhere back there." She gestured towards the rear of the pile of bodies. "So we get the pleasure of waiting to see who finds us first." Beyond the wall a sound like rain on a roof announced the first load of dirt that would bury them alive.

As a burst of fire came from just beyond the hill where the engineers' command post was located, Wendy became aware of what Tommy was whistling under his breath. Then she recognized it as a current pop hit. The singer who had popularized the lyrics was considered to be going through a mid-life crisis and the song was a cool, subtle composition about her relationship with a man young enough to be her son.

The diva was not particularly exhibitionistic so the lyrics were subtle double entendres. The substance of the aria was, however, clear.

"Do you boys ever think of anything else?" she asked in exasperation.

"There was a study done back when," Tommy answered calmly, continuing to look towards the sound of distant fire, "where some psychologists determined that a teenage boy thinks about sex every fifteen seconds on average. The old joke is about two kids who hear about this and wonder what they are supposed to think of the other fourteen."

Wendy snorted in response.

"Besides," he continued, "violence and sex are inextricably linked, at least in men. Similar endorphins and hormones are released during violent confrontation and sex, they both use the same areas of the brain, and one has a tendency to trip the other. Tell me you're not thinking about sex more today than normal."

"Okay," she thought about it, "you're right. So why?"

"I don't know, I suppose there are lots of theories. Survival reaction is what the Darwinists say, a counter-reaction to death say the philosophers. A joke by Mother Nature. Take your pick." Another salvo of shells rumbled overhead. "Shit, I wish we could communicate with that battleship."

"Why?"

"We could bring the fire in closer and really get the Posleen slowed down." There was a sudden series of tremendous sonic booms. The room rocked and plaster fell from the damaged ceiling as firecrackers detonated in the distance, intermingled with the sound and glow of exploding aircraft.

"I guess the fighters are back," said Wendy, brushing plaster dust out of her hair.

"*Peregrine squadron, Peregrine squadron, this is Tango Five Uniform Eight Two, over.*"

"*Tigershark Five, go ahead Uniform,*" gasped Captain Jones as his fighter rocketed across the Rappahanock on final. "*Ground Control's listenin'.*"

"*Peregrine squadron. Drop everything you have on the intersection of Williams Street and Kenmore, say again Williams and Kenmore, over.*"

"*Roger, that, Uniform.*" Jones risked a quick glance at his terrain map, but was unable to find the designated intersection. "*That's gotta be for Showboat, we're hot for the interchange.*"

"Roger, Peregrine . . . Good luck."

"Shark Five."

Luck would have no place in this mission if Jefferson Washington Jones had anything to say about it. He might have gotten his high school equivalent when most of the other fighter jocks had been out of college, but he had years of experience with the bad and ugly. Over the years he noticed that there was rarely such a thing as a no-win situation. Sometimes you had to really try, but he had never been in a situation he could not think his way out of and this one was no exception.

The flight paths downloaded to the Peregrines all had the I-95/VA 3 intersection in common, but they continued on to varying other locations from there, as if everyone in the squadron was going to survive. When the mission was changed and the flight paths downloaded, he immediately set to reprogramming.

While his flight path still went over the Posleen positions at the interstate, it deactivated the terrain-following gear and followed a manual profile that was much closer to the mapped terrain. As long as there were no unexpected obstacles the plane would *probably* not fly into the ground and the new flight path had far fewer sight angles than the standard terrain-following path would have taken.

But the computer did not like it one bit.

"Terminal flight path entered," the cockpit voice system chirped. The sexy contralto was standard equipment on all the Rapier series. "Terminal flight path requires command override."

"Override." It might look like suicide to the computer, but that was why there was still a person in the cockpit.

"Confirm flight path data. Press set three times."

He did.

"Last warning, terminal flight path entered. Suicide is a permanent solution to a temporary situation. Are you sure you want this flight path? Press set three times if you do, otherwise press cancel."

He pressed set three more times. Since the cockpit system was not designed to get in the last word, it let him get away with it.

"Like it ain't a suicide mission already."

Passing over the old mill district, he pressed the bomb release button on the joystick. The system was set to "pickle at drop point" as long as the trigger was depressed, so all he had to do was hold on and pray. He thundered across Mary Washington Hospital, sparing a brief thought for the patients as lasers and plasma searched for him to either side and hung on for dear life as the fighter dove for the deck. As he came up on the interchange he suddenly realized that he had failed to compensate for the trees.

The robust stealth plane survived the lurch as its underframe snapped off the last few oak tops surrounding the interchange and then dropped into the open. Around him, as far as he could see in the odd mixture of moonlight and ground fires, the ground bucked and heaved with wounded and dead Posleen.

The centauroid bodies were a carpet of dead and dying, the ground soaked with their fluids. Thousands, tens of thousands of the centaurs had crossed the light-years only to find a final resting place under the hammer of sixteen-inch guns.

"HOOOOWAH!" Kerman shouted over the squadron frequency, as other pilots cheered the sight of the carnage from the battleship's fire.

Jones's fighter immediately performed its programmed hard bank to the north. As its wingtip dipped to within inches of the masses of alien flesh, the weapons bay popped open and deployed a totally unnecessary CBU-52. The cluster bomb opened out almost immediately and scattered two hundred more bomblets across the decimated Posleen adding insult to the masses of injury.

As the plane snapped through a programmed set of low-level evasion maneuvers, Jones could see other flashes to the south that told of squadron mates less fortunate. He finally cleared the treeline on the northeast side of the interchange—chased by a last spiteful burst of laser fire—and returned to terrain-following mode. Now all he had to do was survive the unknown dangers between here and Manassas and he would be home free. Until the next mission.

✦ CHAPTER 38 ✦

The Potomac River, Near Potomac Creek
United States of America, Sol III
0548 EDT October 10th, 2004 AD

Video from the side cameras of all the Peregrines was downloaded to the *North Carolina* along with the orders to fire on the intersection of Williams and Kenmore Streets. The captain ordered the video piped over the closed-circuit TV system, while the tactical officers huddled over their maps.

"Okay, Williams is VA 3, but where in the *hell* is Kenmore?" asked the peeved S-2. Standard tactical maps never denoted street names. This was because calls for fire never used them as references. Except in real life.

"Well, it has to be further into the city," noted the chief gunnery officer. The lieutenant commander turned to his fire direction chief. "Pull the fire in some, and spread it out. Target all the major intersections on the way into town, one battery each."

"Aye, aye." The warrant officer began punching commands into his computer as the officers went back to arguing. Suddenly one of the communications technicians jumped up from her station.

"Sir," she said, coming to attention next to the chief gunnery officer, "permission to speak, sir."

The officer rounded on her testily. "What?"

"I've got a way to get a map of Fredericksburg, maybe, sir."

"How?"

"Off the Internet. I've got a laptop in my locker. I can hook into the Internet and get it."

"Shit," said the S-2, "good idea, why didn't I think of it? Or maybe

297

put in a priority call to the Defense Mapping Agency?" He caught the eye of the communications officer and gestured him over.

"I think Expedia would be faster, sir," said the tech, diffidently.

"Can we still get Internet access?" asked the gunnery officer.

"The Posleen have destroyed all the standard systems in the area around us," said the communications officer, "but we might be able to punch through a short-wave transmission. What's this all about?"

"We desperately need a map," said the gunnery officer. "Your tech here thinks she can get it off the Internet if she can get her laptop and connect to Milnet."

"Okay, girl, good work. Go get your laptop. If the Marines stop you, tell them to call me."

"Yes, sir," said the tech and jogged out the door.

"How are you going to get through?"

"Patch a line to Norfolk. I'll get one of my techs on it."

"Okay."

"You know, we're going to have company before too long," commented the S-2, poring over the updates to the dispositions map. He noted the red marks showing Posleen in close proximity. The Peregrines had come within five miles of the ship on their way out. "That should get interesting."

Like everyone else in the ship, he was becoming bored with the continuous main gun fire. After cheering the first few rounds it just got damn loud and monotonous. He could hardly imagine what it was like for the gunners.

"Briefly," laughed the fire control chief.

"Yeah," noted the gunnery officer, "if only they'd *all* come down to the water and get baptized."

"You wish," said the S-2 with a grim chuckle. The Posleen were not going to like their reception from the *North Carolina*.

It was by far the most monotonous job on the ship. The Electrician Class Two was one of the close-approach lookouts, the eyes and ears of the ship. Since the environment the ship had been refitted for was projected to be extremely hostile, a duty that traditionally involved exposure to salt spray and fresh sea air was now performed in a crowded, air-conditioned compartment.

And instead of hefting a pair of heavy binoculars and spotting the occasional leaping porpoise or diving bird, the technician ceaselessly scanned a bank of twenty monitors hooked to low-light cameras. Five across, four down, numbered sixty through seventy-nine, back and forth, top to bottom, bottom to top, every odd monitor, every even monitor, back and forth, top to bottom, for eight long hours.

Then, after a rest period that seemed shorter and shorter all the time, it was back to scanning monitors, each of which now showed the same monotonous scene of a nighttime Potomac riverbank.

When they first sailed up the river, civilians had poured out of the woods. Some had their own boats, but many just lined the bank hoping to be rescued. They had been picked up by boat parties or the Marines and now huddled in the forecastle awaiting a return to port. But since that first flurry of activity, the shoreline had been undisturbed.

The tech had just picked up a Pepsi and taken a sip when a centaur appeared from the trees lining Marlboro Point Road and immediately opened fire with its shotgun.

The light shot did not even reach the ship—which was moored nearly a mile out in the broad river—and was unnoticed in the next crash of the main guns, but the lookout lurched forward in his station chair and keyed a mike.

"Posleen report, monitor sixty-eight, starboard abeam."

"Posleen report, monitor ninety, port forequarter," sang the soprano of a seawoman handling the portside monitors. The hull rang as the first hypervelocity missile struck the case-hardened steel of the bridge.

"PosRep monitor seventy-three, seventy-five, sixty-nine . . . PosRep all monitors."

"CIC, this is Lookout Control," the chief petty officer managing the compartment called over the intercom, "we have a full court press."

"Go to full auto on all Thermopylaes and Mark 49s, engage the zone defense system," ordered the captain, panning his monitor along the shoreline suddenly packed with Posleen.

The defensive systems officer flipped a cover up and inserted a key in a slot. With a twist of the wrist, the close-in defenses went to fully automatic mode.

The original Close-in Weapons System, codename Phalanx, was developed in the 1970s as a defense against antiship missiles and other close air threats. A sophisticated radar guidance system was coupled with a rapid-firing Gatling gun. The guidance system was mounted atop the gun and the single housing looked for all the world like a little robot. The conical white weapons sprouting up on the decks of Navy ships all over were immediately dubbed "R2D2s." With the transition from a stance of the Navy fighting humans to the Navy fighting Posleen, the weapons appeared, like most of the Navy, to have become obsolete.

However, the same bright boys at Naval Sea Systems Command

who pointed out the relative invulnerability of World War II battle-ships to Posleen ground weapons noted one other point about fighting the Posleen swarms. While the swarms might be difficult for weapons systems to distinguish when they were just moving or standing, once they fired it was a different story entirely. The conical white radome then disappeared, replaced by a heavy-action turret borrowed from the Abrams tank and a turret targeting system borrowed from the Hummer-25. Atop the turret was an infrared spike detector.

As the Posleen God Kings in their saucer-shaped craft came down to the river, they immediately opened fire with their pintle-mounted heavy weapons. The lasers, hypervelocity missiles and plasma rifles scored deep ridges in the battleship's plate, occasionally penetrating to the surface magazines of the vessel's secondary weapons. When they did, thundering explosions would rupture forth from the embattled dreadnought. But with the turn of a key, the tides of war changed sides.

The Thermopylae turrets—so christened for a famous defense in ancient Greece—swiveled outboard and the infrared spike detectors immediately found targets. It was the most robotic of actions, as each weapon noted spikes in their area of responsibility, double checked their safe systems, swiveled in two axes and fired.

Every fifth tungsten ten-millimeter penetrator was a tracer, and the shells were so close together that the tracers seemed one continuous beam, a curved orange laser searching out the impudent fools who had dared to challenge the Navy's battlewagon. The plasma cannons and lasers caused huge thermal blooms each time they fired and the signature was distinctive against the cold night background. Six CIWS on each side locked on to the targets in their area of responsibility and serviced them with the greatest of efficiency.

Each thermal spike was fed back from the CIWS and noted by the onboard defensive computer. It, in turn, swiveled the five-inch secondary cannons outboard and loaded them with canister ammunition. Its algorithm called for a certain number of spikes over a certain vector. At that point there was a seventy-five percent certainty of hitting significant numbers of Posleen normals.

The certainty levels reading was displayed on the defensive systems officer's monitor while the captain was cross-feeding. Each waited for the heavy guns to engage, but the certainty level first rose, then started to fall as the heavy weapons of the God Kings were silenced one by one.

"Turn the certainty to sixty-six percent," said the captain, swinging back and forth in his command chair, arms crossed. He had never agreed with the standard setting on the defensive systems.

"Aye, aye," said a tech, and tapped in the command.

Immediately twelve five-inch double turrets fired canister rounds filled with flechettes along the average bearing-to-target in their area. Then they started to sweep from side to side, pumping out a beehive round every second and a half.

"Lordy," whispered the EL-2 lookout as the centaurs were slaughtered. The dead began to mound in heaps as the turrets swung from side to side, the weapons sweeping across the normals like huge brooms as the Thermopylaes picked off leader after leader.

As the certainty level dropped from lack of targets, each time a God King or one of the HVM-toting normals fired at the armored dreadnought it would be answered by a storm of fire. As trailing God Kings came up, they began to concentrate the fire of their companies on the secondary turrets that were decimating their ranks. However, the dead continued to mound as the Posleen swarmed to the sounds of the guns.

Althanara was only a scoutmaster, but he knew a losing situation when he saw one. The heavy fire from the direction of the water was bad enough, but the description he coaxed out of the net interface was worse. He gestured to his oolt and turned to the rear.

"Where are you going you coward!" shouted Stenarnatta, the battlemaster he had attached himself to. "The Net will cast you down as a Kenstain if you do not return NOW!"

"Kill yourself if you desire," he snarled. "I'm going to attack that thing with a Po'osol!" He gestured at the shotguns that his oolt carried. "These *abat*-spit guns are useless."

"Fine," snarled the battlemaster, "run away. *Kenstain!*"

The scoutmaster turned his back on the soon-to-be-destroyed battlemaster and trotted his company to the rear.

"We're down twenty-five percent on monitors on the port, only fifteen percent to starboard," noted the defensive systems officer. "And we're down twelve percent overall on secondary systems; we took a bunch of casualties in turret five. They're whittling us away and we're taking heavy fire from Fairview Beach since we can't bring the broadside to bear."

"So far so good," said the XO.

"Sir," snapped the regional alert communications technician, "incoming alert from CONARC!"

Althanara double-checked the complicated controls of the ship. Normally the devices were left on automatic, although a few Kessentai did make a study of their use. He, however, was barely out of the nest, on his first conquest. Well, if the Net granted him the victory of this horrible battle then the debts for his entire company might be set aside. He might even be able to get a few decent weapons from this damn battlefield.

He entered the last command into the *Alld'nt* damned equipment and fluffed his crest. "May the demons grant me luck."

High Knob Planetary Defense Center was as open as a strip mine. The plan of construction had all the PDCs opened in a cone from the top down, then the various equipment installed. Last the centers would be covered in concrete, steel and native rock.

But the plan had only gotten as far as installation. When the guns had not arrived in time, it had thrown everything behind. Thus the defense center, which was designed to be complete in another month, was wide open at the top and had only one of its slated nine guns installed.

Since they were relatively defenseless, they were under strict orders not to engage landings. What they were being held back for were the "airmobile" operations the Posleen initiated at seeming random that had repeatedly hammered human forces. It was hoped that engaging a lifting lander would not call down the devastation that had been wreaked on other defense centers around the globe.

Euro Fortress Command, a joint operations unit centered on France and Germany, had chosen to engage the initial landings. The massive European defenses had been created from the fortress lines that both countries had constructed as historical enemies. The line of fortresses, representing tens of millions of man-hours' effort, had been shredded by the first wave of the assault. Whereas during World War I and World War II the fortresses had been proof against days and days of conventional shelling, twenty-kiloton kinetic energy weapons had opened the forts like so many tin cans. Rebuilding the centers would require a miracle from a beneficent deity. China and India had also used their incomplete fortresses to engage the landings, with like results. In one day better than half of the planetary defense centers under construction had been totally destroyed. Only the United States and Japan of the "primary powers" had refrained from engagement.

The control was now going to be loosed. When Posleen landers engaged their antigravity systems, distinct emanations were detectable. The command center for the fortress, which, being on the ground floor, had been completed, detected the emanations of the rising lander immediately.

"Lifting lander, Westmoreland County, Virginia," sang out a female technician, studying the readouts. The final box of the form blinked and cleared. "The box says it's a standard lander, not a command ship."

"Roger," said the operational commander, a bird colonel. He shunted the information to Continental Army Command along with a request to engage. The answer had already been fed into the computers and he got a nearly instantaneous response. "Weapons free. I say again, weapons free."

The one-hundred-millimeter grav-gun was fully automated and required no crew. There was, however, a crew of three detailed to respond to mechanical malfunction or to man it if the central fire control failed. The procurement process had insisted on a backup "local" control system that seemed as useful to most of the personnel assigned as teats on a boar hog. If the central control was out, aiming the weapon was going to be a matter of luck.

The weapon defied most conventional Air Defense Artillery concepts, as could only be expected of something designed to engage space cruisers and not lightly built aircraft. Instead of swiveling gears to track and aim it, the support struts flexed in a sinuous fashion that was mildly nauseating to watch. The struts also were only required to maintain its position against gravity; the grav-drive system had no recoil.

In addition, instead of sending up a hail of exploding "flak" like most antiaircraft weapons, it fired single free-flight bars of depleted uranium, accelerated to .3c in the path up the twenty-meter barrel. One hundred millimeters in diameter and two meters long, the bars would go through a command ship long ways when they hit. Besides the massive kinetic explosion such an impact would entail, as they passed through the atmosphere the bars created a standing relativistic wave in front of them that generated a blast of gamma and X rays sufficient to cook anything in the ships.

However, instead of nine such weapons there was a single gun. And, instead of the fortress being "buttoned up," a mass of concrete and steel, with concentric, compartmentalized defenses and multiple firing points of the main guns, there was sunlight coming in from both directions in the firing area. Both the armored outer door, which should have protected the compartment from impacts on the surface of the fortress, and the armored inner door, which should have protected the compartment from internal blasts, were missing.

Basically, they were naked as a jaybird.

Which was why the three-man crew decided there were better places to be as the gun swiveled and pointed down and to the southeast. The last one out grabbed the helmet for his skin-suit and then pelted after the others. Without his helmet the mass of radiation that was about to be generated would cook his brains.

The lander was currently below the horizon. But the Posleen had never heard of "nap-of-the-earth" flying; hugging the ground made no sense to them. The ship finally crested into view, visible both through the Galactic-supplied sensors and the various radars scattered across the surrounding hills.

"We have lock," stated the control tech. Although there was a manual override, the system was designed to be automated. The tech only need keep his thumb on the firing tab and the weapon system would do all the work. The thumb was currently ready to flip off the safety cover.

"Engage," said the operational commander. The tone was level and disinterested. It was the professional tone of the truly terrified.

The tech flipped up the cover and depressed the firing stud.

The gun gave a final, organic quiver and fired one round.

Althanara had finally cleared the obscuring trees. He began the rotation of the ship to align the main plasma cannon as his secondary weapons opened fire on the Po'osol floating on the water. The great ship was continuing to fire, oblivious. The thresh obviously did not recognize the threat. But as the heavy plasma cannons and lasers of the secondary defenses began tracking across the floating ship it rocked with explosions. Just wait until the antiship HVM was able to target.

"Sir, damage control!" said the damage control officer. "We've lost number three, five and seven turrets. Four of the six Thermopylaes are out and Main Turret C is welded to the deck!"

The captain fanned himself with a clipboard and swore fluently. The temperature in the bridge had risen fifteen degrees in transmitted heat and he could hear the screams of burn victims transmitted through the foot-thick walls of the bridge. "What the *hell* was that?"

"Lander, sir," said the defensive systems officer. He pointed to a screen. "It's up on anti-grav firing on us with its secondaries." As he said it there was another series of wracking explosions punctuated with a roar that tossed the multithousand-ton ship like a terrier.

The captain held onto the arms of his command chair as the ship rocked in the waves it had generated in the explosion. He had felt the distinct *thud!* of the hull hitting the bottom. Which meant it had been driven at least twenty feet downward by the explosion. "*What the hell was that?*"

"We're holed!" said the damage control officer tapping frantically at his keys to get data. "Something punched right through the ship!

We lost number three boiler, number two engine, two five-inch magazines and, Jesus, *sickbay*!"

The captain spun on the defensive systems officer. "Can you see it?"

"Yes, sir," said the officer, pointing at the screen, "but . . ."

"Then *try to hit it!*"

"Yes, sir," said the officer, punching commands as fast as he could type. The remaining Thermopylae began to point skyward as the five-inch turrets followed.

The same communications technician who had found the firing locations on the Internet suddenly lurched to her feet, laptop in hand, and ran to the main-gun control center. Pushing another tech out of the way, she ripped out a standard computer plug and hooked it into her computer. Preempting the displaced technician's station chair she started loading a program.

"Come on, come on, come on you son of a bitch," she chanted. Never had a simple DOS program taken so long to load.

"Yahai!" shouted Althanara, as the ship rocked in the water. Somewhere would be the magazines. Once he hit those it was all over. However, even as the next HVM loaded, the ship began to spit fire back.

"What are you doing, girl?" asked the gunnery officer. He was fairly sure there was a rhyme or reason to the tech's actions, but the kid had taken his main guns off-line. As he asked he saw the repeater panel indicate movement of the guns. "Or should I say, 'Why are you doing it?'" he asked in a deadly voice.

"Trying to save our ass, sir," the tech said in a distracted voice. A solution light blinked on the computer and she hit the enter button. All six remaining main guns of the ship fired at one point in space.

Althanara had just raised his arms in celebration when he realized the fire from the ship was not a palpable hit. He did not, however, have time to panic. Before the thousand-pound shells of the ship had made it halfway to the target, the uranium bar from the distant Planetary Defense Center arrived.

The round penetrated from the bottom of Athanara's ship and exited the top. Along the way it passed through the matter-antimatter converter and the antimatter storage tanks. Puncturing the plasma conduits of the HVM launcher on its way out was merely a formality.

The expanding ball of nuclear fire that had been a lander caught the main-gun rounds in mid-flight and disintegrated them. The shockwave and thermal pulse caught the Posleen along its path and incinerated them as well. From the exterior it was impossible to tell which round had arrived first.

This incident would create a running debate in history. The argument over whether it was the PDC round or those of the battle-ship that had destroyed the lander would be argued from boardroom to bar for years to come. The optimistic assumption was that it was the battleship's guns that had caused the destruction. Medals, com-mendations and lucrative defense contracts would be based on that, false, assumption. That, however, was for the future. The present held only the result of the action. The shockwave that finally reached the battleship.

It was tests of the hydrogen bomb at Bikini Atoll that finally broke the power of the battleship. On that morning of hydrogen fire a fleet of empty ships was sunk by a single weapon. However, the blast from the already depleted lander was far less than the blast from the Bikini Bomb. And the lander was rather farther away.

When the shockwave from the nuclear blast washed across the ship the damage was great but not catastrophic. The wave of fire searched down through the great rents in the fabric of the ship, but was sty-mied by the same blast doors that were containing the flooding water. It exploded a few more exposed magazines, killed a handful of damage control personnel and tore the ship loose from her moorings. But it did not sink her.

Sunk or not, the *North Carolina* was done for the day. One tur-ret welded to the deck, huge gaps torn in her armor, and belching smoke and flame from the punctured engine rooms, she raised her other anchor and turned to the southeast. Let one of the other battlewagons take the position. "Showboat" had some cleaning up to do. The Planetary Defense Centers, however, were still in the midst of it.

Sten'lonoral fluffed his crest. The world below, which was supposed to be of relatively low technology, was aflame with war. The evidence was obvious even from space as flashes of nuclear fire and kinetic bombardment sparked on the surface.

His oolt'ondai was passing over a large sea and coming up on a continent, still in orbit, but descending, when a little-used sensor chimed.

"Antiship surface weapon detected," the androgynous voice stated. "Request permission to engage."

Sten'lonoral leaned forward and inspected the readout. It was so much gibberish but he did not want this supercilious *Alld'nt* piece of crap to know that. "Very well, you have my permission to engage."

The signal was sent to an outer lander with a kinetic energy weapon launcher. The large weapons platform shot the massive hyper-velocity round out like a pumpkin seed and continued on its path.

The kinetic round took a moment to orient itself, nosed over and dove for the planet. The drivers in its body accelerated to a fraction of the speed of light then cut out. At those speeds additional aiming was unnecessary.

"Sir!" shouted a technician, as the round of congratulations swept the PDC. "Incoming K-E-W!" All eyes swung to the sensor screen but that was all they had time for.

The warhead was massive but contained no explosives; all its power was in the kinetic impact. On impact with the base of the bowl, directly above the thinly shielded control center, the potential energy of its descent converted to light and heat.

The fireball was mostly contained by the cone shape that had been carved out of the mountain, so the damage to the surroundings was mitigated. The few watchers had the amazing image of fire gouting out the side of the mountain forever imprinted on their brains, just before the kinetic blast erupted out of the top of the mountain. The mushroom cloud was all that they needed to see to know the fate of the poor souls in the command center.

◆ CHAPTER 39 ◆

**The White House, Washington, DC, United States of America, Sol III
0558 EDT October 10th, 2004** AD

"And the *Missouri* is on the way?" asked the President, shaking his head at the carnage.

"Yes, sir," said the secretary of defense, looking at his briefing papers, "and the *Massachusetts.* The *Missouri* will be on station within two more hours; she's just coming upriver. The *Mass* was steaming near New York City and won't be there for another twelve hours."

"And the Planetary Defense Centers are out of action?"

"Pretty much, Mr. President. We're caught between a rock and a hard place. When there's a take off, we have to engage it. But when we do we lose a PDC. High Knob makes four that we've lost. But if we let the landers move at will, they'll slaughter us."

"What about Fredericksburg?"

The SecDef turned to the High Commander, "And?"

"And they're still holding out, but that won't last long. We've effectively exhausted the Peregrines, so we're about out of reconnaissance assets. No reconnaissance assets mean no calls for fire although we've got some experimental stuff on the way. My guess is that once Fredericksburg is finalized they'll turn outward to the north and south."

"And we won't try to stop them between the James and the Potomac, right?" asked the President of the United States, somewhat bitterly.

"Yes, sir. Fighting them with a battleship is one thing, and even then we saw the sort of damage we can take; the *North Carolina* will be off-line for months. But engaging them in open terrain, with hasty defenses, is something completely different. The forces still are not as ready as I'd like—heck they're not ready, period, not for open field maneuver. Let us pull back behind the terrain defenses, like we planned, and pound them with artillery. That's the way to kill Posleen.

"Now, down in Richmond they're planning a forward firesack. But they have the terrain for it: Washington doesn't. So we pull back behind defenses and let them break their teeth, then we sally and mop them up. I'm glad we reactivated those battlewagons, though," he turned and looked at the video again, "damn me if I'm not."

"What about C-Decs taking off and counterattacking?" asked the President.

"General Horner has released the Planetary Defense Centers to fire on Posleen ships now that the main force is down. The centers are not fully operational, and they only have a few heavy grav-guns each, but they should be able to take out any landers that take off between the mountains and the sea. There's a little curvature problem in Maryland, but I don't think the Posleen will be able to use it effectively. The PDCs are still under strict instructions not to engage actual landings. We don't want them torn up like Europe's."

"Maryland," said the President.

"The Twenty-Ninth's forces got mauled, but Tenth Corps sent an extra division and that should do the job. If not, First Army has already ordered all the East Coast corps to send forces to Virginia. The Posleen in Maryland aren't going anywhere, Mr. President."

"But in Virginia . . ."

"In Virginia we have another problem. Once we concentrate sufficient forces across the Potomac and the James we'll begin to retake Virginia. As I think we've demonstrated, there are two aspects to waging war with artillery when it comes to the Posleen. The first is that you have to see them to kill them. That means that they can see you. If they can see you they can usually kill you. So we need troops in prepared positions to call fire on them. The second is that, given observers, they are extremely *easy* to kill with artillery fire. They are the definition of troops in the open. That is an artilleryman's favorite target. The second point, however, is that you have to be able to see them to kill them, and that means that we eventually will have to advance against them.

"When we do, I want our troops massed and fully prepared, with good artillery coordination in effect. Any harum-scarum attack in the glow of the good work put in by the *North Carolina* would be premature in the extreme, sir. We shouldn't throw away a relative success now."

The President nodded in thought. "Jody," he asked, turning to the press secretary, "what are the networks saying?"

"So far they haven't gotten any reporters into the area so there's not much they can say. There have been some sharp protests about the military not allowing them on the interstates because they've been taken over by the federal government, but so far that hasn't made the news. The only thing they are getting is whatever video we give them from the front."

The President nodded and shifted in his chair as if uncomfortable. He looked at the television again and said: "General Taylor, give me your opinion of the Forward Defense argument."

Taylor froze with his mouth open until he recognized how stupid the expression made him look. In a crystalline moment he saw the future laid out before him and realized that in good conscience, despite the futility, total and complete honesty was the sole option. "I think it's a crock of shit, Mr. President."

"Why?" asked the President, eyes narrowing.

"The proponents ignore every wargame ever played around it. Their contention is that the Posleen can be defeated in decent terrain because it permits maneuver of armored and mechanized forces. But when we've actually gamed it out, the Posleen can move nearly as fast and are more maneuverable than armored or mechanized forces. The Posleen may use primarily unaimed weapons and depend on mass fire, but between the heaviness of their weaponry and the aimed fire of the God Kings, mechanized forces in vehicles within one thousand meters of Posleen are slaughtered.

"If they are out of their vehicles and in prepared positions—not fortresses, just dug in—standard Army units have about a ten-to-one advantage over the Posleen. That is based on game theory and observational evidence from Barwhon.

"However, projections place Posleen forces at over one hundred to one for the total invasion.

"In this case we are talking about the five divisions in northern Virginia that will have time to dig in. Sort of, not well, just foxholes and bunkers and a little concertina. Locally emplaced minefields, some claymores, some Bouncing Bettys and M-833s. A division runs about sixteen thousand troops in its current configuration. About seven thousand of those troops actually fire weapons at the enemy."

"I know all those figures, General," snapped the President.

"Yes, sir, you do, but frankly neither you nor General Olds have done the math."

"I never said I'd spoken to General Olds," the President said.

"No, sir, you didn't; however, he is the most senior proponent of

Forward Defense and he is a player in the Washington scene," the general retorted angrily. "I understand you did consult with him during your election campaign, which, since he was a serving officer, pushed a line that most officers don't prefer to push. Have I made my point, Mr. President?"

"Go on," said the President through clenched teeth.

"Yes, sir. Now, all I ask is that you do the math. If the math works out I will be the most vocal supporter of Forward Defense you ever heard. Are you ready, sir?"

"Don't get pedantic, General."

"Certainly not, Mr. President." The High Commander glared at the Commander in Chief for a long moment. "Here's the numbers. There are five divisions. Five. Give them the absolute benefit of the doubt, all the forces are in place. There are *four million* Posleen. Assume that the majority do not head towards the larger target and turn north; we still can assume that they will split. Can I make that assumption, sir?"

"Yes," answered the President, tightly.

"That is two million Posleen. Fifty-four hundred shooters per division. That includes all the infantry, cav and artillery. Five times fifty-four hundred is twenty-seven thousand. AID, twenty-seven thousand goes into two million how many times?"

"Seventy-four," said the artificial intelligence device supplied to him as a courtesy by the Galactic Federation.

"Every shooter has to kill, not slow, not wound, *kill* seventy-four Posleen for a forward defense plan to work. That won't happen even with massive artillery support; it's just not in the cards. Those Posleen can pin the divisions with a fraction of their force and go around or they can overrun them and keep going.

"If they choose to simply overrun our divisions, by straight math they will lose a quarter of a million troops. That sounds great until you consider that that is about *ten percent* of their forces! If, when, our troops get flanked the defense ratio goes out the window and the Posleen gain a two-to-one advantage *over* our troops, at which point it is all over but the screams."

General Taylor wiped his face for a moment, trying to find an argument, any argument, to stop the insanity he knew was about to occur. "Now if you can tell me how five divisions can stop two million Posleen, I will be happy to give 'cheerful and willing obedience to your orders' that I know are coming. If you can't, all I ask is that you consider the effect that the loss of *eighty thousand* soldiers will have on the American people's morale," he ended quietly.

"Why eighty thousand?" asked the secretary of defense. "You said there were twenty-seven thousand."

"There are sixteen thousand men and women in a division, Mr. Secretary. Given the road network and movement speeds of the divisions versus Posleen movement speeds, I would estimate that eighty to one hundred percent of the corps would be overrun."

"Don't you think you are underplaying the effect of armor and artillery on the Posleen, General?" asked the President. He actually appeared to be listening to General Taylor and considering his arguments. But after nearly a year's experience with the chief executive, Taylor was fairly sure he was not changing his mind.

"The Posleen three millimeter railguns go through Bradleys the long way and about one in ten carry a three millimeter. One in twenty carry an automatic hypervelocity missile launcher, which will take out an Abrams with a frontal hit. While they are 'unaimed,' what the term actually means is that the weapons don't have sights.

"However, the Posleen seem to be naturals at firing from the hip. And don't forget that those numbers discount the God Kings, whose weapons are automatically targeted and frighteningly accurate. They're accurate enough to act as antiaircraft fire against stealth fighters, for God's sake. There will be some five thousand God Kings in that mass. That's nearly a division of God Kings alone. And a God King is worth about five troops even if they are in the defense."

"I thought they dealt with them through sniper fire," commented the secretary of defense.

"That works in an ambush, *sir*, or where there is an intense conflict in limited terrain. But the God Kings are not all stupid. Most of them move in random evasion patterns that are hard as hell to hit and that is a lot of targets for snipers, even four or five at a time. The problem with Posleen is always a situation of target overload."

"Artillery," said the President.

"Probably our best bet," the infuriated general admitted, "but artillery is a wounder not a killer. And the Posleen can take more wounding than humans. I want you to consider something, Mr. President. That video we just watched showed a mass of casualties from the battleship rounds, the most effective weapon we have in our arsenal. AID, have you calculated the casualties visible in the films of the battleship action?"

"Yes."

"How many casualties?"

"Eight thousand, plus or minus four percent."

"And that is what percentage of the total Posleen force?"

"Point one six percent or one point six mils."

"Less than one percent, Mr. President, Mr. Secretary, actually, close to one-tenth of a percent."

He looked at the two civilian controllers of the military and saw their recoil of shock. "Don't look so surprised. We have to do that same thing, kill just as many Posleen, nearly one thousand more times. And the *North Carolina* took a lot of damage even before the lander tore her up. So the question is where are we going to get all the battleships we need!"

"So you're saying that we can't stop them with artillery?" asked the President.

"Sir, every indication is that the Posleen don't retreat or suppress under fire. The only option is to kill them before they overrun you. While artillery reduces their numbers, it can only stop them with masses of firepower that are not realistic in this scenario. What I mean is we don't have that many tubes on hand. The artillery is useful for reducing their numbers. But it does not have the consequential effect that it does with humans. It does not make them stop and hunker down or retreat. They just wade through it, the stupid bastards, and if it kills all but one of them, that stupid bastard is too stupid not to charge the guns anyway.

"Unfortunately, what has generally happened on Barwhon is that artillery fire kills maybe thirty percent of maneuvering Posleen and then the other seventy percent hit the defenses like a tsunami. In this case, that would be, AID?"

"One million, three hundred and seventy two thousand plus or minus six percent assuming recognized ratios for bonding scatter and rear area security."

"How many God Kings?"

"Three thousand four hundred and thirty, plus or minus ten percent."

"Number of Posleen per shooter."

"Fifty-one, plus or minus ten percent."

"This is not like fighting humans, sir," the High Commander concluded. "We need time to create fixed defenses and mass huge amounts of troops. If those troops are forced out of position and have to run, the other problems of training and maintenance come to the fore. If we had the time, the training and the room, I would send out some fast units with fast logistics support and mobile artillery to slow them up. I don't enjoy sitting on my hands. But, as it is, our best bet is to rig the Occoquan, mine the roads and retreat like hell until we have the Potomac between them and us.

"Once we have the whole First Army on the north bank of the Potomac and the Eleventh ACS in place and once we have masses of engineering support with convoys of concertina and cement trucks, we can start moving into northern Virginia again.

"Then we'll use firetraps to reduce their numbers until it is survivable to send in regular forces. We'll put the ACS out front and when they run into really heavy forces they'll backpedal onto fortifications that we'll make as we go.

"That is the plan, sir, and it's a good one. The only sticking point is that we have to lose Arlington Cemetery, but we will by God get it back!" the High Commander ended passionately.

"You're not retreating in Richmond?" asked the secretary of state.

"No, sir, that is a somewhat different scenario," the commander pointed out. His AID helpfully brought up the appropriate map on the wall-sized view-screen. "Very different in fact. Richmond is easier to evacuate across the James; they have fewer people to move and damn near the same roads infrastructure as south D.C. and Arlington. The point that General Keeton is defending has good terrain features and clear lines of retreat. Richmond itself has more in the way of terrain features than Arlington and there are some structures that Richmond has that improve the defense plan. For that matter, the firebase they are building is the nucleus of an outer fort like we intend for Fortress Forward and will hold almost the whole corps artillery and divisional artillery batteries.

"From Libby Hill they can pound the Posleen with relative impunity; the Posleen aren't going to make it up those hills in the face of massed fire. Although Arlington Cemetery offers some of the same benefits it is not as steep a slope and it would take too long to make it that way. Also, the really critical installations are in the areas the Posleen would hold." Taylor shook his head at the thought of trying to hold Arlington.

"I reviewed General Keeton's plan when CONARC announced his support and found it tactically and operationally sound. General Keeton has clearly stated that this is intended to slow the Posleen and he expects to lose Richmond eventually. Really all it is intended to do is give them a serious bloody nose. That being said, using his corps in that manner will have a far greater impact on the Posleen than meeting them in hasty positions in open field combat. The Richmond plan calls for employing fortifications that will stop them physically, leaving the soldiers with nothing to do but kill Posleen. The defenses also create an open and fixed target for massed artillery." He pointed to the appropriate positions on the view-screen, the icon of battalion after battalion lighting as the AID followed the Twelfth Corps forces. "This will have the Posleen in a trap of interlocking fire.

"If they complete all the defenses before the Posleen arrive I suspect that they will take care of the southern force for us. Schockoe Bottom will be the graveyard of the Posleen."

"And there is no way to replicate that in Washington?" asked the secretary of defense.

"Not easily, sir, and not with the same surety. As I said, the only really decent terrain feature in the critical area is Arlington Hill and it has a relatively light slope. Slope is a big factor with the Posleen. Replicating the complete defense is just not on, none of the other features, such as the floodwall, interstate embankment cuts or the valley channels, are replicated."

The President nodded his head when it was clear that General Taylor was done. "General, that is a very well-reasoned presentation."

"And it didn't change your mind one bit, did it, sir?"

"It made me fully aware of the risks, which I admit certain individuals had glossed over. Let me ask you something, since it's unvarnished-truth time. What is your opinion of Generals Simosin and Olds from the point of view of carrying out a Forward Defense of northern Virginia?"

General Taylor looked that one over carefully before he responded. "General Simosin is probably one of the best defensive generals in the business for heavy troops such as Tenth Corps. If we tell him, 'center your defense south of the Potomac' I think he will do as good a job as anyone on earth could. I don't think he's going to come back with much in the way of the corps and I would request that such an order be a written Direction of the President. I don't want to lose him to political splatter when he crawls back with fewer troops than are necessary to bury his dead."

The President took that like a man. "What about losing you to political splatter?"

"If it's a Direction of the President, there's not going to be much splattering on me, especially when you include phrases like, 'against the advice of my most senior military advisors,' " said Taylor with a thin but determined smile. "And frankly I could give a damn. I'm worried about the poor sacrificed bastards in Tenth Corps, not political fallout."

The President's face hardened at the implied insult. "And what about General Olds?"

"Well, if he joggles Arkady's elbow too much I'll send Warrant Kidd up to New York with a direct order to terminate him with prejudice. I am dead serious, Mr. President, pun intended."

The President leaned back in his chair and considered his senior commander with his hand on his chin, forefinger lightly tapping his cheek. "You're really against the Forward Defense, aren't you."

"I think it's a Goddamned nightmare, sir."

The President nodded his head. "Yes, it is, and I appreciate your candor, believe it or not. You maybe got too strong, but that is the vice of your military virtues, General, and I respect those virtues. Now, let me tell you about political fallout, 'splatter' as you call it." The short politician knew better than to try to overawe the general with physical presence. He simply leaned back in his chair, steepled his fingers and fixed the officer with a blue, basilisk stare.

"Political fallout occurs when an administration tells the American public that it is going to throw away the most historic cities in our country for military expediency. Political fallout occurs when the politicians ignore the desires of their constituents for whatever reason seems appropriate at the time. Political fallout occurs when politicians get so wrapped up in listening to their own thoughts, ambiguous polls and advisors that they forget to listen to history. And I intend to do none of those things."

Edwards leaned forward suddenly and tapped the black top of the table. The situation room was absolutely still as he dictated the future of the nation in a few words. "The people in those divisions are American citizens, citizen soldiers. And their families and loved ones are American citizens. And those people sent me a clear and certain mandate to defend the United States with my last breath. And, General, we are going to start right here."

"Yes, sir," answered the general gravely.

"Not because of any political expediency, but because the citizens of the United States want us to defend those cities and towns. And if we do not perform the will of the people, we have failed in our mandate."

"Yes, sir."

"Are you going to carry out these directives to the best of your ability?"

"Yes, Mr. President," answered the High Commander, back straight. "I have always carried out my orders, even when I had clear and strong objections. It is my duty."

"Very well, here is my direction. The United States Ground Forces will defend against Posleen incursions further into northern Virginia. Such defense will take place south of the Potomac, certainly, and all available forces will initially defend in and around the area of Quantico Marine Base. Most of the corps is stationed there so they won't have far to go.

"I will put that in writing and I will address the nation and both read the written directive and present both views as evenly as possible, giving full credence to both views. But in the end, it is my responsibility to call the hard shots. Are you clear on this directive?"

"Yes, sir. What is the primary intent? Beyond the defense of northern Virginia. What is the main target for defense?"

"Don't lose an inch of ground is the idea. The last place to lose is Arlington, but defense is to be as forward as possible given constraints of movement and time. Initial defense by the majority of Tenth Corps will be south of the Occoquan. You are clear on that?"

"Yes, sir, in and around Quantico."

"Very well, General. Winston Churchill once said 'war is too important an endeavor to leave to generals.' I don't completely agree but I do agree that there is a reason for civilian control of the military and it is for reasons like this, not to prevent coups. Good luck, and may God be with us all, especially those poor souls in Fredericksburg."

As the general left the Situation Room, the President glanced at the secretary of defense, who was still fuming. "General Taylor doesn't think much of Forward Defense, does he?"

"No, Mister President, he doesn't," agreed the secretary, with gritted teeth. "I can't believe you let him say those things to you."

Edwards nodded his head. "He's become quite popular. There has been a noticeable turnaround among the forces under his direction."

"So," said the secretary, "what you're saying is we have to put up with his bullshit?"

The President leaned back and gripped the arms of his chair firmly. "What I'm saying is, your friend Olds had better know what he's talking about."

◆ CHAPTER 40 ◆

Fredericksburg, VA, United States of America, Sol III
0614 EDT October 10th, 2004 AD

Another wash of firecrackers slammed into the hill as a barrage of sixteen-inch cluster rounds landed and Tommy picked up his AIW. "Okay, let's go over it one more time."

"We fire a few shots from here," said Wendy, tiredly, "then move back to Alesia's."

"You go first, let me take any of the fire that might come through when we run. I'd trade armor with you, but I don't think you could move fast enough in this."

"Okay." She looked at the shoulder-to-knee padding. "I don't think so either. At Alesia's, we set off the claymore in here." She pointed to the mine set up in the middle of the room pointed at the door. "When they attack Alesia's, we go to the basement, get in the tunnel, pull the safe in front of the hole using the pry bar and set off the claymore in Alesia's when they come through that door."

"Okay. Good enough." A burst of fire came from the machine gun post catty-corner across the intersection from their position. A hail of flechette rounds answered the fire and the wall of the building sparkled in ricochets. The M-60 coughed once, twice, then was permanently stilled by a hypervelocity missile. The kinetic explosion sent a shock wave across the street that hammered the breath from their lungs.

"Oh, God," Wendy coughed on the cloud of dust blasted into the street, pulling the rifle into her shoulder, and placing it on the pillow.

"It's time to dance," whispered Tommy and snuggled the AIW into

318

his shoulder. He switched to grenade launcher and took up slack on the trigger.

When the first rank of the Posleen phalanx entered the intersection of Charles and George Streets it was met with a storm of fire. Wendy fired a series of laser-aimed bursts that were surprisingly accurate for a beginner while across the street a pair of youth militia fired rapid individual rounds from their vintage M-14s. The real killers, though, were the five 20mm grenade rounds that Tommy Sunday used to fill the intersection with dead Posleen. By walking the fire rapidly from one side of narrow George Street to the other, he created a flesh barrier of dead and wounded centaurs that, for a moment, balked their trailing fellows. Unfortunately, the second rank could see the location of the defensive fire.

A tungsten and steel rain of flechettes hammered the openings through which the two youths were firing and ricochets bounded though the stone-walled room. Tommy dove back and down in a roll away from the windows.

"Move!" he yelled and bounded towards the back door of the shop, forgetting to cover Wendy with his armor.

Wendy lurched towards the door, then stumbled as her right leg refused to support her weight. She looked down and, in the gathering daylight, saw a dark stain on her calf from a ricocheted flechette. She used the Galil to prop herself up and limped towards the door.

Tommy leaned out the door, rifle training left and right as he slid in another clip of grenades. "Come on!" he shouted above the din of fire on either side. When she did not bypass him he looked back in the room. The problem was obvious.

"I can make it," Wendy cried, stumbling on half-seen furniture as tears of pain clouded her eyes and the world swam in gray.

He looked at her and for a moment time seemed to stand still as his mind raced over alternatives. His hand twitched once towards the Desert Eagle at his side, then in sudden decision he hefted the assault rifle in his left hand and swept her over his right shoulder. As pounding started on the front door of the shop, he sprinted for Alesia's Antiques.

Bill Worth coughed wrackingly in the rubble of his demolished book shop, the cough sending fresh waves of formless pain through his body. The heavy wooden rafter pinning his legs and his general condition indicated that he would not be in the most dignified of positions when it came time to meet the gentlemen from off-planet.

However, whatever John Paul Sartre might have thought, one did not always choose one's destiny. If this was how he was to meet the latest visitors to Fredericksburg, so be it.

From a vague feeling of weakness and the spreading stain under his chest, he suspected he might not be greeting the visitors in person anyway. To take his mind off the vagaries of fate, he tried to sight-inventory what was left. A book by his right hand caught his eye and he tugged it over despite the discomfort it caused somewhere in his nether regions. Not immediately recognizing the binding, he opened it to the title page and was pleasantly surprised by his unexpected discovery.

"My goodness," he whispered, "an original Copperfield! Wherever have you been hiding, young man?"

Thus, the words of Dickens served to soothe him, like the gentle friends that they were, until grayness overwhelmed his vision.

"Tommy?" said Wendy, coming out of her daze into darkness as a hand clamped over her mouth.

"Shh!" he whispered fiercely. Somewhere above there was loud crashing. A thump through the ground told a story of distant detonations.

She recognized the smell of the tunnel and realized, shamefully, that he must have carried her all the way down here instead of fighting. She was feeling better all the time, the wound a distant discomfort but no more. She felt at it.

"I injected it with a local," he whispered. "You were in shock, that's all."

"Sorry," she whispered back.

"It's okay; it takes some people that way." He pushed an object into her hand. "This is a Hiberzine injector. Hold it down where our thighs are close together. If we get buried when I set off the claymore, or when the Big One comes, you can inject yourself and maybe make it until we get dug out."

"Okay, what about you?" she whispered.

"I've got one too, but if I get knocked out by debris, inject me, and I'll do the same for you. Now hang on." He picked up the claymore clacker and squeezed it three times rapidly.

With the first compression came a tremendously loud explosion and the sound of complicated destruction. The safe covering their hiding place rang as a series of heavy weights fell on it. There were further sounds of settling material and finally silence.

"I took a couple of seconds to set some more explosives in place after I got you in here," he whispered. "They pretty much dropped the bottom floor into the basement and sealed us in."

He paused for a moment. "Now we just wait to find out if we survive the Big One."

The reinforced concrete top of the pump house had been blown into the interior and more dirt piled on top of it to within four feet of the top. Colonel Robertson, his RTO, two engineer privates and a civilian grading contractor now waited in the resulting fighting position for either the Posleen to reach them or the fuel-air explosion to end the defense once and for all.

Colonel Robertson took a moment to watch the nascent sunrise while one of the engineers kept watch. The other engineer, the radio operator and the civilian were playing liars' poker. A few birds, more hopeful than realistic, were participating in a limited dawn chorus. Except for the cold, and the fact that he was about to die, it was a beautiful morning, clear and with a good chance of a perfect fall day. Too bad he was going to miss it.

And Major Witherspoon lay among the dead in the Command Post, half of his head scooped away by a railgun round, as the Posleen pounded at the church door. The wounded and medics clutched their weapons and waited in silence. The ghosts seemed to gather around, in their blue and gray and camouflage, waiting for their fellows to come join them.

And Chief Wilson stood on the ground floor of the Executive Building wearing her breathing apparatus. At her feet was a car battery and in her left hand was a clamp, opened wide. She carefully transferred the clamp to her right, making sure it stayed open at all times, and worked her hand before transferring it back to the left. As she did so, she saw movement through the doors.

Since they knew the Posleen were east of 95 now, Kerman, Wordly and Jones had permission to avoid the interchange and each intended to stay among the trees where the Posleen had far more trouble finding them. As they rocketed through the dawn, the Gs, the slamming of the plane, the route, seemed as familiar as a daily commute. As they crisscrossed the Rappahanock they took each G shock with aplomb, passing on up the valley towards the rapidly approaching town.

"*Lay it on the ridge,*" said Kerman.

"*Tigershark Five.*"

"*Three.*"

They spread apart and, from three different axes, dropped napalm along Prince Edward Street in a crossing maneuver to shame the Thunderchiefs. Kerman could see no tracers, although there was plenty of Posleen ground fire.

"Ground control, Tigershark Two. Negative human activity Fredericksburg."

"Copy Two. Concur. One more pass, over."

The three performed a synchronized fifteen-G bank over Belmont Manor, drawing sporadic fire in the morning light, and approached from the rising sun.

"Lord, take me down to the river . . ." Morgen whisper-sang, wishing the sun into the air as she sat on the bank of the Rappahanock. She saw a set of dots, banking through the rising sun and closing fast . . . " . . . and wash me in the blood of the lamb . . ."

Even Posleen normals can learn, after a fashion, and they had slowly learned that a quick way to not pass one's genes on to the next generation was to simply open a door in this gods-forsaken town. This was the first company to reach the town's single high building. Or rather the remnant survivors from the company that opened the door to the headquarters of the military technicians, the lucky ones that were behind a hill.

They had, however, heard the reports, seen the results, the remnants of the building and the signs around it. So, although they could not read the words "Welcome to Historic Fredericksburg, Home of the Two-Twenty-Ninth Engineer Battalion" emblazoned on the paper banner flapping above the door in the auroral light, the lopsided and runny twin-turreted castle was as clear to them as a skull and crossbones sign would be to a human.

As the remaining thirty out of four hundred approached the door, they slowed. Every step of their advance had been contested, every building mined, yet here was the largest structure in the town and it was undefended save for the sign. They peered through the shadowed windows, discerning a figure within. Their God King had carefully remained all the way across the street. At a barked command from it, the lead normal stepped forward and opened the door.

Chief Wilson was almost glad. The agonizing night at long last was at an end and whatever was on the other side would no longer wait. Everything that could be done, to preserve life a little while longer, to make safe the innocent, had been done, and now, for the first and last time, she would take sentient life. Most would be Posleen, but many would be human. And she was one who felt that at the bottom they all were brothers. However, she was sure that the humans were just as ready for this long night to be over, as content to enter into a longer but hopefully more peaceful one.

"Gentlemen," she said to the Posleen filing through the doorway, "welcome to historic Fredericksburg," and dropped the clamp.

With the closest simultaneity that an experienced engineer NCO could achieve, sixty one-hundred-gram charges of Composition Four, located on window ledges, detonated. The detonations simultaneously ignited the liquid propane gas still being pumped to the interior and ensured oxygen was provided to the environment to sustain the reaction.

In a pair of milliseconds, every window in the seven-story building imploded, as the air for three blocks in every direction was sucked down to near vacuum by the reacting propane.

As the propane consumed the oxygen, the inrushing air served to compact the highly energetic reaction until virtually the last molecule of the propane was consumed, at which point the superheated air erupted outward with cataclysmic force.

For Morgen Bredell and Colonel Robertson—along with all the surviving humans and Posleen above ground in historic downtown Fredericksburg—it was a sudden moment of breathless vacuum as a hurricane of wind rushed towards the city center and ice picks drove into ear drums, an almost unnoticeable pause and then darkness as the shock wave slammed outward leveling everything in its path.

"*Nuke!*" shouted Jones at the sun-bright dome of fire, automatically snapping his fighter into a hard right bank away from the formation as Kerman snapped into a hard left. Wordly was left with the unsurvivable up and yanked his stick back in a twenty-G climb at nine hundred knots.

His fighter was immediately acquired by God King saucers from Marlboro Point to Spotsylvania as well as landers and C-Decs. A pyramid of light beams followed his exploding fighter as it climbed into the sky, a high-tech Vesuvius, a bright triangular firework in the dawn to punctuate the erupting town.

The shockwave propagated outward, leveling the Public Safety building, historic downtown, finally demolishing the cut Chatham bridge, ripping up rails from the railroad tracks and tumbling them through the air.

Wendy screamed as the ground bucked like a bronco, brick and dirt raining around her. She had one arm over her head, and noticed that Tommy had his over her head as well, so the only thing protecting her ribs when a melon-sized rock fell on them was the body armor. As the rubble fell around her, she inched the Hiberzine injector towards her thigh. . . .

To Shari and the fire fighter in the bunker, the effect was only a slight tremor, the combination of the blast shadow from the railroad embankment and the tons of overburden serving to reduce the concussion to a minor nuisance. They stopped their gin game for a moment, said a prayer, swiped at the tears again and returned to the distraction of cards.

Jones hit the afterburners as soon as his ass was to the blast and settled into his seat as the fighter rocketed towards its maximum speed. The fighter began to buck from ground-effect and then the buffet increased as the shock wave started to catch up. Finally the buffeting slowed as the shock wave receded and he reduced speed and turned back towards the town.

Or where it had been. For five hundred meters on every side of the tall building offset from the city's center the ground was as flat as if scoured. The quaint buildings that had survived multiple bombardments in the Civil War were erased down to the cornerstones. The largest remaining structure was a nub of grain elevator south of the train embankment.

The ridge where they had previously dropped napalm was wiped as clean, the churches gone, but the sheltered valley beyond was still intact and there was sporadic fire as he rocketed across. He banked sharply north, avoiding the open area around the interstate, and called base.

"*Ground control, this is Tigershark Five, over.*"

"*Tigershark, Ground.*"

"*You copy this uplink, over?*"

"*Roger, Tigershark.*" A single turret volley from the battleship landed in the swale from which he had taken fire. "*Return to base, Tigershark.*"

"*Tigershark Five.*"

"*Two,*" echoed Kerman, unexpectedly.

The last survivors of the Peregrine squadron turned to the north and headed for Andrews Air Force Base.

"Are you all right?" asked Tommy, sitting up as brick chips, mortar and dirt cascaded off him. He flicked on a portable fluorescent light.

"I'm alive," said Wendy, staying horizontal, but kicking some of the debris off her legs. She pushed aside the stone that had glanced off her side. "How all right am I supposed to be?"

"Jesus," said Tommy, shining the light up at the intact arch above them. "I can't believe this held," he continued, looking at the sealed tunnel at both ends. He pulled off his helmet and scratched his head vigorously then wriggled out of the body armor.

"What if the Posleen find us?" asked Wendy, gesturing at the doffed armor as he detached the side connections and laid it out flat.

He shook it to get the last brick and stone chips out and flopped down on the field-expedient mattress, hands cradled behind his head. "At this point, if the Posleen want me, they can just eat me, okay?"

Wendy snorted, sat up and shook the bits off as well. She took off her own body armor and stretched, wincing at her bruised ribs, then lay down and put her head on his chest. He wriggled over to let her get on the armor-mattress. After a few moments, they both sighed as the tension came off the day.

Tommy's breath began to deepen as the strains of the long night took their toll. At some time in the future—he feared many times in the future—he would think about the destruction of all he held near and dear. But for now it was enough that, for a moment, there was peace, if only the peace of the dead.

Just as he was drifting into sleep, he felt a pair of fingers slip under his T-shirt. He froze, suppressing a snore and a moment later, one of these fingers began playing with the hairs around his navel. Wendy leaned forward, her breasts pressing into his chest and put her face against his ear.

"Tommy Sunday," she whispered, flicking his ear with her tongue, "if you don't take off your pants right now, I'm going to cap you with your own Glock."

◆ CHAPTER 41 ◆

I-95 near VA 639, VA, United States of America, Sol III
0629 EDT October 10th, 2004 AD

During the early morning hours, work had virtually stopped on the Richmond defenses. Occasionally the crash of explosions could be heard in the distance and the portable TVs receiving broadcasts from Continental Army Headquarters held everyone enthralled. However, with the breaking dawn the enormous boom of the FAE in the distance and the uplinked video broke the spell and the tired cavalry troopers and civilian grading contractors returned to preparing the I-95 fighting positions. Meanwhile teams of women and teenagers emplaced claymores and other mines along the verge. It looked to be a hot reception for the Posleen.

"Let's get to it, boys and girls," said Sergeant First Class Mueller as the extended break ended. "It's us next."

"Are we ready?"

"Yes, Mr. President. Obviously, given the time of day and all the transmission problems there is not a major audience. But there is a higher share than normal because of the emergency."

"It'll have to do." He turned to the secretary of defense. "What is the situation with Tenth Corps?"

"They've turned around and are headed back down to Quantico. It's a bit confused but I'm sure they'll get straightened out in time."

"They'd better. What about Ninth Corps?"

"They're headed for Manassas. The whole First Army is heading into northern Virginia, with the exception of the Fifty-Fifth Armored Division, which is assaulting a landing in Maine."

"Maine. Maine and where else?"

"Arkansas, California and Oregon all have at least one landing of a battlegroup," answered the FEMA representative referring to her notes. "Several other states have already dealt with individual landers. But only Fredericksburg has been hit by a full globe. Not counting Fredericksburg or areas that haven't turned in complete reports, we have over fifteen thousand civilian casualties. Most of those are in the immediate area of landings. About two-thirds are mortalities." She almost continued with a report on the evacuation of northern Virginia.

A bad situation had gone completely catastrophic when Tenth Corps was forced to shut down Interstate 95 and the Beltway to turn around. The corps was out of the way now, and most of the lanes on both sides of the highways had been opened to traffic, but the monumental traffic jam had stalled cars all over it. Instead of pushing more traffic through than normal, the interstates were almost deserted. Millions of Virginians were now on foot, heading towards the Potomac bridges.

"Mortalities," repeated the President with a grimace. "Great. How 'bout just telling your President that he lost fifteen thousand American civilians in the depths of the night."

"And an almost irreplaceable engineering battalion. And a city, sir," said the secretary of defense. "On national television no less. There, feel better?"

"No." The President turned to the makeup artist. "Are we done?"

"Just about, Mr. President. You want to look your best, don't you?"

"That's going to be hard," he commented looking at the text of the speech. It was not the best copy he had ever seen, but it was fairly good given the time the writer had to create it.

"You need to look good, Mr. President," said his Chief of Staff. "Presenting just the right face at this time is very important. You can't appear worried or haggard. It will send the wrong message."

"Would someone please tell me something new? I can do without the pointless reminders."

"The Eleventh Mobile Infantry Division commander called," said the secretary of defense, reading an e-mail hardcopy from CONARC. "As the senior Fleet representative, he asked that we hold off on using the Third Battalion of the Five Hundred Fifty-Fifth. He recommended that we use First Battalion instead."

"Did he give a reason?" asked the President with a look of confusion. "General Olds didn't want them because they're on block leave, right? And isn't the commander stuck in California?"

"Well, Mr. President," said the secretary. "He pointed out that they are fully trained and tested, unlike the Third. Third Battalion is only halfway through their initial training cycle, sir, and has not had an FSTEP."

"So why did General Olds prefer to bring them all the way up from Carolina instead of using First Battalion?" asked the president. The answer had just reinforced the question. "Isn't that the battalion that's officially assigned to him?"

The secretary of defense looked uncomfortable. "I think you'd have to ask General Olds, sir."

"I'm not asking, Olds, Robby. I'm asking my secretary of defense! Is it that divided chain of command thing, again?"

"I wouldn't venture to guess, Mr. President," the SecDef answered, tightly.

"Guess," the President snapped, tired of the prevarication.

"I think it might be a matter of General Olds's opinion of the First Batt's officers, Mr. President, rather than their readiness," commented the President's military aide.

The President turned and looked at the normally silent brigadier general. Since his function was specifically to handle information flow and keep his opinions to himself, the President was surprised to hear him say anything.

"Why do you say that?"

"I was present for the conference on Fortress Forward, Mr. President," the brigadier related without a change of expression. His face might as well have been carved from mahogany. "General Olds several times expressed openly his distrust of the ACS concept in general and specifically of some of the officers of the battalion assigned primary responsibility for his area of operations."

"Did he state which officers?" the President asked.

"No, sir, but the person giving the ACS brief to which he took particular exception was Michael O'Neal."

"The Medal Of Honor winner?" the President asked, surprised. "Did he indicate what he had against him?"

"Again, Mr. President, let me clearly state that he expressed reservations about the ACS program and some of the officers in the battalion attached to his Army. He did not state that it was Captain O'Neal he particularly found offense with, although that might have been taken from the context."

The President looked at his secretary of defense. "He's your friend. You want to explain that?"

The secretary gave the military aide a long measuring look which the general returned without a blink. The brigadier had commanded the Special Forces Sniper School for three years and could stare down a cat. "Jim Olds is an experienced and combat tested officer who has certain strongly held opinions, Mr. President," the SecDef explained. "Many of those opinions are about the nature and function of an officer corps within an Army. He also has a strong opinion about how this war should be prosecuted and how funding should be distributed. They are opinions that the majority of the ACS community disagree with.

"Given those facts, I doubt that General Olds is particularly happy with one of the companies in his command that consumes a disproportionate share of funding being commanded by a former sergeant. Or the influence that that former sergeant has had on its preparation and training."

Mike fishtailed the Tahoe through the median, climbed out of a ditch and pulled out under the nose of a five-ton truck. The vehicle braked with a blare of horn as Mike cut into the lane and then swung the Tahoe back onto the median as the way became clear. The pickup pounded down the rough median, swerving around trucks, buses and Humvees pulled off the road for breakdowns and bouncing in and out of ruts cut by previous passersby. It seemed like he had been traveling up the twisty mountain interstate his whole life. He was barely over the border of Virginia and the traffic was only getting heavier.

He glanced at the heads-up display of the Eastern United States with unit movements denoted on it and grimaced. Murphy's Law was settling in with a vengeance.

"Captain O'Neal," chirped his AID, "incoming call from Lieutenant Colonel Hanson . . ."

"O'Neal?"

"Yes, sir."

"Caught in traffic, I see." The colonel was getting good at drawing information from his AID.

"Yes, sir."

"I'm stranded in Los Angeles. I'm hopping AMTRAK in about thirty minutes, but . . ."

"Shelly, display continent tactical." Mike glanced at the virtual display. Green and red zones were scattered across the United States, with grounding and routing arrows superimposed. "It'll be at least a couple of days, sir. Unless the Sixteenth Cav can clear that infestation in Kansas."

"Yep. And airlines are well and truly grounded. There were scatter landings in the interior and all it takes is one lander in the wrong spot."

"Roger that, sir."

"How long for you?"

Mike saw another MP post coming up, the Hummer-25 already training its barrel on his hurtling truck.

"Damn near as long at this rate, sir. I'll see what I can do."

"Well, I talked to Major Givens, and unless either I or Major Rutherford makes it back in time, that'll leave the battalion in command of the S-3. Who do you think I said should fill in as S-3?"

"Great, like I want to plan this operation." Mike didn't mention his questions about Nightingale's abilities or his own capabilities. It would be a hell of a test of both. "Did you see the Tenth Corps go into defense?"

"Yes, lovely. I wonder what's going on there?"

"I don't know, sir, but I have to talk my way past a roadblock." He started slowing as the MP team leader got out of the Humvee.

"Okay, good luck. I don't know if it will help, but I'm ordering you to reach the unit as quickly as possible. Using any means you deem necessary."

"Roger, sir. Well, good luck to you as well."

"Thanks. Out here."

"Shelly, get me First Sergeant Pappas."

"First Sergeant Pappas is not near his AID," answered the AID.

Mike wrinkled his brow. "Is he on post?"

"When last located. But he is not in range of his AID. His AID is in his office. He is not."

Mike, who went virtually nowhere without his AID, shrugged in puzzlement. "Okay, get me Lieutenant Nightingale."

"Lieutenant Nightingale is not near her AID."

"What the hell is this?" the commander grumped. "Is anybody with their AIDs?"

"Lieutenant Arnold is available."

"Well, get me Tim then."

After a moment the weapons platoon leader answered. "Captain O'Neal?"

"Yeah, Tim. Look, I'm stuck in traffic on I-81. I don't know how long I'll be. Tell Top that I want an assessment of Nightingale. If she's not up to the job he's to tell Major Givens on my say-so. I don't care if she remains technically in command, but I want Gunny Pappas to run the show. Clear?"

"Uh, yeah. Yes, sir."

"Do you know where the gunny is? He's not by his AID."

"Not exactly. I'll see if I can track him down."

"Okay. I'm gonna bend heaven and hell to get back as fast as I can, but I don't know if its gonna work."

"Yes, sir. Take care."

"Right. Out here. Corporal," said O'Neal, rolling down the window and holding out his Fleet ID, "my name's O'Neal, Fleet Strike . . ."

"My fellow Americans . . ."

The President personally hated that phrase but it was the only acceptable one for such a usage. He stared at the TelePrompTer and firmly quelled all doubts. Though he knew that the country was about to pay a terrible price, it was a price he was sure the American people would call for, a price that duty and honor called for.

" . . . you have by now all witnessed the terrible events which have occurred overnight. In the space of twelve hours thousands of American citizens have lost their lives and one of the most historic cities in our nation has been erased from the face of the Earth.

"I call upon you now, as Americans, to face this challenge as we have faced every challenge in our great history, with honor, courage and a sense of duty towards all mankind.

"The current military plan in a situation such as this is clear. Since the Posleen are here earlier than expected, and in overwhelming local strength, the proper military reaction is to retreat to better terrain, to retreat behind the James and Potomac Rivers to the north and south, into the Appalachians on the west, until such time as sufficient military forces are assembled to defeat the enemy on the plains of battle.

"This is a good and just plan, one caring, as American generals always have, for their soldiers. If there were insufficient time to evacuate the civilian populace the decision would be to stay and slow the Posleen until the civilians could evacuate. But there is enough time to evacuate these areas. Manassas, Arlington and Alexandria, all of northern and central Virginia, is evacuating even as I speak." He took a pause, not for any reason of drama, but gathering courage for the words he was about to say.

Throughout the country, at radios and, where they were functioning, televisions, Americans leaned forward waiting for their chief executive to continue, knowing that such a reaction, such a decision was anathema to the politician.

"Unfortunately, sometimes the proper military response is not the correct action for the country as a whole. Many mistakes have been made in history because of taking the proper military choice. It is for this very reason that the military is under civilian control in the United States and virtually every western nation. If we had taken the proper military choice we would have dropped nuclear weapons in Korea. The proper military choice led to the Battle of the Bulge. The proper military choices nearly lost World Wars One and Two to the Germans.

"I have, therefore, decided to override the 'proper military choice.' I have ordered the Tenth Ground Forces Corps, the Corps of Northern Virginia, to go into defensive positions south of the Occoquan River in the area of Quantico Marine Base. Their purpose is to stop Posleen incursions aimed towards Alexandria, Arlington and Washington, D.C.

"In addition, the soldiers of the Ninth Corps, the Pennsylvania and New Jersey Corps, should arrive in time to take positions south of Manassas, Virginia, a name well known to us all. It is also remembered in some parts of the country by the name Bull Run. It is a land saturated in the history of conflict.

"I have done this, over the strong objections of my most senior commanders, because I believe that is the desire of the American people and I believe that the justifiable military reaction misses one small factor.

"We have been attacked," the simple statement came out as almost a snarl, while his expression changed hardly at all. "For the first time in nearly two hundred years, the United States has been invaded. And I don't like that. If these . . . things communicate among themselves I want them to get one communication loud and clear. If you attack the United States, you are asking for a bucket-load of trouble. If you land on *these* shores, the only things you are going to get for your pains are chaos and death!

"The video from Fredericksburg, horrific as it is, clearly shows what Americans, surprised and facing overwhelming odds, can do to these creatures on their own turf. As your President, I cannot simply throw away northern Virginia, not and face myself in the mirror in the morning.

"I have made this decision, knowing that it means the death of many of the soldiers sworn to the service of their country.

"To the soldiers in the field, I have only this to say.

"Obey your orders, care for your comrades and take the field knowing that few things can face a human who is in the right and just keeps coming.

"Good luck. Pile 'em up like cordwood."

Mueller watched the female technician hooking wires up to the demolition circuit board. "Where are we with the stringing?" she asked. Her hands moved with a graceful haste, barely pausing as each circuit was connected; her fingers seemed to blur in the morning light.

"We've strung all but the outer edge, and the engineers have placed all the detonators. We're still putting up the claymores, but they'll be done by the time you're ready."

"I wish we had enough Pyronics for this job," she said, testily. "I hate working with this lowest-bidder military stuff."

"Hey, MILSPEC is the class of the world!"

"Hah! Tell it to the amateurs, kid. I've worked with every type of detonator in the world and five gets you ten one of these blasting caps fails when I do the systems check. These dang military caps are too dang sensitive."

"Okay, I've got ten bucks says you're wrong."

"It was an expression. I don't drink, swear or bet. I have enough excitement in my life as it is."

"What do you usually do?"

"Well, I used to drop buildings for a living, but lately I've been a home demolition contractor." She set the last circuit in place and hooked up the meter. "How certain are you that they haven't hooked up any of the blasting caps?"

"Not certain enough."

"Good answer. I wanted to see if you had any sense." She stood up and arched her back, rubbing at her lumbar. "I prefer doing this with a table, too."

"We must all make our little sacrifices for the war effort."

"Sure. Personally, I gave up chocolate. I'm gonna go do the circuit. Stay here and make absolutely certain no one touches the board. I don't like all these amateurs running around."

"I thought I was one of them."

"Yeah, but that way I only have to worry about one."

"Let me make you a deal. Since I am in charge of most of the 'amateurs,' especially the civilian ones, and I really shouldn't be tied to this spot, let me get a guard who knows darn well not to touch anything and only understands simple commands so he gets it right."

"Whatever."

Mueller came back a few moments later with one of the cavalry troopers providing security for the construction site. With a screen of Bradleys and Humvees five miles down the road, Mueller was personally convinced that the Posleen would be spotted well before they reached the ambush. But the military's standard operating procedures were developed from numerous situations where people were personally convinced of one thing or another and totally wrong. So—despite anyone's personal conviction—Colonel Abrahamson was providing security to all of the ambush preparation sites.

This was the ambush site most distant from Richmond and

presumably the point of first contact for the Twelfth Corps. At this point, near Road 656, there was a perfect site for a long-range armor and mechanical ambush. An overpass ran along a very slight ridgeline perpendicular to the interstate. North of the overpass there was a straight stretch nearly two miles long. Half a mile from the overpass a group of trees crowded the road at either side and ran down the median. In the midst of the trees a shallow and apparently unnamed creek crossed the interstate in a box culvert.

Now, both sides of the interstate just behind the overpass had been cratered and dug out for fifty meters towards Richmond, creating a shelf in which a platoon of cavalry vehicles crouched with their twenty-five-millimeter cannons pointed northward. They would be able to fire hull-down, protected from most of the Posleen fire, until the Posleen were close enough to be a threat. When the cavalry started taking casualties they could drive away protected by the slight ridge.

And the wooded patch was lined with two thousand claymore mines.

Each mine was a narrow curved box, with thin "legs" on the bottom, projections for detonators on the top and the convexly curved front labeled, humorously in the opinion of most military personnel, FRONT TOWARDS ENEMY. The directional antipersonnel mine consisted of a plastic cover encasing a thin metal backstop, a pound of Composition B explosive and seven hundred fifty small metal ball bearings, just a little larger than a standard BB. On detonation the ball bearings would spew out in a cone, tearing apart anything in their path. At fifty meters, the recommended stand-off for maximum effect, the mines were designed to create a zone of total destruction thirty meters wide. Fifty meters was just about the width of the right of way and there was one claymore spaced every two meters, or six feet, for two hundred and fifty meters on either side of the road, on both sides of the interstate. When the daisy-chained mechanical ambush was detonated, nearly a million and a half ball bearings would fill the air, each traveling faster than a rifle bullet.

"Specialist Rossi," said Mueller, introducing the cav trooper, "this is Amanda Hunt, the lead demolition person for the claymore ambush."

"Ma'am," said the specialist with a nod of the head and a wave of the hand at his helmet. He knew better than to salute, but wanted to acknowledge her civilian rank.

"Ms. Hunt is going to go check the demolition circuits." Mueller pointed at the circuit board. "This is the controller for the ambush. One of the things she is going to do is check to make sure none of the detonators have been connected. This is like the claymore clacker, so she would like to take it with her. But she'd have to hook it back up and that takes time. So, you are hereby ordered to remain at this post until personally relieved by Ms. Hunt, understood?"

"Yes, Sergeant."

"I've coordinated this with your squad leader and your platoon leader. Now, I don't think that this will happen, but in the event that we are attacked while she is out there, you are to remain at this post until relieved by Ms. Hunt, understood? You are not, I repeat, not to return to your fighting vehicle, but remain here. Understood?"

"Yes, Sergeant." The trooper was clearly unhappy with the order.

"In the event that your platoon pulls out before Ms. Hunt returns, you are to destroy the circuit board. Do not attempt to use it, do not let anyone else, not your platoon nor any of the engineers, use it. Understood?"

"Yes, Sergeant, understood. Why?"

Mueller smiled. "Because I might be out there, and I don't want any idiot cooking off two thousand claymores because somebody saw a horse run across the road. And if Amanda isn't back, it means that some or most of the detonators are not hooked up. If she makes it back after you destroy the box, she can probably get most of them to detonate anyway.

"I would order you to stand your post until the Posleen are on you. That would do the same thing, would mean that she and the engineers weren't still trying to hook up claymores. But I'm not going to expect you to remain when your platoon pulls out. You're behind the overpass embankment and the drainage ditch runs right into the fighting position, so even if she doesn't get back when we're taking fire, you can still hold out until the tracks start to move, so stay here until relieved. Understood?"

"Understood."

"Repeat it back."

"I am to remain at this post, letting no one but Ms. Hunt have access to this circuit board, until relieved by Ms. Hunt personally and no other. I will remain under those orders, unless my platoon retreats from its position, at which time I am to destroy the circuit board and retreat with my platoon."

"Ms. Hunt?"

"Okay." She looked deeply skeptical. "If I ain't back though, your boss better make damn sure he waits as long as he can."

As she drove away in her pickup Mueller looked the specialist in the eye.

"How long you gonna stay?"

"Till she gets back or the Posleen are swarmin'. I'll get a radio from the track, I'll still be able to call fire right up till then."

"Right." Mueller looked down at the departing civilian contractors. Their grading work done, they were headed to the next ambush. It would probably be less elaborate than this one, but the Posleen were going to be greeted as many times as possible as they advanced.

"Any word from the scouts?"

The cav scout pulled a device out of his thigh cargo pocket and tapped the keypad. The box was the size of an old "brick" cellular phone and had a hand strap on the back for ease of carrying. This was useful, for example, when under fire. The LCD display flashed as he scrolled through options and finally settled on a screen.

"Nah, the Posleen they're watching are still in some sort of security distribution around their lander. There's some sort of armor indicator, maybe one of their God Kings. But they still don't seem to be moving this way."

"Nice," said Mueller. "What is it?"

"You've never seen one?" said the surprised scout.

Mueller held up his wrist where the GalTech AID was wrapped as a thin bracelet. "I use an AID."

"Oh, well it's a combination of the IVIS and the ANCD," said the scout, using the military acronyms for the InterVehicle Intelligence System and the Army-Navy Cryptographic Device.

"So it's both a tactical dispositions locator and a code book?" Mueller asked.

"Yeah. Your position is broadcast by it to command vehicles that gather the data and pass it on. And you can pull down signals information from the intervehicle network. So, like, if I want to call up that battleship, I just search for . . . what was its name?"

"The *North Carolina*."

"Right." The scout tapped keys for a moment and grimaced. "It doesn't want to give me Navy information. Why the hell do we practice Operational Security when the Posleen don't use the information?" he asked rhetorically.

"Where's it getting its location data from?"

"Triangulation from the vehicles. They're getting it from reads off of other vehicles that get hard position data from those position markers that are scattered around. We hit one on the way up here and the guidance system has us just about where we are—sitting under the overpass—so it seems to be working." He tapped the device again. "I can put in a call for fire to the artillery battery that's attached to us, but I can't get up to the Navy."

"You can do a call for fire?" asked the Special Forces NCO.

"Yeah, in case it, you know, like drops in the pot." The trooper shook his head. "I hope I don't have to, though. That means the chain of command is down to me, you know? How's that thing work?" he asked, gesturing at the AID.

"Pretty much the same." Mueller held out his wrist. "AID, battlefield schematic out five miles." A holographic projection of the battlefield in three dimensions appeared in front of the two soldiers. As they watched, units, friend and foe, were sketched in. "A little easier, though."

The trooper shook his head again. "Why'd you ask me?"

"I was actually thinking you might say something like, 'Oh, yeah, I heard on the radio. . . .'" Mueller lowered the device and it decided the demonstration was over and switched off the schematic. "Little did I know you were going to pull out your own handy-dandy battlefield computer."

The trooper smiled. "I really love this thing."

"What's the brief for the front-line scouts?" asked Mueller, wondering if everyone had gotten the same word. "Are they staying out of sight?"

"Oh, yeah. They're not gonna stick their dicks in there, man. The quickest damn way to get the Posleen to follow you is attack them."

"Yeah, it's kind of like leading a pig." Mueller felt the glimmerings of an idea.

"Huh?" asked the urban-raised cavalry specialist.

"The best way to lead a pig is to poke it in the nose," said the NCO with a distracted smile.

"Oh. Well, until the colonel says different, we're staying out of sight."

"Yeah, best thing for it."

"I thought you'd know that."

"Why?" asked Mueller, warily.

"Well, wasn't it a Special Forces team that got shot up on Barwhon?" asked the specialist.

"Actually, it was a mixed special operations team: some Special Forces, Marines, a SEAL."

"And they stuck their dicks into a Posleen camp, killed some God Kings and got their butts kicked, right?" the specialist asked archly.

"More or less."

"So we don't want to do that, do we, Sergeant?"

"We didn't want to either," Mueller admitted, grimly.

"So why did they do it?" asked the scout.

"We got orders from higher to snatch some Posleen for medical experiments. We didn't exactly like it and we liked the result even

less than we thought we were going to. We lost two absolute legends
in the special ops community—Sandra Ellsworthy and Arthur Tung—
and when we made it back to the Himmit scout we were at Death's
door from fatigue and vitamin deficiency."

"Hold on, by 'we' you mean you were *on* that team?" asked the
cav trooper, his eyes round.

"Me, Ersin and Mosovich. We were the only survivors."

"Jesus, sorry, man. I, well, you know . . ."

"Yeah, you didn't know. It's all right. But the only reason we went
into the camp was on orders. The real bitch of it was the whole
mission was out of date by the time we did it. They wanted a Posleen
to study, but by the time we got back with it there were captured
Posleen and frozen Posleen bits out the ass coming in from Diess.
Total and complete fuckup."

Mueller paused, his face hard as he remembered the results of
following incompetent orders. The general whose bright idea it had
been had never even commented, not even obliquely apologized. Just
handed out the medals, tapped them on the shoulders and went on
to his next star. "Anyway, the point is, I agree with the scouts staying out of sight." He looked down the road. "AID, how's the installation coming?"

"Engineers report all claymores installed, all wire run and all
blasting caps are in place and ready to be connected. The engineer
teams are ready to start connecting the circuits when Ms. Hunt gives
the command."

"Okay, tell the engineer lieutenant to move all the civilians back
to the buses and on to the next ambush. What's the status on claymores for that?"

"Tractor-trailers are unloading them as we speak, however, we have
received only seven hundred, since the rest have been diverted to the
defenses on U.S. 1 and U.S. 301. If time permits, more will be sent
forward when a shipment arrives from the plant. The factory is
emptying its storage as fast as it can move the material out."

"Where's Ersin?"

"Master Sergeant Ersin is with the forward scouts."

"Hell. Well, tell him to be careful."

Mark Ersin adjusted the focus on the purely optical binoculars and
let out a soft sigh. He and the cavalry scouts with him were wearing ghillie suits, coveralls sewn with dangling fabric strips that made
them almost impossible to see against the scrub pine they were nestled
in. But Ellsworthy had been wearing a similar suit when she bought
it. Up against Posleen sensors, a ghillie suit was cold comfort.

The Posleen, a God King and about thirty normals, had obviously been left behind as security for the lander. The numbers were far under the normal number of troops associated with a God King, though, and Ersin was nervous about where the rest might be.

The lander loomed on what had previously been a tobacco farm. A tractor jutted out from under one edge. The God King and normals had begun surveying duties soon after the scouts came on site and, with the exception of the arrival of a small anti-grav tank that was parked on the interstate, no changes had occurred.

"*Three Five Echo Two One, this is Nine Eight Bravo One Seven, authenticate Whiskey Tango, over,*" came a whisper over the scout's radio.

"What?"

"*I say again, Three Five Echo Two One, this is Nine Eight Bravo One Seven, authenticate Whiskey Tango, over,*" the transmission repeated.

"AID, who is that?" whispered Ersin.

"Master Sergeant Ersin, that is the Twenty-Ninth Infantry Division's division artillery fire direction center."

"What? Direct?" asked the NCO, his faintly Eurasian face wrinkling in puzzlement. His nose twitched like a rat sniffing cheese.

"Yes, Master Sergeant."

"What's the authentication?"

"I've got an ANCD here," whispered one of the cav troopers, pulling a box out of his thigh pocket.

"Don't worry about it," said Ersin.

"Authentication is Mike."

Ersin picked up the handset and keyed it. "*Niner Eight Bravo One Seven, this is Three Five Echo Two One. Authenticate Mike, over.*"

"*Echo Two One, require fire mission, over.*"

What? "*Say again, Bravo One Seven?*"

"*Echo Two One, do you have the enemy in sight?*"

"*Roger, over.*"

"*Require fire mission, over.*"

Ersin wrinkled his brow and took a deep breath. "*Bravo One Seven, this is Echo Two One. Negative, say again, negative. Stay off this net in the future. Out.*"

"*Echo Two One, this is Bravo Five Nine Actual, over.*"

"Okay, AID, who's that?" queried Ersin, angrily.

"The Division artillery commander."

"Shit." He thought about it for a moment then keyed the radio anyway. "*Bravo Five Nine Actual, this is Echo Two One. Negative fire. I say again, per corps orders, negative fire. Get off my net. Out.*"

"*Echo Two One, this is Bravo Five Nine. This is an order. Call fire, I say again, call fire, over.*"

"AID, contact corps, send these transmissions with explanation. Do it now. *Bravo Five Nine, require electronic authentication and link.* AID, don't accept the link."

"I have to. Bravo Five Nine outranks you."

"Not really, haven't we been transferred to Fleet Strike?"

"Your team has not been officially transferred yet."

"Okay, what about divided command authorities? I fall under CONARC, not corps and we are under a corps command not to fire."

"Most recent orders of a superior officer overrule previous orders. That's Ground Forces General Regulation One Dash One Zero Five. Link confirmed, Posleen positions transmitted." There was a brief pause. "One-Five-Five fire on the way. Your position was noted as well. They are using close support rules as stipulated by doctrine."

"Goddamnit! Have you contacted corps?"

"I am unable to contact corps at this time due to message traffic. Material transferred to e-mail and sent to queue."

"Get me Sergeant Major Mosovich," he snarled at the recalcitrant machine as the sky began to scream.

"*He what?*" shouted the normally mild-mannered Twelfth Corps commander.

"General Bernard ordered his artillery to engage the Posleen positions near Virginia 639." The corps operations officer looked like he had taken a drink expecting water and gotten unsweetened lemonade. In a way he had.

"Send the corps provost to the Twenty-Ninth Infantry Division headquarters. Order him to place General Bernard under arrest for insubordination and disobedience to direct orders. Send General Craig to take command."

"Craig isn't from the Guard, sir."

"Fuck 'em. This is the last irresponsible action I am allowing that rat-fuck division command and staff to undertake. Tell George to put a leash on those idiots. Contact Division Arty, tell them that the order is countermanded. Relieve the commander, have him report here, replace him with his XO pending final disposition. Tell the XO he can figure on finding a new home unless he justifies staying in command."

"Yes, sir."

"Get me Colonel Abrahamson. He needs to know we may be kicking off early."

◆ CHAPTER 42 ◆

There was thirty dead and wounded on the ground we
wouldn't keep—
    No, there wasn't more than twenty when the front begun
    to go—
But, Christ! along the line o' flight they cut us up like sheep,
    An' that was all we gained by doin' so!

We was rotten 'fore we started—we was never disciplined;
    We made it out a favour if an order was obeyed.
Yes, every little drummer 'ad 'is rights an' wrongs to mind,
    So we had to pay for teachin'—an' we paid!

An' there ain't no chorus 'ere to give,
    Nor there ain't no band to play;
But I wish I was dead 'fore I done what I did,
    Or seen what I seed that day!

—from "That Day"
Rudyard Kipling

Dale City, VA, United States of America, Sol III
0728 EDT October 10th, 2004 AD

"Does anyone know what the fuck is going on?" asked Specialist
Keren, rhetorically.

"You heard the Pres, so shut up and dig," said Sergeant Herd, but
it was without heat. Everyone was confused and uncertain.

The Fiftieth Infantry Division was a new unit. Its unit colors had

341

been in storage since World War II when it had performed undistinguished service in the Pacific theater. It had nearly participated in the battle of Leyte Gulf. It had performed heroic rear area service during the battle of Tarawa. It had nearly invaded the Japanese mainland and gone down in Army history. Unfortunately, it was only a blip in Army history and an unnoticed blip until the present emergency. And Ground Force personnel had responded appropriately.

The current service personnel transferred to the unit were, by and large, the soldiers and officers that relieving units were just as happy to see the backs of, and the new recruits had only those personnel and a smattering of rejuvs to use as guidance. A few officers and NCOs stood out, but in many cases only because of average performance rising out of an abyssal morass of incompetence.

Mortar platoon, Alpha Company First Battalion Four Hundred Fifty-Second Infantry, Third Brigade, Fiftieth Infantry Division, was, if anything a cut above the rest. Specialist Keren had, admittedly, been a sergeant before and would probably be a private again but that had very little to do with his competence as a mortarman. He had a bit of a drinking problem, and with it came a coincidental habit of telling officers what he thought their mothers did for pocket money, but that was no problem in the field. And he was the high point of the "trained" privates. A couple of the newbie privates were on the mental level of Oscar the Zoo Gorilla. And the platoon sergeant had spent the last fifteen years improving his knowledge of metalworking in a machine shop. And the platoon leader, despite the overabundance of first lieutenants, was a recent graduate of the Pennsylvania Army National Guard Officers Training School and would soon, almost certainly, require a razor.

But, for all of that, they had established a unit camaraderie that was sorely lacking throughout most of the division and they had managed to hold together during the occasional riots that had broken out and they had trained, even when the rest of the battalion had screwed off or gone AWOL half the time. What magic element infected them, whether it was Keren's sarcastic outlook on their chances in the event of real combat, or the platoon sergeant's careful attention to every last detail of personal and equipment needs or the platoon leader's puppy-dog eagerness that was too infectious to ignore and too ingenuous to kick, the unit had come together. True, they were far below the pre-emergency norm for the American Army, and they had a lot of training to catch up on, but they were as good as it got in the Fuckin' Fiftieth.

Unfortunately the current situation would have strained a veteran unit.

First there had been the mad dash to saddle up, with nearly half the battalion officers gone and over fifteen AWOLs in Alpha company alone. Then going into the defense when it became apparent that they might be in the interdiction circle. Then the orders to move out to positions north of the Potomac, which was just fine with most of them. Last came the sudden about-face.

Up until then operations had progressed with remarkable smoothness. The occasional unit got lost or at least off on the wrong road and stuck in civilian traffic, and a couple of units had run out of fuel because their bowsers could not find them. And there were not enough lowboys—the tractor-trailer rigs that were normally used for any movement that would not involve conflict—in the entire world to move all the armored fighting vehicles being shuffled on the eastern seaboard. So the division had to move in its APCs, Bradleys and tanks and plenty of them broke down; some of the units in the division had not done maintenance in months. But, basically, all things considered, up until the turnaround everything was going as smooth as silk.

Moving a corps is something like moving a large family. Telling such-and-such a unit to go to this location and repeating that ad nauseum will not work. The units invariably do not have enough fuel to complete the movement, even as simple a drive as from Alexandria to Quantico: a forty-five-minute drive by car on a good day. And telling the units to go here or there, centering hundreds of fighting units with their support on a small area, means that thousands of vehicles are all trying to use the same roads at the same time. While that works just fine for commuters, military units rarely recover well when they lack cohesion. Individual vehicles simply follow the vehicles in front and rarely does every vehicle commander follow a map. Mixing units leads to one unit with extra vehicles and one unit with virtually none. Just having mom and dad go out to the car and sit after telling the kids to pack and load the car is a recipe for disaster.

In a normal movement or even a "planned" emergency every unit is given a destination, a route to use and an estimated time of arrival. In addition there are specified points to refuel, rearm and be served hot chow. Good commanders send that information down the line and the subordinate units brief their individual drivers and vehicle commanders. At a minimum almost every driver and vehicle commander knows where they are going, the route to follow and any planned stops along the way. (There are always exactly ten percent that do not "get the word.") Then the unit moves out and invariably everyone except the drivers, the officers, senior NCOs and overeager junior NCOs goes to sleep. On arrival it is the overeager junior NCO's job to wake everyone up. That is how they become senior NCOs.

When the President gave the corps its marching orders every officer from the High Commander down to the company commanders knew in their bones that the result would be utter chaos. And they were right. With no time for the staff to prepare any of the units and with the units effectively backwards to the way they should have been arranged, the night had been an unending madhouse.

The platoon had just heard a valid report that the Fiftieth Infantry Division had less than seventy percent of its vehicles in the correct location. This after what would have been a simple five-mile road march if they had driven directly from their laagers in Quantico.

Unable to determine precise points for every unit to move to and through, the Corps had been forced to give general orders to the subordinate divisions along with a general axis of movement. These were the orders that the divisions then transmitted to their subordinate units. They had had varying success.

Some divisions, notably the Thirty-Third, had tried to give every subordinate battalion its precise destinations and axes of defense using the correct and proper codes for such vital information. The result had been utter confusion on the part of the battalions. Through simple errors inherent in any complex unpracticed endeavor—especially when undertrained communications personnel were attempting to use necessarily complex encoders and decoders—battalion commanders found themselves with orders scattering them all over the map. In some cases the orders had them outside of the continental United States. Several commanders referred the obviously incorrect dispositions to the brigade commanders, who should have been detailing their tactics in the first place. The brigade commanders tried to contact the division for clarification.

In the midst of all of this the corps's communications protocols changed, not all the correct protocols were transmitted to all the units and suddenly half the corps was out of communication with each other.

The mortar platoon had three of its five fighting vehicles in what the platoon leader was fairly sure was the right place. After switching back and forth on their PRC-2000 radio they finally established contact with the platoon sergeant and the first squad track. The same method finally got them in contact with the company net; the company commander's RTO was flipping around to the old and new frequencies trying to find its units.

The information from the company was mildly encouraging. They were in more or less the right place. Some of the company's line platoons were in more or less the right place. And the company commander was fairly sure that he would be able to contact battalion "soon." A request for refueling and chow, however, was answered with an unsettling "we'll have to get back to you on that."

Now fairly sure that there were some gun-bunnies—riflemen that is—between them and the Posleen and fairly sure that they knew where they were and where the gun-bunnies were, they were preparing for their first taste of war. All they had to do was set up to fire, an exercise that should take a maximum of twelve minutes according to Ground Forces Standard. Keren had been digging for over a half-hour, waiting for word that the platoon leader was ready to lay the guns "in-parallel." Until that was done, control orders from the Fire Direction Center would be meaningless; the guns needed a starting point to work from.

"You know, I like Lieutenant Leper. I mean . . ." Keren tossed another shovel of dirt out of the fighting position he was digging next to the mortar track. He might not need the hole, but if he did he knew he was going to need it bad and in a hurry. Most of the platoon thought he was an idiot.

"Can it, Keren." Sergeant Herd knew he had the best gunner in the battalion, maybe in the division, but he also knew he had to keep him firmly in check.

"No, really, he's a nice guy and he tries hard. . . ." continued the specialist. He tossed another shovelful of dirt out of the hole, and looked around to see if he'd hit anyone with it. No. Damn.

"What," snorted Sheila Reed, the ammo bearer and track driver, "you think you could do better?"

"Shit, I *know* I could do better," Keren responded, tossing the next shovelful higher. A drift of the wind caught it and threw dust onto the rest of the crew lounging on the track. His chocolate face creased as they cursed him.

"Go out there and do it, then," said Tom Riley, the assistant gunner.

"Fuck no, Sergeant Ford is out there. You know what a bastard he is."

"Fuck Ford," said Herd, suddenly interested. "He can do Fire Direction, but anybody that can punch numbers can do that. Do you really think you can lay in the guns?"

"I can tell what their problem is from here," Keren said, throwing the D-handle shovel out of the hole and dusting off his hands. "They can't get the deflection head leveled up. It's not like a one-twenty, where you only have to level side to side. A deflection head you gotta level all the way around." He hoisted himself out of the hole and looked at his squad leader.

"Go on. Tell Ford if he has a problem to take it up with me." Sergeant Herd knew the specialist was probably right. Having volunteered before the invasion was ever heard of, the gunner had been in the service six years already and knew his way around a mortar platoon far better than anyone but the platoon sergeant. If he said he could get the platoon laid in he could get them laid in.

Keren pulled his sleeves down and settled his cap on his head. Regulations called for wearing the Kevlar helmet at all times in the field, but his Kevlar was in the track—where it did some good keeping you from banging your head—and that was where it was gonna stay. Since most of the men and women in the platoon were wearing BDU caps he fit right in. Those who were not wearing BDU caps were wearing either floppy brim "boonie" caps or were coverless. The only people in sight with Kevlars on were Lieutenant Leper and Sergeant Ford. On the other hand Keren's LCE with his pistol, ANCD and food and water did not leave his body.

"Okay Zippy," he said, referring to Riley by his nickname, "get ready to lay that bastard in."

As he neared the pair Sergeant Ford turned and glared at him. "We don't need your help, Keren, so get lost."

"Already am Sergeant, happens any time I leave the barracks. Sergeant Herd told me to come over and see if I could be of assistance."

"Sergeant Ford," said Lieutenant Leper, "maybe you could go and see if you can reestablish communication with battalion TOC."

Ford glared at the specialist and stalked off towards the FDC track.

"Specialist, I seem to be having a little trouble with leveling this up. I've watched Staff Sergeant Simmons any number of times and I thought I knew how but . . ."

"Yes, sir, I understand," Keren said, tactfully. "These things are a real bugger to level." He grabbed the leveling knobs and centered them, then looked at the bubble and stomped one leg of the tripod down. Using both hands he manipulated all three knobs, two at a time for a few seconds and spun the sight around.

"Direction of fire is twenty-eight hundred, right, sir?" he asked.

"Twenty-eight hundred mils, right," said the confused lieutenant, looking over his shoulder to ensure that the recalcitrant bubble was in fact centered. To his amazement it was. "How the hell did you do that so fast?"

"The same way you get to Carnegie hall, sir." The specialist manipulated the head to twenty-eight hundred mils and spun it towards his track. *"Two gun aiming point this instrument!"* he shouted.

"Two gun, aiming point identified!" Riley answered. The gunner on the other track scrambled off the ground where he had been dozing and dove into the track. A moment later his head popped through the top.

"Deflection, one-seven one seven five! Close enough."

"Deflection, one-seven one seven five!"

Keren spun the sight towards the other track and read off the numbers. *"Three gun!"*

"Three gun!"

"Aiming point this instrument!"

"Aiming point identified!"

"Deflection one-nine one one eight!"

"Deflection one-nine one one eight!"

He waited until the guns called up, secretly pleased that the assistant gunner on his track got up faster than the gunner on Third Track and repeated the process twice more for each gun until they were laid in parallel and he pronounced himself satisfied. "They're in. Only way to know if they're actually aligned is to fire them in series, sir. But they're as laid as I can get them."

"That was amazing. How did you get the bubble to level so fast?" the officer asked, still surprised at the casual display of skill.

"My first platoon sergeant taught me that trick, sir. If the bubble seems like it should go one way, you have to grab two knobs. Twist one to push the bubble and twist the other in the opposite direction. Also you should be looking at the bubble from your normal sighting angle, rather than trying to crane down from on top. That keeps you from chasing the bubble."

"I'll remember that. Thanks."

"De nada, sir. No offense but we really needed to get laid in."

"I know. I think the company is really going to need us this time." The young lieutenant was obviously trying very hard not to look scared. For an officer to look frightened was bad form and also he had been told it was guaranteed to push the troops over into panic in a situation just like this one. Unfortunately he was trying so hard not to look scared that he was looking terrified instead.

"Sir," said Keren, taking pity on the poor kid. "We're three klicks behind the line and we've got a battalion of line dogs in front of us. What do we have to worry about?"

"Is it that obvious?"

"Hell, yes. Want some unsolicited advice, sir?"

"No, but you're going to give it to me anyway, aren't you?"

Keren grinned. "Wouldn't be a specialist if I didn't. Walk back to the FDC track. Tell Sergeant Ford, who is an asshole and everyone knows is an asshole so they won't take offense at you, to go to the tracks and make sure that all the .50 calibers have been cleaned, oiled, check head space and timing and get some of the ammo bearers cutting fire lanes for them. Get some mines out, that sort of thing. Pull it out of a book. Then sit there and look regal while you pore over a map you already have memorized. Don't pace. Sip water from time to time. Make like you're asleep. Maybe read the manual a few times."

"And that is supposed to inspire the troops?" The lieutenant gave a tired smile.

"No, but it's better than watching you run to the latrine every fifteen minutes, sir," the specialist quipped. "Yeah, the newbies and, hell, even the sergeants are looking kind of light around the gills and they could use the example and some work to take their minds off what's coming up the road. Act like it's just another exercise, a nice, cold day in the country."

"Good suggestions, Specialist. So, why in the hell are you just a specialist?"

"You didn't hear that, sir?"

"No."

"I told my last platoon leader his mother was a whore with AIDS who squirted him out in a public toilet and forgot to flush, sir." He looked momentarily chagrined. "I was kinda drunk at the time. But he really was an asshole," he finished, as if that completely explained the incident.

"I'll bet."

"*Roger, out.*"

Captain Robert Brantley carefully hung the microphone back on its clip, settled his Kevlar on his head, adjusted the chinstrap just so, picked up the squad automatic weapon he had appropriated, checked the chamber to ensure it was clear and climbed over the cases of ammunition in the Bradley fighting vehicle and out the troop door. Descending to the loam of the forest floor he caught the eye of his first sergeant and made a circular motion with his arm signaling "rally on me."

As the sergeant ambled over, the commander took the time to observe the company digging in. At least he watched the few members of the Second platoon who were in view. The order had been clear and, for once, unquestioned. Two-man fighting positions, interlocking fields of fire, M-60E machine gun positions with extra cover, sand-bagged front parapets, everything rikky-tik. Except for a few small points that it was no one's job but the company commander's to consider.

"How's it going?" he asked the first sergeant when he arrived. The first sergeant was a transfer, a large NCO with a beer gut that a few years before would have had him out of the Army. The company commander could have accepted that without qualm—armies had functioned for ages without professional runners being the norm—were he a competent NCO. Unfortunately he was not.

The first sergeant was a nice, quiet simpleton who had apparently risen to his present rank through a series of superiors who were okay with having a nice, quiet simpleton as an NCO. How that had happened in the pre-Posleen Army, Captain Brantley was unsure. The Army he'd left ten years before generally shuffled material like this out by around staff sergeant rank.

"Uh, okay, sir," the first sergeant said and saluted sloppily. He pulled his BDU blouse down to straighten out the wrinkles and tried to buckle his equipment belt. The maneuver only served to heighten the effect of the beer gut. "Umm, First platoon has most of their people now, but we still ain't heard from Third. An' we still ain't seen any sign of Bravo, so Second doesn't have anybody out there on their left."

"How very good. Well, the mortars are finally up and ready to support but they only have two guns. How are the positions coming? And do we have any word on hot chow?"

"Well, we're not as far along over in First platoon as we are here. And I can't get the XO on the horn, so I don't know about chow."

Captain Brantley refrained from sighing. He remembered his first sergeant in the company he commanded during his last hitch. An NCO who was one of the last with service in Vietnam, he could track a mess section down no matter how "lost" they got and if he did not find the mess section he would get pizza delivered. By helicopter if necessary. Since the time of Wellington, at least, if not Gustavus Adolphus, the importance of a prepared meal before a battle had been highly emphasized. Brantley was not particularly happy going into battle with two-thirds of his company, nobody on his left flank and soldiers who were subsisting on MREs and junk food they had packed along.

"Okay, take the command Hummer. There's a McDonald's up at the interstate. Get a hundred and twenty hamburgers and thirty cheeseburgers." He pulled out his wallet and handed the first sergeant enough cash to cover the purchase. "If they'll take it, try to give them a chit for the food. If they're closed, get the makings out of the building. Take Specialist Forrier with you." He gestured with his chin at the RTO lounging on the troop ramp of the command Bradley. The kid got into enough trouble that he would probably jump at the chance to do a little authorized scrounging.

"If you can't find any hot food there, keep looking, find a deli, a restaurant, anything. Got it?"

"Yes, sir." The first sergeant looked hangdog. "I don't want to leave you, Captain. We don't know when they'll get here."

"Just make sure you're back with some real chow before they do. And make sure you have communications in place; I want to be able to get ahold of you if I need you back here."

"Yes, sir. Maybe the XO will turn up with some chow."

"Maybe. Get going, First Sergeant."

The NCO saluted again and headed for the command Humvee. Give him his due; if you gave him clear instructions he carried them out to the best of his ability. As that headache was placed under control, Captain Brantley saw the Hummer of the battalion commander rolling in through the pine forest.

A tall heavy-bodied officer hopped out of the Humvee before it came to a full stop and strode rapidly towards the waiting company commander. Although he looked about twenty-two, Lieutenant Colonel Hartman was nearly sixty, having retired as a battalion commander in the First Infantry Division in the early '80s. A solid professional officer, he had taken command of the battalion only four months before and had worked steadily to bring it up to a highly trained level he could be proud of. Unfortunately, the Posleen did not seem to be in favor of giving him the time to correct the unit's multitude of deficiencies.

As he approached his Alpha Company commander—the only commander he had he considered worth the spit to insult them with—he was rehearsing how to break all the bad news.

"Captain Brantley."

"Colonel," the officer said with a nod. "I would offer you a hot cup of coffee, but we seem to have misplaced the mess section."

"That's not all we've misplaced," the battalion commander alleged with a patently false grin. "Let's take a walk."

When the officers were far enough away from the unit that they could not be overheard, the colonel maneuvered to place Brantley's back to the soldiers in view. That way they would not be able to see his face when he heard the news.

"Okay," the colonel said without preamble, "there is no good news. None. The bad news is as follows. I know you don't have Bravo on your left. That's because there is, effectively, no Bravo Company. There are enough tracks to make up a platoon in Bravo Company's area of operation. All the others are either lost or hiding. We may be able to find a few more that are simply lost, but most of them are on the run to avoid the battle. They ran, it's as simple as that. Before the damn battle was even joined."

He shook his head but did not let the overwhelming sense of shame and anger cloud his features. Even from here he could see the occasional glance from the soldiers digging in and he was not about to let them know how badly they had been screwed.

"Your First platoon has turned up intact intermingled with the Twenty-First Cav and since they're already there they have been 'detached' for the duration as infantry support to the Cav."

"Oh, shit." The company commander shook his head and tried not to let the hysterical laughter that was bubbling to the surface over-come him. "Jesus, we are fucked."

"The battalion trains—including all the spare food, mess section, ammunition, repair units and general logistics—somehow got on the Prince William Parkway and are halfway to Manassas. That's where breakfast is."

"I'd be happy to load up and go after it. I mean the whole company."

"I'm sure you would," the battalion commander said dryly. "I have seen some consummately fucked-up exercises, but this is arguably the worst."

"This isn't an exercise, sir," said the Alpha commander, all the humor evaporated. A cold wash of chills came over him and his mouth went dry. "Charlie Company?"

"About where you are, effectiveness-wise, with the exception of Captain Lanceman being among the missing." Something about the commander's lack of expression seemed to denote a lack of regret at the captain's absence.

"I put the XO, Lieutenant Sinestre, in charge and he has most of the company, but he is missing his mortars. I sent them Bravo's mortars and I'm detaching Bravo's personnel to you as your 'Third Platoon.' However, there are two more problems."

"And they are, sir?"

"The battalion has no reserve, this way, but worse we have no one on our right flank."

"Where's Second batt?" the company commander asked, shocked.

"Somewhere around our mess section, thirty miles away near Manassas. That was the location they received to dig in. Brigade is running around like a chicken with its head cut off, so I'm arbitrarily going to extend the battalion. Third batt is on our left, but there's a divisional boundary on the right. I've got the scouts out looking for the Thirty-Third, which is supposed to be out there somewhere, or even the Forty-First. IVIS says there's no one between here and the Potomac, but I just can't fathom that. There has to at least be someone around the interstate!"

"Run that by me again." Arkady Simosin felt like a half-dead corpse. As many times as he had participated in exercises—from a junior officer leading a tank platoon up through exercises with multiple corps—he had never seen such a tremendous mishmash as had happened during the night. His corps had utterly jumbled units and, apparently, directions and intentions. Now he was finding out just how badly. His staff had assembled to tell him the bad news with the Chief of Staff as official sacrificial lamb.

"As you know, sir, the corps battle plan called for the Forty-First to establish strong positions between the Potomac and the I-95/U.S. 1 area, the Thirty-Third to mass in the area of the roads and the Fiftieth to establish strong positions to the west of the roads, with a cavalry screen to the west and Nineteenth Armor in reserve. This plan was developed on the presumption that the Posleen would drive up the 95/1 axis towards Alexandria."

"Tell me something I don't know," snarled the general. His accent went briefly Brooklyn Slavic, always a bad sign. "You said something about the Forty-First being out of position."

"Badly, sir. The Twenty-First and Fiftieth divisions are the only ones on the correct east-west axis. The Forty-First is set up seven miles to the rear and the Thirty-Third is set up four miles to the rear of where they are supposed to be. We have logistics trains forward of our combat teams and combat units. Currently we have three divisions echeloned instead of massed which is going to invite . . ."

"Defeat in detail." Arkady grimaced and glanced at the screen of his PC. "That's not what this says. It just notes that they are not at full strength."

"It perceives that a percentage of each unit is in the right location and, given the current chaos, that is their actual axis, General. Unfortunately, most of each division is in the area I just gave you. Those are the locations that they received to set up in or, in some cases, chose to set up in."

"Okay." Simosin flogged his tired brain for a solution. "Call the Twenty-First. Tell them to hold in place. If the Posleen make contact they are not to decisively engage but they should try to slow them down. Pull the Fiftieth back to where the Thirty-Third is actually axised. Pull the Forty-First forward to that axis. Get as many units properly joined up as possible in the time allotted along that axis."

"That will put us almost on the Prince William, General," noted the G-3. "Well north of the President's stated intent."

"North or south of the Prince William?"

"South of it, sir."

"Good, the President will have to suck it up; having that road at our backs will give us a way to move reinforcements back and forth and to retreat if necessary. Move the corps artillery north of the Occoquan; they'll be able to range for close support. And move all the logistic elements except ammunition and food north of it too. Tell the division commanders to make their own judgement on where their artillery should be placed. They should know that if it's north, if those bridges go down their artillery will be out of contact.

"What is the status on the bridges?"

"They're cored, mined and ready to drop, General," said the Ninety-Fifth ID Assistant Division Engineer, a major-promotable. As the most senior noncommanding engineer left in the corps, he had been seconded to act as engineering liaison to replace the absent corps engineer. "They will drop them when the last of the units are south and the refugees are north or when the Posleen come into close-contact range."

"Well, we'll just have to try and make sure that doesn't happen. Okay, get to shuffling units. We still have time to straighten this out, people; we just have to keep our heads on straight."

◆ CHAPTER 43 ◆

Near Ladysmith, VA, United States of America, Sol III
0912 EDT October 10th, 2004 AD

The Twenty-Ninth Infantry Division artillery fire was like a slight tap against a hornet's nest. Slowly at first, practically one at a time, the hornets began to wander out, looking around for whatever had kicked their home.

Ersin held onto the ceiling grab bar and the seat in front of him as the Humvee left the ground for the fifth time, this time striking a streambed with a tremendous splash that threw water over the hood of the all-terrain vehicle. Above him the twenty-five-millimeter chain gun burped. How anyone could expect to hit anything while airborne was beyond him but the gunner in the seat next to him grunted in satisfaction.

"Better get us hull-down, Tom," the gunner shouted over the howl of the engine as the vehicle dug itself out of the stream. "I got the God King."

He turned to look at the Special Forces master sergeant on the seat next to him and laughed. "I knew all that time playing Death World was going to come in handy someday!"

Ersin glanced out in time to see the trees behind them begin coming apart under the hammer of Posleen guns. In response the Humvee cornered so hard his clamped hand came loose and he slid across the compartment and slammed into the gunner. The wide stance and advanced traction of the combat vehicle permitted maneuvers that would roll any normal off-road vehicle.

"Sorry!" he yelled to the gunner as he forced himself back across the seat.

"No problem, Sarge." The gunner tapped the four-point harness holding him in place. "That's why we changed out the belts in this thing." He glanced at his monitor and shook his head. "Nothing in sight."

"Another klick to the interstate!" shouted the vehicle commander over the howl of the diesel engine. "I told them we're coming in!"

"Just make damn sure they're ready to pass us through the lines!" Ersin tapped his AID. "AID, get me Sergeant Mueller."

"He is standing by, Master Sergeant Ersin."

"*Mueller?*"

"*Yeah, Ersin. I understand we got company.*"

"*How's it coming?*"

"*We're hooking up the blasting caps as fast as we can.*"

"*Well, you got hostiles at about a klick, klick and a half from the IP. Hurry.*"

"*Roger. We need to keep them from coming down U.S. 1, they're not as far along.*"

"*How the hell do we do that?*" snapped Ersin.

"*Do you know how to lead a pig?*" asked Mueller.

"*No.*"

Mueller explained.

The master sergeant gave a feral smile in return and spared a glance out the back window. The Posleen were not to going to like their reception by Twelfth Corps.

"You sure about this, Sergeant?" asked the Bradley gunner, as the TOW launcher rotated outward.

"No, but it's the orders. Edwards," he continued to the driver, "you be ready to put your foot in it as soon as you get the word."

"Okee-dokee, Sarge," said the driver of the Bradley. In sheer nervousness she gunned the throttle.

"Now, Irvine, you gotta . . ."

" . . . launch the rocket off-axis. I got it."

"Hopefully, that way the lander won't fire right at us. When the Posleen turn this way, we'll lead them down 632."

"What happens if they do take us out, right away, that is?"

"Four track will wait for the ground response and take it under fire. Not that we'll care," he ended, parenthetically.

"I got family in Richmond," responded the gunner. "Target," he said, indicating that the target was in sight in his scope.

"Right." The vehicle commander looked through his repeater. The missile launcher was pointed into a tobacco field. With any luck the gunner would be able to turn the wire-guided missile and get it on a course to hit the Posleen landing ship before it was destroyed by counterfire. The alternative, firing directly at the lander, had been determined to be suicide on Barwhon. At that point, the thinking went, the Posleen would send their forces towards the launcher. Towards them, that was, as they retreated down the country road.

Since their vehicle was nearly three thousand yards from the lander, the only Posleen weapons they had to worry about immediately were the automatic weapons on the God King saucers and the defensive fire of the lander itself. Not that either system was very survivable for a tin can on tracks like a Bradley.

If the plan worked, the Posleen would be exposed to sniping flank attacks by cavalry units scattered throughout the woods and fields and it would give the ambush sites more time to prepare. "Confirm, target identified. Fire."

"Man," whispered the gunner as he closed the firing circuit, "I really wish they'd used an Abrams."

The United States Ground Forces were in the unusual situation of having incomplete battlefield intelligence. Knowledge of an enemy's abilities and intentions is better than half a battle won or lost. For years the pre-Posleen Army had worked on systems to insure that future commanders would have an almost Godlike view of the physical and electronic battlefield. Satellites would look down from their Olympian orbits while closer pilotless drones and deep-viewing reconnaissance planes with sophisticated radar and visual systems gave precise moment-to-moment information on enemy movements.

The coming of the Posleen had ended for all time the concept of "sundering the fog of war."

The satellites were already gone. Most of them had been destroyed during the ponderous atmospheric entry of the Posleen battleglobes and the rest were picked off at leisure by the automated sky defense systems of the landers. The same defense system created a virtually impregnable information bubble around the Posleen forces. To find the Posleen, small units were forced to maneuver forward until they made contact. It was a return to the bad old days of information warfare; the days of skirmishers and scouting parties. The term "Dark Ages" was used frequently.

Given Posleen psychology, if they saw a target, it would be taken under fire. Once taken under fire, if there were any survivors the Posleen would give chase. If they gave chase they were bound to run into defenses, defenses which were still not prepared. The whole concept of the defense and the information war had been predicated on cavalry or infantry patrols making contact but not being seen.

Now those slowly probing patrols were converting to skirmishers. In most cases the results were poor. On the north edge of the Posleen bubble, in the Tenth Corps area of operations, a reconnaissance platoon of the Twenty-First Cavalry found out the hard way that Posleen can be fast and brutal in movement-to-contact.

Probing forward on U.S. 1, the two Humvees and two Bradleys would bound forward in echelons. First a Humvee would move, then a Bradley. When they were in place with troops deployed, the next echelon would dart forward, twenty-five-millimeter chain guns constantly questing for heat signatures.

As the Bradley of the second echelon was bounding forward, without warning a company of Posleen came out of a side road at a trot. Before the standing echelon could even call in the sighting, all four hundred normals opened fire at under five hundred meters.

The moving Bradley was the first to be hit, as a three-millimeter railgun tracked across the personnel compartment. The tungsten rounds penetrated the thin magnesium armor and began tumbling through the compartment, chewing up the troops within. Their moment of horror was brief, however, for within seconds of one another, four of the twenty hypervelocity missile launchers in the Posleen company found the armored cavalry vehicle. When the slugs of gadolinium traveling at .3c struck the vehicle with near simultaneity, there was not enough left to do a chemical analysis.

The forward Humvee was gone seconds later, victim of massed fire from 1mm railguns and shotguns, and the rear echelon, taking fire from nearly a hundred 3mm railguns and HVM launchers, lasted only moments longer. The entire battle was over before the standing unit could send out a sighting report, before they could even move out of their positions.

The dense smoke and crack of HVMs from the skirmish, however, was not lost on the next echelon of scouts. The backup company a thousand meters behind the point went into a hasty defense and called in a sighting report. Their platoon of Abrams main battle tanks turned to the rear of a nearby strip mall. With a brief, almost unnoticed, crash 120mm cannons shivered the remaining display glass from the inside. The shadows of the buildings effectively hid the massive combat vehicles within.

Arkady Simosin watched the main IVIS display start to light up with Posleen sightings and knew they were doomed. The Fiftieth Infantry Division had just reached its defense points and started digging in. The slower Forty-First was not even completely in place. One look at the number of sightings, and the rapidly blunting blue arrows as cavalry forces were pushed back, told him that the Posleen were coming to dinner and they would not be denied. He punched a button on his command panel and an officer in helmet and LCE answered.

"Corps Arty," the officer started to say and stopped when he saw who the caller was. "Yes, sir."

"I want you to target those sighting reports at will, just as if they were valid calls for fire," he told the artillery officer abruptly.

"They're only guesses, General," protested the colonel.

"Yeah, but by the time they fire on them, every single one of those roads will be packed with Posleen. Can the battleships range to here?"

The officer looked off-screen at another display. "Yes, sir. It can easily range to the interstate points, and all the way along the cav's front. Right now we only have the *Missouri*; the *Massachusetts* is on the way. But they're not linked into the tac net; we have to give them vocal calls for fire."

"That'll do. Feed them those coordinates. I want to pound the follow-on forces as hard as possible. Do it."

"Yes, sir." The officer punched a series of keys. "So ordered."

"Out here." The general cut the display and leaned back. He zoomed the IVIS out to cover all of northern Virginia, punched in another series of commands and grunted. At current rate of advance, the ACS battalion was still six hours away. And he was fairly certain that one battalion was not going to be able to make a difference. The Eleventh Mobile Infantry Division was getting closer, barely ten hours away, but it was a division in name only, with a brigade and a half of troops fully suited and only partially trained.

He punched another button and called up the Chief of Staff.

"Okay, I've had a really bad idea."

"Yes, sir?"

"So far we have failed miserably at every movement we have tried to make, but I think we need to get ready to make another one."

"What, now, sir?" asked the COS, upset and startled. The corps was barely getting into its positions and he could not believe the general was preparing to move.

"Not now. I said prepare for one. With the way they are boiling out of there, we might have to turn this into a battle of maneuver. If so, I want to be as prepared as we can. This battle is in play mode; it's up to company commanders now. So get the staff working on a plan to pivot the corps to a north-south axis, anchored on the north by the Occoquan. Start the Nineteenth towards the west; they'll anchor the left flank. If we find ourselves being pushed out of position we'll need to pivot towards Manassas and slow their rate of advance towards Ninth Corps."

"What about the Forty-First, General? They'll be swinging in the breeze."

"Plan it with them on the north flank, but I agree that they will have problems completing the maneuver. However, they can retreat towards the Occoquan bridges or, barring that, they can move down to the Potomac and be Dunkirked under the cover of the battleships."

"You're assuming that we won't be able to stop them, sir."

"You are correct. At a tactical level we cannot maintain visual contact with them long enough to get good calls for fire, at least not so far. We will have to see what happens when they come into contact with the prepared positions. If we had had more time, more room to trade for time, we might have been able to pull this off. But without good trenches, wire and bunkers, I think they'll overrun us. We'll see."

"Aiming point this instrument!"

"Aiming point identified!"

The missing platoon sergeant and One Gun had linked back up during the move and Keren was back where he preferred to be. The L-T had handled the sudden move—and the linkup with the missing tracks—with remarkable smoothness. As the hammer came down the lieutenant seemed to be getting more and more into harness, like a young horse that never really shines until up against a competitor. He was laying in the section under Staff Sergeant Simmons's direction and doing it well. The guns were up almost before anyone knew it and almost simultaneously the released troops dove into their tracks to check the IVIS displays.

Red enemy marks sprinkled the entire front of the Twenty-First Cav, only six miles down the road, and the hammer of missiles and artillery could be heard from the distance.

"Look," said Keren, scrolling the display to the west, "it's solid along their front all the way to the edge of the division."

"So?" asked Sheila.

"I doubt that they just end there because the divisional front does," snorted Riley.

"Huh?" The ammo bearer was only seventeen and straight out of basic training. Most of the symbols on the display were still foreign to her.

"The Posleen are probably out around the cav's flank," explained Sergeant Herd. "And there," he continued, pointing to a unit marker in movement down Gun Truck Road, "is the response."

"Only a company," muttered Keren.

"They're stretched thin covering a three-division front," pointed out Herd. "Besides," he pointed to a mass on the primary roads, centered on the cavalry division's forward units, "that's the main thrust. If the Posleen are off the roads, they're slowed down." He turned towards the front of the track and began a fuel and maintenance report.

As the rest of the squad began maintenance or personal activities, Keren stayed to track the scout company as it rushed down the twisting backroads towards the threatened flank of the division. Before it was halfway there it flashed the purple of in-contact then dropped off the screen.

"Shit!"

"What?" asked Sergeant Herd standing up quickly and banging his helmetless head on the overhead of the crowded track. "Damn! Cocksucker!"

As the sergeant cursed every piece of metal ever designed by an engineer with the express purpose of making an infantryman's life uncomfortable, red enemy icons began popping up to the rear of the westernmost regiment of the Twenty-First. A fuel convoy, driving forward to refuel the thirsty vehicles of the embattled division, went purple then winked out. Other logistics units began to report contact as the main reserve of the division started a movement to the west.

"Posleen have turned the cav's flank," said Keren. "They must have bypassed the security companies and they're in the rear area."

"Shit." Reed hung upside down from the top of the APC watching the inverted screen. "Better get ready to rock and roll, boys and girls."

◆ CHAPTER 44 ◆

The Pentagon, VA, United States of America, Sol III
1024 EDT October 10th, 2004 AD

"This is Bob Argent reporting from Continental Army Command. With the unauthorized firing of artillery by units of the Twenty-Ninth Infantry Division, the Posleen have started pouring out of their positions around Fredericksburg like ants out of a kicked hive." The reporter looked like hell. It was obvious under the makeup that he had gotten as little rest as the soldiers he was reporting on. Under normal circumstances a replacement would have been sent in to cover for him while he got some sleep. But the veteran reporter would have none of it; this was the news event of the century and he was at the nerve center.

"I have with me Lieutenant Colonel Guy Tremont, aide to General Horner, the Continental Army Commander. Colonel, how do you rate the chances for the Tenth Corps forces, that is, can they hold?"

"Well, Bob," the colonel said with a somber smile, "Tenth Corps is a very heavy corps and if any five divisions can do the job they will. We have great faith in General Simosin here at CONARC and everyone feels that if any general can command a defense like that, it is General Simosin."

"What about the confusion overnight? We understand that many of the units got lost."

"Define lost," said the colonel, with a shrug. "It's central Virginia, they always knew where they were. In many cases there was great confusion about where they should be, but that happens any time that there is a sudden change of plan. Tenth Corps has recovered and is in position to handle the threat."

"Is that an implied criticism of the President, of his sudden change to defend forward of the Potomac?"

"No, definitely not. The President is the Commander in Chief; his word is law for the military. If he wants us to defend in close, we defend in close; if he wants us to defend in Pennsylvania, we defend in Pennsylvania."

"So you think that the Tenth Corps will be able to stop the Posleen?"

"There is no surety in war, and certainly no surety when the situation is as chaotic as this one, with the threat arriving before expected and by surprise. The Tenth will do the best that any unit can do. If they succeed, so much the better. If they do not, and have to retreat, there is another bullet in that gun. The Posleen still have to get through the Ninth Corps coming into position near the head of the Occoquan reservoir. One or the other should stop them."

"According to the IVIS displays, they are already starting to turn the edge of the cavalry . . ."

Jack Horner nodded his head solemnly at the accurate statement.

"So you're still in favor of broadcasting the IVIS?" asked General Taylor. The two were conferring about how many and what units should be moved into the area, but they had taken time to watch the hastily briefed interview.

"Yes, and when the ACS get here, I'm going to broadcast forty channels of raw video for the networks to monitor, edit and distribute; every platoon leader at a minimum. There is no indication that the Posleen use operational intelligence and under the circumstances I think that the American people have a full right to know what is going on."

"Well, the President agrees with you," Taylor commented with a nod.

"I wish I could have gotten him to agree with me on the locations to defend," said Horner, with a tight, humorless smile. "If we had even moved up to where the Ninth is digging in, it would have made this almost survivable. Especially with the Tenth up and the Ninth in a second defensive belt. As is, I'm afraid they're going to chew up the Tenth then go for seconds on the Ninth. The Tenth has its right flank swinging in the breeze."

"He should have extended his line with the reserve."

"No, watch how Arkady uses the reserve; I think that might save the corps. At some point the Posleen would have turned the flank. They'll turn the flank of the whole corps if he's not careful. But the Nineteenth is already moving to intercept."

"Okay, it's Arkady's battle, let's let him run it. What's the story on Richmond?"

The Posleen scout companies moved southward on the broad highway towards the distant city skyline at a tireless ground-eating lope, columns of phalanxes on either side, heads swaying from side to side searching out potential trouble. A unit of the thresh had been spotted, but they were still too far out to bother engaging, their tracked *tenar* that had given so much trouble over the last few hours hull-down and at maximum engagement range. The lead God Kings considered firing but decided to hold off until their companies were in good range.

There had thus far been no sign of the twin-turreted military technicians and the scout leaders breathed silent words of relief. Bad enough to fight a fast and slippery enemy that fired from ambush and disappeared into the brush taking countless oolt'os with them, but at least there were brief targets to engage, an enemy to combat. The military technicians and the explosives that coasted through the air on ballistic paths were impossible to fight. As long as neither of them made an appearance the battle was a foregone conclusion.

Finally they were getting in range of the thresh, close enough that massed fire would start to strike their hated *tenar,* and the western God King gave the command to fire.

As a hail of railgun rounds and missiles began to spark off the overpass, the cav platoon leader gave Mueller a quick thumbs-up and dropped into his command Bradley, the hatch quickly shutting behind him.

Mueller checked the monitor from the ambush site and decided to give the Posleen a little more rope with which to hang themselves. The lead companies, which he considered fair game for the cav, were still in the ambush zone. Let a few more Posleen pass out of the ambush zone and fill it with the heavier armed follow-on companies. Behind him the driver in the Humvee left for his use started the engine, ready to get out of harm's way as intended.

Mueller nodded as the first God King on either side passed completely through the ambush zone. Their companies were engaging the cav well, coming forward at what would be a canter in a horse, and apparently confident that they had this battle won. Wrong. He smiled ferally and engaged the firing circuit.

At the speed of light the current flashed to the far side of the half-kilometer mechanical ambush and then simple chemistry took over.

Since Amanda Hunt and the engineering platoon leader who helped set up the ambush were both pessimistic people, there were three fairly independent methods of detonation for the claymores. It was one of the reasons the ambush was so time consuming to emplace. First, the entire ambush was "daisy-chained." Each claymore had two points for detonators to be attached. The first claymore had a detonator on either side, one for wire reception and the other for radio, and was wrapped with detonation cord. One line of detcord ran from another radio detonation sequence, another line ran from a secondary wire detonation sequence, the third ran to the next claymore in line and the fourth and last ran to the third claymore in line. At each succeeding claymore the same sequence was set, with the exception that the succeeding claymores only had the wire circuit on one side and an "inbound" detcord on the other. Second, the wire backups on all the claymores were circuit-delayed to let the primary daisy-chain sequence carry the detonation.

As it turned out, the backups and redundancies were virtually unused except for one point on the east side where a stray twenty-five-millimeter round had severed the detcord daisy chain and, surprisingly enough, did not set the whole ambush off. Elsewhere the entire sequence ran like a Swiss watch, a tribute to Ms. Hunt's consummate professionalism.

When the first claymore detonated, it in turn fired the detcord that was wrapped around it. This cord, like an exploding fuse, carried the explosion the few meters to the next claymore in line which exploded and sent it to the next. With a series of trip-hammer explosions sounding like the world's largest machine gun, five hundred yards of roadway flashed white and the air filled with dust and smoke.

As the air cleared, it revealed both sides of the roadway packed with dead and dying Posleen, a monstrous abattoir of torn yellow flesh. In many cases of the outer centaurs, only the finest of forensic analysis would be able to separate one mangled centaur from another. In less than a second, over sixty-four hundred Posleen, normals and God Kings, a full B-Dec command, was wiped off the face of the earth.

The lead companies checked, shocked by the destruction behind them and fighting the conflicting stresses of justifiable fear of what they might face and the God King bondings driving them on. As they checked, the first artillery started to fall.

The Posleen in the phalanxes following the erased companies checked as well—shocked and terrified by the sight in front of them— but only for a moment. As some units began to pour around the organic roadblock, other units began gathering the dead and transporting them back to the nearest landers for processing. The Posleen firmly believed in the doctrine of waste-not-want-not.

The lead companies moved back up to a canter to try to close the distance to the enemy through the beaten zone of the artillery but the combination was just too strong. The time the Posleen had used up on Fredericksburg had been put to good use by General Keeton and his staff. Most divisional artillery and all the corps mobile artillery units had been moved forward to support the ambushes while their revetments on Libby and Mosby Hills were being prepared. Over a hundred 155mm artillery pieces—each with a thirty-meter "footprint"—were firing into a zone only one hundred meters wide and five hundred deep.

Between the accurate fire of the Bradleys and the massed artillery, the lead companies of Posleen were erased in seconds before coming within five hundred meters of the cav scouts.

The cavalry had not escaped unscathed. The plasma cannon of the western God King had accounted for two Bradleys and a lucky hit by the massed HVM for another. But the reinforced platoon, the artillery and the ambush had accounted for over seven thousand Posleen in less than five minutes. The destroyed tracks were quickly replaced on the line with vehicles from the reserve platoon while medics worked on the traumatized survivors.

It takes approximately three minutes for a Posleen to gallop a kilometer. The forward edge of the ambush zone had been placed at a kilometer and a half from the cav unit while the surviving Posleen forces were an additional half a kilometer back. The cavalry company commander called for fire to be adjusted outward as the follow-on Posleen companies charged forward.

For the first five hundred meters the centaurs slipped and slithered in the offal-moistened soil of the verge. The unholy slurry slowed their movement through that beaten zone and increased their time in the zone of fire. However, within a few minutes Posleen battle units were up on the interstate and pounding forward towards the cav unit.

Despite the long gallop and the massed artillery fire, it was obvious that the tide of Posleen would eventually break through. Even as the lead elements drove forward—melting like a sugar cube in water—more forces poured around the distant bend. It was an unending stream of centaurs.

The company commander ordered his reserve up to the line and prepared to retreat as the Bradleys and artillery began to pound the assaulting Posleen.

Meanwhile, Mueller took one look at the charging army of centaurs and decided that this was a better fight for the cav. He picked

John Ringo

up the circuit board—also being a great believer in waste-not-want-not—and trotted to the waiting Humvee. With a sigh of relief, the driver pulled out as soon as he was on board.

◆ CHAPTER 45 ◆

"It's going well," said Colonel Abrahamson, watching the bank of monitors set up in the main conference room of the R.J. Reynolds Corporation.

With the security of the north bank of the James questionable, corps command had relocated south of the river and the Reynolds company had graciously offered its facilities. The fact that the building was now the most heavily defended in south Richmond was surely besides the point.

Whatever the rationale, the logistical and information management facilities were top-notch, befitting a Fortune Five Hundred company. The administrative employees who had shown up were immediately press-ganged by the various corps staff to handle the massive management headache involved in creating the Richmond Defense from scratch in the midst of a "murthering great battle."

John Keene had gotten a start on that early by calling in the top five engineers involved in Richmond's previous defense design and winning them over to the new plan. Despite their personal desires they could all see the rationale of the plan and they were as familiar with the terrain as could be hoped.

He gave each of them a specific task to organize, and blanket authorization to dragoon anyone and anything they felt that they needed to accomplish it. One of the corps Chief of Staff's planning officers was slated with the unenviable task of managing the flow of materials. Working from the same office complex in Shockoe Circle where Keene and Mueller had paused in their survey, he set to work

367

coordinating the flow of personnel, equipment and supplies to the various projects.

A radio and television appeal for anyone with construction or demolition equipment had generated massive response. Five assembly points in and around Richmond were designated and practically before the police traffic control could get set up, jams of lowboys with front-end loaders, backhoes, power shovels and earth movers were at each site.

Along with them came concrete and dump trucks, construction personnel and virtually anyone who felt that it was time to volunteer. Some of the volunteers—those who somehow impressed the military and civilian personnel arriving to inventory and segregate the response—were immediately put to work sorting out the sheep from the goats. Within two hours, starting from scratch, the complicated task of receiving the equipment, determining what was where and determining where it should be was running smoothly. In the meantime the engineers had called upon their engineering firms and other firms for support, and by the time that the requested equipment was arriving at the construction sites, the engineers had sketched out plans and movement paths and were surveying the areas to be graded and cut.

It was from this appeal that Amanda Hunt, the volunteers stringing claymores and the grading contractors who had dug the cavalry positions had sprung.

It was quickly determined that the biggest time factor was not going to be cutting out embankments to make walls or backfilling the mile-long floodwall—there was enough heavy equipment in surplus to backfill it twice over in six hours—but rather rubbling the three newer concrete factories along the James and turning the rubble into a hasty wall.

The preferred method for rubbling a factory was to lace it with explosives and drop it in one piece. Unfortunately all the personnel who were adept at that task were either rigging the bridges over the James or laying the ambushes on the roads to the north. The civilian specialists on the ambush teams were about to be called back when a junior officer on the corps staff had a brainstorm.

Less than an hour later a brigade of the Seventy-Fifth Armored Division rolled across the Mayo bridge and through Schockoe Bottom. Since it was also determined that the two- and three-story brick buildings would offer far too much cover to the, hopefully, trapped Posleen, the brigade paid little attention to roads.

After nearly a hundred seventy-ton M-1E tanks rolled, literally, through the area, there was hardly a building left standing. A couple of the bars were intentionally spared in case they still had liquor in them.

When they reached the area of the concrete factories, each battalion singled out a building. Each tank was given certain points to take under fire and clear fire lanes. The area around and behind the factories was evacuated and the brigade opened fire.

High Explosive Anti-Tank (HEAT) rounds were used for breaching lower floors, while senior NCO tank commanders used Discarding Sabot Armor Piercing Rounds, "silver bullets," to destroy key structural members. These members had been thoughtfully highlighted by the engineering group with orange spray paint.

Under the pounding assault the buildings gave way, finally crumbling to the ground like slumping giants. One of the factories retained much of its structural integrity even after the lower floors gave way, but that was dealt with by a few rounds and a battalion road march, right center, front. Satisfied with the start to their day, the brigade rolled back across the James to their laager point and a chance to get some rest before the big game.

The furious pace of work continued throughout the night of distant battle and a new day dawned on Richmond transformed.

The towering interstate and highway bridges that loomed over Schockoe Bottom were either mined, ready to blow, or had had their concrete surfaces cut in such a way that cranes, standing by with lift cables in place, could lift them up, leaving a bridge of only narrow concrete beams for the Posleen to cross.

This late idea was suggested in the hope that the bridges could be salvaged. There were over twenty bridges that would have to be cut and the cost of replacing all of them after the conflict would be staggering. Although the Posleen could cross such a structure, they could only cross in a trickle, one line of centaurs to a beam, making them easy meat for the human defenders. Afterwards the bridges would have to be repaired, surveyed and recertified, but that was far less expensive than the cost of replacement.

The north-side floodwall had been backfilled, its gate controls reversed to lock from the river side and the riverside road regraded and reinforced for heavy vehicle traffic. Mayo Island had been transformed into a command bunker by piling and interconnecting prefab concrete slabs and covering the temporary structure with dirt and rubble. The upper portion overlooked the whole floodwall and it was from this location that the Forty-Ninth and Sixtieth Infantry Division commanders would maneuver their troops.

The island also now held the reserve—a brigade of the Sixtieth Infantry Division—that would respond to any breaches of the wall.

It was anticipated that eventually the defenders of the wall would have to retreat, and the Mayo Island forces were also intended to establish a base of fire to enable a safe and secure escape route. The Mayo bridges, both to the north and the south of the island, were also mined and ready to drop.

On the east side of the city, all along the I-95 corridor through Richmond, road embankments had been joined and rubble had been piled creating a continuous wall that would be well-nigh impossible for the Posleen to climb. To make it even more difficult, angle iron welded with sharpened rebar, saw blades and anything else sharp and metal that came to hand had been piled in front of the embankments and laced with concertina wire.

Above these embankments temporary "Jersey" walls, easily recognized as the low temporary walls seen around highway construction, had been emplaced, creating a continuous barrier from behind which the infantry and armor of the Seventy-First Infantry Division could pour fire into the passing centaurs with relative impunity. While the three-millimeter railguns and HVMs of the Posleen would easily breach the wall, the majority 1mm and shotguns would bounce off. Although there would be casualties, the defenders had an excellent position.

With two brigades of the Seventy-First "up" and one back as reinforcement, any temporary breaches in the lines would be easy to fill. All along the route, the towering buildings overlooking the defenses held snipers, their .50 caliber rifles zeroed onto the interstate. Their job was to dispense with any God King that might try to overfly the defenses.

On the north side of the city the roads and buildings had been blockaded with a physical barrier of cross-piled Jersey walls and stacked cars. Thousands of personal automobiles had gone into creating virtually impenetrable multivehicle-deep barriers. Buildings had been sealed and faired over or had concrete slabs piled in front of them to prevent any entry by the Posleen on that side.

The Sixty-Fourth Infantry Division awaited the Posleen in this sector, bunkered into second-floor rooms with heavy sandbag emplacements.

The roads leading out of Schockoe Bottom had been blockaded using all of the previous methods and, in addition, engineers and armored fighting vehicles of the Forty-Eighth ID had dropped the James Monroe building across Broad and Franklin Streets. The multistory government building formed a massive barrier of mangled concrete and steel which was further laced with concertina barbed wire. The building demolition had not been the precision undertaking usually associated with such an endeavor. In fact, it had impacted against the Consolidated Laboratory building. If the city survived, that building might have to be replaced. But better to replace a building than a state.

Despite the obvious structural damage, the Lab building along with the Corporation Commission, the Ferguson building and the DOT annex was packed with the troops of the Forty-Eighth Infantry Division. With a perfect view of Schockoe Bottom and plunging fire, the unit was poised to pound the Posleen as soon as they came into view, while their armored fighting vehicles manned the barricades. The joke among the troopers on the Lab building was that since the morgue was just downstairs, they would not have far to go.

Around the perimeter of Schockoe Bottom other tanks and engineers had been at work removing the construction efforts of the last few decades to create hasty fighting positions. The James Center, the First Union Bank, Riverside Plaza and even the Federal Reserve had given of their structures to create a wall of rubble around the heart of the city. Behind them, troops from the Seventy-Third Infantry Division held a long, light line, designed to pin the Posleen in place for destruction by the troops along the floodwall.

At Riverfront Plaza, the wall finally necked off, joining with the end of the floodwall. The "neck off" point of the defenses would probably come under heavy attack, so it was reinforced with tanks of the Seventy-Fifth Armored Division in the heaviest revetments possible to construct. Although the Posleen could spread onto Browns Island, all of the foot bridges but one had been removed. It was intended to act as a bleed off for their forces.

The main reserve for the defense, the majority of the Seventy-Fifth Armored, was laagered at the Ethyl Corporation building, overlooking the island. From those positions they could pound the Posleen with direct 120mm canister fire, effectively sweeping the area like a broom. The sole remaining footbridge led all the way across the James and was defended by a battalion of the Twenty-Second Cavalry. The idea was to lure the Posleen into thinking they were getting across the river, while simultaneously setting them up like ducks in a shooting gallery. The battalion had been issued extra manjacks, just to make sure.

In addition to their personal weapons, fighting vehicles and automatic weapons teams, every fire team in the various divisions had a Protean manjack. Accepted only the year before, the Proteans were the brainchild of Hester L. Jacobs, a man well-hated by Ground Force procurement officers everywhere.

Ground Forces had intended to field manjacks, automated infantry weapon systems, all along, but that was where the process had sty-mied. In the truest fashion of every light weapon developed by a committee, the procurement system finally developed specifications for the manjacks that transformed them from the original concept of a light, relatively simple automatic weapon on an automated tripod, into a virtual mini-tank.

Jacobs, on the other hand, already had developed a weapon system that met the original concept. Sure of his product, the former Marine gunnery sergeant had launched an all-out assault on the Ground Forces procurement program. Jacobs visited numerous infantry field officers and NCOs and, in violation of a slew of regulations, demonstrated his system for them and got written suggestions and testimonials.

In a short time, from the point of view of hundreds of infantry lieutenants, captains, first sergeants, sergeant majors and colonels, he had perfected a battlefield weapon system.

With those testimonials, and presentations on the cost difference and what it meant to production numbers, between his system, already up and running, and the systems being developed by the major corporations, behind schedule and over budget, he pigeonholed congressmen and senators night and day, to the point where those elected officials nearly had him arrested for harassment.

But his arguments finally started to sink in and, in a rare burst of logic. The Congress overrode the military procurement bureaucracy and ordered them to accept the Jacobs Industries Protean Manjack as it was.

The manjacks were heavy, bulky and awkward to carry in their large formed-plastic cases, but they might be the weapon that turned this tide. Each manjack consisted of an M-60F machine gun, the newest version of the venerable platoon automatic weapon that had first seen service in Vietnam, and a removable automated firing system. The firing system contained a mechanized tripod and a simple autotarget system. Place the weapon on a vector, let it "read" the area—get a laser picture of the zone of fire—and if the "picture" changed, if anything broke the continuously sweeping infrared lasers, it would fire down the broken vector. The weapon could be produced for one-third the cost and in a fifth of the time of the first "correct" version to be fielded. Already, in less than a year's time, there were sufficient manjacks for all the forces and more were being installed in the fixed defenses.

Since the M-60F contained the latest in barrel technology, the barrels actively dissipated heat. Thus the weapons could continue to fire as long as the ammunition held out. To assist in that, each team had hooked the machine guns up to a "battlecase," boxes preloaded at the factory with twenty-five-thousand rounds of 7.62mm ammunition. The boxes were backbreakingly heavy, one hundred rounds of M-60 ammunition weighs seven pounds, and awkward to maneuver into some of the manjack positions, but once in place they gave every team three times the throw weight of fire they could otherwise expect. In addition, the boxes could be ganged together, so that if one box ran dry, the weapon would be fed from a second. The joke went that if you used up two boxes, fifty thousand rounds of ammunition, you were officially having a bad hair day and could take the rest of the day off.

But the armor, the infantry, even the manjacks, were really only there to hold the Posleen in place.

To truly make the Posleen's day miserable, and for the long-term defense of Richmond, over fifty percent of the construction equipment had been detailed to the Mosby and Libby Hill defenses.

The two hills towered over Richmond, dominating the landscape at least as much as the city skyline, and loomed doubly over the Schockoe Valley that separated them from the city. While the sides towards the James and Schockoe Bottom were extremely steep, far too steep for the quadrupedal Posleen to negotiate, the north and east sides were another matter. Among other things they had roads leading up to the numerous homes and monuments on the hills.

All of the roads were initially left in place, but demolition of the slopes began immediately. Where a slope was merely steep, it was made vertical by a combination of explosives and graders. The many abandoned buildings again went into the defenses, the rubble used to create hasty fighting positions for the cavalry troops detailed for security. The cavalry, in the meantime, began covering their front with antipersonnel mines, concertina barbed wire and "tanglefoot," barbed wire stretched tight at knee level, designed to slow the advance of ground troops. Between the slopes and the obstacles, assaulting Posleen should be effectively stopped, sitting ducks for the heavily armed defenders. Their cavalry fighting vehicles were well back to avoid taking fire, but they were ready to go if ordered to sally. The line would be held by troops with rifles, grenades, machine guns and the ubiquitous manjacks.

The outer edges of the defense boasted a brigade of cavalry. Then in the next ring was the massed artillery of the infantry divisions. Over one hundred tubes of 155mm artillery were packed on the hills. In a few cases, the artillery was placed so as to cover straight open steep roads, such as Broad Street, which ran through downtown Richmond, through Schockoe Bottom, and up into the Montrose Heights area.

When, inevitably, the Posleen charged up that street, they would eventually be met by batteries A and B of the One Hundred Ninety-Third Artillery, firing 155mm canister rounds into them from revetments at point-blank. If they were able to overcome the defenses anyway, the road was mined to blow out a crater large enough to make the approach impenetrable.

In the inner ring were better than half of the infantry division's mortar platoons, set up in their tracked vehicles. Since they were invisible to any reasonable angle of fire from the Posleen, the feeling was that they might as well stay in a mobile configuration in case they had to move off the hills for some reason. They were behind the artillery because mortars have no direct-fire capability. However, as John Keene had pointed out, mortars carry more explosive-weight-to-size than rifled artillery. Because the mortars were fired from smooth bores, they did not have to be able to withstand the rotational force placed on an artillery shell. A 120mm mortar round has the same explosive power as a 155mm artillery shell.

Mortars are a lot of bang for very little buck and there were over one hundred packed onto the hills. In addition, the mortar vehicles, unlike the unarmored mobile artillery vehicles, were designed for close defense. And the mortarmen who crewed those vehicles were trained and heavily armed for it; a mechanized mortar platoon had twice the throw weight of a mechanized line platoon, including just as many manjacks. If the Posleen penetrated the outer defenses, penetrated the cav and the depressed artillery's point-blank fire, they would still have to penetrate the band of mortar infantrymen and women to take the command and supply facilities.

Libby Hill, Mosby Hill and Montrose Heights were a seething fortress of artillery, eagerly awaiting the arrival of the centaurs. Troops in the open are the artilleryman's meat and drink.

While there were heavy defenses along the north and east, the west side of the city was virtually undefended; only scattered cavalry units were there as sentries. The defense plan depended on the Posleen turning towards the east and Schockoe Bottom. Barriers were being erected along the I-95/U.S. 1 corridor, designed to physically and visually distract the Posleen away from the westerly route. And when the Posleen approached, all of the roads to the west would be cratered by the heavy charges being emplaced. General Keeton was prepared to move the Seventy-Fifth Armored up in defense if small numbers moved in that direction, otherwise—if the Posleen did turn westward en masse—the "good" plan would have to be scrapped.

The alternative plan was to use the Libby Hill defenses to create a curtain barrage along the Posleen axis of assault. While the barrage would kill many Posleen, it would not be nearly as effective as the slaughter possible in the fire-trap. Deception and luring plans, some of them wild, others reasonable, were being designed to draw the Posleen in the more favorable direction.

For the inevitable moment when the north or west flank was turned, the Corps had worked out precise and simple retreat routes to the south side of the James. The heavy road infrastructure and plethora of bridges helped. Each unit had a designated route which was color-coded; city road crews had worked through the night putting up the new signs.

As the primary defense points came on-line, the freed construction crews hurried to the south side of the James and began construction of fighting positions designed to maintain a permanent assault on Posleen in the Richmond area. Craters and trenches began sprouting throughout the south Richmond area as many of the people in the refugee enclaves came forward to help.

Ramps and scaffolds began to sprout behind the south floodwall for direct fire from infantry and even tanks. At the same time pits for mortars and larger positions for artillery began to form throughout the city, wherever there was any sort of angle of fire. In many cases abandoned buildings were demolished to both improve angle of fire and donate their material for the defenses.

There were three tiers of defense, and every one had written its signature on the skyline of the city. As Keene had said, the city was writing a new chapter in her history. But she was also getting a facelift.

"I can't believe it is going as well as it is," said the corps commander.

"Well," said Colonel Abrahamson, scratching his head before redonning his Kevlar. "I don't know exactly how to put this. It's complex but not complicated. Every individual action either is something the military has trained for or is being done by civilians who are experienced and highly motivated. With the exception of my battalion's job, it should be a simple, set-piece siege. It's the poor bastards in Tenth Corps I feel sorry for, sir."

"Yes, I would have liked a little longer to prepare, you're never prepared enough. But this is effectively a World War I scenario. Easier really, there's no artillery for us to worry about. But General Simosin's divisions are about to get hit by a blitzkrieg, and they have no time to prepare."

"The President shouldn't have ordered them so far forward, General," the cavalry commander commented in a voice so neutral it was gray.

The corps commander nodded his head. It was the first overt

comment he had heard in the negative about the President's decision. "Possibly. I suppose ordering them to defend before Alexandria made sense, some sense, but he should not have ordered them to set up almost on the Posleen's door." He shook his head again. "God save their poor brave souls."

◆ CHAPTER 46 ◆

It started with a crackle of manjacks. The observation post was a regulation one-hundred meters out from the company and in view of the Second platoon but, being barely in view and after the stresses of the night with multiple moves and digging in not once but a total of four times, as the division moved again and again and the battalion adjusted lines, reassigned areas of responsibility, moved the company forward and back, the two-man team had fallen asleep. They awoke to the rattling burp from the manjack set up beside their foxhole and the cracking whistle of railgun rounds in return.

In his foxhole, Captain Brantley dropped the half-eaten remains of a hotdog loaded with chili, onions and relish, and rotated his shoulders. To the captain's amazement the first sergeant had made it back. And although he had not found an open restaurant, he had found enough supplies and cookware to feed the entire company on hotdogs, hamburgers and a really horrible concoction of canned baked beans and chili. After nearly two days on MREs, the troops consumed it so fast that the first sergeant's party had to make seconds and even thirds in the ten-gallon pots hung over sooty fires.

The commander had been a history major in college. To him, the scene was reminiscent of the Union and Confederate Armies in the War Years. The same scene was replicated over and over in the woods and fields around his position. The soldiers digging their foxholes had turned up Civil War era "Minié" balls as they dug and the ghosts in their tattered gray and blue seemed to hover around them, urging them into battle. He heard them now, rattling their ramrods and

377

whispering in his ear of the terrible sights to come and he wrapped the whispers around himself like armor.

He looked at his thin line of troops—the few in view in the thick pine scrub—and knew despair. What the situation called for was defense in depth, pillboxes and wire, trenches and no-man's-land. What it had was a thin screen of infantry, dug-in deep, with a few mines and claymores out front, hoping against hope for the strength to stop a force a hundred times their size.

The one bright spot was artillery support. With the shift in emphasis from human-human to human-Posleen combat, the Army had radically changed its approach to artillery equipment. Although the bulk of the Army would remain mechanized infantry, the lack of counterbattery ability—the ability of one artillery unit to fire on another—by the Posleen meant that the division and corps artillery did not need to be armored. Thus the M-222 "Reaver" was born.

Modified from a South African mobile artillery piece, the Reaver was a six-wheeled all-terrain vehicle mounting a 155mm howitzer. It had the speed to keep up with mechanized forces and the ammunition capacity to support them effectively.

Three full batteries of these artillery behemoths were in places to support the division and the resultant firepower exceeded the artillery of three divisions of the latter twentieth century. The Posleen might succeed in overrunning them, but they should take massive casualties in the process.

The captain had previously ensured that he was authenticated on the automated central firing network, so he calmly picked up the microphone and called in his first ever real-world call for fire.

"*Central, Central, this is Echo-Three-Five, fire mission, over.*"

He paused and waited a moment for a response. Usually, the newly fielded Central Artificial Intelligence Targeting Artillery Fire Remote Command and Control System, or Central for short (the military, for once, had universally decided *not* to use the acronym), came back practically before you could unkey the microphone. In this case it seemed to either not receive the call or be overloaded.

"*Central, Central, this is Echo-Three-Five. Fire mission, over.*"

"*Echo-Three-Five, this is Central, call fire.*"

Better. "*Central, Central, fire concentration, Echo-Two, say again, Echo-Two.*"

There was another pause. Fire was building on the line, but these Posleen seemed to be the equivalent of scouts and there had yet to be a call for a medic. He waited a moment longer then called again.

"*Central, Central, this is Echo-Three-Five. Say status fire mission, over.*"

"Echo-Three-Five, no fire mission in status, over."

"What?!" he shouted and stared at the radio in his foxhole. His RTO looked around, puzzled.

"What's wrong, sir?"

"The—" He realized a need to maintain a calm demeanor. Even if the one ace he thought he had in a hole was starting to look like a deuce. "I'm having a little trouble with the artillery net, I keep getting stepped on." It was a bald-faced lie, but better than the truth.

He had used Central several times in Exercise Without Troops, map exercises and field problems and it had never shown a bit of problem, once you got used to the syntax. The system had been designed by the Advanced Technology Research Board, a board formed in reaction to the "GalTech" group, and was the brainchild of the former Ground Forces High Commander.

As a concept it was deceptively simple; rather than having fallible humans make numerous transmissions in the call for fire chain, let computers do the work. Practically "off-the-shelf" voice-recognition software would "recognize" calls for fire, given by authenticated individuals and in the proper form, register them and pass them to a central computer. The computer would determine priorities, make the fire calculations and both send out fire commands and update the units calling for fire on the status of their request.

Combined with the Inter Vehicle Information System and the Ground Tactical Positioning System, it would eliminate "blue on blue" or "friendly" fire and distribute the available fire more equitably and efficiently. As a salve to the technological nay-sayers, there were both system overrides that commanders could invoke and real human beings in the chain. And it was just about time to invoke one.

He poked his head up to get a look at the situation and called again. *"Central, Central, this is Echo-Three-Five. Final protective fire, I say again, final protective fire. Command override, priority one. Over."*

Nothing.

"Sir?" said his RTO, as the first medic cry came from Second platoon, "where's the artillery?" One of the medics in the next foxhole crawled out towards the line, just as a centaur group broke through the firelanes and into view. Shotgun rounds flailed the foxholes, momentarily suppressing the company's fire and smashing the luckless medic into red paste. Captain Brantley dropped back into the foxhole just as the radio crackled back into life.

"Echo-Three-Five, authenticate Whiskey-Tango."

I already did that! The captain dug into his rucksack and dragged out his ANCD. *"Victor! Over!"*

"Say, again, syntax not recognized, over."

"*Central, this is Echo-Three-Five, authentication Victor, over.*" He ground his teeth, seemingly drawing patience out of the air.

"*Echo-Three-Five, say again full callsign, over.*"

"*Juliet-Mike-Echo-Three-Five,*" he said, very slowly and carefully.

"*Juliet-Mike-Echo-Three-Five, welcome to the net, say request, over.*"

"*Central, this is Echo-Three-Five, fire mission, over.*"

"*Echo-Three-Five, call fire, over.*"

"*Central, this is Echo-Three-Five, fire mission, concentration Echo . . .*" He popped his head up and took a quick look towards the front. The Posleen had begun to thicken, their fire beating down the company's with the exception of the manjacks. As he watched, a God King plasma cannon removed one of those, reducing the fire pressure. A lane was being cleared through the minefield by the simple expedient of pushing the Posleen normals through it. He saw two blown up in the brief span he was up but there were thousands behind them, a mass of yellow centaurs so great they were pushing down the trees, turning the forest into a plain.

"*Fire mission, concentration Echo-One. Final Protective Fire, priority one. Say again, FPF, Echo-One, Priority One, over.*"

There was a brief pause and panic set in as he feared he would have to start over from the beginning. There was no time.

"*Echo-Three-Five, this is Central. FPF on the way. Splash in two-five seconds. One hundred rounds.*"

Captain Brantley switched to the platoon local net. "*All Echo units, all Echo units, final protective fire, One-Five-Five close. Twenty seconds! Incoming!*" He clamped his hands over his ears, hunkered down and smiled at the RTO. "Here it comes! Better late than never!"

"Yes, sir!" shouted the RTO, quickly stuffing earplugs in and dropping into the hole. The captain noticed that his Kevlar helmet had a furrow across the left-hand side. *Good troop,* he thought.

The commander was still smiling when the first 155mm round dropped in his hole.

"*Juliet One-Five, Juliet One-Five, this is Whiskey One-Five, over!*"

Keren turned from the fire control computer and picked up the microphone. The rumbling impact of heavy artillery to the front had been going on for nearly two minutes, meaning that the captain must have called for Final Protective Fire, but there had not been a command over the net for fire from the mortars. Now Third platoon was calling and he still could find no request for fire. At least the L-T had sent Sergeant Herd off to recon their secondary firing position. Maybe if they gave him an hour or two he could be ready to lay in the guns.

"*Whiskey One-Five, this is Juliet One-Five Papa, go ahead.*"

"*Juliet, we're getting pounded by this goddamn artillery! The fuckin' CP is gone and so is Second platoon. It's got the horses stopped, but it's killin' us! Get 'em to stop! We can't reach anybody!*"

Oh, Jesus. Keren used his free hand to wave at the platoon sergeant and lieutenant, talking quietly by the Three Track. "*Whiskey, sorry, confirm friendly-fire call!*"

"*Yes, confirm damnit! Blue fire! Blue fire!*"

Keren swung around and keyed the Central Fire Net. "*Central, Central, blue on blue! Say again, blue on blue! Check fire! Check fire!*" At his shouts, every head in sight turned towards him and the two leaders started running towards his track.

"*This is Central, to calling station, say callsign and authenticate.*"

"*Central, this is Juliet One-Five, check fire for Echo-Three-Five, say again, check fire, check fire, blue on blue, check fire.*" He waited for a response as the thunder of artillery in the distance and the express train rumble overhead continued. A checkfire for "friendly-fire" was supposed to occur immediately, *then* authenticate. The cumbersome authentication problem was programmed to occur after friendly artillery stopped killing human troops.

"*Juliet One-Five, authenticate Alpha Sierra.*"

Shit. Fuck this. Something was obviously screwy with Central, he should not even have had to state his callsign. He punched numbers on his ANCD. Since it was for a fire direction track, it held all the "phone numbers" for the entire division. The platoon leader started to reach for the ANCD and stepped back at the involuntary feral snarl that crossed the specialist's face.

He now knew why Keren had gotten demoted; the officer suspected that if he had tried to take the ANCD, the private would have simply shot him where he stood and not even noticed.

"*Charlie-Five-Papa-Five-Four,*" Keren called, using the callsign and frequency of the artillery battery tasked to support his company. If Central was the problem, then simply take it out of the loop. "*This is Golf-Four-Juliet-One-Five, check fire! Check fire! Blue on blue, say again, blue on blue! Check fire! Check fire!*"

"*Calling station, say again callsign, check fire confirmed! Say again callsign!*"

Thank God. "*This is Golf-Four-Juliet-One-Five. Check fire!*"

"*Confirmed.*" The rumble of artillery died away overhead as the unit called back. "*Juliet One Five, authenticate Whiskey Romeo.*"

"*Roger, stand by . . . authentication Del-Ta.*"

"*Juliet, this is Papa, that fire was confirmed by Central, over.*"

"*Roger, well, we don't have a fuckin' company anymore, Papa. I don't*" *know what's wrong with Central, but you just wiped out Alpha Company First Batt."*

"Jesus. It's a damn authenticated order! And . . ." There was a pause, *"Yeah, and the target point is forward of the company on our IVIS! What the* fuck, *over?"*

"What do you have for the company coordinates?"

"Juliet, this is Whiskey, over!" came another call from the Second platoon.

"Hang on Arty!" Keren swung to the other radio as the platoon sergeant picked up the microphone and continued the questioning of the artillery unit.

"Go ahead, Third."

"We still need fire! The Posleen are massing for another attack!"

"Roger. Stand by." Keren picked up the intervehicle transmitter and almost called for the pre-laid Final Protective Fire, then looked at the fire control computer. Obeying an instinct he did not want to define, he dove across the compartment and rummaged behind a seat in the Humvee until he found an overlooked piece of equipment.

"What are you doing with that?" asked Lieutenant Leper, trying to keep up with three nearly incomprehensible situations at once.

Keren continued sketching in positions and locations on the mortar plotting board. It was nearly two years since he had last picked up the obsolete piece of equipment and this was turning out to be a lousy time to try to remember how to use it. But with the problems with Central, and the fact that the new Mortar Ballistic Computers interacted with it, he was damned if he was going to depend on anything else at that moment.

"Just checking something, sir."

"Well, check fast."

"Mortars, this is Third platoon! We need some damn fire, over!"

Keren picked up the mike without taking his eyes from his calculations, *"You want it on the Posleen or on your heads?"*

"Keren!" said the lieutenant.

"Sorry, sir," said the specialist. He pulled out a calculator, looked up a trajectory in a book and made a final calculation. His shoulders slumped. "Shit."

"What?" asked the platoon leader. The platoon sergeant looked over as well, telling the artillery to hold on.

"This FPF is fucked, sir," said Keren, scribbling furiously again. "Our computer-calculated Final Protective Fire would have landed right on the company command post. And the mistake is somewhere in the computer."

◆ CHAPTER 47 ◆

The Pentagon, VA, United States of America, Sol III
1342 EDT October 10th, 2004 AD

Major George Nix suspected that he was at the pinnacle of his career. As Tactical Systems Manager for the Continental Army Command he got to control every aspect of information going to and coming from the Continental Army commander. For him, it was equivalent to being a colonel with a brigade or a Navy captain with a ship. From here on out, even if he was called a commander or a manager, he would not be involved in day-to-day hands-on managing of systems, and that was his love. To gather and redistribute data efficiently and effectively was, to him, the epitome of the military intelligence field. After all, accurate military intelligence was half the battle and good orders were the other half. All the actual fighting was just the cherry on the cake, so to speak.

So when the first reports came in of garbled orders, like everyone he took it to be the confusion of the moment, "the fog of war." But as more and more reports came in, an alarming pattern of data invalidation began developing.

For him, the final straw was an overheard argument between the CONARC and the Tenth Corps commander. CONARC had been informed, out of channels, that Tenth Corps had given conflicting orders, some of them vocal orders from General Simosin himself. General Simosin's response was so angry, so absolutely sure, that Major Nix, who had dealt with the general several times over the years, could not decide which data to trust.

Given a conflicting set of statements, only additional, preferably objective, data could decide the answer. Major Nix set out to find that data. He was no cyberpunk, but he could get the job done.

He started with order logs. All electronic commands issued over Battlenet were stored on the Cheyenne Mountain Secure Server. He first called up the initial deployment orders for every unit in Tenth Corps. After that he called up the logged unit responses. A short query indicated that twenty-five percent of the units gave an invalid response. Logically, the higher commands receiving an invalid response should have replied, but there were only three replies to invalid responses. In addition, a plot of the logged responses had the units scattered all over northern Virginia. If the encryption codes had been invalid, the units would have either gotten no communications or map references scattered all over the world. Puzzled, he queried the unit local servers.

It was a little-known fact that communications within the local commands were also stored locally. Unlike external communications, which were stored in Cheyenne, these communications were purged after each exercise. Mostly it was interdepartmental e-mail that would not be stored under any normal conditions, or comments between the staff and their subordinates. Like "back channel cables," the information was in no particular style and often had nothing to do with the exercise or even the military. In addition to local communications, however, the precise information presented on the command screens was stored. Since, logically, this would be the same as the commands stored at Cheyenne, the information was considered of low priority and only existed as a debugging tool. However, until purged it was available and purging only occurred during a stand-down maintenance cycle. To Major Nix's surprise, most of the Corps's databases had been purged, but Thirty-Third and Fiftieth still had some intact files at battalion level and the data conflicted with Cheyenne. Not in every case, but in several cases what the operators at battalion level saw was not what had been transmitted from their division.

Tenth Corps had been hacked.

Jack Horner stared at the electronic map of northern Virginia and shuddered. Across the map were red penetrations and friendly-fire markers. Now he knew how an officer as experienced and capable as Arkady Simosin could have let the battle fall apart like this.

He turned to Colonel Tremont. "Begin the evacuation."

"But . . . sir!"

"It'll take hours to do it in an orderly fashion, and if Major Nix is right . . ."

"I am . . ."

"We don't know how this is going to go. I don't know if Ninth Corps is where that map says it is without sending you out on a goddamned horse to tell me! If we are penetrated, we have to assume the worst-case scenario for this battle."

"Yes, sir."

"So start the evacuation of the Pentagon. Now!"

"Yes, sir."

"Now, Major, explain this. How pervasive is this penetration, and who did it?"

"I don't know, and I don't know, sir, but here are the best guesses. I tickled Second of the Four Fifty-Second's battalion computer into sending me all its files including a complete copy of its core programming. I ran that through some analysis tools and it isn't good. I've got a bunch of file snippets that look . . . questionable, but this is the beaut." He pointed to a line of incomprensible text on the screen of his laptop.

"What am I looking at, Major?" asked the general, smiling tightly. He looked like a gray tiger about to teach a deer why it should learn to drink looking backwards.

"This is a portion of IVIS control code. It is telling the IVIS system to go to an external file each time it sends a position fix. I don't know what the external file is, but I can guess."

"It tells it whether to tell the truth or not."

"Yes, sir. And if it's in IVIS . . ."

"It's in everything."

"Yes, sir. These friendly-fire incidents . . ."

"Shit." The general swung around. "Operations, send out a priority order to all field artillery units. Do not use the Central System for fire control! Go to voice communication for all calls for fire."

"Umm, sir . . ." interjected the major.

"What?" snapped the enraged general.

"Their targeting computers might be corrupted as well. And the units might not know where they are, precisely, without IVIS. It's happened before."

"Monsoon Thunder," said Jack, with an angry shake of his head. "But this time we're the side being hacked. Maybe renegade cyberpunks? Who's that guy, got the Medal, quit and then disappeared?"

"No, sir," said Major Nix, positively. "If it were King Arthur, we'd never know it until you were out of the picture. His MO was to assassinate the command elements *then* confuse the troops. No, sir, I think it's someone else. Because there's this bit of code." He flashed another line on the screen. In this case, it was only ones and zeros.

"Binary, so?"

"It's Galactic binary, sir, a translation program for a quantum algorithm."

"Galactic? Could it be Posleen penetration? They use similar code, don't they?"

"It could be, sir, but it doesn't feel that way. I'm no GalTech expert, but this line looks a lot like some of the code in the AIDs." He gestured at the one encircling the general's wrist. "My guess is it's someone with renegade GalTech. I think that that external file was an AID program running somewhere that gave more or less random units false data and then carefully backed up all the lies.

"The key is that the files in Cheyenne do not match what was received at battalion, but battalion's responses were ignored. I suspect that the 'response' was crafted by this program to be what the higher unit originally sent out, and the IVIS code was there to maintain the distraction as long as possible. In addition, all of this was masked by legitimate 'fog of war' incidents. This is sophisticated as hell; I don't even know if cyberpunks could pull it off, not for this many units. I would have to finger renegade Galactics. At this point it is way out of my league. We need some Darhel investigators, or maybe Tchpth."

"Darhel," said the general, distractedly. "They're the programmers, the Tchpth don't program. Damn, this means all of our automated systems could be corrupted. Even the ACS could be vulnerable. There goes our ace in the hole."

"I don't think it's global, sir, but I can't tell how widespread it is. I definitely think we should go to full manual backup on call for fire and movement orders. We can probably wait and see on logistics."

"Right, put it out along with an alert about the problem. And good work, Colonel."

"Major, sir."

"Not anymore."

The officer blinked. "Thank you, sir, but I need to send out that warning."

"Get on it, and send an order to Tenth group telling them to retreat through any available route."

"Gee, thanks for the information," muttered Keren. The cheep for arriving orders from the now-useless ballistic computer distracted him momentarily from plotting the next fire mission. He quickly read the terse code and went back to his board.

"Last volley, Keren!" said the platoon sergeant, throwing personal gear into the armored personnel carrier. A stray Kevlar helmet bounced once on the deck and cracked cleanly in half.

"*Mortars, this is Third! You better be ready to pull out, we are about to bypass your position!*" The call was an effective punctuation.

"*Roger, Third.*" Keren took one last glance at his charge sheet and stored the board; this one was easy enough. He stood so he could look out of the Mortar Carrier and called, "*Deflection Two-Eight-Zero-Zero!*" All the communications wire was stored and the commanders had their heads out of the hatches, the better to man their machine guns. Company was expected and it deserved a professional reception.

"*Elevation fourteen hundred! Charge one!*" Nearly the lowest charge and highest elevation possible, the mortar rounds would not be going far. "*Five rounds, traverse, at will and run like hell!*" Everyone had been instructed on the route to use to reach their secondary positions. At the command the drivers all started the big diesel engines, like race-car drivers at a tracked Indy race.

Keren could see tracers from the Bradleys' 25mm Bushmasters through the trees. A bright flash indicated the erasure of another fighting vehicle from the remnants of the company. He was just as glad that the sight was obscured by trees.

"It's okay, Keren," shouted the platoon leader. He climbed in and dogged the troop door just as the first round went downrange.

As the mortar tracks began firing, the driver of the FDC track pulled out. It would take only moments for the rounds to be expended and then all three mortar tracks would "run like hell." Better to already be on the road than contributing to the log jam.

"Don't matter," continued the lieutenant, grabbing a stanchion. He smiled grimly. "We're fine as long as we're not on charge zero!"

Arkady Simosin looked at the scrawled-over paper map of Prince William County and sighed internally. He refused to succumb to despair, despite what the map was telling him. His units, his beautiful divisions, were so much scrap scattered through the woods. But there were still troops to save.

"Reinforce the order from CONARC, regarding the retreat." He stared at the red arrow of Posleen, charging up the I-95/U.S. 1 corridor. Unlike the horses they resembled, Posleen seemed inured to fatigue. They would be to the Occoquan bridges within the hour.

"Send a message to the Thirty-Third and Forty-First to pull back to the beaches. See if we can get some craft down to the water to pull them out. The battleships were never tied into the fire net and they've been accurate so far. They might be able to cover the withdrawal. Get on that stat."

"I'll handle it," said the planning officer.

"Okay, all the rest, turn them towards Manassas, modify the original pivot plan. Tell them to retreat as fast as possible, Nineteenth Armored to take the back door and slow the Posleen." He glanced at the map again. "The Thirty-Third, Forty-First and Fiftieth DivArty should be able to make it across the bridges. I'm sure they'll hurry. Have them follow the back roads along the Occoquan. They should be able to provide some fire from there.

"The units are to retreat until they are in reserve of the Ninth Corps, in the area of . . ." He looked at his chart and smiled grimly. "Bull Run National Battlefield Park. We will reorganize there."

He paused and looked at his staff. "Gentlemen, we all know that a retreat under fire is the most difficult maneuver of all to effect. This is, effectively, a rout. We have to get to Manassas before our troops do, and get them stopped behind Ninth Corps. We will use the units that are still combat-effective to reinforce Ninth Corps and stop the Posleen on that axis. Prince William County is as far as they go!"

◆ CHAPTER 48 ◆

Occoquan, VA, United States of America, Sol III
1344 EDT October 10th, 2004 AD

Lieutenant Ryan tried not to listen to the quiet murmur of the troops around him, but the rumors of defeat were reinforced by the continuous rumble of artillery vehicles crossing the I-95 bridges. A few armored personnel carriers even rumbled across the VA 123 bridge, tearing at high speed to the north. It was clear from every sign that Tenth Corps had had its butt kicked and was escaping as fast as it could. Even as his platoon continued its preparation for the Posleen, the rumble of falling artillery came closer and closer.

He had moved his command post to the high ridge on the north bank of the Occoquan. Screened by a thicket of beech saplings—their palmate leaves turning brilliant yellow in the autumn chill—he had a clear view of the town, including the opposite ridge and both bridges. The last orders he had received were to blow the bridges when the Posleen were in sight and remain in position to cover the old dam. Until an infantry unit could be found to replace him, his platoon was responsible for preventing the Posleen from crossing that vital defense work.

In preparation for the oncoming tide, the engineering platoon had been busy little groundhogs. A slit trench ran the length of the top of the ridge, with V-cut positions for riflemen stretched along its length and intermittent reinforced positions for machine guns. The slope was a mass of concertina and barbed-wire tanglefoot and the road running across the south slope was mined for demolition. Should they somehow force a crossing it would be extremely difficult for the inflexible Posleen to establish a bridgehead without the road.

When an artillery battery began firing from just behind the ridge, with impacts on the south edge of the town sending woodwork flying into the autumn sunshine, Ryan decided that knowing how to contact artillery might be a good thing. A brief scroll through his ANCD, however, indicated that there might be a problem. He did not have listings for Tenth Corps units.

Since the platoon had been drawn from a training establishment, their chain of command did not include any of the local tactical forces. The ANCD listed a vast number of training units in the Belvoir local area and even higher command frequencies that few platoon leaders would have under normal tactical conditions. But, unfortunately, there was not a single artillery unit listed. The closest thing to an artillery unit was the cryptic entry: "Continental Indirect Fire Net."

With a shrug, he flipped his PRC-2000 to the listed frequency and keyed the mike . . .

Since the prohibition on automated indirect-fire, the Fire Direction Center had been stymied. Even when automated fire was allowed, so few units had direct contact that the Fire Control could only order fire on rough guesses of enemy location. Even worse was the lack of feedback. Nothing got a gun crew hopping like the word that they just destroyed an enemy.

So when the crewwoman heard a faint whisper in her earphones, she clamped her right hand over the earphone and responded instantly.

"*Unit on this net, unit on this net, you are coming in faint and broken. Say again callsign.*"

"*Oscar-Fi—is—Romeo—*"

"*Unit on this net, you are broken. Say again, or boost signal.*"

"*St—by.*"

"*Roger, this is Oscar Five Uniform Four Seven, standing by.*"

A few minutes later the calling unit came back in, still faint but clear.

"*Oscar Five Uniform Four Seven, this is Mike Eight Romeo Six Seven, over.*"

"*Romeo Six Seven, this is Uniform Four Seven. Authenticate Victor Hotel.*"

Pause. "*Authentication, Bravo, over.*"

"*Romeo Six Seven, welcome to the net, over.*"

"*Roger, adjust fire, over.*"

"*Adjust fire, out.*" She began to enter the order as she hit the foot trip to switch to intercom. "*Fire mission!*"

"Target, Posleen in open, coordinates 654894. Can you range, over?"

"Romeo, what map sheet are you on, over?"

The lieutenant stared at the private next to him and realized that he was no help; they were both trainees.

"Sergeant Leo!"

"Yes, sir?"

"I got an artillery unit that needs to know what map sheet we're on!" The platoon leader looked at the military grid map covered in incomprehensible signals. "Where the hell is it?"

"Why do they need the map sheet, sir?"

"You want me to take the time to ask?"

The NCO forced his way through the troops between himself and the lieutenant and ran a practiced eye over the map.

"There it is, sir, in the upper right. Occoquan. That was next week's course," he finished with a wry grin.

"Right." The lieutenant keyed the mike. *"Occoquan, over."*

"Umm," the fire direction technician checked her map and eyeballed the range. *"Roger. say your position and condition, over."*

"Ridge to north of Occoquan River, overlooking 123, dug-in, coordinates 654897."

"Roger, stand by."

"L-T, we got movement on 123!"

Lieutenant Ryan lifted his head out of the slit trench and peered into town. Down Main Street, "Old 123," trotted a swarm of yellow centaurs, their God King prominent in their midst. He had been surprised by the female voice, but now just wished she'd get her fanny in gear.

"Sergeant Leo!"

"Yes, sir?"

"Drop the 123 bridge!"

"Yes, sir. What about the footbridge?"

"Let's keep that up for a while."

A group of centaurs came around the shoulder of the hill, trotting down 123. At the sight of the intact bridge they broke into a gallop. Almost simultaneously there was a thundering racket from downstream where the I-95 and U.S. 1 bridges went up simultaneously.

"Purple Heart Bridge indeed," muttered the lieutenant.

"What was that, sir?" asked one of the waiting engineers.

"Nothing, I think I've got some artillery on the way."

"Great! That battery behind us?"

"No, I don't have their frequency. Somebody else, I don't know what."

As the 123 bridge blew up, the two hundred pounds of Composition-4 explosives lifting concrete chunks and the first rank of centaurs into the air, the radio crackled with a transmission.

"*Say again, over!*" shouted the young officer, ears ringing. Despite orders and pointed suggestions, he wasn't wearing earplugs.

"*This is Uniform Four Seven, ranging round incoming. Danger close, say again, danger close!*"

The lieutenant lifted his head up to see if the view had changed. No, he was still over three hundred meters from the center of town. "Danger Close" for 155mm was only two hundred yards. What the heck.

"*Uniform, this is Romeo Six Seven. We are three or four hundred meters from impact area, over.*"

"*Roger, incoming five seconds, danger close, I say again, danger close. Hunker down and cover your ears, soldier-boy! Splash in five seconds!*"

"Sir, what's that?"

The lieutenant looked up and followed the private's view to a rapidly descending dot. As it lowered it loomed larger and larger. The precise size was hard to determine, but it was the biggest shell the young officer had ever seen or could possibly imagine. It looked like whatever it was was firing cars.

"*Incoming! Everybody down!*" the lieutenant screamed and demonstrated by throwing himself to the bottom of the slit trench.

The impact of the shell rivaled the explosion of the much closer bridge. The officer stumbled to his feet, partially stunned and shaking off good Virginia loam to survey the damage. The round had impacted on the far ridge, near where the now silent artillery had fallen, and the damage area was wider than that of the damage from the full battery behind him. The area was covered in dust and smoke from the explosion, but he could make a reasonable guess at adjustment. With the "footprint" of whatever it was, "close" was going to be good enough.

"*Jesus Christ*, sir," yelled Sergeant Leo, "who the hell did you call?"

"*Romeo Six Seven,*" the radio crackled, "*Did you observe the fall of shot?*"

The shaken lieutenant picked up the microphone. "*Uniform Four Seven, roger. Down seven five meters and fire for effect. And careful with that seventy-five meters! What unit is this, over?*" It was lousy communications discipline to ask, but he felt like he needed to know what he had called down upon their heads.

"*Romeo Six Seven, confirm down seventy-five meters and fire for effect. This is the USS* Missouri, *at your service. Hunker down for a nine-gun salute, Romeo.*"

✧ ✧ ✧

Kenallai cursed the evil harvest that inhabited this thrice-damned world.

"Threshkreen, indeed, my edas'antai," murmured Kenallurial as the nearby guns hammered the remaining scouts of Sammadar as they swept down the main street of the small town.

He had convinced his edas'antai that the proper way to deal with this enemy was to observe his methods, then develop ways to combat them. Sammadar had been virtually wiped out assaulting the enemy lines to the south. But when the enemy's own guns destroyed their positions, Kenallurial's oolt'os were in position to exploit the break in the lines.

He had maintained a forward position, capturing rich booty on the way. But on approaching the town, which captured maps showed bisected by a large river, he had slowed, probing forward carefully, and instructing his junior Kessentai, with hard blows when necessary, to remain under cover. Now his oolts held a strategic ridgeline—one without noticeable booty, but a commanding view—and he and his edas'antai observed the destruction of the rival oolt'ondar from a house on the ridge.

Houses were a dangerous prospect on this thrice-damned planet, but the Posleen had slowly begun to recognize the signs. A single oolt'os would be sent to, carefully, open what looked to be the primary door of a building. If there was a beeping sound and a black box with a flashing light, the oolt'os would run like the demons of the sky were after it. Sometimes it made it, sometimes it did not. But at least they were not losing oolt'os by the double hand anymore.

This house had no flashing lights, nor demolition charges. It rested comfortably on the riverward shoulder of the ridge overlooking the town. The sign on the front, in the beastly language of this planet, said something about "Rock Shelf," which certainly described the terrain.

The far bank of the river was steep as the side of a building, with a narrow road winding around to the right. The left was obscured. He could see a four-lane highway bridge downriver, and there was a small footbridge just below the house they occupied.

"We should send forces to seize that crossing!" snarled Ardan'aath, pointing to the four-lane bridge. "Why do we skulk in buildings?"

"Hmmm," murmured Kenallai. The oolt'ondar was feeling unrecognized emotions. Among others, doubt.

"If you wish to try," said Kenallurial, calmly, "go right ahead."

Ardan'aath had not gotten to where he was by being stupid. The thrice-eaten-by-demons puppy had something up his sleeve. "Why don't you?"

"I prefer to live long enough to enjoy the fruits of my conquests," answered the younger Kessentai, with an almost contemptuous snout wrinkle.

Ardan'aath started to say what he thought of such a cowardly approach, but was stopped by the raised hand of Kenallai.

"The argument is done," he said, gesturing out the window.

They watched as Sammadar charged his main force towards the bridge, and as the front two oolt were swept away by the explosions.

"Sky demon shit," snarled Ardan'aath, rounding on the junior Kessentai, "you knew!"

"I suspected."

"Why?" asked Kenallai.

"It is what I would have done."

"And what would you do next?"

Kenallurial looked towards the river below. "I would pound this valley to pieces as our comrades rush to try a crossing." He pulled out the captured map. Ardan'aath turned away from the piece of alien garbage, but Kenallai bent over in interest.

"Look, we are here," he said, pointing to the town. "This river stretches all the way to here," he continued, pointing to the town of Manassas. "That is the first place that we can turn towards the treasures to the north."

"What about this?" asked Kenallai, pointing to a symbol. "Is this not a closer bridge?" Near the possible defense point, but to the side, a bridge crossed.

"What bridge, my edas'antai?" asked the junior, respectfully, keeping his eyes on the map.

"Oh." Once he thought about it, it was obvious that the threshkreen would destroy the bridge before it could be taken by the host.

"But before the Po'oslenar can turn this corner, can take that booty to the north," continued the eson'antai, "there is this stretch here." Near the end of the Occoquan reservoir, a thin line of blue stretched to the south and widened to become Lake Jackson. "The threshkreen can organize here and meet us in terrific battle. Woe betide the force that first assaults them there!"

"It would be an honorable battle," snarled Ardan'aath, "none of this skulking and running about. We could sweep them aside as we did their fellows to the south, as we destroyed their town! As we shall sweep all these thresh into our pens!"

"We would be like Sammadar!" snarled the junior, rounding on the older Kessentai in challenge mode. "Without an oolt'os to our name, reduced to a castellaine! Perhaps that is what you seek?"

"Enough!" snapped the oolt'ondai, stepping between the two officers as they began to close. "Each has his merits! I listen to both, and each decides for himself the actions of his oolt'os. For himself! That is the Way and the Path. Ardan'aath, I listen to this one, for he is often right before the battle. But as battle is joined, do I not take your advice?"

"Aye, my lord," said the older advisor, calmer with the reminder.

"Then, listen to this one. Take not anger from this conference, but wisdom."

"I listen. As to wisdom, when this puppy has seen the burning of the orna'adar, when he has conquered worlds, then will I learn his wisdom." He turned away and stomped again to the window. As he did, a tremendous crash on the southern ridge smashed the remaining glass inward, scattering it about the room and into the God King's crest. With an angry gesture, he shook his crocodilian head to clear it. *"Demons of the sky eat your souls, you gutless thresh!"*

"My edas'antai, we do not have much more time," whispered the junior softly.

"The firing of this valley? You are sure of that?"

"Yes, here is the final quotient. If the thresh defend here," he pointed once again to the map, wondering for a moment about the mind of a species that would make such a thing, the Po'oslenar had no equivalent, "then they will be strong. But if we swing here," he pointed south of Lake Jackson, "to the south, we can come in behind them. They cannot be strong everywhere."

"That will take us hours out of our way, we will not be there before deep night!"

"That is my suggestion. If you prefer to try that footbridge . . ." He gestured pointedly out the window.

The oolt'ondai winced, without looking again. He was experienced enough to recognize a trap when he saw one. "I think not. Ardan'aath!"

"Oolt'ondai?"

"Are you with us?"

"For a long march with no prospect of battle for hours? When battle rages all around us? What use am I?"

"Ardan'aath! Yes, or no? We must move!"

"I have traveled far with you, Kenallai. I continue, despite your dependence on this puppy."

"Then we move!" With those words he led the way out of the room, already at a trot, a terrible fear clutching at his soul.

✧   ✧   ✧

They passed the outskirts of the town of Occoquan, the normals of the brigade in a ground-eating lope, just as the first salvo of sixteen-inch rounds landed in the square.

"Big Mo *pour it on!*" The condition of Ryan's ears, despite hastily jammed in earplugs, had gone beyond ringing to probable permanent deafness. *"I can't hear any response! I think I'm deaf! But you've wiped out hundreds so far."*

The plan had worked beyond his wildest dreams, because somehow the word had gotten around that there was an intact bridge at this location. Through the afternoon, the Posleen poured into the valley, charging for their chance at taking the far bank, and the shorter route to the prizes to the north. But as fast as they charged, the guns of the *Missouri* pounded the narrow defilade where the town had once stood.

Occoquan was no more; not a single house was left standing throughout the entire valley. As the engineer/forward observer walked the big sixteen-inch rounds back and forth, the quaint one- and two-story wood and stone houses had been torn apart under the hammer of the guns. Main Street was choked with rubble and in places the big rounds struck so many times they had pummeled the underlying rock into layers of gravel. The spot where the Occoquan Boatyard had once stood was now a channel, dug by repeated impacts of the big rounds.

The huge shells were briefly visible as they plunged into the maelstrom, each one adding its load of dust and smoke to the surreal haze across the river. Occasionally, the pall was blown away by the light north wind but not fast enough for clear vision. Parties of the Posleen would make their way through the holocaust, taking casualties that would turn back a human force, all the way to the foot bridge and the dam, where they would run into more problems.

The dug-in engineer platoon had festooned the bridge with command-detonated mines. As the Posleen continued to reach the bridge, these were slowly used up, but the base of the narrow bridge was within easy small-arms fire. As the Posleen tried to cross, one at a time, they were brought under a hail of fire from the M-16s and AIWs of the platoon. Three times God Kings had made it through the curtain of battleship fire, but even their heavy weapons had been unable to force the passage.

Trying the old dam was no more use. In an inspired move one of the privates had found a can of grease in the now-erased waterworks and spread grease all along the top of the dam. The engineers rarely fired at the centaurs trying to cross there, instead taking notional bets on how far they would make it. There was a steady flow of white water across the top and the massive Posleen rapidly drowned in the deep water at the base.

The platoon had lost some trainee engineers, and the names of each would lie heavy on his soul, but this day Lieutenant Ryan knew he had done a man's job and done it with style. The sun descending in the west was bringing on the night's bitter autumn cold when the private next to him yelled to get his attention.

The sound barely penetrated the ringing as he called another adjustment, but the hand on his shoulder turned him around. There was a captain in battledress on his stomach behind him, camouflaged face split in a watermelon grin and crossed-rifles on his collar.

"We're here to relieve you!" the lieutenant half-heard, half-lip read.

The battle-shocked lieutenant just nodded his head. Combined with an infinite feeling of relief as he saw fresh, trained and heavily armed infantryman swarm over the lip and drop into the slit trench was a terrible sadness. It was the feeling of a job not completely done, of leaving a battle to another, a feeling similar to survivor guilt. It said "I am alive, and going to safety, but I leave you here to carry on my work and die."

It was a silly feeling in the conditions; the infantry company was better trained for this sort of battle, fresh, more heavily armed, with three times the personnel. If his platoon of trainee engineers had been able to hold the bridge through the day, then surely this unit would have no problems through the days to come. And there must be a sore need for engineers in other battles. But it still hurt.

He nodded his head again at the captain now standing next to him. "*I can't hear anything, sir, just nod your head!*" To which the captain nodded.

"*USS* Missouri," Ryan shouted, gesturing with the microphone, "*Uniform Four Seven! Be careful how close you get.*" The hammer of machine guns in the background was washed out by another salvo of three rounds impacting. "*You're sharing fire with the divisions getting pulled off at Deep Hole Point and over in Maryland, but it's enough.*" He keyed the mike a last time.

"*Uniform Four Seven, this is Romeo Six Seven, over.*"

"*Romeo, this is Mo, over.*"

"*Mo, we are being relieved. I'm turning you over to . . .*" He glanced at the captain.

"Lima Niner Two!" shouted the captain.

"*Lima Niner Two, over!*"

"*Roger, I accept Lima Niner Two to this net, over.*"

"*Well, thanks Mo, this is Romeo Six Seven, out.*"

"*Good luck, Romeo, this is Juliet, out,*" responded the unknown female on the other end of the circuit.

With a smile, the tired lieutenant carefully slid out of the trench and down the back side of the hill to where the remains of his platoon was gathering.

◆ CHAPTER 49 ◆

Richmond, VA, United States of America, Sol III
1320 EDT October 10th, 2004 AD

Time was on the side of Washington. The direct line distance between D.C. and Fredericksburg was practically the same as the distance between Fredericksburg and Richmond. But the dogleg around the Occoquan Reservoir and the resistance of the Ninth and Tenth Corps ensured that the first city to be hit by the spreading incursion would be Richmond.

And in Richmond they were just about done laying in the drinks.

"Won't they spot that?" asked the specialist who had been assigned as Mueller's driver.

"Maybe," said Mueller, affixing the last connection on the sensor pod. The small device was a surveillance tool that had been modified for long-range transmission. Set up in a lightly armored shell, the tiny camera and transmitter looked northward on I-95.

"But we'll be able to fire them up at least once with artillery. If they don't notice them, or do and don't take them out, we'll be able to use them for long-range artillery fire and surveillance during the whole battle."

"Sergeant Ersin?"

"Yeah?" Ersin turned from supervising the installation of a field of mines along the northwest rim. The querying individual was one of the junior engineers assigned to the area. The kid didn't even have his professional license. He was a junior flunky at one of the local engineering firms sent out as a last bit of support. But at least he knew he was wet behind the ears and wasn't afraid to ask questions. He was accompanied by a tall, beefy civilian. Something about the florid face and casual clothes spelled "salesman" to Ersin.

"This guy is trying to explain something to me . . ." the engineer started to say.

"Hi there, Sergeant . . . Ersin, was it?" asked the civilian, brushing aside the engineer and taking Ersin's hand in a hearty shake. "Tolert, Bob Tolert, I represent Advanced Materials Manufacturing here in Richmond . . ."

"If it's about the Golden Girls . . ."

"No, no, different company entirely. We have a line of . . ."

"We're a little busy here . . ."

" . . . military supplies that I . . ."

" . . . and I really don't have time . . ."

" . . . think would be just perfect for . . ."

"You're not listening to a thing I'm saying, are you?" said Ersin in a dangerously calm voice. The scars on the side of his neck and face were flushed.

"Oh, yes, I am, sir; yes, I am," said the salesman, smiling broadly in reply. "You have the most important job in the entire United States right now, protecting our fair city, and these little caltrops my company makes are just the thing to help." The smile was wide and patently insincere. The salesman was obviously figuring on a hard sell.

Ersin snapped forward like a snake until his scarred Eurasian face was inches from the civilian's. One hand snatched the collar of the Dockers shirt and dragged the salesman the last inch. "What did you say?"

Bob Tolert had dealt with difficult customers in his time. However, he'd never dealt with ones who had an instant ability to remove him from the face of the earth. He considered his next words carefully.

"We're under contract to produce something called caltrops for the mountain defenses," he croaked. "I don't even know what they are. One of our foremen told me you might want to buy a few."

"Neither did I," said the civilian engineer. The junior engineer was waving his hands around as if to try to suggest that maybe killing a civilian would not be a good idea.

"How many can we get?" asked Ersin, his smile turning feral.

"He brought some dump trucks with him," offered the engineer.

"Can you let go now?" Tolert croaked. "Please?"

The Posleen scout company trotted in good order down the broad highway. Their God King followed them pensively despite the rearing buildings of the great prize plain before him. His was the fifth company from the oolt'ondar to be in the lead. Between the ambushes of the *tenar* and the ballistic weapons of the thresh the horde had lost oolt after oolt. He was determined to last longer than the rest.

To avoid the ambushes that had plagued his fellows, he had a scout well out in the lead of his oolt. The oolt'os was a superior individual, it could nearly talk. The Kessentai's sole eson'antai had been born from their coupling and he trusted the oolt'os to respond effectively to mildly complex problems. If any of the oolt'os would spot a problem, it would be that one.

So he froze his *tenar* then slid to the side when the point let out a surprised cry. However, the cry was not one of fear or anger and the point almost immediately turned and ran towards him.

In the oolt'os's hand was a strange device. A metal stake, dirt dribbling to the ground unnoticed, topped with a symbol. The metal of the symbol looked like . . . but it couldn't be . . .

The God King let out a cry like that of his scout and practically snatched the golden trinket from its hand. He patted the excited semimoron on the back and gave it bits of thresh from his own hand in approval.

A trailing scoutmaster slid his *tenar* forward, wondering what the excitement was about.

The God King held the implement overhead. "Pure heavy metal," he crowed, waving it back and forth.

"No," shouted the newcomer his crest standing straight up in excitement. "Is there more?"

"Let us find out," he cried and waved to his oolt. "Forward, find more! Follow the road!"

"They're at the first Babe," said Mosovich, adjusting the sixty-power spotting scope. He smiled faintly at the silent pantomime in the distance. "It looks like they took it hook, line and sinker."

"We ought to fire 'em up," said Ersin sourly, leaning back on the head of the hotel-room bed. From the suite in the Marriott they had a clear view of the advancing host. He took a bite out of the dehydrated peaches from his MRE and wrinkled his face like a rat. "That's what cannon-cockers are for." He stopped talking as the absorbent fruit removed all the moisture from his mouth.

"Suck 'em in, General," said John Keene to the air. "Don't shoot till you see the yellow of their eyes." With the defenses completed, he found himself flapping around at loose ends. After considering his options he decided that the best place to be would be with the SF team. Among other things they were the only people in

Richmond he knew weren't gunning for him. They also made fair bodyguards.

He now lay on his back on the floor, nursing the first beer he'd had in two days. He took another sip of the astringent brew and smacked his lips. "Let 'em get in the sack."

"Yeah," said Mueller, assembling a sandwich on the table. He carefully laid out a sliver of ham, layered it with lettuce, then another layer of ham, lettuce, pastrami . . . "We want as many of 'em as possible to reach Schockoe Bottom."

"Fine," snorted Ersin cynically. "Be complicated. All that complicated means is more to go wrong."

"It looks good so far," said Keene, defensively. He sat up and drained the bottle to the dregs. "They're going for it," he finished with a belch and tossed the bottle in the wastecan.

"That they are," agreed Mosovich. "But I don't believe they're going to get to Schockoe without anybody firing. That'd take more discipline than this Army's got."

"Come to papa," whispered Specialist Fourth-Class Jim Turner, snuggling the .50 caliber sniper rifle into his shoulder. For once he was able to use the tripod that came with the beast and he now waited impatiently for the signal to fire.

The interstate highway was marked at regular intervals by survey stakes with colored ribbons attached to them. With the time they had to prepare, each company was detailed with specific areas of fire and those were then broken down to the point where every rifleman, grenadier and sniper had a specific area to concentrate on. The snipers were given larger fields of fire to work with, but even then the section of interstate that was "his" was only two hundred yards long and a hundred deep. There were currently three God Kings, his particular target, in his box. He had already decided to take the rearmost one first and work his way forward. That one was moving faster than the main force, coming up through the host with his normals trailing. As soon as the signal came, he was history.

Jim was of two minds about whether everyone could hold fire until the signal. The order was to stay out of sight but ready and not watch the approach of the enemy. Most of the troops had been ordered to sit on the floor, their manjacks safed, and wait for the order. How many of them were doing that he didn't know. He wasn't. And then there were the fifteen or twenty thousand manjacks set up to cover the whole of the interstate and Schockoe Bottom. The only reason none of them had fired yet was that all the ones the Posleen had come across were on safe. Sooner or later they were going to cross the laser of one that was overlooked. The odds of everybody getting the word *and* getting it right were slim.

On the other hand, virtually everybody had also gotten the word that the Posleen reacted violently to fire. If they didn't wait for the signal and somebody fired on their own, the whole host would target that single individual. So, when somebody did screw it up, it'd be Darwin Awards time. And the NCOs and officers were supposed to be . . .

"Turner, Goddamnit!" said Sergeant Dougherty from the doorway.

"I'm just watching, Sergeant," he answered reasonably. Dougherty was a hard case. She ought to have gone Fleet Strike with the way she ran around all the time like a spike was stuck up her ass. On the other hand, she was fair and, more to the point, right. He wasn't supposed to be where he was. "I'm not gonna fire." Nonetheless he stepped away from the rifle.

"I don't give a shit, get on the floor like everybody else! We've been taking magazines away for less than that!"

"Yes, ma'am."

"You ought to know better. If you can't handle the responsibility of being a sniper, we can find somebody who can! An' don't call me ma'am," snapped the short, heavy-set, dishwater blonde in summary. "I work for a living."

Her back straight and face set in a disapproving frown she stepped back into the hallway to continue her circuit of positions. Time to go find some more ass to chew.

Inevitably everyone didn't get the word.

"How is the road to the east?" asked Artulosten. The returning scoutmaster looked grumpy. Many of his oolt'os were limping and all looked miserable.

"Horrible," snapped Arstenoss. "There is nothing out there, the buildings burned, the roads destroyed or scattered with these." He held up a caltrop. "I've half my oolt injured, many of them made to thresh by these damn things."

The battlemaster took the offending item and looked at it curiously. It was a small bit of metal. He understood its purpose, to present a small knife turned upwards. "How could these kill an oolt'os?"

"They don't kill. But when they are driven into a foot, many of the oolt'os panic and roll. Then they are driven into them all over their body. I had to put nearly two dozen down. I finally said enough and came back. There is nothing of interest out there. I understand that there is a road of heavy metals here?"

"Indeed. This must be a place of great worth. The lead force has encountered no resistance and found marker after marker made of pure heavy metals. They are all on the one road and appear to lead towards the other side of that river." He pointed to where the distant James was partially visible. "That would normally be the objective." He pointed up at the skyline. "And it is packed with thresh, but the host seems content to follow the markers to their source."

The interstate had already started to bend away from the city proper. "Other scoutmasters have returned from the west with much the same news. There is nothing of worth out there now. What would have been of use has been destroyed or removed."

"Those buildings are packed with thresh," noted the scoutmaster, studying his sensors. Every looming skyscraper was patterned with red. "Why don't they fire?"

"Fear of the host," snorted the battlemaster. He gestured to the front where they were preceded by the thousands of Posleen of the vanguard and backward to where another million and a half followed. "They are numerous but not nearly so numerous as the host. They would be fools to fire."

The Posleen normal was responding to a call of nature. Posleen would drop solid and liquid waste without question. But it was time for a birthing, and that required a modicum of privacy lest a fellow oolt'os succumb to hunger. In camp, even a temporary camp, there would be an egg pit where the leather-skinned egg would be dropped until it hatched. And there would be designated nursemaids to remove the hatchlings to the hatchling pens, there to fight for survival until they reached maturity.

But when the host was moving, the best that could be done was to set the eggs aside and let the hatchlings free. Most would die, even more than in the pens. But there was no easy way on the Path and the normal could care less. All it wanted to do was relieve the discomfort and nausea of the fully mature egg.

It trotted away from its group and down off the interstate to the east; the western wall towards the thresh was a sheer bluff topped with barbed wire so there was no going that way. It had to cut a fence, but that was easily done with its monomolecular short sword. There was a small building of nondescript purpose immediately available. It was under strict instructions not to enter buildings without permission, but being out of sight was enough for the purpose. It trotted around the back of the building and started the birthing process.

Its abdomen began to ripple and the ripples spread quickly up its neck. It had almost waited too long. A bulge appeared at the base of its neck and traveled upward like a python swallowing a cat in reverse. Finally it spat up a spotted, leathery egg the size of a small chicken. It licked the last birth juices off the egg, tossed it disdainfully against the wall of the abandoned subsidized housing and trotted back towards the interstate. Mission complete.

The normal's company had gotten far ahead of it. It hurried through the smashed buildings and hacked-down and burned trees along the interstate trying to catch up to its god. As it did it passed through an invisible beam of light.

Everything was wrong with the manjack. It was not on safe. It was pointed more or less sideways into another brigade's area. And the linked ammunition leading to it was bent around the corner of a desk, ensuring that the weapon would fire for the shortest time possible and then jam.

The team from the Seventy-First Infantry Division had set up the weapon and its bitchingly heavy ammunition cases with unseemly haste. They were more interested in getting back to their crap game than whether the weapon was aimed or the belts of ammunition run smoothly. The sergeant who was supposed to ensure that the gun was aligned properly and on safe was enjoying the fruits of her position with a good-looking and limber young soldier. The first sergeant was playing poker with two of the platoon sergeants and a warrant officer from supply. The company commander was at battalion ensuring that the battalion commander knew just how well his company was being run.

In the end it was all the same. The weapon fired twelve rounds and then jammed. The 7.62mm bullets, two of them tracer, drifted with apparent laziness through the air until they reached their point of aim and dug into the soil of Virginia. Since the manjack had never been boresighted, they did not even strike their erstwhile target, which continued on towards its objective oblivious of being fired at.

Specialist George Rendel had just thrown a three and snatched the dice back up. He rattled them a few times and prepared to throw again when the manjack across the room stuttered its twelve rounds. He froze, wide eyes echoed by everyone else in the game.

"We forgot . . ." someone said and the world fell in.

The Posleen were used to fighting enemies who were visible. Most of their opponents had no history of warfare and, therefore, had never heard of such items as camouflage, cover or concealment.

However, they had developed a process for dealing with humans' cowardly tendency to hide themselves while fighting. The God Kings' saucers possessed not only weapons, but excellent sensors. So, even if the position of a firing platform was not clear, the sensors could pinpoint it. When there were hundreds of positions firing they tended to become overloaded with information, but when there was a single target it was easy. And wherever the God King fired, there fired its company.

There were over twenty God Kings in sight of the manjack. All of them fired at the sensor point. And so did approximately eight thousand normals.

A storm of flechettes and missiles slammed into the side of the skyscraper. Since Posleen aim was weak at that range, the storm was diffused over two or three floors and half the side of the building. Hundreds of soldiers throughout the structure were killed and injured by the storm of fire. The only survivors of the laggard company were the company commander, downstairs in the battalion TOC, and the first sergeant and platoon sergeants in their poker game.

The plasma cannons and hypervelocity missiles, designed to defeat plate armor, cut upward through floor after floor, most of them passing entirely through the building. Structural members were cut and the building reeled with the impact of the storm of fire.

Throughout the line, thousands of heads popped up to see why the storm of fire had occurred. Some individuals, more panicked, brave or foolish than their fellows, started to fire. However, in every case other, wiser, heads prevailed and soldiers were ordered, cajoled or wrestled to the floor to prevent creating another target. The single burst had proven the truth of the order and, despite the ongoing hammer from the Posleen, the check fire held.

With no further fire forthcoming, the Posleen resumed their interrupted advance towards their distant El Dorado.

◆ CHAPTER 50 ◆

Richmond, VA, United States of America, Sol III
1417 EDT October 10ᵗʰ, 2004 AD

"This is scary," said General Keeton, staring at the hundreds of monitors set up throughout the battle control room. The large meeting hall in the R.J. Reynolds facility was crammed with intelligence technicians and a few conscripted secretaries. The group was deciphering the data from the video cameras strung along the route of advance and keying it into the battlefield control system. General Keeton was left with the summarized version to work with. The twenty-four-inch monitor appropriated from the head of Reynolds' Management Information Systems department was indicating that the Posleen vanguard had just reached the floodwall and was spreading out to either side of the entrance.

He almost felt embarrassed by the appropriation. The company had been surprisingly enthusiastic in their support of the defense. The local vice president for facilities had organized most of the support and had rousted out the MIS head and dozens of technicians to cobble together the network Keeton was working from. Integrating the military system and the various PCs and Macintoshes that were being used would have taken a military contractor ten years and two hundred billion dollars. The Reynolds' MIS folks, told to just figure out a way, had jury-rigged a fully functional system in hours. It just showed what happened when you gave clear goals, plenty of resources and let competent people get on with the job.

The whole defense was like that. Once the plan was in place, he had barely been able to keep up. So many little details had been handled by people who realized there wasn't time to argue. From

Keene, who had been a veritable whirlwind, directing projects here and there, to Sergeant Gleason from the SF team who had strong-armed half a dozen intransigent hospital administrators into providing impromptu MASH units.

There had been the other side as well. He had generated a simple order. If a situation came to the attention of a general officer in which an officer of captain's rank or above was slowing down the progress of the defense for political or bureaucratic reasons, that officer was to be relieved of commission and sent to the front to dig foxholes. He had fully twenty former field-grade officers and three flag officers wielding shovels. When the defense was all over he was going to have to sort it all out. The generals were likely to be a problem.

In the meantime he had a godlike view of the approaching enemy, a clear view of the thousands of them spreading through the kill-box and enough support in place to fight for days. And he'd only had to deal with three problems in the last hour. Remarkable.

But it was about time to give the signal to open fire. He suspected he was just about to be very, very busy.

He keyed the headset microphone that connected him to the Tactical Control Officer. "Okay, ADC. Open the ball."

The technique was called time-on-target. Depending on the distance to the target and the type of weapon, it takes a certain amount of time for an artillery shell to reach its objective. Some artillery, like mortar, fires at a high angle. These projectiles describe a high arc and take a relatively long time to reach their target. Some artillery is fired on a flatter angle and takes less time to reach a target.

This phenomenon was known, but up until World War II no one had paid much attention to it. However, early on during that war a senior American artillery officer had determined that a better "punch" could be gotten if the initial salvo of an artillery barrage arrived more or less simultaneously.

After thinking about this for a relatively short time, he decided to try having guns fire at timed intervals. With proper planning, all of the rounds would arrive within seconds of each other. The technique was discovered to work quite well, as surviving Germans were happy to attest after the war. And a new technique in the old, old game of artillery was born.

Arstenoss shot a spiteful plasma bolt at the towering wall. The lead Kessentai had loaded their *tenars* with heavy metal and retreated to the rear. The treasure could be bartered for prime genetic samples and fiefs, disdaining the necessity to fight for them. Now the host had reached this demon-bedamned wall, with the symbol of those thrice-damned and soul-chewed military technicians on it, and there seemed no way to follow the trinkets onward. The few God Kings that had floated their *tenars* above the wall had been removed from the Path. To make matters worse the trinkets had been getting larger and larger as the road progressed. Demons only knew what the eventual horde would look like. Faced with the potential for riches and the sudden blockage, tens of thousands of the host were packing into the valley, looking for more treasures or for the cowardly thresh to at least show themselves. A small bridge had been found to the east and many Kessentai were leaning that way, but it was both heavily defended and very small. It would take days for the host to cross the river and take the thresh from behind. Occasional blasts of fire out of frustration would drift up towards the dots of positions in the towers without eliciting response.

"We'll have to go over it," said Artulosten thoughtfully as the Posleen normals packed around his *tenar* jostled it on its ground-effect. The tens of thousands of oolt'os were reassuring. Surely nothing in the universe could stop such a host. "If we get a number of the Kessentai together, we can assault over it and take the gate from the far side. Then . . ." He stopped as a sound over his shoulder made him look back and up. It appeared that the top of the towering hill to his left had exploded as a ripple of purple fire and smoke exploded upward. His sharp eye caught a flicker of objects lifted on the columns of fire. There were hundreds of the things. He froze in indecision, unsure what action would help the situation. A human would have screamed "incoming." That action would have been just as useful as paralysis.

There were five divisions of infantry involved in the defense of Richmond. Three of those divisions had contributed their mortars and artillery to the Libby and Montrose Hill firebases. The relatively low velocity and high arc of mortars ensured that they would be the first to fire. The 120mm rounds arced gracefully upward to apogee then tilted over and headed down. It would take twenty-three seconds for the one hundred fifteen rounds to reach their targets. Before they were one-third of the way a second salvo was fired. And a third. At the third salvo the ninety-seven artillery pieces finally fired.

The Posleen were packed practically shoulder to shoulder in Schockoe Bottom. Many of them had started to try to climb the obstacles into the city. Others had started pressing against the wall of rubble across Williamsburg Road. A stream was headed towards the Belle Isle footbridge. None were prepared for the incoming salvo.

The devastation was impossible to describe. Within seconds of each other two hundred rounds of artillery landed in a space that could be occupied by four football fields.

The center artillery fire, well away from the infantry positions along the wall, was set to variable timed fire. VT rounds exploded above the Posleen force, scything downward in an oval pattern of death. Posleen caught under the hammer of the guns were torn apart by the artillery bursting charges, their yellow blood flying in an unnoticed mist from the fury of the charges.

The mortar rounds were, if anything, more effective. Using a proximity fuse they exploded a mere meter off the ground. The circle of death that spiraled outward slaughtered packed centaurs by the dozen. And another salvo hit. And another.

The infantrymen and women packing the buildings and defenses around the Bottom had been told that they would know when to fire. "Fire when the artillery goes off." For a few moments they were shocked into immobility as the black puffballs of VT and purple flashes of proximity rounds struck the world with a jackhammer of the gods. But as the stunning overpressure of that first devastating time-on-target passed and the guns set into the steady rhythm of eight rounds a minute the forces arrayed along the line popped up, took the safeties off the various weapons and started hunting targets.

The manjacks started going off before the first rifle. The entire kill zone was still packed with dazed and wounded Posleen, stumbling here and there under the thunder of the guns. As one would cross the interlocking target beams of the manjacks the robotic weapons would fire. Often the same Posleen would break three or four beams at a time, so densely packed were the weapons. The 7.62mm rounds, admirably designed for killing the centaurs, would tear the luckless alien apart, adding the slime of its juices to the ichor-soaked ground.

Much of the battlefield was already obscured by the smoke and dust thrown up from the artillery when the first infantrymen looked over and through their defensive walls. But there was the occasional flash of a centaur, most of them reeling stunned through the hammer of the guns. Such were taken under fire with glee; everyone had seen the news from Fredericksburg and the news media had already started on the interviews of survivors and relatives. They engaged the yellow centaurs with a fiery rage.

The snipers, arrayed higher in the buildings with their tripod-mounted .50 caliber sniper rifles, were having a field day. The surviving God Kings throughout the mass were trying to rally their forces, trying to return fire, trying to retreat out of the sudden abattoir that Twelfth Corps had made out of Schockoe Bottom. But the snipers were having none of it. The occasional flash of a plasma cannon or HVM, the white light so different from the black-orange of the artillery or the orange-purple of the mortars, revealed them clearly. Then, disdaining their target zones, dozens of snipers from as far as a kilometer away would return fire. Any God King saucer pulling out of the maelstrom of dust and smoke in the valley of death was targeted immediately. The plunging fire of the .50 caliber rifles smashed the centaurs off their vehicles, smashed through their inertial drivers, smashed through their energy crystals and added their devastation to an afternoon of fire and smoke and death.

General Keeton's monitor had a battlefield schematic and four waterfall graphs. The graphs were controlled by the Galactic AID that had been supplied to each corps commander and higher. One graph tracked casualties among the human defenders, the actual soldiers with rifles in their hand, who would keep the Posleen from coming out of the Bottom. The second tracked live Posleen in the fire-sack. The third tracked total Posleen that had entered the fire-sack. The fourth tracked total Posleen numbers.

Despite the fact that human numbers were less than a hundredth of the Posleen, they were on the same scale. The number of defenders was limited, the Posleen seemingly unlimited. When he had taken too many casualties he intended to retreat across the James.

That, however, looked a long way off. The graph indicating Posleen in the sack had climbed and climbed and climbed. Then, when it was apparent that they were about to stage a breakout, the Corps scale ambush had opened up. Now, there was virtually nothing left alive in Schockoe Bottom and human casualties had been next to nothing. If he had lost two hundred troops, excepting that company erased by one idiot's actions, he would be surprised. His total losses to date, as far as had been reported, were two hundred fifty killed in action, four-twenty wounded in action. And the Posleen had lost better than forty thousand.

However, there were still darn near two million left to kill. And the portion of the host that had not entered the kill zone was spreading to either side, despite the caltrops and craters.

Couldn't have that.

"Send out the sally," he whispered.

Lieutenant Colonel Walter Abrahamson wrapped a yellow silk scarf around his face and waved his hand overhead in a "wind-'em-up" signal. This was not, technically, the place for a cavalry battalion commander to be, in the hatch of an Abrams leading a do-or-die charge into the face of two million enemies. On the other hand, be damned to where he was supposed to be. The mission was to give the Posleen a sharp enough poke in the snout that they charged back into the fire-sack. He could have left it up to his company commanders. Should have. Had been ordered to. Sure. Like hell. Where else would a lifelong cavalry officer be?

"*Stew, you better be damned sure those cannon-cockers have got the word, over,*" he shouted into his intervehicle microphone. Despite the sound-proofed helmet the thunder of sixty jet-turbine driven main battle tanks revving their engines was an aural Vesuvius.

"*No problem,*" said his fellow battalion commander. The Second Battalion of the Twenty-Second Cavalry regiment had been relegated to defending the Libby Hill defenses and the other officer was bitterly envious of his comrade. "*I'm in the fire control center now. They've got the word. They'll cease fire when the gates start to open. Even the mortars will be landed by the time you get through.*

"*Just in case, you might want to go through buttoned up, though,*" he joked.

"*Yea verily,*" shouted Abrahamson. He waved to the civil engineers manning the gates. The hasty job done on the locking mechanism meant a hastier job done on the opening system. The gates, multi-ton concrete and steel behemoths, had been hooked to bulldozers to open them. The two structural engineers waved to the drivers and started moving them forward carefully. If the gates warped there might not be a way to get them closed again. And when the cavalry came back they were *really* going to want to be able to close the gates.

"*Okay, tell 'em the gates are moving back,*" he yelled and switched to intercom. "Move us up to the entrance," he said as he hit the switch to drop him into the belly of the beast.

As the gates rolled back they revealed an alien world. The artillery still falling in the bottom churned an indescribable stew of yellow Posleen corpses blended indiscriminately with the shattered brick of the former buildings. There was no living thing in sight. The hammer of the artillery combined with the fire of the infantry had done what practically never happened in battles: the combination had killed all of the enemy. Even in the most intense battles of World Wars I and II there had been a few survivors. Not here. The slaughter of the Posleen in Schockoe Bottom had been efficient, remorseless and complete.

"Pull forward slowly a hundred meters," he said over the intercom. "Then stop and wait for the squadron to get on line."

"Yea, though I ride through the valley of the shadow of death I will fear no evil," said Private First-Class Mills, the tank's gunner.

"For I am the baddest motherfucker in the valley," laughed the colonel, ending the military version of the psalm.

"Amen," whispered Private Hulm, the driver. The young private was as stunned as everyone else by the grounds-eye view of the devastation, but he gunned the big tank and pulled it slowly forward into the devastation.

The surface of Fourteenth Street was coated in a layer of slime and the rubbercoated tracks of the behemoth threw up a fine spray that looked like orange mud. With the exception of the occasional shattered carcasses of God King saucers, there were no obstacles. The occasional nearly intact Posleen corpse was ground beneath the treads of the tank without notice or comment. The seventy-ton armored juggernaut didn't even lurch.

PFC Mills swung the turret to the side. *"Target. Moving saucer."*

The colonel checked his repeater display by reflex. The saucer was skewed to one side, crabbing to the north and out of the firesack. As soon as it left the overwhelming haze it would be a target for the snipers dotting the towers, but it also could be a threat.

"Confirmed," said the colonel. *"Engage co-ax."*

"Roger, co-ax," responded the gunner, switching to coaxial fire instead of main gun. *"On the way."*

The M-1E was a modification of the venerable Abrams main battle tank. Designed for fighting the Posleen, it had improved frontal armor and thermal damping to make it more survivable when hit by hypervelocity missiles and plasma cannons. It also took a leaf out of the Russian Army's book.

The Russians, their tank markets faced by overwhelming air threats, had modified their tanks to double as antiaircraft platforms. They had mounted a twenty-three millimeter cannon on each side of the turret and slaved the fire control to the tank gunner. With a little luck, the mass fire from a battalion of tanks might take down an attacking aircraft.

The Americans had looked at the idea and scoffed. Until the coming of the Galactics. The Posleen depended on mass assaults, but their weapons were also phenomenal. A conventional platform to combat them would have to be able to survive plasma and hypervelocity missiles but still be able to kill large numbers of troops. Rather than try to develop an entirely new platform, the army had taken the Russian idea and improved it.

On each side of the turret of the M-1E was a pod of four 25mm Bushmaster cannons. The cannons turned with the turret and could swivel up and down for targeting. The targeting computer of the Abrams, still the most advanced and capable of any tank made by man, was modified to accommodate the new weapon, making it incredibly accurate. But it really wasn't about accuracy. It was about massive firepower.

The gunner chose "HE" from a menu of ammunition options. Then he stroked the trigger.

The Bushmaster cannon had a maximum fire rate of twenty-five hundred rounds per minute. There were eight cannons targeted on the lone God King. The single stroke of the trigger fired a burst of seven from each cannon. The fifty-six rounds, each with nearly a pound of explosives and notched wire for shrapnel, exploded across the saucer, shredding it and the riding God King.

"Target eliminated."

The gunner continued to search, but with the exception of the sole God King, no targets showed themselves. The tank moved through the lifting cloud of dust and smoke as the stench of the dead Posleen became thicker and thicker and the other tanks of the squadron spread to either side.

The artillery had stopped as promised and Colonel Abrahamson decided to pop the hatch and look around. The alternative was staying inside, and the atmosphere couldn't be any worse outside.

It was. The stench of the Posleen increased five-fold as he raised himself out the hatch, but he controlled his desire to heave and looked around. The squadron was spreading out and he was happy that he had talked the colonel into the earlier reconnaissance mission. The squadron was fairly well trained, for this day and age, but the battles to the north, small-scale as they were, had helped immeasurably to put some polish on it. And it had gotten rid of some deadwood.

Now the unaccompanied tanks spread out into an extended V formation without a hitch, aligning on their pennon-flapping company commanders and platoon leaders. He had decided not to bring any of the Bradleys or Humvees for this mission. They knew, generally, where the enemy was and he did not intend to press home an attack. The Bradleys were slower than the Abrams and more vulnerable, while the Humvees were completely unsurvivable.

No, this was a straightforward heavy cavalry charge: Run out, lower lances, hit the barbarians and charge back through the gates. The barbarians always chased after you. But the general had better have everybody off the Mayo Bridge when they came back. Anybody in Walter Abrahamson's way was going to be paste.

The radio crackled. *"Bravo troop, in position."*

"*Charlie troop in position.*"

"*Alpha, rrready to rock-and-rolll.*"

He smiled. The Alpha commander was a bit of a personality, but he knew his business. Abrahamson stopped noticing the stench as the moment came upon him. He looked through the haze towards the distant and unseen enemy and nodded his head. "*Roger,*" he said over the radio. "*Move forward to phase-line Shenandoah. And may God defend the right.*"

◆ CHAPTER 51 ◆

Ravenwood, VA, United States of America, Sol III
1923 EDT October 10th, 2004 AD

"*Mortars, throw some rounds on the other side of that bridge we just passed over.*"

So much for fire control procedure, thought Keren bouncing along in the back of the commandeered Suburban.

Military equipment has a life of its own. The military spends billions of dollars every year not on procurement of new equipment, but on maintaining the equipment they have. Armored fighting vehicles, next to helicopters, have to be the worst. They have thousands of moving parts, none of which, it seems, have sealed bearings. The tracks of an AFV are only good for a few hundred miles, a fraction of the life of a tire and a thousand times as expensive. Maintenance is not a haphazard requirement, but a vital necessity.

Unfortunately, the divisions committed to the defense of northern Virginia had only begun to become coherent when the Posleen landed. Training had been sorely lacking. Maintenance had been worse.

Of the four armored mortar carriers the platoon had possessed at the start of the bugout, only two remained. The Fire Direction Center track had been the first to succumb, dying of a failed track bearing before they were five miles down the road. But the Three Gun track had been destroyed soon after, casualty of their one close brush with the Posleen.

The FDC section had packed into the Two Gun track, still humming along like a top, thanks in no small part to Keren's efforts before the battle, until they found the diesel Suburban by the side of Prince

416

William Parkway. The SUV had turned out to be victim of simple lack of fuel, and a few five-gallon cans of premium military diesel fixed that.

But hundreds of other tracked vehicles had failed to survive, and the troops from those Bradleys and M-113s were strung along both sides of the road, marching as fast as they could to try to outrun the oncoming horde. Both gun tracks were covered with personnel, and wounded were packed all around him in the Suburban. *This really is "Needs must when devils drive,"* Keren thought.

But the problem of friendly-fire was on his mind with the last call for fire. He looked out the window. If there were this many personnel along the road here, the roads had to be packed back there.

"*Boss, are there friendly troops in the area, over?*"

Their mortar platoon leader was the last officer in the battalion and had taken command of all the line tracks he could find. A few tracks had bugged out, others had died from mechanical failure, but seven remained from the battalion, with about half the crews for them, and the lieutenant had picked up replacement personnel as he went. The deal was simple, you could ride if you would fight. If you wouldn't fight, you could walk. After the last Nineteenth Armored Division unit was destroyed, the scratch unit continued a nearly single-handed rear-guard throughout the afternoon and simultaneously replaced all its casualties. Along the way, "Puppy-Dog" Leper had been forever changed.

"*Not any more. Engineers just blew the bridge with the last few stragglers on it. The horses are bunching up on the other side. Fire 'em up, Keren, ten rounds per gun then move on back.*"

"*Roger.*" He popped up through the sunroof and waved to the gun tracks on either side. "*Fire mission, hip shoot!*" As he did he noticed a Humvee in the woods to one side, with a soldier leaning against the hood. *Well, if the stupid bastard can't figure out to run like hell, that's his problem.*

Arkady Simosin silently watched the last unit crossing the Davis Ford bridge. Whoever it was had fought a hell of a rearguard action after the last of the Nineteenth Armored expended itself. "The Last Charge" would probably be forgotten in the throes, but the final company of the armored unit had shattered a flanking movement that would have cut off half the survivors of the corps. It had been a heroic and ultimately suicidal charge.

He had come to the conclusion that military disasters follow certain prepared scripts. There is ample warning of the danger. There are critical moments, even after the disaster is clear, where proper orders and actions can correct the situation. And there is a reactionary political response in aftermath.

Given the modern speed of information transfer and decision making, it appeared that the reactionary aftermath was not even going to await the end of the battle. He looked again at the bald prose ordering him to turn over his command to his chief of staff and report to First Army Headquarters in New York. The e-mail continued with the comment that a replacement was on the way. He knew the general, a crony of General Olds; Olds would have done better to leave the COS in charge.

So, he thought, *this is what a thirty-year career comes to.* Better than the poor bastards caught in the political-correctness witchhunts of the '90s.

He crumpled up the flashpaper and dropped it on the ground, adding one last bit of litter to the battlefield. He turned and climbed in the Humvee as the first crump of departing mortar rounds filled the air.

◆ CHAPTER 52 ◆

***The White House, Washington, DC, United States of America, Sol III
2045 EDT October 10th, 2004*** AD

"That's it," said General Taylor, glancing at the e-mail brought in by a communications technician. He looked over to where the President was hunched into his chair. "All the remaining units of Tenth Corps are through the Ninth Corps lines."

"How many are left?" asked the Secretary of Defense, staring at the electronic map on the wall.

"Of infantry, armor, engineers and other front-line units, there are less than two thousand accounted for."

"Okay," said the President, in a harsh voice, "put another way, how many did we lose?"

"Over twenty-five thousand . . ."

"*Twenty-five—?*"

"We sent in a *heavy corps*, Mister President," said the general, in tones to bend metal. "Five heavy divisions with full support. Of front-line troops we've gotten back less than one battered brigade! We lost half the total number of casualties in Vietnam; five times the estimate for the first day of the Normandy invasion. We killed approximately nine thousand Posleen, according to the last and only reports we received. All that did was add to their goddamn supplies."

"If it hadn't been for the hacking . . ." said the secretary.

"If it hadn't been for the hacking," interrupted the general, "we would have killed more Posleen. We still would have taken these losses."

"We'll never know," said the secretary.

"Yes . . . we . . . will, Mr. Secretary," responded the general, suddenly tired of the whole game. "There's Ninth Corps." He gestured towards the screen. "It's had hours to dig in, lay wire and mines, which Tenth didn't, and it has nearly secure flanks, which Tenth didn't, and it is not being hacked, which Tenth was, and it is not going to be pasted by its own artillery and mortars, which Tenth was, and we are going to lose them, too! Oh, they'll kill more Posleen, but it doesn't damn well matter, Mr. Secretary, sir, because the Posleen can afford to lose a *million* troops to destroy one of our corps! This is just the start of the damn war! The only way we could win it from the beginning was to kill over a hundred Posleen for every guy assigned to a gun! And we just took about twenty casualties for every Posleen killed! At that rate we'll lose every goddamn soldier in the eastern United States to this single landing!"

The High Commander suddenly realized that he was shouting at the secretary of defense. On the other hand, no one seemed to care if he was. He also realized that the secretary was not the one to be shouting at.

"What if we recall Ninth Corps?" croaked the President, looking up at the map for the first time in nearly an hour. His eyes burned. He had spent twenty years trying to get into this chair. It had cost him most of a stomach, a marriage and his children. And one mistake was all it took.

The general shook his head in resignation. "Too late." He looked down at the briefing papers. The critical information on maintenance was damning. "The Posleen can move faster than those units."

"Tactical mobility is one of the American Army's strong suits," said the secretary, his tone resounding with surety.

"It is when you have well-trained, experienced units," said the High Commander, raised back into fury by the fatuousness of the remark. "It is *not* a strong suit when you have undertrained, inexperienced, unsure units. Patton's Third Army could have done it easily. Waffen SS? No problem. The Allied troops in Desert Storm? Fuck, yeah. Give an order, pull out, run to the next position, be it a mile or a hundred miles, reassemble. No problem, Can Do.

"Here we have troops that have only had a filled chain of command for five months. Units that were rioting three months ago. Units that are a year behind on scheduled maintenance, almost two years behind on training. Units where half the vehicles break down in the first fifteen miles. Units that will have a hard time holding *fixed* positions, much less maneuvering.

"No, sir," he continued, looking the President square in the eye. "The best we can hope is that Ninth Corps does more damage to the enemy than Tenth did, before the bastards pull them down."

"And Richmond?" asked the secretary of defense.

"Well, sir," said the general, "if we could only get them to turn around and attack Twelfth Corps."

"How's it coming?" asked General Keeton.

John Keene spun around in his swivel chair and stared at the commander with a blank, distant expression for a moment. Then he shook his head and focused on the reality of the moment.

"Sorry," he said, ruefully, "I was elsewhere."

"I could see that. How's it going?"

"Remarkably well. Good news: by the end of this battle, we'll hardly have to do a thing to prepare Richmond for the long-term projects." That was good for a weary chuckle.

"And what about being prepared for this particular set of visitors?"

"Well, the weakest points are still there. If they turn to the west, we are screwed and if they turn to the east we have great difficulty. But we think we have a good plan for centering their focus."

"What's that?"

"Gold."

"Gold?"

"Yep. The Posleen are notorious looters and they seem to be particularly interested in heavy metals and gems. It seems crazy, because you can get gold and diamonds much more easily from an asteroid belt than you can from a hostile city. But they really seem to crave it. Anyway, the Federal Reserve Bank here had a rather large supply of it. We . . . came up with a designation for Fourteenth Street as 'Gold Avenue' so to speak and have put what looks like some sort of ornamentation, made out of pure gold, on the street every fifty yards."

"Oh, joy . . ."

"Yep. So, there will be a line of ornaments, on little stands, every fifty yards all the way up to the floodwall gates."

"And that means that they'll follow the yellow brick road and want to keep following it."

"Right. And just to add a little fun to it, we had a choice of five different sizes, so the first twenty were small, the second twenty were larger, and so on. By the time the front rank gets to the wall and the word gets around among them, we hope they're in a frenzy. We had quite a bit left over, so as an added bonus we put out larger ornaments from time to time. But only along Fourteenth Street. If they use the logic . . ."

"They will really want to cross that bridge when they come to it."

"Yes, sir. And if the word gets around, most of them should head for Schockoe Bottom."

Something about the facile explanation started to bother the corps commander. The general looked a little questioning for a moment. "How did you get the ornaments made so quickly?"

"Well, there is *quite* a bit of industry in the area," Keene temporized.

"Or perhaps I should be asking what kind of ornaments they are?" asked the general, his suspicions now fully aroused.

"Well, we didn't have much of a choice . . ."

"What are they, Keene?" asked General Keeton.

"Well, you ever been behind a tractor-trailer, and noticed how on some of them, on the mudflaps, there are these shiny silhouettes . . . ?"

Ersin watched as the private hammered in the last iron stake topped with a golden silhouette of two busty females in a reclined position and shook his head.

"Yah know, boss," said Mueller, "somebody's bound to have a cow about this."

"And the defenses at Libby Hill are as complete as was planned for this battle," continued the High Commander. "Later on we'll build concrete bunkers and such, but the Twelfth Corps is going to have it as good as it gets on such short notice. And we're bringing in the Thirteenth and Fourteenth Corps from the Carolinas. Richmond is going to be a graveyard of Posleen," he stated definitively.

"What about their data security?" asked the secretary of defense.

"There was a cyberpunk team in Richmond on an unrelated mission," answered the High Commander. "They checked the Twelfth Corps's IVIS and FireTac systems. Both were infected by a virus that apparently noted the detection and performed an autodestruct.

"They're picking apart the remnants right now and scratching their heads like everyone else. But as far as NSA, the Cybers and CONARC's own Data Security department can determine, Twelfth Corps is fully mission capable, including all automated systems. On the other hand, they've also zeroed every weapon in the Corps on particular targets and are only awaiting the Posleen to open fire. They really don't need FireTac or IVIS."

"So you're saying that *this* battle should go as planned?" asked the secretary, sarcastically.

"I did not plan the previous engagement," said the High Commander.

"No, General," said the President. "I planned that engagement, as I made plain on national television. What can we do about Ninth Corps?"

The general shook his head again. "We can pull out some of the supply personnel, but not many. I mean, there's a reason for every person who is that far forward. We don't have a terrain obstacle to interpose between Posleen and our support as we did with Tenth, so our downside is actually higher.

"If . . . when, the Posleen break through the defenses, they'll be able to engage the support elements, including artillery and supply units, that they weren't able to assault at the Dale City defense. Casualty estimates on this battle are double or triple the Tenth Corps battle."

"And there's nothing we can do?" asked the secretary, incredulously.

"First Army has committed all of the Tenth Corps units that are reasonably cohesive to reinforce Ninth along with Tenth's Corps and division artillery, which was mainly behind the Occoquan. He was sending the Eighth and Eleventh Corps in to reinforce them, but he was countermanded by CONARC."

"Why?" demanded the secretary.

"If Ninth can hold with all six divisions, two corps of artillery, and fixed, prepared positions, we'll send them in to reinforce. If it can't, and I do not expect it to, it is futile to throw away another sixty thousand troops. Besides," he concluded, "First Army is strung from here to Boston. We're parceling them along the Potomac at crossings. We might have to use them to extract the refugees."

"What about the ACS battalion?" asked the President.

"They are on their way. They should be there about three hours after the battle is joined. At that point the plan is to send them around Lake Jackson and hit the Posleen in the flank."

The overloaded tractor-trailers carrying the Third Battalion Five-Fifty-Fifth Mobile Infantry Regiment had left the secure Interstate 81 hours before. The laboring trucks packed with half-ton suits had crossed the outer Blue Ridge before descending into the Virginia horse country. This was no-man's-land. Even the police had evacuated with the last civilians, heading to the Blue Ridge and safety.

To the troops, packed like sardines in the trucks, it had been a nightmarish ride. Although they each had hundreds of hours in their suits, lying on their backs under, in some cases, a dozen suits while swaying from side to side for hours in a tractor-trailer had been a shattering experience. There were several cases of troopers panicking; in one case the spasmodic gyrations of the panicked troop tore open the side of the truck, spilling two squads of ACS troopers out on the interstate to the general detriment of any vehicle that hit them. Between panic and motion nausea, the unit was in poor shape when the convoy ran into a Posleen ambush outside of Warrenton, VA.

The Posleen were not even skirmishers. The God King had gotten his fill of fighting humans when he lost almost his entire oolt to the guns of the *North Carolina*. Having lost all interest in engaging artillery he struck out in the direction of least resistance. He was one of the rare Posleen that was not spoiling for a fight.

Along the way he lost a few more oolt'os to random armed humans. They mostly fired at long range and from cover, but were remarkably accurate and persistent. And the oolt learned quickly not to bother with the residences. The few that did not explode in his face yielded only scraps of food and occasional bits of light treasure. Many had been cleared of anything of value. The God King and his forces followed U.S. 17 northward through the rolling hills of Spotsylvania, Stafford and Fauquier counties, past country farms, mostly deserted, and occasional clusters of houses. Nowhere did he encounter significant storehouses, but on the other hand he also did not encounter significant resistance; he felt it was a fair trade.

At the junction of 17 and 15/29 the group encountered a large abandoned vehicle. The cargo area revealed a vast storage of multiple types of foodstuffs. The side of the vehicle sported a picture of a food beast he had already encountered. The beast yielded a flat and tasteless food. The similarity in taste to the threshkreen caused some of the Kessentai to speculate that these might be the threshkreen's nestlings. The disparate sizes and conformation argued against it. But the Posleen had seen stranger methods of reproduction.

However, the cargo vehicle had many other types of food, many of them oddly spiced and prepared. Some of the material, sporting a picture of a white avian, tasted remarkably like nestling.

Other than the storehouses of the thresh it was the finest booty taken so far. Obviously, the cargo vehicles were to be captured whenever possible. They had found three more on the way north. Only one contained more foodstuffs but the others had useful mixed supplies.

Thus, when the four vehicles hove into view, the oolt'os followed their carefully conveyed and simple orders to open fire on the motive portion of the lead vehicle.

When the tractor-trailer containing Alpha Company and part of the battalion staff jackknifed, the heavy and refractory suits tumbled through the light sidewalls of the trailer like buckshot through paper. The troopers were thrown through the air and tumbled along the ground for multiple meters. The trailing trucks slammed on their brakes and, as soon as they slowed to a survivable speed, the truckers dove out and took shelter in the roadside ditch.

Most of the troops tucked themselves into balls as they flew through the air, the inertia of the thousand-pound suits carrying them hundreds of feet in an uncontrolled tumble. Since the Posleen company was more or less in line with the inertia of the vehicle, several of the troopers and the battalion intelligence officer were carried into its midst.

The GalTech Armored Infantry Design Team had been composed of knowledgeable and careful individuals. They were people who had either experienced or extensively studied a variety of calamities. To a man, or in one case, woman, they were pessimists where combat was concerned; Murphy was an old and dear friend that they kept always at the forefront of their brains.

In addition, the conditions that the company was in were remarkably similar to an insertion technique briefly considered during the initial phases of development. Thus, when these particular conditions arose, a series of planned and legacy software reactions occurred.

Inertial compensators did not slow the suits, but rather served to remediate the effect on the users. The apparent roll was significantly reduced, while the visual conditions were matched to the apparent inertial effects. Thus, instead of feeling like bowling balls, the luckless troopers found themselves wrestling with molasses. But the reduction allowed them to see what was coming and, at least partially, prepare.

Three of the troops tumbled into the midst of the Posleen were from Alpha weapons: Grim Reaper suits. Realizing that they might need close-range support on the way, the platoon leader had switched out all four weapons points for flechette cannons.

Composed of twelve-barreled light flechette guns, each flechette cannon could spew forty thousand lethal steel slivers a minute. Of course, like all Grim Reaper systems, they could also run through the onboard munitions in less than six minutes of combat. Grim Reapers always preferred to be close to their ammo sources.

Two of the weapons troops, through a combination of luck and gymnastics, ended up on their feet and practically side by side in the midst of the Posleen. Most of the Posleen lining their backtrack were dead, or well on their way, but the final group that cushioned their stop was struggling to their feet even as the Reapers opened fire.

Dropping all four cannons to horizontal, the two suit troops went back-to-back and began to spin in place, throwing out a horizontal steel rain of destruction. The steel razors shredded any Posleen in their path, the yellow centaurs tearing apart under the fatal onslaught of the hypervelocity flechettes.

Unfortunately, there was no way for two troops to cover the entire circuit. Posleen on every side hurled themselves on the explosive dervishes in their midst, monomolecular blades rising and falling in awful cadence. In moments the luckless Grim Reapers were taken apart like lobsters.

However, their sacrifice was not in vain. The violence of their entry into the Posleen force had thrown it off balance just a moment too long. The moment's breathing space was enough time for many of the troopers of the ambushed ACS to regain their feet and their wits.

Before the Posleen could regain the upper hand, fast-thinking troopers whipped their grav-guns to level and opened fire.

A hurricane of silver lightning crashed into the remaining Posleen. The God King had lost most of the oolt at Market Crossing. When the tsunami of fire crashed into it the remainder was washed away in seconds; the few scattered defensive rounds of the Posleen disappeared into nothingness.

The faithless and luckless God King attempted to escape the tidal wave of relativistic fire, but was picked out of the sky by a cone of fire from dozens of troops. The detonation of the energy matrix was muted by the kinetic explosions of thousands of rounds intersecting on the point in space once occupied by the vanished saucer. Of the God King, naught was left but a whiff of putrescence on the wind.

Lieutenant Colonel Calvin Bishop pulled himself up out of the wrecked cab of the third truck and sat on the mangled door. His AID was already cataloging the damage and he grimaced at the digests. The battalion was mostly intact—the losses were actually minimal—but the ambush on top of the devastating ride over the Blue Ridge had combined into nightmare.

He was in the middle of nowhere, thirty miles from the battle and already four hours behind schedule. He wasn't sure his lone battalion could exactly turn the tide, but if they made it to the Ninth Corps's line in time they might be able to extract the corps. It had become something of an instant tradition among the ACS.

He took a brief moment to contemplate the situation and began to snap orders to his company commanders. They had a battle to catch.

✦ CHAPTER 53 ✦

Monsignor O'Reilly carefully considered the items to carry with him. With the Posleen rapidly approaching his small house in Arlington, he was rather certain that he would be on foot for the majority of the next several days.

There were so many things to choose from. His collection of books and manuscripts dating back to the twelfth century. His antiques and archaeological treasures gathered throughout the world. Complex electronics to decipher the secrets of ancient and modern times. On the other hand several of those would have to be thoroughly destroyed.

Finally, recognizing that the only true treasure to the cause resided in his cranium, he packed a bookbag with some socks, easy-to-prepare food and bottled water. He took a last look around the comfortable room, set the autodestruct sequence and walked out the front door. He didn't bother to lock it.

He debated whether to walk or drive the half mile to VA 123. He finally decided to drive. The traffic might have cleared and, if it had not, every little bit of energy savings would help. He shouldered the bag and started towards his late-model Buick, but froze as a dark-tinted Suburban with its lights off appeared out of the darkness and pulled up in front of his house.

He thought for a moment if there was anything incriminating in the house or on his person. He quickly decided that there was not and just as quickly decided that it probably wouldn't matter to his visitors. He braced himself for what would come next and barely flinched when the back door was flung back to reveal the Indowy Aelool and Paul des Jardins in the light from the interior.

"Get in," snapped Paul, all trace of the dapper dilettante vanished.

O'Reilly considered the situation for a moment—it was a common trap—then hurried over to the SUV. "Just because it's a tank doesn't mean you're going to be able to negotiate traffic." The heavyset driver pulled away without a word and headed away from VA 123.

"We have made arrangements," said the Indowy. "We will be picked up by a Himmit stealth ship along the Burke Run."

"There's another problem," said des Jardins, gesturing towards the Indowy with his chin and turning to look out the window. The large bag at his feet could only hold weapons and O'Reilly smiled gently. You could take the boy out of DGSE but you could never take DGSE out of the boy. The hand inside the fine Saville Row suit undoubtedly cradled some lethal bit of French hardware.

"Indeed," continued the little Indowy. "We intercepted a termination order originating from the Tir Dol Ron's office."

"Intercepted?" asked the Jesuit incredulously.

"The Bane Sidhe is very ancient and very well-represented among the Indowy," stated the diminutive alien. His batlike face wrinkled in a complicated fashion. Scholar or no, the expression was far too complex for O'Reilly to decipher. It seemed one part satisfaction and three parts exasperation. "Our ineffectiveness at direct action stems from many of the same sources as the Darhel's. And our response has ever mirrored theirs: Let humans do the dirty work."

The former DGSE agent snorted. "To our discredit."

"I am aware that the difference is often not one of execution but of goals," admitted O'Reilly, wryly. "However, how does this termination order effect us? Is it for a member of the Société? Or of the Franklins?"

"No," admitted the Indowy with another grimace. "The individual affected is unaware of the actions of the societies. However, the Bane Sidhe are in the individual's debt. Furthermore, we believe that the individual may represent a strong destabilizing factor to the Darhel."

"One individual is not worth risking the Société," stated the Monsignor definitively.

"Not normally. However, this individual has repeatedly demonstrated traits that make him outside the norm. And the Bane Sidhe ask it. We have aided the Société much. This is *nothing* compared to what we have done for the Société!"

"What about you, Paul?"

"All of our *Marion* teams are in the Northeast right now. Otherwise we would be handling it."

"So, you think it worth the risk. Where is it that you need help?" asked the Jesuit, warily.

"We need Team Conyers."

The monsignor smiled thinly and tried not to let the surprise show on his face. He hoped like hell the *Darhel* did not have the Mother Church so thoroughly penetrated.

The robe-clad monk knelt in the dirt of the well-tended vineyard and carefully tasted a grape. His mouth worked as he swirled the juices around, gathering every last nuance. The harvest would have to be gathered soon or there might not be one. The grape lacked that last bit of sweetness, but the lack might be to the good. Surely the wine of such a bitter time should not be sweet. The gentle wind of the night was a boon to his soul. The night was still the same, even as the world had come apart around them. The sheltering night had not changed.

He rose to his feet with the grace of a dancer as one of the senior brothers approached. The senior brother gestured for him to follow and headed towards one of the outbuildings of the monastery without a word. The monk saw others being gathered and realized that there must have been a special calling. The senior brother turned aside as he entered the building.

The assistant abbot would retire to his cell and pray continuously until the team returned. He remembered his own days on the teams and feared that many would not be at the next vespers. A call from the Société was so often a death sentence. They were like the French Foreign Legion in a way; the only thing that mattered to the Société was the mission and damn the casualties. To the Benedictines, the importance was the ritual and the art. That is why, contrary to popular myth, the special troops of the Catholic Church were not Jesuits. Shao-Lin did not own the monopoly they thought.

The monk perused the briefing under red "battle-lights" as his black- and gray-clad brothers assembled the instruments of their arts. The mission was complex but not terribly so. The gravest question was time. And of course going in with no communications and limited intelligence.

The monks had special dispensation to speak during briefings. There were, however, no questions. They took up their equipment, changed their clothes and loaded into the darkened vans without a word.

O'Neal stared at his opponent across the dimly lit green expanse. The next move would decide the outcome of the contest. The stakes

were high, but Michael O'Neal, Senior had been in tougher spots.
There was always a way out if you tried hard enough, thought about
the situation and acted with precision and violence. But he usually
had better cards.

"Raise you five," said Cally.

"Call."

"Two pair, kings high."

"Damn!" said Papa O'Neal, throwing his cards down. The pair of
aces lay forlornly on the table as if mocking his inability to win a
simple hand of poker against an eight-year-old. It was well past
midnight and he should have had her in bed long before. But with
news coming in from the fighting and her father on his way to the
front, Mike Senior was waiting for her to fall asleep naturally. So far
she was showing all the stamina of a professional gambler.

"One more hand like that and you'll be doing the dishes for a
month," Cally said with a laugh.

"Yeah, well . . ." He tried to think of a retort but just gave up. What
could he say?

His pager went off and he pulled it off his belt. The device was
hooked into the property sensors, not his phone; just because he was
in his sixties didn't mean he couldn't use modern technology. And
it showed that they had a visitor. First motion sensors and then metal
sensors had detected movement on the long road into the farm.
However, the device that monitored for subspace transmissions was
quiescent.

So, not Posleen then. Maybe the sheriff coming up to make sure
he wasn't making moonshine. Or at least not at the house where it
might get found and be embarrassing. Best not to offer him a taste
of the latest batch. Although it made little or no sense at this time
of night.

"We've got a visitor," he said.

"Friend or foe?" Cally asked seriously. She tossed down the cards
she had been shuffling.

"Don't know," he said. "I guess we ought to go look."

It was an unremarkable Ford Taurus. Probably a rental. The driver
was a male. There wasn't much else Papa O'Neal could tell, even with
the high-definition light-amplifying binoculars. He waited in the front
room of the house, screened by the light curtains over the windows,
until the car pulled up to the front and stopped.

The driver revealed in the glare of the security lights was a male,
early twenties and alone. He looked faintly Hispanic—mostly because
of his swarthy complexion—but could have been any of a hundred

races and mixtures across the world. He was wearing an old and battered field jacket. It had a Special Forces patch on the right shoulder but was otherwise unadorned; "sterile" in the parlance of the special ops community. He also looked familiar, but O'Neal could not place the face.

Mike Senior opened the front door and stepped out, watching the stranger warily. There was no reason for a total stranger to come to the house. Come to think of it, he had never had an uninvited visitor. With the exception of the law. But it wasn't like he had much choice.

"Mike," the guy said on first sight and his face broke into a broad grin. "Long time, 'mano!"

Papa O'Neal's face creased in thought but his expression remained wary. "Do I know you?"

"Shit." The stranger shook his head in apparent chagrin. "How 'bout this: 'Sometimes you get the feathers, sometimes you get the bones.' "

Papa O'Neal tilted his head sideways and his mind wandered down a lot of years of memory. Then his eyes widened. "Harold?" he asked, incredulously.

"So that's the deal man. Got a new life, new identity and I've been workin' for the Man ever since. Just call me Lazarus," he ended with a lopsided grin.

"You work for the Company?" Mike asked, leaning back in his cowhide-covered chair.

"No," Harold said, with a shake of his head. "There really are groups nobody *ever* talks about." He suddenly leaned forward in his own chair. "You *know* what fucked us, man. It was the bean counters in the States. The peaceniks and the politicians in uniform that would never let us do our job the right way. You *know* man, you did the job we were supposed to do!"

"Sure, Harold," said Mike Senior soothingly. "But that was then, man. Different world. Different enemy."

"No," said the visitor with a shake of the head. "The enemy's still the same. The rear-echelon bastards that sit in their air-conditioned offices and fuck everything up for the poor bastards that have to do the job."

"Harold," said Mike Senior, with a gesture at Cally. She was on the other side of the room from him, behind the visitor's chair, trying to work the puzzle box. He was indicating that Harold might want to watch his language, but he also hoped it would calm him down. He did calm down, but something else happened and it snapped Mike's attention down to earth like a bolt of lightning. A sixth sense he had developed in more really bad places than he wanted to dwell on told him that something had changed in his visitor. And he didn't think it was for the good.

"Look, Mike," said Harold, leaning forward and his voice dropping, "there's a place for you." He nodded seriously, his eyes boring into the sergeant who had trained him so many years before. "These are the people who know how to get the job done. Sometimes there are problems, the REMFs that don't know when to crap or get off the pot. And sometimes they need a little lesson. You dig?"

"Harold," said Mike Senior, suddenly wishing that he knew what the hell was happening, "this is my place. I'm old, man. Real old."

"Don' matter, man. So am I," said the visitor, spreading his arms, "and *look* at me! They want experienced people. And with the call-up they are getting damned hard to find. Your name popped out of the computer and it was like a sign from God."

"I was wondering why you looked so good. Rejuv?" asked O'Neal.

"We got all the support anybody could want," said Harold. He leaned forward and swept his hands across in a negative gesture. "Whatever you want, we can get it. No questions. Whatever you want."

Mike nodded seriously and finally realized where they were in the conversation. This was not an offer that could be refused. Harold had told him that he was involved with a group that was outside constitutional bounds, had access to full Galactic medical technology and could obtain any weapon or support. The fact that nobody had ever had an inkling that such a group existed simply pointed out the fact that no one had ever talked about it. Ever.

Since he had no intention of joining such a group, it would require that he never be able to talk about it.

Leaving Cally in the room was a deft touch on the part of his former pupil. Harold assumed, perhaps correctly, that Mike would not want to kill him in front of the girl. Harold, on the other hand, would have no such qualms. One of the problems with being in the military is that you don't always get to choose your acquaintances or trainees. In the case of Harold, Mike Senior had always secretly despised him. The man was the Compleat Sociopath. If he shot a five-year-old girl by mistake the only thing he would feel was recoil.

This left Mike Senior in a bit of a pickle. And it was one he wasn't quite sure he was going to survive. Harold had just as much experience as he did and he was physiologically years younger. Since Harold knew that there was a chance Mike Senior would turn down the job, he was undoubtedly armed and prepared to kill Mike and Cally. He would also be prepared to ignore or end any distraction.

If Mike even offered to get up it would probably terminate the interview. With prejudice.

The only thing that he could do was play along. Of course, Harold would suspect that he was playing along. That was what would make it so interesting.

"Well," said Papa O'Neal, steepling his fingers—the moment of thought had been a flash; there should have been nothing to betray his sudden insight—"That's an interesting offer." Just as he said it, his beeper went off. Again.

Harold leaned forward so fast it made a cobra look slow and his hand moved towards his side but Papa O'Neal simply sat very still and hoped for the best. When Harold also froze Mike smiled thinly. "Beeper."

Harold laughed. "Huh. Yeah. Yours?" The assassin leaned forward with his hands on his thighs.

The weapon was either on his side or in a skeleton holster on the back. And who the hell could be coming to call? Papa O'Neal lifted up his shirt, exposing the beeper. The gesture looked totally normal as he pulled it off his left side. He could only hope and pray that Harold still thought he was in the dark.

Harold's hands remained in sight on his thighs. Side then. Papa O'Neal made a show of checking the beeper. "It's my son," he lied. "He's on his way to rejoin his unit."

The sensors showed another vehicle. This one had a heavy metal signature. Either a large truck or a van with metal in it. The last time he had seen a signature like that was when he and his buddies came back from Dahlonega after a weekend shooting against the Rangers. It actually looked an awful lot like a van full of door-kickers. Since he didn't expect reinforcements, he had to assume that it was friends of his visitor come to ensure the real orders were carried out.

"As I said," Papa O'Neal continued, "that's a very interesting offer. Especially the rejuv. That is what we're talking about, right?"

"Yeah," said Harold relaxing ever so slightly. "That's part of the package."

"Well, God knows I've done some wet work in my time . . ." he said when Cally interrupted.

"Grandpa, did Daddy give you the key to this puzzle box?"

"No, honey," he snapped, not taking his attention away from the visitor. At normal speed the van would just about be clearing the woodline. They might unload under cover and try to sneak up. Or they might barrel-ass right up to the door. If the second, they would be here in less than a minute. Which meant that time was about over for the conversation. "Figure it out yourself."

"I'm kind of in a hurry," said Harold as if reading his mind. "I think I need a yes or no. Now." He leaned forward and his right hand drifted downward.

"Well, I never did like the balance on that Galactic piece of shit," Cally said to no one in particular. There was a sound of a slide drawing back.

Mike Senior closed his eyes just in time to block out the blood and brains from Harold Locke's head as an exploding .380 round from Cally's Walther PPK opened it up like a melon.

He wiped his eyes, lunged to his feet and spit the soft-boiled-egg-like brains out of his mouth. "Good work, girl, but we got company."

"I know," she said. "That's why I hurried. I was hoping he'd give some more away. Bunker?"

"Yeah." He paused for just a moment as she carefully safed the small pistol and started towards the command bunker. "How did you know?"

"Your right hand twitches when you've got losing cards. That and you lied about the beeper." She didn't mention her first reaction. Why she had started trying to open the puzzle box right after they came in. It was because the man had looked at her like Grandpa looked at a chicken he was about to harvest.

He nodded his head and smiled. "I don't think you learned that from your father, did you?"

"No," she said, thumbing towards the door out in obvious emphasis. "But Dad didn't teach me how to play cards. Mom did. Let's go."

◆ CHAPTER 54 ◆

Rabun County, GA, United States Of America, Sol III
0325 EDT October 11th, 2004 AD

The team leader's head came up at the crack of the pistol round and he shook it violently. There were two protectees though. One was a young female and the profile on the assassin did not make that a pretty picture. There was still a mission; the question would be how to proceed.

He waved for the point to stop and turned to the technical expert. That worthy was deciphering the readout from the Galactic-supplied life sensors. He made a motion for three humans, one terminated. One male, one female alive. Male and female were moving.

The team leader checked the location and gave the point hand signals to move to the opposite side of the house and do a covert entry. He waited impatiently for more intelligence.

Mike Senior finished strapping Cally into the Kevlar battle armor and threw his own on. Cally had pulled down her British 7.62 Bullpup and the sight of her with pistol and rifle made him think of other ways to spell her name. The drying blood flecked through her blonde hair was a sight to behold.

"You're a mess, Grandpa."

"You don't look so hot yourself," he snorted, fixing the last two straps in place and picking up his MP-5. The friction sling rode smoothly and he hopped up and down for a second to ensure there weren't any rattles. "And the living room is going to be a bitch to get cleaned up."

"Sorry about shooting him, then. Not."

✧　　✧　　✧

The point monk checked the window for entry. He popped up a microcam and scanned the bedroom beyond. It looked like a spare, bed made, no one around, no personal items, no mess. Next he checked the window for tell-tales. It had magnetic alarms but they were easily bypassed. There were motion sensors in the room, however. He bypassed the window alarms, jimmied it and made a slow entry into the room. As long as you moved very slowly, the sensors would not detect you. If they were set to detect motion that slow, they would false-alarm on every breath of air. He moved into the room, the camera on his shoulder faithfully repeating the picture back to the team leader.

"They're in the downstairs guest bedroom," said Papa O'Neal. The command bunker was connected to the kitchen by a short tunnel. From it he had a commanding, and camouflaged, view of the approaches. He also had readings from the sensors scattered throughout the property and house. The sensors were not connected to alarms, so they were set on the highest possible threshold. Detecting false alarms from reality was something of an art. However, the bedroom also contained a small sound mike and camera. Occasionally kinky but old habits die hard.

"Who is it?" asked Cally, sliding her Bullpup behind her back and checking the mine controls. She got the fun part; her job was detonating them on Papa O'Neal's command. Well, she might let Papa O'Neal try a few. If he was nice.

"Hmm, lemme see," answered Mike Senior. "Black body armor. Black ski masks. Black weapons. Black boots. Gee, Santa Claus?"

"Police?"

"No, they'd have it across their backs in great big letters," said Papa O'Neal, gesturing at the picture of the point moving stealthily down the hallway. "They're good, though. Shame we're gonna have to kill 'em."

The point froze at the entrance to the living room. The body slumped across the rawhide chair was not one of the protectees. It appeared to be the target. He began to relax out of his crouch.

"That's odd," said Papa O'Neal.

"What?" asked Cally, running a circuit check. The detonators were designed to take a low-voltage test current without actually exploding. Only two circuits were dead. Very good. And there was one claymore placed directly behind their visitors. As soon as Papa O'Neal gave the word, one special operations team was toast.

"He just relaxed. If he was backup for Harold he should be more tense, not less."

"What else could he be?"

"I don't know. But it's odd."

The team leader looked at the tech with a puzzled expression in his eyes. Then he shrugged, picked up his cell phone and consulted a scrap of paper.

A red light over the phone in the bunker began to blink. Papa O'Neal looked at it with a puzzled expression and picked it up.

"Michael O'Neal, Senior?" asked a faintly accented voice on the phone.

"Yes," said Papa O'Neal, warily.

"Are you and Cally O'Neal in good condition?"

"Yes."

"In general, if I might ask, where *are* you?"

Mike Senior chuckled evilly. "In a command bunker watching you and your point scratching your heads. Smile for the cameras!"

"Ah," said the commando, cautiously. "We were ordered to respond to protect you from one Harold Locke, an operative of . . . An operative who had been given a contract on you. You are in good health?"

"Yes."

"Oh. That is good. We will withdraw then."

"Okay," Papa O'Neal agreed warily. "You'll understand if we don't invite you to tea?"

There was a dry chuckle. "Of course. Question: Do you want us to dispose of the body or would you prefer to yourself?"

It was a good question. If there was an investigation the body would be a mountain of evidence pointing right at Cally. The fact that he was an assassin would not even be worth bringing up in a trial. There was no proof.

The question really was: Did he trust these people not only to dispose of the evidence but to do so as perfectly as possible? In the end the answer surprised him.

"Yeah. Thanks. Come to tea some other time. With a few less friends."

"God be with you, Mr. O'Neal."

On that odd farewell the group broke into activity. The point opened the front door of the house while three other black-clad troops slung their weapons and trotted forward. Two vans pulled up within seconds and, as the four in black on the inside bagged the body, another group in white exposure suits exited the second van. These individuals lugged in a variety of materials, mostly cleaning supplies and equipment, and began a thoroughgoing cleaning of the room.

Once practically every scrap of blood and brain was cleaned up, they closed the curtains to the room and doused the lights. Papa O'Neal could not determine precisely what went on, but he had a pretty good idea. Many modern investigation techniques involved materials that fluoresced or are visible only under ultraviolet light. Undoubtedly the team was cleaning up these otherwise invisible bits.

When the lights came back on it was to reveal the last of the group exiting a perfectly cleaned room. The only thing suspicious about it was that most living rooms do not look like a factory clean room. The body bag had already disappeared into the maw of the evidence van. Once both groups loaded up the two vans pulled out without, as far as Papa O'Neal could determine, a single word being exchanged. One of the white-suits had donned mufti and drove the rent-a-car. From the time the point man entered the living room, less than an hour had elapsed. The only face they saw was the white-suit and he was wearing dark sunglasses and a beard.

"Damn," whispered Cally. "Who were those masked men?"

"I dunno," answered Papa O'Neal with a broad smile. "But they sure knew what they were doing." Fellow professionals were *so* hard to find.

◆ CHAPTER 55 ◆

The Pentagon, VA, United States of America, Sol III
0424 EDT October 11th, 2004 AD

Jack Horner stared at the map-screen and wondered what in hell he was supposed to do. The roads out of the Arlington pocket were jammed with refugees. Turning the corps around had thrown the whole evacuation plan into a cocked hat and it had yet to recover. Although the interstates had been cleared of stalled vehicles, the side roads had become so gridlocked that virtually no one could get on the major arteries.

Most of the evacuees had panicked when the Tenth Corps had been destroyed. They did not understand that it would take the Posleen hours and hours to move around the Occoquan Reservoir and that Ninth Corps was in the way. Quantico—which had become the graveyard of the corps it once hosted—was a bare thirty minutes from Arlington. Faced with a nonmoving traffic jam, many had turned off their cars and started walking.

These vehicles now created a nearly impassable obstacle to movement. Many of those on foot had made it to the interstates where they were being picked up with buses. But many were wandering aimlessly northward on back roads, imagining that the Posleen were right behind them. These lost souls would eventually find their way to the Potomac bridges and safety. But many would be caught on the wrong side. Too many. The current guess was hundreds of thousands.

Normally, in exercises, he would be sending in flying armored columns about now. Their purpose would be to slow up and misdirect the Posleen while military police backed by light armor would be rounding up, and in some cases driving, the refugees.

439

Unfortunately that would have been the task of either the Tenth Corps, which was no more, or Ninth Corps, which was fading fast.

Part of Eighth Corps, the One Hundred Fifth Infantry Division, had arrived in northern D.C., but they were scattered hither and yon. It would take them a while—quite a while if recent history was anything to judge by—to get all the armored vehicles off the lowboys and the units assembled. And the idea of flying columns with those troops was a joke. Three months before he had sent an entire MP brigade from Fort Bragg to Fort Dix to put down a mutiny by the same unit. They were just as likely to run back to New Jersey as throw themselves between the Posleen and civilians.

And then there were the landings. Over fourteen B-Decs had exited hyperspace in the last twenty-four hours. Four had been totally destroyed by the remaining fighters and frigates. But that had been at the cost of three frigates.

The PDCs were still in their cleft fork. Designed to stop the landings, they were unable to perform that function, instead being held back to stop liftoffs on the part of the landers. Despite that, Europe had lost twelve of their total of twenty Planetary Defense Centers. China had lost eight, America four.

But the landings were occurring everywhere. There had even been one in *Phoenix*, for Christ's sake. With more Posleen coming in from God-knew-where, he could not totally strip any area of its local defenders. But he needed to get troops from somewhere.

He knew that the maps and graphs were not reality, but they were all he had to work with. The chart of Ninth Corps strength was dropping like a waterfall as more and more Posleen charged into the gap between Lake Jackson and the Occoquan. The icon of the Second of the Five-Fifty-Fifth was nearly to the staging point behind Lake Jackson, but even a flank attack would hardly stop the Posleen at this point. Hell, it might just point them to the way around. So far they hadn't tried that.

There was only one mobile unit left at Indiantown Gap, the closest base to Arlington that hadn't been emptied. Harrisburg had a brigade of the Twenty-Eighth Mech to defend the area. So. Time to dump out the tacklebox. And call a few people out of hiding.

The gentle rocking of the five-ton truck as it negotiated the stop-and-go traffic of the interstate was at first maddening and then lulling. But Michael O'Neal was heading to the sound of distant musketry as fast as he could.

Every time a unit stopped for a rest or the truck he was riding on broke down he hitched a ride with another unit. Usually the Fleet uniform alone would guarantee a ride. Once he had traded on his name. Once it had been necessary to get a higher chain of command involved. But it was slow going. He wasn't worried that the Posleen would go away; they were going to be around for weeks at least. But he was worried about the company being thrown into battle with Nightingale in command. It was his nightmare come true.

So he was nearly asleep when the AID chirped.

"Incoming call from General Horner."

Mike sighed and didn't bother to open his eyes. "Accept."

"Mike?"

"General."

There was a pause. "We tried."

"I know."

Another pause. "We've got a situation . . ."

"Refugees."

"Yeah," the general sighed.

Mike flicked his eyes open. At this point the AID could practically read his mind and a hologram of the battlezone suddenly appeared in the troop compartment. The soldiers who were awake stirred uneasily. Suddenly, without a word of command from the Fleet Strike officer, a hologram of the battle over the eastern United States was floating in the darkened interior of the truck. The lights from the next truck in the convoy partially washed it out. But then the AID polarized that area and created a shadow zone.

It was as advanced as radio to an aborigine and just as alien. As superficially sophisticated as the soldiers were, the technology was still stunning.

The AID sketched out probable movement rates for the scattered evacuees in Arlington. Then the time for the Posleen to reach them, assuming that the Ninth Corps lasted as long as anticipated. Then it sketched in the best possible movement time for the MI battalion. The three washes of color clearly missed proper intersection.

"We'll be too late," Mike said quietly. Everyone expected the cavalry, yellow flags flying, to come rushing in at the last moment. Well, this time the cavalry was just too far away and scattered to the winds. After all his careful preparations, it was coming down to too little, too late.

"I'm ordering the movement anyway. I've got a gut that the worst point is going to be around the Fourteenth Street bridge."

"Yeah," Mike nodded, "makes sense. It's almost the last one in the line going east, it's a chokepoint and everybody knows where it is." The bridge was overlooked by Arlington Cemetery and led directly to the Lincoln Memorial.

"Yeah. I'm expecting that once the refugees are in contact, that will be where the biggest backup is. And the Third Infantry is planning on holding the south side as long as they can."

"Let me guess."

"Yeah, the CO more or less said that the Posleen could have Arlington Heights over his dead body."

"And he meant it literally." The Old Guard was fanatical about Arlington. Much more so than about any passing President or minor monuments. However, the unit was primarily ceremonial and had virtually no heavy weapons. "Well, I suppose one more stupid symbolic action won't hurt any more than all the others."

"He's our President, Captain O'Neal," the general said quietly. The rebuke was clear but Mike could tell the general's heart wasn't in it.

"Your President," Mike said just as quietly. "We renounce our citizenship when we join the Fleet. Remember? Sir?"

The statement was greeted by silence.

"Have you told the battalion they're moving, yet?" Mike asked, changing the subject.

"No, I'm going to call Major Givens right after we get done."

"I need to be there, General." Mike flicked the hologram away with a wave of his hand and puffed out a breath of air. The fog from his breath was misty white in the light from the following truck.

"Well, I don't see how, Captain."

"Helicopter."

"Are you nuts! The Posleen'll destroy it before you're halfway to Indiantown Gap! Hell, look at the ambush of Second batt!"

"Fluke," snapped Mike, pulling up the map again. This time he took command of the display, tapping on vectors and assigning threat levels. "Shelly, cross-link this to General Horner."

At those words, heard throughout the compartment, the troops realized who the Fleet captain had been arguing with. Their heads ducked as if he were going to be hit by lightning at any moment. Mike paid them no mind.

"We're almost to Winchester. Have a bird meet me there. Blackhawk, Kiowa, I don't care. We'll stay low by slipping through the gap at Harper's Ferry. I'll intercept the unit somewhere on Interstate 83."

There was silence on the other end as Horner studied the schematic. The hologram had the plotted positions of Posleen and probable fields of fire. If an aircraft stayed below one hundred feet, all the lines ended well short of the route he had sketched in. "You're assuming two things that are not true. One: that the Posleen will not take off. If a lander lifts it throws this whole thing away. Two: That there are no more landers coming in. We've had three landings in the past hour."

"And if one is coming in, or lifts, the schematic changes. Shelly will keep it continually updated. That's what she's for. We land if we have to until the threat is past."

"I don't like this, Mike. I feel it is an unnecessary risk of a vital asset."

Mike swallowed a lump in his throat. He considered Horner an alternate father but he was never really sure what the general felt. That was about as good a compliment as any son could want. "Were you talking about me, or the helicopter?" he joked. "Never mind. I'm not vital, sir. But I do think that it would be a good idea if I was in on this operation."

Again there was a long silence on the line. "I'll get you the helicopter. I agree we probably don't have much time."

◆ CHAPTER 56 ◆

Brentsville, VA, United States of America, Sol III
0446 EDT October 11ᵗʰ, 2004 AD

"L-T," Keren hissed.

Lieutenant Leper lurched awake, AIW in hand. Keren grabbed the barrel and pointed it upward and away.

The lieutenant shook his head a few times, then peered blearily at Keren. "What time is it?" The inside of the Bradley was pitch black.

"Four thirty, L-T. The ACS just got in. They're assembling up behind us. The colonel, he'd like to talk to you. I told him you was sleepin' . . ."

Leper snorted. Knowing Keren he'd done more than just tell the colonel. "It's okay. I was just back when we lost Three Track."

"Yeah. Like you said, L-T, we're fine until we're on charge zero." Keren shuddered. Mortar platoons aren't *ever* supposed to see the enemy. Those that do rarely survive the experience.

The lieutenant lurched upward and automatically checked his AIW. He jacked a grenade into the chamber, checked that both the rifle and grenade launcher were on safe and scrambled across the scattered gear and sleeping bodies to the troop hatch.

It was black as pitch outside, the stars glittering in the clear sky. They added nothing, however, to the illumination. Leper could hear the chuckle of Kettle Run nearby. The run took a turn to the north as it approached the Occoquan reservoir, then looped back. The remnants of the company were assembled in the middle of the loop astride Brentsville Road.

He regretted not grabbing a pair of night-vision goggles. The power

444

had been sundered to Manassas and the surrounding area, so the backscatter that was so difficult to avoid, that contributed at least an erg of illumination on the darkest night in the eastern United States, was entirely absent. He could barely see his hand in front of his face.

He took a step forward and his Kevlar ran into a metal wall.

Leper could vaguely make out a looming presence. "Lieutenant Leper?" the apparition asked.

"Yes," said the lieutenant, rubbing his forehead where the Kevlar helmet had gouged him.

"Lieutenant Colonel Bishop, Fleet Strike."

"Yes, sir," said the tired lieutenant. Two hours sleep after all that they had been through was simply not enough.

"What's the situation, Lieutenant?"

Leper tried to digest the question and had a sudden urge to scream at the fresh, technologically sophisticated officer. *What's the situation? The situation is we're all fucked!* The word from Ninth Corps was that they couldn't hold out much longer. How anyone was going to retreat with the Posleen right at their heels was a good question. It was going to be ten times as bad as Occoquan. Then at least the Posleen had been scattered. In this case they would be massed and right up the corps's backside.

And his units were on the wrong side of the Ninth Corps. Since they were guarding the south flank, if the corps broke the Posleen would be swarming in *behind* them. And that was just a matter of time. There was a pretty strong rumor that MP units had been stationed behind the line with orders to shoot deserters.

None of it would matter for much longer. When the levee broke, none of it would matter a hill of beans.

"We're holding the south flank of the corps, sir." Actually they were holding the south flank of Lake Jackson. Lake Jackson itself was anchoring the south flank of the corps. "The area has been quiet. We had one God King come this way with one of their companies, but we took care of it without significant casualties."

There was less than a brigade in total holding the line. Most of them weren't even infantry. Clerks and cooks and the officers' band. Everything that was left of Tenth Corps less DivArty.

The casualties when the Posleen company hit had been less than a platoon's worth. On the other hand, this was all that was left of a corps. There was some sort of calculation there that he didn't want to think about. Would that platoon be the equivalent of a battalion to a corps? And if so, should they be considered the same as the loss of a battalion? "So far so good?" he finished.

"I understand that you were in the retreat from the interstate?" The question was asked without any emotional overtones, but Leper felt Keren bristling behind him.

"We were the rear guard. Sir," the lieutenant said in an absolute monotone.

"What do you estimate the Posleen forces as?"

"Sir?"

"How many of them are there, Lieutenant?" the colonel asked with iron patience.

The exhausted officer goggled at him for a moment. "Is this a trick question?"

"No." The blank of faceted plasteel was nearly invisible and even if it weren't there was no way to see the officer's expression. The question was nonsensical.

"Sir, there are more than the stars in the sky, more than the blades of grass, more than the trees in the forest. One good look is all it takes. They fill the world from horizon to horizon and every fucking one of them is trying to kill you!"

The armor was still and silent for a pause. "So, how did you survive?"

Leper blinked rapidly and thought about all the ones that didn't. "I don't know," he admitted. "I oughta be dead." He closed his eyes and shook his head.

"We lost—oh, Christ. Forget losing the company and the Old Man to the artillery. We lost 'em like a river loses water! Sometimes I'd have fifty, sixty troops. The next thing you know, we'd just stop for a second to . . . to get a breather, to . . . to reconsolidate, hell, to find out who the hell was hanging on the vehicles. And then *they'd* come. And . . . and the next thing you knew we were back on the road, running as fast as we could. And we'd have maybe two squads. And that'd happen over and over." His hand was over his eyes now and he shook his head continuously.

"I don't know how many went through my hands, Colonel. I don't know how many I lost along the road. I don't know how many we passed. Some of them just gave up. Some of them were injured. Some of them were just tired of running. I don't know their *names*!" The lieutenant drew himself up and tried to clear his eyes.

The colonel reached up and removed his helmet. The solid pyramid of plasteel came away with a sucking sound. A tap of a control and the suit began to glow a faint blue, just enough to give some vision.

"Have you been debriefed at all?" the senior officer asked in a gentle, surprised voice.

"No, sir," Keren answered for the lieutenant when the officer just shook his head. "When we rolled into Ninth Corps territory they got rid of us like we had the plague. They just told us to come over here and get our shit together. And don't walk on the grass."

The colonel nodded his head at the answer. "Well, Lieutenant, I think you did just fine." The tone was firm and believable. The colonel put his hand on the lieutenant's shoulder. "Son, that was hell. I know. I've been in hell too."

The lieutenant looked up at the officer and took a deep, shuddering breath.

"My company had a week-long firefight in Dak-To. We would lose a couple and then get a resupply then lose them as often as not. I never knew who the hell was in the holes. At the end of the whole thing the VC just melted back into the jungle. I had fifteen left in the company that started the battle, including me. I had worked my way through nearly two hundred troops in those weeks. I'd use them like pouring water in a well. I didn't recognize any of those names. Nobody else in the company did either."

"No records, sir," said the lieutenant, quietly.

"No. And that will probably haunt you. But there is still a job to do. Are you gonna do it?"

"Yes, sir."

"You got observation posts out?"

"Yes, sir. So far nothing except the one company."

"Patrols?"

"No. I've got one going out in a couple of hours. The Posleen have got to find this edge sooner or later. But we only got finished digging in a couple of hours ago. If I sent out a patrol right now, they'd go out a couple of hundred yards and rack out."

"All right," said the colonel. At least the lieutenant had a grasp on reality. "Just as well you don't have a patrol out there. We're gonna pass through your lines in about ten minutes. Then we're gonna stroll on down Bristow Road and try to take the Posleen like the monkey took the miller's wife. It might work and it might not. But there's a chance that we're gonna be coming back about as fast as we went out. You gonna be here?"

"Yes, sir."

"Good. Glad to hear it. How 'bout you, Keren?"

"Maybe," said the private. "Depends on who gets here first. If it's the Posleen, you better be ready to walk back to the mountains."

"Fair enough," the colonel said and put his helmet back on. The blue glow of the armor faded after a moment as he rolled his shoulders. " 'Bout time to go, don't you think?"

✧   ✧   ✧

Ardan'aath snarled as yet another road to the north was bypassed. "Can we not turn yet?" he raged. He pointed to the north with his plasma cannon, where the thunder of artillery and rockets could be clearly heard. Beams of light and orange tracers could be seen ascending into the sky. "*There!* There is where the battle is!" He fired a spiteful plasma burst towards the distant battleline.

"Soon," soothed Kenallai. He glanced at his eson'antai. "Soon?"

"Soon," agreed the young Kessentai, fluffing his crest in thanks. "Up ahead is the road. Arnata'dra has already turned up it."

"Finally!" snarled the older Kessentai. "The battle will be over before we can make this stupid turn!"

"Ardan'aath," said Kenallai, "look you at the results of charging these thresh head on! There are more oolt'ondai dead at the feet of these thresh than Po'os in the Swarm!"

Ardan'aath fluffed his crest in anger but had to agree. The thrice-damned harvest of this world was damnably capable at battle. He had finally reviewed the information from Aradan 5, when no one was watching. The metal-clad thresh would be formidable foes. He had begun to consider how to fight them and had a few ideas. He hoped he would not be forced to test them.

It was more than ten minutes. The Fleet Strike battalion had only gotten their suits a month before. While the First of the Five-Fifty-Fifth averaged over a thousand hours of suit time, most of Second Battalion had less than three hundred hours. It took time for the officers to decipher the icons of their forces, to set up the formation, to finalize briefings and recharge the suits before going in harm's way. They had been doing all of those things while the colonel talked to the local commander. But it still took more than ten minutes.

In the end, it took more time than they had.

As the first scouts approached the Tenth Corps line, their sensors started to scream.

"Colonel," said the S-3, traveling between the two lead companies and the reserve.

"See it," barked Bishop. He had two "up" companies in movement with the third waiting to see if they ran into anything. If he had thought there were bad guys out there it would be the other way around. "Stop Bravo and Charlie. Have Charlie dig in with the Mech guys. Tell Bravo to cover Charlie until they're dug in. Send Alpha to the right to probe for a flank."

It was a normal out-of-the-book reaction of a combat veteran officer. But it was a tactic for fighting humans, not Posleen.

✧   ✧   ✧

The scout's eyes were flared wide to drink in every bit of luminance. The battle to the north occasionally caused painful flares in
his vision, but he paid it no mind. He paid mind to few things, he
was focused on the link between himself and his god and the question
of where the thresh were. He hungered for them, for the approval
of his god in the gathering and the harvest. Well down the hierarchy was self-preservation or pain.

He paused, dust-flaps lifting off his nostrils to scent the air. Behind
him his pack-brothers paused as well, scenting. The smell was an acrid
mixture of chemicals and organic respirations. He turned to look
towards his god.

Arnata'dra studied his readouts for a moment and then cross-linked
them to Kenallurial.

The Kessentai studied them for a moment and winced. "My
edas'antai, we have a problem."

Kenallai studied the readout for a moment and flared his crest.
"Indeed."

"We could attempt to bypass them . . ."

"Gutless babe . . ."

"Stop!" Kenallai studied the readout again. The signatures were
clearly the metal-clad thresh and already they were extending their
line. The next thing would be to drive forward on his oolt'ondai. In
addition they were supported by regular troops lightly dug in. They
appeared to be the warriors, thank the spirits of the land, rather than
those bastard military technicians. But there would still be explosives
and the ballistic weapons.

"No. There is a time to maneuver and a time to strike. We must
drive into the rear of the thresh. Drive hard. If we maneuver around
these thresh, the main body will attempt a retreat. We will drive
through these and destroy the resistance in the pocket. The Net will
recognize the worth and grant us extensions to our fiefs."

"Yes, my edas'antai."

"Ardan'aath."

"My oolt'ondar?"

"Destroy them."

Ardan'aath *had* studied the reports from Barwhon and Diess. These
threshkreen were tricky and capable, more of a challenge in their way
than the Po'oslenar in *orna'adar*. But there were only three things
present to fear. The ballistic weapons, the fact that they dug like *abat,*
and the metal-clad thresh.

The only way to deal with the ballistic weapons was to close with the thresh. Once his oolt'ondar was among the harvest, the ballistic weapons were forced to cease fire. And, if he was among them, they could be dug out like the abat that they were. The metal-clad thresh remained the only problem. However, they too were vulnerable to the Posleen blades and, as usual, they were few. He could overwhelm them with numbers, especially if he extended his line and concentrated on them.

Everything called for a wide front charge. It could not have been more perfect.

"Telaradan! Forward! Assarnath! To the left. We shall eat their get! Forward! Spread out. And kill the metal thresh first! *Tel'enaa, fuscirto uut!*"

"Dig in!" The Charlie Company first sergeant was striding down the line of suits, pushing them into position or juggling firepower. And giving a few hasty lessons.

"*No!* God dammit!" He yanked a cratering charge off the belt of the trooper who was shoveling dirt with his armored gauntlets. The suits could move a massive amount of dirt in a surprising hurry, but the digging charges were still faster. "Use your foxhole charges!" the NCO snarled over the company push, snatching another off a belt and slapping it into the gauntlet of a confused trooper.

"Here they come!" one of the outpost troops shouted and jumped out of his shallow hole to try to make the security of the lines. He almost made it to safety before his chest erupted in red. In the darkness a parachute flare floated upward with a hiss. There was a pop overhead and the field in front of the infantry company was lit like day. It was covered in centaurs.

The first to fire was the Third platoon machine-gun post. The orange tracers drifting lazily through the still night air towards the unexpected company seemed to trigger a firestorm.

"Three gun! Traverse flares. Preset five!" shouted Keren.

The gun crew startled awake and stumbled to the gun. When the remnants of the Corps were reassembled there were enough gun tracks to scatter them around. As a reasonably intact unit, Alpha Mortars had received two orphan tracks to replace their maintenance losses. They had also been offered an FDC track. Keren had demurred. The Suburban was much more comfortable.

At Keren's suggestion the platoon had left their mortars set up to

support the company. Three gun's mission was to fire flares and all
that they had to do was begin dropping rounds.

The assistant gunner, the person who actually fires the mortar, had
actually slept curled around the cold metal of the weapon. At the
cry from FDC she simply rolled upward with a round in her hand.
Before she was fully awake she had the round in the tube and firing. It was a regular HE round instead of a flare, and the setting of
the gun sent it flying almost a mile downrange, behind the charging Posleen. But it was the thought that counted.

The next round was a flare.

Lieutenant Leper ran forward towards the front-line CP. He was
not only in charge of the mortars, but of the company as well. That
being the case he had completely scrambled normal procedures. The
mortars were well forward with his CP closer to them than the line.
He had planned on straightening things out in the morning, but the
Posleen hadn't given him the time.

As he reached the large hole scraped out of the Virginia loam, he
got his first clear view of the enemy and despaired. The company
was in no shape to face that mass; the Posleen must outnumber them
a hundred to one. It looked like a full Posleen brigade was charging them at a gallop.

He dove into the hole and reached for the radio.

If there was one thing that Keren had learned along the way, it was
that there was no such thing as too much information. Which was why
he had one radio set to the company frequency, another on the fire
control frequency and two "off the books" radios that he had picked
up along the way set to battalion and brigade. So he was the first person
in the company to hear the lieutenant condemn them to death.

"*Papa One Five, this is November One Five, over.*"

The distant crack of railguns and the hammer of machine guns
was echoed in the transmission.

"*November One Five, this is Papa One Five, over.*"

"*Papa One Five, we are in contact with approximately a regiment
of Posleen. I do not estimate that we will be able to hold them off, over.*"

"*Roger, understood. ACS support is on the way. Over.*"

"*Papa, they are already here. I still don't estimate we'll hold. The
Posleen look fresh and they are charging the line even as we're talking. The ACS is spread out and looks pretty confused. I don't intend
to do the bug out boogie, but I don't see us stoppin' these guys, either.
Tell corps to get ready to run. Over.*"

"*November One Five. All of corps's reserves are on the line. You are
ordered to hold. Over.*"

"You're dreamin', Papa. November out."

"Tango Three Six, this is November One Five, over."

There was a pause. The fire control center for the defense was busy; they were still scrambling to replace the central fire net.

"Calling unit say again callsign, over."

"Tango three six, this is November One Five. Final protective fire call, designation One-One-Bravo. Posleen in close-contact. Final protective fire. Over."

"November, be advised we are tapped out for artillery at this time. We are in final protective mode for the entire Ninth Corps, over."

"Well, if we get overrun you're gonna have visitors pretty damn quick. So make up your mind. Out."

"All guns!" yelled Keren, out the back of the Suburban. "Final Protective Fire! Continuous fire!"

Specialist Nick Warren crouched in his foxhole and tried to count kills. The foxhole had been built for interlocking fire, with a mound of earth in front of it and the firing slot angled out to the right at a forty-five degree angle. The idea was to fire at everything from the side and not be shot at by the horses you were shooting at. Which was fine except that the whole wall was being hammered by railgun and shotgun rounds. Dirt drifted around him in streams as the pounding fire tore apart the sandbags on the outer layer, then began to destroy the packed dirt of the fill.

His zone of fire was packed with horses. There were so many that he had stopped bothering to aim. If he missed one the bullet was sure to hit the one behind. He would run but he had done that once and knew what it brought. The horses could run you down faster than you could escape. There was nothing to do but kill them and keep killing them and hope it was enough. He had to keep them off the other holes and hope that there were enough guys left to keep the horses off his. He wished he'd saved some grenades, they'd be a treat. But he was out of gun grenades and the hand kind both.

His bolt flew back on an empty chamber and the plastic magazine dropped out. He was patting his ammo pouches trying to find another magazine when he heard a sound like a machete hitting a watermelon and looked over his shoulder.

The other soldier in the foxhole was down, half her face torn away by the railgun round that had finally punched through the wall of sandbags. He couldn't even remember her name, some chick from headquarters company. He had a moment of shame at his first thought, which was joy that he could see she had two magazines left. But he didn't have much time to dwell on the shame. There was a sudden shower of dirt, heavier than the earlier ones. He never even saw the blade that clove into the back of his head, slicing through the Kevlar helmet, bone and brain like butter.

There just wasn't enough concentrated firepower. Fighting Posleen had often been described as trying to stop an avalanche with a fire hose. It only works if you have enough fire hoses.

The Posleen were on a narrow front, crossing an open beaten zone. They were, in fact, a perfect target for a prepared veteran unit with backup or even an intact, dug in, green ACS unit. But without massive artillery fire, without an intact ACS battalion, without more troops and tangle-foot and barbwire and mines, Ardan'aath drove his forces forward in a wild charge that overwhelmed the defenders in bare minutes.

Bravo Company of the ACS was the first to fall, left exposed on the flank of the mechanized company. Their lines of silver lightning stretched out to the charging Posleen and tore them apart like paper. The same carnage would have shocked a human force into immobility. But there were over twelve thousand Posleen charging down the narrow front and dozens of God Kings. And Posleen just don't stop.

The Posleen focused on this danger first, striking the company with direct-fire. The armor was usually proof against anything but a plasma cannon or an HVM. But as the mass of fire pounded them, occasional three-millimeter rounds would find a weakness. And there were over six hundred HVM launchers and nine hundred heavy railguns in the force. Between those and the God Kings the exposed ACS company was eliminated without killing more than five or six hundred of the enemy.

The dug-in forces fared better, but not so much that it mattered. The first to be silenced was the partially dug-in Charlie Company as their grav-guns and Grim Reapers were picked out for special attention by the heavy weapons of the Posleen brigade. Charlie Company put up a hard fight but the whistling centaurs drove forward against the wall of fire, piling up windrows of their dead in an effort to close with the armored humans. It finally came down to hand-to-hand as the Posleen reached the foxholes of the unit and overwhelmed it in a charge with monomolecular blades.

In the meantime the lighter railguns and shotguns of the Posleen normals concentrated on the foxholes of the mechanized unit, in most cases hammering them so hard they were unable to respond. Anyone who jumped out of a hole and started to run was cut apart by massed fire. When the Posleen reached the firing line it was all over. The forlorn troopers were butchered in place like so many sheep. A few made it away in the confusion, but for all practical purpose the unit had ceased to exist.

"We cannot leave those metal thresh wandering around," said Kenallurial, gesturing at the display. Inside he was bitter with envy. He knew his worth, but a successful *te'naal* charge like that one would be spoken of for a thousand years. That it was his trickery and thought that brought them here would be forgotten.

"Ardan'aath will dispose of them in good time," said Kenallai calmly. "Look at the thresh run," he continued, gesturing at the schematic. The remnants of the Tenth Corps were pulling up stakes and backpedaling towards Manassas as fast as they could. "Like *abat* from a corpse."

"We should press them," said Kenallai. "We must not let them stop and build defenses before the great prize to the north."

"We will, my eson'antai, we will," the oolt'ondar said, fluffing his crest. "Don't be so envious."

Kenallai turned away at that insight, tapping the display to bring it wider. This was a fine land, rich and with much booty to be won. There would be fine fiefs to be had. If only the Net recognized his contributions.

In the distance there was an end to the screaming and a fading sound of diesel engines.

◆ CHAPTER 57 ◆

Cally rubbed the orange solvent into the Cordura nylon, trying to get the last stains out. "I wish those white-suits had stayed around long enough to clean this stuff."

Papa O'Neal chuckled, working a bit of bone out of a crevice. They had both taken fast showers to get the bits of the late Harold Locke off, but the armor had picked up quite a bit of evidence. Getting it cleaned up was a priority.

"Yeah, well, I guess we're just going to have to use a little elbow grease." He took a puff off his pipe and scrubbed at another spot of blood.

"Who do you think they were, really?" she asked in a serious tone.

He stopped looking for spots on the black cloth for a moment and leaned back. It was a good question. "Honey, I don't rightly know. They were obviously here to save our bacon. Now, I've got a lot of friends in the business, but nobody that could call up a team like that. And they knew Harold was coming to call. Now, they might have figured on being able to cover things up so whoever sent him didn't figure out what happened. That's more or less what happened. If the question gets bandied around we can take quiet credit for it."

"But that still begs the question of who sent 'em."

She nodded her head and went back to working, but he could tell from the expression on her face she was thinking about something. "Penny for your thoughts," he said.

"I think it was somebody that thought they owed Daddy a favor."

He started to open his mouth to dismiss the suggestion and

stopped. Mike Junior had told him about the present of the combat suit. At half a billion credits, one of the suits was, to say the least, no small gift. Somebody who thought they owed him a half-billion-credit suit might think they owed him a quick response from a special actions team. Instead of dismissing the thought he nodded his head in agreement. "Okay, I can buy that."

She nodded in turn and picked up the toothbrush as a sonic boom hit.

Both of them looked upwards and cursed simultaneously.

"Oh, fuck!" said Mike Senior.

"*Batshit!*" echoed Cally.

Michael O'Neal, Sr., looked at the wet, orange-scented armor in his hands and shook his damp head. "What the hell else is going to go wrong today?" he asked with a slightly hysterical laugh.

The team leader pressed the fingers of his hand into his forehead, as if to press in an idea. There were no safe houses nearby where the team could to go to ground. Even if the lander did not land on them, the team would surely be stopped, the vehicles might be commandeered by the local response teams. And then the shit would well and truly hit the fan. Their hastily prepared covers would not survive investigation.

There was only one possible path to obscurity.

"Turn around," he snarled to the driver. The monk obeyed without a word, swerving right and spinning the over-powered van into a fishtail. "Go to the O'Neal house." He pulled out his cell phone for the second time in an hour.

Papa O'Neal had the local weather radio turned up loud as he and Cally battened down the hatches. There was a protocol for a landing, one that they had not been able to perform for their unexpected visitors. Shutters were closed across the windows, even the ones that had cracked at the sonic boom. The horses were brought into the barn. The cows could fend for themselves. Circuits were rechecked, ammunition was laid out, spare weapons were set up to hand.

The phone ringing was almost drowned out by the radio, the automated voice now chanting a mantra of landing warnings. But Cally heard it and ran to pick it up.

"Hello?" she said.

"Miss Cally O'Neal?" asked a faintly accented voice.

"Yes."

"May I speak to Mr. Michael O'Neal, Senior?"

"May I ask who's calling?"

"Recent visitors," said the voice with a note of faint humor.

"Oh. Hang on." She ran outside and clamped the cordless phone against her side. "*Granpa!*" she shouted.

He looked up, startled, from where he was fixing one of the defective firing circuits.

She waved the phone overhead vigorously. "He'll be here in a second," she said to the "recent visitor."

There was a pause as they waited for the senior O'Neal to trot up the hill. Cally could hear a background of a growling engine. Their visitors appeared to be in a hurry.

"Might I ask a question?" asked the accented voice in the interim.

"Sure."

"How to say it? The other visitor. He appeared to be . . ."

"Me."

"Ah. That would explain it." The voice sounded somehow satisfied with the answer.

"Here's Grandpa. Bye."

She covered the mouthpiece again and smiled. "Our visitors seem to be coming back to tea."

"Oh, shit," said O'Neal, Sr., shaking his head. "Be careful what you ask for."

"Hello?"

"Mr. O'Neal?"

"Speaking."

"This is one of your recent visitors. We find ourselves somewhat at a disadvantage . . ."

"Come ahead. Put the vehicles in the garage. I'll move the truck out so there's room. And hurry. If our friends get here before you I'm activating the minefield and you're on your own."

"Of course. We're nearly there."

In the distance there was a thump of artillery and a rattle of machine-gun fire. The Posleen lander had managed to land squarely between the Fifty-Third Infantry, defending Rabun Gap, and the main positions of the supporting Tennessee Volunteers. And only two miles from the entrance to the O'Neal valley. In all likelihood they would bypass the small entrance to the valley. The turn was deliberately obscure.

On the other hand, the way the day had been going . . .

Papa O'Neal rotated a shoulder to get the armor seated better. Either it had picked up ten pounds of water in the cleaning, or he was getting too old for this shit. He smiled at the black-masked commando coming up the walkway and held out his hand. "Mike O'Neal. And you are? I didn't quite catch the name before."

"Call me Raphael," said the team leader. He took the proffered hand as his team hurried up behind him. The "white-suits" were following them. Although the black-suited commandos were armed, the white-suits were unarmed and without armor.

"You want to outfit them?" asked Papa O'Neal, gesturing with his chin at the white-suits.

"It would be fairly pointless," said "Raphael." "I doubt they could hit the side of a mountain. But if you have some little hidey-hole it would be perfect."

"Well, can't say as I'm sorry you came back," admitted Papa O'Neal. "We can do with the extra firepower if the Posleen come up here." He gestured towards the house and started walking.

"I take comfort in the fact that we are not the only ones assailed by these visitors," said the visitor dryly. "Surely we are not forsaken by God if they also land upon the Muslim."

Lieutenant Mashood Farmazan sighed as he gazed down at the enemy host through the ancient Zeiss binoculars. The Posleen group was a remnant of the mass that had descended upon Turkmenistan. The force had slashed through the impoverished country, spreading out from their landing around devastated Chardzhou and destroying every unit thrown against them. The force that was marching towards the Iranian border was still tens of thousands strong and had cut a bloody swath through Bagram-Ali and Mary following the Old Silk Road. Fellow forces had leveled ancient Buchara and now pressed storied Tashkent. This force was presumably headed for Teheran and the riches it hoarded.

He would like to say that this was as far as they were going. The terrain at this pass through the Koppeh Dagh was very favorable for stopping their advance. However, he was the commander and sole officer of the single understrength battalion that now stood between the Posleen and the Fars plateau.

The unit was part of the First Armored Division, the Immortals. The division traced its roots to the fabled days of the Medes and Cyrus. It had, however, fallen upon hard times since the days of the Shah. The current regime seemed to question the integrity of a unit that traced its genesis to Zoroaster.

But the predecessors of the division had blooded their teeth repeatedly on barbarian invaders in these very mountains. Smart barbarians took the long way around through Pulichatum and up the flank of the Dasht-e-Kavir to capture Mashad. Or to the north to the passes along the Caspian. Only very stupid barbarians came through the little village of Bajgiran. Up through the serpentine Bajgiran Pass. Through the easily defended pass.

Since this was a well-known fact, the majority of the division, along with two other regular infantry divisions, was assembled outside Mashad. Reserve divisions and the Islamic Guard were assembling around Gorgan. Mazandaran might be lost but the enemy would be stopped well short of Quramshar.

The only unit available to defend the inconsequential Bajgiran pass was a "battalion" of clap-trap M-60s from the days of the Shah. The total number of working tanks was less than a company and those were held together with baling wire. And a single unprepossessing, politically unconnected, overly intellectual officer to command what was a battalion in name only. Such were the defenders of Bajgiran.

The village nestled in the high mountain valley behind him. A typical village of the uplands, the green winter rye was just starting to sprout on the fields and a stream chuckled between the fields and a large stand of poplars. The village itself was a huddle of ancient mud and brick houses nestled at the base of the soaring gray mountains, with a few more modern structures scattered among them. Even these dated back to the heydays of the '70s. Nothing much ever changed in the upland villages.

Roads were paved or cobbled, then faded back into dirt tracks. Empires waxed and waned, power structures rose and fell in distant Teheran or Isfahan or Tashkent, whichever owned them at the time. But the muezzin called the faithful to prayer five times a day, regardless. And the goats ate the sparse grasses of the mountains, regardless. And the snows of winter came, regardless. And the occasional invader came through, regardless. Then the fields would be uprooted by battle until a new tax collector was appointed. And life, for most, would go on.

Lieutenant Farmazan had had the most difficult time persuading the local mullah that such was not the case with this invader. He had shown the old man pictures from distant stars. They had been dismissed as fairy tales. He had shown him the edicts of the revolutionary counsel, requiring evacuation in the face of the oncoming horde. They had been dismissed with a long exposition on the Koran and the inconsequence of mortal rulers. He had shown him videos from distant America where battles ranged on land, air and sea. A well-known place of perfidy was the response. Such could only be expected in such a Gomorrah. Finally, nearly tearing his hair out, the lieutenant had invoked the demon Tamerlane.

At this dread name the stern old mullah had blanched. The Mongol invader had reduced the fabled Aryan empire of old to a shadow of its former self, killing every single lord, leader, official or member of the intelligentsia. The only Persians that were left after Tamerlane swept through the country were the peasants. And most of them had been killed or enslaved.

After hearing further descriptions and having the similarities pointed out, the mullah relented. With histrionic wailing and gnashing of teeth he had begun chivvying the poor farmers and artisans of the remote town out of their houses and down the long road towards distant Mashad. The last forlorn figure was still visible at the final turn of the plateau as the terrible host on the plains hove into view.

The lieutenant had been able to scratch up a few artillery pieces and some rounds to go with them. The artillery was laughable, mostly ancient 105mm cannons. The guns were dated at the time of the last Pahlavi. They harked back to lend-lease from the United States during World War II. Along with them were some dilapidated British five-pounders. The sturdy cannon were the mainstay of British artillery for decades but were now so antiquated that most countries considered them museum pieces. None of the weapons would be allowed in any real army. The tubes were practically worn to bare metal and the trunnions could crack at any moment.

With this scratch force of half-trained conscripts, antiquated weapons, limited ammunition and short rations he was supposed to stop an alien army that had cut through half a dozen Turkmen brigades. He hoped that they might turn to the north where the remnant of the Turkmen army was digging in to defend Ashkabad. They might, but somehow he doubted it. His luck just didn't seem to be falling that way.

He supposed it could be worse, although how he was unsure. As he thought that, fine flakes of snow began to fall on the arid, gray, rock-strewn mountains. He sighed. Was there anyone in the world more accursed than he?

Pham Mi shook his head and took the rifle out of the young recruit's hand. He quickly disassembled the venerable AK-47 and shook his head. The militia recruit hung his head in shame as the veteran pointed to the rust on the bolt.

"Stupid child," snapped the scarred Pham. He hit the young man on the head with the extracted bolt. "You may wish to die, but your comrades wish to live. Clean this, then join the women digging the positions."

It had been years since Pham had fired a shot in anger. Many,

many years. He had not been in the Democratic Army during either the defense against China or the incursion into Cambodia. However, as the leader of the People's Militia for his village it was his responsibility to slow the advancing enemy as much as possible. The leadership did not expect him to stop them. However, the actions of all the aroused People's Militias would definitely hamper the enemy. They had hamstrung the enemies of the People again and again. This was their thousand-year history. And this day would be no different.

A hundred women from the village were working on the slit trenches and bunkers while the men of the militia worked on their weapons and equipment. He had to snort at that. Most of the weapons were antiques, relics of the great struggle against the French and the Yankees. The equipment, however—the boots, backpacks, ammunition harnesses and uniforms—were all American.

The equipment was used, assuredly, and much of the material in the crates and crates the militia received was damaged beyond repair. There was much, however, that was not. Only the Americans would be so spendthrift as to throw away perfectly good equipment. And only the Americans would be so strange as to give it to a former enemy for free.

In addition, there were several crates of excellent American mines. The weapons were familiar as an old friend; he had cut his teeth in the militia removing such from the American lines for later reuse. This was actually the first time he had seen them packaged for shipping and he marveled at the interlaced packaging. The Americans apparently expected them to be shipped in a hurricane.

With the weapons, ammunition, equipment and, especially, claymores and "Bouncing Bettys" the People's Militia would seriously sting the enemy. The force from the small-scale landing would undoubtedly make it past the large-scale ambush. And, despite the rhetoric of the local commissar, they would take Dak Tho. But the militia would continue to sting them. And sting. Until they were no more. It was the least they could do. America had its own problems; they would not be coming to help. Humorous as that would be. To wish for a battalion of the "puking chicken" soldiers to drop from the sky. Truly humorous.

"Oh, this is truly humorous!" snapped Sharon O'Neal.

"What've you got, mum?" asked Michaels over the radio.

Sharon shook her head inside the bubble helmet of the battle suit and snarled, "The clamps on Number Four launcher are bent!"

The fast frigates had never been designed for war. But human ingenuity had managed to work around some of the problems. The answer in this case was external Missile/Launch Pod Assembly systems for antimatter armed and driven missiles; the frigates could fit six of the big box launchers, each of which stored four missiles. However, because the frigates also lacked storage space, there was only room for two extra M/LPAs, and attaching them meant that a team had to go out of the ship, presumably in the midst of a battle.

Despite careful husbanding of the weapons, Captain Weston had finally used up all twenty-four missiles. Although there were still occasional emergences, she had determined that it was worth the risk to try attaching the spare stores. Which was why Sharon, two human techs and an Indowy were EVA with a box launcher. And a warped clamp.

Michaels studied the picture of the clamp in the monitor. "We've got a spare that will work, mum."

"No," snapped Commander O'Neal. "We'll shift to Number Five."

"We lost the feed to Five, mum," Michaels reminded her.

Sharon shook her head and snarled at the tiredness that was clouding her thinking. Even with the near miraculous Provigil, combat fatigue crept up on you. She had to remind herself from time to time that she wasn't functioning at top form, even if she thought she was.

"We reloaded Three," she said. "Two and Six are gone." The blast from the Posleen nuke had been *too* close. It was probably what had done the damage to the current launcher. If it had exploded forward of the ship, where the deflector screen still was not fixed, instead of under it, the entire crew would already be talking to the angels.

"And we're getting intermittent faults from Three, mum," Michaels finished. "I think it's repair the bloody thing or go with one launcher."

Sharon nodded. She knew her preference but it was really a decision for the captain. As long as they were EVA, the team was sitting ducks. "Captain Weston?" she asked, knowing the AID would switch channels.

"I was listening," answered Weston, her voice raspy from hours of giving commands. Sharon winced at the fatigue in the officer's voice. They all were on a thin string. "We need all the launchers, Commander. Sorry."

"That's fine, ma'am," answered Sharon. "That was my call as well. Bosun?"

"I'll break the clamps out of stores, mum."

"We'll get started on getting these removed." She shook her head again. Working EVA was hard under any condition; working EVA with the specter of suddenly being a target was for the birds.

She turned to the Indowy technician, to ask his help in removing the device, but stopped as her eyes widened.

It was a sight she never expected to see with her naked eyes, and one she expected she would never see again, as the Posleen Battle Dodecahedron translated out of hyperspace. The tear in reality caused localized energy buildups that caused distortion of the stars behind it, so the ship seemed to almost appear out of "cloak," with a ripple like water. The surface of the ship sparkled for a moment more with static electricity discharges and then it was *there*, fully emerged and seemingly close enough to touch.

"*Emergence*," yelled the sensor tech, startled out of a fatigued half doze. "Angle two-nine-four, mark five!" His eyes bulged at the distance reading. "*Four thousand meters!*"

"Lock-on," called Tactical, the weapons tracking lidar and sub-space detectors locking onto the gigantic signal.

"Fire," snapped Captain Weston, automatically. Then her eyes flew wide open. "*Belay that order!*"

But it was an eternity too late. The weapons tech had been on duty for eighteen straight hours and fire orders were a reaction that bypassed the brain. His thumb had already flipped up the safety cover and depressed the switch.

A pyrotechnic gas generator fired as the clamps holding the missile flew open. The gas pushed the eighteen-foot weapon far enough away from the ship that it was safe for it to kick in its inertial thrusters and antimatter conversion rocket.

Safe for the ship. But not safe for the weapon installation team. Or the pod of antimatter missiles they were installing.

◆ CHAPTER 58 ◆

The White House, Washington, DC, United States of America, Sol III
0526 EDT October 11th, 2004 AD

"Mr. President, it's time to leave," said the chief of the Secret Service Detail.

Thomas Edwards stared at the view-screen on the wall of the Situation Room. The occasional flickers of red across Fairfax County were getting closer and closer to the Fairfax Parkway. A solid bar represented the advancing Posleen chasing the remnants of Ninth and Tenth Corps up U.S. 28. He assumed that once they reached U.S. 29 and I-66 they would turn east towards D.C. and the nearest bridges. Unless the scattered forces could outrun the Posleen to the bridges, none of them would survive.

He had watched Monsoon Thunder. He knew all about retreats under fire. And ignominious defeat. He had been sure that those well-supplied and prepared corps could face the Posleen and live. All of his advisors had been sure. And he and they had been wrong. Completely and totally wrong. And it had led to the worst military disaster in American history.

And that was not the worst of it.

The view-screen also showed that the roads were packed with refugees. Most of them were in Alexandria or almost across the Potomac, but the distance between them and the enemy was reducing on a minute-by-minute basis. Soon the first reports of refugee columns overrun by the Posleen would come in. And he could do nothing about it.

"I'm sorry," he whispered to himself.

"Shit happens, Mr. President," said an unexpected voice.

The President looked at the doorway. The Secret Service chief was accompanied by Marine Captain Hadcraft, commander of the Guard Force. The hulking combat armor seemed totally out of place in the White House.

"Shit like this doesn't happen," snapped the President. "Not here. Not to us."

"What? You thought because this was *Earth* it would be different?" asked the captain with a faint note of scorn. "Well, welcome to *our* world, sir."

The President turned his chair to look fully at the Marine, who was being glared at by the Detail chief. Since the Marines were really loaners from the Fleet, there was a certain amount of friction between them and the Secret Service, friction that contradicted tradition.

The Marines had protected the American President since the days of John Adams. They had a longer and deeper tradition of it than even the Secret Service. But the Service had always treated them as the hired help. It was the Marines who held the perimeters while the Service took the close-in Protection detail.

With the splitting of the Marines to the Fleet, the Detail had assumed that they would take over full responsibility for Presidential protection. Instead, personnel were rotated out of Fleet and detailed to the Presidential Protection Unit. And that created two rifts between the Detail and the Marines. The first had to do with cost and the second with divided loyalties.

American ACS personnel who had distinguished themselves in combat on Barwhon and Diess and had good records could apply for placement to the PPU. The cycle was two years and it was, blessedly, out of combat.

On acceptance, the troopers would be sent, along with their suits, back to Earth. After a brief "refresher" course at Parris Island, they were sworn in as United States Marines, outfitted with new Marine Dress Blues and sent to D.C.

Then they could chase the girls, or boys as the case might be, turn their noses up at the garritroopers of the Old Guard and generally start to decompress.

However, they were still Fleet personnel. The suits and personnel were actually on loan from the Fleet. And the Federation did not cut the United States any slack on the cost. The reason that the American President, of all the chief officers in the world, was the only one that had a full company of guardian ACS was that they were horrendously expensive. The suits cost nearly a half billion credits apiece and were amortized by the Darhel over twenty years. Add to that the inflated Fleet Strike salary levels and the monthly cost for the company was nearly as much as a division of regular troops.

Then there was the problem of divided loyalty. The Fleet did not in fact require a person to renounce their citizenship, but had a strong sentiment against nationalism. And Fleet oaths were overriding. Under the laws of the Federation, the Marines were still under Fleet orders and answered only to the Fleet, just like any other ACS unit.

The Marines knew better. Some of them had applied to get away from Barwhon, where the hell of battle in the swamp ate away at the soul day by day. But most were there because they were, at heart, Americans and proud to defend the country's chief executive. But the incredible cost of the unit and its ambiguous loyalty was a cancer that ate at the Detail.

The President thought about all of that as he contemplated the Marine captain. The captain was the holder of the Silver Star and the Fleet Cross. The Star was an award retained by the Fleet in deference to the heavy American influence. The Cross was the equivalent of the Distinguished Service Cross.

No one had been so openly scornful of him in months. It just didn't happen to a President. On the other hand, this was a Marine who had "seen the elephant". He was entitled.

"Yeah," husked the President. His smooth, well-trained voice was gone after hours of talking. He had been awake for nearly thirty-six hours and felt like a week-dead corpse. "Yeah," he repeated, clearing his throat. "I did. Everybody told me that the terrain and the situation was right. It was just a matter of trying."

The suits, in deference to their position, displayed the seal of the President when in noncombat mode. But with the faceted helmet on, a seal revealed no emotion. The only hint was in the tone. "As I said, welcome to our world, Mr. President. We come back here to "The World" and listen to the commentators and bunker generals talk about how 'mobile warfare' and 'focal terrain' will defeat the Posleen. And we laugh. And get drunk.

"ACS troopers get drunk and stoned a lot, Mr. President. 'Cause we're always the ones who clean up the battlefields after the generals fuck us. And after all the fucked-up calls on Barwhon, this one takes the cake."

President Edwards held a hand up to the Detail chief, who was about to explode. "So. What do you think I should do? Resign?"

"No," said Hadcraft in a firm tone. "Running doesn't get you anything but a blade in the back. Another lesson of Barwhon. If you have to, you have to. But for what it's worth, I think you should stay.

And I'll say that in public. But you'd better learn fast. This kind of mistake can only happen once."

The President nodded his head. "So it's time to leave?"

"Yes, Mr. President," said the Detail chief, with a final glare at the Marine.

"Where are we going?" asked the chief executive disinterestedly.

"Camp David, Mr. President," said the Detail chief.

"But there's a teensy problem," noted the Marine. There was a note of grim humor in his voice.

"We can't stay here. Because of all the bridges, General Horner won't guarantee that there won't be a crossing. But we've had landings all over, Mr. President," noted the Detail chief with a harried sigh. "We just had another one in Pennsylvania. So, I don't feel that moving you is absolutely secure."

"And don't forget," noted the captain in a wry voice. "There's a division between here and there. And some of them might not be as forgiving of presidential errors as I am."

The President held up his hand again to the Detail chief. "So, what's the answer?"

"Put you in a suit," answered Hadcraft.

The President blinked rapidly in surprise. "I thought that only one person could wear a suit."

"Well," said the Marine, turning his hands palm up. "There's a long story there."

"Make it short," said the President.

"Okay," sighed the captain. He walked over and sat on the edge of the conference table without asking permission. The President noted that crumbs from the secretary of defense's last meal danced off the table top and hung momentarily in the air. He finally realized that the suit's antigravity system must have activated to reduce the impact of the half-ton suit on the relatively fragile table.

"The first thing is, suits are fitted to a person," said the captain. "And once they've been 'hardened' to that shape, it takes an act of God, or at least an Indowy master-craftsman, to get 'em changed. That's why we try to make sure that people are gonna stay generally the same shape before we fit 'em. You can change slowly over time, that's okay. The suit will adjust *itself* to a slow change. But sudden weight gain is really bad. So is loss. The underlayer can expand and contract itself a fair amount, though, so generally we're okay.

"But somebody can put on another person's suit. If they are generally the same shape."

"I take it that I'm generally the same shape as someone in the Unit?" asked the President, dryly.

The suit was silent for a moment. The President was sure that if he could see the face of the officer it would show a certain amount of chagrin.

"It's not something that we talk about, sir," Hadcraft continued, reluctantly then stopped.

"What?"

The suit finally did the palm-up gesture again. The President realized that it might be the only gesture open to a combat suit user. "More than half of the Unit is chosen on the basis of the physiology of the sitting President. We always realized that if the shit hit the fan we'd want the protectee in armor."

"Oh." The President looked at the Detail chief, who was trying hard to hide a stunned expression. "Well, Agent Rohrbach?"

The Secret Service officer shook his head. "You guys planned this?"

"Hey, Agent," said the Marine with a grim chuckle, " 'expect victory and plan for defeat' is the only way to *survive* on Barwhon. So, yeah, we planned this. Believe it or not we take our responsibility to the Pres very Goddamn seriously."

The suit did not change position an iota, but something told the Secret Service agent he was being regarded. He nodded in acceptance of that important point.

"Anyway," continued the Marine after a moment, "we've got an open suit. Sergeant Martinez was on leave and won't make it back anytime soon. Home of record is Los Angeles."

"I take it that Sergeant Martinez is my size," said the slight President with a chuckle.

"Yeah," answered the captain. "That ain't the other problem."

"So what is the other problem?"

"Well, there's two more. One major and the other minor."

"Tell me the major first," said Rohrbach, humorlessly.

"Okay. The way these things work is that they 'read' our nervous signals. It generally takes about thirty hours for them to get fully worked in. And the program that drives the pseudonerves is an autonomous AID that picks up not only our neural signals but also our 'personality.' And it's built off of a completely different algorithm than the AID's," the Marine continued, pointing at the President's AID on the desktop. "So the 'gestalt' is capable of taking over control of the suit if the human inside is injured and doing all sorts of things that an AID would be constrained against. Like, surgery, combat, all sorts of things."

"Hold it," said the Detail chief. "You mean there's a self-directing computer in there with some sort of 'personality'? How is it going to react to the President being in there?"

"We don't know *how* it's going to react," admitted the Unit commander.

"No," snapped the Detail chief. "No way!"

"What," asked Hadcraft in a tired, cynical voice, "you want to truck him through a landing in one of your fuckin' Suburbans?"

"Wait," said the President. "Just stop. Captain, can we . . . talk to this personality? Tell it what's happening? Reason with it?"

"Yes, probably and I don't know. You see, we don't even notice the gestalt. The thing is *us*. Do you carry on a conversation with your spleen?" he asked rhetorically.

"So you're going to try to talk to it before I try it on?"

"Yes, sir. And if we think it's too dangerous, we won't proceed," he continued, more to the Detail chief than to the President.

The President held up his hand to forestall the protest of the Detail chief and nodded his head. "Okay, we'll try it. I agree that wandering around in a Suburban given the situation is not a good idea. You mentioned there was one more minor problem?"

"Uh, yeah," said the Marine, with a chagrined tone.

Roselita Martinez was apparently a very angry woman. If there was such a thing as ESP, President Edwards was experiencing it. The rage of the suit transmitted up a link that was supposed to be unnoticeable two-way communication. The reason for the gestalt's rage was ambiguous. It missed its proper user. It hated Posleen. It hated "brass" and had one in its belly. But it loved the protectee. It adored the protectee. It had to protect the protectee. It was very confused. It was very angry. It was very, very angry.

"Mr. President," said the captain. The voice sounded odd, incredibly crisp and relieved of all background noise by the transmission technology.

The President tried to turn his head against the enveloping jelly in the helmet. He could barely move against it, but the viewpoint of the helmet shifted wildly as he struggled against the Jell-O. The way it flew around was dizzying.

"Mr. President," said the captain again, grabbing the suit and turning it. The President finally got the viewpoint settled down and focused on the officer. The view was cluttered by dozens of indecipherable readouts. "Just keep looking forward and walk carefully. If the viewpoint starts shifting all over just look forward and close your eyes."

"There's all sorts of readouts," the President said, closing his eyes as the viewpoint started to swivel again.

"AID, tell the suit to clear the view and reduce sensitivity to view shift by fifty percent," said the captain. "Sir, we don't have time to get you trained to the suit. We have to leave."

"Okay," said the President, fighting against the waves of anger flooding through him. He took a deep breath. "Okay, let's go." He started to shake his head and was stopped by the gel of the underlayer. The viewpoint nonetheless shifted side to side. How anyone got used to this insane device was a mystery to him.

◆ CHAPTER 59 ◆

"How the hell do you guys get used to this?" asked Captain O'Neal, fighting down the nausea as the OH-58 Kiowa banked past Harper's Ferry and dropped down to follow Interstate 70 towards Baltimore. The road was packed with military vehicles, most of them at a standstill.

"Get used to what?" asked the pilot, keeping a close eye out for wires. The requirement to stay below one hundred feet was nerve wracking. You never knew where some stupid electric company was going to stick their lines. And half the time it seemed like they weren't on the damn chart.

"Never mind," muttered Mike, wishing he was back in a suit. Even the interface using a set of Milspecs was limited. He craved the total immersion of the suit like the drug it was. But he had other things to worry about right now.

He leaned back in the seat of the small helicopter and let the information flowing from the Virtual Reality glasses sink in. The interstates were completely overloaded, as were the side streets. But the mission was to get the battalion to D.C. before the Posleen. There seemed to be no way, but that was an illusion.

Back under the hammer of necessity, doubts and fears started to fall away. "Impossible" was a word that left his vocabulary as the information started flooding through his synapses. The Posleen had torn his world apart and ended the Golden Age he had grown up in. Such a species would not be permitted to continue to live, breathe

471

and breed. Earth was their last stop. He nodded his head as the final piece of the plan fell into place and keyed the AID.

"Shelly, get me Major Givens." It was time to start the dance.

Bob Givens was an experienced officer. Therefore, he knew that what he was in the grip of was a classic military disaster, not a nightmare. There was a simple difference. You woke up from nightmares.

"I know, Sergeant Clarke. I agree," he said to the battalion operations NCO. The sergeant first class was one of the few battalion staff NCOs that was not scattered to the four winds. And the NCO had a legitimate complaint. The tasking from Continental Army Command was clearly impossible. The roads were packed with military units scrambling in every direction and refugees heading for the hills. Getting to Washington in anything under twenty hours would be a miracle. "But those are the orders."

"How in hell does General Horner expect us to perform them, sir? Did he give a hint?"

"No, but we'll have to figure something out."

"I'll start getting transportation laid on," said the NCO. "But I'm damned if I know how it's going to cut through the traffic jams."

"Major Givens," chirped his AID. "Incoming call from Captain O'Neal."

Givens's shoulders slumped. He shouldn't be ashamed of his delight that the captain had finally initiated communication. The colonel had told him that if O'Neal made it back he would be taking over operations while Givens took command. And God knew he needed all the help he could get. There was only one company commander present and half the first sergeants were still out. There were no other battalion staff officers. He was just about to shanghai senior lieutenants from the companies to take up some of the administrative slack. Having a captain back would be a bonus even if it weren't O'Neal. But it was. And although Givens was an experienced and capable field-grade officer, he still had a germ of hope that the doughty captain would have thought of a miracle.

He picked up the AID and decided that humor would be the best approach. "Dammit O'Neal, where the hell have you been," he said with a smile in his voice.

O'Neal's mind felt like a whirring machine and he neither acknowledged the humorous greeting nor misunderstood it. "I've been fighting my way up I-81, Major, just like the Eleventh Division."

"Good to have you back. Where are you?"

"In a Kiowa headed up I-70. I'm planning on meeting you in Baltimore."

"Well, you'll probably get there before we do."

"Yes, sir. But not long before you do."

"I estimate that it will take us nearly twelve hours to get there through the traffic, Captain. Sergeant Clarke is calling for trucks right now."

"Trucks, sir?" said O'Neal in a bad Hispanic accent. "We don' need no stinkin' trucks."

The command track lurched to a halt and the following MP Humvee drove up to the man standing by the side of the road. The vehicle commander dismounted and saluted the boyish-looking colonel. "Colonel Cutprice?" he asked. The BDU uniform had only rank insignia, no nametag, no United States Ground Force identifier.

"Yes," answered the colonel, shortly. He had spent two weeks going through rejuv processes and he was still sore as hell. And cooling his heels with the rest of the officer "heroes" while they watched "The Jig and The Kraut" screw things to hell had been worse. In all honesty it did not seem to be Taylor and Horner's fault things had come apart so badly. They had inherited most of the problems and had been working to remedy them. But the vision of those fine boys being slaughtered through bad strategy and lack of training had been hard to take. It was goddamn Korea all over again. And Kasserine. And Bull Run. And the Somme for that matter. The goddamn Perfumed Princes just never ever seemed to learn.

"The general would like to speak to you," said the MP, leading the way to the back of the track and opening the door.

Horner was sitting in front of a video communicator smiling like a tiger. The colonel the smile was directed at was not enjoying the call.

"Colonel, when you receive orders from those units they will take priority over *any* other orders below the level of this command. *Is that clear?*"

"Sir . . ." the colonel started to respond.

"*Goddamnit I asked if that was clear!*" Horner shouted, finally losing his normally placid temper. "If I do not get a straight answer I will have an MP unit over there so fast it will make your head swim! I have a half a dozen colonels loading ammunition and driving *trucks!* Do you want to join them?"

"No, sir, but . . ."

"*Yes or no?*"

"Yes, sir," said the recalcitrant colonel. "I'll pass on those orders."

"Good, now get off my monitor," snarled the harassed general. He swung around and pinned Cutprice with a glare.

The colonel, however, had been glared at by the best of them, and it washed off him like dew. He stood at attention and looked six inches over the general's head. "Colonel Cutprice, reporting as ordered."

Horner looked at him for a moment and spun around again. He rummaged in a desk and came out with a small medal. "Take this," he said, tossing it to the colonel. "Wear it."

The device in question was a blue field with a rifle on it. Around the field was a wreath and it was surmounted by two stars. The Combat Infantryman's Badge signified that the holder had been in infantry combat; actual firefights where people were trying to kill you and you were doing your best to "do-unto-them" first. The stars signified that the combat had occurred over the course of three wars. There were very few people breathing entitled to wear one.

"Stand at ease, damnit," snapped the general. "I heard you weren't even wearing a goddamn nametag. So I acquired that for you. Do you feel like you need anything else?"

"No sir," said Cutprice quietly. He shifted his feet shoulder width apart and looked at the general, as the command allowed. The door behind him opened and closed again and someone came up beside him and came to attention as well.

"Sergeant Major Wacleva, reporting as ordered, sir," said the soldier. Cutprice gave the individual a quick glance. He was a short, skinny young man with sergeant major's stripes on his collar. Given his apparent age he had to be a rejuv and he looked faintly familiar.

"At ease, rest even, both of you," said Horner shaking his head. "I think you've met."

"Have we?" asked Cutprice.

The sergeant major just smiled, extracted a pack of Pall Malls and tapped one out. With a flick of a lighter the room was filled with the pungent odor of unfiltered cigarette. "Yeah," he answered in a surprisingly deep voice. It was almost gravelly, which was unusual for a rejuvenated individual. "We did meet. Briefly." He blew a smoke ring. And coughed.

"Oh, shit!" said Cutprice with a laugh. "You're trying for new lungs *already*?"

Horner just shook his head. "I want you two to get the rest of your respective groups together and get down to the Washington Mall. Most of the units that survived Lake Jackson and the rout are there.

I want you to see if any of them are fit to fight. I've got an ACS unit on the way and an intact division assembling. I'm worried about the Posleen capturing a bridgehead. If they do, it will be fight or die time."

"Yes, sir," said Wacleva. "We let 'em get over the Potomac and it's gonna screw us."

Horner nodded. "The big problem will be that we probably won't be able to dislodge them before the main landings. That means all the production and control that is in this area will be lost. There's actually not that much that was vital in the area between the James and Potomac. Not that we're not going to take it back. But losing the area north of the Potomac this soon will kneecap us.

"So, go get your band of brothers," he continued with a faint, real, smile, "and get down to the Mall. Find some that have a spine left and get them organized. Get ready to use them, too. 'Cause I got a bad feeling about the Potomac."

He smiled again. "Fortunately, besides your 'band of brothers' there's another card up my sleeve."

In the dawning light O'Neal waited on the Crosby Road overpass of I-695, the Baltimore Loop. The smell of jet fuel from the departed Kiowa still filled the air when the first of the apparitions came in sight.

The armored combat suits were delivered and stored in large Galactic-supplied storage containers. The silvery "Morgues" looked like oversized shipping containers and held forty suits. They came equipped with a Federation Class Two fusion plant or antimatter generator for recharging.

The Morgues were designed for the suits to be readily accessed, each suit stored in an interior pod, the double row of pods aligned down both sides of the large container. When the troopers suited up they went into the container, tossed their uniforms in the provided laundry bin and loaded up in the pods. The struggle of naked bodies in the narrow corridor normally led to a certain amount of playful grab-ass, but it was an efficient process. The suits exited through portals in the sides of the container.

The Fleet Strike Armored Combat Suits included a full suite of inertial compensators and drivers. Given enough power, the suits could and did "fly" under the combination of compensator and drivers. The process, however, was power-intensive. A normal combat suit could only sustain about ten minutes of flight, a command suit twenty to thirty, compared to three days of use before having to recharge if conditions were perfect.

However, as stated, the Morgues had their own onboard power source. And they were designed for high-intensity charging.

Mike thought the silvery containers probably caused their fair share of accidents as they floated down the interstate. The speed was not much, not more than seventy or eighty miles per hour, but it had permitted the battalion to cover the distance from Harrisburg to Baltimore in an hour. And it would permit them to continue on to D.C. in no time at all—once they picked up a stray captain.

The giant boxes floated noiselessly to a halt around the overpass and began to drift downward to the roadway. The control on the way down, managed by forty AIDs in each container, was spotty and most of them dropped to the roadway with rumbles that shook the early morning air. Many of the remaining residents rushed out to see if the sound was landing Posleen. When they saw the strange and obviously alien objects scattered down the road many of them took it as a final sign that it was high time to head for the hills.

The nearest conex began to spit suits and Mike let go of a deep sigh. He had not even realized how uneasy he had been until that moment. A soldier without his unit is like a man with one arm. He was finally home.

The first suit sprinting towards him was the unmistakable outline of Gunny Pappas. He grinned wryly as the NCO slid to a halt. "What kept you, Gunny?"

"Goddamn, am I glad to see you, boss," said the NCO, quietly. "We've got a hell of a situation on our hands."

"Yeah, same here. How's the XO holding up?" he asked, almost afraid of the answer.

There was a momentary hesitation. "Lieutenant Nightingale is doing fine, sir," the NCO answered baldly.

O'Neal stopped and turned towards the NCO. He wished, not for the first time, that he could see the first sergeant's face. "Does that mean that she's marginal?"

"No," said Pappas instantly and definitively. "She's made a hell of a lot of improvement. I think she'll be fine."

"This is going to be the real deal, Top," said the captain with steel in his voice. "I can't take any chances. She'd better be ready."

"I know that, sir," answered the NCO. "She's ready. I'd say that . . . anyway. She's ready."

O'Neal tilted his head to the side and wrinkled his forehead. "Say that again?"

"She's ready, sir. She'll do fine. I'll make sure of that."

Mike had thousands of hours in and around suits. They had virtually no body language, but virtually was not the same thing as none. And the first sergeant's body language was contradicting his words. O'Neal placed both hands on his hips. "Top, what the fuck is going on?"

The gunny paused for a moment then made a negating gesture. "It doesn't affect the efficiency of the company or my analysis of Lieutenant Nightingale, sir. You gotta take my word on that."

Mike shook his head and sighed. "Okay, Gunny. I'll take you at your word." The other suits were a small security force. He wasn't sure if someone had ordered it or if the troopers had taken the responsibility themselves. "What's with that?" he asked.

"The landers are everywhere, sir," grumped the first sergeant as he gestured towards the container. The subject of whatever nonsubject they had just not discussed was obviously dropped. "We actually got jumped by a lander on our way down."

"Any casualties?" asked Captain O'Neal. He stripped quickly and unselfconsciously, tossing his gear in the bin. The stuff would get sorted out if and when.

"No, sir," said the sergeant. "We mounted sensor balls all over these things so we could see where we're going. We spotted it coming in and landed our ownselfs. The horses had a kinda hot reception."

Mike shook his head with a smile and headed for his pod. The container popped open before he even reached it and the suit was opened up like a lobster as he stepped up. "Missed me, did you?" he chuckled. He slapped Shelly into her interface slot and stepped into the future.

◆ CHAPTER 60 ◆

Keren started awake and yanked the wheel to the left as the Suburban drove off the road.

"Sorry, man," said the driver, shaking her head to wake up. He didn't even know the girl's first name; her nametag read "Elgars." She was wearing a Thirty-Third ID patch, which put her miles away from her unit. How she had made it to Lake Jackson and then out of the rat-fuck when the Ninth Corps came apart was a mystery. He had picked her up when he saw her by the side of the road with a disassembled AIW, carefully oiling the parts. It was obvious she'd decided she had had enough running.

"Where the fuck are we?" asked Keren, his voice rasping. He'd had barely three hours of sleep in the last forty-eight. The division was supposed to be supplied the new antisleep drugs but, like a lot of things, that hadn't worked out. The platoon was subsisting on caffeine. And it was starting to fail.

"We just passed the Beltway," said the female soldier in a husky contralto. "But we got a problem."

"Yeah," Keren agreed. "What else is new."

Interstate 66 was the major thoroughfare through Fairfax County, Virginia, leading into the nation's capital. The Army had maintained a stranglehold on it for the movement of troops and material until the Posleen cut through the Lake Jackson defense. Since then, between panicked civilians who would not take "no" for answer, routed units from Ninth and Tenth Corps and desertions among the MPs tasked to maintain control, the interstate had become a solid grid of flee-ing vehicles.

From where they were currently parked, the roadway gave a clear picture of the surrounding secondary roads. At first the press of vehicles indicated to Keren that taking the platoon off the interstate would be no better than pressing on. But then he changed his mind. The major thoroughfares were thoroughly blocked, but many of the neighborhood roads were open.

"The good news," he whispered, "is that this is gonna slow the horses up some." He picked up the radio and extended the whip antenna out the window. "Reed, you there?" he said.

"Yep," came the response on the frequency-clipping radio.

"Looks like we gotta take to the side streets," he said, pulling out a DeLorme gazetteer. The multipage map of Virginia had repeatedly come in handy when the smaller scale tactical maps ran out. But now he needed even more detail.

"We're gonna cut the corner on Sixty-Six and head for Arlington," he said over the radio, trying to find a good route on the map. "There's bound to be some sort of units assembling around there. Reed, I want you to take the front. If there's a couple of cars blocking the way, try to push 'em out of the way with your track. If we can't push through a blockage we'll go around. We'll take to the back roads and back yards if we have to. Go through houses and buildings."

"Gotcha."

"Okay, turn off and take out the fence. I'll follow, then Three Track then One Track. Stay together but put your foot in it. The damn horses can't be far behind."

Kenallurial looked at the report and his crest stood straight up in stunned amazement.

Ardan'aath looked over his shoulder and grunted. "Apparently, the Net recognizes your worth." The senior Kessentai chuckled at the figure on his own monitor. "And mine as well."

The area surrounding Fredericksburg had been designated as "secure" by the information Net and the distributed processors were beginning the assignment of resources. How the Net decided what area was to be distributed to what Kessentai was not understood by the aliens; the technology predated their recorded history. But it was generally fair and the best way to distribute initial booty. Often, it was the only way to prevent an early descent into *orna'adar*, the apocalypse of post-conquest worlds.

There was even trade and wagering based on future conquests. Ardan'aath owed quite a chunk of the area he had been bequeathed to the late Aarnadaha; a matter of a wager on offspring hatched during the voyage. The debt was now void. All debts were voided by death.

"And as we take more of these lands from the thresh," said Kenallai, joining the conversation, "the amount will grow. At this rate we'll be the richest Kessentai in seven systems. You are going to need a castellaine soon."

Kenallurial flared his nostrils in agreement. His previous service as a scoutmaster had granted him a bare minimum of range. A small farm, a bit of land for hunting and a minor factory. All of them were managed through a proxy castellaine. There had been no need for the expense of one of his own with such meager resources.

The results from the last three days' work was not a minor fortune but a major one. With the income from the miles of arable land, several industrial areas and four chemical processing plants he could retire. The choice was retire or refit. Ardan'aath, for example, had the most heavily armed oolt'os in the host. He had been involved in five conquests and his only interest was the Path. That being the case, he poured his riches into outfitting his oolt'ondar and eson'antais. The result was that he took fewer casualties and was able to take more land; paying for better refitting. His entire oolt was now armed with three-millimeter railguns and the oolt of his "subordinates" were nearly as heavily armed.

Kenallurial's plan had always been to retire from the Path so that he could start a long-term genetic modification program. But he had not expected it to be so soon.

"This is amazing," he murmured, his mind awash in plans for the future. He had already begun collecting prize genetic samples from the smartest of the normals. His plan was to design a complete line of superior normals, standard Posleen nearly as intelligent and independent as God Kings. The line could fill in that fuzzy gap in labor caused by the shortage of *Kenstain,* the cowardly "castellaines" who were used to manage the absentee estates of the *Kessentai* battlemasters. The income from that prize would be enormous. Especially if his newly acquired skill in cybernetic repair transferred to even a fraction of the offspring.

The income would be enough to equip a dozen eson'antai, to go forth and conquer other worlds. And they would owe him for the equipment, as he had owed Kenallai. That debt was settled before the landing, so he was clear.

"And the greatest prize lies ahead!" Ardan'aath boomed. His crest fluffed once again, finally standing straight up in excitement.

"As long as it is not as bad as the 'prize' to the south," said Kenallurial, gloomily. But quietly also.

Kenallai rattled his crest in response.

Colonel Abrahamson led the way up the dirt ramp. The jaunty yellow scarf around his throat was dark with soot and oil, stained with human and Posleen blood. He strode with determination, but the set of his shoulders spoke of overriding fatigue.

The trailing General Keeton paused for a moment, causing a backup in the gaggle that followed him, and stamped the soft earth. The ramp, and the rest of the wall of earth along the interior side of the Richmond floodwall, was loose and uncompacted, barely useable for foot traffic. The first serious flood would wash it away but it had served its purpose and served it well.

General Keeton shook his head at the thought of all this effort disappearing in the first hard rain and continued up the slope. At the top of the ramp he looked at the wall and shook his head again. It looked *chewed*. The top of the smoking concrete and rebar was missing chunks and wedges, some of them leading down to the uncompacted fill. The bodies of the Sixtieth Infantry Division dead and wounded had already been removed, but the dark staining of the soil and gouges of melted soil were eloquent testimony to the casualties the division had suffered. As were the flickering fuel fires and smoking armored vehicles along the support road.

Survivors of the brigade in this, the hardest hit sector, were moving around performing all the usual after-battle chores. Ammunition parties were coming up from the trucks at the base of the wall and technicians were moving down the wall repairing or replacing manjacks. All of the soldiers staggered about like drunks, but the progress was steady.

The general walked over to stand by the cavalry officer, who had moved to the wall and now stood quietly looking out over the valley beyond. As far as the eye could see there was a carpet of dead Posleen and smashed saucers. The general leaned over and looked down. Sure enough, there was the *ramp* of Posleen dead he had been told about. The mass of centaurs ran for at least a hundred yards here near the Fourteenth Street gates. How many bodies were in that pile alone was impossible to calculate. Most of them had been pounded into paste by their fellows in a vain effort to surmount the fateful obstacles envisioned by John Keene.

" 'They just came at us in the same old way,' " he quoted quietly. The morning was quiet, with the exception of the distant boom of artillery targeting concentrations of the shattered enemy.

"Hmm," murmured Colonel Abrahamson in slight demurral. "The third wave was a little different. They were finally starting to use some sense, or there were more God Kings using sense than in the other attacks. They hit us while we were still headed out to them."

"That was when you lost your track?" asked the general.

"Yeah. Got a little hairy there for a bit." They had slowed the Posleen by calling for a full artillery concentration on his own position. He would go to his grave remembering the sound of One-Five-Five shrapnel pinging off his tank like steel rain while the vehicle took hit after hit from hypervelocity missiles. Why none of the missiles had penetrated the main crew compartment would remain a mystery. But he had lost his driver, six other tanks and a dozen troopers in the counterambush. The remaining Posleen had still chased them back to the Wall. That wave nearly overran the defenses, when a half million blood-mad Posleen crowded into the killing zone, taking the hammer of the guns on the chance that some of them could surmount the Wall or the obstacles along the sides. The final straw was when nearly two hundred God Kings had sailed over the Wall all along its length.

Snipers from the skyscrapers had shot through the flying roadways above the defenses or from the far side of the James while the defenders hammered the assaulting saucers. The casualties had been fierce as plasma cannon played along the berm and hypervelocity missiles slammed into the ammunition and fuel bowsers cached behind the defenses.

But in the end even that was not enough. The human defenders soaked up the charging God Kings, taking the casualties and dishing them out, supporting the fire from across the river. And the God Kings had died, one by one and in bunches. As had the forlorn normals in the pocket. And in the end the survivors stumbling out of that hell of death were less than one battalion. A paltry few hundreds of the half million that had entered the valley of death.

Keeton was of two minds how to respond. He almost sallied the Seventy-Fifth Armored to drive into them one more time and lure some back. On the other hand, the defenses were in sorry shape and the Posleen seemed to be headed back north.

Better to chase them in good time, with prepared units. For all he believed in Bedford Forrest's aphorism about "keepin' up the skeer," he also knew that facing the enemy in prepared positions was one thing; chasing them back up I-95 and U.S. 1 was another. The Eleventh MI was nearly on site. Let them go out in the open and play tag with the Posleen. That was what combat suits were designed for. He would husband his forces instead. It looked like being a long war.

"They're still trying to flank us," said Colonel Abrahamson, apparently reading his mind. "They still might."

"Maybe," agreed the general. "They've still got the numbers for it. And I'll worry about that if it looks like they're coming back in a serious way. And then I'll send somebody out to poke them in the snout."

"Somebody else, I hope," the colonel said, dryly.

"Somebody else," the general agreed.

"Good," said the exhausted officer. "It's about time somebody else had some fun."

◆ CHAPTER 61 ◆

"Gee, isn't this fun?" snorted Papa O'Neal.

The Tennessee Volunteers had thus far failed to live up to their name. The landing was small, only a single lander. That meant no more than six hundred Posleen, probably closer to four hundred. But the force had gone one way and run into the unVolunteers. Then it had recoiled the other way and run into the Rabun Gap defenses. Now it was milling around more or less at the head of O'Neal's Hollow. And the first trace of entering scouts had appeared on the sensors.

"That was how you knew," said "Raphael" quietly, watching the sensors.

"Yeah. You guys made a signature like a rocket." Papa O'Neal chuckled.

"Hmm." The special action team leader nodded. "My fellows are confused by your granddaughter. They don't know what to make of her."

"Well," said O'Neal, dryly, "it's more what she makes of them."

"You ever use one of these?" Cally asked the black-masked commando, gesturing at the General Electric mini-gun. Since she would be handling the demo, putting one of the commandos on the 7.62mm Gatling freed Grandpa up to handle overall actions.

At his negative head shake she touched a control. "That arms it," she said as the barrel advanced with a whine. "Butterfly triggers just like a Ma-Deuce, but the safety is on the side." She pointed to the appropriate button then released it. "Other than that it works just like a hose. Fires eight thousand rounds a minute. Looks sort of like a laser going downrange. Just walk the fire onto the enemy." She stood on tiptoes to look out the slot of the bunker but declined to fire. The Posleen weren't in sight yet and they still might just go away.

The commando nodded and stepped forward. He carefully put the safety back on and advanced the barrels again. A single round flew out and dropped into an open blue plastic fifty-five–gallon drum.

"Keeps you from getting awash in brass," said Cally, gesturing to the huge box of ammunition under the weapon. "It'll only catch 'em on a narrow traverse, but it helps."

The commando nodded again and looked out the slit.

Cally tapped her foot a few times and rotated her shoulders to relieve the chafing of the armor. It was a lot more comfortable when it was dry. "You sure don't talk much."

The mask turned towards her and brown eyes regarded blue. He cleared his throat. "We kin talk," was all he said.

The accent was faint, but completely different from the team leader's. Cally nodded and put that and a few other facts together. "Can I ask you one thing?" she asked.

He nodded.

"Can I see your left hand?"

The head of the commando tilted slightly to the side but then he pulled the thin black Nomex glove off his hand. He held it up for a brief inspection, rotating it so that she could get a good look and then waggling his fingers. He obviously thought it a silly question. He put the glove back on.

Cally glanced at the hand and smiled. When he was done with his little pantomime she looked him straight in the eye and made the Sign of the Cross.

As the commando's eyes flew wide she smiled again, turned and left the bunker without a word.

"Oh, this is truly good!" snarled Monsignor O'Reilly, reading the missive on his Palm Pilot.

The message was written in Attic Greek, encrypted half a dozen ways, and used code phrases. The message was, nonetheless, clear.

"What?" asked Paul, looking up from the card game he was engaged in with the Indowy. The Himmit stealth ship was in two hundred feet of water in Hudson Bay. And the Indowy had explained that it would stay there until the majority of the Posleen were destroyed and clear areas declared. Himmit would risk much on occasion, but they believed that discretion was better than valor.

"Our team is trapped at the O'Neal farm!" he snarled.

"Calmly, Nathan, calmly," soothed the Indowy. "The O'Neals are an inventive clan. The team will be well taken care of."

"Bit of a turnabout for the books." Paul smiled, taking a card off the stack on the table. He grimaced. "Your move." The cards were difficult to read in the odd blue-green light. This Himmit ship, unlike some, had never been converted for human use.

The table was too low and the bench he sat on was designed to be used by lying on a hairy belly. The air was thin, the gravity too heavy and the lighting set to Himmit norm, which meant that it was mainly in shades of violet invisible to human eyes. The result was an odd blue-green that made everything look as if it was under deep water. There were odd sounds at the edge of hearing; the Himmit communicated in hypercompressed squeaks that were barely in the human audible range. There were strange chemical smells and occasional odd slurping noises. All together it was one of the most uncomfortable environments the widely traveled des Jardins had experienced.

Aelool looked to the Monsignor, who finally gave a resigned gesture. "It is not as if there haven't been breaches before," the little alien said.

"Hmm," said the Monsignor, irritably. "But there are reporters swarming nearly as thick as the Posleen. There are already reports that there is a well-defended farm near the landing. And the local commander says that the reason they haven't attacked Posleen yet is to see how the farm fairs. He says he's afraid of hitting the farm with friendly-fire, but it sounds more like he trusts the *O'Neals* to take care of the attack. One old man and a young girl up against a Posleen company?!"

Paul smiled sardonically. "Well, they are Irish, no?"

Nathan's eyelids dropped, giving him a sleepy look and he stared at des Jardins's back. "This is a small ship, Paul, and the lighting is really getting on my nerves. Don't push it."

"We gotta push it, sir," said Captain O'Neal, looking into the Virtual infinity of data. He was in a trance of data assimilation as graphs and maps cascaded past. The data included snippets of live video from the front lines, where reporters were finally encountering the enemy firsthand.

In many cases the locations of advancing Posleen had to be assumed. Here a company not responding, there a transmission suddenly cut off. But the picture was firming up. The battalion was still well short of the District while the Posleen were well into Fairfax

County and nearly over the border into Arlington. They had spread up to the Potomac on the north side and were moving rapidly down the Beltway towards the crossing to the east of Arlington.

The movement was unconscious, but it was creating a pocket in the Arlington area. All the survivors were being pushed towards the downtown D.C. bridges, just as General Horner had anticipated.

"Agreed, Captain," responded the acting battalion commander. "Any more suggestions?"

"No, sir. Not at this time." The movement of the canisters was as fast as the AIDs could handle the information load. Not only did each suit have to be controlled, but the overall load had to be balanced among all the suits. The current speed of an average of eighty miles per hour was the fastest they could do. The alternative, exiting the containers and running, would be even slower. The maximum sustainable speed for suits was about forty miles per hour, if the roads were open.

The roads, however, were packed with military units and refugees. First Army was finally getting its combat power concentrated, with units flooding into the area of the Potomac from all over the northeast. Like the units of Ninth and Tenth Corps, most of the forces were undertrained and their equipment was in pitiful shape. But with any luck they would be fighting from fixed positions.

Mike glanced at the exterior view and his eyes narrowed. Somebody had had a rush of sense, and the lead units were mostly artillery. By the time they were in contact, there would be a mass of artillery available. Command and control, however, was spotty.

"But I'll figure something out. I'll get back to you soon, sir."

"Okay, Captain. We need a good plan if this is going to succeed."

"Roger, sir. Shelly," he continued, looking back at the feeds. "What are you getting from D.C.?"

"It's a bit of a dog's breakfast, sir," responded the AID.

Mike smiled. The device had been getting more and more attuned to human interaction, even starting to use some slang.

"There's a mishmash of units," she continued. "Some of them are ordered there, like the engineers that are rigging the bridges and the One-Oh-Fifth I-D. But most of them are from Ninth and Tenth Corps."

"Any sign of leadership?"

"There are small units that are coherent. But nothing over a company."

"Hmm. Bring up an appropriate scenario. Assume the Posleen take a bridge intact." If the Posleen did not take a bridge, the battalion could wait for Eighth Corps to get its act together, then cross the river at leisure to sting the Posleen. It was only if one of D.C.'s bridges fell that time would be critical.

"Is there a scenario in the can for this?" Mike thought there was, but there were so many developed "games" scenarios it was impossible to keep track.

"*Bridge over the River Die*," responded the AID. "On the basis of probable Posleen numbers at contact and probable friendly support I would recommend responses for difficulty level six."

"Yeah," whispered the officer, reading the scenario as it scrolled down the left of his heads-up view. He remembered it now. He had gamed it at least three times. It wasn't one of his favorites, but it had some interesting surprises. The similarities to the current situation were remarkable. Even the buildings were similar; the writer of the scenario had clearly envisioned Washington as a target. That was not in the description and Mike had never noticed the similarities. But it was obvious now. "Who wrote it?"

"A teenager in Fredericksburg. Thomas Sunday, Junior."

"Oh. Damn." Fredericksburg was, of course, gone. What a waste of a good mind. The writer had obviously had a good grasp of suit tactics. Losing him this early in the game sucked. "Shit happens. Shelly, can this one. Set it to level eight. Now, what are we missing for an eighth-level response?"

"Command and Staff. A level of response of that difficulty requires everything to hit the ground running perfectly."

"What's the first and most obvious lack? Take them in order downward."

"Artillery command and control. We do not have a Fire-Support Team."

"Right. Who do we have in the battalion with significant fire control experience?"

"Besides yourself?" she asked dryly.

Mike rolled his eyes at the ceiling. *Save me from an AID with a sense of humor.* "Besides me."

"There are four NCOs in the battalion with fire control experience and one lieutenant."

"Who's the lieutenant?"

"Lieutenant Arnold, your mortar pl—"

"Pass," he said. "I want Arnold right where he is." *In case he has to take over from Nightingale.*

"Then one of the four NCO's."

"Who is senior?"

"An E-6 in Bravo Company. Staff Sergeant Duncan."

Mike wrinkled his face in the flexible gel. He was unable to place the name in his own company's roster. And, as far as he knew, with the exception of Sergeant Brook in the Mortar platoon none of Bravo's NCOs had ever been in fire control. "The name rings a bell," he continued, "but not from Bravo Company."

"He joined Bravo Company while you were on leave."

Mike thought about the roster for a moment and grimaced. "Gimme Gunny Pappas."

The AID chirped after a moment and the Gunny's voice came over. "Yessir?"

"This new NCO that joined while I was on leave . . ."

"Duncan?"

"Yeah. Let me guess. He got put in charge of Second Squad of Second Platoon."

"Yup. Only squad without a staff sergeant. Wasn't much I could do."

"Agreed. So, how is Stewart taking it?"

"Fairly well. Duncan's a real experienced NCO as you know. Generally he lets Stewart continue to run the squad and helps Boggy with training. Stewart's actually started to pump him for information and support. They work well together."

"Hold it," Mike said after digesting this. "'As I would know'? Is this *Bob* Duncan?"

"Yeah. Sorry, boss, I assumed you'd know." The Old Man was damn near omniscient normally. "Shelly didn't tell you?"

"No. Damn. Shelly, bring Sergeant Duncan in on this conversation."

"Yes, sir." After a moment there was another chirp of connecting circuits.

"Captain O'Neal?" asked the quiet voice.

"Duncan! Who the hell let you into my company?" Mike snapped in a serious voice.

There was a pause. "Well," responded the quiet baritone, "they wanted me to take a commission as a captain. They said there was this really screwed-up company that needed straightening out. I told 'em I wanted to infiltrate it first as an NCO. And here I am."

Mike and the first sergeant both chuckled. "Like I said," said Pappas. "He's a real screwball."

"Yeah," said Mike with a smile in his voice. "I've noticed that before." He thought about the situation for a moment. He had some of the best experience in the battalion in the three way at the moment. He thought about bringing in Sergeant Bogdanovich, but she was undoubtedly busy with her platoon. There were four other combat veterans that he knew of in the battalion, but none of them were officers. From the point of view of suggestions, this was as good as it got.

"We've got a bit of a FUBAR situation in D.C." He ran over the outline of what they could expect. "There's combat power to spare. But nobody has any sort of decent control and most of the line units have just been through a rout. The first problem on Shelly's list was artillery support. We don't have a Fire Support Team. And the automated system has been taken off-line. We need someone to coordinate artillery support."

"Me," stated Duncan.

"Right. If I had a FIST captain, it would be him. We don't. So it's you."

"Is the arty gonna go for that?" asked the first sergeant. It was a realistic question. Duncan would effectively be ordering artillery battalions. Colonels do not normally listen to sergeants.

"I'll take care of that," said Mike. "Shelly, send General Horner an e-mail. Tell him we are assuming control of the defense of the bridges of D.C. under Standing Regulations for the interaction of Federation and Local forces."

"Oh, shit," whispered Duncan.

"Did you just say what I think you said?" asked Gunny Pappas in an incredulous voice.

"Yep. We now own the forces in D.C.," said O'Neal in a definite voice. He suddenly realized that Major Givens might have liked to be informed. He had just sent a message to an Army General telling him that a lowly battalion, commanded by a major, was taking command of one of his Armies. If it was anyone but Jack Horner it would be impossible, whatever the standing orders. "Shelly, slug this plan to him so he understands what we're doing."

"Yes, sir."

"Are they going to listen?" asked Duncan.

"That is where you come in. The first order will be to reestablish the automated fire control network. The AIDs will stomp any virus they find so security won't be an issue. Get that up. After that, we *will* have control. Without direct orders to the contrary, the cannon cockers will follow the computer guidance. And the computers will follow our orders."

"Then what?" asked Duncan. He knew his own AID would be taking in the details.

"Shelly?"

"The next problem is Command. We are short three of four combat company commanders."

"Pass. Nightingale can carry the company," said O'Neal. *Lord, hear my prayer.* "Same for Alpha's XO. We'll use Bravo for the shock company and Alpha and Charlie for support."

"This scenario will require all three line companies to interact perfectly," the AID demurred.

"If needs be, I'll take direct command of the suits. Start preparing a program to lead every trooper in Alpha and Charlie by the hand. We can slug them to replicate the actions of Bravo troops. That will give us three times the firepower for each Bravo shooter. Delta's Reapers will be under control of fire-support. They won't be a problem. Next."

"Communications."

"Handle it."

"Captain, I cannot handle the entire communications strategy!" the AID responded. The tone was almost hysterical. "There are too many variables."

"Define the problem," Duncan interjected.

"We will require the support of forces in the area to accomplish the mission," his own AID responded, unexpectedly. The device had a slightly different voice than Shelly, more of a contralto. "Captain O'Neal, you yourself specified level eight difficulty. Given that, we will need the majority of the forces in the area for base of fire. We will need a complete fire control network. We will need communications to higher headquarters for logistical support. And we will need to maintain communications intelligence monitoring. We AIDs cannot handle all of that alone. We will be heavily tasked to maintain local coordination. Especially if you have to take direct suit command."

"Agreed. Okay, okay." Mike suddenly wished he could scratch his head. Inside the pod he couldn't even pop the helmet; there was no room. "Pass for right now. Next."

"That's it," answered Shelly. "With the forces in the area or approaching it we will have the force necessary to retake and destroy any two bridges that are no more than six miles apart."

"Okay. Duncan, Pappas, I'm open to suggestions on the communications problem."

"Debbie," said Duncan, "how are you planning on communicating out of the battalion? That is, who are you planning on talking to?"

"We would normally communicate with the local commander. However, there isn't a local commander. The units are fragments." Suddenly on all three screens a map of the area around the Washington Mall popped up. It was scattered with dots and blobs of all the colors of the rainbow. There was little or no rhyme or reason to the colors. "Each of the different colors represents a unit which has made it to D.C. It is based on a spectrum of units from each of the divisions involved. Therefore, units that are from vaguely similar units would have vaguely similar colors."

Mike made an okay sign with his hand. It was the body signal the ACS had developed to replace nodding the head. "Okay. Nice picture."

"Thank you."

"And of course," he continued, "that's not what's there. These units are randomly mixed."

"Correct. A complete higgledy-piggledy. A mishmash. A hodgepodge . . ."

"Yes, thank you. We get the picture. So that is the communications problem. You'd be required to find the frequency of each unit and broadcast to it."

"Correct. We actually have the frequencies of all the units that have communicated. However, there are others that are not communicating at all. They might not even have radios."

"Are they all at the Mall?" Duncan asked.

"Many of them are," Shelly answered. "It is a prime destination. The units from Ninth Corps are trying to find transport to their bases. Tenth Corps units are just lost."

"Christ," muttered Gunny Pappas. "What a rat-fuck."

"Dantren," Duncan said, cryptically.

"Yeah," Mike agreed. "Remarkable how the Posleen keep doing this to us." The first expeditionary force to Diess had had its mobile units trapped by advancing Posleen in an Indowy megascraper. The siege had been lifted by then-Lieutenant O'Neal's platoon. In that case the hard-hit American and British units had been reduced to scattered squads.

"What about artillery?" asked Duncan, taking a closer look at the unit data on the screen. Most of the units seemed to be from front-line combat forces.

"Artillery and Service and Support units generally have stayed together better," answered Shelly. "Although many of them have crossed farther upriver, those that were caught in the Arlington pocket have mostly crossed the river and are assembling in the area of Chevy Chase and Rock Creek Park. The remnants of Ninth Corps's Artillery are actually assembling at the Chevy Chase Country Club."

The first sergeant snorted. "Hate to see the bill for that."

"Yeah," snorted O'Neal. "Anybody sends me a bill, I'll tell 'em to stick it where the monkey put the peanut. Duncan."

"Sir?"

"This is going to hinge on fire-support. Get with those units. Get them to not just assemble but get ready to fire."

"Yes, sir," he said dubiously.

"If you get any guff, call General Horner, directly," Mike said definitely.

"Okay," Duncan answered in the same tone.

"Do it."

"Yes, sir."

"Gunny."

"Sir."

"Start setting up some commo with those units on the mall. Figure out a scheme for assembly and get them assembling. Get the units you can cajole to start making signs for assembly areas. Use the color scheme you've already got."

"Yes, sir."

"Try to put some spine into them. We're going to have to get support. Remind everyone and anyone that if the Posleen cross the Potomac, we'll be running all the way to the goddamn Susquehanna."

"Right."

"Ask your AID for help."

"Not a problem, sir."

"Okay. Good." Mike desperately wished he could rub his face. "Okay, Shelly. Anything else."

"Just one thing," she responded.

"Yes?"

"This scenario will require forces that are willing to stand and fight. That is not a normal characteristic of routed forces."

"Well," said Mike softly. "We'll just have to hope that the survivors were not just the ones with the fastest horses, but also the best aim."

◆ CHAPTER 62 ◆

The Suburban lurched as it crossed the toothpick remains of a backyard fence.

The fastest way through the neighborhoods of scattered one- and two-story houses was often the yards. They had had to turn around at Glebe Road and backtrack up Wilson Boulevard until they found a section not completely blocked by cars. The choked roads had overflowed to the point of bursting and the abandoned vehicles were scattered through the strip malls and fast-food restaurants along the major thoroughfares. Once they got across Wilson they stayed as much as possible on yards and side streets, only attempting crossings at the least likely places.

They could have abandoned the vehicles. There were military vehicles scattered throughout the region. But if they left the tracks they would lose the mortars and the .50 calibers. All in all, Keren was willing to chance the Posties catching them to keep the firepower.

But the circuitous route had other problems.

"Where are we?" asked Elgars, leaning out the window and looking back at the two following mortar carriers. Surprisingly, none of the vehicles had broken down in the harum-scarum run from Manassas. Apparently all the deadwood had been left in Prince William County. "You got any idea?"

"Not really," said Keren, handing her the map. They had switched drivers when the going got bad. She was fine on streets but he had much more experience at off-road.

She found the last notations he had made, back at Wilson Boulevard. "That doesn't tell me much."

He picked up the microphone. After the third time he had pushed it out the window, Elgars had found a roll of duct tape and fixed it so the antenna stuck out the moonroof of the vehicle. It worked remarkably well and he wondered why he hadn't thought of it. Probably because the only time he hadn't been running for the last three days was when he was dead asleep.

"Reed."

"Yeah?"

"Find a road sign."

"Right."

The mortar carrier made a hard left, kicking up a rooster tail of soil from the manicured yard. It trampled a pink plastic tricycle then slipped into the space between neighboring houses. The wooden fence between them turned to splinters as the vehicle ran down its length. As he cleared the house he made another abrupt turn to the right.

The houses were halfway down a block. The mortar platoon proceeded to the end of the street where the ubiquitous green sign finally fixed their location.

"Jackson and Sixth," said Reed over the radio.

"Damn," said Elgars. "Not bad. We're nearly to Arlington Cemetery."

"How far?" asked Keren, peering ahead. There were skyscrapers ahead, which was not good. The damn things drew Posleen like flies. He keyed the mike again. "Anybody see a big hill? Should be at our nine o'clock."

"I got it," said somebody from the Three Track. The squad was from another brigade, added on to their nearly intact platoon at Jackson Lake. They still didn't feel like family, but at least they kept up. "Between two buildings. You probably can't see it from there."

"Okay," Keren said, "that's our objective . . ."

A tremendous explosion tore the face off a skyscraper to the south and a tracer kicked up and out crazily.

"Holy Shit!" shouted Reed. "*Posleen!*" The .50 caliber on the top of the mortar carrier tracked to the south down Sixth Street and began to spit fire.

"*Goose it!*" shouted Keren over the radio, putting action to words as he dropped the Suburban into gear. "Don't just sit there!"

He turned into the road just as the mortar carrier began to move. A hypervelocity missile evaporated a section of roadway to their right as the Suburban slid crazily into the intersection. Elgars had her AIW out and was climbing into the moonroof. Out of the corner of his eye he saw the other tracks cutting across the parking lot on the corner but he put his foot down and accelerated towards the distant hill.

He had just passed forty when Elgars kicked him painfully in the shoulder.

"Stop!" she yelled as another HVM flew by. The shockwave of its passage shook the heavy vehicle like a terrier and the missile itself demolished a gas station on the corner.

"*Fuck you!*" he shouted back and started weaving. The silver lance of plasma cannon came from nowhere and he saw the Two Gun track erupt in fire. "Goddamnit!" The mortar carriers were firing their .50 calibers but with the way they were jumping over curbs there was no chance in hell of hitting the Posleen leader that must have fired that accurate blast. He was barely in sight in the rearview, at nearly a thousand yards. The distance was the only thing saving them from the notoriously inaccurate Posleen. Distance, however, helped not a bit with God Kings.

"*Stop or we're all FUCKED!*" Elgars shouted again. Her feet were braced on the backs of both front seats and the rifle was rock-steady.

He stomped on the brakes and reached in the back for his own AIW. He was no expert, but unless they took out that God King, they were all toast. Two rifles were better than one. The 7.62 rifles had the ability, technically, to hit something at that range. He'd never been able to hit the broad side of a barn at over five hundred yards. But, hell, the horse might sing.

The vehicle had barely lurched to a stop when there was a single crack from overhead. "*Go!*"

He looked in the rearview as a storm of fire erupted towards them. The Posleen normals of the company were attacking berserkly. But they were firing at everything in sight, not just the vehicles, and the fire was scattered. There was enough to begin slamming into the Suburban, but the God King was clearly dead. His saucer was barely in sight drifting off to the side. Keren dropped the Suburban back into gear and floored the accelerator. The smoke from the burning gas station was just ahead and if they made it to that obscurement they might just survive.

"Holy Mother of Acceleration, don't fail us now!" shouted Elgars as she began pumping out grenades. The 20mm rounds pounded out like a metronome, weaving a dance of destruction in the wake of the retreating platoon.

The platoon had torn through Fort Myer as if it weren't there. Headquarters of the Continental Army Command and one of the most famous facilities in the United States, it was now a ghost town;

it seemed that the only sentients in the world were the platoon and the pursuing Posleen. The mortar unit had a blurry view of the commissary and the clinic as they rushed past and then they were at the wall around Arlington Cemetery.

Knowing the barrier was coming up, Keren had slowed to let the tracks catch up. He picked up the mike again. "Three Track. Run that thing over," he said, pointing at the wall.

"Idn't there a gate?" asked the person on the radio in One Track.

"You wanna take time to find it?" asked the Three Track commander and waved at the wall. The vehicle snorted forward and put its nose against the low stone wall. With a burst of power a wide section of the wall came down.

"Now, goose it. Three Track, FDC, First. Go!"

Keren fell in behind Three Track as it began to weave a way up through the headstones. The specialist looked around at the white markers drifting off into the distance and shook his head. He suspected that the residents would understand the unseemly nature of the platoon's passage, but dislike the running away part. Well, sooner or later they were going to find a real unit to rejoin. And they could stop running.

Three Track turned right on the first road and followed it around the hill. The trees in the area shielded them from sight, but until they were on the back side of the hill, Keren wouldn't feel happy. Mortars are never, ever, ever supposed to see the enemy. It was drilled into them from basic training. Unlike artillery, they could not fire directly at an attacker. Used correctly, though, their big 120mm rounds could be devastating.

They were just approaching a traffic circle when an officer came striding down the hill towards them. The lieutenant colonel was in Dress Blues and carried an MP-5 submachine gun. He walked out in front of the leading track and held up one hand for them to stop. After a brief conversation with the vehicle commander, he strode back to the Suburban.

Elgars laid down her AIW and reached for the 9mm that was half-forgotten in Keren's holster.

Without turning his head he said: "No."

"Why?" she asked. A brief glance in her direction revealed pale blue eyes as dead as a shark's.

Keren gestured up the hill to his right. A line of foxholes could be seen running up the ridge towards the Tomb of the Unknowns. The soldiers in them were hunkered down waiting for the approaching centaurs. Their AIWs and crew-served machine guns were plainly in evidence.

"You want to take the chance that all of them are willing to have this guy fragged?" he whispered as the officer approached.

"I'll think about it," she said, leaning back into the passenger's seat. "We'll see." She was as determined as any of them to put a river between themselves and the Posleen.

Keren fixed a military expression on his face and saluted as the officer approached. It was not precisely correct under the circumstances, but it never really hurt to salute.

"Colonel," he said, "Specialist Keren, Mortar Platoon, Alpha Company First Battalion Four Fifty-Second Infantry, Third Brigade Fiftieth Infantry Division."

The colonel was tall, slim and almost painfully handsome. He looked more like some movie star in a truly screwed-up war movie. He returned the salute with parade ground precision. "Lieutenant Colonel Alexander." He looked at the Suburban. The vehicle had been some yuppie's pride and joy before it fell into the clutches of the Infantry. Now it had only one remaining window, the side and rear panels were pocked with flechette strikes, the left rear quarter panel had been mostly torn off by a close encounter with a mortar track and the engine compartment was spurting steam.

"Where did you acquire the vehicle, specialist?" he asked in a dry and deadly voice.

Keren blinked rapidly. It was the last question he had expected to be asked. Hell, the platoon had stayed together, unlike most units. They had practically no NCOs left, the tracks were on their last legs, they had no officers, no spare ammo, no communications. And this stupid bastard wanted to know why they stole a truck.

There was only one option: Lie.

"Sir. Our Fire Direction vehicle was struck by friendly-fire in the Occoquan Defense. My company commander personally commandeered this vehicle, which was out of fuel on the Prince William Parkway. We used it for an ammunition carrier and to transport wounded in the withdrawal. We were overrun again, in company with an Armored Combat Suit battalion, at Lake Jackson. We lost our company commander, our platoon leader and all of our NCOs in the first contact at Lake Jackson. I've been using it as an FDC vehicle ever since. Sir. We are the last unit in. We have been performing a fighting withdrawal under fire. I could not have done that without a vehicle. Sir."

And the colonel could believe as much or as little of that as he liked. If the bastard made any more complaints, Keren would just let this hard-faced bitch do her thing. And then the platoon could just perform another fighting retreat.

The commander of a unit like this should have been a grizzled veteran as well as a martinet. Keren knew that was what the President's Marines were. Every swinging dick was a veteran of Barwhon or Diess. And they still had lovely drill. So it only made sense that the commander of the Old Guard would be the same. But the fruit-salad on the Dress Blue uniform said otherwise.

Keren wasn't one of those guys who spent all their time memorizing the medals they wanted to get someday. But he had seen fruit-salad before. And he knew a few things to look for. He didn't recognize the highest award on the colonel's chest, but it was probably a Legion of Merit. And that pretty much said it all. An L-o-M was the sort of award a really proficient paper-pusher got for thirty years' slavery in the Pentagon.

After careful but covert searching of the dangling medals, Keren determined a few lacks. There were no Silver Stars. There were no Bronze Stars. The colonel was infantry, he had the crossed rifles, but no Combat Infantry Badge. Expert Infantry Badge, yes. Expert Marksmanship Medals, yes. Master Parachutist Wings, yes. Combat Jump Star, no. His chest full of medals broadcast as plain as day that the colonel had never heard a shot fired in anger.

Patton might have shown up at a time like this in a dress uniform. He probably would have been in BDUs, but Georgie was funny. The same with MacArthur. If he had been ordered to hold Arlington Cemetery to the last man he probably would have had the entire unit in Dress Blues. It was an impossible task and everyone was going to die anyway. Might as well go out with style. But both of *them* had seen the elephant.

Keren's face was a polite mask but he knew the deal. This guy was a piker. He was scared shitless and throwing away his unit to prove he wasn't a coward. When the time came he would probably be running down the hill for the bridges. And praying like hell the engineers wouldn't blow them before he was across.

The colonel favored him with another cold look and nodded. "Very well. I am aware that there have been certain exigencies of service in the last two days." His face twisted into a sour expression that ended as contempt. "Your division has been on the run for quite a while."

Keren suppressed a deep angry breath as a last tiny trickle of adrenaline made it into his overloaded system. After a brief pause he nodded. "Yes, sir. We have."

"Well." The officer smiled coldly. "Lucky for you. Your running days are over." He gestured up the hill towards the barely visible Tomb on the hill. "Move your . . . unit up there. And dig your mortars in. They will be a useful addition to our firepower."

Keren nodded respectfully and reached for his map. "Yes, sir. Sir, might I point out two items of mortar doctrine . . ."

The officer's face hardened. "I am quite aware of mortar doctrine, specialist. I gave you an order."

" . . . which point out that in close contact mortars are to be maintained on the mortar vehicles. We can be in operation in four minutes after we stop if we stay in the vehicles, sir. It will take time to dig in." He looked the officer right in the eye. "We were in contact less than two miles from here, sir."

The officer's face tightened at that. He could not have missed the hypervelocity missile impacts, but apparently he had hoped that the enemy was farther away. "Where?"

"The Posleen unit was at Arlington Hall, sir. Their God King was using a plasma cannon. You did see the fire, sir?"

"Yes. Specialist, we don't have time to argue . . ."

I've got all the time in the world, you jackass. If you put us on that hilltop we've got maybe fifteen minutes of life left. "Sir, we were heading for a traffic circle on King Drive. One-hundred-and-twenty–millimeter mortars have a minimum firing distance of nearly eight hundred meters. I cannot provide Final Protective Fire for your unit from the hilltop." It was a bald-faced lie. The distance was a third of that. But he was betting that this officer wouldn't know it.

And he was right.

"Very well," the officer snapped. "But if you attempt to move out of position once we are in contact, I will have your vehicles destroyed. Your running days are over, Specialist."

"Yes, sir!" said Keren. "What is your fire control frequency?"

The officer was desperately attempting to not look over his shoulder towards the encroaching Posleen. So his sudden look of shock was comical. "Uhhh . . ."

"We're on Sixty-Three Seventy, sir," said Keren, helpfully. He pulled out his leader's notebook and made a note. He tore the sheet of paper out and handed it to the colonel. "Here, sir. We'll go set up then?"

"Yes. Go, I'll . . ."

"Call us."

"Yes."

Keren saluted again and picked up the mike. "Three Track. Hold up. I'll ground-guide into position." He was glad that the receiver was turned down and to his ear.

"*What?* We're stopping?" said Three Track. One Track responded similarly but the response was garbled by Three's response.

"Yes, we're going to the roundabout. I've got the map and the colonel has our frequency. I'll lead in. Get ready to get set up." He smiled at the colonel and saluted him without taking the mike out of his hand. Then he put the Suburban into gear and gunned it around the big mortar track in front of him. The rear wheels of the big SUV tore the carefully tended sod and threw a rooster tail of loam back along his backtrack. He looked in the rearview to where the colonel was still standing, holding the little slip of paper. *What a dumbfuck.*

"You dumbfuck," snarled the specialist, leaning in the window. Third squad's leader was not happy about stopping. Keren glanced up from his board and saw first squad's leader headed over to the Suburban as well. The sergeant was from another battalion in Third Brigade and outranked Keren. But he was originally a rifle team leader and did not know much about mortars. He also was not much of a leader. He had been happy to defer to Keren throughout the entire flight. Keren finished setting up his board just as the sergeant arrived.

"Yeah, maybe," Keren admitted. Then he jerked his chin towards the hill. "There's Dragon antitank missiles up there. And maybe those big goddamn sniper rifles. If we try to run you want one of those up your ass?" He looked third squad's leader in the eye. "The fuckin' Posties are gonna be here anytime. You think maybe we better be ready to fire?"

The squad leader was a big man, with fine blond hair that was cut down to the stubble. The stubble on his face was nearly as long. His nostrils flared as he clenched and unclenched his hands. Then, with a glance up the hill towards the rifle positions and a curse, he turned around and stomped back to his track, shouting for them to get the gun into action.

First squad's leader was an older guy, balding, fat and black as an ace of spades. He stood with his arms crossed as the other squad leader stomped away and looked at Keren somberly.

Keren looked back. "Yeah?"

"How long we gonna stay?" the squad leader asked.

Keren shook his head in resignation. "The smart answer is until they," he said with another jerk of the chin towards the battalion, "have got it well and truly stuck in the horses. When they don't have any time to spare for a mortar unit that is running away."

The sergeant nodded his head. "In other words, we gonna run at the worst possible time." The statement was toneless.

Keren looked down at his shaking hands as they spun the board. "I've never been accused of being smart," he answered. "Stubborn, yeah. Stupid, yeah. A pain in the ass. Oh yeah. But not smart."

The sergeant smiled faintly and nodded his head. With that he started walking back to his track.

◆ CHAPTER 63 ◆

"Mr. President," said Captain Hadcraft, "this is stupid."

The commandeered Bradley Infantry Fighting Vehicle crabbed sideways as it fought its way up the road embankment. The platoon from the One Hundred Fifth Infantry Division had been reluctant to give up the vehicles. But the combination of a direct presidential order and a platoon of Armored Combat Suits had won out. Now the suits had transportation that was all-terrain to an even greater degree than the Suburbans they had started out in.

But that wasn't going to help a bit if they were overrun by an angry mob.

U.S. 29 and U.S. 50 on the north side of D.C. were being ruthlessly cleared of vehicles. Anyone who had not made it to the Beltway by this time was ordered out of their car, truck or van and the vehicle pushed to the side by dozerblade-mounted tanks. The refugees from this and the battles to the south were being trucked to parks around the Veterans' Hospital where a tent city was forming.

The Presidential Unit had been headed by the area when this came to the attention of the Commander in Chief. And he had ordered that they detour immediately.

The problem from the point of view of the Secret Service, and the Marines for that matter, was that the President's approval rating was not the highest at the moment. By a result of a direct presidential order, the United States had just lost more soldiers in a forty-eight–hour period than at any time in the last century. There was a formless anger about this that had already been observed on

503

the still-functioning Internet. What form it had was directed at the President. Add to this the anger of people forced from their homes and it meant a good chance these people would attack the Chief Executive.

The President turned the helmet over and over in his hands and finally shook his head. "Maybe. I've never been called smart. Stubborn, yes. A pain in the ass, yes. But not smart." He looked up at the Marine officer hunched forward on the crew seat. Bradleys were never designed to accommodate combat suits and it was obvious. The squad in this one was crammed in like sardines. He looked directly at where he figured the captain's eyes would be. "But these are my people. This is part of the job. Put it to you this way; when one of your soldiers is in the hospital, do you go see him?"

The suit was unmoving, but the President imagined there was a tiny change in the set of the arms. "Yeah."

"Same deal. And sometimes they're angry at you."

The captain turned his palms up in admission.

The President turned the helmet over in his hands again, watching as the mobile gel flowed and humped. It looked like something from a bad horror movie and he was supposed to put it on his head. "I gotta see these people. If I blast past them on my run to Camp David, it'll be a slap in the face this administration might never recover from." He looked up and his face hardened. "So tell the driver to head over there."

The refugees were a milling mass. Thousands of people, individuals and families, had been transported to the area by truck and bus and dropped on the golf course. A company of MPs was futilely trying to get the people sorted out and tents erected, but by and large the people stood, sat or walked around as they wished. The MP company commander had set aside a platoon for a reaction team and they occasionally had to enter the mass to break up fights or stop incipient riots. The management was becoming more and more like dealing with prisoners of war as time went on.

The Bradleys and Suburbans of the presidential caravan swung up Arnold's Drive towards the Soldiers' Home then pulled to a stop. Because all the Marines had not been able to fit in the Bradleys and SUVs, one squad had clamped onto the outside of the fighting vehicles. These individuals dropped to the ground before the tracks had stopped turning, their grav-guns dropping into place as they searched for threats.

The milling refugees had watched the caravan approach with mingled curiosity and trepidation. The Suburbans indicated that it might be a higher government official, although the usual limousine was missing. But the armored fighting vehicles, tanks to most of those watching, were a scary reminder that the government was not always a friend. Already treated as effective prisoners by the necessities of the situation, seeing heavier firepower, and especially the half-saint/half-demon Armored Combat warriors, was a mixed blessing. When the Marines lowered their weapons, searching for an exterior threat and not thinking about the effect on the civilians, the mob surged backward.

Newsies had swarmed to the refugee camps like flies to jam. It was apparent from several of their fellows' transmissions that reporting on the Posleen advance was tantamount to suicide. That being the case, the next best press was governmental incompetence and bullying. Since the "government" had not been able to instantaneously provide food and shelter for fifteen thousand refugees, it was obviously incompetent. Along with the deaths of nearly a hundred thousand soldiers in northern Virginia, this was proving to be a scoop of legendary proportions. Or so it appeared.

In the wake of the Posleen destruction of the satellites, most standard television signals had been lost. Although cable companies were scrambling to connect their networks back up through the Internet, most people had switched to the nationally mandated broadband for their primary media link.

While the regular media still had a significant share of that market, many viewers had become savvy enough with the still-developing medium that they were seeking out their own news venues.

Major "alternative" news sources were sustaining such massive loads that servers were failing left and right. However, enough of them remained up for the viewers at home to zero in on each individual's concept of "newsworthy." For once a major war was being sent into homes virtually unfettered.

Viewers had a choice of live feeds from Inter-Vehicle Information Systems that clearly indicated where the fighting was going on, or even live video from combat suits headed to or involved in the fighting. An encounter between First Battalion Five Hundred Eighth Mobile Infantry and a small landing outside Redmond, Washington had the highest audience rating in history, surpassing even the final hours of the Battle of Fredericksburg. The fact that it occurred at primetime had something to do with it.

And the highest rated "show" for the battle was not on any of the networks. The output of a website dedicated to Armed Forces news and issues was the most common "hit" on several major search engines for "combat news." This relatively minor website had nearly sixty million simultaneous connections for the full three hours of the battle. The entire event was "commentated" by text box overlays, unit descriptions and explanatory graphics.

The "commentator" was a former Army colonel who was too old, even with regen, to have been recalled. His expert analysis was compiled by a team of communication-savvy internet geeks, then interactively viewed by over a hundred million people in the United States alone. Not only did he determine in advance the precise outcome of the battle, he was correct within two suits of the total friendly casualties. The video was enhanced with audio clips from the battle and erudite commentary on the similarity to battles ranging back to the campaigns of Sargon. Sun Tzu was frequently quoted, leading to overloads in most of the search engines that had led to the site. And their primary advertiser, which was Barrett assault rifles, experienced the largest ordering frenzy any site had ever seen. They and all their linked sales outlets immediately went into terminal overload.

But the "major media" ignored these quiet inroads on their market share and continued to concentrate on the tactics that had worked for them in the past.

So when the crowd surged back from the Marine Guards, the reporters crowded in. The screams of the hysterical refugees, already driven to the brink of despair by the loss of their homes and the possessions that they had accumulated over the years, were faithfully broadcast across the world.

The Marine captain put his hand on the President's chest as the rest of the company deployed. "Not until it's safe," he growled. The President, still holding the hated helmet, just nodded his head. The sound of the plasteel armor slamming through the troop doors and the diesel engine overrode any note from outside. But a moment later the detail chief put his head in the door.

"Sir," he said, his face tight. He was in a dilemma. The crowd was about to turn into a riot and the only person who might stop that was the President. But by the same token, doing so would be nightmarishly dangerous.

Captain Hadcraft put his hand up to his helmet, then cursed. Since he had been on speaker it was faithfully reproduced. "Sir," he said, grabbing the President by the arm, "we got another problem."

The President ducked to keep from smashing his head on the troop door. The suit was already trying to adjust to his shape and style of movement, but occasionally it interpreted his sharp, precise movements as a command to jump. Fortunately that had not happened while he was in the crew compartment with his helmet off. Now it propelled him out and down the troop ramp in a near sprawl.

As he came around the back of the AFV it was immediately apparent what the problem was. He looked back and forth for a moment from the Marines with lowered weapons to the surging crowd and the news cameras.

"Christ," he whispered, "what else is going to go wrong?"

He thought for just a moment and the capacity for rapid and effective action that had stood him in good stead in his climb up the political ladder came to the fore.

"AID, the suit can act as an amplifier, right? Like that suit unit did on Diess?"

"Yes, sir."

"Okay, tell the damn Marines to raise their weapons." He dragged himself up onto the roof, unable to find the footholes he knew should be there.

He reached the top of the vehicle just as the Marines raised their weapons. He dropped the helmet, raised his hands and said, "Amplify."

"*My fellow Americans!*" were the words that boomed out of every suit at tremendous volume. The tornado of sound, the words and the familiar voice shocked the crowd from motion into inertia. The President put his hands on the hips of the suit and leaned forward. "*I came to see what I could do to* help!"

The President was in the midst of the crowd and the Secret Service was frantic. They could barely keep up with his rapidly moving suit as it shook hands and gave bone-crushing hugs. The smell of the crowd was completely different from any he had ever worked. It was not just the lack of baths. There was a stink of fear to them that was palpable along with the effect of not having latrines. Unless they got this camp under better control disease would begin breaking out. The thought of cholera and typhus in modern America was mind-boggling. Especially on the steps of a hospital.

"We're doing all we can," he said, nodding at another problem. He stopped at the sight of a mother with a sleeping child in her arms. The little boy had a large gash on the side of his head, only partially healed.

"Ma'am," said the chief executive carefully. The woman had her eyes closed, rocking back and forth. "Your son's hurt." There was no response as the woman continued rocking and the President looked over his shoulder. He didn't know what any of the suits were but surely the company had medical supplies. "Captain Hadcraft," he snapped as the Detail finally caught up with him through the press of the crowd.

"Sir."

"Do we have a medic?"

"You mean a corpsman, sir? No, they're not on our roster."

"Any medical equipment?"

"Just the suits, sir."

"Get in here," he finished, stepping towards the woman. "Ma'am?"

"Sir," cautioned Agent Rohrbach with a hand out to stop the executive as he stepped forward. The massive man reached out gently and touched the woman's arm.

The woman's eyes flew open and she hissed at the agent. "He's dead!" she spat. "Dead! Leave me alone! He's dead! Dead!"

The President and the agent both stepped back as the woman started to cry. "AID?" the President queried, "can you . . ."

"The child is not dead, sir," the device stated definitely. "His vital signs are not even bad. He does, however, appear to have some cranial damage." The sensors of the suits were better than an MRI at that range. "He is probably unconscious and in a coma. But not dead."

The crowd was pushing forward again to get a look at what was going on, and the reporters were forcing their way to the fore as Captain Hadcraft arrived. He didn't even ask a question, just stepped forward with an injector and caught both falling bodies. The mother was handed off to one of the Detail as he cradled the child to his chest and headed back to the tracks.

"Captain?" the President started to ask. The action had been so fast and smooth there had been no time for reaction and the suit was halfway back already.

"I'll take him to the VA hospital, sir. You get the situation stable."

The Commander in Chief shook his head and smiled. Having good subordinates was a treasure. The crowd was still pushing forward but there was enough room for a conversation. It would have been better to be up on something to be able to see more people and be seen but this appeared to be as good as it got.

He looked around and caught the eye of one woman who looked composed. "What do you need? Tents? They're here and more are coming. What else?" His stare was like a laser, daring her not to answer.

She looked startled for a moment then responded. "Food. Most of us have hardly any. And there are already fights over it. And we need more protection. It's like hell in here." Her eyes went wide at that and she looked around.

"Okay." He nodded. "I'm going to do something about that right now. But . . ." He looked around. He needed to address the crowd but there was no podium or stand or anything. "AID, I need to get higher."

"There is a way. I can simply lift you up on antigravity. However, it might be viewed negatively."

The President shook his head. Lifting himself up like Christ would not be a good image. "Well, I can't damn well stand on anyone's *shoulders*." The suit weighed half a ton and it was fully loaded with ammunition.

"If you wish I can reduce the effective weight of the suit to nearly zero. Then you could stand on Agent Rohrbach's shoulders. I also can stabilize it so that you don't fall over."

"Do it," the President said, catching Rohrbach's eye. "You heard?"

"Yep," said the burly former football player dubiously.

As he felt the weight come off, the President swarmed up on the agent's shoulders. The Detail surrounded their chief to keep the crowd from jostling him.

He looked around for a moment and decided that the only way to start was a joke. "*Hi, I'm from the government and I'm here to help you!*"

Some of the crowd looked nonplussed but there was actually a slight chuckle.

"Seriously," he continued, still amplified but not as loudly as the crowd stopped pushing forward. "Help is on the way. I, personally, am not leaving until it gets here. *But you need to help too!* There are tents over there that need setting up. I'll get more soldiers over here to help, but there's enough of you here that with a little organization you could have had them set up already.

"Food," he said and stopped. "AID?" The conversation was still amplified.

"Sir?"

"Is there a large mess unit available that can be diverted over here? One that is close?"

"Yes, sir. The primary supply company for the Thirty-Third Division is assembled less than four miles away."

The President looked out over the crowd. "I'll get them on the move over here. And other units to the other camps. You have given to your country your whole life and now is when you get some of your own back.

"But you have to *help*. Work together! Take care of each other! There's a hospital right over there," he said, gesturing over his shoulder. "If there's someone who is injured, help them get there. Let the strong aid the weak until we can rebuild and repair our lives!"

"When can we go *home*?" a voice floated out of the crowd. There was a rumble of discontent at that.

The President's face went grim. "I didn't want most of you to have to leave! So I made the biggest *screwup* in American history. *I am never going to do that again!* When forces are assembled and prepared we'll go home. When all the units are ready. When *we are damn well going to kick those Posleen bastards' asses* we will go home!" The cheer that raised was faint-hearted but the best that could be expected under the circumstances. He didn't bother to mention that most of the homes would probably have been destroyed. Those that did not have mines would be first looted, then demolished by the Posleen as they converted the area to their use.

"I screwed up big time," the politician admitted. "And as soon as there's a moment's peace I am going to submit myself to the Congress for impeachment."

The shock of that statement was so great that one news cameraman actually dropped his camera and several microphones were dropped.

"But until then, I'm going to hang on. I'm in contact with Generals Horner and Taylor. I don't know if you know it, but we've totally smashed the invasion in the south, using the tactics that were planned on before the landing. General Keeton and Twelfth Corps have done a tremendous job.

"But here in northern Virginia, the battle isn't over yet. We still have random landings going on and no real force in this area. So I'll stay here until more support arrives."

At that the Detail chief on whose shoulders he was standing began to curse quietly and fluently.

"According to plan I was headed to Camp David and then to a defense bunker," he admitted, shaking his head. "But seeing this, I can see where I'm really needed. Generals Horner and Taylor can run this battle without me joggling their elbow. After we've got this area squared away I'll go to the other camps to make sure they're okay."

He looked around the sea of uplifted faces one last time as the mob seemed to drink energy from him. The group was totally mixed. There might have been a few more black faces than others, but there were white men in suits next to black laborers, Hispanics next to Orientals, Hindus shoulder to shoulder with Pakistanis. In the face of the alien horror, little differences like Shiva versus Allah were temporarily forgotten.

And all of them were looking to him for the strength to make it though the bad times. Whatever mistakes he might have made, however bad it had been and would be, he was their President and he was standing by them in need. It was nearly worth a meal.

"Now I'm going to detail my Marines to show you how to get these tents set up and latrines dug. They'll be getting people to help.

Everyone is going to end up with a job. And every job is important. I've got to go get some supplies and support headed this way."

"We are *Americans*. Black, white, brown or yellow, we are the descendants of survivors! And we have proven again and again that we are the *toughest* people in the world because of it! Now is the time to *prove* that!" To the sounds of cheering he jumped down off the Detail chief's shoulders and shook his head.

"What a *screwed*-up situation," he whispered to the agent.

Rohrbach just rubbed a shoulder and frowned.

◆ CHAPTER 64 ◆

Alexandria, VA, United States of America, Sol III
0923 EDT October 11ᵗʰ, 2004 AD

Keren frowned as he tapped out a cancer stick. He lit the Pall Mall with a butane lighter and leaned back in the comfortable driver's seat of the Suburban. He had the plotting table balanced on the steering wheel, a fresh cup of really lousy coffee and a cigarette. It was as good as it got. Of course, that wasn't all that good.

"Those'll kill you," said Elgars in a quiet voice. She snapped the freshly cleaned AIW back together and gestured for him to pass over the pack. "Gimme."

Keren snorted and fished the pack back out.

Elgars looked for a car lighter but the Suburban had only an empty socket marked "12-Volt Power." The vehicle also had no ashtray and a cute little trash hamper now stuffed to overflowing with Meals Ready To Eat wrappers. Keren passed her the lighter and she lit the cigarette and propped her feet up where the windshield used to be.

"So," she said, getting her weapon laid across her lap just so. "What happens now?" She took a deep pull on the unfiltered cigarette and coughed wrackingly. "Aw, Jesus! That's awful!"

Keren blew out a cloud of blue smoke and laughed again. "Yeah, ain't it. Well, in a while the horses are gonna show up. And they'll call for fire," he said, gesturing towards the hilltop. "I've set up all the probable avenues of approach on this." He tapped the mortar plotting board. "When they call for fire, I'll tell the guns. They shoot the mortars, the bad guys die. Everybody who matters is happy."

"Uh-huh," said the soldier who had fought her way out of two bloody defeats. "And when the yellow bastards just keep coming?"

Keren took another puff, blew it out and propped one boot up in the shattered driver's window. "Well, then it gets interesting."

"*Mortars, what's your callsign?*"
Keren picked up the handset. "*Golf One One.*"
"*Golf One One, this is Third Regiment fire control. Adjust fire, over.*"
Keren shook his head and snorted.
"What?" Elgars asked, picking up her rifle. She had fallen into a cat nap in the fifteen minutes or so they had been waiting.
"Hang on," he chuckled and composed his voice. "*Roger, Third Regiment, adjust fire, out.*" He unkeyed the mike and snorted again. "They wanted to know our callsign, which is used to keep the 'enemy' from knowing what unit is calling. But they sent their own unit in the clear."
"Oh," she said and frowned. It was obvious she didn't think it was important.
"Elgars, *everybody* in an infantry unit should know correct radio procedure. It's basic infantry training. But they don't. What does that tell you?"
"Oh," she said again and nodded. "They don't know shit?" she guessed.
"Yeaaah," said Keren, nodding. "Makes this real damn interesting, don't it?"
"*Uhmmm,*" the radio said and was silent again. "*Golf . . .*" It went silent again.
"One One," offered Keren. "*Or just say, 'mortars.'* "
"*Golf One One, fire mission, over.*"
"*Go ahead.*"
"*The Posleen are at the intersection of Washington and Fifty. And there's more by the annex.*"
Keren shook his head. The humor, though, was gone.
"What?" said Elgars.
Keren keyed the radio. "*Roger, stand by.*" He spun the plotting board: "Could you try to find something called 'The Annex' on that map, please?" he asked Elgars.
He picked up the microphone for the gun frequency as she said, "There's something called the Navy Annex. It's over by the Pentagon."
"*Guns. Deflection two seven three seven, elevation eleven hundred, charge three. Four rounds.*" He dropped the radio and spun the board again. "Where by the Pentagon?"

The Posleen normal stared up at the symbol. It was not one of the familiar ones. There was the crossed projectile weapons; they were familiar and easy to deal with. There was the two-turreted building of the military technicians. There were orders to avoid that symbol at all times. This was a new one. It appeared to be picture of a world with some device on it and rope around the device. Perhaps it was a symbol of a group that chained the world. The normal looked over its shoulder towards its God King. That worthy ordered it to open the doors with a gesture of its crocodilian head.

C-9 was an atomic catalyst explosive. The President's Marine Guard Force had easy and unquestioned access to Galactic weaponry and explosives. They also were veterans of Barwhon and Diess. Since they were well aware that the Posleen first looted, then destroyed, most of the buildings they captured, they saw no reason not to advance the timetable. Well, the destruction timetable. And there was a whole lot of tradition attached to Henderson Hall. So there was no damn reason at all to give it to the horses. It just wasn't a Marine "thing."

Keren had discovered that there weren't many safer places than under the steering column of a Chevy Suburban. So when the white flash to his left transferred palpable heat to his skin, he dove for the floorboards.

The shockwaves from the series of triphammer micronuclear explosions rolled the Suburban over onto its top then back up onto its springs. Shaken, Keren took a moment to compose himself and make sure that the worst was over, then dragged himself up into his seat and looked to the south.

From the area where the Pentagon had been faintly visible a pall of smoke was rising. The trees across Arlington Hill had been stripped of most of their fall leaves and the tops of some of the southerly ones were sheared off. Several fires had started on the south edge of the hill.

He did a quick inventory to check the damage. One of the PRC-2000s, the one set to support the regiment, was smashed. The other had apparently jammed under one of the seats and physically survived. He'd check to see if it still transmitted in a minute.

The interior of the vehicle was trashed. All the personal gear that had accumulated in the back along with half-eaten meals, open drinks and other debris had been thoroughly mixed. On the other hand, it wasn't much worse than it had been before the explosion. There had been less spaghetti sauce on the royal blue headliner. But not much less.

Elgars was apparently alive. The soldier was braced against the door cradling her left wrist with an expression of agony on her face.

First things first. Elgars wasn't dripping blood, so finding out if they still had wheels was paramount. Keren turned the key and after a couple of cranks the engine caught. There was some blue smoke but all the gauges dropped into the green and the engine kept running. He cautiously put the Suburban into gear, but the grinding sounds were no worse than they had been.

He looked over at Elgars. "Broken or just sprained?" he asked.

"Broken, I think," she said through clenched teeth.

He nodded his head. "Hang tight for a couple of minutes." The last question was whether the radio would key. The blasts had looked like nukes, which meant Electro-Magnetic Pulse. EMP was supposed to destroy all electronics. But the truck had started, which came as a surprise. Now if the radio had just survived.

"*Guns, you there?*" he asked.

"*Roger, FDC. What the fuck was that?*" asked the sergeant from One Gun.

"*Dunno,*" answered Keren. "*Can anybody see any of the bridges?*"

"*Yeah,*" answered Three Gun. "*I can see the Arlington Bridge. It's still up.*"

"*Okay, I gotta switch freqs. I'll be right back. Is everybody okay?*"

"*We're here,*" answered One Gun.

"*For a while,*" Three added.

Keren switched frequencies to the regiment's and set the remaining radio for ease of switching back and forth. "*Regiment, this is Mortars, over.*" No response. He turned to Elgars. "Hang on a sec." He crawled into the back of the vehicle and started turning over the mass of rucksacks, clothing, candy wrappers and sleeping gear. After a few moments' search he found a medic's kit he had picked up on the retreat. In it, as expected, was an inflatable splint. A few moment's later he had Elgars' wrist splinted and was back on the radio.

"*Regiment, this is Mortars, over.*" He unkeyed the radio and took a deep breath. The fires on the hill were getting worse, the small blazes joining and catching the dry grasses of the graveyard. A few of the trees on the south side were smoldering as well. If it spread much farther they were going to have to leave, good timing or not.

"*Mortars, this is regiment,*" came another voice. The previous caller had clearly been young and extremely confused. This was an older voice, full of assurance.

"*Regiment, we have fires spreading towards our position. We will have to move soon. Do you need fire, over?*"

The bleak humor of the responder was clear. "*Mortars, we need a hell of a lot more support than you can give us. What's your ammo situation, over?*"

Keren didn't know who this person was, but it was a completely different cat than the colonel in command. "*Not so hot. We've got about fifty mortar rounds a track left and we're about out of Ma deuce.*"

"*Roger.*" There was a pause. "*Gimme a volley of twenty rounds of variable time per gun on the big twisty intersection right by the Marine Memorial. Seems the Marines didn't rig that for some strange reason. It's grid 1762-8974 if you're using a military map.*"

Keren's face split in a grin. "*Roger. But who the fuck is this?*"

"*Major Cummings. I'm the S-3.*"

"*Well, Major, nice to talk to a professional for a change. Stand by.*"

"*Yeah, likewise mortars,*" said Major Alfred Cummings, lowering the radio. Not that it was going to matter. Alpha Company was heavily engaged by the Posleen mass coming down from the north. In Andatha this would have been the time for a shower of artillery, cluster ammunition for preference. What really pissed him off was that he knew there were artillery units in range, but he didn't have the frequencies or codes to call for fire. Just another cock-up.

The post was supposed to be a sinecure. A comfortable unit for a company commander who had seen just a little too much combat. He and a few NCOs were there to add a tone of reality to the purely ceremonial guard force.

But now it was a different beast. The colonel had decided to make this stupid stand. Naturally, when the C-9 went off and the pressure went on, he didn't make the grade. Major Cummings had hated polluting this holy ground with that coward's blood, but he was sure the ghosts would approve. Some of the boys had run into the coffins as they dug in. Most were intact, but a few had spilled. He told them to dig on, dig on. The soldiers, sailors and Marines who were buried on this hill would have no argument with a little jostling. They understood.

And that boy on the radio had understood. The major could tell. That was a good troop. He smiled as he heard the crump of the mortars firing in the background. Only two tracks, which was a shame. Mortars were hell on the yellow devils.

"Sir," said Sergeant First Class Smale. "Them's mostly through Alpha Company. Bravo an' Charlie's holdin', and thems that's gonna stays from Delta, they's up at the Tomb."

"But we're being flanked."

"Yissir."

"Should we pull out?" he asked. It wasn't much of a test, the sergeant was another veteran.

"Nah, Major. Whut's da fuckin' point? Landin's right and left. Might as well die here as anywhere. Better than fuckin' Andatha." The NCO turned to the side and spat.

"Yep. But no reason to take everyone with us."

"*Golf One One, this is Echo Niner Four, over.*"

Keren picked up the mike as he carefully watched the hill to his west. "*Golf One One, over.*" It was the S-3 by the voice.

"*Golf One One, the explosions from the complex slowed the tourists down on that side. However, we are being pushed back to the north. We anticipate losing the bridge shortly. I recommend that you move out on completion of the fire mission.*"

Keren smiled and his eyes misted slightly. "*Roger, Echo Niner-Four.*" He wondered how to ask the next question. "*Will we have company?*"

The smile on the radio was evident. "*Not unless you're slow and our out of town visitors catch up. I think this is all the farther I'm gonna go.*"

Keren nodded. "*Well, there are worse places.*"

"*Roger, that, Golf, and I've been to most of them. Looks like only one to go.*"

Keren smiled. "*Roger, Echo. See you there. Golf One One out.*" He flipped frequencies. "Can you still use your rifle?" he asked Elgars. The private was white-faced with pain, but had the weapon trained towards the fire to the north.

"Yeah. When the hell are we getting out of here?" As she asked that there was a large but distant explosion to the southeast. "And what the hell was that?"

"Probably a bridge going. And we need to be across one before we're the main course." He keyed the mike again. "One Gun, how many left on that volley?"

"Just about done. We sort of lost track."

"Roger. Three?"

"That was the last."

"Roger. Button up and do the boogie. We've been waved off by the Regiment." At the words the Three Gun track jerked to life. The driver apparently did not think it necessary to take the gun out of action. Keren had never turned the Suburban off, so he put it into gear as well. One Gun still wasn't moving.

"One Gun, you mobile?"

"Roger." The track spat one more spiteful round skyward and lurched into movement. "We're outta here."

"Let's just hope the engineers know we're coming," whispered Elgars pessimistically.

◆ CHAPTER 65 ◆

Lieutenant Ryan was not lost. It was impossible to be lost on the Washington Mall. You always knew right where you were. What he did not know was where he and his platoon were supposed to be.

After Occoquan the platoon had been unable to find anyone in their chain of command. The trucks that had brought the rifle company to replace them had left immediately. Without transportation they had walked northward, hopping the occasional ride. Their target had been Belvoir; however, just short of their goal they were directed away by MPs and told to join the bits and tatters of units headed for Washington. They eventually found transportation but the bus drivers had no better idea of where they were supposed to be than anyone else.

By default they had ended up on the Mall. Most of the remnants of Ninth and Tenth Corps were there, electronic intelligence units without divisions, mess halls without battalions, the occasional artillery or infantry unit that had made it out of the rat-fuck to the south. There was no attempt at organization; units set up wherever they stopped.

Lieutenant Ryan parked the platoon near the D.C. War Memorial and sent Sergeant Leo out on a scrounging mission, hoping that he'd actually come back. The sergeant had and reported that anything anyone wanted was available, for a price. Since nobody had orders to release anything, the only way to get it was black market. There had been one mess hall that had set up, but it had run out of food in no time. Now it was cash on the barrelhead or go hungry.

However, Leo also reported that engineer units were on their way to rig the bridges for demolition. When they showed up the platoon might be able to attach themselves and at least get some rations.

Lieutenant Ryan passed around the hat for donations. After that was unsuccessful he and Sergeant Leo shook down each of the engineer privates individually. This time Lieutenant Ryan left Leo with the platoon and went out on his own. While he fully recognized that the older soldier could probably negotiate a better deal, that assumed that he came back with the rations.

Their combined two hundred dollars was enough to secure two cases of MREs. His Academy ring got them a heated tray meal. Water was still flowing in the city so that was no problem. As the platoon shared a tray of lasagna, the lieutenant pointed out that it was better than Ranger School. Within a day or so they should be able to find a unit to attach to so the food only had to last that long. Sergeant Leo pointed out that he had managed to *avoid* Ranger School at least three times.

The approaching sounds of battle had drawn many of the insanely curious towards the Potomac. But Lieutenant Ryan had drifted that way in hopes of finding the engineers who were sure to be rigging the Arlington Bridge. The MPs who were holding back the curious let him through without comment when they saw the engineer tab. He could see figures moving carefully along the bridge, stringing wire. It looked like about a platoon of engineers, and he knew he was almost home. There was a single figure leaning on a Humvee supervising the activity. Lieutenant Ryan walked up to him and saluted.

"Ryan, sir. Second Lieutenant, Corps of Engineers," he said to the officer.

The officer was a short, broad colonel smoking a cigar. He looked the lieutenant up and down for a moment and then took the cigar out of his mouth. "What can I do for you, Lieutenant?"

"Sir, my platoon apparently has been lost by higher. We were deployed from Belvoir and couldn't get back in. We're out of rations and don't know where to report." The young officer paused as if unsure how to go on. "I don't know what to do, sir. I'm not even through the basic course!" he ended on a rising note. He caught himself as he almost began to babble. Just because things were a little fucked-up was no reason for an academy graduate to lose control. It could always be worse.

The colonel took another puff on his cigar and regarded him evenly. "Where were you?"

The lieutenant misinterpreted the query. "We've been camped on the Mall, sir."

"No," said the colonel, flicking an ash. "Which bridge were you blowing? That's what all the Belvoir Boys were doing, right?"

"Oh. Yes, sir. My platoon was tasked with the Virginia 123 bridge at . . ."

"Occoquan."

"Yes, sir," the lieutenant finished lamely. "How'd you know?"

The colonel finally let a smile violate his face. "You're the 'Lost Platoon,' Lieutenant."

"Sir?"

"Where's the rest of your unit, Lieutenant?" asked the officer without answering either query.

"Back on the Mall," said the thoroughly confused lieutenant.

"Well, I'd offer you my Humvee, but you're just going to have to walk a little longer. Go find them and tell them to get their asses over here. I've got to get on the radio."

"Yes, sir," said the lieutenant. The colonel saluted in dismissal and the tired and still confused lieutenant started trudging back to the platoon's bivouac.

"*Castle Six this is Castle Five, over.*"

The officer who leaned in and snagged the microphone ahead of his RTO was a mountain. Nearly seven feet tall and proportionately broad, his uniforms required custom-tailoring from raw material. The crew-served M-60 machine gun slung across his back looked like a toy. "*Castle Five, this is Six actual, over.*" The voice was a deep, rich bass.

"*Six, we found the 'Lost Platoon', over.*"

The ebony face creased in a broad smile and the general gave a thumbs-up to the distant and unseeing colonel. "*Great! which one was it?*"

"*Ryan.*"

"*Well, the West Point Society is going to be pleased as punch to hear that.*"

The smile in the distant officer's voice was evident. "*Only the cream, boss.*"

"*Well, only the stuff that rises to the top,*" corrected the general, a graduate of a 'lesser' school. "*How's it going otherwise?*"

"*Pretty well. I'm gonna have to put those poor kids to work one more time, but we'll be ready.*"

"*Roger. We're about done laying in the champagne.*"

"*Sorry I'm gonna miss the party.*"

"So'm I. But we all must have the occasional sacrifice. Good luck, Tom. Out here."

The general looked around and smiled. Most of the forces that had been sent out to mine the bridges over the Occoquan had come back immediately. They had then been sent back out in a less harum-scarum fashion to prepare other sites for demolition and to establish fighting points. After those tasks were complete they again returned to their base at Fort Belvoir.

With the destruction of Ninth and Tenth Corps the general had put his personal plan for Ragnarok into place. The ammunition dumps of Fort Belvoir, filled once again for the training of recruits, had disgorged an amazing variety of explosives and mines.

Since he had at his disposal the equivalent of a brigade of Army Combat Engineers, he was determined that the Posleen would have a very hot reception. On the other hand, he was no fool and had no intention of being a hero. The force of trainees and their instructors were put to work turning Belvoir into mechanical hell.

Mining and booby-trapping is a matter of art. The point is not just to kill the enemy, but to frighten and shock them. Simple overwhelming force is usually the best bet. But with all the munitions and time available to them, the general felt that the "Home of the Engineers" could do a little better than that.

He dug out a computer program a nasty-minded engineer had come up with and tried it out. The program was called "Perfect Hell" and was a minefield design aid. It created a fiendish series of concentric self-activating fields. The purpose was to first suck a force in, then thoroughly trap it. Feed in an inventory of available materials and personnel and it spit out a design and a timetable.

He had run the available parameters and almost choked on the solution. It turned Belvoir into a nightmarish set of mine nets. The nice part about it was that it designed with the Posleen in mind. They could drive their forces right across the mine zone, but it would cost them thousands and thousands of "troops" to clear it that way. Of course, if he had to come back and take it out it would not be pretty. But that was another bridge.

He'd started the installation and the brigade had worked like demons. However, as each section was completed he sent the trainees down to the fort's marina, where they were ferried across the Potomac.

He now waited with a few remaining senior officers and NCOs. For the last hour they had talked about old times and watched the monitors that had been scattered along U.S. 1. He was currently outside getting a breath of air. But at a yell from inside the boat house he strode back in rapidly.

"They're in sight," said the Belvoir operations officer. The colonel was leaning forward, hand on the shoulder of the tech managing the monitors.

The general grabbed the back of the colonel's battle dress uniform and pulled him gently back. "You can't make 'em come on any faster. And that's practically the only private we've got. She's more important than any three of us."

The colonel shook himself and laughed deprecatingly. "Sorry, soldier," he said.

The tech nodded with a smile and switched screens. The new screen was from a sensor ball placed on the sign at the main entrance. The mine fields started just on the other side of the sign. The staff officers leaned forward like spectators waiting for a crash and the general had to laugh. The operations officer was actually washing his hands in anticipation.

"Sir," said Belvoir's sergeant major, keeping one eye on the screen, "I made a little foray on the officers' bar." The sergeant major held up two bottles of Moët & Chandon. "I thought we might want to toast the first blast. Or something."

The general laughed again. These guys were really getting into the spirit. "Sure, why not," he said then turned back to the screen at a gentle "Shit" from the operations officer.

The mass of Posleen on the screen had stopped. A single Posleen was forward of the rest and it had stopped cold fifty meters in front of the Main Post welcome sign. The mass of Posleen behind it was not a single company but thousands. They had been concentrating on the drive up the U.S. highway and now milled in front of the sign, shuffling back and forth and fidgeting.

A God King came forward and then another. Their alien saucers were drifting from side to side constantly, apparently to make it harder for snipers. Several of them gathered in front of the sign and appeared to engage in an argument. Slowly the saucers stopped moving back and forth as alien teeth were bared and crests lifted and fluffed.

Another one came forward, finally, who apparently was senior. This God King took one look at the sign and backed away. Much further away. It then called the other God Kings over and continued the discussion. Another argument ensued which was finally cut off by the senior God King. At his gesture most of the God Kings and their forces simply turned around and trotted back to the south away from the facility.

One leader was left with a single company. He watched the others retreat, then took a last glance over his shoulder and headed after them.

The jury-rigged control room in the boathouse was filled with stunned silence. The general leaned forward and tapped the tech on the shoulder. "Switch to U.S. 1 north," he said quietly.

There another force was trotting, a single company in the lead without a "point" individual. The God King was close to the front in the midst of the company and others were visible farther up the road. The company trotted down U.S. 1 to the main entrance and swung in. However, just as it neared the MP Post, which was where the booby traps started on this side, it too stopped, piling up in its haste. The God King came forward for a brief look and his crest went straight up in the air. He appeared to shout something and lifted his saucer out of ground-effect. Before the regular Posleen of his company could even get turned around, their leader was back on U.S. 1 and accelerating to the north.

The general was never sure where the laughter started. Some said it was the sergeant major. Some said it was the female technician's infectious giggle that set it off. Some insisted it was the deep, bass laugh of the United States Army's Engineer. Whoever started it, it turned out to be impossible to stop for nearly ten minutes as monitor after monitor showed untouched Posleen units in full retreat.

For years afterwards, in the midst of the worst of news, the few lucky souls who were in that control room could look at one another in brief encounters and crack the other up by a simple widening of the eye or a gesture of a crest lifted in total fear. Utter, total and abject fear. Of a twin-turreted castle. Of "Fort Belvoir, Home of the Engineer." Of the Sapper.

◆ CHAPTER 66 ◆

Washington, DC, United States of America, Sol III
1045 EDT October 11ᵗʰ, 2004 AD

"I think we shall stay well away from there," commented Kenallai. The notice had been ferreted out by one of Kenallurial's "Companions." With the fief of the military technicians finally neutralized, perhaps they would be fewer in number.

The crossed-rifle warriors were becoming more and more of a challenge, however. This last group, outnumbered and with pitiful weapons, had seriously mauled the oolt'ondar that assaulted them. Their last stand atop the hill had been worthy of song and there was still discussion as to which was the Kessentai. Given that there were more than enough thresh to be had, including many on foot that were yet untouched, they might declare the entire group piled on the monument at their center Kessentai and give them a single Kessanalt.

The place that they had stood made no sense. There was a fairly good shelter on the ridge, but it was well away from the monument they had chosen to cluster upon. And the entire ridge was covered in stones. He had set Kenallurial to determining the purpose of the ridge as he and Ardan'aath surveyed the problem to the east.

"So, old friend," he said, gesturing to the bridge below. It was still intact but they had learned what happened when they tried to cross one. "What shall we do?"

"That I know not," admitted the old oolt'ondai. "If we set claw on that structure it will take us to the *Fuscirt*."

"Yes," agreed Kenallai. "*Fuscirto uut* these 'sappers'!"

"I have, perhaps, two answers, edas'antai," said Kenallurial, drifting up silently from behind.

Ardan'aath turned away as Kenallai queried with a lifted crest. But the older Kessentai did not go so far as to not hear the suggestions of the younger.

"This place is a 'graveyard,' a place where certain of the thresh are placed after death."

Kenallai tilted his head to the side in query. "I don't understand."

"It was difficult for me to comprehend as well, edas'antai. However, instead of recycling their dead, the thresh apparently place them in boxes in the earth." He gestured at a headstone. "This lists who they were and when they lived."

"That is," the Kessentai wrinkled his snout in distaste, "that is disgusting."

The younger Kessentai lifted his crest in assent and snorted. "Nonetheless it appears to be the case. Furthermore, these in this place are not just thresh, they are all threshkreen."

At that Ardan'aath turned and looked at the serried rows of headstones drifting off in every direction. "Oh, *abat* shit," he whispered.

Kenallai looked at him questioningly. "What?"

"I will make you a bet. Most or all of them are not just threshkreen. I will bet you they are *Kessanalt*."

At those words both of the other Kessentai were flushed by combat hormones. Kessanalt was accorded to only the most potent, the bravest. To be surrounded by unrecycled souls of Kessanalt was like some nestling nightmare. At a visceral level they were suddenly surrounded by the larger and fiercer teeth that drove all the Posleen to become as secure as possible.

"*Fuscirto uut!*" said Kenallai. "First metal threshkreen. Then where the Kessanalt go to die. What is next?" he finished rhetorically. "You said you had two answers?"

"Yes, my edas'antai," Kenallurial agreed. "I perceive a possible way to capture the bridge."

"Ah!" exclaimed the oolt'ondai. "And will it work?"

"It might," admitted the younger Kessentai. He told them what it was.

Kenallai watched a descending ship as it headed to the other side of the river. If they did not make the crossing, the latecomers might make a bridgehead. He could call his Oolt'pos forward to make the crossing. But many of the large command ships had been destroyed doing just that and it would take precious time. No, better to try the crossing with his eson'antai's idea.

"Look at those *abat*," snorted Ardan'aath. "We do all the work and they come wandering in to take our prize."

"They are landing on the other side of the river, Ardan'aath,"

Kenallai retorted with a snort. "They seem to be landing in a *grat's nest* to me."

The sonic boom overhead was hardly noticeable after all the artillery and demolitions they had endured. But Keren still looked up.

"Oh, fuck," he said as the Suburban bounced across the torn grass to the south of Washington's Monument. The lawn had already been abused by various tracked and wheeled vehicles and was rutted and worn. They had seen the units scattered across the mall and the monuments area and wondered where the hell their assembly area was in the whole sea of tents, trucks and fighting vehicles.

"Just another lander," said Elgars. A couple of ibuprofen had apparently helped with the wrist.

"Yeah, but it's gonna land on some poor bastards who are gonna have to do something about it."

"You mean it's landing in a hornet's nest."

"Yeah. But it's gonna kill a bunch of hornets."

Sergeant Carter had never set up a squad tent in his entire military career. But, not surprisingly, the AID had precise directions. So, while one squad was laying out the grid for the tent city, he and his squad were showing a group of civilians how to set them up. The rest of the company was explaining field latrines in another area or standing guard. The guards were still by the Bradleys, rather than around the President, when the Posleen ship landed.

The ship slowed to practically zero and drifted, light as gossamer, over to Fifth Street. There it set down and dropped its ramp.

The crowd had started to panic at the first sonic boom. The now familiar sound went straight to the reptile hindbrain and triggered a flight. Unfortunately everyone had a different idea of which direction to run in and the result was a riot.

The riot stopped when the ship arrived. As the shadow drifted across, the mob noted distance and direction in its mob mind and headed the other way. The effect was to sweep the Detail along with it.

The President, on the other hand, in his half-ton battle armor was simply buffeted. Once he was knocked over as he stood his ground but as the crowd thinned he regained his feet.

The golf course between the Posleen ship and him was scattered with injured and dead from the panicked mob. Most of them were children or the old. As the ship drifted to the ground the President shook his head. He looked around at all the poor people who had been killed and injured in this last incident and put them squarely

County and nearly over the border into Arlington. They had spread up to the Potomac on the north side and were moving rapidly down the Beltway towards the crossing to the east of Arlington.

The movement was unconscious, but it was creating a pocket in the Arlington area. All the survivors were being pushed towards the downtown D.C. bridges, just as General Horner had anticipated.

"Agreed, Captain," responded the acting battalion commander. "Any more suggestions?"

"No, sir. Not at this time." The movement of the canisters was as fast as the AIDs could handle the information load. Not only did each suit have to be controlled, but the overall load had to be balanced among all the suits. The current speed of an average of eighty miles per hour was the fastest they could do. The alternative, exiting the containers and running, would be even slower. The maximum sustainable speed for suits was about forty miles per hour, if the roads were open.

The roads, however, were packed with military units and refugees. First Army was finally getting its combat power concentrated, with units flooding into the area of the Potomac from all over the northeast. Like the units of Ninth and Tenth Corps, most of the forces were undertrained and their equipment was in pitiful shape. But with any luck they would be fighting from fixed positions.

Mike glanced at the exterior view and his eyes narrowed. Somebody had had a rush of sense, and the lead units were mostly artillery. By the time they were in contact, there would be a mass of artillery available. Command and control, however, was spotty.

"But I'll figure something out. I'll get back to you soon, sir."

"Okay, Captain. We need a good plan if this is going to succeed."

"Roger, sir. Shelly," he continued, looking back at the feeds. "What are you getting from D.C.?"

"It's a bit of a dog's breakfast, sir," responded the AID.

Mike smiled. The device had been getting more and more attuned to human interaction, even starting to use some slang.

"There's a mishmash of units," she continued. "Some of them are ordered there, like the engineers that are rigging the bridges and the One-Oh-Fifth I-D. But most of them are from Ninth and Tenth Corps."

"Any sign of leadership?"

"There are small units that are coherent. But nothing over a company."

"Hmm. Bring up an appropriate scenario. Assume the Posleen take a bridge intact." If the Posleen did not take a bridge, the battalion could wait for Eighth Corps to get its act together, then cross the river at leisure to sting the Posleen. It was only if one of D.C.'s bridges fell that time would be critical.

"Is there a scenario in the can for this?" Mike thought there was, but there were so many developed "games" scenarios it was impossible to keep track.

"*Bridge over the River Die,*" responded the AID. "On the basis of probable Posleen numbers at contact and probable friendly support I would recommend responses for difficulty level six."

"Yeah," whispered the officer, reading the scenario as it scrolled down the left of his heads-up view. He remembered it now. He had gamed it at least three times. It wasn't one of his favorites, but it had some interesting surprises. The similarities to the current situation were remarkable. Even the buildings were similar; the writer of the scenario had clearly envisioned Washington as a target. That was not in the description and Mike had never noticed the similarities. But it was obvious now. "Who wrote it?"

"A teenager in Fredericksburg. Thomas Sunday, Junior."

"Oh. Damn." Fredericksburg was, of course, gone. What a waste of a good mind. The writer had obviously had a good grasp of suit tactics. Losing him this early in the game sucked. "Shit happens. Shelly, can this one. Set it to level eight. Now, what are we missing for an eighth-level response?"

"Command and Staff. A level of response of that difficulty requires everything to hit the ground running perfectly."

"What's the first and most obvious lack? Take them in order downward."

"Artillery command and control. We do not have a Fire-Support Team."

"Right. Who do we have in the battalion with significant fire control experience?"

"Besides yourself?" she asked dryly.

Mike rolled his eyes at the ceiling. *Save me from an AID with a sense of humor.* "Besides me."

"There are four NCOs in the battalion with fire control experience and one lieutenant."

"Who's the lieutenant?"

"Lieutenant Arnold, your mortar pl—"

"Pass," he said. "I want Arnold right where he is." *In case he has to take over from Nightingale.*

"Then one of the four NCO's."

"Who is senior?"

"An E-6 in Bravo Company. Staff Sergeant Duncan."

Mike wrinkled his face in the flexible gel. He was unable to place on his ledger. He could have ordered them dispersed, put into scattered and controlled groups. Then all those poor children who were lying broken on the ground wouldn't have been there. And if he had had the sense that God gave a donkey all the poor children who were scattered across Prince William County would still be alive.

He shook his head one last time and looked into the depths of the hated helmet. He really, really hoped that the gestalt knew what it was doing. He could feel it pulsing against his control and he was about ready to let it take over.

He put the helmet on and waited for it to open pockets over his eyes, nose and mouth before opening his eyes. "AID?"

"Sir?"

"When the first Posleen appears, begin taking your control from the gestalt."

"Yes, sir."

"I will attempt to not make distracting movements and sounds. However, if I move in a major way, AID, you follow Sergeant Martinez. Clear?"

"Clear," said the AID. There was a strong but complex surge from the gestalt. He took it as agreement.

He reached behind him and lowered the M-300 grav-rifle. As the heavy weapon dropped into place, a series of screens blossomed across his vision. The information was surprisingly comprehensible for a change. Range and bearing tracks crawled across as he shifted the weapon back and forth. A crack appeared at the top of the ship's deployment platform.

"Well, guys," he whispered to the electronic entities, "it is up to you. Do your President proud." At least he would be able to look his ghosts in the eye.

◆ CHAPTER 67 ◆

Washington, DC ,United States of America, Sol III
1046 EDT October 11ᵗʰ, 2004 AD

The gruff but friendly colonel had left, after ensuring that Ryan's platoon of trainees was firmly attached to the local force. He had been replaced by a much more dour captain. Lieutenant Ryan felt like he'd wandered into a play in the middle of act three. The colonel and the captain seemed to communicate in some sort of code. But he could tell that the captain was not pleased to make his acquaintance. His only comment was something to the effect of points for the WPPA.

Now, Lieutenant Ryan had not been in the Army long, but he knew what the "West Point Protective Association" was. Since it was normally invoked to save the career of a West Point graduate, he had to assume that he was in deeper shit than he thought over "losing" his platoon. The good work they had done at Occoquan had been forgotten, of course, and the only thing that would be remembered was that he had wandered around the Mall all day looking for a home. It didn't seem fair but, then again, the Army rarely was. All the "atta-boys" in the world were erased with one "oh-shit."

However, whether the captain liked him or not, Ryan felt it was his duty to point a few things out to him. So he screwed up his courage and approached.

"Sir?" he said, diffidently. The captain turned from where he had been surveying the work on the Arlington Bridge. The location was perfect for getting a good overview, since the back side of the Lincoln Memorial looked directly across the bridge. It did, however, have a few down sides.

"Yes, Lieutenant Ryan?" he asked in a supercilious tone. Captain Spitman was a tall, broad officer whose black eyes were piercing.

"I was just wondering, sir," said the lieutenant, hesitantly. He cleared his throat. "This location is ... sort of exposed." Some of the engineers on the deck had been blinded by the flashes of the Pentagon's destruction. It only highlighted how exposed the position was.

The captain's face tightened. It could just have been a question from a junior officer requesting greater knowledge, but the captain obviously took it as an attack. "And I suppose that that observation is from your mass of combat experience, Lieutenant?" he snarled.

The fact that the reaction was completely overboard was lost on the lieutenant. Ryan's first reaction, which he suppressed, was sarcastic. He wanted to say, *No, it's from having my head somewhere above my waistline.* The location *was* exposed. The first Posleen approaching the bridge would be looking right at them. And if they were even slightly on the ball they would shoot the shit out of this half-ass "command post."

But he controlled himself manfully. "No, sir. I was just wondering."

"This is the best location to control the rigging and detonation of the charges, Lieutenant. We have three separate methods of detonation leading to the command center. I would hate to have one of those out where anyone could blow up the bridge at whim. Furthermore, it permits me a clear view of approaching Posleen. Last but not least this is well beyond the standard range of engagement for Posleen forces."

The lieutenant nodded in agreement at this fatuous explanation. It immediately called to mind Law Seven of Murphy's Laws of War: *If the enemy is in range, so are you.* "Very well, sir. Thank you very much for that explanation. I was wondering, I have a few issues to discuss with my platoon sergeant. By your leave, sir?" He finished in a ritual request to be excused.

The captain grandly waved him away and went back to watching the last few wires being rigged into the circuit board. The bridge did indeed have three backup systems to drop it. One of the three would be guaranteed to work. Of course, they all terminated at the command post, so it was a point failure source. A minor item that had been glaringly obvious to the trainee lieutenant. A minor item that was pointed out in all the "how not to do it" parts of the manuals. But that had somehow completely escaped the engineer company commander.

✧　　✧　　✧

"*Echo Three Golf One One, this is Whiskey Four Delta One Five, over.*"

Keren glanced at the radio with a puzzled expression and handed the mike to Elgars as he pulled out his ANCD. The device was about to expire, and he had no idea where to find another.

The platoon had stopped on the back side of the Washington Monument mound. It put them hull-down to any Posleen at the level of the Potomac, but they were still in view of Arlington Hill. There were no more fireworks from the Hill, so he had to assume that the Old Guard major was raising one with absent companions. But, for the time being, the platoon was out of it.

They had set up with the guns ready to fire, and Keren had automatically laid them in and set up the plotting board, but now they were just resting. Eventually he was planning on finding somebody in the mass who had some idea what was going on. But for now he was content just to chill. They had done their bit and more.

So the radio call, an unknown station trying to log onto their net, was unexpected.

The ANCD listed the caller as the Fiftieth Division Artillery Fire Direction Center. But the hacking on the first day of battle made him cautious. He took the mike back from Elgars. She stepped out of the Suburban with a whispered, "Gotta go."

"*Whiskey Four Delta One Five, this is Echo Three Golf One One. Authenticate Victor Charlie, over.*" There was no such authentication line. It was a trick.

"*Golf One One, there is no such authentication, over,*" said the confused voice on the radio. On reflection the voice sounded a bit rote. It could be a very good voice processor and Keren was suddenly glad he had used the old trick.

"*Sure there is, Delta. Figure it out or get off my net.*"

There was a brief silence on the radio. Keren suddenly realized that Elgars was striding steadily towards a cluster of soldiers about seventy meters in front of the platoon. From the set of her shoulders there was a problem and as he watched she drew his 9mm Beretta out of her BDU cargo pocket. He had assumed from her words that she meant to find a latrine; that was obviously incorrect. He flipped frequencies.

"*Sergeant Chittock,*" he yelled. "*Get somebody out there to cover Elgars!*"

The private had walked into the midst of the group and up to a beefy soldier showing the admiring crowd his .50-caliber sniper rifle. As Keren looked on in horror she placed the barrel of his Beretta on the back of the soldier's head and thumbed back the hammer. It appeared that she was about to pull the trigger.

One of the group lunged towards her but stopped at a burst of overhead fire from the .50-caliber machine gun on Three Track. The heavy machine gun would chop the entire group into hamburger if the gunner dropped the barrel a few inches lower. The tracers drifted past Washington's Monument and towards the distant enemy.

By this time the crews from the two tracks were deployed and had their weapons out. The array of leveled rifles and grenade launchers convinced the crowd that making an issue of the lady's informal declaration of war would be inadvisable. Sergeant Chittock apparently talked Elgars into walking back to the Suburban. She was carrying on a continuous harangue directed at the now white-faced holder with the sniper rifle. Several of his former admirers were not looking so admiring.

Keren switched frequencies again as the milling crowd, herded by the platoon's weapons and covered by the two machine guns on the tracks, made its way towards the Suburban.

"*Whiskey Four Delta One Five, this is Echo Three Golf One One, over.*"

"*Golf One One, this is One Five,*" said a different voice than the previous. "*What is this authentication problem? And where have you been?*"

"*Delta, we got some shit going down here, sorry. Authenticate Victor Charlie or get off my net.*" Keren was rapidly tiring of the game but he was bound and determined not to get screwed by orders from nowhere again.

"*Echo Three Golf One One, this is Whiskey Four Delta One Fiver. I authenticate Khe-Mother-Fucking-San. Now are there any other stupid radio tricks you want to play?*"

Keren smiled. "*Negative Delta One Five, welcome to the net.*"

"*Roger, what is your position and status, over?*"

The group of individuals, covered by the rifles of the platoon, had nearly reached the Suburban. Sergeant Chittock was now carrying the sniper rifle and the Beretta. Things had definitely gotten interesting. Keren was spot-on for a bit of boring in the near future.

"*Delta, I'm going to have to put you on standby soon. We've got a personnel problem that has gotten out of hand. Our location is on the east side of the Washington Monument mound just short of Fifteenth Street. We're a one-twenty mortar platoon with two remaining tubes on tracks. We have approximately twenty rounds of H-E left per gun and some flares and Willi-Pete. We badly need resupply of diesel, beans and bullets. We've been in the goddamn last rank of the goddamn retreat since fucking Dale City and we are about done in. That is our status. Over.*"

"Roger, Golf One One," said the voice, cooly. *"Understood. We'll try to scrounge up some supplies for you. Get back to us when you're under control. Out."*

Keren nodded to the unseen fire center and flipped back to the platoon frequency. The confrontation outside had been reduced to fluent cursing on the part of the female soldier. Keren got out of the Suburban and lifted his palms in a calming gesture as Sergeant Chittock handed him his Beretta back. "Okay, one at a time. What the fuck just happened?"

"This son of a bitch . . ." "This lying cunt . . ." "She said he . . ."

Keren lifted the 9mm and fired it towards the Potomac. "I said one at a time. Sergeant Chittock?" He held the pistol barrel up and pointed downrange. If anyone was wondering why a Specialist Fourth Class was ordering around a sergeant, they weren't asking.

The sergeant's round and normally friendly face was creased in hard lines. "She says this is her rifle and that this soldier and some of his friends raped her an' took it off of her."

Keren thought about that. He had seen Elgars in several moods and easily rapable was not one. "Okay." He turned to Elgars and held up a finger in warning. "Calmly," he emphasized, "explain."

She took a deep breath and crossed her arms. "I was a sniper with the Thirty-Third. Bravo Company, Second Battalion Five-Ninety-First Infantry. We were in Third Brigade. My platoon got attached to the Twenty-First Cav in that rat-fuck at Dale City. I was on the west side when it all came apart. I ended up with these clowns." She jerked her thumb at the beefy specialist who had been holding the sniper rifle. "I don't know where the rest of them are, but he was with a truck unit. I stuck with them at Lake Jackson 'cause I didn't know where the fuck to go. He was always wanting to try my rifle and he tried to cop a feel a couple of times. I didn't think about it. That kind of shit happens all the time.

"Then when it came apart again, I had just decided to catch some rest. We were in the back of a truck headed up the road to Manassas." She paused and took a deep breath.

"I woke up with two of 'em holding me down and Pig-Breath here pulling down my pants. When the three of 'em were done they dumped me by the side of the road with that piece of shit rifle and *one fuckin' magazine.* I guess they thought we were the back side of the retreat." She took another deep breath. "Which was where you found me." She looked at Keren with eyes smoldering. "I want my fuckin' piece back and Pig-Breath charged! I'd prefer castrated, but I wanna stay out of Leavenworth myself."

Keren nodded at her when he was sure she was done and turned to the beefy specialist. He noted in passing that his nametag read "Pittets." It was obvious where Elgars had derived the name Pig-Breath.

"What do you have to say?" he asked evenly. He was ninety-nine percent certain that Elgars was telling the truth. But since for some ungodly reason everyone was looking to him for judgement, he had to be impartial.

"This cunt is lying," snarled the heavyset specialist, flexing his fists. "I'd never met her before she walked up and stuck a fuckin' gun to my head. She just wants my rifle, the bitch, and I can't believe you're letting her fuck me over like this!"

Sergeant Chittock grabbed Elgars by the collar of her BDUs just in time and got an elbow in the stomach for his pains. But she subsided after she realized who she'd hit.

Keren nodded again. He rubbed the stubble on his chin in thought and nodded a last time. "What's the serial number of the piece?" he asked Pittets.

The beefy specialist blinked a few times. "Why the hell would I memorize a serial number? I don't see what that . . ."

"BR 19784," Elgars hissed. "It stands for Barrett Rifles. And my initials are scratched on the bottom of the receiver pan. A-L-E." She smiled thinly. "If I've never met you, I've never met the rifle, right, Pig-Breath?"

Keren looked at Sergeant Chittock, who was searching the rifle for the serial number. He stopped, then looked up at Keren and nodded.

Keren's face tightened. He looked at Pittets. "Wrap him up with hundred-mile-an-hour tape and strap him to the side of One Track. We'll turn him over to proper authorities if we ever find them. If he makes too much noise, put a piece of tape over his fat mouth."

"Hey," shouted the specialist as willing hands dragged him towards the Mortar Carrier. "You can't do this! I've got rights . . ."

Elgars hefted the rifle and tried to support it with her broken left wrist. She grimaced and let the barrel drop.

"Well," said Keren with a grim expression. "You've got it again. What the hell are you going to do with it?"

She slid the butt to the ground and opened the bipod one-handed. "Well, first I'm gonna give 'im a good bath," she said. "Then I'm gonna zero 'im back in." She lowered it onto its bipod and sat crossleg alongside. "What I don't know is how I'm gonna reload the magazines."

"Well," said Keren with a faint smile. "I guess you're gonna need some help."

◆ CHAPTER 68 ◆

Washington, DC, United States Of America, Sol III
1048 EDT October 11th, 2004 AD

"Is there something we can do to help, L-T?" asked Sergeant Leo. The Old Man looked as despondent as the NCO had ever seen him. Even worse than when he thought they were gonna run out of chow.

The lieutenant sat on the steps of the Lincoln Memorial looking at the reflecting pool. It was another perfect fall day, as all these awful days of death and devastation had been. It was as if nature was laughing at them all for their silly games of war. The only effect of the kinetic bombardments, so far, had been to make for some spectacular sunsets and sunrises.

Lieutenant Ryan had chosen the perfect spot to capture the reflection of the Monument in the water. He was vacillating between hysteria and depression, both riding on a knife edge. He was an academy graduate whose first professional responsibility had, from his point of view, gone better than anyone had any right to expect. Lucking onto the *Missouri* had permitted him to slaughter the Posleen. And his platoon had performed like veterans under fire.

So they got lost from their unit. It wasn't their fault. There wasn't a unit to rejoin. So now they were talking behind his back about how the WPPA was going to have to recover his career. After turning most of a division of Posleen into paste.

And now this.

He'd only been in combat for a few days, but he felt he'd developed a "gut." And his gut call was that the Posleen were gonna wipe out the only controller for the demolition charges. That meant that they would capture the bridge. At that point the fucked-up units on the Mall would shatter like glass. And the Posleen would own America's core.

Losing the Mall would cut the heart out of the States. Hell, it would have a major effect on the expeditionary forces. Americans complained about their government all the time, but that was not the same as hating the symbols on this historic piece of ground. And all because a single stupid officer wouldn't pay attention to what a manual, an experienced junior officer and good common sense told him.

But Ryan was an officer. And a professional officer at that, a product of the long, gray line.

"I'm fine, Sergeant." He stood up and took a deep breath. There was a hint of smoke smell from the fires to the south where the Marines had mined the Pentagon with micronukes. He fixed what he thought was an expression of reserved contemplation on his face.

I was right, thought Leo, *we're fucked*. The last time the L-T had gotten that constipated-possum look was just before they latched on to the *Mo* and got all the fire-support any rational human being could want.

Leo knew what was bothering the L-T and agreed. He was, after all, a demolition *instructor*. And the captain was totally fucked-up. When the L-T mined the 123 bridge, Leo had been ready to help on the design. But the L-T figured just the right amount of demo and not only had three ways to blast, but different firing points for all three. That was way over the limit to conservative, but the Old Man was a belt-and-suspenders kind of guy. Which was just fine by an NCO missing two fingers from his left hand. Cutting corners around demo was a baaad idea.

"How are the men?" the lieutenant asked. He stopped whatever he was going to say next and his breathing deepened as he dropped into thought.

Leo cocked his head to the side. "They're fine, sir. We got a resupply of chow and ammo. Hell, we even managed to scrounge some wheels." He leaned over to look at the officer who had suddenly stopped paying attention. "Sir?" He looked the way the L-T was looking but all he could see was the reflecting pool and the Monument.

The lieutenant closed his eyes for a moment, then they flew open. "Get them up here," he snapped. "Full loadout. Now!"

"Yes, sir!" said the sergeant and started trotting down the steps before he wondered why. But he continued on. The Old Man was nobody to cross.

The lieutenant strode across the echoing room dedicated to either the greatest humanist or the greatest tyrant in American history, take your pick, and stopped at an innocuous side door. He had visited the Memorial as a kid and wondered where it went. Someone had already shot the lock off and he stepped into the small room beyond. The staircase he had fully expected to see dropped into the stygian depths and he smiled. Fuck with his country would they? Fuck with *engineers* would they?

The last of the platoon was starting down the stairway when the first gout of plasma slammed into the Memorial.

The wash of ionized deuterium caused the marble face of the Memorial to sublime. The gaseous carbon mixed with the carbon from the squad on the portico and was blown away in the wind from the superheated air. The flight of God Kings was at first unnoticed, but the rapidly approaching saucers could be seen all along the Mall as their cannons continued to wash the area between the Memorial and the bridge.

Kenallurial shouted in pure joy as his *tenar* flared out. So this was the *te'naal* battle madness that was spoken of. He felt whole for once, concentrated wholly on the task. The thresh burned beneath his guns, and that was good. The far side of the bridge was taken and the hated military technicians had been overcome for once. He detached Arnata'dra to begin clearing the demolitions as he charged the huge building.

There did not seem to be an entrance on this side, but that was no barrier. He floated the *tenar* up to the level where the hated technicians had been set up and landed. There was no sign of their devices, but wires still lingered, melted to the face of the rock in places or dangling on the ground. Without knowing their purpose he was loath to touch them; that was Arnata'dra's province.

He raised his talons in triumph. Let Ardan'aath belittle this accomplishment. A bridge across the river was in the hands of the Host. Let the thresh despair.

◆ CHAPTER 69 ◆

So this is despair. Jack Horner looked at the two messages in the light from the hatch of the swaying Bradley. The ACS battalion was at the intersection of U.S. 1 and Capitol Avenue. They were barely ten blocks from where the President was under attack.

They had been planning on leaving their canisters when they were almost at the Mall. The incoming lander, however, had forced them to ground. Once they were on the ground they were not a target to the lander, but anything flying was fair game. They were assembling even as he read the conflicting messages. If he sent them north to the refugee camp that was under attack they would still not be able to save the President, who was probably already dead. They might be able to save a few more civilians, but the President's Guard was probably going to do the job just fine.

So that meant south. But by the time they got there the Posleen were going to be deployed. Which meant that most likely the battalion would be overrun just like those poor bastards at Lake Jackson. It was precisely the sort of place where he had told his subordinates to use regular forces to stop the Posleen, not the ACS. The suits were a finite resource. He should use the Hundred and Fifth to try to stem the tide. Using the ACS would be the wrong strategic decision.

But the Hundred and Fifth wouldn't stop the crossing. They were weak as a twig even with the "band of heroes" that he could throw in. They would break just like the other units; you can't stiffen a bucket of spit with a handful of buckshot. And then the Posleen would be across the Potomac. And that meant backing up to the

Susquehanna. And ceding Maryland and Delaware to the Posleen. And
the Washington Mall. When it came right down to it, it was the
battalion or the monument. And he just could not make the professional choice.

He shook his head and tapped his AID. "Nag, get me Major Givens
of the ACS."

Mike watched Major Givens giving unseen thumbs-up signs as he
tapped one armored boot on the ground. O'Neal had six different
battle maps up on his display and the lander to the north, President
or no President, was not the problem. Standing around and discussing
it was just making it harder. He popped off his helmet, clamped it
to his side and took a whiff. The one thing the suits did not replicate well was smell. There was a hit of wood smoke from the mess
around the mall. Some less savory burning smells in there as well.
Probably the Pentagon. And the slight waft, even from here, of
unwashed humanity. Soon, soon, there would be the stench of slaughtered Posleen. Or his name wasn't Michael Leonidas O'Neal.

There was no room for failure; the choice was success or the
ferryman. He inhaled the last fresh air he was going to smell for a
while and felt his center finally click into place. No doubt. No fear.
No failure. He'd sworn it on the graves of his dead.

"Captain O'Neal," Major Givens finally said, cutting him in on the
conversation, "we have two problems."

"The Marines can handle the refugees, sirs," Mike said, cutting him
off abruptly. "We need to get to the Mall. Now." He opened up a
belt pouch and extracted a can of Skoal. The transceiver in the helmet
seal broadcast his words faithfully.

"Mike," said General Horner. "They're going to be spread out . . ."

"Not a problem," he said shortly, taking one gauntlet off and
clamping it onto the outside of his suit.

"Mike . . ." said General Horner over the circuit.

"Jack. Do *not* tell us our job. We don't have time for this." He
tamped the can down hard and turned his head to the side to listen. The firing to the north, felt and heard in the background, reached
a crescendo and died away as a large number of grav-guns opened
fire. It sounded as if they were finally clear of an intervening obstacle.
And as if the users were very, very angry.

"Captain . . ." Major Givens said.

"No," interrupted General Horner quietly. "Major, the captain is
the expert. If he says let's go, then you better go."

"We have . . . fourteen seconds to continue this conversation," said
Mike stonily, with a glance at a projected hologram. He had

programmed the time he thought it would take the Posleen to get assembled into a countdown timer along with the minimum time to make the movement. The battalion was ready. All they needed was the word.

No doubt. He'd gamed this a thousand times before. It would work.

The suits were also useless for pinching snuff. He popped the can with his left hand and pulled out a pinch. "General Horner," he continued formally, "Fleet Strike is *not* giving Washington to the Posleen."

No fear. They were invincible. The Posleen would kill individuals. But as a unit, the only way to fail was to fail to try. This was a strightforward "Horatio at the Bridge" action. He had forty scenarios prepared. Any of them would work.

"General?" asked the acting commander. The officer was used to clear plans developed in advance. While he could change them on the fly to an extent, he was not a "seat of the pants" warrior. He found himself simultaneously in command and out of his depth. It was a most uncomfortable feeling.

"Do it," said Horner. He had no idea what the plan was. But he knew Mike O'Neal. If Mighty Mite said the sky was green, Horner would double-check the forecast and then get a second opinion before doubting him.

"Okay, Captain O'Neal," said the commander, "what's the plan?"

"I'll have to tell you on the way, Major," said O'Neal. "We haven't got any time at all." He then belied his own words by inserting the pinch between his cheek and gum. He carefully closed the can and put it away, then reclamped the gauntlet and helmet. He spit out a few stray bits of tobacco and keyed the frequency to the battalion broadcast.

No failure. He hadn't *read* the book, he'd *written* it. "Okay boys and girls. Lets go kill us some E-Ts."

"Man," snarled Keren, "it seems like we never have any time together. All we've been doin' is killing Posties!" He helped Elgars up and got the big rifle hoisted over her shoulder.

"Well," she smiled grimly, "maybe later."

"Sure." Like there was going to be a later. He could see the Posleen pouring across the bridge and the God Kings popping up and flitting around the Memorial. The whole damn pack of demons was over the river and all hell was out for noon.

Elgars trotted towards the Monument, supporting the weight of the bouncing rifle with her right hand. Keren shook his head one more time and headed for the Suburban. He was glad she finally got her gun back. He suddenly realized he'd never even found out her first name.

A blast of fire came from the area of the Memorial, but he never paid it any attention.

The area under the Memorial was not exactly a warren of tunnels, but it bade a fair resemblance. And, as the Posleen were discovering, engineers above ground were nothing compared to engineers in tunnels.

The ball bearings from the claymore bounced off the walls and ceiling of the stone-lined tunnel and tore the front rank of the assault apart. A few tossed grenades finished off the rest and the engineers lunged forward to retake their positions. The first private in kicked closed the brass-fitted door at the end of the corridor and threw the bolt.

"Set the charges!" shouted Sergeant Leo, spooling out the wire and preparing the blasting caps. "Move! Move!" He handed one to each of the chosen privates as they emplaced the charges to blow the tunnel. These young men, and one woman, had experienced a crash course in demolitions over the last three days. The survivors had become experts.

He rounded the corner and nearly ran into the L-T and the security team. The security team held everyone that, in Sergeant Leo's opinion, really needed to become a rifleman. They were the survivors who had not learned the lessons of demo adequately. They were used for support of the "real" sappers. Leo intended to suggest each one of them get a small medal then send them over to the infantry.

"We've got the corridor secure," said Lieutenant Ryan, gesturing over his shoulder. "Once you blow that tunnel, there's only one way in and one way out. And they'll have to dig us out."

"Well, we're about done," said Sergeant Leo as the sappers came around the corner. He counted each one past then leaned around the corner for a visual check. The look drew a violent response as flechettes spanged off the rock walls and ricocheted down the side tunnel. There was a cry of pain from one of the engineers as a ricochet caught him in the thigh.

"*Fire in the hole!*" shouted Leo as he twisted the hand-dynamo generator up to speed then pressed the firing switch.

There was a blast of heat and a wash of marble dust. As the platoon coughed on the dust there came a complicated sound of settling from overhead.

"Uh-oh," said one of the privates, quietly.

"Yeah," said Lieutenant Ryan. "I think we might be in a little trouble here."

Elgars's jaw dropped as the statue of Lincoln in the distance settled slightly to the left. "Holy shit." But that was only one bad sight among many.

The area around the Memorial was rapidly filling up with Posleen. The assaulting God Kings had been joined by their units and the forces were deploying outward, opening the wings of the Host to capture the city. Starting with the Memorials.

She filtered out the shouting and sounds of panic behind her and set the familiar stock into her shoulder. It was a long shot up the entire length of the reflecting pool. The laser range finder gave a reading of forty-two hundred feet to the steps of the Memorial. As she shifted her sights to the side, trying to decide which one of the God Kings to gift with her attention, there was another gout of dust and fire from the interior of the monument. At least one other group was willing to fight. Behind her she could hear the fading engines of those either smarter or more cowardly.

"I am didee-mao, asshole!" snarled the specialist in charge of the Three Gun track. The driver put words to action, backing out of their position and spinning the track in a shower of carefully tended turf.

Keren stepped up to the spinning treads, daring to be churned into paste. "Austin!" he shouted.

As the specialist turned to look, a grenade came flying through the air and landed in the crew compartment in the rear.

Trailing blue air, the gunner and ammo bearer dove out of the compartment, falling to the ground in a heap. The driver took her foot off the gas and piled out as well, as the heavy-set squad leader tried to struggle out of the TC's hatch.

The assistant gunner had been deep in the belly of the beast when the grenade came flying into the compartment and rolled to the front. With nowhere to go he picked it up in the vain hope of throwing it back out. And howled in rage.

"*The fuckin' pin's still in!*" he shouted swarming up the side of the crew compartment bent on killing a café au lait gadfly.

He was met at the edge of the compartment by a cocked Beretta. Keren punched the barrel of the gun into his nose hard enough to draw a spurt of blood and followed his tumbling body into the interior of the track.

Austin tried to train the .50-caliber machine gun to bear on the raging Keren. But the pintle mount was designed to prevent accidents just like that. Keren kicked the squirming assistant gunner in the crotch, turned and triggered a single round into the squad leader's face.

It was a shot he never could have made on a range. The bullet entered just below the squad leader's nose. The top of the specialist's head was lifted up into the air in a spray of blood and brains. He slumped backwards over the front of the Mortar Carrier and landed on the still-quivering driver.

Keren pulled himself up on the top of the Mortar Carrier and pointed the pistol at the gunner and ammo bearer just starting to get up from their crumpled heaps.

"You will get into this vehicle," he shouted. "And you will lay in the fuckin' gun! Or I will personally kill every one of you sons of bitches! Is that clear?!"

"The fuckin' horses are over the river!" the gunner shouted, then looked at the unwavering pistol. He wondered where Austin was. Then he saw the faint trail of smoke from the barrel and made a rapid guess.

"*I am not giving the horses the goddamn monument!*" screamed Keren, leaping off the track and striding over to shove the still-warm gun into the face of the recalcitrant gunner. "*We have run and run and run and we are not going to run anymore! Are we clear on that? Or do you need the same lesson?!*" The barrel intersected the cheek-bone of the gunner hard enough to leave a bone bruise. The gunner closed his eyes as urine trickled to darken his BDUs.

The ammo bearer raised one shaking hand to wave at the pistol. "We . . . we're clear. Okay?"

Keren jerked up and strode to the front. The slight specialist pulled the driver out from under the former squad leader with a single jerk. The female private was stuttering and shaking uncontrollably. Keren shook his head and dragged her back to where the gunner and ammo bearer were just starting to regain their feet.

"Get . . . the . . . gun . . . laid . . . in. Now. And don't *ever* try to cross me again."

The gunner nodded as the specialist strode away.

The ammo bearer shook herself and hissed. "We could shoot up that piece-of-shit Suburban. See it make it through some Ma-Deuce fire!"

The gunner slapped her across the back of the head so hard it knocked her to the ground. He sucked his knuckles and kicked her. "Don't even *think* about it. What if he *lived*? And One Gun would eat us alive. Now get in the fuckin' track."

As Keren strode towards the Suburban he noticed that One Track had been watching the whole show. Sergeant Chittock was on the .50 caliber and the weapon was pointed more or less towards the Three Gun track.

"*Point it that way!*" he raged, pointing towards the Potomac, "*and get ready to fire the gun!*"

Chittock just watched him as he headed to the SUV. The rest of the crew flew to getting the weapon trained towards the enemy; nobody was going to get in the way of the sulphurous specialist. As Keren reached the truck Sergeant Chittock caught his eye with a lifted chin. The specialist stopped and looked towards him with fury in his eyes. But Chittock just saluted, very precisely. Keren stopped and nodded. Then returned the salute, just as precisely. As he stepped into the truck he realized that the stench of urine he was trailing was not from the gunner of Three Track. *We're all fuckin' cowards,* he thought. And picked up the firing board.

◆ CHAPTER 70 ◆

Washington, DC, United States of America, Sol III
1053 EDT October 11th, 2004 AD

The private bit her lip and caressed the unfamiliar rifle on her lap. There was still a shortage of the Advanced Infantry Weapon, so rear area units were issued the venerable M-16A2. She had shot it in the abbreviated basic course, but once she reached her permanent post the situation was so messed up the chain of command was not about to let soldiers have weapons. So the first time she had actually had one in her hand since basic was three days before, when the ammo supply unit scrambled out of Fort Indiantown Gap.

She looked at the selector now and considered her options. There was the easy one, which was to go along with the actions of the driver. That made a lot of sense, really. Who the hell wanted to drive a truck full of ammunition *towards* Posleen.

But then there was the fact that they'd been ordered to go resupply a mortar unit by the Washington Monument. The platoon had shot out all their ammo, which meant they'd at least been fighting. And they were probably still there, whatever Lee thought.

Let's see, she thought. *How hard can it be. It says "semi" right there.*

"Turn around," she whispered. The voice was barely audible over the scream from the overstressed engine of the five-ton truck.

"What?" snarled Private Lee. The stupid bitch was always whispering shit. Just like she never pulled her goddamn weight when they were unloading. He'd thought half a dozen times about dropping her off as a present for the fuckin' horses. One of these days...

"Turn around." The voice was a bare whisper again, but something

544

about the quiet click as the rifle was taken off safe penetrated the thunder of the engine.

Lee turned to look at her with disbelief in his eyes. "Are you fuckin' *nuts*? Point that goddamn thing somewhere else before I make you eat it, cunt!"

The slightly built private looked like she had swallowed a lemon. Her mouth was dry with fear, but she slowly lifted the rifle until it was pointed at the temple of the driver and snuggled it into her shoulder. Take a breath and let it out, just like the drill instructor said.

With a jerk she pointed it to the side and shot out the driver's side window. The blast from the rifle tore the glasses off the driver's face and peppered his face with burns. "*Turn us the fuck around, you bastard,*" she screamed, "*or I will spread your brains all over this cab.*"

As the truck rocked through a U-turn she felt that that was insufficient. "*There, was that loud enough for you? Asshole!*"

There was a snort of diesel behind Elgars as a Bradley troop carrier spun around and started disgorging troops. The squad spread out down the mound, using the reverse of the gentle slope for cover. The guy in the lead was real young for a lieutenant colonel, but as he dropped to the ground not far away she saw he was wearing a dress uniform Combat Infantryman's Badge with two stars. Either the "fresh-faced" kid had been in three wars already and was working on his fourth or he was a "PX Ranger." From the calm expression on his face and the expert way he surveyed the battlefield she was fairly certain which one it was.

The Bradley spun on its axis again and moved to the other side of the Monument, well away from the squad. The mound was just a bit higher than the top of the vehicle but that was no problem. The barrel of the Bushmaster cannon canted upward and fired a burst of tracers.

Elgars watched with glee as the rounds drifted up and then down, splashing without particular note into the Potomac. She nodded her head as the lieutenant colonel "squad leader" whispered into a radio, directing the fire of the gun.

"Hey!" she called, catching his eye. "Those mortar tracks behind us are on sixty-three-seventy!"

He grinned and gave her a thumbs-up then started switching frequencies.

There was a *thonk!* from the rear and she realized that a 60mm mortar team had set up right behind her. The squad leader, another "fresh-faced kid" with master sergeant's chevrons, was lifting his head up to spot the fall of the shot then adjusting with hand and arm signals. It was the crudest of fire control, but with the mass of Posleen forming on the sward it was effective. Elgars saw a splash of Posleen thrown away from the fall of the one-pound shot and nodded in satisfaction.

At least she wasn't gonna die alone. She could see more people moving up to the mound, many of them obvious rejuvs by their rank and assurance but others just simple soldiers responding to the threat to the nation's soul. She understood the call. As screwed up as her life had been, she was still an American. And the thought of the Posleen taking the White House, or the Capitol or even the stupid Monument was just more than she was willing to accept.

If she fired at a God King without more covering fire she was doomed. But maybe if she didn't fire at a God King? Just one of the "normals?" She had to re-zero the damn thing somehow. She used the splinted forearm to support herself as she took a calming breath.

"Duncan?"

"Yeah, boss?" the NCO responded, his breathing deep and regular.

Certain anomalies of armored combat suits had modified long-standing military practices. One of them was the ubiquitous "jody" calls, chants paced to a running or marching beat. When ACS units ran, it was at a long open lope, the rhythm of which had so far resisted every attempted choreography. The standard ACS "double time" was approximately a four-and-half–count beat that carried the unit forward at nearly thirty miles per hour.

What had been discovered, however, was that certain popular music, especially "hard" seventies and eighties rock and roll and the rhythm-similar "raker" rock of the turn years fitted the pattern with remarkable congruity. Thus, units usually pumped one or the other type of music through to the personnel, helping to set the running beat. A fair simulation is to imagine listening to "Thunder Road" by Bruce Springsteen while running on the moon. Long-forgotten, and in many cases dead, artists were staging a quiet comeback among Armored Combat Suit units.

Although the physical strain was lower than a standard training run, it was fairly equivalent to a "long slow distance run." A well-trained unit in peak shape could generally sustain the pace for two to three hours. This gave the ACS an approximately sixty-mile range using the same technique, the difference being that a unit doing a "long slow distance run" usually did it in PT uniform, whereas the ACS did the same thing in battle armor.

This time the movement was a relatively short distance. The battalion, less Bravo Company, was in a four-column formation, running down Seventh Street in Downtown D.C. to the beat of Heart's "Crazy on You." All Duncan had to worry about was coordinating two corps' worth of artillery while doing it.

"Status." The voice on the other end was cold and distant. Mighty Mite was obviously in his prebattle trance.

"Up." It was not that the run was taking away air. This was barely breaking a sweat. But that was all the Old Man needed to know. It was all he wanted to know.

"How much?"

Well, usually. "Three battalions of One-Five-Five and scattered mortars."

There was no answer and Duncan realized that the Man was gone. It was just as well. The tubes were there, but he was still slamming out the plan, his fingers flying across a virtual map. Each of the units that had responded positively was available for fire as an icon along one side of the map. Dragging an icon onto the target point called up a dialogue asking for fire type and quantity. After the first the others called on the same locations took the first as a default. It was a simple method of developing a fire plan, but the complex plan the Old Man had laid out called for several separate fire plans with contingencies. Setting it up was taking time but he kept slamming it out. To the sound of the drums.

"Gunny."

"Yes, sir." The NCO angled across the formation as they passed the MCI building. He accelerated ahead, driving the pace and elongating his stride to get to the front. He pushed it up to nearly fifty miles an hour down the nearly empty street. An advance party of real runners had moved ahead to seal the Mall end, preventing a general retreat up the route. But he had to get to the Mall ahead of the battalion. He needed to have a heart-to-heart with a couple of units. Sergeant First Class Clarke had done wonders getting the cluster fuck on the Mall organized, but that was just organization. Some of the units were willing to stand and fight. But most were running again. He was zeroing in on a few that were critical to the plan. If he couldn't get them to stand and deliver the Old Man might as well throw in the towel.

"Status." The captain was at level four again. It wasn't like anybody had to protect him or keep him from tripping over the curb, he reacted faster in a trance than when he was "here." But it was mildly unsettling to hear a voice with no more emotion than a new AID.

"Coming along. They don't want to deploy forward."

"Push it. Get some units to the Watergate. Any units. Stat."

Pappas swallowed the sigh. "Yes, sir." There was no point arguing; he knew the plan and the requirements. But *doing* the plan was something else. He put one foot down on the hood of a Mercedes and soared off it, pushing the speed up even further. If he was going to get somebody to the Gate, he had to step on it. It was going to take direct, personal attention. The fucking Mall was a mess. The Posleen were organized and ready to roll. It was gonna be a slaughter.

Ardan'aath snarled. "This puny bridge is creating a total hash of our units! The entire host is pushing forward without any control! It will take forever to sort out." He drifted his *tenar* to the side, watching his junior Kessentai trying to reform the oolt'ondar. His own oolt'os were somewhere in the mess as well, but they would find him. Most had been with him through worlds. They would find him in Hell.

"Well, at least we *have* a bridge," said Kenallurial, blowing a snort.

Kenallai raised his crest to forestall fresh argument. "We are exposed here," he said, just as a wave of explosions tracked across the oolt to the south. The blasts were small, the charges weak. But it killed several oolt'os outright and others were rendered as a loss.

The exuberant young commander waved off the blasts. "The fire is coming from near that structure," he said, gesturing to the distant obelisk behind him. "It is random. The thresh cannot hi—" His chest exploded in yellow as a .50-caliber bullet punched through his neural path and out through his chest.

The head of the young Kessentai flew upwards and yellow blood spurted from his mouth and nostrils. He slumped onto his *tenar* controls and his talons scrabbled at them as he appeared to be trying to say something. The crocodilian mouth appeared to shape the first syllables of the name of his lord, father and master, then he slid out of the cradle and to the torn ground, his fiery eyes going cold and glazed.

The sensors on a half dozen *tenars* screamed and weapons automatically swiveled towards the source of the fire. The weapons vomited a mixture of coherent light, relativistic missiles and concentrated plasma. A corner of the Monument was gouged out as the fire continued into the spot where someone had had the temerity to assassinate a God King. In a moment it was joined by the fire of dozens and then hundreds of Posleen normals, following the aiming points of their gods.

Of all that host, only one did not fire. Kenallai sat upon his unmoving *tenar*, staring down at the body of his eson'antai. As the fire slacked off the oolt'os came forward to start the rendering, but he held up his hand.

Finally, finally, he understood the thresh and it made him fear. Suddenly he was forced to wonder if there was not a better way than to make such a one into an evening's meal. Not even a special meal, but simply one bit mixed into the ration chain. Was there not something to such a one as this brilliant Kessentai? Something that lasted beyond the moment the thrice-*Fistnal* threshkreen put a bit of metal through him? Was there not something that lived on?

And he finally understood something else. Sometime, somewhere, someone in the Host had felt as he had. Had felt this for an eson'antai, for a beloved comrade, for a beloved enemy. And had fought for a change. For a bit of tradition that lifted out of the continuous cycle of conquest and *orna'adar*. For something higher.

He had never felt that calling. But he understood it now. Understood it at last.

He reached down to his feet and snapped loose a staff. There was only one per Kessentai, in keeping with tradition. Some cast them away as scoutmasters. Most had cast them at one time or another. Three had been cast on the long ride to this hellish spot. But never by him. He had never understood the need. Now he did. Finally. He finally understood his son, who had cast his at the blasted heath of the first conquest on this blasted planet. This thrice-damned, never to be mentioned, horrid, horrid little planet.

And he finally understood the thresh. And feared. For they felt this way for every single death. To the threshkreen, all the gathered thresh, all the wasted thresh, all the thresh on the hoof were Kessanalt. Each and every one. And *every single* threshkreen felt the anger he did now. It was terrifying to suddenly realize how thoroughly they had erred in landing on this white and blue ball.

"We are doomed," he whispered, as he tossed the staff onto the body. He looked to the oolt'os. They were of his personal oolt and all fairly intelligent. They should be able to follow the instructions. "Carry him to the hill." He pointed to be sure they were clear on which hill he meant. "Place him on the pile of threshkreen that are upon the top of the hill. Take the staff. Report back to this location when you are done."

Ardan'aath drifted his *tenar* up behind him. "We have to get moving." He pointed to the distant obelisk. "We've killed that one, but more will be back."

Kenallai turned to the older Kessentai. The commander could not expect him to suddenly change as he had. He had not had the vision. "Do you realize how thoroughly we have failed?"

Ardan'aath did not even turn his head. But a twitch of crest betrayed his discomfort. "I never expected you to be one to throw the staff," he said dubiously.

Kenallai flared his nostrils in agreement. "Well, I have. And I will tell you. We are caught in the *grat's* nest. There is no escape."

Ardan'aath took a deep breath. "I will give you a moment to decide. After that you can take the field or return to the rear."

Kenallai flared his crest in bleak humor. "You idiot. There *is* no rear. I will take the field with or without you. And be damned to your threats. But it is because we have no retreat! This is the end! We have thresh dug-in like *abat* in this damn building," he continued, gesturing to the monument behind him. "We have the force to the south, which has *destroyed* the host there and we are faced with this force here while the host trickles across the *river*. We are *fuscirto uut!*"

Ardan'aath gestured in negation. "You are made soft by the teachings of that young fool." He gestured towards the obelisk-topped mound. "They are few and already running."

The sensors screamed again as another God King slumped off his *tenar*. This time the fire raked from one end of the mound to the other, tearing across the front of the obelisk. But even as the fire tore into the engineering work, another target dot appeared on the OAS Annex. And another on the Agriculture Building. Then a group of oolt'os splashed away from the explosion of the first 120mm mortar round.

The .50-caliber rifles were not only powerful, they had enormous range. The snipers were taking shots from nearly a mile. Most of them were falling among the normals, causing unnoticed casualties. But the occasional shots, better or more lucky than the others, were hitting the leaders. And drawing massive response. But as more of the weapons joined the fray, the response of the God Kings was becoming more diffused.

Kenallurial fluffed his crest. "We have come far together. But now it is time to sever our relationship." He nodded at his old friend. "I go to the field. And I shall not return."

He turned his *tenar* and sent it floating down towards his waiting oolt. The heavily armed company would scythe into the distant defenders. But he already knew it was for naught.

Suddenly a targeting dot appeared at the top of the obelisk and a moment later the *tenar* of Ardan'aath evaporated in actinic fire as a bullet penetrated the crystal pack.

The low-grade nuclear explosion washed the steps of the Monument clear of Posleen. Kenallai had already moved away from his former comrade when it happened and he controlled his *tenar* as the shock wave threatened to drown it in the shallow reflecting pool.

He was beyond cursing. He winced at the gouge riven across his back by a bit of shrapnel and looked to the distant obelisk.

"That is just about enough," he whispered. "To the *Alld'nt* with this." He gestured to the members of his oolt'ondar. "Off your *tenar!*" He suited action to words, climbing off his own saucer and removing the plasma cannon from its pintle mount. The heavy power pack was lovingly placed across his back as the other God Kings dismounted and began gathering the oolt'os of the late Ardan'aath. "If we are among the oolt'os the *fuscirto uut* thresh cannot pick us out!"

He turned to the east and the distant monument as another line of explosions tracked across the mass of oolt'os gathered before the pool. "*Let us to battle!*" he cried. "*It is a good day to die!*"

The cough tore wrackingly through her chest and more blood spotted the white dust. The falling limestone cap stones had pretty well flailed her ribcage and put the final whammy on her left arm, but it had been a good shot. She had stayed in place long enough to see the God King saucer blow. Her eyes were still mostly blind from it. But it had cost her.

She knew all the long goddamn run up the stairs that it was stupid. But the thought of the shot, when she'd managed to avoid getting killed after the first one, was just too good to pass up. A shot from the top of the Washington Monument. It was a sniper's wet dream. And it had been a good shot. She knew it the moment the stock slammed into her shoulder. Perfect, right through the fuckin' X-ring. Despite the heaving breath. Despite the pounding heart.

The heart still refused to stop pounding. Only, now it was pounding blood out on the marble floor. But it was worth it. It had been a perfect moment. And her life had had damn few perfect moments. It had been a *good* shot. . . .

◆ CHAPTER 71 ◆

They might not win, but they were taking their best shot. Keren had tossed aside his board and was down to breaking rounds. The guns were traversing their fire, walking the explosions across the front of the oncoming Posleen force. Two more gun tracks had joined them and the four mortars stitched a seam across the enemy.

Three Gun seemed to have settled down now that more ammo and support had shown up. He wished that the backup driver of the ammo truck would pitch in or at least put down her rifle. But he had become familiar with the look in her eye and wasn't going to be the first to suggest it. And it wasn't as if they needed the help.

The troops helping wore every damn kind of unit patch. There were cavalry, infantry and a mass of combat-support types. They didn't really know what they were doing, but the hands made the job much faster and the mortar rounds were finally piling up quicker than the guns could pour them out. About half of them had come with a cavalry bird colonel. The guy looked like he was seventeen, which just meant he was another rejuv. As he strode around directing the support force he displayed the most incredible command of invective Keren had ever heard.

And these were just the dregs, the ones without decent weapons, or any at all for that matter. Most of the volunteers had joined the cavalry troop on Monument Mound. Some of them, they were just tired of running. Some of them figured if they didn't stop the horses here it was all over; might as well die here as anywhere. But plenty of them seemed to just be pissed about where it was. Sure, take

Virginia, who cares. Take Arlington Cemetery. We'll take it back. But the Monument? Fuck that. There were a bunch of obvious rejuvs; most of them arrived together and seemed to know each other. He didn't know who they were or where they had come from; they weren't from any regular unit. But they were coming out of the woodwork now, leading any damn soldier that showed an ounce of willingness.

He had seen plenty of the soldiers on the Mall run. The tent city that had been setting up was nearly empty. And most of them weren't here. But a good few were.

They were black and white and oriental and Hispanic. Men and women. Most of 'em stank from days of running. Plenty of 'em looked like they could use a good meal, or a night or two with no guard duty and no nightmares.

But they were here. And they were helping. The ammo truck carried a mixed load and the volunteers swarmed over it, throwing down cases of .50 caliber to feed the guns on the tracks, breaking open the mortar rounds and running forward to feed the infantry positions.

The infantry, in the meantime, was laying down a curtain of fire. At least six hundred soldiers had crept up the mound and now fired at the oncoming Posleen. They were belly down with just their heads and rifles showing. An occasional HVM would strike a section and open it up or the odd round would strike an individual, but more volunteers would creep forward to fill the gaps.

Sure, most had run. But plenty more stayed. And the horses would have the Monument over their dead bodies.

"First Sergeant, I don't care if you are Fleet. I don't care if you have orders from God Himself. I am going back there over my dead body. I'm not even going to think about it. There's no way to win and I'm not going to be a stupid hero." The tired and dirty first lieutenant was the last officer the cavalry company had left. Of course, he was in charge of less than a platoon of Abrams so it wasn't like he was overtaxed.

Pappas thought about the statement for a moment. "L-T, I need your tracks at the Watergate. I'm getting part of an infantry battalion headed that way and there's a buncha artillery support. But I really, really need your tracks, too."

"No. And what's more—fuck, no," snarled the lieutenant, tired of arguing with the remorseless NCO. The upstart Fleet bastard had been nagging him for nearly an hour before the horses crossed the river. If they hadn't crossed he might have stuck around, but as it was there was just no reason. No reason at all. No force on Earth was going to stop the Posleen tide now that it was over the Potomac. They might as well head back to New York city as stick around and get eaten.

The officer dug at the plasteel fingers holding onto the coaming of his TC hatch. "Get off my track." The lieutenant switched on the intercom. "Pauls, move out." As the Abrams sprang to life, the other four tanks fell in behind it, moving down the Mall to the east, towards the Capitol and away from the fighting around the Arlington Bridge.

Pappas sighed and leaned forward. Steel fingers removed the helmet from the struggling lieutenant's head and pulled him in close. The writhing officer found that fighting against them was like fighting a mechanical clamp.

"AID, whisper mode," said Pappas, calmly. Then he whispered to the lieutenant. "You said that it would be over your dead body. Turn this platoon around or I will squeeze your head until it pops. Literally." Pappas palmed the back of the officer's head and applied a calculated amount of pressure.

The officer writhed in the iron grasp and whined from the pain. It felt as if his eyeballs were going to burst. "You can't do this the whole way there!" he shouted. One shin banged painfully against the thermal repeater but the lesser pain went unnoticed.

Pappas face hardened and he yanked the officer out of the tank. "AID, broadcast to all tank units. All units. Stop right here. We have to have a little talk." The tanks continued to the east. Instead of stopping they actually increased speed. "AID, did that get to them all?"

"All tanks have active carrier waves and I shunted it to the intercom."

"Right," snarled Pappas. He pulled out a roll of spacetape and secured the futilely protesting officer to the turret. Then he walked across the tank to the driver's hatch, his EVA clamps holding him to the skin of the armored behemoth. He knelt by the driver's hatch and pounded on it. "OPEN UP!"

There was no physical response, but he could have sworn he heard a faint "*No!*"

He tapped a spot on his forearm and a two-foot blade sprang out from the underarm of the suit. The blade had been suggested by Duncan, and the Indowy fitters had been more than happy to oblige for the whole company. Now it came in handy as the monomolecular vibroblade slid through the Chobham armor like butter and sliced the hatch lock in two.

In short order Pappas had the remaining members of the platoon lined up at attention. Two or three were bruised and at least one had a broken arm. There was a cooling spot on the turret of one tank from a glancing armor-piercing round and there was a gunner who would require serious medical attention. But most of them were there.

"I tried to do this the easy way. I am now going to have to do it the hard way," he said in an iron tone. "This unit is guilty of desertion in the face of the enemy. The life of every member of this unit is forfeit, under both the Uniform Code of Military Justice and the Federation Procedures for the Prosecution of War." He stopped and looked at the figures. Most of them were still defiant. Despite the regular hangings for desertion before the Posleen landed, the bug-out in this case had been so widespread that it was unlikely they would be charged. What they did not realize was that they were no longer under the control of American Law.

"You were given an order by a duly designated noncommissioned officer of the Fleet Strike Forces. As such your offense falls under Federation law." He stopped again and lowered his voice. "What that means is that you have just entered hell."

He picked up the securely bound lieutenant and held him again by the back of the head. "This officer ignored a direct order. He led this retreat. He is primarily at fault." Pappas closed his fingers and the skull of the officer exploded. The corpse of the lieutenant catapulted to the feet of the lined-up troops along with a splatter of blood and brains that covered the arrayed troopers in gray matter. The nearly decapitated body kicked and thrashed on the ground as undirected nerve impulses continued to fire for a few more moments. Most of the troop looked stunned, a couple looked satisfied. Then about half doubled over in nausea.

"I want you to understand something," Pappas snarled. "The Posleen *might* kill you. If you try to run again, I *will* kill you." Pappas lifted his M-300 and fired over the head of the platoon. The blast of relativistic teardrops took out a section of the Longworth building, scattering debris into the street. "This weapon will go through your fucking tin cans long ways. You *will* be more terrified of me than of the enemy."

"*Mortars, they're over Seventeenth Street and spreading out,*" said the cool voice on the radio. Keren had seen him from time to time, pulling out the occasional wounded or dead, calling for more volunteers, even, for God's sake, giving marksmanship lessons. And he didn't sound any more flustered now. "*Can you get us any more fire-support, over?*" The voice was young, but the assurance wasn't. Rejuv again.

"*Negative,*" responded Keren over the radio in the Three Track. His hands dripped blood to the steel deck as the blisters took another beating from the rounds. The members of Three Track had finally had it, slipping out one by one in the crowd of volunteers. But it didn't matter. There was a halfway intelligent gun bunny dropping rounds. And two chicks with signals intelligence patches cutting charges. And a dozen more men and women preparing rounds. The bastards from Three didn't matter a damn. "*I've tried all the arty freqs. Nobody.*" Not even the Fiftieth Division control. The bastards had probably run.

"*Well,*" said the guy on the radio in a voice that was both resigned and positive, "*Gotta die somewhere.*"

Keren twisted the traverse and dropped the range a crank. "*Guess it's that time.*"

"Yep," said the guy on the other end. "*Well, I always said every day after the Chosin was one I wasn't meant to live. Thanks for the support, Mortars. Out here.*"

Keren shook his head in wonder. Maybe the guy was talking about Valkyries or something.

Mike had some important decisions to make. As the battalion stepped out, crossing the Twelfth Street Phase-line he was still in a quandary. But, after thinking long and hard, he finally came to a decision.

"Duncan?" he asked.

"We're up! Where do you want it?"

"Question. What tune should I use?" he asked. The firing from the distant Monument was clear. The forces had to be thinking they were doomed.

"What?"

"I'm thinking 'Ride of the Valkyries.' "

"*What?*"

"Or should I go with tradition?"

"What tradition? . . . Oh."

"Yeah, tradition wins. Pity, really. This is such a Wagnerian moment."

Keren looked up and snarled as the guy hanging rounds froze. Then, when he saw his slack-jawed face he looked to the rear. The tune was familiar. At first he could not for the life of him place it. But then, as the approaching unit began singing, it came to him and he started to laugh so hard he thought he would die.

Colonel Cutprice looked up at the sound behind him and started to laugh. Just when you thought you had lost the game, sometimes life handed you an ace. Some of the riflemen on the mound turned to snarl at the misplaced mirth but then, as more and more of the veterans began laughing, they looked to their rear and smiled. They weren't sure what the joke was—the song was familiar from basic training but otherwise a mystery. But the old guys obviously got whatever the joke was.

And to the strains of "Yellow Ribbon," the anthem of the United States Cavalry, the men and women of the First Battalion, Five Hundred Fifty-Fifth Mobile Infantry Regiment, the "Triple-Nickles," began to deploy.

◆ CHAPTER 72 ◆

Teri Nightingale was not happy. The plan that battalion, which meant Captain O'Neal, had downloaded was unnecessarily hazardous and invited defeat in detail. It also left Bravo Company with an unsecured flank. The hazards of that were obvious to a blind man. But not to the world's greatest expert in combat suit tactics.

He also had sent Ernie out on a forlorn hope. Trying to hold that force coming across the bridge with a few infantry troops and some cowardly tank crews was impossible. They would be slaughtered. And that would be the end of Ernie Pappas.

She was not happy with the direction that relationship had taken. She had never intended to actually go to bed with him. But when the captain had turned her training over to the NCO, she felt a certain amount of flirtation in order. A good report from the NCO, much as it galled her, would go far towards restoring her position in the captain's eyes. Since the captain wrote her evaluation report, her career depended on keeping this NCO happy.

Flirtation had, unfortunately, quickly led to more. And now she was not sure she could end the relationship without causing the exact opposite of the effect she had been striving for. It was a hell of a predicament. Much as it bothered her to consider it, Sergeant Pappas's death would certainly permit her to be free and clear.

Her own death, however, might quickly follow. She swallowed at that thought and caught her breath. For the first time she seriously regretted her change from Intel to Infantry. A career in Intel would have meant slower promotion, but one of the costs of being in combat arms was the chance of dying. That had never been real to her until today. Despite the reality of the training systems, the possibility that Teri Nightingale might cease to exist was a shock.

That possibility was much on her mind as the company double-timed down New York Avenue. Confident in his company and assured by the first sergeant that the XO was capable of handling the load, Captain O'Neal had assigned Bravo the most difficult assignment. It required moving across Washington at an oblique angle and taking the Posleen forces in the flank. It also left them out on a limb, unsupported by the rest of the companies in the battalion. And to get to the point where they were truly in trouble required a head-long charge towards the distant enemy.

Second platoon was in the lead as they approached the back side of the White House. Lieutenant Fallon had pushed his point out well in advance of their location, but they were running without flank-ers, an invitation to ambush. That was not a comforting feeling to the XO.

"Lieutenant Fallon," she said, carefully controlling her voice, "hold up at the intersection of New York and Fifteenth Street. I don't like this running blindly towards the enemy. We need to get some scouts forward."

"Ma'am," said the lieutenant, diffidently. "With all due respect we're behind schedule as it is. We need to be in position to support the battalion's assault."

"I am aware of the plan, Lieutenant!" snapped the acting com-mander. "But if we get ambushed it will not help the battalion either!"

"Yes, ma'am," said the officer, tightly.

The company stopped in the open area to the east of the Trea-sury annex and automatically trained weapons out. The unit had been moving in tactical formation, the suits spaced twenty meters apart, weapons trained out to either side. If any Posleen unit had ambushed them it would have been toast.

Wilson tapped a grav-gun to get the rifleman on the correct axis and walked over to where Stewart was standing, one foot tapping a rhythm on the concrete. He leaned into the squad leader and set his communicator to private mode.

"Manuel, we're not supposed to be stopped here," he hissed.

"No shit," snapped Stewart. He did not even correct the use of his former name. The alias James Stewart was a bit of comedy that the gang had managed to keep secret to everyone but the first ser-geant. But right now he was worried more about the colossal screwup the company was engaged in than in keeping his former existence a secret.

"Well, do something!"

"What would you have me do?" he asked in exasperation. "Off the XO?"

The response was resounding silence.

"Oh, great," Stewart responded. "Do you have any idea what a *really* bad idea that is? No? You think that Rogers or Fallon would just pick up the ball if we shot Nightingale? Or, maybe, they would have to deal with whoever shot her first? Bad, bad, *bad* idea."

"Okay," relented the former gang member. "But what the hell are we going to do?" he asked plaintively. "We were supposed to be in position by now, not standing by the White House with our thumbs up our butts!"

"*Muy trabajo*, buddy. I know that, you know that, the L-T knows that. The only one who doesn't know it is the fuckin' XO. So, when the Old Man figures out what's going on he'll kick her ass and get it in gear. *No problemo.*"

"Sure, sure, *Jim*," snapped Wilson. "No problem for us. But the rest of the battalion is going to get corncobbed."

Stewart snorted faintly and smiled in his armor. "Why, Juan, I didn't think you cared about anybody but the gang!" The sarcasm was gentle and ironic.

"Well." Wilson looked at the symbol across the street. "I guess maybe I figure this is as much my turf as anybody's. And you know damn well that if you're standing still, sooner or later the Bloods are gonna find you!"

Atalanara had been part of Kenallurial's charge across the Potomac. But, unlike most of the other Kessentai, he had marshaled his oolt by the bridge, ready to cross. So the force had made it across relatively intact. Seeing the massive confusion near the Memorial he had struck out on his own.

A very junior battlemaster, he had no interest in facing well-prepared forces. His first movement to the north along the great river had been rebuffed by fire from thresh dug-in among the buildings of a large complex. Although the complex had looked desirable, he doubted his ability to drive the force of thresh out of their positions.

Taking a side street he sent teams of oolt'os into the buildings lining the roads. They reported nothing of value. Some of the buildings had fine artwork or well-made equipment, but nowhere were the heavy metals, refined chemicals or production facilities that he craved. Such a find would assuredly be assigned by the Net to the first to capture it. And it would permit him to equip his oolt with much better weapons.

Of course, the threshkreen had already helped in that regard. The oolt had exited the lander equipped mostly with the cheapest of shotguns along with a few missile launchers. The *tenar* that he had started off with sported the company's sole 3mm railgun.

The *tenar* was the same, but it now was mounted with a gigawatt laser and a new sensor suite. The Kessentai that had "improved" his vehicle would never miss the equipment. And their oolt, scattered in death from the threshkreen's ballistic weapons, had yielded a mass of weapons. So, now, the normals of the company were armed with a decent mix of weaponry. He had been able to double the number of hypervelocity missile launchers in the company and most of the remaining normals were now armed with railguns. True, many of those were 1mm rather than 3mm. But there were several plasma cannons to make up the lack. There was not a single shotgun left in the oolt; he was as well armed as a senior battlemaster. Now if he only could avoid using all that might!

The map that Kenallurial had been using indicated that there was a "Treasury" around here somewhere. The translation of that term had been more than satisfactory. That would be a prize worth fighting for.

"Okay," said Nightingale over the leader's circuit. "I know you're wondering why we've stopped. I'm not happy with running around without scouts further out. We don't know what is out there and we could get hit at any second."

"In that case," said Lieutenant Rogers, angrily, "we should be *moving*, not stopped. And, in case you haven't noticed, the rest of the battalion is about to engage the enemy. They are expecting us to hit them in the flank and cover the holes on that side! Which we are not doing standing around with our thumbs up our butts!"

"Watch your tongue," snapped Nightingale. "I understand your concerns, but we need a good op order on this." She paused for a moment. "This plan is not complete. We don't have good intelligence on the enemy's dispositions."

"Ma'am," said Sergeant Bogdanovich, "that is the Infantry. We're always the people who are gathering the intel the hard way. And this isn't about intel, it's about assault. We have to *move*."

"We will move when I am *ready* to move," said Nightingale angrily. "And not a moment sooner!"

"Boss," said Arnold, over a side channel.

"Yeah," sighed O'Neal. "I see it." Bravo had stopped at the

intersection of New York Avenue and Fifteenth Street. Although it was not where he would have had a pre-rally, a stop made sense. If they had moved on. But they hadn't.

The battalion had finally cleared the detritus on the Mall and was preparing to cross Fifteenth Street. The forces on the Mound were getting hammered so he had brought the unit up to a lope. As they cleared Fifteenth, Alpha Company opened out like a fan. The edges of the company were already taking fire from distant God Kings and as soon as they cleared the mound it was going to be a firestorm. He needed to get Nightingale going. Fast.

"Top," he said, letting the AID switch him automatically.

"Yes, sir," said the first sergeant. According to the schematic he was not far from Bravo, in the company of a platoon of tanks. "I got a more or less intact battalion to move over to the Watergate. They got a brush from Posleen but beat them off. I'm taking these tanks over and there's some more forces that might trickle along behind. If we get artillery and not *too* many bad guys we should be fine."

"That's great, Top," said Mike quickly. "Just one problem. Look where Bravo is."

Mike waited a moment then snorted faintly at the fluent swearing that the AID faithfully broadcast.

"Shit," the first sergeant finished. "I'm sorry, boss."

"You get one suggestion," Mike answered. He was not terribly happy with the situation he was in. Pappas was normally to be depended on for a logical evaluation of personnel. In the case of Nightingale it had obviously failed and he was beginning to suspect why.

Pappas thought about the question furiously. If he left the Abrams unit they would take off like a scalded cat. But if he tried to persuade Nightingale over the radio it would be a waste of breath. He could see as clearly as the Old Man that she had frozen, whatever she was telling the company. There was only one choice, as painful as it was personally and professionally.

"Relieve her, sir," he said after the brief moment's thought. "Put Rogers in charge. If they're stopped and get hit by a Posleen company, you'll have a hell of a time getting them started again."

"Concur. Out here," said O'Neal, coldly.

Pappas knew he was going to get his ass kicked at some time in the near future by the little fireball. But that was only if they survived the upcoming battle.

Atalanara was nearly there. All he had to do was take this "Treasury" building and survive the battle. If he could, he would be set for all eternity; the treasury of such a rich nation would be bulging with loot. As he cleared the intervening bulk of the Old Executive Office Building the long-sought building came into view. And so did an oolt of metal threshkreen.

"*Posleen!*" shouted a private in First Platoon and sent a stream of relativistic teardrops towards the Posleen company that had appeared around the corner.

The fire was obscured by the fences and trees at the back of the White House as well as the bulk of the government office building. This gave the company enough time to react to the sudden appearance.

"Okay," said Nightingale, looking at her readouts, "we can do this." She tapped her gauntlets together and thought for a moment. "Okay, First platoon. Dig in and prepare to lay down a base of fire. Second, swing to the right and prepare to hit them in the flank. Third, get ready to pass through First to lay down more fire. Mortars—"

"*No, no, no, no!*" shouted Stewart over the command channel. "*Kick their ass don't piss on them! The battalion is about to get fucked because we're out of position!*"

"Stewart," the officer snarled. "One more word out of you and I'll have you court-martialed!"

"He's *right*, Nightingale," snapped Rogers as he stepped into line with his platoon and opened fire at the Posleen. The force was actually moving into the Executive Building, using the mass of the structure as cover and concealment. And the fire coming back was heavy. But they could bypass this resistance and move to their positions with minimal casualties. If the intel-weenie *bitch* could ever get off the stick. Giving vent to his frustration he sent a code to the platoon to open fire with grenades.

The small antimatter grenades sailed out in a volley, the spheres smashing through windows and bouncing off of walls before detonating. The arc-light bright flashes tore off the front of the building without noticeably impeding the Posleen fire. Whoever the God King in charge was, he was starting to learn human tactics.

"Cease fire with grenades!" shrilled Nightingale, horrified by the damage done to the building. It was on the grounds of the White House for God's sake. The consequences were going to be catastrophic.

"Nightingale," came O'Neal's voice, snapping across the company general circuit. "You are relieved. Move immediately to the area of the cargo canisters and remain there until further ordered. Lieutenant Rogers, you are in tactical command. Move immediately down G Street to Nineteenth. Take your positions along Constitution. You have three minutes to effect this maneuver. If you hit resistance punch through. *Kick their ass, don't piss on them!*" he finished in unconscious mimicry of his most junior squad leader.

"Yes, sir!" said the new acting commander. "Bravo Company! Follow me!" He locked his grav-gun and mortars on the building sheltering the entrenched Posleen and began a cascade of fire as he trotted off. By the time he reached the end of Lafayette Square he was at a full loping run, accelerating past forty miles per hour.

Stewart was right behind him with Lieutenant Fallon at his side and the rest of the company charging behind them. The hurricane of destruction from the company chewed away the north end of the Gothic structure, shattering the concrete and stone around the Posleen and covering them with cascading debris. Stewart realized halfway down the street that making the requisite turn was going to be nearly impossible. If they turned to the left it would take them towards the fire.

They had the Posleen suppressed at the moment, but when they turned the fire would break up, permitting the aliens to pick the suits off at the corner. However, if they turned right it would put the Posleen behind them. That was no good either since it would give the enemy a clear shot at the company for several blocks.

However, as they reached the end of Lafayette Square and faced the need to decelerate, he realized that Rogers had no interest in turning.

Accelerating past forty miles per hour, the combat suit of the acting company commander smashed into a building at the end of the street without slowing. The concrete and stone wall shattered at the impact of the thousand-pound suit, leaving a vaguely human-shaped hole as the officer disappeared into the depths to the echoed sound of destruction.

Laughing like madmen Stewart and Lieutenant Fallon lowered their heads and prepared to enlarge the hole.

◆ CHAPTER 73 ◆

Washington, DC, United States of America, Sol III
1121 EDT October 11th, 2004 AD

Mike had one eye on the repeater from Stewart's suit as the battalion reached the Mound and he laughed as well. The two forces arrayed against one another were shaping up. The Posleen had the advantage of numbers but, since they had to pulse the forces across the Arlington Bridge, it would be difficult for them to gather enough forces to dislodge the defenders. If, that was, the humans killed them fast enough.

The humans were at an apparent disadvantage. Most of the units were barely recovered from a rout. There was no central command. And there was no vital rationale to defend this spot. The location was not clearly critical terrain.

But Mike could see that few agreed with that analysis. As he passed the line of figures hunkered down on the mound and firing steadily he could see others picking up weapons from the dead and thickening the line. The mortar tracks were firing their guns steadily and adding the weight of their .50-caliber fire to the mix. Snipers were interspersed with regular infantry, and officers and NCOs were moving among the troops cajoling, correcting or ensuring that everyone had enough ammo. The fact that they had barely slowed the Posleen advance was apparently lost on the soldiers on the mound. They were done running.

The Posleen, on the other hand, were advancing. The lead companies were already past the Reflecting Pool and nearly to Seventeenth Street. Mike was surprised that there were no saucers in the mix, but he quickly surmised by their regular order that the God Kings must have dismounted to make themselves less of a target. The force was not, however, solid. There was a large force advancing on their position, but just as many or more were still milling around in the area of the Memorial. If they stopped this force butt-cold they could deal with the others at leisure. If.

This was where having Bravo in place would have helped tremendously. Not only could Bravo have taken the force with enfilading fire, but the plan called for the battalion to wait for Bravo so that the shock of their first strike would turn the Posleen towards the Monument and into the killing field he intended to make of the monument area.

The mound was now within effective range of the Posleen weapons and the forces on the mound were starting to take serious casualties from the fire of the approaching wave.

"Forward!" shouted Kenallai. "If we take that monument we break their backs!" He did not know what the obelisk was that had drawn the threshkreen to it. Perhaps it was a power generator or some other important structure. Whatever it was, it was obviously vital and he intended to capture it.

He had the pleasure of seeing the thresh begin to fall, some to the plasma cannons in the host around him, or thrown up and away by strikes from railguns. Still others were hit square on by the massed HVM fire of the force around him. They were being whittled away and in a few more moments the host would be upon them. And then they would feed.

Duncan took a suck on his suit rations and grimaced. The Old Man seemed to love fried rice, but it wasn't his favorite. He punched in the last few fire commands and looked around for a good spot to sit. There was a badly beat-up Suburban sitting forlorn on the torn lawn of the Mall. He walked over and sat on the tail as he monitored his readouts. It looked like the ball was about to begin. The fuckup with Bravo had cost them a few minutes and the poor bastards on the mound a few casualties. But no plan worked perfectly. As it was, this one was close. He compared the Posleen positions to his readouts and smiled. They were not going to like what happened next. But he was gonna love every fucking minute of it.

Mike checked the feed from his rifle and smiled. The Posleen were making headway against the fire; there weren't really enough guns to stop them. The fire, however, was having another, more salient, effect.

It would be useful if the whole host became focused on the Monument. Not vital, but useful. And it had required taking some casualties to let the Posleen live long enough to draw attention away from the north. Now if Bravo would just get in position they could fuck them all, not just the few.

Stewart slid into position with a sigh. The Pharmaceutical Institute building on the corner of Twenty-Third and Constitution had a wonderful view of the Potomac and the Memorial, even on the ground floor. Well, normally. Now it had a wonderful view of more Posleen than he had ever wanted to see in his life. The position was horribly exposed and if the captain's plan screwed up in even the smallest detail it would be a death trap. But it was also the best possible place to kill Posleen. And he found that he was looking forward to that.

His squad had slipped in the back way and was now preparing to dig in. There had been a few scattered normals on the ground floor, but without their God Kings normals were cold meat and had been dispensed with quietly. The suits were in place with their deception holograms on, waiting for orders to trigger their cratering charges.

Mike glanced at his readouts and waved at the rejuv colonel who seemed to be in charge of the mound defenses. The officer had not even asked why they were just sitting there, out of sight, while his soldiers were taking all the casualties. Which meant he knew why, more or less. At the gesture he started shouting to the riflemen along the slope to retreat. He had to pull some back by main strength.

Mike smiled and punched in a few last-minute commands. The moment had to be timed perfectly, not because it would effect the outcome of the battle, but because it meant the difference between winning and winning with style.

"Duncan," he whispered. "Now." And stood up.

"The thresh flee!" Kenallai shouted in glee. He waved to the force. "Forward! Take the hill! The Host shall be invincible!" He did not believe it, however. He knew full well the fact that the Host was doomed. But the more damage he could do to the thresh that had taken his eson'antai the better.

The first of the host were at the base of the hill when the sky rang out with thunder.

✧　　✧　　✧

Over the crest of the mound came a creature from nightmare. The beast was a dragon of a hundred heads, every swiveling head spitting silver fire. It was preceded by a horrible caterwauling and the thunder of drums as the silver lightning of its breath tore the host apart.

The Posleen of the host were shocked by the appearance of the fell beast but they held their ground. There were tens of thousands of their fellows behind them and their massed might was sure to bring it down. The breath flying down from the height was opening huge rents in their wave but they drove forward against the fire, clawing to engage the beast talon to talon.

Atalanara had retained his *tenar* on the stumbling retreat to the Mall. The damage from the metal threshkreen had been bad enough but to find that the "treasury" was filled with nothing but paper and the offices of castellaines was enraging. Now he simply hoped to rejoin a force with a decent oolt'ondai who might be able to explain this strange world to him.

As he crossed Virginia Avenue on Eighteenth Street, just short of the Mall, a monitor on his new sensor suite chirped.

"Incoming artillery fire," it relayed in its androgynous tenor. The term was familiar. It meant the hated ballistic weapons of the thresh. "Time on Target, fire. Forty rounds."

That sounded like quite a lot. He started looking at the surrounding buildings, wondering if it would be better under cover. Forty rounds would be very bad.

"Sixty rounds. One hundred and twelve. One twenty. One sixty three. Two twenty-four. Two fifty-eight. Splash."

The fire was a complicated curtain barrage. The technique had been developed in World War I as a method to prevent movement of forces across no-man's-land. In this case it was being used to drive the Posleen into the anvil of the ACS.

Duncan had had the full authority of the Continental Army Commander and the artillery of two decimated corps. Most of it was 155mm mobile cannon. The variable time and cluster rounds dropped in a veritable curtain of death along Constitution Avenue, heaviest in the opening leading to the Watergate, but everywhere in incredible density.

Forces squeezing out of the press towards the north ran into this wall of death. The few that stumbled out were hit from the side by the silver lightning of the ACS now firmly dug-in on the ground floor of the pharmacy building and the distant fire from the Watergate.

Duncan switched to the next stage of the game, which was smoke. Four batteries were tasked purely to obscurement missions and they began to lay a curtain of white along the Potomac. This effectively stopped the Posleen across the river from determining what was happening in the cauldron. Then he started to walk the curtain barrage down from the north.

Kenallai looked at the approaching wall of steel rain. Then he looked to the east where the strange beast wrestled with the first ranks of the host. Steel-rain. Beast. Steel-rain. Beast. His crest slowly lifted until it was straight up. He looked at the Kessentai gathered around him and started snapping out orders.

"Alrantath, take your oolt'ondar to the right. Tenal'ont, take the left. All the rest, form behind them and my own oolt'ondar. Call to all the Kessentai in reach! Cry unto the oolt'os! Upon my signal, we shall lead the host in a te'naal charge the likes of which has never been seen!"

Mike had expected the Posleen to move towards his position, had, in fact, depended on it. But not with the immense unanimity they displayed. The word that came to mind was stampede as the huge mass, the AID counted it as a quarter million, turned ponderously to the east and made a concerted bolt for the monument and freedom from the steel rain. He stopped the battalion and started snapping out orders. As usual, timing would be everything.

Lieutenant Rogers swore fluently. This was the moment that Bravo had been placed for, but the reality exceeded the Old Man's expectations by an order of magnitude. He wasn't sure that the original orders, to wait until the enemy was within two hundred meters of the battalion before he opened fire, should be followed or not. He finally decided that they were still extant. It would just be a *lot* more exciting.

"*Forward!*" shouted Kenallai, firing his plasma cannon over the heads of his personal oolt. The ranks of his own forces had been swelled by the majority of Ardan'aath's oolt'os and the reinforced company was leading the charge.

The fire of the beast was a silver waterfall, tearing the host asunder, but the return fire of the host was as deadly. Already many of the heads had fallen to the ground and were lying quiescent. They were finally reaching the point where the mass fire of the host could have good effect and within moments the horrid creature would be another trophy to brag upon.

❖   ❖   ❖

"Jesus Christ!" shouted Major Givens, stumbling backward under the hail of railgun rounds.

The God Kings were interspersed in the body of the Posleen forces, effectively hidden by the intervening normals. However, every now and again they would target a particular suit. When they did, thousands of normals would follow the lead of their gods. Even catching the edge of such a hurricane of destruction was enough to damage the suits, and the luckless individual at the center was usually toast as a storm of 3mm railgun rounds and hypervelocity missiles struck their suit.

The exception, thus far, had been Captain O'Neal. Twice he had been targeted by God Kings. In both cases he was able to evade the majority of the fire, including the initial fire of the God King, while still managing to crank out a stream of orders.

The diminutive suit seemed to be everywhere. Whenever the fire of the Posleen forces appeared sure to destroy a section of the line, he was in the thick of the fighting. He was moving the suits in a complex pavane designed to avoid the majority of the damage. Whenever a section became bogged down, he was sure to be there first, loosening up the movement, directing the fire, calling for support.

Givens realized he had been still for too long and began his next movement. Even the acting commander followed the baton of the little hobgoblin.

"Why aren't they digging in!" shouted Lieutenant Nightingale. She had set her helmet aside, but she continued to follow the course of the battle on a computer-generated hologram. "He's killing them! The sadistic little bastard!"

"Teri, you need to get a grip," Pappas snapped over the communications circuit. "If he had them dig in, it would ruin the illusion. Right now, the Posleen believe they are fighting a dragon. As soon as he's sucked as many as possible into the kill-box, he'll go to ground. Until then, he's doing his job, as an officer, and accepting the casualties to further the mission."

"That is insane!" she shouted. "He is butchering the battalion for . . . for *nothing*!"

Pappas sighed quietly and decided he had more important things to do than continue this pointless argument. "Lieutenant Nightingale, I think you need to find another job. There are realities about combat I don't think you will ever grasp." He tapped a control on the suit for privacy. "AID, unless I have to, I don't want to talk to Lieutenant Nightingale again."

"Very well, Gunny," said the female contralto. There was a slight pause. "Does that mean I'll be seeing more of you?"

Mike skipped past a private from Charlie Company and pointed to the right. "The bouncing ball is that way, Private Vargas. Follow the bouncing ball."

The suit followed the directions, sidling off to the right just as a cone of railgun fire tore through the space where it had paused.

"Nah, nah, nah, nah," Mike called, broadcasting the taunt over both speakers and the battalion broadcast frequency. He stopped and directed the holographic dragon head he projected to stick its tongue out at the advancing Posleen mass. "Youuu caaan't touch meee!" he taunted again, the cry this time going out in Posleen. As the fire of the division twisted towards his location he popped out a string of grenades and sidestepped. "Nah, nah, nah, nah," he taunted as the storm of fire swept by.

Gone were the fear and uncertainty. Gone were the question and doubt. The high of combat, the joy of battle had taken him and he was once again in his element. There were at least four ways to win the current scenario and do maximum damage to the Posleen. Each of them projected nearly identical casualties for the battalion. Given the choices, he had chosen the one with the maximum style. Even now with the casualty graph climbing and the whole mass of the Posleen force charging them. Whatever the outcome of the battle, they'd fought it "their way."

But the time for stylish destruction was coming to an end. The Posleen were getting close enough that they could overwhelm the battalion with their massed fire. They were still steering away from the curtain barrage to the north, but it was time to teach them that there were worse things than artillery.

He skipped to the left and hopped over a crossing trooper as he considered the timing. With human troops it was usually better to withhold your heaviest fire until they were within two hundred meters. At that point, human troops felt that no matter how much fire there was, they still had a chance of overrunning the position. So they would come on in droves, through any sort of maelstrom. If your intent was to kill as many as possible, and his was just that, then waiting until they were that close was best.

With Posleen, this magic distance was still unclear. Simulations refused to recognize it, instead opting for an almost suicidal determination on the part of Posleen forces. But he had seen them break and run, even up close. So. When to start the *real* massacre?

He decided to let the music choose. They had started out the battle with Led Zeppelin's "Immigrant Song" pounding in the background. The tune had become something of an instant tradition for the American ACS units after Diess. That had segued to the Rolling Stones' "Paint it Black" and that was good. But not quite what he was looking for. Something . . . more. When the next song started, he smiled ferally.

"Lieutenant Rogers," he whispered over the comm, trotting sideways towards his predesignated position.

"Sir," responded the camouflaged acting-company commander.

"Prepare for enfilading fire on my mark."

"Roger, sir."

Mike tapped a series of Virtual icons floating in the air in front of his face. The AIDs accepted the commands, considered the current conditions and prepared movement orders for all the individuals in the battalion.

"Execute," he whispered as the first bars of Black Sabbath's "The Mob Rules" began to boom out through the battalion's suit speakers.

Kenallai exalted as the mass of the Host approached the beast. Despite the beast's awesome fire and the writhing, difficult to strike heads, the host had passed through the worst of the fire. In moments they would take the beast and drive on to the prizes to the east. They were close enough that nothing could stop the Host now. Some of the dragon's heads had already fallen, their fire stopped. The rest would fall soon enough. However, as the Host closed to perfect range, everything changed.

Before the eyes of the front rank of the Posleen the creature dissolved into an oolt'ondar of metal-clad thresh. The thresh were visible for only a moment, however, for as fast as they appeared they disappeared into holes dug by special charges. A moment later their guns poked out of the holes and the only thing visible was the guns and the scattered few bodies of metal thresh.

Even as they were greeted by this horrid sight, worse horrors fell upon them.

"Bravo Company, fire," said the officer, quietly.

The three companies of the battalion formed a box. Each of the suits could keep up a continuous stream of fire for over thirty minutes with onboard munitions. When a unit of ACS was faced with a unit of Posleen the usual method of engagement was face-to-face. By waving the fire of the individuals back and forth, the Posleen were, more or less, washed away with fire hoses.

However, the current situation was perfect for enfilading fire. By firing the grav-guns straight forward at knee-height each individual suit-trooper created a "beam" of destruction. If a Posleen touched one of the beams, they died. And the fire of the three companies was interlaced.

When the beams of fire from Bravo Company reached out, they slaughtered Posleen by the thousands, driving all the way through the mass of the host. The terrain was nearly flat and there was nowhere for the centaurs to hide. Driving towards the Monument, towards the submerged suits of the majority of the battalion, meant crossing the beams of fire from Bravo. Turning and driving towards Bravo meant crossing not only the fire of the battalion, but that deadly curtain of steel rain which was still falling.

Then the companies started panning their fire.

It hadn't been the direct fire of the horrid weapons of the threshkreen that had struck him down. If it had he would have died instantly. The terrible weapons of the threshkreen rended oolt'os and Kessentai alike in a single burst. When one struck it was as if they were hit with a missile, their bodies exploding outward. To be tapped with even a glancing blow was fatal.

No, it had not been the terrible weapons of the thresh, but a weapon of the host that had laid him low. When one of those terrible beams had struck the power-pack of his bodyguard's railgun, the resulting explosion had broken his back and buried Kenallai under rendered Po'oslena'ar. Now he caught glimpses of the terrible rendering going on on either side.

His personal oolt and the Kessentai of his oolt'ondar were scattered in death around him. There lay brave Alltandai, swift and fell. Behind him lay Kenallurial and Ardan'aath. Before him lay only death.

The battlemaster turned his head from side to side, looking at the piles. Finally it was too hard to hold up and the broad head settled to the ground. It was as well. The host was doomed. The thresh would destroy them somewhere. Somewhen. Better that he not be there to see it. Strange that it was getting dark.

Dimly, he heard the sounds of the other, older, nestlings out in the dark, screaming as they fed. But here beneath his mound of treasured dead he was surely safe. Tonight they would feed on another.

Might they always feed on another.

The mounding centaurs began to form a wall and the windrow finally obscured the view for the battalion.

"*Up and at 'em!*" Mike snapped, suiting actions to words as he stood up out of his hole. He marked the next point for the battalion to move to on the dispositions map. "Move to the Seventeenth Street phase-line with rolling fire," he continued. "Duncan, we need a rolling barrage."

The line of the battalion was slightly broken up by the windrow of bodies, but the Posleen force was no longer a threat. The survivors had fled into the pocket and very little fire came the way of the battalion as it advanced. Nonetheless they kept up regular fire, picking out any individuals or groups that looked to cause trouble.

The worth of the suits was finally being proven as they followed the fire. Although the barrage would eventually devastate the Posleen force, the fire that the battalion was taking was enough to wipe out a conventional infantry force or even tanks. But the suits shed all but the fiercest flame. In some cases the fire from the Posleen force was so great it was like walking into a rainstorm, but it had as much effect. Only the three-millimeter railguns could penetrate the suits, if a round hit perfectly, and the rest of the 1mm and shotgun rounds were no problem. The occasional HVM that fired out of the mass or the fire of a God King's plasma cannon would remove a luckless trooper. And then it would be silenced by mass fire. The battalion was still able to advance with "acceptable loss."

Mike pushed the battalion forward until they were on a line with the end of the Reflecting Pool and dug-in one last time. There, with any conceivable Posleen assault broken up by the topography of the monument area and with the Posleen forces pushed into a relatively small area, the final phase of the artillery battle could get underway.

The three companies locked their forces into grazing fire across the paths out of the pocket and Mike called for the final fire plan.

No more bad guys seemed to be coming over the hill, so Keren took the long walk up the Mound. The smoke across the Potomac was fading, but there was a solid core of it around the Arlington Bridge and the Memorial. It was an eerie sensation to look out over the battlefield. The view was famous from movies and TV shows, the green lawn, the Memoria, the cherry trees. Now it was torn by fire and the tracks of armored vehicles, with white obscurement smoke drifting in the light wind, the scent of burning and slaughtered Posleen carried upon it.

What was going on in the pocket around the Lincoln Memorial was invisible, but it didn't sound good. The occasional red-cored puff of VT could be seen above the curtaining smoke and there was a continuous clatter from cluster rounds, sounding like the world's largest Chinese funeral. And that was exactly what it was. The Posleen were being forced into a sausage grinder.

The aliens, without any real internal communication, could not see what was happening in the smoke. And the few who survived for a moment were pushed willy-nilly into the caldron of fire by the pressure from behind. What was happening, however, was clearly evident to the armored combat suits. Their all-weather, all-conditions systems made it all too clear.

The Posleen were literally being ground by the fire. The Variable Time fire would explode overhead, scything down a cluster of Posleen. Then the cluster ammunition would butcher the downed group. As wave after wave fell, the earlier ones would be chopped into smaller and smaller bits under the hammer of the guns. The ground was running with yellow blood, the flood pouring into the Potomac, tinging the brown waters an unwonted sienna.

And it was unrecognized by the oncoming tide. Thousands, hundreds of thousands, millions of the centaurs poured across the bridge in a continuous flood. A few made it through the caldron. A very, very few.

These few were picked off by the interconnected grazing fire of the battalion. The intersecting bars of lightning looked like a light show, but they were lines of death for the Posleen. Bravo had been split, with half the company firing across the Mall while the other half fired at an angle across the opening to the north.

The battalion had been similarly split, with half firing to the south side of the memorial and the other to the north. Posleen in the pocket trying to escape to the north ran into the intersecting beams of Bravo and Alpha Companies. Those trying to escape towards Inlet Bridge ran into the fire of Charlie Company. And all of them ran into artillery.

A few of the survivors made it to the Roosevelt Park, on the south side of the pocket around the Tidal Basin. These shell-shocked survivors were all that told the Posleen something bad was happening.

The forces massing to cross in Arlington could clearly see these battered and bloody remnants of the horde. From that, some few began to deduce that entering the smoke was a bad idea. These few told others. And they told others. Then they started taking notes on the color of the river. North of the bridge, brown. South of the bridge, yellow-brown with lots of yellow streaks. Those few who had made a study of sensors studied them. And came to conclusions. And turned away from the inviting bridge.

But . . . most stayed. The Posleen were, by and large, a not very bright species. On that horrible afternoon of blood and slaughter they went through a brutally Darwinian evolution. The few, the smart ones, the ones who used their eyes and the sensors wrested from the long-gone *Alld'nt*, turned away. The many, the stupid and ignorant, those for whom being the warrior was the all and be damned to the technological claptrap, crossed the bridge.

The few survived. For the day.

Mike watched the slaughter stonily. He had come to understand the Posleen in a way that many humans did not. Sometime in the past of the species tinkering had occurred. And that tinkering, rather than some "normal" process, had led them on the long journey to this field of death. Led them on the quest for newer, fresher worlds to conquer.

Understanding them meant that he could not hate them. They were trapped in a cycle they had not created. But he could be a professional about destroying them. And there was a small, professional satisfaction in the carnage before him. He keyed the AID. "Give me General Horner."

"Captain O'Neal," said Horner.

Mike thought he sounded more tired than ever. Maybe they could both get some rest. "General, I would like to report that we have the infestation stopped at the Potomac. As soon as forces are reassembled we can begin reducing them in northern Virginia."

"That is good, Captain," said Jack.

"So, formal, sir?" he quipped. It was a heady high to have succeeded so totally in the sight of his old mentor. "It's okay, General. We've taken too much damage, but we'll take it to them next."

"Yes, we will, Mike," said Horner. "Captain O'Neal . . ." he continued with a catch and stopped.

"Jack," said Mike with a smile, "it's okay . . ."

"No, it's not, Mike. Captain O'Neal, I regret to inform you that your wife, Lieutenant Commander Sharon O'Neal, was lost in action this morning at approximately oh-five hundred hours."

"Oh, shit!" said Mike, in a near wail. "Oh, fuck!"

"I convey the regrets of the new President."

"Oh, goddamn, Jack!"

"I've ensured a qualified contact team is on the way to the farm." Horner waited through the silence, not sure what was happening on the other end. "Mike?"

"Yes, sir," said Captain O'Neal in a toneless voice.

"Are you going to be okay? I, you can ask for some time, if you want it."

"No, sir. That will be fine," the captain said in a monotone. "I'll be just fine."

"Mike . . ."

"I will be fine, sir."

"If you're sure?" The general knew that this was not going to be the end of it. But there were other demands on his time. Other needs to fill.

"I will be just dandy, General, sir," said the captain in an icy voice. "Just dandy."

And he was, as he watched the remorseless destruction of the centaurs. As he led his battalion in the part of the anvil. For the anvil never cries for the iron.

◆ VISIONS ◆

The sensor wand was much more sensitive than the detectors on their suits. And Minnet was a maestro. For all the damn good it was doing.

The cold, pouring rain was washing the remaining soil and grit off the ridge. It had already formed gullies around the bits of buildings and roads, uprooting ancient flagstones and undercutting the three-hundred-year-old foundations that were all that was left of Fredericksburg, Virginia.

Minnet took another bound forward on the search grid and second squad bounded with him, grav-guns tracking. In the last two weeks they had hammered the Posleen in the Rappahanock Pocket into gravy. But there were still a few around. And dead was dead.

Using the untouched Fort Belvoir as a base, the battalion had split up into companies and had ravaged through the remnant Posleen. When a unit found a concentration they would call for fire then finish off the survivors. If the Posleen force was too large the company could either join up with other companies or fall back on Belvoir. The Army Engineer had been only too enthusiastic about turning his base into a giant fortress. The work was still ongoing, with concrete slowly replacing compacted dirt, but the facilities were more than adequate for the purpose. When a couple of thousand Posleen came up to the walls topped with a giant wooden effigy of the Engineer Corps symbol, they got the point. Just before the battleship rounds started falling. In the south the same was being done by a brigade from the Eleventh MID. With much the same result.

So now the Posleen were down to nuisance levels. The new President was even considering letting people back into northern Virginia. Those who wanted to.

Most of the refugees were already being installed in the Sub-Urbs. The vast underground cities were still under construction, but there was enough done to take the trickle of Virginians. With their homes mostly destroyed and the area still under threat of the Posleen, most of them opted to take the government settlement payment and start a new life. It was better than seeing the wrack of their once-beautiful state.

That was left to the ACS. As usual. They had carefully swept the battlefields of the Ninth and Tenth Corps, hoping against hope for a survivor. All they found was the occasional warrior staff, with a hero beside it. Usually the story was unknown. The biggest surprise had been on the first day of sweeps. They found nearly a whole company of the Third Regiment and a single God King all piled on The Tomb. And *two* staffs. There must have been a hell of a story there. But there was no one left to tell it.

Now they had come to the center. The detector would sniff out any living human, no matter how damaged, no matter how buried. But so far they were coming up empty.

"Hey, Sarge," called Wilson, waving for Stewart to join him.

The small NCO bounded over towards Wilson. He looked at his map and shook his head. He should have been standing on the site of the oldest Presbyterian Church in America. Instead there was a scoured flat waste. And one upthrust warrior staff with a small device dangling from it.

"What kind of unit was it here?" asked Wilson.

The question was probably rhetorical. They had been briefed. But Stewart answered anyway. "Engineers. A light battalion."

Wilson plucked the device off the staff. "Well, they must have been some bad news juju," he said grimly. He handed the scrap of cloth to Stewart.

Stewart popped off his helmet and turned his face up to the pouring rain. The cold fall would probably be sleet by morning. But now it worked admirably to wash away the tears. The bloody scrap of cloth was a tab from an engineer officer's uniform.

"Bad fuckin' juju, man," he agreed, his voice thick. He wiped his eyes and put the helmet back on. The nannites scurried to carry away the intruding water. If they had been human they might have clucked in approbation.

"*Contact!*" shouted Minnet, swerving to the side. He bounded twenty feet through the air and landed on a section of crumpled road.

The point was damn near ground zero of the fuel-air explosion. How anything could have survived was a mystery.

Stewart caught a flash out of the corner of his eye and started to track on it before he realized that it was the captain. The officer was taking full use of the almost unlimited power available through the antimatter generator in his suit. He now flew towards the reported contact. The lidar on Stewart's suit clocked him at over four hundred klicks an hour. When they all had those it would make things a *lot* easier.

"Where?" said O'Neal, landing next to the sensor-toting private.

"Right under your feet, sir. Two forms. In hibernation or so it tells me." The private dropped and started to pull up the mixture of concrete, asphalt and glass that overlaid the find.

O'Neal laid a hand on his shoulder. "Hang on." He slid out his monomolecular fighting knife and cut into the mixture. A few slices and he had a cube of the overlay which he threw to the side.

The rest of the squad dove in and before long they were to a brick ceiling.

"What the hell is this, sir?" asked Stewart. The captain was tracking again, which was good. It had looked rocky the first day. But he seemed to be coming around. If he didn't, there wasn't a hell of a lot they could do about it.

"Dunno," said O'Neal, flipping through his database on Fredericksburg. "There's no mention of structures like this." A quick sonic pulse indicated that it was a single layer of brick. Mike lifted himself on his AG drive and took a slice out of the ceiling.

The gray light and cold rain fell on two dust-covered forms, one male, one female. The two young civilians lay in each other's arms on a mattress of body armor. To either side were automatic weapons. The sensors unnecessarily confirmed that the weapons had seen use.

Mike lifted himself out of the hole as the squad dropped in to extract the two. He snorted a few times then gave a deep braying laugh. Shelly had enough experience to know when he was talking to himself so the laugh was not broadcast. Nor was the statement, "Those poor Posleen bastards."

"*Contact!*" shouted another sensor wielder, closer to the river. "*Big contact!*"

This time the construction was a concrete bunker. Mike first wondered how the hell the engineers had managed to make it during the battle, but a brief study indicated that it was an earlier construction. Although what was not obvious.

"Whatta we got?" asked Pappas, kicking the wall of the concrete monstrosity.

"Lots of signal," said the sensor wielder. "All hibernating as far as I can tell. If there are any conscious, it's lost in the mass."

"How many?" Mike barked.

"Don't know, sir," said the tech. "Lots."

Ampele deployed his cutter and tackled an exposed corner. He was standing up to his knees in the rising river, but he didn't seem to notice. It took three cuts to get a hole in the thick concrete walls. He lifted his head up to look in and received a shotgun blast full in the face.

The blast, gnatlike to a suit of combat armor, hardly fazed the phlegmatic Hawaiian, but he dropped down anyway. Better to let whoever was on the other side of the shotgun realize what they'd shot.

Mike lifted himself on compensators and flew over to the opening. "This is Captain Michael O'Neal of the Mobile Infantry. We're friends." He lifted up until he was opposite the hole.

Inside there was a woman in what appeared to be a soiled waitress's uniform. She had stringy, unwashed blonde hair and a wild expression in her eyes. Having been trapped under a building one time, Mike could well appreciate her frame of mind; he still got a bit panicky in the dark. So he could never afterwards decide if he was brilliant or stupid to take off his helmet.

The woman took one look at the human face and burst into tears.

Mike lifted himself up so he could see in and almost recoiled in horror. The room was filled with bodies and they at first appeared to be corpses or even vampires. Their skin was waxy with red-flushed cheeks. Their lips were swollen and flushed and their eyes were open and glassy. But the same effect was caused by Hiberzine. It was just that he had never seen hibernation patients piled willy-nilly in a sarcophagus before. He shook his head and offered his hand to the woman. "Are you alone?" he asked solicitously.

The answer was another flood of tears but the woman took his hand and slid through the hole. "Ah, ah," she gasped for a moment then caught her breath. "There was a . . . a firewoman with me at first. But she . . . she couldn't take the walls. I had to . . . to . . ."

"Sedate her," said Mike. He shook his head again. Strength was an odd commodity. Like hope, it sprouted in the strangest places.

Aberdeen Proving Grounds, MD, United States of America, Sol III
1626 EDT October 13th, 2004 AD

Keren watched the video for the umpteenth time. The networks, overrun with incredible images of heroism and cowardice, competence and idiocy, had settled on this one to wrap them all up in a nice neat network package.

The crowd surged back. The lander had dropped perfectly; just far enough that none of the humans were injured, but too close for them to run far. As the giant landing door dropped the panicking crowd washed away from the single, still armored soldier in its midst.

The foreground held a crying child, her forearm obviously broken. If any parent had been in that crowd they had been swept onward, as had the guards of the figure standing in the background, perfectly poised against the foreground of the sobbing child. As the door dropped, silently in this version, the grav-cannon on the back of the figure dropped forward. The figure took a perfect position, a picture from a Fort Benning textbook of a rifleman firing from the standing position. One hand cradled the grav-cannon while the other pulled it into the shoulder. One foot was cocked slightly backwards with feet shoulder-width apart, body slightly canted towards the target.

As the Posleen descended from their craft, harvesting swords held high, the figure opened fire.

Cheyenne Mountain, CO, United States of America, Sol III
1423 EDT October 14th, 2004 AD

She had never planned on being President. Her position was to balance the ticket. And she sure as hell did not want to be President stuck in a concrete bunker in the middle of a mountain in Colorado.

But she had to admit it made more sense than a combat suit in the middle of D.C.

The cabinet was scattered to hell and gone. And so were the staffers. And there was no conventional transport faster than trains. Trains. They were reduced to using trains.

But the Galactics weren't. The Tir Dol Ron would be here any minute, courtesy of a Himmit stealth ship. She supposed she could probably avail herself of one as well. But reassembling a staff was still going to take months.

She had had damn little staff with her when the landings started. And not many more had made it here so far. One of those, though, had turned out to be a goldmine. The girl was a total airhead about everything outside her narrow specialty, but she had an immense understanding of the Galactics and their punctilious protocol.

Which might make or break the war.

Washington Monument, Washington, DC
United States of America, Sol III
1430 EDT October 14th, 2004 AD

"It is you people, and other soldiers like you, who will make or break the war to come," said General Taylor.

Immediately following the battle, the two colonels and their sergeant majors had gathered the survivors of the Battle of The Monument and made a list. The six hundred or so that survived, along with a dazed platoon of engineers extracted with some difficulty from the Memorial, were now gathered at the site of their triumph to be decorated.

The tall black general looked around at the group with a penetrating eye. "Many of you, in years to come, will belittle that moment. That is a fundamental nature of true heroes. But I tell you now, this battle will be remembered with Bunker Hill and Lexington and Concord. Not only because those were battles that formed a great nation, as this was a battle that saved one. But because they were small skirmishes that presaged a great and terrible war. And the survivors from those small skirmishes formed the core of the great army that arose from their ashes." He smiled faintly.

"But enough of the words. We all know there ain't no extra pay, and rations will be catch as catch can. But we still got plenty of medals!"

Rabun County, GA, United States of America, Sol III
1820 EDT October 14th, 2004 AD

The reporter from the local station shook water from the hood of his raincoat and looked at the camera.

"And three, two, one . . . Good afternoon, this is Tom Speltzer from WKGR, reporting from Habersham, Georgia. It seems like there are plenty of medals for the soldiers, but it wasn't only soldiers that beat the Posleen.

"I'm talking with Mr. Michael O'Neal, of Rabun Gap, Georgia, and his eight-year-old granddaughter, Cally O'Neal." The reporter turned and proffered the microphone to the elder O'Neal, standing in the pouring rain like a statue.

Mike Senior's camouflage raincoat shed the water like a duck and the hood worked much better than the reporter's. And he wasn't about to let the newsie bastard in the house.

"Mr. O'Neal, can you tell us what it felt like to have the Posleen assault your home?"

"Well, first of all, they never got to the house. We had 'em pretty well stopped down in the valley," he said, gesturing towards the distant entrance.

"We?" asked the reporter, surprised. "You had help?"

"From me!" piped up the little girl. "I ran the demo!"

The reporter's face took on that special look of false pleased surprise that adults affect when children interject unnecessarily. The report was going out live nationwide and he just had to shut the kid up as fast as possible. But what the hell was demo? "Really? Did that help?" he asked.

"Blew the shit out of the bastards," Cally said, ingenuously. "Must have killed half the damn company. We had the whole fuckin' woodline strung with claymores and I just blew the fuck out of them."

The camerawoman suppressed her laughter but expertly caught the frozen look on the reporter's face as he attempted to come up with a response to this.

"Cut to the old guy," snapped the producer. "Ask him about the name."

"And Mr. O'Neal, there's another O'Neal that has become famous, again. By exactly the same name . . ."

"That's my daddy!" said Cally excitedly. "He really rolled those centaur sons of bitches up, didn't 'e?"

The reporter had assumed that out of control runaway train expression again. Mike Senior decided to twist the knife. He worked the wad in his cheek around and spit. "I teached 'im ever'thang he knows," he drawled, looking right in the camera. And hoping like hell the damn monks could keep their vow of goddamned silence and not laugh their asses off. There were enough damn problems in the world without having to explain them.

In the background, a green Army sedan appeared out of the woodline, headed to the house. In the cold Georgia rain.

Walter Reed Army Hospital, Washington, DC
United States of America, Sol III
2015 EDT October 15th, 2004 AD

Keren knocked on the door of the room and nodded at the nurse who was just leaving.

The room smelled of disinfectant. It was an odor that raised the hackles on the back of his neck. To the lizard hindbrain, it meant that things were bad and going to get worse.

He looked down at the figure on the bed. There were three medals pinned to the pillow; apparently something had made it into the database before it all came apart at Lake Jackson. He shook his head and sat down.

"You really missed a good party," he whispered, pulling a bottle out of the recesses of his coat. The gold bars of a second lieutenant winked for a moment in the light over the bed. "The general was buying. Damn, he can drink. And that old snake of a warrant officer that followed him around. And the general told this story, damn it was funny, 'bout how come the warrant follows him around. It's all about an alligator and two bottles of bourbon."

So he told his friend the story. And he told her a couple of others, about how General Simosin and General Ford finally had it out and Ford accused Simosin of incompetence in front of a TV camera and Simosin dragged it all out in the open how Ford had opposed integrating the old-timers and screwed around so bad that there was no damn way anything could have gone right. So now Ford was out and Simosin was back at Tenth Corps and General Keeton was First Army.

And he told about the meeting between the new Prez and the Darhel. How the Prez had threatened to recall all the expeditionary forces unless the Darhel ponied up all the grav-guns we could stand. And how the Tir had finally agreed that all equipment would be at no cost and that husbanding the humans was the most important thing in the universe. But the pipeline was still plugged and the Fleet was takin' forever and most of the PDCs were smoking holes. . . .

And he told how some rag-head had made a stand to equal theirs, taking a bit of this unit and a bit of that and somehow putting enough steel in their spine to hold a vital pass against a whole swarm. Or so they said.

But India was a madhouse and nobody knew what was happening in the Africa swarm. And the one in Kazakhstan was just wandering around trying to find its way out of the plains. . . .

But finally the bottle was empty and it was time to leave.

"Well, Elgars. They say you might be able to hear me. And they tell me you might come out of it someday. I left the e-mail to my . . . our unit with them. They're taking all the survivors from The Stand at the Monument and making a special unit. You're included as one of us. You and all the other . . . wounded. And the dead. So, you can, you know . . ."

He stopped and wiped a tear away. "And I watched Pittets hang. You'd be happy to hear that. They didn't tie it the way I asked, I wanted him to kick for a while. But he's gone. And you know about the decorations." He tried to think of something else to say but nothing came. "I gotta go," he said, looking at his watch and trying not to look at the lovely face behind the tubes, as the machine sucked in and out.

"The Galactics, they're picking up the tab now. So there's no reason to, you know ... to take you off. And they'll be moving you to a Sub-Urb. They've got plenty of room and really good facilities. So they're gonna leave you hooked up in case ..."

He wished now he hadn't finished the bottle. He could use a little taste. He took her hand one last time. "Thanks for that shot on Sixth Street." He nodded at her, one soldier to another. "I know it saved you, too. But it still saved my ass." He nodded again, hoping that she would do the thing with grabbing his hand, but there was no response. "Well, bye, Elgars. Take care." Finally, he turned and left the room. Behind him it was silent except for the suck and whir of the machines.

> Beyond the path of the outmost sun though utter
>   darkness hurled—
> Further than ever comet flared or vagrant star-dust swirled–
> Live such as fought and sailed and ruled and loved and made
>   our world.
>
> They are purged of pride because they died, they know the
>   worth of their bays,
> They sit at wine with the Maidens Nine and the Gods of the
>   Elder Days,
> It is their will to serve or be still as fitteth Our Father's Praise.
>
> 'Tis theirs to sweep through the ringing deep where Azrael's
>   outposts are,
> Or buffet a path through the Pit's red wrath when God goes
>   out to war,
> Or hang with the reckless Seraphim on the rein of a
>   red-maned star.
>
> They take their mirth in the joy of the Earth–they dare not
>   grieve for her pain.
> They know of toil and the end of toil, they know God's Law
>   is plain,

So they whistle the Devil to make them sport who know that
    Sin is vain.

And ofttimes cometh our Wise Lord God, master of every
    trade,
And tells them tales of His daily toil, of Edens newly made;
And they rise to their feet as He passes by, gentlemen
    unafraid.

To these who are cleansed of base Desire, Sorrow and
    Lust and Shame—
Gods for they knew the hearts of men, men for they
    stooped to Fame,
Borne on the breath that men call Death, my brother's
    spirit came.

He scarce had need to doff his pride or slough the dross
    of the Earth—
E'en as he trod that day to God so walked he from his birth,
In simpleness and gentleness and honour and clean mirth.

So cup to lip in fellowship they gave him welcome high
And made him a place at the banquet board—the Strong
    Men ranged thereby,
Who had done his work and held his peace and had no
    fear to die.

Beyond the loom of the last lone star, through open darkness
    hurled,
Further than rebel comet dared or hiving star-swarm swirled,
Sits he with those that praise our God for that they served
    His world.

AUTHOR'S AFTERWORD

On September 10, 1998, my father died of a stroke while watching a rerun of *Seinfeld*.

It was the first cool day of the fall after an awful, sticky summer of blazing heat, repeated heart attacks and kidney failures. The day had been his first good one in six months and fall was his favorite time of year, so it was doubly auspicious.

There is no such thing as "a good day to die." But there are better and worse. Taking the alternative of D-Day or the Battle of the Bulge or the Hurtgen Forest or Iwo Jima, where so many of his fellow age-mates died, an apparently fast stroke while laughing at Jerry's antics is fair.

I mention my father for two reasons. The first is that I keep his generation in mind while writing my books. The societal conditions that provided the soldiers for the American Army in WWII were unprecedented in history. It was a society that was as technologically adept as any in the world, but that had fallen upon hard times so that there was a great need for work. Also those hard times had hammered out some of the impurities in the metal already. What was left was pretty good iron that was turned to steel by 1944.

Which, if a similar situation were to occur today, would not be the case. Personally, I like the present day. This is, unless anyone is confused, a golden age. With all the ills of a golden age. (Read *The Decameron* and tell me that there is a new ill under the sun.) But, given the choice between a decadent golden age and a stoic time of privation and war . . . give me the golden age.

But—there is always a but, isn't there? But, if a situation were to occur today which called for a national will to survival, it would be difficult to replicate that "Greatest Generation." First we would have to go through the sort of pre-tempering that occurred with the Great Depression, getting out all the "lesser" impurities. Only then would we as a nation be prepared for the greater tests.

And I personally don't think we would have the time. So, I always keep my father, and his generation, in the forefront of my mind.

The second reason that I mention my father is that he turned me on to Kipling. I spent about a day of my week's leave after Airborne school at home (hey, there were girls and bottles out there pining for me). And just before I left, my dad handed me this really beat-up old book. He told me that his dad had given it to him before he went to England in 1944 and that it was time to pass it on. I didn't really think anything of it at the time (girls and bottles) but later, after I settled in at my permanent party, I pulled it out and gave it a look.

The Mandalay Edition of the Works of Rudyard Kipling, Departmental Ditties, Barrack-Room Ballads and Other Verses/Five Nations and the Seven Seas by Rudyard Kipling. Doubleday, Page & Company, Garden City, NY, 1925. Note the last poem is "To Wolcott Balestier," the dedication to *Barrack-Room Ballads.*

For the longest time I thought I was the only person in the world who still read Kipling. Then an old Vietnam Vet first sergeant (a guy I didn't even know could read) dropped a quote. Then I heard a general "kipple." A battalion commander. A sergeant. A visiting SAS sergeant major presented a bound collection to our battalion CSM. And I found out a little secret; there are damn few warriors in the world who don't like Kipling. There are some who don't know about him, but the ones who do are fanatics. It's almost a way to separate the sheep from the goats.

For anyone who has never read Kipling, if you like my books get a Kipling collection. Rudyard could say it as no one before or since has been able to say it. He speaks to the heart and soul of the soldier. In the end, we're all Tommies (or M.I. or Sappers or Oont drivers) at heart.

And that is the other reason I bring up my dad.

William Pryor Ringo, Captain US Army Corps Of Engineers (ret.) P.E.
Born: July 24, 1924
Died: September 10, 1998

> Me that 'ave been what I've been—
> Me that 'ave gone where I've gone—
> Me that 'ave seen what I've seen—
>
> . . .
>
> *Me!*

GLOSSARY

Aarnadaha	Posleen Senior Battlemaster (Brigade commander).
abat	A nearly impossible to eradicate small pest on Posleen landers.
Adenast	Federation world on the far side of space from the Posleen invasion.
Aelool	Indowy Master Craftsman.
AFV	Armored Fighting Vehicle. Heavily armed personnel carrier or tank.
Agincourt	Fast Frigate in Earth Defense Region.
a-hoo-wah	Motivational or "battle" cry.
AirCav	Air Cavalry. Helicopter-borne scouts.
AIW	Advanced Infantry Weapon.
Alld'nt	Demons or sky gods of the Posleen pan-theology. Reputed to give great gifts but to also cause great harm.
Alrantath	Posleen battalion commander subordinate to Ardan'aath.
Althanara	Posleen Scoutmaster.
Anarlaralta	Posleen Scoutmaster subordinate to Alrantath (eson'antai).
Andatha	Region on Barwhon where majority of US expeditionary force is engaged.
APC	Armored personnel carrier. Lightly armed, lightly armored metal box on tracks.
Aradan	Posleen name for the star the Federation calls Diess.
Ardan'aath	Posleen brigade commander. Allied with Kenallai.
Arnata'dra	Posleen Scoutmaster, subordinate to Kenallurial.
Ashkabad	City in Turkmenistan.

Atalanara	Posleen company commander, allied with Kenallurial.
AWOL	Absent Without Leave.
Barrett Firearms	Manufacturer of a (really cool) .50-caliber sniper rifle. Based in Murfreesboro, TN.
Barwhon	Tchpth settled planet. Cool and wet with almost continuous swamps, lakes, rivers and bogs.
battlecase	Large ammunition box for feeding a manjack.
BattleDec	Short for Battle dodecahedron. A Posleen conglomerate ship consisting of an inner dodecahedral command ship (C-Dec) and twelve landers.
Battleglobe	A large Posleen conglomerate ship consisting of multiple hundreds of B-Decs.
Battlemaster	Posleen grade. Equivalent to captain-full colonel. Although all Posleen God Kings (Kessentai) are nominally independent, in general junior officers look to senior officers for direction.
Battlenet	Human Command Network for Continental Defense.
B-Dec	*See* BattleDec.
BDUs	Battle Dress Uniform. The US Ground Force standard camouflage field uniform.
Belvoir, Fort	Headquarters of the US Army Corps of Engineers. Located just outside of Washington, D.C.
Beretta	Standard 9mm sidearm of US Ground Force.
berm	An elongated pile of dirt used for cover.
Blackhawk	Military medium lift helicopter designated UH-60.
bowsers	Military tanker trucks.
Bradleys	Armored Fighting Vehicle (AFV). Crew of two, holds eight infantrymen. Armed with a 25mm chaingun and a TOW-2 Missile Launcher.
Bragg, Fort	Home of the Airborne. Located in central North Carolina.
Bullpup	Design of assault rifle. Places the ammunition magazine behind the firing hand thus shortening the overall length of the weapon.
Bushmaster	25mm chaingun mounted on a Bradley Fighting Vehicle.
caltrop	Four-pointed spike device designed so that one point always faces up.
castellaine	The manager of a Posleen estate.
cav	Cavalry.

C-Dec	Command Dodecahedron. Holds the senior God King of a Posleen "B-Dec" conglomerate and its most heavily armed normals. Is usually the center ship of a B-Dec. Has interstellar drive. Holds 1400–1800 Normals and 3–6 God Kings along with some light, simple armor.
chai	British Navy word for tea.
circumvallated	Surrounded by fortifications.
clacker	Detonation device for a claymore directional mine. So called because when compressed it makes a distinctive "clack" sound.
claymore	Directional mine. Consists of a convexly curved box with two ports for detonators on the top. The rear is a thin metal plate, then a sheet of explosive, then 750 ball bearings.
CONARC	Continental Army Command.
COS	Chief of Staff.
cratering	Detonating explosives so as to cause a large crater. This is primarily used as an obstacle.
CSP	Combat Space Patrol.
Cyberpunk	Elite information warfare unit. Extremely secretive.
Dantren	Indowy Megascraper Deushi Megalopolis. Refuge for mobile forces.
Darhel	Galactic Federation race.
DataNet	Posleen information network. Very similar to the internet except without any indexing tools.
defilade	Maneuvering to obtain cover from terrain
detcord	Explosive cord. Similar to fusecord, but explodes instead of burning.
didee-mao	Vietnamese: Retreat.
Diess	Indowy Planet. Under assault by the Posleen.
DivArty	Division Artillery.
Dunkirked	Evacuated by water.
edan	Posleen: Battle madness.
edas'antai	Posleen: Primary genetic sponsor. Father.
emphysemic	A person who has emphysema.
enfilading	Fire from the flank.
esonal	Posleen: Ovipositor.
eson'antai	Posleen: Primary genetic derivative. Son.
Farbase	Primary military base on the moon. Hidden on the backside in a crater to reduce chance of detection by the Posleen.

Fars	Primary plateau of the country of Iran.
FedCreds	Federation Credits.
firebase	Heavily defended base where artillery is concentrated.
FireTac	Artillery Coordination Network.
Fistnal	Posleen: Damned. (Lit. "Eaten" reduced from "Eaten by sky demons.")
flechette	Finned metal dart.
flikker	To turn in the air like a hummingbird.
Fredericksburg	Town in central Virginia.
Fort A.P. Hill	Military base in central Virginia.
fuscirt	Posleen: Demons.
fuscirto	Posleen: Demons. Part of a wordy curse that translates more or less as "Demon Feces."
Galil	Name of an Israeli assault rifle.
GalMed	Galactic Medications. General name for a wide variety of medications the Federation has supplied to Earth.
GalTech	Galactic Technologies. General name for a wide variety of technologies the Federation has supplied to Earth.
Gamalada	Clan of the Po'oslenar.
Gatling	Type of automatic weapon that has multiple barrels.
ghillie	Type of camouflage suit used to break up the outline of an infantryman or sniper. Introduced by Scottish gamekeepers (or poachers alternately) during WWI.
Ghurka	Elite Nepalese Mercenary Infantry.
Glock	Type of pistol.
grat	Rare but extremely unpleasant pest of the Posleen. Resembles a very large ant and forms colonies.
Hiberzine	Galactic drug that causes almost instantaneous unconsciousness and places the user in a state of virtual suspended animation for up to 180 days. Combines pharmacological substances with nannites. Dosage is managed internally to the substance so that there is no chance of an over- or underdose.
Himmit	Federation race. Racial cowards and long-ranging scouts.
Hummelstown	Town outside of Fort Indiantown Gap.
Humvee	High Mobility Multi-Use Vehicle (HMMV).
HVM	Hypervelocity Missiles.
Indiantown Gap, Fort	Military post in Pennsylvania near Harrisburg.

Indowy	Galactic race. Short bipeds with apparently innate ability with technology and tools.
Irmansul	Galactic planet under threat of invasion by the Posleen.
Isfahan	Town in central Iran. Famous for its rugs.
Kasserine	Town in Morocco where the US Army suffered an early defeat in WWII at the hands of the German Afrikacorps.
Kenallai	Posleen: Senior battlemaster. Equivalent to a colonel or brigadier general.
Kenallurial	Gene derivative of Kenallai. Equivalent to a lieutenant or captain.
Kenstain	Posleen: Term for a castellaine. Castellaines are a lower "caste" God King and are formed from God Kings that have either voluntarily stopped fighting or were incompetent or cowardly.
Kessanalt	Posleen: Battle honor.
Kessentai	Posleen: God King (translates literally as "Philosopher" or "Thinker").
Kevlar	Aramide fiber used in body armor. Also used to refer to the helmets made of it that are worn by US Ground Force personnel.
Kiowa	Scout helicopter.
klicks	Short for "kilometer."
laager	Grouping of tanks or other fighting vehicles.
lidar	Laser detection system.
Maglite	Type of flashlight often preferred by police and special operations personnel.
Manassas	Town in north-central Virginia.
manjack	Automated machine gun.
Mashad	Major city in northeastern Iran.
Mayport	City and naval base in northeastern Florida near Jacksonville.
McCall, Camp	Small military base near the much larger Fort Bragg.
Milnet	Military internet interface and analogue.
Milspecs	Galactic Technology glasses. In appearance simple "wrap-around" sunglasses. Provide full light enhancement ability.
Minié	Type of bullet used by both sides during the Civil War.
monomolecular	Single very large molecule. A substance that is not only incredibly strong but also almost infinitely thin and therefore sharp.

Montrose Heights	Large hill overlooking Richmond, VA.
Mosby Hill	Large hill overlooking Richmond, VA.
MRE	Meals-Ready-To-Eat. Military combat rations. Come in plastic packaging.
Myer, Fort	Military base near Washington, D.C.
nannites	Very small mechano-electric machines that are used for a wide variety of purposes by the Galactic Federation.
NCO	Noncommissioned Officer.
Nomex	Fireproof fabric.
Occoquan	River, town and reservoir in northern Virginia.
oolt	Posleen: Group or company. (Lit. "Pack")
Oolton	Posleen: Battalion or brigade. Used interchangeably. (Lit. "Big Pack")
oolt'ondai	Posleen: Battalion or brigade commander. (Lit. "Big pack leader")
oolt'ondar	Posleen: Battalion or brigade.
oolt'os	Posleen: Posleen normal. (Lit. "Pack member")
Oolt'pos	Posleen: Command Dodecahedron. Holds 1400–1800 Normals and 3–6 God Kings along with some light, simple armor.
orna'adar	Posleen: Final battle or Ragnarok. A scramble for dwindling resources that leads to destruction of the world and extinction of all the Posleen on it.
Panatellas	Long, thin cigars.
Panzergrenadier	German Mechanized Infantry.
PDC	Planetary Defense Center.
plasteel	Galactic armor material.
Po'oslena'ar	Posleen: "The People of the Ships."
Po'osol	Posleen: Lander. Holds 400–600 normals and one God King.
Posleen	Enemy aliens. Yellow-grey centauroids. Thirteen to fifteen hands high at the shoulder. Arms jut from a combination shoulder. Sauroid head with multiple teeth is mounted on a long, snake-like neck. "Hands" are four-fingered talons with an opposable talon, similar to a fish-eating bird of prey. Feet are foreshortened talons adapted for running and slashing.
Proteans	Term for current generation of manjacks.
Provigil	Anti-sleep drug.

tanglefoot	Barbed wire stretched taut at knee height designed to catch and "tangle" assaulting enemy troops.
Tchpth	Galactic race. Pseudoarthropods with a remarkable resemblance, other than being blue and red, to a Dungeness crab. Renowned scientists and philosophers.
Tel'enaa	Battle Demons. Part of a wordy curse. (Demons of battle eat and defecate their souls!)
te'naal	Berserk charge.
Tenal'ont	Posleen company commander.
tenar	Posleen God King's saucer vehicle. Has a heavy weapon mounted on it and a suite of sensors.
terawatt	One trillion watts.
Thermopylae	A famous defense in ancient Greece. Also, a primarily automatic close defense system for battleships.
thresh	Posleen: Food.
Threshkreen	Posleen: Enemy. (Translates literally as "food with a bite.")
Thunderchiefs	Air Force aerobatics demonstration team.
Tindar	Clan of the Darhel.
Tir	Intermediate rank Darhel.
Tir Dol Ron	Darhel senior executive.
uut	Posleen: Fecal matter.
Zoroaster	Primary god of the religion that preceded Islam in Persia.

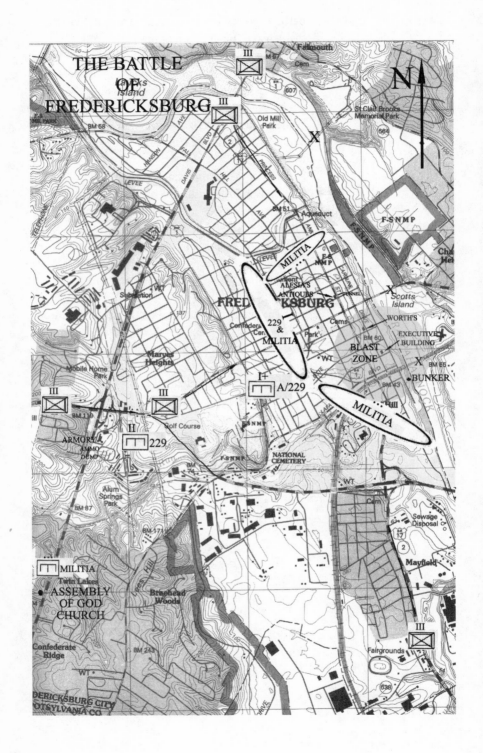

OCCOQUAN DEFENSES

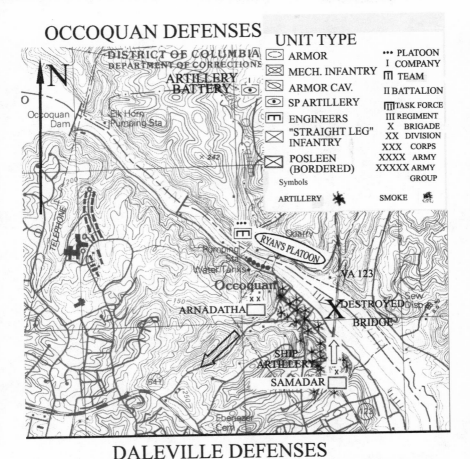

UNIT TYPE

Symbol	Unit Type		Echelon
	ARMOR	•••	PLATOON
	MECH. INFANTRY	I	COMPANY
	ARMOR CAV.	⊓	TEAM
	SP ARTILLERY	II	BATTALION
	ENGINEERS	⊓⊓	TASK FORCE
	"STRAIGHT LEG" INFANTRY	III	REGIMENT
	POSLEEN (BORDERED)	X	BRIGADE
		XX	DIVISION
		XXX	CORPS
		XXXX	ARMY
		XXXXX	ARMY GROUP

Symbols

ARTILLERY   SMOKE

DALEVILLE DEFENSES

TO OCCOQUAN

50th Retreats And Screens

19th Armor Adjusts to Screen

41st And 33rd Retreat

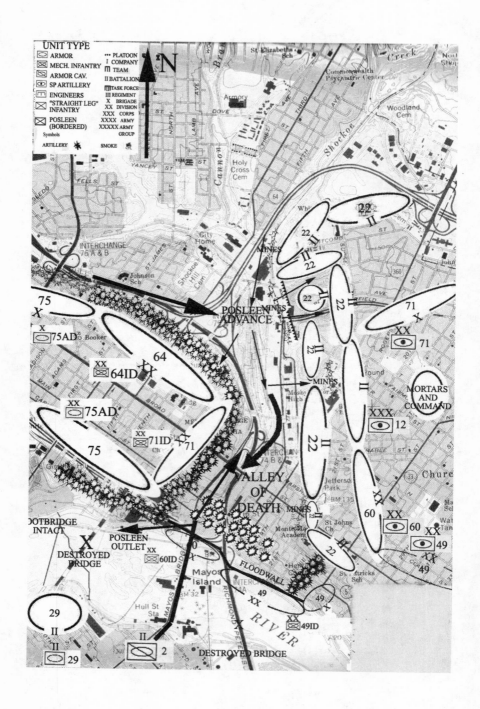

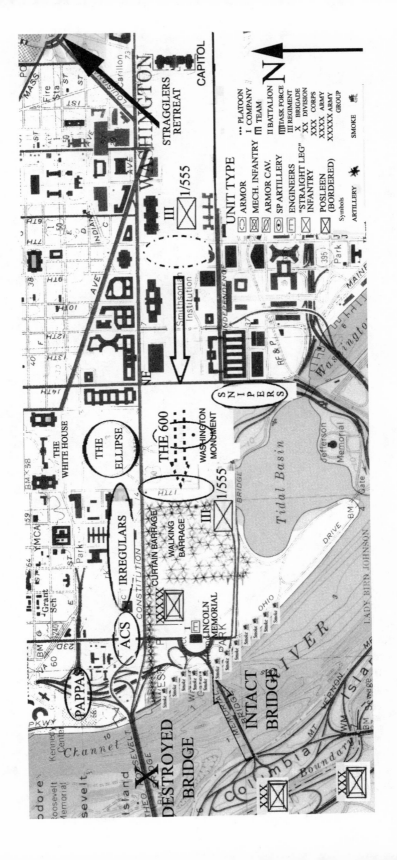